1400

6

BOOKS BY

REYNOLDS PRICE

REYNOLDS
PRICE

THE
SURFACE
OF
EARTH

A SCRIBNER PAPERBACK FICTION BOOK
Published by Simon & Schuster
New York   London   Toronto   Sydney   Tokyo   Singapore

SCRIBNER PAPERBACK FICTION
Simon & Schuster Inc.
Rockefeller Center
1230 Avenue of the Americas
New York, NY 10020

First Scribner Paperback Fiction Edition 1995

SCRIBNER PAPERBACK FICTION and design
are trademarks of Simon & Schuster Inc.

Designed by Harry Ford

Manufactured in the United States of America

3 5 7 9 10 8 6 4

Library of Congress catalog card number 74-32615

ISBN 0-684-81339-4

Parts of this novel appeared, in earlier forms, in
Esquire, Harper's, Shenandoah, Southern Voices, and
The Virginia Quarterly Review.

FOR

CHRISTOPHER BEEBE

AND

WILLIAM SINGER

But You, the Good which needs no good,
rest always, being Yourself Your rest.
What man can teach another man that?
What angel an angel?
What angel a man?

AUGUSTINE, *Confessions*, XIII, 38

BOOK ONE   ABSOLUTE PLEASURES

BOOK TWO   THE HEART IN DREAMS

BOOK THREE   PARTIAL AMENDS

ONE

ABSOLUTE PLEASURES

MAY 1903

"**W**HO told Thad she was dead?" Rena asked.

"Thad killed her," Eva said. "He already knew."

Their father—from his rocker, almost dark in the evening—said, "Hush your voices down. Your mother's on the way. And never call him *Thad*. He was her dear father, your own grandfather; and of course he never killed her."

Kennerly said, "He gave her the baby. The baby killed her. So I think he did justice, killing himself."

"Shame," their father said. He drew at his cigar. "I hope none of you lives to face such a choice." Another draw. "But one of you will. Then remember tonight—the cruelty you've talked against the helpless dead."

He had started directing his answer to Kennerly—Kennerly was leaving home in a week: a job, his life—but he ended it on Eva. His middle child, his choice of the three, the thing in the world (beside his own mother, dead twenty years) that he'd loved and still loved, for sixteen years.

Dark as it was, Eva met his eyes and waited him out. Then she said, "What's shameful, sir, in wanting the truth? We're all nearly grown. We've heard scraps of it all our lives—lies, jokes. We are asking to know. It's our own story."

Her father nodded. "It would kill your mother to hear it."

They all were silent. The street beyond was empty. Hector the dog surrendered to Kennerly's scratching hands. Their mother's voice came from the kitchen, still talking—"Mag, you can take this bread on with you and bake fresh for breakfast if you get here in time. You'll get here, won't you?" —Some grumble from Mag, amounting to Yes. —"And you too, Sylvie? We got to iron curtains." A younger docile voice said "Yes'm."

Rena and Kennerly also looked to Eva. She was running this.

Eva said "Safe."

Their father said, quickly and as near to whispering as he ever came,

"Thad Watson married Katherine Epps and, much as he loved her, he wanted a son. Three, four years passed—no son, no daughter. Katherine told him it was God's will, to calm down and wait. *Wait* was the one thing Thad couldn't do; and within another year, Katherine had a baby and died in the act. It had been a hard labor; and Dr. Burton had sent Thad out to wait in the yard, anywhere out of sight. He waited on the porch, really sat and waited for once in his life."

Eva said, "How do you know that?"

"My mother was there, helping what she could."

"Which wasn't much," Kennerly said.

"Not much. What could you have done with God set against you?"

Kennerly said, "I could have asked Him why."

"You'd have stood there and talked, and she'd have died anyhow. My mother gave the ether, little bits at a time on a clean cotton rag. So she died at ease—no pain, not a sound, no signal to Thad twenty feet away. When the doctor had listened to Katherine's still chest—Mother said he listened for the length of a song—and seen Mother safely washing the baby, he washed his own hands and put on his coat and stepped to the porch and said, 'Thad, I lost her. But I saved you a girl.' Thad waited on a minute. Then he stood up and looked Dr. Burton in the face as calm as this evening and told him 'Thank you' and headed indoors. The doctor assumed he was going to Katherine—there were plenty more women in there with her to meet him—so he stood on the porch to clear his own head. It had lasted all night; it was past dawn, May. The next thing he heard was a single shot. Thad had walked to the bedroom, straight through the women—never looked to your mother, herself nearly killed in Katherine's labor—and taken his pistol off the mantelpiece and walked to the bed where Katherine lay—they had still not washed her—and blown his brains out and fallen on her body." He drew at his cold cigar. "Now you know."

"It was Mother," Eva said. "The baby that killed his wife was Mother?"

"You knew that," he said. "But never say *killed*. She was innocent as if she had come from the moon, and her own father stopped her life in its tracks before she could move. Part of it anyhow."

Rena said, "Why would he do that, Father?—not wait for his child?"

A long wait. No answer, though voices still rose and fell in the kitchen.

"He knew his life had stopped," Eva said.

Kennerly made his sound of disgust.

"—Thought it had," their father said. "Then why not take the ruined baby with him?"

Nobody offered an answer to that.

But Eva said, "Did you ever see them, Father?"

"I remember him—I was ten when he died—and I must have seen her any number of times. But I don't have a shred of memory of her. A perfect blank. Your mother even—I still have to look at pictures of her to see her as a girl, and she all but lived with us."

Rena said "Why was that?"

"She was a quiet child."

They all waited silently and listened to her come slowly forward through the house; stop in her bedroom (the left front room) and brush at her hair; then stand in the door and say, "Eva, take a chair"—Eva sat on the steps—"You're too dressed-up anyhow. Commencement's *tomorrow*."

"Yes ma'm," Eva said.

Their mother went on to her usual place—the far corner swing where Kennerly waited, gently rocked as though by a breeze.

Eva stayed still.

Her mother stared at her—the side of her face; she was lovely, brown curls in swags to her shoulders. "Eva, go change. You'll smother in that."

Eva looked to the street. "I'm breathing," she said.

"Rena, make her go change."

Rena budged, vibrated by the words themselves; but she also watched the street and stayed in place.

"*Eva*, look here."

Eva turned and looked and before her mother could speak, even study her face in the dusk, Eva said "Be good to me—" She looked to her father.

Their mother said, "What is that supposed to mean?"

Hector barked once.

Rena said—and pointed—"Mr. Mayfield."

He was almost on them, having come up the stone walk that quietly; and everyone but Mrs. Kendal stood to welcome him, though she spoke first—"Did she fail, Mr. Mayfield?"

"No'm, she passed," he said. "She barely passed." He was at the steps and paused there, three feet from Eva. So no one but Eva could see the smile that rose in his face as he turned to her father. "Ninety-six in English. One hundred in Latin. Be proud, Mr. Kendal."

"Thank you, sir," he said. "She'll graduate then?"

"Far as I'm concerned, she's graduated now; could have two years ago. Knows more than I do," Forrest Mayfield said.

"Too kind," Mrs. Kendal said. "Sit down and rest. Have you eaten your supper? You'll be starved and blind from reading children's papers."

"No I'm not," he said. "Good young eyes like mine—I can see in the dark."

"You're thirty," Mrs. Kendal said, "and thin as a slat. You'll lose your looks. *Then* where will you be?" She got to her feet. "Mag's still in the kitchen. Come on and eat.'

"Thank you, no," he said. "I'm thirty-two and I've got to move on. Just wanted to tell you the fresh good news."

"Are you leaving for the summer?" Mr. Kendal said.

"Yes sir," he said, "when I get myself together."

"To your sister's again?"

"Not at first," he said. "I'll wander a little."

Mrs. Kendal said "To where?"

He smiled again, though entirely dark by now; spread his arms wide and sang it as music—"To my heart's true home."

Mrs. Kendal said "I thought so," and all of them laughed.

He joined them but then he looked to Mr. Kendal. "But you've got all I ever wanted, here." He gestured round with one arm again, a single place in which to gather, people made in the place, made by the place and grown firmly to it.

"I love them," Mr. Kendal said. "Thank you, Forrest."

Through all that, Forrest had shuddered with fear but showed only calm, the only lie he told them till then. And when he left, he had not lied again.

2

HE had hardly vanished when Eva rose from the steps and walked to the door.

As she passed, her father said "Proud of you. *Proud.*"

Her mother said, "I hope you are going to change."

Eva nodded. "Yes ma'm." Then she turned the doorknob and looked back quickly at them all. She settled on her father and said to him "Thank you." Then she opened the door and said "Rena, come help me."

Her mother said "Spoiled."

But Rena stood and followed her.

They were silent in the hall and on the dark stairs, Indian-file; but when Eva had entered their own shared room (the back left room), Rena gently shut the door behind them and said "You've decided" to Eva's back.

"I decided long ago."

"You're leaving," Rena said.

Eva turned, nodding. "Tonight. This minute."

Rena said "Wait—" not meaning to stop her but to hold her an instant longer, for study.

Eva said "No" and took a step forward.

"Go," Rena said. "I just meant *why?*"

Eva touched her sister at the damp elbow-bend. "In a year or so you'll know."

"I'm eighteen months your junior," Rena said. "Eighteen more months won't answer me why you are killing us like this."

"You're glad," Eva said. "Mama'll surely be glad. Kennerly's leaving—"

"Father will die."

"No he won't," Eva said.

"He loves you more than the rest of us together."

Eva thought through that. "Even so," she said, "my life is separate. I'm going to *that*. He's been through worse than this. He'll live. I'll write him."

Rena said again "He'll die."

Eva touched her again, on the back of the neck, and smiled at her fully but stepped on past her to the door and opened it.

"Your grip?" Rena whispered and pointed to a brown leather case on the wardrobe.

Eva shook her head No.

"I've promised," Rena whispered. "Silence till tomorrow. They'll kill me then."

Eva smiled. "No they won't. They'll be glad of news. Now wait in here for as long as you can—till Mother calls us. Try to give me time."

Rena went to the wide bed they'd shared for years and sat on the edge, both hands on her knees. "Will I ever see you again, do you think?"

Eva listened to the sounds from the porch—still safe—then came back across to the bed and touched Rena. On the part in her hair. Then kissed the spot she'd touched. "That's up to Father," she said. "Help him." Then she was gone, no sound on the stair.

3

FROM the foot of the stairs there were two ways out—the front door, the porch, Mother, Father, Brother; and the kitchen where Mag and Sylvie still tinkered. No choice. She aimed herself there and went, still silent, ignoring the pieces of her life on all sides, snags in a river. But she stopped in the kitchen at the corner washstand and lifted one dipper of water from the bucket and drank it dry, from thirst and the fresh need to say one more goodbye in her home. When she lowered the dipper, both women were watching—Mag from the sink where she picked over white beans to soak all night, Sylvie from the midst of the room where she stood like the black greased axle of the whole dark house: Eva's age, one more piece of the permanent furniture of old safe life that Eva now abandoned. She took a step toward Sylvie—the door was beyond her—and said in a low voice, not whispering, "Take anything of mine you want."

"Who going to give it to me?"

"Tell Mama it's yours; tell her Eva said it's yours."

"She'll laugh," Sylvie said.

Eva pointed backward and overhead. "Go up now and take any stitch you want. Rena's waiting there."

Mag turned full around. Her face took the lamplight, darker than her daughter's. "You go," she said. "If you going, go."

Still facing Sylvie, Eva shut her eyes once and forced out the tears that Mag had pressed from her. Then she looked again and cracked her lips to say, "I'll send for you, Sylvie"; but waves of expulsion still pumped from Mag. Silent, Eva scissored one step to the left and was out the door.

Sylvie said "She gone."

"Thank Jesus," Mag said.

Sylvie said "I loved her."

"Me too," Mag said. "But she gone now. She out of my mind. Scratch her out of yours. What she don't know—people worth loving grow on trees in the ditch."

"Yes'm," Sylvie said and watched the shut door where dark air still churned in Eva's empty place.

4

FORREST Mayfield was drowning in gratitude, kneeling above his wife, taking the last of what she freely offered—the sight of her body in morning light laid safely beside him on linen marked only by proofs of their love. Till half an hour ago, at dawn, he had never seen more of her than head and arms—what showed to the world at the limits of her clothes. So he'd loved her because of her face and her kindness, the mysterious rein she accepted from the first on his oldest need—free flight outward from his own strapped and drying heart, that he be permitted after decades of hoarding to choose one willing girl and love her entirely, the remainder of his life. Almost no matter that she love in return, only that she wait and endure his love, his endless thanks; acknowledge them with smiles. Now she was here—by her own will, unforced, still offering (though the room had filled with light) her entire brilliant body, perfect beyond any dream or guess and visibly threaded with the narrow blue channels that pulsed on, warm from their first full juncture.

The memory of that—crown of this past night—was the deepest flood he swam in now, the union and its rising preparations: that she met him as promised at the edge of the field behind her home (had got there before him and the Negro he'd paid to drive the hired buggy six miles to the train—standing, arms at her side, her hands clenched, dark; and when he had said "Your grip? Your clothes?" she had said, "I told you if I came, I'd just be yours. Nothing with me belongs to another soul. This one dress was thrown off by my Aunt Lola"). Then she'd sat beside him silent through the ride to the train, only nodding Yes or No to his muffled questions, and walked silent to the train and mounted one step and then turned to their driver, who carried Forrest's trunk, and said "You know Sylvie" and opened her clenched hand and gave him a five-dollar goldpiece and said, "This is Sylvie's from Eva; to remember Eva." Then once on the train, they had spoken of nothing but the school-year behind them as though they were vanishing now for the summer to separate worlds and would meet in the fall again, master and pupil. And then two hours later, here in Virginia, had accepted their marriage at the trembling hands of an old Clerk of Court and his housekeeper-witness who said to Eva as the clerk took the money, "God above help you." Then had walked with him two hundred yards in the dark to this old hotel and, once concealed by a black pine door from whatever slim dangers the world still held, had welcomed him. Not at once, in a rush, but gravely in her own time, the reins in her ringed hand still firmly clutched. When the porter had lit their lamp and gone and the door was bolted, he had stood in place and looked through the three yards of dimness toward her, by the bed—the light was behind her, she shone at the edges—he had said "I thank you." She had smiled— "For what?" —"For standing here." She had said, "I am where I want to be" and slowly drew the wide green ribbon from her hair and began on the numerous buttons of her dress, looking down at them, till—finished and her undergarments folded—she stood bare and faced him. In her place, he in his. *Simplex munditiis* was all he could think—Horace, "To Pyrrha," *Plain in thy neatness* in Milton's translation which Forrest had thought nearly perfect till now when his own version came: *Simple in courtesy.* Inaccurate for Horace but true for this girl. Then she had said, "I'm sorry to ask it, but can we just rest for a while now?" He had said, "Tired or not, you may call me *Forrest.*" She had nodded, smiling, and entered the fresh bed; and when he had blown out the lamp and stripped, he joined her and lay on the cool edge, separate, till she reached out and took his hand before sleep. By then it was nearly three o'clock. She held him three hours—not turning once, only flinching now and then as she sank one layer deeper toward rest—and he never shut an eye but waited in the dark, appalled by his joyous luck, his hopes; inventing for the thousandth time their life. Then first-day woke her, nacreous light like a fog seeping in; and she turned her head and studied him a long minute, gravely as though he had things still to teach or maybe because she was still half-dreaming; but when she spoke she said "I am rested."

And when he had drawn their long-joined hands from the covers and thanked them with slow dry kisses and had slowly uncovered his body, then hers—all but stopped by the simple plainness of the answer this new sight promised to all his needs—and had knelt above her in the space she offered between smooth knees and bent to the work he had craved since birth, then she'd welcomed him. Had shut her clean eyes and with two hands as powerful as ice in stone had implored him into the still-sealed door of her final solitude, final secret—only looking outward again at the instant of violation when she smiled and drew herself further around him and he said, "You must know: it's as strange to me as you."

All was shared space now, shared news, shared messages freely exchanged of gratitude, trust.

Pitiful fool. He had not seen because he had not looked, had never known he should learn to look—at her true final stronghold, the delicate skull that seemed in their struggle to press forward toward him (another fragile gift) but in which her mind in every cell was howling its terror, loss, loneliness.

Her three hours' sleep had been no rest but a punishment and, worse, a revelation—vision of the ruin she had willed on her home. In the dream that lasted every minute of those hours, she witnessed this—her father, this same night, in their sleeping house, flat on his back beside her sleeping mother in their high black bed, his face tilted slightly forward in the total dark, eyes wide open and straining to pierce the floors and walls between his room and Eva's. When the eyes had succeeded and for whole minutes ransacked the empty side of the bed (beyond sleeping Rena), he shut them and slowly rolled his huge body leftward till he lay full-length on her sleeping mother—who remained asleep as he fastened his open mouth over hers and drew up each shallow breath she exhaled till she lay empty, dead. Then he rose and walked in the dark—no help; he was competent in darkness—to the next bedroom and performed the same smothering theft on Kennerly, who could have refused but—awake, his own wide eyes on his father—accepted the death. Then up the stairs to Rena, who fought him uselessly until her whole head and body vanished under his, not only drained of breath and life but absorbed into him, food for his need. Then he rolled over off Rena's vacant place and lay on his back in the midst of the bed and stared up again—in darkness still, through plaster and lathing—and said "Eva. Now."

Forrest had separated from her and covered them both with sheet and quilt. She was on her back. He was on his left side, lying at her right, facing her profile. Now he must see if speech were still possible, feasible, between them—*words* after what they had finally swapped. He looked on, working for suitable words—it must be a question—till he felt convicted of mooning and said, "What will we do when we stand up from here?"

Eva faced the ceiling but her voice was kind. "You are making the plans."

He lay flat and thought; then beneath the cover, he touched her flank. "We will buy you three dollars' worth of clothes, send my sister a wire to say we're coming."

"Don't tell me," Eva said.

His eyes asked her meaning.

"Make all the plans and lead me through them, but don't tell me first."

He thought that through and decided to smile. "*Made*," he said, "made years ago" and took her hand again and drew it out to kiss before rising.

But, his fingers round her wrist, she pulled her arm inward toward her body.

Thinking she drew back from reluctance or pain, Forrest turned her loose and nodded, smiling, and half-turned to rise.

But her hand strained out and took his shoulder and with more strength, even than before, drew him down and over her body—now cold to his touch—and quickly in. Then with her hands on the back of his head, she fastened his mouth over hers and endured in silence the gift she required.

5

May 12, 1903

My dear Sister,

I am sending this letter care of Kate Spencer in the hope she can get it safe to your hands. If so, you will know when you finish this sentence that I am well and happy as I dreamed. I only hope you have not suffered for me or that, if you have, the cloud is past and that when you read the following description you will think whatever you have suffered worth the pain and can live in the trust of someday having what I have now.

I will not write down all the story of the night I last saw you. This letter may yet fall into cruel hands and several more of those who helped us on might suffer for their kindness. Suffice to say that within three hours of kissing you goodbye, Mr. Mayfield and I were husband and wife, joined forever in that waiting bower of trust and joy made for us by our long delayed union. For the same reason I have just expressed, I cannot here answer in any detail the main question you put to me weeks ago; but a short answer is—Yes, two become one and are better for it.

I can tell you more of that if and when we meet. Surely there is not any real "if" between us—not with you, I know; but please tell me quickly

*that Father and Mother and Kennerly have healed and wish us well in the
life we needed, and hope to see us as we do them. Tell me that, Rena—
that my hopes are met by loving hopes at home. I have prayed each hour
that they be so met. I have not yet thought of another answer or another
prayer and will not until you have set me right or joyously confirmed my
only dream that is still unfulfilled.*

*So write by return of post, no fail—if only the one word Yes or No.
The address below is care of Forrest's sister; and when I have seen the
word "safe" from your hand, I will tell you the rest of how I live through
these first happy days.*

*You and everyone there are in my thoughts and will always be. Please
tell them that, whatever the result.*

Your loving sister,
Eva Mayfield

Care Mrs. James Shorter
Bracey, Virginia

May 12, 1903

Dear Thorne,
   *I am alive, as you will see by this, and only wish that I had some
surety the news would come as a pleasure to you. It has been the only blot
on my recent days—the thought that you and your dear mother and two or
three more of my colleagues at the Academy might have put me down in
your books as a liar, a cheat, a traitor to friendship and solemn duty.*

   *The fact that my hand writes such words here will be sign enough that
the words themselves are only bare counters for the doubts I've had, the
moments of anguish, all of which come to me in the hard form of pictures—
your mother's head shaking side to side at me, No; or your own eyes calm
above slow lips opening to say "Forrest, leave us." Am I piercing the veil of
distance, seeing truth? Or only, as so often, vainly flailing myself? You can
answer me that, dear friend of the past, much hoped-for still.*

   *But in the event there is no answer yet—that you and yours have
waited in friendship through slander and rumor for mine and Eva's facts—
here they are, set down with God as my witness. You may tell them to any
man who claims to know different; he knows a lie.*

   *I have loved her for the best part of two years now, since she entered
my classes two falls ago. Your question will be Why? And my truthful
answer, an answer I have searched and tested for months, is "I do not
know." You have seen her, known her far longer than me—all her life; I
have chiefly envied your memories of her in simpler childhood—so I need
not offer descriptions of her loveliness. I have known, as you have, grander
beauties who entered rooms with their armaments blazing or drew at me
like great magnets in the earth—and left me less moved than a toddling*

child. Eva filled—from the moment I saw her, it seems—every valley in me and bore in herself the press of every height. No one has done that before for me, ever—even my mother, despite her early death from the strain to be all in all for my sister and me after Father's leaving—and it came to seem as the months raced on and no error was made, no flaw revealed, that no one would ever do it again, that if I should scorn this offered chance, there would never come another; and I should be sentenced (self-sentenced as always) to the gradual parching of solitude, concealment, self-contemplation, which I'd felt already at the rims of my heart. And of which I told you.

So in April I seized at the chance, and won. Did you notice at all? How can you not have? The day we took the two classes to The Springs, after the meal when everyone else had gone off to change in the woods before bathing, she and I found ourselves—with no prior intent, I gravely believe—alone together in the ruined springhouse. We were separated by all the trapped air, by the clogged springs at our feet, by the cold half-dark; but we drew at one another like moons at the full. Thorne, I did not touch her—a solemn oath. I said "Eva Kendal." She said "Yes sir." I said, "May we live together all our lives, beginning now?" and she said "Yes sir." I could not touch her—we heard the sound of someone approaching—I did not even move a step closer toward her. We had sealed our lives at four yards' distance—and none the less indissolubly for that, is my strongest prayer. Then you stepped in, having worried at our absence and come to see. But what did you see? Till that hour, I had opened my heart to you fully—no secret held back, no hunger not stated—yet, though you stood a moment in the bright doorway, staring, you never spoke a word to me of question or caution in those few ensuing weeks. Thorne, tell me that also—is there some imperfection in our bond (mine and Eva's) that to you it appeared transparent as day, as the water of those springs we loomed above (had we bent, as perhaps we should have, to clean them)?

And in those weeks, of April and May, we barely came closer than we stood that moment with you as apex to the triad we formed. Nor said much more than "Remember?" —"Yes." Till the week of our leaving when, with no word to Eva, I made what minimum of plans were required for transport and marriage, for ending my work and withdrawing those roots of devotion and thanks I had sunk in the ground of your home, Thorne. Withdrawn never—transplanted, I hope. And then two days in advance of the absolute end of my duties—all my examinations given, hers all taken—I asked her to see me at the end of the day. She came and stood before my desk—I sat, I remember now—and said "Are you tired?" She said "Of what?" and her face gathered in on itself in fear. I said "Of work." "Oh," she said, "Yes. I thought you meant our plan." Till then I had not known she saw it as a plan, that we'd worked in silence to a single end. So in two minutes more I told her the plan and asked did it suit her, and she said "Yes sir." I said, "Could you live if your family disowns you?" She said, "Mr. Mayfield, I am sixteen years old"—meaning, I think, that she knew her own mind. So I told her again the place and time and signal, and she nodded unsmilingly and turned to go. She had got within two, three steps of the door—it was open; people passed in the hall every second—but I said to her, "Eva, why are you doing this?" She waited and met my face straight on and said, "Mr. Mayfield, I don't know that. I only know we promised, and I'm keeping to the promise if you want me to." The room was darkening, a cloudy day; but she also faced the windows and had never, in all my looking, seemed so needed, as urgent as the silent air I drew. Nor had her lean face, her wideset eyes that can hold on me whole long minutes, never shutting, seemed so perfectly preserved from error, from the chance of speaking either lie or delusion or destructive innocence. So I said, "I do. I want you to keep it." And she nodded and left; and I didn't see her till two nights later when she kept it, firmly.

And now we are here at my sister Hattie's, discovering each hour the degree of accuracy in our wager—miraculous luck. I am borne up, Thorne; there are arms beneath me where before—thirty years—there was vacancy, a shaft into dark single death.

Forgive me then. And beg your mother to believe the truth—that I never defiled the trust of her house, that my one room there was honored to the end. Believe—please, both of you—that all I have done was done from long and desperate need but also from careful study of the sustenance offered to that need: study of the danger of my crushing that food in the act of acceptance, of consuming it utterly. That I have hurt the present feelings and the memories of people who had trusted me fully, I bear as my heaviest burden. That I meant them permanent wounds, even harm, I passionately deny. Who, in the world, is harmed by the troth of two single souls unbound to others? Who would deny them their impulse to join? Who could not see that, far from diminished, the lives of our friends and families, perhaps of the world, stand to be enforced at their very foundations by the simple news that Eva and I are sworn to love?

And speak to me soon. When I know if you've so much as read on to here, if you care to know present and future as well as past, then I'll write again with word of both. Till then, for the past at least, loving thanks. But I will not believe Time suffers herself to be broken in three. She is whole and extends her whole self always—then, now, then. Thorne, you are found in all my time—your name, the sight of your generous face, your low kind voice.

In strong hope,
Forrest Mayfield

May 15, 1903

Dear Eva,

I got your letter and nobody but me has seen it or knows about it but Kate who'll be quiet, and nobody will. You ask me to say whether we have all healed and wish you well and want to see you. You always saw more than I ever could in Mother and Father, so I'll let you get those answers yourself by direct application. I've done enough, Eva—almost all I contracted for—and I'm relishing the peace now.

But I will tell you what happened the rest of the evening you left. You may not need any other answers. I waited in our room and read fifteen chapters of First Corinthians before they sent Kennerly upstairs to get us. He said "Where is Eva?" and I said, "Gone, with Mr. Mayfield, for good"; and he said "Thank Jesus." Then he sat in the rocker while I finished chapter sixteen; and then he said, "What do we do now, Rena?" (and him the one with the job and the life—he has already gone to it). I said, "I have promised to lie till morning, so you must too" and he agreed.

And we honestly tried. When Mother came up half an hour later, we were both sitting reading; and when she asked for you, he said you had gone up to Kate Spencer's house to borrow something. She took that, long enough to climb back down and tell it to Father; but in thirty more minutes—and no sign of you; we were back on the porch—he stood up and went in and got his hat and Mother said, "Where in the world are you aimed?" and he said "To the Spencers." So we sat through that—Mother talking every second—and then when we heard Father coming back alone, just his feet on the walk, I thought in my heart, "I'm about to kill him." But I waited and he came up and stopped at my feet—I was on the steps—and, far as I could see in the dark, sought my eyes and said, "Rena, I don't intend to harm you." I said "Yes sir." And he said "Is she gone?" I said "Yes sir." Mother said "With Forrest?" and I said "Yes." Everybody was quiet. Nobody moved for quite some time. Then Mother got up and kissed Kennerly and me and went in to bed, not a word to a soul. Then Father went in and, though I never saw him light a lamp, undressed and went to bed, I guess. The other thing he could have done was sit all night in the dark and study (we heard him and Mother saying two or three things, the noise not the words; but their voices were calm and they quickly stopped). Then we went in ourselves and closed the doors—they had left it to us, first time in our lives—and slept through till morning.

Breakfast went as usual till toward the end when Sylvie was passing the last plate of biscuits, and Father told her to get Mag and come in. So the two of them came; and when they were standing by the sideboard, he said, "There is one new rule; everybody please obey—we are going to give her a rest in our minds. Won't mention her name, speak of her for a while." Everybody nodded and Mother shed a tear. And that same night we went to the commencement. Your name was called.

Since then most everything has gone as planned. Brother left for his job and writes that he hates it but we knew that. Father works hard. Mother has not felt well, but it's already hot here. I am loving the weather, and bed is cooler with just me in it. I will write again if anything happens.

> *Your sister,*
> *Rena Kendal*

May 16, 1903

Dear Forrest,

I accept with thanks your word to Mother and me that you did not abuse our home.

To the rest of what you offer and ask, I can only say that—as ever—you are begging for both the cake and its consumption. You have indeed gone toward something—its present name is Eva. You have also gone from a number of things, whose names are trust and—more necessary to life—the world's belief that love is a rational flame, consuming only what offers itself precisely as fuel, not the innocent or unwilling combustibles which I accuse you of igniting: Eva's mother and father, her sister, me.

Yet not I but the Time of which you speak will be your judge, and you err in referring to Time as she. Any child you taught two months of Latin will know Time is neuter. And neuter Time in its future aspect will uncover—in your face, your heart, and in those of your chosen—the true origin, intent, the end of your act; and any sane sighted man will be easily able to read off the news: sentence or praise. He need only be present, and that I will not be.

> *Believe me,*
> *Thorne Bradley*

May 17, 1903

Dear Mother and Father,

I am married to Forrest Mayfield, and at present we are living with his sister in Bracey, Virginia. She is a recent widow with two children and is the one who raised Forrest when his own mother died, so we will be staying on here through the summer at least till Forrest can get a post at a school.

Out of all that I might want to tell you or you might ask, let me say five things—

What we did was as much my wish as his. I was never forced or even led but walked with him, side by side to now.

My wish did not come out of any weakness in my gratitude to you but out of my needing what I knew you'd forbid.

I am not now, and have never been, expecting a child.
I am happy.
I am hoping, as strongly as for all but our happiness here, that you can find it in your heart to wish us well; to say you have forgotten the few days of shock, and that you can entertain at least the memory of my face and word of my name.
If you have a kind answer to that last thing, may I hear it soon?

Your daughter,
Eva Kendal Mayfield

Care Mrs. James Shorter
Bracey, Virginia

October 5, 1903

Eva,
Flora writing this for me. Me and her out here taking in the fair and thinking we would send you this postal with the news. We won it throwing balls. No news but to say everything here the same. Don't answer me back. You know my mama.

Goodbye again from
Sylvie

November 23, 1903

Dear Mrs. Mayfield,
I am Undine Phillips, Mrs. Walker Phillips; and I write this on behalf of your brother Kennerly, who has roomed here with me since late in the spring. I write in pain and oddly to a stranger, but I've thought and prayed and believe it my duty to say this much.
Your letters to your brother have arrived here since July, but he has not received them. I have laid them each time on the front-hall table where I lay all the mail, and he has not touched them. In July when your first had waited three days and he had walked past, I remarked the fact to your brother who said it was not for him. I said that it bore his name and address; but he said nonetheless he could not take letters from Bracey, Virginia. As others have come, I have laid them out; and they too have been refused.
So I've taken the liberty of keeping them safe in the table drawer, with the thought he would change. I admire him so highly; he is such a fine gentleman, so helpful to me. But this afternoon when he saw your latest, he came straight to me on the backporch and said would I kindly return it to you with no message. I said I could not consider throwing myself into such a private matter unless he explained; he had never ex-

plained. He said you were his sister and offended his parents by early marriage. I knew of his devotion to your parents.

Since I offended my own mother briefly by marrying for love—and had a grand life till he died last year, not an hour's regret—I accepted the sad task. Hence these lines.

I enclose all the letters that have reached my house—three, unopened—and I take the further liberty of going beyond my commission and adding a message, one which I trust your brother will come to himself in time: that you and Mr. Mayfield know long years of unbroken love and care. You have after all only followed Christ's command—cleave then and prosper.

Truly yours,
Undine Phillips

DECEMBER 1903

HATT Shorter stood at the foot of the bed on which Eva had lain for the past three hours, shoes on, fully dressed, face up, eyes closed (at the sound of the noon train, she'd put on her thin coat and walked to the post office; waited half an hour, then walked back in silence and come straight here). Hatt said "No word?"

Eva shook her head No, not looking up.

So Hatt moved round and sat at the end by Eva's feet and touched her far ankle. "May I speak now?—you noticed I've held off."

Eva said "Yes" and sat up enough to prop herself and look Hatt in the face—a long face, smooth for its age and the work it had volunteered to bear in thirty-six years or had not refused.

Hatt smiled as best she could, her hand in reflex flying up to cover the gaps in her teeth. "I've stood by and watched for eight months now; and was glad to do so, glad if that was a help. *I* know what you've been through; and can make a good guess at what's still waiting for you—tearing up every root the way you done, leaving your mother and coming off here in the night with a stranger to live with strangers (two of them, loud boys), and your own people punishing you with silence, and Forrest in his silliness giving you this child." Hatt waited a moment, long enough to stare at her own flat belly and draw a little wind into her own empty spaces. "It was *happiness*, Eva—not silliness. Believe him in that much. And whether he took it from you or whoever—some sow in the road—it was past time he got it. Believe *me* in that. From the day our mother died when he was twelve till the day him and you stood yonder in my door, I never knew Forrest to look less than hungry—for what *I* couldn't give him, God knew, I trust, with my own life sucking hard at me, every pap on my body (and I've felt covered, Eva; pardon me for truth)—but that day in May and many days since, he has looked like some boy fed in Heaven; and whether you are actually his nourishment or not, he thinks you are. He has told me so, many times in private; and I won't lie to you—it comes hard to me to know that the one boy I really failed to love enough has found love and brought it up under my nose for me to smell in my own destitution. But the whole thing has been far harder on you. I've granted you that and I've tried to guess at little ways to help you, and you've thanked us all and carried on kindly; but Eva, you're a soul in misery—am I wrong?"

"No," Eva said.

"It's your mother, isn't it?—no word since leaving her?"

"I never loved my mother," Eva said.

Hatt waited again and, this time, studied Eva. "That has got to be a lie, always is."

Eva nodded. "Till now. I hated her till now."

"What's different now?"

"That's what I don't know. Nobody will tell me."

Hatt said, "What's the one thing you want to do?"

"To hear them say 'Come.' "

"To you and him both or just to you?"

Eva waited. "Either one."

Hatt said, "That is what I was waiting to hear. Listen, Eva—*I know*—they are not going to ask you. And in your condition you can't go alone. Make Forrest take you."

"My people wouldn't have us."

"Are they human beings?"

"Yes."

"Then send them a wire and say you and Forrest are coming for Christmas on such and such train and to meet you please since your health is poor."

"What if they refuse?"

"Then go to a hotel and sit two days—they'll know you're there—and if they still refuse, come back to me. You'll have your answer."

Eva said, "If it's that—the answer you mentioned—I'm not sure I could live on with that."

"Sure you could," Hatt said. "People don't just die. Has it ever dawned on you what a strange thing it is that so few people ever die broken-hearted? They'll moan eighty years but they won't end their pain."

"No," Eva said. "I never thought that."

Hatt said, "You work it out sometime. It's too hard for me." She smiled, leaned over; laid an ear to Eva's belly and rose, smiling wider. "Wait till *he's* here though. Don't worry him now—a strong boy's heart if I ever heard one."

Eva said, "You were serious?—about me going home?"

"Yes," Hatt said, "but the both of you got to go, not one."

"Then will you tell Forrest?"

"No."

"He obeys you, Hatt."

"But it's you he loves. You got to make him do it."

Eva pushed back against her pillow silently until she lay flat-out again. She shut her eyes and said, "Let me just think now. This all matters."

Hatt touched the extended ankle once more, cold through its stocking. She reached behind her and took the blundering apprentice afghan Eva had knitted for Forrest's birthday and spread it across her. Then she stood and went to the door and looked back.

Eva's eyes were still shut, but her brow and the ridges of her cheeks worked intensely.

From the porch came the shuffling of the boys home from school.

Hatt said, "You think. You're the one here with sense. Only one in this place, in all these hills." Her own face was fierce, seen by no one.

2

She had stayed on upstairs for the rest of the day. Hatt had shamed the boys and sent them out into drizzling cold to hunt a Christmas tree; and then they played—a distant muffled din. And when Forrest had returned at five and passed a few inaudible sentences with Hatt and climbed up to Eva, she had said little more than the simplest answers to his simple questions—her head? the baby's movements? would she feel up to joining a tree-decorating in the front room after supper? Her answers had been No.

So Forrest had brought her a supper-tray (by now she was in her gown, in bed) and watched her eat it, then had gone down and eaten with Hatt and the boys and helped them awhile with the Christmas tree, then had climbed back up to sit at his table near the foot of the bed and mark a set of papers on Cicero.

He sat as always, sideways to Eva. ("Facing you," he'd said, "I'd just see you; and with my back turned, I'd exhaust myself looking round to check." "Check for what?" she'd said—this was months before—and he'd said "That you're there" and had quoted her something new he'd found: St. Augustine, "*Volo ut sis,*" *I want you to be*. She'd said "I be" and he'd settled for that, never asking "For whom?") And in her present misery, her wish was to turn her face to the wall and sink to oblivion, instant and long. But the light of his lamp was warmer than the dying stove; and falling on his profile, it offered her a clear chance to comprehend. She felt that, actually said to herself, "Why is he in this room? Why do I stay?" For months she had known the answer to the first, his answer at least—that she filled his life—and watching him now, she knew he believed himself and would always. Change or deceit had less chance in his face than in Jesus'.

What was unknown still was her own full reply—could she bear his presence? Could she go on doing this undoubted service, unending charity, for a smiling stranger? He was strange to Eva. Not mysterious or threatening, never likely to surprise, but simply and terribly strange through *not pertaining* to her. In all these months of stifling nearness—all the happy unions of bodies; she knew they were happy, could think of them calmly: their beautiful competence in one shared action—her heart had never accepted his offer; the offer he had made in the springhouse last April, to which she had spoken a ready Yes: *May we live together, beginning now?* Some days her answer was a flat No that slammed in on her like a runaway cart or that rose like sudden sour cud in her throat and demanded spitting. Always in direct reply to his presence, the looks of unassuaged gratitude he would still fasten on her. And always till now she had swallowed the answer, maintained silence, but looking away at whatever was handy (which was desperately little in this house like a robbed ship with skeleton crew; Hatt had stripped it the day of her husband's death of all that might remind her of him, till the healing of time—every picture or book that had borne his breath: even her sons in the scrubbings she gave them, the square clothes she sewed, were having their father's shapes leeched from their own in the general erasure).

Forrest looked up now from his work and faced her.

The No rose. She held it by smiling, lips shut.

"Answer quick," he said, "—the one thing you want most, that anyone could give you."

Eva no longer answered anything quickly; there were choices of answers, all true and contradictory. The one that came first now was "Stand up from here, dress, vanish in the night." But a question followed in her silent head—"Vanish to where?" No answer yet.

"Cheating," he said and smiled. "Tell me. Now."

She said "To die."

He stared on a moment, then adjusted the lamp for a little more light, then began to stand.

"No. Stay," she said.

He stayed but he said, "I am not meant to stay. I am meant to help you."

She nodded but held out a hand, palm toward him. "Help me there," she said.

Then they waited, studying their helpless faces, for actual minutes.

He said "Please answer."

She said, "I am not as old as I thought. Get me word from my home please."

He nodded but said what he'd never said before in the face of any question—"How? Tell me and I will."

She said, "Wire them tomorrow and say that we're coming when school lets out and will stay all Christmas."

Forrest said "No."

"You said you would."

He nodded. "I lied. No I was wrong. I will not do anything to make you unhappy."

"You have brought me here." She thought she meant this room, and she gestured slowly round it; but then she knew she meant this house, town, his presence.

"You told me you were old enough to know your mind, and you claimed you wanted to be with me. I have to be here."

"Why?" Eva said.

"Because, but for you and that baby growing, Hatt is what I have. Has been for years. She's destitute now as I was once."

"She's got those boys."

"Those boys don't make money."

Eva said, "Forrest, you are lying to us both. You are here in this house, like a whale's dark belly, because you're afraid."

"Of what?" he said. He could smile a little.

"Of asking to go elsewhere to work and meeting refusal because of me."

"That may be," he said. "May partly be."

"You have got to *test* me, Forrest," she said.

"I've never stopped," he said. "You pass each one."

"You are speaking of love again. I'm not."

"Then what?" he said.

"The world. Strangers. I think I am strong, but how can I know?"

"You are," he said.

"Oh for you," she said. "I am speaking of me."

"You are," he said. "And you know that the question is—am I?"

"We can try together," Eva said. "Against my father." Till then she had not blamed her father or seen him as the foe.

"We'd lose," Forrest said. "*You'd* win, I know, but the two of us would lose. Then where would I be?"

"Back at the start, alone but for Hatt."

"Correct," he said, the last question answered. He was bare to her now as a stove-in turtle. He looked down from her so as not to ask mercy.

But she gave it—or tried. "Tell me now please. I need to know."

He nodded and began to deliver it slowly but still to the floor in a low voice flatter than his normal tone, determined to spare her unfair demands. "My father and Hatt's was some sort of scoundrel. Drink, women—what? I never really knew. I was too young to ask when Mother died; and if Hatt knows, it's one more kindness she's done me—to keep it hid. It must have had something to do, though, with appetite. My own memories of him are very dim—I was five when he vanished the final time—but they all represent some form of famine. Anyhow when he'd left—"

"Wait please," Eva said. "Explain the famine."

He looked up quickly to test her seriousness, then down again. "This is my main memory. However he acted in his spare time, he seemed to work hard on the days of the week. And he'd spend Sundays with us. I remember several Sundays—every one, it seems, but surely just a few; maybe no more than one. But that one Sunday then, summer and hot, I was laid out on my little narrow bed in the cubicle I had at the top of the house; and it was barely light. He came in silent in a cotton nightshirt with plumcolored stripes and lay down on me; I was stretched on my back. Laid his whole weight on me—a tall broad man. Expected me to bear it. Well, I did and it woke me—I had not heard his footsteps—and when I looked up for the first sight that day of what the world offered, there were my father's eyes staring down at me, four inches from mine. Could he see from that close? I could and I looked; and that's my memory—the neediest eyes I've seen, asking me. I waited still—"

"Asking what?" Eva said, the dream of her wedding night long buried in her, far beyond memory.

He looked up and faced her fully. "Tell *me*. I'm the one must know."

She thought awhile, taking Forrest's offered face as text; then she shook her head. "Tell on please," she said.

"About him?"

"Yes."

"There's nothing else. Nothing strange as that."

"That was enough."

"Plenty," Forrest said. "Then in what few other memories I have, I turn round from staring out at the road or look up from playing and catch those same eyes fastened on me, never on Hatt."

"Why?" Eva said.

"I've wondered. I guess she was too old by then. He knew she was hopeless, could never save him. She was nine when he left. So she knows more than me but I've never asked. Sometimes she tells little pieces though. She remembers him leaving. I don't at all—why? I lived right there. But Hatt says—or *said*; she told me just once long years ago—that he left in the night with everything he owned which was two books, two shirts, his pants. And when Mother woke there was just a note laid on the washstand beside her. She'd always slept lightly—a leaf could wake her—but she missed his leaving."

Eva said "The note?"

"Hatt saw it right before Mother burned it—*Gone. Tell the children I kissed them. Also you. With thanks, Robinson Mayfield.*"

"Any news after that?" Eva said.

"Not a piece—that got through to us anyhow. Mother may have known every step he trod, but she kept it to herself through her seven years alone. And took it with her."

"Leaving you what?" Eva said.

"Very little. Hatt thinks I loved our mother. I did, I guess—I was lost when she died—but I knew then and since that I'd chosen Father; and he'd have loved me if he'd had a chance. Hatt may not remember or may say she can't; but when Mother died and she came to wake me and say we were alone, the first thing I said was 'Now he'll come back.' And in fact our only living relative wrote a letter in the effort to hunt him but he'd vanished successfully. He wanted to. That has been the hard thing in my life—thinking of that: that after coming to me and begging for God knows what as food and getting no gift, then he wanted to go. Go away from us, three people with names which he meant to forget. Compared to that, Mother's death was easy and Hatt's quick marriage—she married at sixteen, three weeks after Mother died; the first man that asked her: James Shorter, a fool. Everything else was easy. And now even that is fading for me. I trust you know why."

She nodded. "Thank you."

"*You*," he said. He was aware that, through all that last, he had gone on facing her. It occurred to him now to look away again before proceeding, though he also thought clearly, "I am no claim on her, not this face and eyes. Have never been on anyone." But as he gazed downward, he saw Eva move.

Not her whole body. Not even her arms. Her perfect hands rose from the cover above her flanks and waited steady in the air, open for him.

Forrest was held by the doctor's ban; but she waited still, open still. No one had ever asked him before for a thing that mattered, except his drowning father. Now this girl.

She was smiling, to be where she was and with him. For now at least.

He went. And slowly, carefully found that the ban was as useless to her as himself. Useless and needless. Every entrance was free; every channel conductive to the center of joy that had waited in darkness but blossomed enormous and rank in their sight now. So, bare in the cold, oiled with their sweat, they strove all night round their swelling child who rocked with their laughter. Or they slept at intervals to wake to themselves. Once he, once her. Their lovely self, young and savable. Equal in gifts. Christmas of the heart.

MARCH 1904

Blood poured from Eva.

It was all he could see as he entered the room—called by a Negro sent by Hatt to the school, and his own heart near rupture from the two-mile run in freezing rain.

Her legs up and spread, gown bunched round her waist, and steady blood pouring from the wide slack wound.

"*Mine*," Forrest thought. "Made by me." Then he thought "Again," with no sane cause; and seized in both hands the frame of the doorway to hold himself up, to hold back from fleeing the room filled with people like spokes round the hub of Eva dying. Hatt at the washstand bathing a silent child. Dr. Moser with his dirty mustache, in his shirtsleeves, blood to his elbows—silent above Eva, his hands at the wound. Pauline, the Negro midwife, at the bedhead, a bottle of ether and a rag in her hands.

Eva strained up and saw him. She had shrunk, since he left her four hours ago, to a dry death's head—skin like a chalky lacquer on her skull. Not dry but draining, rushing to empty. Her lips said "Come." Her hands were hid in her hair and did not move.

He went through the others toward her. Pauline drew back. No one else looked up from the urgent work. No one spoke. He could not.

Eva spoke. Her voice was appallingly intact as though every other part could leave but her voice remain. Her hands stayed in her hair; but her face and eyes found him and she said, "It was nobody's fault, remember. Mine if anybody's. Never yours, Forrest."

He again said "Thank you."

Dr. Moser snorted through his nose and looked up as if Forrest—convicted, last appeal exhausted—had been blessed by a doting lying mother.

Forrest said "Are you hurting?"

"Yes. Dying."

They looked to the doctor. He did not deny her.

Eva said "*You* stay."

"I'll stay," he said. She had never told him of her grandmother's death, her grandfather's suicide; and so he believed she spoke of the present, that he not leave the room. He realized the sizable distance between them. He was still on his feet, had not yet so much as knelt at her side. He took off his overcoat and dropped it behind him; then moved to kneel, wondering where to find and hold her hand.

Dr. Moser said, "No. Get out of here. Quick."

Forrest looked.

The blood on the doctor's hand was dark, browning, dry.

Eva's eyes had sunk and shut. Every tooth was plain through the skin of her lips, tight as if blown by a monstrous wind. The room was filling with a high steady sound—some durable thread being spun through her nose, which mounted round him, excluding air.

Forrest left, for his life.

2

For thirty minutes he sat in the kitchen in a black straight chair with a cardboard seat, his arms extended on the table before him among the remains of interrupted breakfast, his own eyes shut. In all that time, aside from shallow breaths, he moved once. The fingers of his left hand had come down beside a cold half biscuit; and he'd raised that and chewed till the small dry bite swelled and galled on his tongue, the mouth of his gullet—alive from his spit and an agent of punishment. He spat it in the same hand and flung it to the floor and scrubbed the hand dry on his rough serge trousers, still wet from the run. Otherwise he existed only in his head—in a square space, a room two inches wide behind his eyes— where over and over he spoke a silent phrase: *I kill what I touch.* Every other thought was a variant of that—that if he had failed this second time, he could not try again but must do the world the grace of withdrawal, though again he did not think of death: withdrawal from human intimacy. And that in itself, a return to solitude, seemed now the least of his causes to grieve—the world lived alone, his world at least. In thirty years of steady searching, he had never observed a calm contingency—two human beings in a single space as easy as dogs, as mutually helpful—but only the mute or howling lonely: his father wandering perhaps to this day, his mother dissolving in soaked earth a mile from where he sat (a mile from Eva's body), his sister Hatt, the Kendals from whom he had stolen the last bond that held them in harness.

He was interrupted once by black Pauline coming for the black iron kettle that had groaned on the stove behind his wait. He had seen her movements; but he did not know her—she never faced him squarely, volunteered nothing but the surface of her act: *This kettle is boiling; I am taking it somewhere where water is used.* So he asked her nothing and waited on for the doctor or Hatt or a voice through walls and floors to call him. Call what?—*Come?* or *Go? Go farther, forever?*

It was Hatt who came, and to end the wait. When he saw her face, he knew it held news—held news back from flooding, like a wall.

She shut the door behind her, pressed against it a moment; then went to the stove and moved the second kettle, still steaming, to the back. Then she came to the table and stood above him. "What's his name?" she said.

He shook his head, baffled.

"The boy, your boy."

At first he thought he could not remember, then recalled that they had never decided. Eva had said, "I'll make you a bargain—a boy, you name it; a girl, I do." But he had said, "No both of us, when we see what we get." He searched Hatt's face—still a holding wall, blank—so he said, "We were going to name it together."

"It's a him," Hatt said. "Then he'll have to wait for Eva to speak again."

Thirty-three years—he could still not fathom Hatt's tone or purpose. For all he could read in her face or voice, she might be referring to an Eva resurrected on Judgment Day to name a nameless boy. "When will that be?" he said.

She took the chair opposite. "Once she has slept."

"She's asleep?"

"Yes," she said.

"You are telling me Eva is alive?" he said.

Hatt nodded, pointed behind her upward. "When I came down, she was. Her and the boy both." She stood but as though against enormous weight, the exhaustion of one more day half-done. "I got to go back." She went to the stand beside the stove, raised a dipper of water, took a long drink and attempted to swallow but was forced to bend to the low slop-pail and spit it there with a noise she'd have given a week of her life to strangle down. A little low howl. Then she rose and was facing the mantel clock, loudly ticking noon. "Are you hungry?" she said.

Forrest said "No."

"Thank Jesus," Hatt said.

3

By four o'clock the rain had stopped; but the yard and the bare trees were locked in ice, and full dark was shutting down like a lid. Forrest had stayed out the whole four hours in his one school suit, no overcoat—splitting pine quarters into sodden kindling with a dulling axe and stacking it beside him till now there was more than enough to last till spring, into early May: warmth, leafshade. He could not believe these trees overhead would leaf again; that they would not refuse and stand in their skeletons, black through summer. He had spoken, again, once in the time—to meet Hatt's boys as they slogged up from school and send them on to the Palmers' for supper and maybe the night. Whitby, the younger, had said "Is she live?" and Forrest had said, "She was at noon. I am waiting to know"; and they had obeyed and wandered on. Then he'd begun again chopping with his back to the upstairs window as before—Eva's room—and listened for nothing but a knuckle rattling on the loose pane to tell him.

It came at four and though he was in the midst of a swing, the cry of the wood, it took Hatt only two slight taps to call him. He picked up the split halves and stacked them and turned.

Hatt beckoned with her whole hand. Her face was obscured; she stood far back and the window was misted.

Forrest drew out his watch and checked the time. Then he wiped the blood of his hands on his trousers.

4

Hatt met Forrest at the top of the stairs. "She is asking for you." She pointed behind her—the open door; the hum of desperate waiting poured through it.

"The doctor's gone?"

"Downstairs in the kitchen. Pauline's making coffee. He wants to see you too, when Eva's done."

"Is she all right?" Forrest also pointed.

"Oh no," Hatt said. She lowered to a whisper. "She is walking the line. Which is why I called you—doctor agreed. She may have wishes. Messages. Go."

He had held the dark pine stair-rail through that. Now he used it as a sling to force him up and on through the door. He stopped by Eva's head, an empty chair there on which he sat.

Her hands were still hid, beneath the cover now; and her face was in danger at least as grave as when he'd last left her. But though she was past spending energy to smile, her eyes at once knew him—crouched a little farther in, then fixed on his face. "Don't contradict me. I am not strong enough to help you now, but I want to know in case I die; so name the boy."

He thought five seconds. "Robinson," he said.

She nodded. "Why?"

"My father," he said.

"All right," she said. She did not say the name. "Now listen again. When I go to sleep or die or whatever, you write a letter to my mother please. My *mother*, no one else. And tell her what's happened—whatever that is by the time you post it—and tell her if this child had been a girl, I'd have named it for her. You'd have let me, wouldn't you?"

"You know I would. We could do it now, name him Robinson Watson Mayfield. Wasn't that her name?"

Eva shook her head. "She wouldn't want that. Don't cross me please."

Forrest smiled—"I won't"—and bent to kiss the spot on the cover which seemed to be her hand. Right hand.

"Have you seen him?" she said.

"Not really," he said. "I've been waiting for you."

"You feed him," she said. Her face was no fiercer than usual.

Forrest looked behind him to the wicker cradle pushed near to the stove. "They've fed him; rest easy. Pauline and Hatt."

"They're feeding him off of *me*," she said.

"Dr. Moser's here, drinking coffee downstairs. What they've done was his orders."

"You too," Eva said. "All of you feeding this man off me till I'm brought to here, facing death, young as I am. I am not ready. Hold him off."

He had thought she spoke of their sleeping son, and he said "All right." But she did not know or did not remember that she had a son. It was Forrest's father who roamed her weakness, now and as she slept and for days to come. Whenever he turned in his flight to face her or came to this bed to press her and beg, he wore the face of her own lost father and spoke in his voice—"Eva. Now."

5

March 11, 1904

Dear Mrs. Kendal,

Eva is near death. Forgive me for saying it so harshly first; but I do it, as I'll alter my hand on the cover, in the sole hope of telling you before you consign this paper to flames, unread. And in further hope of reviving the care of her parents and kin for one who has only intended them kindness.

This morning she bore your first grandson, in strong good health; but suffered the issue of so much blood as to leave her weakened most danger-ously for the trials of fever which lurk for her now. Her perfect mind is already assaulted; but as I spoke with her an hour ago, she made two wishes entirely plain—that I name our son now in case of her death (so she know his name—it is Robinson, my father's) and that I write you at once and tell you this news and add her words: if this first child had been a girl, Eva herself would have named it for you. And with my full consent.

Mrs. Kendal, I have never told you and Mr. Kendal I was sorry; and I do not believe that Eva has. Will you understand that at first—in May and in all the months till now—I did not think I was; and neither did Eva if I read her aright. But now I am. And if Eva were strong enough to write, I am almost sure she would sign this with me. Isn't that indeed the message she sends you as reported above?

Beyond saying that, I will end for now, having made no drafts on your time or mercy—only fulfilled my promise to one in danger and voiced my own delayed regret to your family, that I now know myself to have injured. And pledged my intent to engage in repair of all my damage if life now will only give me the chance.

Faithfully yours,
Forrest Mayfield

Care Mrs. James Shorter
Bracey, Virginia

March 24, 1904

Dear Forrest,

I do not know that Eva is alive; but if so, I trust you to use this wisely It is heavy news and could press her gravely if she herself has not already gone.

Your letter to my wife, with Eva's message, arrived on the 14th. Our Sylvie always goes for the mail after I have left home; so I did not see it, and my wife did not tell me that night or the next day. She did not tell another soul. But on the 16th at ten in the morning, having already finished a dress for Rena and laid it on the bed in Rena's room and written a letter of calm news to Kennerly (no mention of Eva), she went to the kitchen and with Mag standing not six feet away, preparing dinner, she mixed a strong solution of lye in a water glass and drank it down.

She was gone well before Sylvie fetched me back, and not until that evening when Rena put on the new dress to meet callers did we have your news. She had folded it into the pocket of the dress with no word of comment or message from herself.

It was all her doing, Forrest. You are not to suffer for it, whatever her aim, nor is Eva nor your child. Her own life was ruined by the carelessness of others before she had drawn a hundred breaths; and never in all the available years did she rise from that. I miss her dreadfully and mourn her choice of eternal separation from the one who had pledged her eternal troth, but that is my grief which I will not share.

Now tell me what these days have held for you, and the look of the

*future. I assume you have found a post in Bracey, and I trust that your life
is rooting there near its natural home.*

*This letter like yours makes no requests. Only the first—that you use
it wisely. I pray you know how.*

Truly,
Bedford Kendal

April 3, 1904

Dear Mr. Mayfield,

*Rena has showed me the letter you wrote her, which came here yester-
day. She did not feel she knew what to tell you or how and had no wish to
disturb Father now, so I answer for her. I think I know how.*

*No Rena cannot visit Eva now or soon. You must not count on Rena
or any of us for any kind of help in the visible future. We regret Eva's
weakness and well understand that she may wish to reforge the links she
ruptured, but we have our hands full here with the pieces of her latest
harm on us and cannot spare time or strength to come there and cheer one
who cheered herself at our hard expense.*

*You know of Mother's death; Rena says Father wrote you. It has been
more than two weeks now. We move along.*

*But so you don't low-rate the damage done, I can tell you that Father
went out this morning just before daybreak when I was asleep and shot my
old dog Hector with his pistol, one time through the left eye, and came
back to bed. When I had left home in May, I turned Hector over to
Mother's good care; and she quickly grew fond, despite his bad habits. He
settled his feelings on her in return, so had barked a good deal since she
disappeared. I tried every way I knew of to calm him—let him sleep in my
room the first few nights, even put paregoric in his evening scraps; but he
started up awhile before light this morning, and Father found the way.*

Will that show you what I mean?—why none of us will come.

Truly,
Kennerly Kendal

MAY 1904

May 1, 1904

My dear Father,

I have just been told the news of Mother—this afternoon, a Sunday, our third warm day. I was also told that you understand my own long weakness, the only cause this time for my ignorance and silence, and so will have pardoned me of that much at least.

The weakness itself is far from gone—I lost much blood—but the health of my boy and the sight of sun and the green light of leaves were making slow but daily amends when this last stroke landed.

What am I to do? Is anyone with you but Rena and the help? What I want to do is come home as soon as possible for a visit. In spite of this blow, Forrest seems to think I am making headway; and it looks like to me that by the time he has finished his school term here, the baby and I will be safe to travel; and the three of us can come down there and help you.

Say Yes to that please. I have lived in pain a good part of twelve months because of my choice that has harmed so many when I meant it to help. And now Mother's dying with no further word to me. How is someone to live with that on her heart, as well as a new son, a needful husband? I think you are my only hope again, Father; the one to excuse me. And I think, though I know you have gone without me for a whole silent year, that if you can extend me forgiveness and welcome—just simple permission—then I and my family can go on healing in the shadow of your own certain recovery, and aid in the work. The thought that we might find our true place beside you, and spend our lives, is now my dream.

Soon, I pray.

Love from
Eva

May 7, 1904

Dear Eva,

Father has gotten your letter and thought it all over and asked me to write you.

He thanks you certainly for what is kind. But as to your plans, he foresees troubles which he does not desire. An example would be that, whether or not he resents Mr. Mayfield, there are many here that do—worse than ever, right or wrong, since Mother's being forced to desperation. So he not only thinks that there's no hope at all of a life for you three in this place again but also that in his own strained condition he does not want to be tested for patience and charity.

Those are truly his words. I will add on my own that, so far as help goes, there is plenty of that. Though they wouldn't stop Mother in her last decision, Mag and Sylvie are here and Kennerly who came home of course for the funeral has only left for long enough to close down his job and move back here and be Father's man on the farms and in timber. I will go on another year and finish my schooling, and then I will no doubt be staying forever. I have no other plans; and no one has them for me, thank God.

So study the above and think what it means; and if you have further intentions, write back.

> *Your sister,*
> *Rena Kendal*

I do not guess I would know your face. Or you mine, either. It has been a year.

2

FORREST had taken Kennerly to walk on the hill behind Hatt's while Eva finished packing. In an hour, at noon, they would sit down to dinner; then drive to Bracey in the Palmers' buggy for the two-thirty train that would put Eva, Rob, and Kennerly at home by dark. Kennerly the escort and nurse, here for that.

At the top of the green rise, Forrest stopped and turned and faced the long valley. He shaded his eyes with a hand against the sun and said, "Leaves are due to be full-grown today." It was May fifteenth, a peaceful Sunday.

The nearest tree was a quarter-mile down, at the edge of Hatt's yard. Kennerly studied that, face bare to the light. "Never make it," he said. "Dying anyhow."

Forrest said "How's that?"

Kennerly pointed to the tree, ran his long white finger up and down in the air as though stroking its bark from crown to root. Then he turned to Forrest, who was uphill from him; and said, "Better take that down tomorrow; kill all your others. May be too late."

Forrest said "How's that?"

"Blight," Kennerly said.

Forrest said, "Tell Hatt when we get back then."

"This is not yours?" Kennerly said and pointed back, gestured round in an arc.

"No my sister's," Forrest said.

"Will you get it one day?"

"Oh no. Her boys. It was her husband's place."

"Where's the Mayfield place?"

Forrest looked again and pointed across to the opposite hills, alone above the river. Blank green hills, to the normal eye.

When Kennerly had studied, he said "That graveyard?"

Forrest said, "Yes. My mother's in there. Her family's graves. The house is gone."

"Who was she?" Kennerly said. "No Mayfield, was she?"

"A Goodwin," Forrest said. "Anna Goodwin."

Kennerly still stared out across the river.

So Forrest looked too. He squinted and strained but could not see the graves, though his eyes were famous with his students for keenness.

Then Kennerly turned. "What's yours?" he said.

Forrest smiled and said "Pardon?"

Kennerly gestured again at the view. "What's yours in all this?"

Forrest could see the house at least, the black roof in sunlight—the spot on the eaves beneath which, now, Eva folded and stowed, obliterating her traces, her touch. She had brought to it nothing but the clothes on her back—and her whole live body droning like a hive with her hope and purpose. She was packing it all round the core of the child to take with her now, leaving what? *What?* He could only think of the mattress-ticking on their mutual bed—the side turned down, still dark with her dried blood, stiff with its salt. *That much*, he thought. But he said to Kennerly, "Your sister and your nephew. A few books and papers. A change of clothes."

Kennerly smiled for the first time since stepping from the train the night before. "Good thing you're such a big reader then." He climbed past Forrest on up the green hill.

Forrest said, "You have got three-quarters of an hour. Go alone. I am heading to the house. Eva'll need me."

Kennerly said "She won't."

"Still—" Forrest said, already walking down, eyes downward to navigate the rocky ground. So he did not see what was freely offered, even to him—Eva dressed and ready at the bedroom window, untouched by the heat which the black roof soaked, her eyes raised higher and set on Kennerly, his on her (both steady, all but smiling), Rob swaddled thickly, suckled and sleeping, cocooned in his mother's arms, making his own life in every cell, waiting to blossom solely for her.

3

In the night Hatt dreamed of her dead husband James—a calm visit from him, rare as it was real, and like many of her dreams, a simple memory. She lay, in the dream, in their bed but alone. She was young, sixteen. He was older, thirty. They had just been married, her mother having died three weeks before and she needing company and care for herself and her brother Forrest. The bed where she waited was in James's house and had been shared by him and his first wife who'd died eight months ago. What Hatt waited for, she wasn't certain. She had heard tales, rumors from schoolmates, Negroes; and half-hoped that all of them were true except that she could not imagine performing such complicated work with her own lean body, dense as ironwood. Or that James would be any sort of good teacher. He did not have children (the house was empty of all but Forrest in the attic room); and his wife had died with cancer of the breast—both sides eaten like bread toward her heart, then that eaten too. Still she was there and warm and trusted that she was safe—her whole life had not made her suspect the world of secret intent to take and dissolve her: not her vanished father, her broke-down mother, her lonely brother. He was polishing shoes—James, by the one lamp. His first, then hers. No use to clean hers; they were cracked past saving. But she did not tell him. Let him work all night—it was nine o'clock. Let him work till day. Then she would stand and fry his breakfast and send him to the depot. He was freight agent there. But he finished, stopped, folded his soft rag carefully, laid it in his shine-box and looked up toward her. When he found her eyes, he said "Go to Forrest." He'd said it kindly and she'd flinched with pleasure at the chance to leave, but she did not understand his reason. "Why?" she said. "He is crying," James said. She strained to hear—nothing, silence. "He's not," she said but thought "I will ruin my chance to go." —"I think you will find me right," James said, standing and beginning to unbutton his shirt. So she rose and went in her nightgown—no robe; she didn't own a robe. In the dream she traveled the distance in darkness—the long hall, the steep narrow stairs to the attic—but even unlighted and in a strange house, she went surefooted because of her destination: Forrest, all she had. Surefooted, barefooted (she also had no bed-shoes). *To no use at all*. Forrest was not there, neither crying nor quiet. She walked to his narrow bed, felt it along its whole length—unused. She had made it for him with clean sheets that day; and he'd gone without touching them—tired, abandoned and abandoning.

Hatt waked herself then with the lingering certainty that her actual hands had searched her own bed for her young brother. She listened—only sounds of James's old house breaking up; and through her open window a single whippoorwill volleying: for what? She stood; found her shoes; and still with no robe, made her way toward Eva and Forrest's room (her own boys were in the attic now, asleep as the dead). The door was open, to Hatt's surprise—even as a boy Forrest slept shut-in, could not be persuaded in the hottest August to open his door and catch chance breezes. His secrets to save. She had come again in darkness, and she waited on the sill for her eyes to search him out in the great bed. But they wouldn't—pitch black. So she spoke his name clearly, her daytime voice. No answer. She moved toward the bed and reached and met cold bedsprings. No cover, no body, no mattress—stripped.

She rose and shuddered in the power of a fear that had not come near her for twenty years, the fear of her dream; and in her struggle to suck air for antidote, she caught the first rank smell of burning. It entered the back window, propped half-open. Hatt stood on Eva's rag rug by the bed and thought, "I have never done one thing to help him. Not once in his life. He has barely asked but wherever he's at, whatever he's doing, is punishment on me—deserved and righteous." Then she walked to the window and bent to its crack and saw, by firelight, Forrest in his good clothes, a pole in his hand with which he was struggling to force the remains of a goosedown mattress to vanish in smoke. The air that struck Hatt was strong as a flat hand, as harsh with burning feathers as with fear, as the face she imagined and set on her brother there, dark and abandoned.

But when she moved, it was toward retreat, her own room and bed. If he chose to burn house and her to the ground, James's sleeping sons, she would not stop him now.

He did not of course. At dawn when she went down (she'd slept again, lightly but dreamlessly), he was waiting in the kitchen, washed and hungry though generally silent; and in all the years that remained of her life, Hatt never alluded to her knowledge of the night or the loss she'd suffered but bore them as penalty, imposed and paid.

4

AFTER supper on her second night at home, refusing Rena's help, Eva took Sylvie upstairs and showed her how to arrange the room, to hold the crib and her own small trunk (Hatt's, James Shorter's really). The room was the back room, shared by her and Rena through their whole childhood. It had been Rena's idea that they would share it now; and they'd tried the first night, but nobody slept—Rob from exhaustion, Rena from the strangeness rising in her, Eva from relief. So Eva had suggested in the morning that she move to the downstairs parlor, set up a bed there for temporary quarters (the parlor was only used at Christmas). But Rena had said "No"; and when Eva pressed her for a reason, turned and said, "All right. Call Sylvie; we'll air it for you. But it's where Mother's body lay two ' days waiting till the ground thawed enough for a hole. Call Sylvie now." Eva had only held her tongue and gone to the shared room and nursed the baby; and in half an hour, Rena had come and said, "You and Rob stay here. It's yours. I'll move in with Kennerly awhile." Eva had thanked her.

Now when Sylvie had done all Eva asked and was turning to leave, Eva said, "Couldn't you two stop her, Sylvie?"

Sylvie stared at the floor. "No ma'm."

Eva said, "You didn't know what she was planning to do?"

"Yes, ma'm, I knew. Been knowing two days since I brought her your letter."

"The letter was from Forrest—Mr. Mayfield, Sylvie."

"Yes ma'm. I knew."

"How?"

"I knowed her all my life. I could watch her."

"And you never told a soul?"

Sylvie faced her. "No ma'm."

"Explain me that, Sylvie."

"She got her right, Eva. You ought to know that. You took your right and walked off with it; she was thanking you."

"How do you know that? Did she tell you something?"

Sylvie waited. "No ma'm. I could watch her. I knew."

Eva sat on the foot of the bed. Rob was snoring three feet away.

Sylvie said "I hadn't thanked you."

Eva thought and said "What?"

"For my goldpiece you sent me."

Eva nodded. "You save it. There'll be no more."

Sylvie said, "I spent it, getting me some teeth." She spread back her full purple lips on teeth that, even in the light of dusk, flashed gold. One canine tooth in solid gold. She held the pose, even stepped a foot nearer for Eva's inspection; but wide as the lips gaped, they did not smile.

Rena stood in the door. "You got what you need?"

Eva oared with a hand at Sylvie's presence. "Everything."

Rena said, "Then Sylvie go and wash Father's feet."

"Yes'm." Sylvie went.

Rena went to the crib and, not bending, looked down at Rob asleep, darkening. "No question who his father is," she said.

"No there's not," Eva said. She had still not risen. "Please don't wake him, Rena. Anything but that."

Rena turned and said, full voice, "Why not? He has just got a little while to learn half his family. He shouldn't sleep through it."

"He won't," Eva said. "He has got time enough." She lay back flat across the bed.

Rena walked to the table and lit the lamp—the plain glass lamp they had always had, whose chimney they had each cleaned thousands of times and never broken, even as girls. She ran the wick up just short of smoking and turned toward Eva and drew from the pocket in her black work-dress an envelope.

Eva tried to see Rena's eyes, thinking quickly "She has gone past me. She has seen worse than me. She has earned Father now"; but the light only struck Rena's strong wrists and fingers, extending to Eva.

"I swear before God I have not read this. It was never sealed but I've saved it for you." Rena's hand was out but she did not move nearer. Eva must meet her in this, must accept.

Eva rose and looked. Even standing and the light blocked, she could read the lines of her mother's tall and mannish script on the face of the envelope.

Rena offered it that way, refusable. *Rena. In the event I succeed, put this directly into Eva's hands.*

It was in them now.

Rena said, "Please remember; that was my duty, Eva."

"I'll try," Eva said. It was in her hand but extended from her at her farthest reach as though she had aged and her eyes contracted farsightedly.

"She doesn't say when you should read it," Rena said. "Maybe wait till you're stronger."

"I may not ever get stronger," Eva said. "Especially if I wait." She sat again, the paper still with her, touching only her hand.

Rena reached toward her sister. "Let me keep it awhile. I'll keep it safe. I've come too soon."

"No," Eva said. She was fixed on Rena, her face a target. "You've come when you wanted to come, to ruin me. Have the plain grace at least not to lie."

"It may just be a goodbye," Rena said.

Eva said "Please go."

Rena went down silently.

Eva sat awhile, revolving in her head the chances of being spared this next. She could light the dry paper at the lamp and hold it till it took full flame, then fling it out the window to the black tin roof to finish there. She could save it, as Rena had said, till she strengthened. She could go to her father now, hand it to him, ask him to decide. No. It bore her name. For all she had seized that was rightfully her mother's, she could give this at least—simple attention. She set down the paper on the edge of the bed and stood and went to the crib and leaned—drowned asleep, his head pressing left away from her, fists clenched shoulder-high, mouth slack and open as if swept by wind, as if he flew or were drawn through air toward some destination different from this. His father all in him. She knew that to touch him now was a risk—to have him awake and howling for hours— but with both hands round his thickening trunk she lifted him, not to her, not against her own warmth but into the air; then quickly across to her bed, laid him there in the center in his cotton summer blanket. She stood back above him and waited—sleep. He had not only lasted the move but clearly had stopped the journey of his previous dream. He was here, enduring his infancy. She took up the envelope; drew out the paper, folded once, and opened it. Then she ran her spare hand under the blanket, found Rob's foot, stripped off its knitted boot and held it while she read.

Eva, I assume that you are alive and will go on living. And if so, I know that should I succeed awhile from now in my aim to die, then I'll never know your fate for certain. I will be in darkness and you may be elsewhere. Or may go elsewhere, if you last this crisis and have a life. But I wonder, will you? Will there be another place that can bear the soul you've made yourself? Even now, it is not for me to say; and everyone will tell you that I died wild or crazy. I have never been clearer, in my mind or my acts; and so it is my final wish to tell you what I see this morning, at the brink of death. Nobody else I knew needs or wants it; and as I have said, I may be wasting time—you may have gone already, may even be awaiting me, calling me to you. I may see you yet, and will say it to you there.

But, here, what I know is—I do not want to live in a world that will harbor and succor a heart like yours. Or that, in my lifetime, has held two such. You do not know the history of your grandfather—my father Thad Watson (if you live, and care, ask your own poor father)—but in short he killed my mother, then himself; and joined with you now, is crushing me. Because you have both torn the lives of others by seeking the sole satisfaction of body. That fleeting food is only found—or only hunted—in other bodies: my mother, Forrest Mayfield. And those who offer themselves as scenes for that foul catch richly earn their fate. I would not reverse it. My mother, your pitiful cheated husband. My one regret for what I do now is the hurt with which I endow your father. Of all the humans that I have known, he is so far the strongest, most courteous, as to brook no rival in life or story. He knows my gratitude. I've taken that care through all these years, to thank him each day for that day's goodness. So he will stand, despite this blow. He will know its target, know it is not him. He can proudly recall that once he had got the children his tender heart required, he asked me my wishes and I said, "May we live as brother and sister?" and though he did not answer then or later by actual word, he answered by deed, by a loving negligence which, if I could wish one blessing on you, would be my choice—that you understand. We have lived untouching for fifteen years in pure devotion—and are paid by you with the sight of your life, the public sight of your inflamed flesh tracking down its assuagement in a heart as simple as the one you seized. I cannot bear it. Or will not at least, despite your demand for my constant witness. My father had the goodness to leave before I could raise my head to see his face. You have not, or had not two days ago; but wait at the door of our lives and beg entry. So, Eva, I precede you with something like pride, the scent in my nostrils—the first time in years, in maybe my life—of something like what other people have told me was actual gladness.

Show this to no one.

Your only
Mother

Eva knew she had suffered unmeasured assault. The questions that followed now in her silence were not of her mother's clarity or sickness or the justice of the wounds she had surely inflicted—those could be answered in calmer times—but of the nature and depth of those wounds, of the damage to herself, its site in her body, the hope of repair. What felt most endangered was the center of her chest, the flat breastbone through which her breath seemed rapidly howling. She took her hand quickly from Rob's warm foot—it did not occur to her to drop the paper—and thumbed that plane of gristle fiercely.

Blood had almost come when Sylvie spoke. "You can't stop him?" She was tall in the door again.

Eva looked up, then heard Rob's wailing and turned to him.

He was red and sweating. He had cried for minutes. His foot pumped wildly in the blanket, caught.

Eva said "What's wrong?"—to Sylvie as much as Rob.

Sylvie said, "We heard him downstairs. Sound mad."

With her free right hand, Eva reached again for his rapid foot; but he kicked in her grasp and his crying deepened.

"Hold him up," Sylvie said. "He hungry, ain't he?"

"No," Eva said. "I fed him at six."

Sylvie said, "Eight o'clock now. He starving."

Eva folded the letter, laid it beside her, found Rob's body in his hot hive of cover, and raised him to her. When he did not calm and Sylvie stood on, Eva said, "I won't have a spoonful to give him."

Sylvie said "I have" and moved forward three steps into the light.

Eva looked up at her as though she now, after all this day, were the sizable mystery, demanding reply.

Sylvie said "I got it" and raised one hand to her own full breast, touched the left breast once. On her tan cotton dress above her clear nipple was the ring of a stain.

Rob had stopped; only reached for air in little sobs, a finger in the soft pit of Eva's throat.

Eva said, "What are you telling me?"

Sylvie pointed to Rob. "I can help you nurse him if you running short."

"How?"

"I had me a baby. Two weeks last Sunday."

"You? What is it?" All Eva's fear seemed a steady piece, an infinite shaft being forced through her chest by relays of hands. Sylvie's now.

"A boy. Come early. Never drew breath."

Eva waited, then said, "You are telling me it died? You had a baby two weeks ago and it died?"

"Born dead," Sylvie said.

"And already buried?"

Sylvie nodded.

"You know the father?"

"He give me some money."

"Are you all right? Did you lose much blood?"

"I guess I'm all right. Got this milk." She touched her breast again.

Eva said at Sylvie what she could have said to the whole long day— "How can I stand that?"

Sylvie said, "You can't feed him, Eva? You pay me to?"

5

THAT same night Forrest took her in his head. The first time he'd touched her entirely since March, first time in his head since before their marriage. He had dreaded such a seizure; and despite his not sleeping the night before, had tried to work, to train his mind to solitude again, however brief. When Hatt had fixed his breakfast and watched him eat it, she had said, "There's a mattress in the attic, old but good if the rats haven't got it. Bring it down and I'll air it today. It's sunny." He had said, "Is it that one I peed on for years?" —"No the goat ate that." She had laughed and he'd climbed to the attic and found it, dusty but whole. Then he'd laid it on the front porch in sun, drawn water, gone to his room and shut himself in; and surrounded by the morning sounds of the boys, had washed and shaved and dressed in worn clothes and worked by main force for more than an hour to transcribe the lines that had formed in his head through the previous night.

TO HADES AS YOU ENTER HIS DOOR
to be placed in your hand

This was called Eva with our Mother's name
Whom here on Earth, through three quick years, I loved.
Deal with her gently in your endless night
And let, from age to age, one shaft of light
Fall down the brown, unmoving air
To plow rich furrows in her hair.
   Then leave her to her myriad sleep
And in the dark and make it deep,
For what are you but Death and young
As love songs sung by golden boys to unseen girls
And raging for her silent curls?
   The vineyards of her flesh were mine,
Where I have fed and pressed the wine,
And sought the rain to heal the drouth,
And will abide no second mouth.

Finished, he'd destroyed his working drafts and hid the fair copy in the pages of his Horace—a poem for her death, now or later, in whatever form that death should seize her. Or had already seized her, from his life at least. Then he had gone down and joined his nephews who struggled with the mule to plow a garden. They'd worked together in full hot sun till dinner, eaten in silence, then worked on into late afternoon. Then he'd come in and washed and changed to good clothes and headed toward town to meet the last post. No chance of word unless she had wired, which she would not do and he had not asked.

Still when he'd found no mail for anyone—nothing even from Hatt's crazy sister-in-law who wrote three or four times a week, inquiring indirectly after James's money (of which there was none)—he'd walked across the road to the depot and asked Mr. Rochelle if there was a wire.

No, none.

As he'd turned to leave, the electric chatter of the black key had started. He'd waited, listening as closely to the code as if the impulses were freely repeating a simple sentence of devotion and promise intended for him should he know its language.

Mr. Rochelle had tapped out a burst of response, then had written for a while and folded the paper.

Forrest had said "Still nothing for me?"

"Not a word," Mr. Rochelle had said and turned, grinning for the first time in Forrest's long memory. "You tell me what you want to hear and pay me a quarter, and I'll send out an all-stations call for an answer. I'll get you something if it's nothing but news of a bridge out in Georgia."

Forrest had also smiled and said "I'm broke" and had gone out the door and past the bunch of waiters on the platform (waiting for Jesus or Judgment Day, no actual train) and half-down the steps to the station yard when a voice said "Mr. Forrest"—a woman's, black. He had turned and searched the dozen faces—Veenie, who'd belonged to his mother's family and who through his childhood had come to help his mother when she could. Or when she came, no more loyal than most.

She had stood to meet him—tall, thin as a slat but straight and her loose dress covered with safety pins (not to hold it together; it was not in rags) so she'd seemed in the sun to stand in armor, all her wealth on her, an ounce of nickel. She had said "You grown."

"You too."

"I'm dead." She had laughed. She was somewhere near ninety. She recalled passing fifty before Appomattox, said her nature had dried up before freedom came. "But they ain't come to get me."

"They won't," he had said.

"Better not." She had laughed. "Who you come for?"

"Nobody, fresh air."

"You ain't still lonesome? I heard you was *fixed*."

"I am," he had said.

"Little young girl?"

"Small," he'd said, "but old enough."

"Them's the best kind, ain't they? Teach em while they blind." She had not laughed then—a serious truth—and her eyes, opalescent with cataracts, had held fast on him. "Where you been?"

"What you mean?"

"When have I seen you?"

"Two, three years maybe. I've been back here since May. Where've you been?"

"State of Maine," she'd said.

"Why on earth Maine? You'd freeze to death."

"Did. Why I'm back. No, Rover's in Maine. Augusta, Maine—building boats. Called me to him, to die in comfort. I stayed one winter and froze both feets and never spoke to one soul that won't my kin. So I'll die here."

"Who you come for today?" he'd said. He had felt surprise at not wanting to leave her—old bore, old rascal. She would find a way to beg money if he stayed.

"Not a soul today. But tomorrow this time if I be live, my great-grandbaby-boy coming to see me." She pointed down at the glistening rails. "I'm here checking tracks to see he come safe."

"Rover's boy?"

"Rover's," she had said; then had stopped and thought. "Lord Jesus, my great-great-*great*-grandson." She'd laughed again. "I started early like your little girl."

He had smiled. "A boy."

"And named for your father?"

"Yes."

She had waited. "He can live that down if he want to."

"I don't know. Maybe my father is happy."

"May be," she had said. "You his mirror anyhow. If he come, you want me to bring him to see you? Tell me is he smart as I think he is."

He had slowly realized she meant Rover's boy. "All right. I'm at Hatt's."

"I know that. If he don't come I'm coming anyhow, to see your girl."

"Then wait. She's down at her home right now."

"When she here, she treat you right?"

"Yes," he'd said.

"Them young ones know how now."

"Yes."

She had laughed.

That night he took her—Eva, consciously, awake in his bed. It had not been his purpose. He had meant to respect her absence entirely—"If she chooses to go, for whatever reason or term, I must let her"—but once the house was black and silent and only he awake, he had found himself considering a question: "Could I live if Eva is gone for good? If so, what was it she gave me when here that made me believe we had grown into one?"

At first the answers came as words—*loveliness, kindliness, need:* her whole offer—but as they passed, they drew pictures with them, illustrative scenes. And soon, though he dreaded it, the picture of their union—borne upward, forward from the rear of his mind like an army veiled, their faces muffled but their hands stocked with power. He let it come. He abandoned himself to the effort to know the name and objective, the diet, of this power. And the effort demanded enactment of the rite—his entering her, her welcoming him. Or abiding him. Demanded its picture, image of the—what?—some seventy times they'd agreed to explore their mutual offer, their dedication to a single life.

Her small body, finely joined at its bends like a skillful garment, which after the first day had always been bare, completely naked—Eva's own choice, executed by her, which he had since followed: proud of the long-boned strength of his own limbs. Her hair spread behind her like a half-lost net in perpetual process of blowing away, of revelation—perpetually held in place round its treasure, her secret head, the shoulders, chest, trunk that flowed down from that vault. More rooms, more guards. To which her round knees, opening like the covers of a heavy book, slowly offered entrance.

Entrance, not knowledge, even explanation. That had been his chore

—not the simple taking and giving of pleasure (natural to them both as the leafing of trees) but the study of what was exchanged and why, the weighing of damage versus repair, wounds versus healing.

It had seemed to him, all year, only healing. But now, in his head, he accepted her offer; and kneeling above, bent to hunt with his mouth—in her dry hair, across the waiting planes of her face, her placid neck, the close breasts (looseheld fistsful of nurture), the high flat belly, the core beneath (barely garlanded) rank with the fragrance of its own demand. By then the instrument of his own search was ready; and again, as generally from the first, with strong hands she pressed him quickly in and, with strong heels crossed in the small of his back, locked him in place.

He thrust. She yielded. And in those minutes—whole minutes!—their act seemed game or dance, solemn, silent, and productive of the minimum joys of a game: the pride in one's self, in the mind's own picture of its body's grace (bowing, ducking, in air), the eye's true image of the all but unacceptable fact of one's partner's *presence*, not to speak of her courteous obedience, her unison. Unacceptable because incredible, unearned, bestowed by a god whose kindness is crushing, unrestrained, not adjusted for mortal capacities. Then the game seemed the oldest memory of all—with Mother and truly wanted there, at last, no rival; no rush to wean, grow, leave. Implored by her to stay forever. He could think that calmly, knowing its truth.

Then she met his thrusts with her own strong heaving—at first, in what seemed a struggle to dislodge him; a cry to which he had all but acceded (there were cries, hers) when he knew his joy had mounted by double. Knew it by seeing her body as his mirror—her face as open as a mine at work: her eyes on his, her haunches approaching his, meeting not retreating. Little cries of his own came antiphonal to hers. No words, no words—he could think of none; she offered none.

So he strained for words through the final miles—words to speak, not his thanks (thanks would come at the end, in the peaceful trough: "Thank you." —"You were welcome") but his present *meaning*, which would be his true purpose and his only chance at knowing her meaning, their use to each other, the omens for their life.

The shock of his loins began its fast climb through his belly, chest, throat, to his crowded skull with, as ever, its threat to kill as it came. Or to burn its bridges, leave the route closed to further passage forever. It arrived. His brain struck like a great bell tolled, the noise poured through him, shuddered on into her; and he knew five words, which he did not speak but would always know—*It is only for me.*

Forrest lay back, ruined, on the bed still musty despite its sunning. Nothing was shared. Nothing gained that could not be gained elsewhere. Nothing lost but the atoms of strife and cry, the sparse clots of joy now cooling on his chest. He touched them respectfully, the second or third time only in his life he had dabbled in his own seed without revulsion. Only months ago, eleven months, Eva's body had consumed precisely this; then ruminant had slowly built it into the fresh body of the child he had not yet known, and might never, though it bore—at his wish—his own father's name. His famished destroying father—still wandering? She would not change that; could not stop the working of his own life in the boy, yeast in the loaf.

6

The two days after that, Forrest worked in the garden—at first with the boys, who were funny enough to ease his mind; then alone once they'd begged off to go up the hill and help the Palmer boys with their summer plan (the building from scratch of a steam-piano). By then—with the sun, the clearing air all flushed through his body, the message of his solitude two nights before, and the customary toughness of his mind (returning now in answer to need)—he was better, firmer on his feet, only the edges of his mind in danger, the pales beyond which lay both past and future. He saw them in place there and honored their presence, their evident power; but he also trusted from his whole life's experience that they would act when they would, not in response to his bruises or dreads. Today they were waiting.

And so he had worked through the axis of the day—the afternoon train, final mail—absorbed in labor, self-contained. When he'd heard the train, he had paused and thought "What's there will wait; what's not will come" and had planted on to the end of his row, a row of gourds. Then his job was finished. He put up his tools and went to the well and drew cold water and climbed to his room and washed and dressed. It was when he had laced his shoes and stood that he thought for no reason of Aunt Veenie's remark—"You his mirror," his father's mirror. No one had ever said it before; and since no pictures of his father survived except in his memory (and Hatt's no doubt), he walked to the dresser mirror and faced himself. He'd shaved that morning but without really looking. Now he needed to look—past the few things of Eva's he'd left there neatly (a hair-receiver Hatt had given her for Christmas, the ribbon she'd worn the night of their marriage, an arrowhead the boys had given Rob). It yielded him nothing, though he smiled, frowned, even worked at producing now with his own face the memory of his father's that distant morning, pressing closer toward him in secret or incommunicable hunger. Nothing—his own familiar face, ready, open as a plate, slightly reddened from his work in the sun. He smiled again—another relief, one more brace—and went down and called toward Hatt in the kitchen "Do you need anything?" and when she said "No but hurry back," he stepped out the front door and down the steps and was trotting down the walk when he heard the gate hinges and looked up—a man, a Negro, serious. Forrest stopped in his tracks, swaying from speed; and the man stopped too in the open gate.

"Mr. Forrest?"

He nodded.

"I'm Grainger," he said. A boy not a man, tall, a light quick voice.

"Grainger *who?*" Forrest said.

"My grandmama sent me," he said. "Miss Veenie." He stood in place but extended his hand. A letter was in it.

Sun was on the envelope. The writing was face-down though. So Forrest searched the boy's face for who he truly was and what was his message. He was maybe twelve—long-boned, long-necked but still on the calm nearside of manhood (in his face and voice; the dry unfulfilled skin of his chest that showed in the open neck of his white shirt, the color of well-used laundry soap or cocoa butter). No visible trace of Veenie's iron roughness. Instead a steady kind of exhalation from the eyes and lips that seemed more urgently his message than the letter. *Hermes, son of Maia and the God, eloquent herald, conductor of souls.* Forrest held his own ground. "What is it?" he said, knowing Veenie could not write.

The boy's hand was firm on the air as a statue's—offering the letter not giving it. But the question released him. He smiled on perfect teeth, stepped forward. "Good news," he said.

Forrest said "You read it?"

"No sir," he said but quickly held it to the sun as if to remedy the failure. His smile bloomed wider. "*Feels* good," he said.

Forrest took the letter from his hand in midair. Eva's script postmarked two days ago; the boy was one step away still smiling, his empty hand slowly returning to his side, no intention of leaving. Forrest said "Wait" and rummaged for his pocketknife and cut the envelope and read the message there, the boy's warmth reaching him across the space—warmth and the clean bitter smell of child sweat.

May 17, 1904

Dear Forrest,

We got here day before yesterday. It seems like a month of years already. We both stood the journey and have been allowed to rest; no visitors yet, though with this house containing so much sadness old and new, I have not found it possible to draw free breath. I had hoped otherwise. Father is kind and caring but broken. Everyone else has been stunned by Mother into states quite foreign to their general lives, as we knew them at least.

So as you will imagine, I am laying plans now for an early return.

*Three weeks more are unthinkable. The plans however are all in my heart.
Do not put them in writing in your next to me—they would be read and
used harmfully—but when the time comes, when I can see Father is strong
enough, I'll signal you somehow and you come for us. Whatever the
greeting, we can stand it together.*

*Our boy looks steadily at the sights around him (has slept very little,
though has barely cried) and permits the attentions of his relatives but
apparently like me is reserving his smiles, the gift of his heart, for his
absent father. Can what I suspect be the actual case?—that he searches my
face (his only source) for your whereabouts? Or as though my face were a
cloudy mirror in which he receives a memory of you? That last is no wife's
dream, I think; for your face—the memory of each hair and line, its various
odors—is worn into me as profoundly as the memory of water in stone. But
happily, gratefully, and in expectation of imminent reunion.*

> *Your promised*
> *Eva*

Forrest looked up.

The boy had waited in place; and his face maintained its smile—
unfixed, fresh as in his moment of giving but confirmed now, fulfilled. "I
was right," he said.

"Yes," Forrest said.

"Do you thank me now?"

"Yes," Forrest said and reached into his pocket for a suitable coin.

When money jingled, the boy shook his head. "Just thank me," he
said.

Forrest tested the last dam against his joy. He held out the letter.
"Why did you have this?"

"My Grandmama Veenie was bringing me to see you, but she stopped
at the office first and asked for your mail; and when you had that—and the
lady give it to her, and I read her the postmark—she said she would wait at
the depot for me, to go on alone and watch you reading and help what I
could if you needed help."

The dam fell; joy inundated Forrest. He could not know that, pressed
almost past bearing, Eva had lied. Or had told the weaker half of the truth.
"You told me your name," Forrest said. "I forgot."

"Grainger," the boy said.

"Thank you," Forrest said as best he could. "Thank you, Grainger,"
he said. And in Eva's absence, with the hand that had reached for money
for the boy, he touched the forehead an arm's reach from him. Warm, dry.
With all five fingers he read at the dome of smooth bone and skin, con-
verting the simple unquestioning presence of a strange brown boy into

tender memory—the feel on these same hands of Eva's body awhile before dawn when, awake himself, he would turn to her and gently lure her up from sleep, the aqueous sounds of her dark interior as she'd bear once again the rescue of day.

The boy's smile vanished while he waited through that—or appeared to vanish. What it did was retreat like water through sand toward a center as dry as Forrest's own. Grainger tried but could not think when he had been touched—any hand on his skin (a wanted hand; Veenie had touched him the day before). He was twelve years old, his own caretaker for seven, eight years. He was happy here, in these tracks, by this man. He thought that clearly, knew he had never felt happy till now. "I love him," Grainger thought. "He will love me for this. He will always love me because of this. This is the place my life will happen."

AUGUST 1904

FORREST rose into darkness on straight arms above her. By careful
study he could see her face in moonlight that came on a breeze through
the window he'd opened—August night—once the lamp was doused. She
was gratified. Her full calm pleasure, even lacking light, reflected his own.
Flood tide again. And again they were freely volunteering the sight of their
separate naked joy to one another—one another only. The almost fatal
pitch of their pleasure had been ample warrant of mutual abstinence, a
mutual wait. She was not wholly silent; above the gentle sounds of subsi-
dence sent up by her body, her dim smile spoke its own firm word. Forrest
read it as "Now we are back again, where our fates intend us. It is happy
here." And himself—what he wanted to say was "Thank you"; but knowing he had said it to the point of foolcry, he said the next thing that rose to
his mouth: "All promises intact." Eva appeared to nod, in her nimbus of
hair—all part of the night, growing into night—though she moved so
slightly Forrest thought the mere breeze might have rocked her.

"I'll meet you in Heaven if not before"—a strange man's voice.

"Heaven or beyond"—a younger man. Then two doors closing, the
turn of locks.

Eva laughed one clear note.

"Drummers," Forrest said. "I saw them at supper—one in shoes, one
in corsets."

"The young one in corsets, I bet," she said and laughed again.

They were lying in a second-story room of the Fontaine Hotel and
Dining Room. It was ten o'clock (the courthouse had struck as they
struggled toward joy). They had been together exactly an hour, the first
sight of one another since May; and for all but three or four minutes at the
start, they had been bare to one another, vulnerable. So no practical questions had been answered yet (no questions had been raised, practical or
not, whatever Forrest fancied).

He climbed gently off her and walked to the washstand. Still in the dark, he felt for one of the two waterglasses and poured one glass full of tepid water and returned to the bed. At the edge he held it out to her.

She clearly shook her head.

So he sat on the edge and drank the glass dry, then set it on the floor and lay flat beside her. "How did Sylvie tell you?"

"Plain as always. I was upstairs with Rob. He had had a whooping spell in the late afternoon—the first in a week and it scared him badly—so I was beside him, just touching his back. Sylvie stopped in the door and said 'Mr. Forrest here.' My hand jerked hard. I was scared I'd waked Rob, so I sat still a moment to help him sleep. Sylvie thought I'd forgot. She took a step in and said, 'Eva, Mr. Forrest your husband is here.' Rob seemed safe. I motioned her over to the farthest corner and asked her where."

"Were you shocked?" he said.

"No."

They waited. Then Forrest said "Tell the rest."

"Sylvie said she had just stepped out of the store—I'd sent her for Father's cereal; we were out—and you stepped toward her, grip in hand." Eva seemed to have finished.

Forrest said "After that?"

Eva lay on, silent.

"Did you ask what I said?"

"Yes."

"What I said *first*?"

Eva rose on her elbows, still looking forward. "She said you asked how strong Rob was."

"I did," he said. "You had not written me for nearly two weeks. I was wild with thinking he was dead and you gone."

"Sylvie said she told you he was coming along. He is. It's a very slow sickness, Forrest. You're lucky he's living; it took all I had in time and strength. I couldn't write too."

"You could have sent for me; sent a wire by Sylvie, any Negro in the road."

Eva faced him in the dark. "I am living in a house where your name is not mentioned."

"Mention it and see what will happen," he said. "I am your one husband, your child's one father. The world is real; they have got to accept it."

"It would just hurt people that are down already."

"Hurt them," he said. "It is not their son. You are not their wife."

"I won't," she said.

"But you've crucified *me* with loneliness, waiting, uncertainty."

"I know I have."

"Then why?" he said.

She sat up fully, hands in her lap, and faced out again—the dark room, silence. Beyond the door, silence. Through the window, silence more strongly than the breeze. She did not know.

"Tell the rest then," he said, "—what happened when you knew I was down here waiting."

"When Sylvie had told me you'd wait till dark for a word, then you'd come, I went straight to Father. He was on the porch waiting for supper. Brother was with him. I asked him to step inside with me—we went to his room—and I said you were down at the hotel expecting word from me. He said, 'All right. Do you want to see him?' I said 'Yes sir' and he said, 'Then go. Get your baby to sleep and Rena will watch him. Sylvie or Brother will see you downtown.' I thanked him and turned to go upstairs; and he said, 'If you plan to take any luggage, I'll harness the buggy.' So I thanked him again."

"You had not thought of it?"

"No," she said. "Not at first." She looked down to Forrest. "Is that painful to you?"

He rolled over quickly and stood, his back to Eva. Then he walked to the window and brushed back the curtain and stared at the dark street.

Eva could see him outlined in moonlight and knew any passer below, looking up, would see his whole body; but she did not warn him. She thought, "He is trying to believe this. He understands; now he needs to believe."

He turned and came back, stopping at the bed, his knees on the side rails. "Yes," he said. "It is all more painful than my whole life till now."

"I'm sorry," she said. She knew he had stated the simple truth. "I did not aim at that. I am here after all. I came to meet you."

"For how long?" he said.

"Till somebody comes to say Rob is whooping or, if not, till dawn."

"Then what?" he said.

"Then whatever you want."

"You know what I want. I wanted you not to leave in May. I wanted you to come back the way you said. I wanted to see you and Rob my son. I wanted to keep my promise to you. I wanted you to let me keep my promise."

"What promise?" she said.

"In the springhouse," he said. "A year ago. Remember that far?"

"Yes," she said. "A year and a half. We were keeping it, I thought."

He had meant to laugh; it came as a moan. "You have broke it to Hell."

Eva waited and thought. "Listen to what I have done," she said. "I have had time in these three months to think; so I know what I say is true for me and will stay true always. I made you a promise a year ago—for far more reasons than I knew then or still, though I think of them nightly; far more reasons than you can ever know, you not having had my sixteen years. I kept that promise to the letter, Forrest; I married you. I left my family in cruelty and followed you. I don't blame you. I thought it was my wish. I took a baby from you and nursed it inside me through nine long months till it tried to kill me. I made a human like you'd make a shed, a good tight shed that will turn wind and water. I killed my mother. I came back here to visit the remnants of my family for pardon. The boy got sick, nearly died; and I've stayed—to nurse him with help; he could not be moved. You know all this."

"Yes," he said. He sat on the edge, quite separate from her. "All but one thing—I know you had reasons; I never understood them. I doubt you do, whatever you say. I doubt any human since Adam understands any full true reason."

"I do," she said.

"And another thing—you talk as if you've done all that in pain. I have never forced you, Eva; not in one single thing. I have thought of that carefully each moment we've had—'She must do this freely, do it from need; *her* need, not mine or anyone else's.' " He paused and sat watching her; she'd faced him through that. He expected reward.

"May I speak?" she said. "You stopped me just now."

"I've begged you to speak for months now, Eva."

"Stop begging and listen. Or ask me questions; don't tell me what you don't know and then say *I* don't. I *know* some answers." She had said it through calmly, the vehemence contained in the words themselves as they rose to her mouth. She stopped and waited for the answers to come. They came but she only said "Forrest, excuse me" and touched his flank.

He bore the touch—her hand stayed there—and he said "For what?"

"For meanness," she said.

"Excused," he said. "Entirely forgiven. But tell me, for God's sake, anything you know about what we've had, Eva; what we can have."

Her hand stayed on him. "I know what *I* had—the fact that you wanted me. The fact that you looked at me across classrooms or the porch at home—your face in a work to hide your meaning but plain to me—as if I were one last crust of bread after long lean years."

"You were," he said. "I told you that."

"That's wrong," she said. "There was nothing scary. You never once made me think you meant to consume me." She thought again. "—As if I were golden, some beautiful work you'd stumbled on and had the grace to recognize: the first person ever. I was very grateful."

"That's all?" he said.

"It's the part I'm sure of."

"Are you grateful still?"

"Yes," she said calmly, though she did not move toward him and he did not draw her. Then she said "Yes" again. "But I also know I was wrong, wrong to think you were all that watched me or joyed in me. There were others, from the start. I didn't know or just didn't see—I've been good at blindness and have suffered for that. I've made them suffer. Some of them still do; need me and suffer, both."

"Who?" he said.

"Father."

Forrest touched her cooling hand that had lain unused by either of them—clasped it; she let him. "I can come here and teach," he said. "They might well let me now that things have calmed, now they see we were serious. Or near here at least, near enough you could see your people every week."

"Just Father," she said. "The others can vanish."

"I'll see Mr. Cooper tomorrow morning. He always liked me. He'll have me back."

"Never," she said. "Too late anyhow. School starts in three weeks. You're promised in Bracey."

"I could try. Eva, Bracey can live without me."

"So can you without me. So have I without you."

"What does that mean in terms of our future?"

"Nothing much, I guess. It is just one more thing I'm certain I know after this past year."

"Then when are you coming back home?" Forrest said.

"I am home," she said. She withdrew her hand and waved gently round her, the local darkness. "Wherever you or I might happen to camp, *home* is here. I'm as sorry as you."

"I believe it," he said. He made no move to reclaim her touch. But he faced her through darkness with scrutiny as fervent as any touch. "What day will you be back in Bracey with Rob, in Hatt Shorter's house, in our own room?"

"When Rob is well."

"What day will that be?"

"A month, six weeks. Forrest, I'm no prophet. You are lucky the boy is alive at all. I know of three babies that have died since June, and of plain whooping cough—Sylvie's nephew for one, Mag's grandson."

"I'll ask the doctor tomorrow morning," he said. "The air in the hills would be better for him, cooler and drier. We could break the trip if necessary. He'd be with the people that love him, Eva."

"My family love him; Rena worships his shadow. Mag and Sylvie love him."

"*We* made him. I want him to be with us."

"Any dogs in a ditch can make a baby. Forrest, you are ruining people's plans again. Don't you see all the trouble of the past long year has sprung from you?—the question you asked me that day at the spring?"

"You answered," he said.

"But I never would have asked."

"You'd have let us die?—our feeling, unspoken?"

"It was not for me to speak," she said.

"Why not?" he said.

"The feeling was yours."

His entire body, the roots of his hair, then knew he had lost; said it clearly in his head—*Your oldest home*. But he did not speak another audible word. He stood and walked to the window again, pulled down the shade against early day. Then he went back and lay down quietly—on his back but economically, drawn to his minimum size, the least bother.

When Eva had seen his eyes shut firmly, she lay back also—on her right side toward him, her natural posture.

They slept till dawn.

Then they hardly spoke—in neither case from coldness or anger but numbness: Forrest numb from loss, the fresh return of his oldest companion; Eva from what seemed the chance she was free, that these chains at least had proved rotten or weak, not chains at all but silk cords cast in luxury and pity, a girl's quick foolish generosity. Forrest stayed on his back when she rose to wash (he had not moved once in five hours of sleep, despite his dreams). His eyes were open but they studied the ceiling—a sepia stain in the form of a sea lion plunging through waves—leaving Eva to dress, unwatched and private as the girl he had first seen, three years before, at the head of his class, poised to recite a perfect lesson, then laugh. He did not even think he was waiting—for her voice saying whatever sleep had brought her (*Goodbye* or *Soon*), least of all for her touch. If he'd thought, he'd have thought, "I'll never need touching. I have had all of that."

She did speak finally. She came to his side of the bed and stood. His right arm could have reached her. She said, "Rob will be awake soon and hungry." She was dressed and ready. Having brought no grip, she could walk out clean. But she waited in place for an answer from Forrest.

He put his right hand back and raised his head with it, enough to face her. "May I see him somehow?"

She genuinely tried to think of a way. There were ways of course, but none came to her. "Please wait," she said. "Make people's lives easy."

That instantly drew "Goodbye" to his lips, but he did not say it. She must say it herself. He had asked the first question sixteen months ago; she must speak the end.

She smiled, shut her eyes once tightly in pleasure, looked again still smiling and turned and went.

When she'd shut the door, he thanked her.

2

HE had luckily beat both the drummers and the heat of day downstairs and so ate cool and nearly alone, only the pad of Negroes behind him, the tired wail of flies, the sounds through open windows of the waking town— harness, hooves, a distant man's voice raised to say "Bless your heart" which Forrest strained to recognize and failed. As no one had seemed to recognize him. He had entered a town of eight hundred people in broad August daylight—a town in which he had lived for three years, teaching several hundred children, whose parents he had finally scandalized—and no one had known him except his wife, for whom he had sent. (Mrs. Dameron, the hotel-owner was away on a visit to Raleigh; he had stayed with her his first month in Fontaine; she'd have known him or would she have turned him away? The clerk anyhow, a strange country boy, had barely read Forrest's name on the register; and when he had said "I expect my wife," had only said, "Good. Room Six. Real clean.") He turned now to ask for a third cup of coffee and saw, behind him, not the coal-black boy who had waited before but a small yellow girl—three feet away, smiling. "Can you get me some coffee?" he said, to her eyes that willed to hold him.

She had it in her hand, having waited for this; and her smile spread full as she stepped forward to him and filled his cup.

He thanked her and leaned to take the sugar.

"I know you," she said.

She was too near for him to study closely (her high odor ringed him). He pushed back his chair. No. "From where?" he said.

"You never seen me. I know about you. Sylvie my cousin."

"Sylvie knows me," he thought—one more human witness. But this girl was offering more than second-hand witness. He drew himself back to the table. "Thank you." She was meant to leave.

"I seen your boy."

"What boy do you mean?"

She pointed the right way. "Up at the Kendals'. Little white boy. Eva's."

He knew it was the only further chance he'd be given. He asked this grinning slut, "When did you see him?"

"Every three, four days. I go see Sylvie when I get off here; I got to breathe *air*." She laughed, set the coffee pot down on the table, and fanned the still air before her face.

"How is he now?"

"He making it now." She moved back two steps and searched Forrest's face. "Do he favor you?"

Helpless, Forrest smiled. "Does he? At all?"

She seriously worked to know the truth. With a beautiful hand she traced one slow sweep across her eyes. "Some little," she said. "Some little through the eyes." She was no longer smiling. "You looking for a place to stay?" she said.

"What?"

"You from up North, ain't you? You looking for a place?"

He stood. His napkin fell to the floor. "Who are you?" he said.

"Flora."

"Flora who?"

"You ask anybody in Fontaine. They tell you."

"I won't though," he said.

3

In the room he packed quickly in his mother's small grip, used by her twice—on her single trip to Old Point Comfort before the war and the final trip on a stretcher in the baggage car to Richmond to die, crowded to death by a growth in her womb the size of a head. He had brought only one change of underclothes, a cake of soap, his shaving utensils—not even his piddling summer work. Though all his life he had flung himself on work in times of misery, work had never received him, never consoled. Still he'd worked—drilling uses for the Dative of Reference, the Subjunctive of Purpose, into wall-eyed children who would spend short lives selling harness leather or lard or plowing, or spreading lean thighs every year on the wet head of one more baby (toothless draining mouth)—and all this summer since Eva's departure, he'd tinkered at English versions of things he loved in Latin. Most of them things he could not show his students— alas: they were poems to galvanize corpses. On his table at Hatt's he had left his latest raid on the start of the sixty-third poem of Catullus, *Super alta vectus Attis*. With well over half his usable goods beneath his hands now, load the size of a baby, and no destination but back to the train, the long ride, his home—his sister's home, sister with whom he could talk of nothing but greens and beets, the growth of her sons, not even their mutual vanished parents of whom Hatt's memories were richer than his— his own pale memory of Catullus' fury came to his mouth; and he spoke it softly, for no reason then apparent to him.

> Borne on swift ship through deep seas, Attis
> Hastened on yearning feet to Phrygia,
> Came to the Grove—dark, crowned by trees,
> Haunt of the Goddess—where rabid fury,

Wandering mind, forced him with sharp flint
To cast down the heavy burden of his groin;
Then knowing all manhood gone from her limbs,
Fresh blood spotting the face of Earth,
She seized the light timbrel in hands of snow—
Your timbrel, Cybele; your mysteries, Mother—
And ringing soft fingers on hollow oxhide, sang
To her sisters tremulous, "Up! Go, Gallae,
Together to mountain forests of Cybele." . . .

He had a destination; how could he not have known it? He set his grip
from the bed to the floor, quickly stripped the stained lower sheet, carefully folded it to minimum size, went to the large white china washbowl,
and put it to soak in all that was left of his shaving water. It was barely
covered—enough though to leave it unfit for whatever searching eyes
would come—Flora's, whosever. Enough to leech out the evidence and
memory—if not from the cloth then his own mind anyhow (the memory's
one home) and for this one morning, this moment at least—of what he
knew in every cell to have been an ending, what every day of his life till
now had promised and constantly, clearly, whispered to his deaf ears,
dumb heart: *Alone. Love that. Love only that. Beyond you is harm, be-
trayal, theft.* He stood now with wet hands in the rented room, hearing the
voice, believing it, and waiting for the prize of consolation—the descent on
his head of the dense balsam wreath of patience, detachment. It did not
descend. Young as he was, he knew it would never. With his long life
behind him—thirty-odd years of hours entrenched in his total memory, not
one forgot—he knew it would never. He took his grip and left. No one saw
him go.

4

HE scared the old Negro, not by intention but because the path was wet
and silent from the hard rain shower toward four o'clock and because,
soaked himself and tired from the long walk, he looked more harmful than
in fact he was.

The old man dropped the plank he had loudly wrenched from the
shed (there were three more at his feet, good dry heart-pine) and said
"Who you after?"

Forrest smiled—"Nobody"—and knew it was the first lie he'd told in
months.

"They ain't here then. They ain't been here. I'm the man here and
the white man give me permission for this." He pointed to the shed's

south wall, half-stripped of siding, the uprights exposed to day. Green light slotted to the dry earth floor.

Forrest looked to the floor. The white flint circles of masonry were there, apparently unchanged. He walked forward to them and found the center of the room to be dark.

Again the old man said "Who are you?"

Forrest bent to see. Both springs were there far down in the shade, clogged with the trash of years, spider silk, but visibly running, their overflow absorbed by buried piping that, miraculously open, carried the water outdoors, downhill. A chained enamel cup stood on the rim of the closer spring. Forrest reached to take it (seeing, as he reached, that its mate was gone, ripped from its chain and nowhere in sight).

"Drink a drop of that, you'll die before night."

Forrest looked up, still smiling. "I may anyhow."

"You sick?"

Forrest nodded and extended his soaked arms. "Pneumonia."

"Not in August," the Negro said.

"Then exhaustion. I have walked fourteen miles since breakfast. I have not eaten since. I am tired, wet, hungry; and my wife and boy have left me. I'm a lonesome ghost." He intended fun.

"You a man. What your name?"

"Forrest Mayfield."

"Where from?"

"Up north. Near Bracey, Virginia."

"That's a *hundred* miles."

"You been there?" Forrest said.

The Negro said "Near it."

"Who are you?" Forrest said.

"Eighty-some years old."

"How long you lived here?"

"Most of my life, last forty years." The old eyes, yellow as piano keys, met Forrest's, unblinking.

"Where were you in April a year ago then?"

The Negro thought. "Bound to been here," he said.

"You were hiding then."

"What you aiming at?"

"I was here that April with twenty schoolchildren, a dozen mothers, three or four teachers besides myself, buggies and horses; there was nobody here."

The man said, "What's the name of this place?"

"Panacea Springs."

He pointed at the springs with a black hand folded and dry as Forrest's grip. "You think that's one of them healing springs?"

Forrest said, "The old folks did awhile back." He squatted by the circles.

"They all dead, ain't they?"

"Who?"

"Them folks and what they thought."

Forrest looked at the old face. It was almost surely smiling. "Dead and gone," he said.

The Negro said, "I know what I'm talking about. I worked at one of them places in Virginia when I was a boy. Won't nothing but water. Make your pecker work. Like anybody's water." He stood while the words worked over to Forrest through cool damp dimness. Then he also squatted and faced Forrest eye-level, eight feet away. Then he broke into high continuous laughter, a boy's voice, young.

Helpless, Forrest joined him.

5

By seven o'clock they had cooked a supper of sidemeat and hominy and kettle-coffee on the smallest stove in the kitchen of the abandoned Springs Hotel, using the boards from the springhouse as fuel. Then—the Negro leading—they climbed the backstairs and walked the long hall to the front of the house, the second-story porch. The old man carried the hot iron pan with their mutual food; Forrest carried the kettle and the two spring cups, having wrenched off the last one at the Negro's instructions. The porch floor was thick with branches, dead leaves, fallen hornets' nests, a child's shoe; but a space had been cleared at the north breezy end. The Negro headed there and, with his free hand, motioned Forrest to sit in the better place—on the floor with his back to the wall of the house, looking out at the tops of thick undergrowth which had reached that high. The man himself sat as easy as a boy with his back to the posts of the lovely railing; and once he had brought out his long folding knife and halved the meat, he pushed the pan toward Forrest. "Half of it yours."

"Thank you," Forrest said and reached out his hand.

"Forgot your spoon." The Negro felt himself on both breast pockets, reached into one and drew out a tin spoon and held it to Forrest.

"Where's yours?" Forrest said.

"Just one," he said. "Just one for company. I got good fingers." He flexed his long fingers, the spoon still in them.

So Forrest took the spoon; and they ate in silence, each consuming exactly half of all the pan held and hot cups of coffee. By then with the thickness of leaves around them, they were nearly in darkness. Lightning bugs had started their signaling. The old man searched himself again, found a plug of tobacco, and again with his knife cut two equal chews and offered one to Forrest. He took it, though he did not normally chew; and the silence continued while they both made starts on the rich dark cud.

The quiet, the general peace, was so heavy—despite the presence three feet away of a strange old Negro, maybe wild, with a knife—that it calmed whatever of pain or fear had survived Forrest's day, the long hot walk. Or not so much calmed as pressed it down by a greater force—his need for rest having found perfect harbor in this place like a happy afterworld for heroes destroyed in the war of love, an Elysium promised in no religion but palpably here, tonight, and his.

At last the Negro rose, spat over the rail and said, "Mayfield—that your truthful name?"

"Yes," Forrest said.

"That name I told you; that won't my truthful name."

Forrest was certain he had heard no name—its absence was part of the peace he'd felt—but he said "All right."

"I don't tell my truthful name to nobody."

"That's all right with me. I'm obliged to you for kindness. I'll be leaving at daylight."

"What you doing here?" the Negro said.

"You invited me to supper."

"In that shed, I mean; by them dirty springs." He spat again.

Forrest also stood and quietly turned out the contents of his mouth to the dark leaves below. Then he swallowed two mouthfuls of bitter spit in the effort to cleanse his tongue and teeth. His back was turned to both the Negro and the springhouse, but his voice was clear and firm. "This is where a young lady and I made a promise some time ago. I came back to see it."

"You seen it, ain't you?"

"What was left of it," Forrest said. "The little you had left." He wanted to laugh but his head turned instead; and he begged the Negro, "Who are you? What are you doing here?"

"Don't blame me," the Negro said. "I never knew you, never heard you was coming. All I thought was, nobody here for thirty, forty years; nobody coming; I'm keeping me warm." Though the heat of the day had barely lifted, he cradled his arms on himself, rubbed his shoulders.

Calm again, Forrest said, "Tell me something to call you."

The Negro thought. "You need to call me, you call me Zack."

"Thank you," Forrest said. Then he sat again by the cold iron pan and looked up to meet the Negro's eyes, hardly possible now with the progress of evening. "Beg your pardon," he said. "I'd have blamed whoever I spoke to today. I'm in serious trouble."

Zack nodded. "Who you kill?"

"That girl that loved me." Forrest felt that his answer was in fact the truth, though he also knew it would throw this old man into some incalculable response. He knew he wanted that—strike, counter-strike.

"And you come back here to the place you found her?"

"Yes."

"They looking for you?"

"No," Forrest said.

"They starting tomorrow?"

"No," Forrest said.

"They already found her?—and they ain't hunting you?"

"They got her. They don't care where I go."

"She white?"

"Yes," Forrest said.

"You crazy, ain't you?"

Forrest laughed a little and nodded—"But safe."

"Where you going tomorrow?"

"Back home. Virginia."

"Who waiting for you?"

"Kin-people, my job."

"That's one more something than waits on me."

"What's that?" Forrest said.

"Dying. Sickness—that do make two." He was smiling apparently; his voice seemed filtered through a broad smile.

"No people at all?" Forrest said. "On earth?"

"Oh I've got people, I'm fairly sure—two questions about them: where they at? they waiting for *me?*"

Forrest said "Who are you?" He waited a little. "I'm perfectly safe. Never hurt a fly. That's half my problem."

"Just killed your woman?"

Forrest nodded. The lie seemed a handsome gift, return for shelter.

"Bankey Patterson," the Negro said, "born what they called a slave round here, somewhere around here some eighty years past. A good while past, leastways anyhow—this place won't built when I was born, not as I recall. What I recall—you seen I'm in my good mind, ain't you?"

Forrest nodded, all dark.

"What I recall—my mama belonged to a man named Fitts that owned this land through here, three hundred acres. His own house stood where we at now—we on his foundation; his house done burned—and my mama had a little place near your springs. They was there same as now, no shed to roof them but dirty as now. Everybody round here cleaned them out once at least as a child and drank a cold handful—bitter as alum, tasted like a fart, a month-old egg—but nobody ever took a second drink and, sure God, nobody ever thought the world would *pay* to drink it. They did for a while—so it look like, don't it?; so word got to me—but I never had to watch it: dances and sick folks, sick folks dancing. I got out of here." He stopped as if at the sudden end of a stock of generosity he'd thought was large.

"When was that?" Forrest said.

"You tell me," he said. "That's most of my study—when things happen; how they got away from me." He stopped again and waited. "You can read. You tell me—if I'm eighty-some now, what was I at the freedom?"

Forrest calculated with his finger on the dark floor. "Forty-some, I guess."

"Seem like to me I was older than that, *feel* like it anyhow. But maybe not. All my children were born after freedom, so I was still plenty good when it come. I never had married in slavery times. I waited it out. I knew I was waiting."

"For what?" Forrest said.

"A fair chance to see my way to the end. The Fittses was good but the Fittses was humans. They didn't own many niggers, didn't need to—rich as they was, little as they farmed—so they sold they surplus off every year or give them away to they children and kin. I had good eyes; I looked and saw; and when I got to twelve and they kept me on—twelve was when they weeded, before breeding time—I said to myself, 'You hold your own. Tend your own heart, else they break it to Hell.'"

"Why did they keep you?" Forrest said.

"My mama fought for me. Some people say I was kin to the Fittses; and they kept they own (I used to be brighter in the skin than now; bright niggers darken—you notice that?). I always aimed, when I got grown, to ask Mama what was the truth of that; but I never did and now I reckon it's past too late." It was nearly full night; he extended his hand though to search it again. "Her husband was Dolfus, lived some miles from here on another place; and when he come to see her once a month on a pass from his master, she make me sleep in the yard if it's summer. But that don't make me call him Father and I still ain't. The thing I *know* is, Mama fought for me. I never heard her do it; but Zack Fitts told me, they youngest boy that I played with. He say my mama come in one evening to where they all set talking in the parlor and tell the master she need to talk. He rise up and go to meet her in the hall and ask what's troubling her (she they head cook, they jewel); and she say 'Bankey.' —'What Bankey done?' he say. —'Nothing,' she say, 'but you want to kill me, you send him off. I dead in two months. My heart dry in me.' Any nigger say that but Mama be beat; good as Master was, he won't stand that. But Zack tell me his papa say, 'Julia, go home and sleep'; and she know she won. So I had me two debts, to Mama and Master; and I paid on them for all them years till freedom come, a good blacksmith. I'm still strong as iron. And like I tell you, I had me a lesson—hold to your black heart else they ruin it. I ain't saying I turned into no steer—too many heifers around for that, and they coming at me—but I tell you what's truth, white man, once I done humped and groveled my way through the two, three years I was getting my nature, I found out that stuff won't all they claiming. You can buy it and sell it or get it free; but it ain't going to cure one trouble you got, not the least boil rising on your black ass."

Forrest said "Why?"

"You tell me," he said. "I big a fool as you. By time freedom come, my mama was crazy; had lost every bit of the sense she had. Times was hard—niggers all turning wild, white folks turning mean, white trash taking over, our master dead, Zack killed in the war, Mistress and her two girls setting out here just staring at the woods like the woods could help. So I'm at the age you say I am—full-grown man—and leave her, leave Mama with Dip her onliest sister and strike out north. Three reasons why—no work round here, nothing I can do for Mama but watch her eat dirt from the road-bank and pick at herself; and some Yankee pass through holding a paper saying ironworkers wanted in Baltimore, a dollar a day. So I walk to Maryland—Baltimore. No such thing. They ain't hiring niggers. I ought to come home; but what I eat if I come here?—old honeysuckle? So I walk down on the map a little and penetrate all round the state of Virginia, doing nigger jobs—a little blacksmithing, a whole lot of digging; everybody back then always digging holes."

"Were you still by yourself? Traveling alone?"

"I left that out. But to answer your question—yes I traveled alone, light as rabbit fur. But a whole lot of time I was standing still or laying down, and then I had company. Two or three wives; three, four sets of children. All named for me."

"Where are they now?"

He looked round slowly, both sides and behind, as though they all might have gathered while he talked, as though by speaking he had summoned not only their memory but their faces, their palpable accusing bodies. "They ain't with me. I ain't with them."

"You've come here hunting them?"

"No indeed. They never heard of here. I never used to tell present folks my past."

Forrest said, "Is the story you're telling me true?" He felt that an answer was urgent to him now; he didn't know why.

"Pretty nearly, pretty nearly—the way I recall it."

"Then go on. Tell the rest, to now."

The Negro waited. "Nothing else," he said. "What you expect? Eighty years of getting up, working, laying down. You want to hear all that, you need eighty years which I ain't got."

"Please. Why are you here, in this old place?"

"Same reason as you—looking."

Forrest said "For what?"

"My mama."

Forrest gave a little chuff through his nose—laugh, wonder.

"She be in her hundreds if you counting right. Nothing but a girl when I was born. She always say I parted her ways while they still was green; I her live first-born. I looking for her."

Forrest said "Why?"

"To see her again, see do she know me, did she ever get well, get her right mind back, let her blame me some."

"Blame you for what?"

"Not fighting no harder for her, when I could."

Forrest said "How could you?"

"Sat and watched her, talked to her, answered her questions. All the stuff I thought was vain."

Forrest said, "Did you fight for anybody?"

"Me," he said quickly and struck at himself, palm on his chest twice, dry hollow thumps. Then he waited and thought and said, "Who the Hell you?—all time doubting me, all time asking *why?* I'm telling you *what,* the *what* I recall, what I need to find. If you here to listen, you listen to *what*. It's all I giving."

Forrest also waited. Then he said "Beg your pardon."

"I don't beg yours. Who you anyhow?"

Forrest told him again—his name, age, home, his work.

"And you killed your woman?"

"What she felt for me, yes."

"But she still living?"

Forrest nodded in the dark.

"And you hunting her?"

The answer reached Forrest from wherever it had waited or freshly burgeoned. In total dark it caused him no pain to give it to this rank old madman, powerless to use its news, powerless to hurt. "No I'm not," he said. "I am heading home."

Bankey said, "I'm there. And I'm ready to sleep. You welcome to sleep in my poor home." He waited, then cackled with laughter awhile, then bowed from the waist toward where Forrest sat, then entered the black house.

6

THERE were two large rooms on the front of the house, the old public rooms. When Forrest stood and followed Bankey indoors, he found him waiting in the hall, hand extended; found him with his own hand in the unrelieved dark. The dry old skin gave a rustle at his touch—hide of a rattler, dragon, hermit; the skin of all Negroes he had ever touched, the tough loving cooks (spiteful and tender) of his own childhood—but he did not refuse it; and Bankey said "You ready?" Forrest nodded which no human eye could have seen and felt himself drawn off to the right, the center of that room, till his toes were stumped by a low soft obstacle. "This your bed." Bankey left him.

Forrest squatted and felt at the mass on the floor. It seemed a pallet made of carpets or draperies; *dirt, vermin*, he thought but didn't care. Again a huge weight, greater than fatigue, was pressing him earthward. So great even he did not struggle to see it, name it, discern its need or diet. He loosened his high shoes and lay and sank. No fear. Surrender.

After hours of pure sleep and lesser dreams, he came to this. He had walked for days, in familiar country, southern Virginia (pine woods, rolling pastures, the trees and the air one enormous bell ceaselessly rung by millions of thirteen-year cicadas); and now tired but calm, he had come to a small town, a boarding house. He had signed his name in the book which the lady kept by the door (the house was her home, small but cool; she was beautiful, a widow in her early forties, well-spoken, fighting with lovely and effortless grace to feed her children, herself, her servants, by the hard expedient of opening her doors to a streaming world—he felt that in the dream). She led him to a room on the back of the house, far from noise; and once she had shown him the wardrobe and basin, she turned to go, then stopped and said "This bed is yours." There were two iron beds, one large, one small; she had shown him the small. He did not ask why, only set down his grip (which by now he had rigged with rope as a pack); but she smiled and said, "You have paid for a room that holds two people. Now we'll wait for the other." Then she turned and left; and he did not see her, had in fact no life at all till evening when from far at the other side of the house a bell rang supper and he washed and went. And had eaten a full meal—steak, pan gravy, corn, greenbeans, tomatoes—when the lady appeared in the dining-room door and, grave as a sibyl, searched the faces of his fellow feeders. It was him she wanted. Forrest knew that at once—there was someone behind her in the darkening hall—but he did not speak. A fellow guest, a young man at his right, was asking him the purpose of his journey. As he offered his face to the lady's search, he was also trying to answer the question, to remember the answer. Just when he knew and was ready to speak, the lady spoke also but not to him. She turned to the person waiting behind her and clearly said, "Mayfield—take the seat by Mr. Mayfield." An elderly man—white hair in clean long locks to his shoulders, the clothes of a wanderer (more nearly a tramp)—stepped slowly forward. As he came he studied only the floor, his shuffling feet; a careful mover forced into care by age and exhaustion. Forrest thought he should rise to help the man; but the young man beside him again asked the purpose of his lengthy trip; so Forrest turned and said, "My health, for my health"; and by then the old man was seated beside him. Silently. Breathing hard from his effort, the latest leg of his own long journey, but no word of greeting and no look, no smile. The old man faced only his plate, empty, white; and when Forrest passed the cooling food to him, he served himself in silence, staring down. The young man beside Forrest asked what was wrong—"You look quite well"—but Forrest was openly watching the old man and knew, though he couldn't look up now to check, that the lady stood on in the doorway, watching also. She was watching two—Forrest, the old man—and still she was grave, not from puzzlement but fear: that something would not happen. It did. Then. The old man separated a biscuit into halves. He was Forrest's father. Forrest saw it; no question of doubt or error. He sensed that the lady was also smiling. Forrest spoke the name—"Robinson. Father." The old man ate the biscuit slowly, still watching his plate. He did not seem hungry. He was eating because he had been led there where eating was expected. Yet when he had chewed it all and swallowed, he turned to Forrest waiting with eyes from the morning which Forrest remembered; but with this crushing difference—their gaze was no longer needy or searching, merely polite. He was trying to think of an answer for this stranger smiling beside him. No one but Forrest was waiting now. All the others were eating blackberry roll (it was mid-July); the lady had gone. The old man—Robinson Mayfield undoubtedly, the father Forrest had not seen for twenty-eight years, for whom he now yearned—that old man carefully said "Forgive me," then smiled. "Maybe so. You may very well be right. I am too tired to say. Too tired, too far." Forrest did not wonder *Too far* from what or why his heart yearned so fiercely tonight for the simple sound of his own name spoken in that old voice. He said "Forgiven" and turned to the food congealed on his plate.

In the midst of that, at the point where Forrest heard the dinner bell, black Bankey came to the door of the room and stood—no light. Since leaving Forrest here, he had been to the kitchen to deposit their pan, then into the breezeway to wash his feet, then back to the front room opposite Forrest's. He had sat in an armchair and tried to sleep (he had not slept flat on his back for years—danger of death) but had failed and succeeded only in thinking: memory, faces he had hoped to see only in Heaven (he was certain of Heaven, though afraid to go). So he'd crossed the hall and listened for the sounds that would locate Forrest and, more, tell his nature—the secret signals of kindness or cruelty which, all his life, Bankey had detected in darkness or light, near or far.

He stood and listened till the end of the dream. There seemed to be sounds of quicker breath, two muffled blows of a fist on the floor; but age had dulled the special keenness of his organ of knowledge (that film of skin on his palms, in his nostrils, across his eyes that received from the world—or had for eight decades—the urgent news: early warning or, rarely, confirmation of clear path ahead, invitation to safety, pleasure, rest); and silence had taken the room again.

So Bankey moved slowly to enter the space, sliding each foot forward with fear and care so as not to touch the body somewhere there asleep, afloat in its secret life, castaway. Bankey thought some of that—and felt it all—and when he knew that his right foot had come to the edge of the body, he stopped and waited a little, thinking. The white man covered in dark beneath him—in reach of all his organs of touch, his harmful instruments—seemed quiet again, entirely quiet. Bankey slowly reached to his own hip pocket, no fumbling now, and found his knife. He opened it silently and in one move, fluid and quiet as a snake—no cracking of joints—he knelt to the floor.

His knees touched Forrest's warm right hand where, abandoned in the dream, it lay open, empty. The knife was in Bankey's own right hand. He extended his left and with perfect aim inserted his forefinger, dry, and touched Forrest lightly on the palm. Misery poured from the hand into Bankey like the jolting current he had known thirty years before when lightning struck a mule he had just finished plowing fifty yards away and slammed through the damp earth to burn his feet. His finger moved on still accurately and stopped at the crest of the sleeping wrist where a pulse thudded up to meet him like cries, deep wide-spaced bellowing. He had not felt active pity for years, maybe since his mother lost her mind and raved; but he felt it now and knew its name and also thought he knew its demand.

He drew back his probing hand, extended the other—the right hand armed with the open knife—and with no need to gauge his force or feel for his target, he pulled the sharp edge once across the wrist. Lightly though, a dry rehearsal. He felt again. The wrist was dry and in that instant of touch, Bankey knew he could not help this man, not give him the peace that lay in his power to render now. He drew back his knife, folded and hid it in his pocket again.

Then knowing there was no chance that he would sleep and die unawares, he lay slowly back on the hard floor. Forrest was just beyond his reach, ten inches more than the length of his arm; and to ease the morning, the strange awakening, Bankey's head was laid at Forrest's feet. At first light Forrest would not have to wake to immediate sight of Bankey's eyes, open and waiting.

He woke a good two hours past dawn, not from any external sound or movement or Bankey's nearness or the light full on him through the tall east window but from satiation, a rest so deep and venturesome as to give him the sense, as his eyes broke open, of lightness and cleanness, of a life unburdened by past or future, all an open *present* like a cleared field in sunlight. A sense of healing that bore in its heart no threat to end. His dream had sunk beneath conscious memory, and the turbulence that rose from its plummet was hope. He could live his life; he knew the way. And so he was happy for twenty, thirty seconds. He had waked on his back; and all he had seen till then was ceiling, the strangely intact unstained white plaster twelve feet above.

But Bankey had waited as long as he could. When he heard the final sounds of waking, he quickly rose to his knees again and was there over Forrest. "I'm going with you."

Forrest looked. All the causes of misery stood in him, large and genuine, his respite ended. "Where am I going?" he said.

Bankey smiled, the first time. "You say. I'm following."

Forrest said "Why?"

"You by yourself now. You need some help, need somebody. I'm free and ready."

Forrest said, "You are looking for your mother."

"Did I tell you that?" Bankey said. "I was. When I came back down here, I thought I was—two, three weeks ago. First day, I come straight here, found this. I knew it was the place; somebody told me years ago the Fittses had sold out to some poor trash that had built this hotel and then gone broke. But before they left, they tore down all that was in my memory except your springs and a tree or two I recognized. All the quarters was gone—my mama's house, Dip her sister's, the shop I forged in. Trees and foul water. So I walked on to Micro—I knew that good, ain't barely changed—and asked this old white man in the store if he heard of Julia Patterson. He told me, 'Sure. Old crazy Julia. Lived back yonder with all them dogs.' I ask was she live. He say he ain't seen her for twenty years; but he say, 'Don't trust me. Heap of folks I ain't seen ain't dead, and some of em come back and cheat me.' I ask him who must I trust; and he say, 'Won't she a Fitts nigger? Miss Caroline Fitts still living up the road.' He tell me where; so I go and there she, old as me and meaner and three-fourths blind. But she knew me the minute she see my face. 'You're too late, Bankey,' she say first thing; 'I'm poor as you' (it looked like she was, but she a big liar). I say to her I ain't here for money, but can she tell me where Mama is? She say to me 'No' as quick as that. —'When she die?' I say. Miss Caroline say, 'Who say she dead? Maybe she living in the Washington White House, cooking angel-food cakes for Teddy Roosevelt. Maybe she living in a shack near here with fourteen hounds, eating dirt and scratching. Either way, you're no good to her now. Too late, Bankey; too late again.' She always been the bitch in the crowd, Miss Caroline; but she tell what her mouth think is so; so I didn't backtalk none at all. I say to her 'True.' Then she say 'Where you living?' and I ask her do she have a suggestion? She say 'No' again; she quick as ever. I ask her, 'Who own that old piece of hotel where the house used to be?' She say 'I do.' I told her I heard the Fittses lost it. —'Did,' she say, 'but the trash that bought it couldn't sit there and work long enough to pay the mortgage so it's mine again.' Then she study me hard, then say 'You want it?' I say 'Yes' to see what she mean. —'Take it,' she say. 'It's mine to give. Take it, use it and when you done, burn it. But don't come asking me for Julia again or money or food. Don't bring me your face another time.' Then she shut the door. I swear to God—two weeks ago."

Forrest nodded. "I believe you. You've got a grand home." He smiled, waved round at the big bright room.

Bankey said, "This don't mean birdshit to me."

Forrest said "It does to me." He had heard all that, half-risen, arms propped behind him. Now he reached for his shoes and laced them on carefully. Then he stood and walked four steps toward the door (nearer to the door than Bankey, still kneeling); then he turned and said, "I'm sorry, Bankey, and I thank you for kindness. I am going home myself—eventually, I hope." As Forrest spoke, he knew he had said that last night; but it came entirely differently now like the mention of a gate, a goal not a terminus. "And, the way I'll live, I cannot use you. I would be no help on earth to you."

"Help won't what I needed," Bankey said. "I *helping* myself." He rose, faced Forrest and extended his arms to demonstrate his truthfulness—his strength well-tended for a man any age, the knowledge of his years intact, unhardened, offered for use.

Though he did not know it and never would, Forrest had taken the thing he could use—the message imparted by Bankey's example, inserted in his sleep: the dream still buried beneath his memory; his own lost father, burnt-out, abandoned. He felt in his coat, withdrew his wallet and extended a paper dollar toward Bankey. "For your trouble," he said.

Bankey shook his head and held his place, his eyes full open, unblinking on Forrest, who said again "Thank you" and turned and, finding his grip in the hall, went quickly out.

7

By the middle of the morning he had got to Micro, a crossroads—two stores, post office, a depot, six or eight squatty houses in sight. A train was in the station, northbound and ready. Two Negro girls in white clothes were boarding. He could be home by evening. But he knew his purpose, or his plan if not its purpose; and he walked past the train with his grip in hand and waved at the sweating conductor to show they could leave without him, which they slowly did.

Then he went in the first of the stores and waited till a game of backgammon had played itself out. Then he bought a tablet of paper and a pencil and asked the clerk, "Ever heard of a Negro named Julia Patterson?"

"Never hear of nobody else, looks like." The clerk was a hunchback five feet high with snow-white hair and eyebrows the black of fresh hot pitch—no smile, no chance of one. "Why you need to know?"

Forrest said, "I don't need to know; I wondered. I heard she was old and pitiful."

"Old all right. Last time I saw her—ten, twenty years ago—she was pushing eighty. But save your pity. I've been at this counter all my life; what I don't see is known but to God. She went crazy right after niggers ran free. They all went crazy, don't you know, but her worse. That didn't stop her though from her main business—way into her fifties, when most women dry up, she went on dropping babies every nine months. Bred em like maggots. Eight or ten head at her shack any time, and her raving round like a hoot owl at harvest. Then she did dry up or—maybe; let me see; yes, I know I'm right—the Klan took a hand. Younguns scattered like tumbleturds in the breeze; some old as twenty, breeding their own. So she just had dogs from there on out, lived alone with dogs, her the mangiest one. Save your pity, friend. Put it on *my* back. I'm a working cripple." He showed his back. "Born with this."

"I'm sorry," Forrest said. "You've earned your keep." And before the man could question him further, he took up his purchase and went into daylight, knowing as it struck him that he needed food, knowing more strongly that he needed to leave.

8

By early afternoon he had walked eight miles; and hunger was gathering behind his eyes, a small clenched fist. But he'd walked on narrow roads in deepening country—no town, only two or three far poor houses, no wild thing to eat (though vines were heavy with hard green grapes, due in late September)—so when his path descended once more to a sandy creek-crossing, he told himself he must stop here and wash. Then he'd be fit at least to ask for food at the next likely house. There was no house in sight, no sense of one near; still he turned off the path and entered the dense woods that banked the creek and walked till the path was well-hid behind him and, in the green dark, there was no sound of bird or squirrel or snake. Only his own loud feet on ground that might well not have been touched till then.

A tight tall clearing—open half-circle with the creek on one side, thicket all behind, and a shaft of green air rising through the hole in high beech trees toward sky, sunlight (which only reached this depth, slowed and cooled as though it had fallen through miles of seawater, millions of tons). Forrest stopped in the center and listened closely for human sounds—none, only water. So he went to the thicket side, set down his grip, untied his shoes, then stripped off the clothes that were now fine nets retaining the dirt and secreted misery of two full days. In fact as he peeled down his underdrawers and caught their stench, he wanted above all to wash every thread in the quick clear water—and had leaned to gather them for that purpose when calm thought told him they would not dry in this light in less than a day. A measure of both his need and his calm, the curious peace that had numbed him all day, was the fact that he stood whole moments and thought, "I will wash them and wait—a whole day, two, in this one spot" and did not see the wait as intolerable. What decided him against it was merely the will for physical motion—to be out of this place and into another, no conscious thought of his movement as either *flight* or *hunt; for* or *from* anyone, anything.

He spread each piece of his clothing to air on clean low bushes (the ground was dry to his tender feet, but there'd been no rain; road dust could not sift in this deep). Then he walked to the edge of the water and studied it. A simple bank of sand, brown gravel; no holes for snakes. Two feet or so of water over sand, round rocks—cold and with strong eddies threading his calves as he stepped to the middle. He looked to the bottom for crawfish, minnows.

Waste. Shameful waste, the shame of which was only his. Sinful waste, an offense in the nostrils of whatever powers witnessed or intended his stopped dry life. The sight of his sex, hung dark from the dark hair of his whiter groin, roped with the veins that (however vulnerable) still bore the blood that could swell him to ready strength in a moment should there be an object, be a present need—that daily sight, familiar as his hands, brought down the frail but roofing shed he had nailed above him in the months since Eva and Rob's departure, a roof made of pride in his gift for solitude (the main gift offered by his whole past life), patches of work, messages from Eva, patches of hope, the thought of (at last) a life companioned, the sight of a son taking form before him, short kindnesses from passers. *Rotten scantlings.* The screened light of day, the eyes of his own mind, had full sight now of his white huddled life—a thirty-three-year-old orphan boy who could teach Latin verbs to country children, whose dick would work in the presence of friction (give pleasure, strow seed), whose hand could chop wood, weed a garden, tinker out a milksop line of verse; but who could not extend that same plain hand (competent, ready) and seize the only food he desired. Seize and *hold*—hold by becoming, in deed and word, pleasant himself to whomever he needed, then deeply delightful, then vital for life. He had never been that to anyone—oh vital to his son in the sense of providing the first warm clot but now (when the boy was six months old and, however weakened, increasingly aware of the passing world and smiling surely) not even so much as pleasant to him. To Eva, what?—a recollection, memory from which all force had leaked.

He stood in the water, swayed by its mild hands, staring at his life, unable to weep but retching from the sour pit of his belly, hacking at the young firm cords of his trunk as though his error were a gorging hookworm, a fluke encysted, a suckfish fastened to the base of his heart which violence could now dislodge and kill.

As though he were not already standing in the life he wanted, the life he required—palpable as this water around him, clean and cleansing.

9

August 4, 1904

Dear Sister,

I am all right and hope that you and the boys are bearing the heat and having cool nights. I have talked to Eva. I have not seen Rob, though I am told he is coming along better now and has a fair chance. Otherwise I now know that your fears were justified. I do not think we shall see Eva again.

Again, as I said, I am all right. I am coming home slowly. So look for me when you see me.

Your grateful brother,
Forrest Mayfield

August 4, 1904

Dear Grainger,

I hope very much that this message finds you. If so, I am pretty sure you are surprised. You would be a lot more surprised if you could see where and how I am writing it. I am about twenty miles northwest of Fontaine, North Carolina, propped against a beech tree beside a creek in which I have just bathed myself. Now I am waiting for my traveling clothes to air before I commence my trip again. My trip is eventually toward home; but I have decided to walk for my health and since, with the heat, that may take four or five more days, I am writing this to mail at the next depot. You will have it tomorrow evening, if Aunt Veenie passes anywhere near the post office.

It is to say that if you still mean what you told me last month, then I am ready to accept. I am also glad. You can help me, Grainger. In the fall I will be moving out of my sister's into some place private to me if I can, and there I will need somebody's help.

If you are ready to leave your people and live in Bracey or wherever I go and if you will work as hard as you promised and grow up clean and honest and loyal, then I will be faithful to tend your needs.

Read this message to Veenie and ask her to guide your choice. If you answer Yes, you must stay with her till I get back and find some suitable quarters. Or maybe in the weeks before school opens, I will need to travel and you can come with me.

Be serious, Grainger, and give me your word as soon as you can. I will send to know when I reach home. I will also hope to hear you have read the books I lent you and can answer questions.

                          Very truly,
                          Forrest Mayfield

AUGUST 1904

THERE was no word from Grainger at home when he got there—Hatt's home strange to him now as a hostel, with an air that repelled him, a literal odor of death in his nostrils, the brown dry odor of generations of choking and throes. The walk had stetched into five full days, more than time for the letter to precede him; but when he asked Hatt for mail or messages, she said "Not a word" with, he thought, a harsh pleasure—he was hers again. She had thought he was hanging on news from Eva; he did not correct her. He went out within an hour of arriving, having only taken time to wash and change, and walked to the post office (still open at six) and checked for his own mail; then asked Miss Lula if she had any mail for old Aunt Veenie—he was headed to see her.

"Nothing since that one you sent her boy, three, four days ago. First they've got in years." There was good-natured triumph on her face; she'd known his hand.

But he would not rally. "He got it then?"

"I gave it to her personally, told her I'd read it to her."

"It was Grainger's," he said.

Miss Lula smiled. "She said that herself, said he could read; if his name was on it, she'd take it to him. I told her it was, with *Master* in front of it and in your writing. So it got here, yes. Or as near here as Veenie. She may have forgotten it and have it in her bosom still. If you don't remind her, it'll stay there till October 1st, her fall bath."

Forrest nodded and left and walked ten yards, meaning to go straight to Veenie's and check; then he stopped and wondered where Veenie lived. He had not been there in twenty years; now that he thought, he had never been there—never had any reason or wish to go. Veenie had simply materialized throughout his youth when his mother needed help. He did remember going with Hatt to the funeral of one of Veenie's daughters and cringing at the spectacle of wild grief and rage which issued from the generally solemn Veenie like the voice and fury of a hurtful spirit, a demon entrenched. But her house, no. It would be on Clay Hill, the north end of town, where loose strings of cabins rode the pitching tumult of red slick earth.

So he headed there and met no one he had ever seen—children born in his years away, in rags that could not conceal their laughter—but he did not need to ask directions. She was in the yard of the third place he passed, in a straight-backed chair that seemed made from cast-up pieces of the Ark, in the shade of a low umbrella tree—though all was in virtual shade by now—and she watched him come up the hill, cross the gulley, with no sign of recognition or welcome. Yet she seemed alone—no one else in sight, no dog or chickens—and in need of company. He charged it to her cataracts and came to within two feet of the chair before he stopped and squatted below her.

She faced him squarely, still no flicker of greeting.

He said "What you doing?"—his voice would name him.

"You really asking," she said, "or passing time?"

"Asking," he said.

"Then what I'm doing is waiting on you, what I been doing four or five days."

"Grainger got my message then?"

"No," she said.

He pointed behind them back toward town. "Miss Lula said she gave the letter to you."

Veenie nodded. "She did."

"Then what?" Forrest said.

"I got it," she said.

"Does Grainger know?"

She shook her head.

"Is he still here?"

She nodded. "Out somewhere playing with some little girl."

Forrest stood—her eyes didn't follow him—and looked in a circle: no other humans. "Aunt Veenie," he said, "kindly tell me why."

Her eyes had found him. "Sparing *him*," she said.

"Sparing him what?"

"You trying to harm him."

He thought she had yielded to age, confusion; so he waited awhile, then went on calmly. "Harm is the last thing I intend. Veenie, you sent him to meet me, remember?—three months ago. He took to me. We worked together those weeks at Hatt's, painting her roof, building new steps. He's a good worker and, like I say, he took to me—"

She nodded. "He did."

"—So when I quit to go south for my wife and boy, he said he would like to serve me for good. I told him thank you but that I was expecting my own folks back and would not be able to pay his keep. Now I can. The letter says that. It offers him work."

"What else?" Veenie said.

"Just that—good care as long as I live. You know my people keep their word."

She made a snorting sound, high in her head as if from her eyes. "I ain't studying that—your people's word; *I* know your people some sixty years before you born. What I'm asking you is, what else you tell him in that letter yonder?" She pointed to her house, its whereabouts.

Forrest tried to recall, tried to guess her concern. "Not another thing that I remember; oh I said I hoped he had read my books."

"Read em all fore you got to the edge of town." She laughed at that, the incredible memory, a picture before her. Forrest joined her briefly; then when she'd calmed she said, "Forrest, listen. Will you give your oath?" She had whispered it, a confidence in an empty world.

"I will if I understand," he said. "Veenie, I do not understand."

But as he spoke, she was rising and going toward the house—six or eight steps, tottering slowly in an arc as grand as a ship underway, before she stopped and waited, listening; then turned and said "You said you would." She paused no longer, going on, climbing steps, vanishing inward.

Forrest waited. He did not want to follow her—her general air of harsh mystery, the edge of harm which even at her age she pressed against him, and (easier to face, his conscious reason) the promised heat and stink of her house. Two other reasons urged him though—the chance of light on her curious claims and, stronger, the chance of Grainger's help in whatever lay ahead for his own remaining life. So he went toward her or at least in her tracks. For all he knew of what lay ahead, the dark low doorway open on darkness might hold behind it a wall of solvent that had just taken Veenie and waited now to take him also, reduce him to essence in punishment. But he went and quickly. And stopped on the sill to let his eyes open.

The room seemed also a relic of the Flood, survivor of many floods beached here. Except for the tin stove painted silver, it all was wood—wood scoured with sand or ashes or lye to a blond near-white so that what his eyes adjusted to from the waning day was not the promised darkness but an excess of light. Veenie herself was the darkest thing—she and the low trunk she knelt before, a black horsehair lady's trunk with brass studs, its rolled lid open. He watched only her, unable to search elsewhere in the room for signs of Grainger, hints of other lives; and hers was the only odor that reached him—not fetid but strong, proud metal of age, an exhalation of the core of force that had brought her this far in a life as low to the earth as a weed, untrammeled and rank. And the posture she held now (kneeling, straight-backed) was clearly no bow but a purposeful, calmly considered self-service. He stared on, silent through her rummaging.

Finally she turned. "Come here to me." It was not the mock-hard voice Negroes kept for laggard children; it was feral but still contained by a purpose.

Forrest felt he was summoned to retribution but also felt, whatever his crime, the justice of the summons; so he went through the bright room (it seemed to take hours) and stopped three feet from Veenie by a bed. A small bed, wooden, short and narrow, cleanly made and spread in August with a quilt—Grainger's surely, his length and width.

Veenie's eyes found him, held onto him. "I had a Bible your grandma give me right at the freedom, saying I would need it; but I never needed it. I kept it in here locked up from niggers and now it's gone." She waited and thought. "You swear anyhow."

"All right," he said. "Tell me what."

She waited again, then turned and reached back into her trunk, searched under more quilts and folded skirts till she found a parcel wrapped in white tissue. With her back still to Forrest, though he could see, she unwrapped it slowly with her careful utterly inhuman fingers—the brown prehensile tentacles of sea-life, blind but infallible. What she had was a picture.

Forrest caught a glimpse before she took it to her chest and rubbed it there—cleaning it? greeting it?—faded and sepia, apparently a man. Was she finally crazy? Should he turn and go?

She rounded on him. "This good enough. Swear on this." She offered the picture on both flat palms.

A man, yes. More nearly a boy—sixteen, seventeen. His dark fine hair parted sharply on the left and pulled back high on a broad smooth forehead. Deep-set eyes that seemed blue or gray—startlingly bright in their recessed sockets, in the picture's pallor, and immensely sad. A long straight nose, a long straight line of mouth slightly down. What seemed the beginnings of a mustache and goatee, more fur than hair, that soft and defensive. A dark coat and vest, light shirt and stock, a watch chain and fob. Short arms—wrists showed at the bottom edge, but the hands were omitted. No visible sign of resemblance to Veenie. If the boy were black, it was just a taint; long lines to Britain stretched back of the eyes. Forrest brought the fingers of his right hand together and laid the five tips on the boy's sad face. Then he nodded his head.

"Say it," Veenie said.

He said "I swear."

"All right," she said. She turned at once to wrapping the picture.

Forrest stood encased in the heat of the room, feeling it for the first time—an element in which all will to movement seemed idle, ludicrous. So he did not move, but he said to Veenie "What have I sworn?"

She went on wrapping. "To never tell Rover, Jess, Gardn—" She broke off the roll of her scattered kin. "What's my baby name?"

"Grainger."

"To never tell Grainger his rightful story."

"Who did I swear on?"

Her hands stopped work. She turned and studied him. "Your daddy, fool. Your Mr. Rob."

His hand flew out. "Show me."

She balked.

"Please. I don't know him."

She gripped the covered picture. "Your own blood daddy."

"I was five when he left."

"Other people was young when he done other things, not young enough though."

Stunned, baffled as he was, Forrest knew his only hope—here with her—was to take one thread of the tangle and hold it; refuse to drop it till it led to help or proof of her lunacy, proof of malice. He chose the face, asked for it again.

She handed him the parcel.

He opened it, careful as she; and tilting the face toward the small side window, pressed the image with his own good eyes for recognition, response, reward. Nothing came. He worked at the eyes especially—the strongest trace left in his own mind—but while he could see again their beauty, their faded lament, he did not feel the stock of images joining: his memory to this. "Where did you get it?" His own voice shocked him far more than the face, a steely tone of insatiable demand.

"He gave it to me."

"I don't believe you." The fat of his right thumb rubbed the face, still no knowledge. "When did he give it?"

"You right. I stole it."

"Who from?"

"Your mama's stuff, when she dead."

"How come?"

"It mine just much as hers," Veenie said. Her own force flowed back into her voice.

"The Hell you say. I've gone these long years with no face for him."

"You got it now."

"Have I?" Forrest said. "How will I know? You may be lying again, again."

Veenie said "I ain't. You his picture, Forrest." She pointed behind him, a fragment of looking-glass propped on a table beside a basin.

But he knew his own face. He studied the picture, touching it over and over, Braille. He was; and for reasons he did not now consider, he had failed to see it—the live present image of this vanished boy, give or take some grief, whoever the boy. A clamor of something—hunger? devotion?

the new chance of joy?—poured out of his heart, an uprush of birds. "Where is he?" he said, his voice low but firm.

"Richmond City last I heard."

Forrest said "When was that?"

"Oh Jesus. Don't ask me."

"Since Mother died?"

Veenie thought that out and nodded Yes. By now her eyes had dropped from his. She watched the legs of the nearest table.

"Since I left home?"

She thought again. "How old is Grainger?"

"Twelve, I think."

"Twelve," she said. "Twelve years ago then; that's the last." She pressed with her thin arms, palms flat as stovelids, to rise and stand.

"Goddammit, Veenie, stay still and *tell* me." He touched her forehead, bald as an old man's—not with pressure but to stress his urgency, the three middle fingers of his left hand: she was cold.

She had borne, fairly often in her life, physical trials harder than this—a beating for theft at seventeen; the hackings of various careless men (no care but for their own hunger), the procession through her tight dry narrows of eleven children; the deaths of nine (death, for her, being physical trial)—but she could not remember, now where she knelt, the last time she'd cried. When was the last death?—she couldn't think: Cassie's? Anica's? ten, twenty years ago? Her face was wet, both dull eyes streaming; and though she struggled to hold herself, before this boy with no claim on her, the rails of her chest could not hold the noise—her mouth and nose gave off high bellows. *A broke-down cow lost far from the herd*; she thought it that way. But she did not think of the boy above her, knowing in her tough heart that he (little he) was not a cause of her present affliction, only a trigger, the blind slewfoot that kicked down the first grit that tripped the rockslide.

Forrest saw her and said in an easier voice, "Remember. I don't understand anything. You're the one that can tell me."

It took her awhile (his hand stayed on her); but she calmed herself enough to say, "Mr. Forrest, I figured you knew all this. I beg your pardon. I ought to been dead thirty years ago."

"You won't die," he said.

"You right," she said. "I pray for it some. Lord good to me when I ask Him right."

"I've asked *you* something."

She stood up slowly; he let her rise. "I know you have. Let me set down here. My knees give out." She shuffled past him to the near small bed and sat on the edge. Then she motioned him over to the second bed, ten feet away, a broad marriage bed. "Sit yonder and rest where I can see you."

He kept his place.

"Sit down. It's clean as your right hand—Grainger's bed. He love to stretch."

Forrest went and sat and bore her direct gaze for the time it took her to find whatever of him she could see and focus on. When she started speaking, he looked to the floor, imagining at least that it was cooler, that the ground beneath (visible in cracks) was cooler still.

"Start with me," Veenie said. "Start with Veenie Goodwin. I one of your mama's folks' favorite niggers cause I breed so good; your mama's granddaddy call me 'Mean But Quick.' First baby I drop, I was still a child—twelve years old, I guess. First baby to live come later though, three years later when I learned how to have em and keep em, both together— come a big fat girl named Mary Lucretia. Your great-grandmammy name her that; I was too weak to study no names, I tell you. Good like I was, I was always weak; took the bed for the best part of two weeks every time. Say I'm lazy; go on and say it. Too late—it's done. Good sleeping rest!" She laughed for herself, not expecting response. Once started now, this was all for herself. He was only the room in which she said it, excuse for reeling it out aloud. "All I call her was Mary Lu, and she the next in what I'm telling. She young as me, maybe younger still, when she have her first, another bitch. Your mama's great-uncle say womens in my line has a bitch first to open the track; then the race is for dogs. He mean men-babies and he near bout right. Mary Lu's was Anica. Then Anica waited till she near dead, seventeen years old; and *she* drop a girl, Elvira Jane. I go on having em all this time; ain't studying being no great-grandmammy at forty-five years old, give or take; but what I'm telling now stop right there. On Anica's girl, Elvira Jane. My old head say she born fore freedom; but she big enough to run and talk when it come, cause it's her that brought it to me and Trim. We sitting in the dark, cooling off from day—March, early planting—and she come running and say the news: 'Miss Pattie say we free. Start moaning.' Miss Pattie—she your mama's own grandmammy; she foreman, overseer, everything else while mens at war—Miss Pattie she think we due to moan. Some did, some didn't. Elvira didn't. She don't remember no hard time at all, but she take to freedom like it got her name wrote on it in ink. So it stop with her." Veenie stopped—a clear end, no pause.

Forrest looked. She still watched him or the space he filled. To give her a moment more of grace, he looked aside—an old wicker fern-stand beside the bed; the socket intended for plants had been lined with flannel, and his books were there, Grainger's cache: *Gayley's Classic Myths of Greece and Rome*; a McGuffey he himself had used as a boy; *The Boy's Life of Washington*; *The Indian Princess* (a life of Pocahontas); Mrs. Ashmore's *History of the Commonwealth of Virginia*; *Tom Sawyer, Detective*. Rob his own son—he thought of Rob, first time in hours. These were rightfully Rob's, should be stored up for him. Some of them bore inscriptions in his mother's bold hand—always *Forrest from his mother, to help him on* and the date, never more.

"They Grainger's," Veenie said. She could see him after all.

Forrest said, "I'm glad to let him use them."

"He'll use em *up,*" Veenie said and waited. Then she said, "Where he at once he know every bit of that foolishness by heart? Where that take him he ain't at now?—under some fig bush rubbing some nigger girl's flat little titties?"

Forrest stood and took two steps toward her. "Where is my father? And why do you know? Give me his picture."

She gave him more, dead at his face, her own eyes not blinking once as she finished the tale she knew and had sworn him to keep. "He Elvira's white man, he Rover's daddy. Why I know he in Richmond some years back—when Rover had his first child in Maine and it was a boy, this boy here Grainger, he wrote your daddy a letter to tell him; and your daddy sent back a five-dollar goldpiece. Rover still got it. Rover always knowed. Elvira told him, told him everything down to where your daddy was boarding at. Worst thing she done; that's saying a mouthful. I told her when she died, God never forgive her. She my own great-grandbaby-daughter; but I stood right yonder"—Veenie pointed to the floor before the big bed where he had just sat, the spot his feet had touched—"and said as she sucked her last cold breath, 'Nobody love you no more. Go on.' "

It was Elvira's funeral he and Hatt had attended. "Does my sister know?"

"Don't ask her," Veenie said. "Don't ask nobody. You swore to me you stop it *here.*" She pointed again to the floor between them. "I may be the meanest nigger left, but you swore to me."

Forrest nodded. "I did."

In the yard, filtered to them through knot-pierced walls, a dog spoke once in pleasure.

A Negro girl said "Come back here."

A Negro boy said, "Go your way. I'm heading home"—Grainger on the steps.

Within, both Forrest and Veenie smiled—he fully; she barely, weak from her story, the backward trek he had forced on a life that aimed only forward: death, rest.

2

THAT evening Forrest had pled exhaustion to Hatt and taken three syrup biscuits upstairs where the trapped heat of day was no added burden to his head and chest that seemed now either released from failure—a shaft onto

hope—or permanently stove, past remorse or repair. He had opened the
window on the hills behind, no lamp for bugs, and eaten one biscuit and
stripped and washed; then had turned back the blankets Hatt offered year
round and slid in between rough sheets—a welcome. His hands had risen
and dropped by his ears, fingers closed but unclenched (he had sought
sleep thus each night of his life there was no one to hold, literal surrender). Sleep had accepted and he'd sunk for an hour through peaceful
depths.

Then Hatt stood over him. No reason to knock now, she'd listened at
the door; then opened it quietly and entered and looked for a long time
(the boys were back on the hill, playing late). Then silent she set her lamp
on the table and touched the covered blade of his left shin and learned he
was bare. His nearness reached her, stirred the silt of her own loneliness. So
she thought he was also desperate and with fresher reason—one more
desertion and no indication that this was the last for Forrest or her. Her
James was gone (but at least into death), and the voices of her boys came
fading through the window. She would never have more of them than
now. Gid had noticed girls; Whitby would soon endure the need. She and
Forrest were back where they'd started at their mother's death, each
other's. Safe. Hatt knew that suddenly—a team of orphans, ground and
gouged for thirty-odd years by the force of others till now they fitted each
other only, stone and socket, anvil and mallet, trapped rocks in a backwater
carved through ages into perfect contingency (she felt that, not thought
it). She sat on the near edge; and when he did not wake, she touched him
again, his complicated knee.

He slowly woke and, though by the candle he could see his sister, he
said "Yes ma'm?"

Hatt smiled. "I am just your elder," she said.

He took the time to wake up fully; she waited, quiet. Then he said,
"You are. Do you know more than me?"

"I think so," she said.

"What?"

"You've give up on Eva."

"I may have," he said. "She has on me. But I knew that."

"Then we're even," Hatt said. "You hungry now?"

Forrest moved his calf against her spread hip—a juncture; he also felt
their congruence. "Where is Father?" he said.

"Dead, to us anyhow." She waited. "Why?"

"He would be old now. He might want to see us."

Dark as it was, Hatt faced him squarely. "You want to see him. But he
left you."

"And you and Mother."

"And I've let him go, you notice," she said. "I think he's dead."

"Truly?"

She thought. "He would be the first to say he deserved to be."

"But you aren't certain?"

Hatt shook her head. "You've been talking to Veenie."

He nodded Yes. "When did she tell you?"

Hatt said, "She never did and I'll never let her. No, through the years I have heard people say Veenie knew a good deal. But I heard it from Mother, so I never troubled Veenie."

Forrest said "When?"

"The year she died."

"Why would she tell you?"

"I was old enough," Hatt said in defense. Then she waited and the harshness settled into puzzlement. "I used to wonder myself, now you mention it—why she would tell an ignorant child. It sure never helped me. But I've been busy so I never dwelt on it; and now when I do, I know she didn't intend it for help."

"What?" Forrest said.

"—One more anchor she was dropping for herself, in hopes of striking bottom. She was trying not to die. She had held it long years. She told who she could."

"You were sixteen," Forrest said.

"I know I was." Hatt thought it ended there; that now she could turn and clarify the present, the news from Forrest. But the old story stood in her throat, alive and claiming its toll, sporadic but great (she was beautiful to Forrest by the one weak light). "I was sewing for you, mending some blouse. She had taught me of course; and she liked to watch me at it, long after I needed supervision. It meant you were safe—me sewing for you; she knew she was dead; you were in skilled hands. And so I asked her some trifling question, to let her share—would the patch be stronger on the slant or straight?—and she gave it to me like a normal answer: 'Hattie, why your father abandoned us was I asked him politely to honor his vow and love just me. His reply was to vanish by night awhile later when he'd let me almost believe I'd won.' Well, I just sewed on, never questioned again; and she died soon."

Forrest waited; then said, "You were too young to ask."

"No," she said. "I understood. I'd had good eyes and ears all along; what are names and dates? No I just didn't care and still don't; I'm busy. I've been kept busy."

Forrest said "Thank you" to turn the rebuke. But then he said, "I'm going to move out of here, find my own place, let Grainger work for me; then hunt Father down and offer him home here again if he'll come."

Hatt frowned deeply in response to pain, not a sign of disgust. "Why?" she said.

But he did not answer. He was trusting as always in dream, dim warning, the urgent promises of sleep.

Hatt actually smiled. "You are grown and free. It'll occupy your mind. It may be best. You were all he loved the time *I* knew him."

Forrest smiled in return. He could not be sure she saw him at all. The light ran to her.

3

August 12, 1904

Dear Rover,

I am a voice from the past, the one you used to say played baseball worse than you crocheted. I gave up trying after you moved north— nobody to rag me—and spent most of those years right up to now teaching school at home and in Carolina. Aunt Veenie or someone may have posted you on my life. Suffice to say I've often thought that you had picked a perfect job, just you and some timbers and tar and the sea. Mingling with children and hoping to aid them is old-maid's work, people life has refused.

Anyhow I am back here in Bracey now, plan to teach here next month, and will be moving out of my sister's house as soon as Grainger helps me fix the old Brame place so I can live there. I will be by myself.

That is one of my reasons for writing now. I would like to keep Grainger down here with me. He would be a great asset in my new quarters, and I would respond by teaching him privately six days a week. I could guarantee him kindness, wholesome food, schooling, enough work to train him for a future life, and sufficient rest. He would also be near Aunt Veenie and could watch her, though as you know she takes less watching than most people half her age and puts up with less. I could guarantee you and his mother he'd be safe, barring acts of God. There is no one here to harm him; his goodness wins all.

My second reason is to ask if you know where Father lives now or whether he's living and, if not, where he lies? My sister and I have had no word for twenty-eight years, and I at least am hopeful now of meeting him again if he's on this earth. Veenie said you might know his whereabouts. I wish him only well—which of course I wish you, Rover; you and all yours. Bring them back someday for a look at their seedbed, a chance to thaw out! I would like to shake your hand, maybe fan a few pitches while we both can still move.

Yours in good memory,
Forrest Mayfield

P. S. When I spoke as a "voice from the past," I only meant your past and mine together. I have no intention, and have sworn so to Veenie, of burdening your boy with the old wrongs of others.

August 21, 1904

Dear Grainger,

    I will write to Mr. Forrest and say you can work there for him if he really want you. I am sending this to you first in care of Miss Veenie so you keep it to yourself, my last word to you about this anyhow. You had a real easy life up here with us, everybody good to you, so you don't know yet what they holding back to hit you with. Count on it coming though and pretty soon now and not letting up. Never failed yet, Virginia or Maine. When it come and I can't tell you how it will look you remember you got a dry place up here and a job I will teach you, nothing all that good but a fair day's trade. Forrest was a good boy when I used to know him but he didn't know nothing then that he could teach a flea that the flea could use and anyhow he living in a hole right now till his people come back or he get new people so you watch out for Grainger and leave fore they tell you to. You still got us here like I told you before and you got Miss Veenie and kin people there so don't stay any place they can't use you and do right by you and give you plenty rest. We doing all right. Your mama say hey and we see you someday, any day you ready.

                                   Your father,
                                   Rover Walters

NOVEMBER–DECEMBER 1904

Thanksgiving night, 1904

Dear Forrest,
No word of you since August, but now I am writing to honor your birthday on Monday next. All good things for you, is my genuine wish; and Rob would join me if he understood. Maybe he does. At least I have told him. He seems to know more every day, although he is still held back by his ordeal—thin and pale and has a spell of whooping every two or three days yet, by which I am much more scared than he: he threatens to leave, and even in his hardest throes of gasping, with his eyes on me (me begging him to stay), something in him seems calm, seems ready for the journey if that is demanded.
Forrest, I am sure that is you working in him—that and his face. You are all in his face whenever I watch him, which is every two or three minutes of the day. No sign of me or any of my people.
An early hard frost here last night. All day we have barely moved from the stove. We hope you are warm and spared affliction and, again, that your birthday brings you your wishes.

Love from,
Eva

Forrest waited three weeks till he knew his intent, that his wish was his need. Then he spent the best part of a Friday evening writing her this.

December 16, 1904

Dear Eva,
Thank you both for your hopes. I have taken what you said as honest and kind, in purpose at least—though I cannot imagine living long enough

to acquire understanding of how, over eight months, you go on extending me an open hand yet withhold all the rest: heart and presence, the sight of my son. Maybe this was all you ever intended—to smile at a distance, in my direction, and witness my answer. Maybe the only error was mine—to breach that purpose, seek to close that gap.

You cannot witness me at this distance though, so here is my news since you left me last.

We have found my father, or his whereabouts. A long chain of circumstances, too long to tell, has led us to his door; and I think I am hoping to see him somehow during the Christmas.

Then I will let you know more about me, for Rob's future use if nothing more, though one of my hopes is—whatever our fate—that you will understand more fully and forgive what you seem to feel I have wreaked on your life.

For now, suffice that I live alone in the old Brame house on the hill back of Hatt's. It is small, four rooms, but is fully mine for as long as I wish. Some meals I take with Hatt, some here. A Negro boy is working for me—young, from a family we know of old—and he is rapidly learning to cook; so I have health and care and the sound at least of another animal, near in my space.

More word soon, I trust.

Ever,
Forrest Mayfield

December 19, 1904

My dear Forrest,

I have just read your letter and am in my room, one hand on Rob awake beside me, inspecting his own hand with grave amazement (he found it last week and is still amazed). It is only the strength of his great discovery—he is late in this, having been so weak—that keeps him from sensing my load of sadness.

I want to see you. I was hoping you had some Christmas plan for us but now you don't.

I know I should say I am glad you are healthy and have a new house and have found your father, but I feel only lonesome misery. I know I should kneel and beg your pardon for my childish meanness in these past months. I do that now and only ask that, in thinking of me, you recall what a child I actually am. Or was till now—a feeble plea but the only one I make and true. Also the fact that, once I was home, there were awful circumstances holding me here which I did not mention to you last August—a message from Mother that hurt, being true; a letter she left me, delivered by Rena who spares me nothing, my personal hound.

All of that though is not an excuse but the start of a partial explana-

*tion, the rest of which will require whole years of my life to come. What-
ever your feeling and whatever your answer, I vow to change.*

*More love from,
Eva*

December 21, 1904

Dear Eva,

*Your second letter was here when I came home yesterday evening
from school. Grainger. my help, had fetched it and propped it in the midst
of my desk; so I read it at once—and many more times before going to
bed, where I did not sleep.*

*What I must say is this. You are now stranger to me than an animal
would be, and what you say in this latest letter is a stroke more cruel than
any human being has ever dealt me (with no claim at all to a martyr's
crown, still I think I can say I have had strokes enough in thirty-odd years
to give me some title to accuracy in the recognition and gauging of harm;
you know my past well enough, you cannot object).*

I was all but repaired. Have you no plain mercy?

*That calls for an answer, an answer which might well need your life;
but so then have you called for more from me. I thought I had given that
once for all, the day we promised ourselves last year. I meant quite literally
all I said, however quickly put. Now recall how I put it. Surely you can.*

*Yet because—for whatever reason—you ask, I say it again. Not in
words this time. Words failed before. But in something you can see and
touch and wear, something weighty and not forgettable. It is in the smaller
of the parcels in this crate—my mother's ring which, despite her sadness
(or whatever she felt), she wore to the end of her life. And would have
worn to her grave for good if Hatt had not gone in an hour before her
burial and reached in the coffin and worked it from her finger and brought
it to me. It has since been mine. Now I give it to you, whatever your
meaning.*

*If you take it and wear it—on your own left hand, above our own—it
will signify our reforged bond and, for me at least, my triumph (with your
help) over whatever blight struck my parents' union. If you will not wear
it, please keep it in some safe place for Rob till the day he needs it or gives
some sign of the adult strength to understand its total meaning in our own
lives, yours and mine, and the previous lives of his father's family. I trust
you to let me know of your choice.*

*Taking it, you take me. If that is your wish, I will come for you on
New Year's Eve, whatever the weather. My Christmas is now involved
with my father.*

The other parcel is for Rob, the nicest express wagon I could buy here,

*a thing my father gave me very early which I also remember—him hauling
me around the house and laughing, saying, "Forrest and I are bound for
bliss!" I don't know if it will have meaning for him yet; but whatever your
own need and choice may be, I trust you will help me in seeing that the
boy has something from me on his first conscious Christmas.*

So, Eva, I'm waiting. But you never doubted that.

> *Love ever from*
> *Forrest*

The initials in the ring stand for Robinson Mayfield to Anna Goodwin.

He placed that letter in an envelope and addressed it to *Mrs. Eva
Mayfield, In the Care of Kendal, Fontaine, North Carolina.* Then he took
the sturdy gun-shell crate which Grainger had got for the purpose in town
and—padding with newsprint, clean rags, and straw—he carefully packed
his three solid gifts: the wagon for Rob (red with removable wooden sides
and rubber tires), the ring for Eva (in the small jeweler's box it had come
in some forty years before), and his letter at the top. Then he laid on a
final thickness of padding (a clean white shirt of his own, slightly worn)
and nailed down the top with broadheaded dark-blue roofing nails—the
blue, as he recalled, of the Atlantic Ocean (his father had carried them
once to Norfolk). Then with Grainger's help he carried it out to the
woodshed in back and hauled out an ancient two-wheeled goat-cart, some
old playtoy of the dead Brame children, and with Grainger in the staves
(prancing, laughing), he saw it downhill to the depot, the train.

2

In Fontaine the next day, eleven o'clock, Sylvie was coming out the post-
office door, no mail for the Kendals. The morning was bright and the
ground was stiff-frozen; but she wore no shawl or scarf, just her dress and
apron, the rag on her head, the shoes that had been her brother Doc's. So
her step was fast, aimed back toward warmth; and in time to her feet, her
mind worked quickly on happy pictures—Christmas, the end of a hard bad
year, the sense pouring through her (just now this morning, the first time
in months, since her baby's death) that what stretched ahead promised
better than the past. She was also in love.

"You. Sylvie"—a man's voice off to her left. A white man.

She looked but did not break step. Old Mr. Rooker on the depot
porch, waving her toward him. She stopped and rubbed her arms against
cold but did not go nearer.

He tried to come to her—an old man, gimp-legged, blue-faced and bald with whom she had purposely had no dealings in her whole life till now; somebody who paid a nickel to touch you. So her sisters had said. He came down the stairs and took four or five lame steps toward her, collapsing on himself like a complicated mechanical toy; then he gave up the effort and said, "*Come* on. I'm ruined, you see."

She went and he turned and climbed back up and waited for her at the top of the stairs. She stopped at the bottom.

"You're Sylvie, ain't you? Mag's Sylvie?"

"*Sylvie's* Sylvie."

Mr. Rooker grinned. "You want a job?"

"Not yours," she said and took a step to go.

"Hold on." He laughed and reached down a short arm toward her; hopeless, it dropped.

But Sylvie stepped again as if in one more try he could touch her.

"Too early in the morning, too cold," he said.

Sylvie turned back, smiling.

Mr. Rooker whispered, "Just a little message; just carry a message."

She took back the two steps to hear his message, but she crossed her arms on her chest as a shield.

"Come on up here. You got to see it. Warm-up a minute." He turned and stumped through the freightroom door.

She followed him in and shut the door behind her. It was warm—hot, stifling, and dry. The big room held two other men—old Mr. Mitchell who wore ladies' silk stockings under his clothes (wool trousers on his skin gave him open sores) and black Harry Brown, bent halfway double from fifty years of hauling.

"You know Bedford Kendal? You know him, don't you?" Mr. Rooker was standing four feet away. "You know that much?"

"Yes."

"Yes *what*?"

"Yes sir," she said. She had stopped the smile.

"Then look at this." He pointed beside him to a crate on a dolly. "This here's for him. Go home and tell him."

"Harry'll bring it." She pointed to Harry, who was studying her.

Mr. Rooker shook his head. "My instructions was different. You going to deliver my message or not?"

Sylvie came a step closer and looked at the crate.

Mr. Rooker moved on her and managed to lay a quick hand on her chest before she could drop back and reach for the door—Mr. Mitchell grinning, Harry Brown laughing with Mr. Rooker. Mr. Rooker said "That won't the message!"

Sylvie stood—door open, neither nodding nor smiling yet holding her ground, having seen enough to raise her curiosity.

Mr. Rooker said "Repeat it."

"You say, 'Tell Mr. Bedford he got him a box. Come down here and get it." She paused. "Is it heavy?"

"N'mind how heavy. Just tell him that—nobody but him, no other soul."

She nodded and turned again to go.

"You got your reward already," Mr. Rooker said, alluding to the spotty dry hand that had brushed her.

Harry Brown laughed again.

But she had slammed the door and was down the stairs, stepping faster than ever and huddled inward now on more than her cold assaulted breasts, on the certain knowledge that the box was for Eva from Eva's husband. She could not read—Sylvie—but she knew two or three words by size and shape: *baby* and *spoon* and *train* and *Eva*.

3

After supper that night they had all adjourned to the sitting room and poked up the fire. The room was actually Rena's now (when Rob had come down with whooping cough, she had silently resigned her own room to Eva—her share of hers and Eva's room—and set up a cot in the sitting-room corner, so short and narrow as to make it easy to conceal her traces each morning early: her few clothes were hid in various corners around the house); but they still sat there because of the warmth, the lack of a better place to go, the weight of the memory of the dead in the parlor. Eva sat till everyone else was settled—her father reading, Kennerly doing the accounts on his knee, Rena talking to Rob. Then she stood and asked Rena, "Will you watch him awhile?" Rena's contented answer was Yes. Eva climbed to her room, with no explanation to anyone and questioned by none. She knew that they knew; it pertained to Forrest, her other life.

She was making a Christmas gift for Forrest by lamplight in these few minutes of evening (daylight hours being taken by Rob and her gradual share of the household duties). She had had no money to spend since June when the three dollars Forrest had given her exhausted themselves in things for Rob; so she'd cut up a fine dresser-scarf of her mother's and for three weeks now had been making the gift, a single big linen handkerchief which she'd hemstitched and edged and was embroidering in silk, *F. M.* There was only the last downward leg of the *M*; and she strained forward now at the delicate stitching (she was good at small work, her mother's instruction). Tomorrow she'd manage to post if off. Or she'd hear by then and deliver it some other way, direct.

Sylvie's step on the stairs. No need or reason for Sylvie this late. Eva did not hide the handkerchief though; Sylvie had seen it (in silence, no questions). She looked up to meet her and found her already in the door, dark, waiting empty-handed.

"You working," Sylvie said, plain statement, a fact reported to no one but them.

Eva nodded and bent to the light again.

"You be done soon?"

"Tonight I hope."

Sylvie said "You better."

Eva looked up but did not ask her meaning.

Sylvie entered and walked past the bed to the dresser. She felt in the dark and found an object which she carefully brought to the foot of the bed, the edge of the light—a silver mirror. She tilted it, studied it, traced on its back with her index finger the confirmation of her earlier knowledge—*Eva*, engraved in lavish script. Then she carefully set it back in its place, never having sought her own reflection.

Eva laughed one note. "What is that meant to mean?"

"That you better get that job done tonight."

Eva said, "I know. Time's bearing down." But her voice was puzzled.

Sylvie was still by the dresser, dim. She whispered from there. "What you get? From him?"

"It's not Christmas yet."

"In the box, today."

Eva said, "I don't know what you mean."

"Can't fool me," Sylvie said. "I seen it."

Eva turned up the lamp to the verge of smoking. "What?" she said.

"The box you got today from your husband."

Eva shook her head slowly.

"It sure God come here. I seen it and touched it." Sylvie pointed to her own eyes; then outward through walls toward the depot, Mr. Rooker.

Eva only waited.

"I coming back this morning, no mail, and that old *feeling* Mr. Rooker, all hands, called me in to the depot and showed me—a gunshell box. He say it for your father, for me to tell him and nobody else. So I told him when he come in the backdoor for dinner, and he just thanked me and set down and ate. I step home this afternoon for a while—Mama still right weak—so I won't here when they brought it up." Her smile was visible. "What you get from him?"

Eva strained for accuracy. "Sylvie, to my knowledge, no box has come. When it does, it will be for Father like you say."

Sylvie shook her head, still smiling. "For you," she said aloud, triumphant. She reached behind her for the mirror again, reckless this time, endangering it. But she got it across to Eva safely, held its back to the light, traced the name for Eva. "Your name on it. I *seen* it, Eva."

Eva kept to her chair but studied upward—Sylvie's face. No sign of harm, intended or accomplished. No readable sign. "You're sure?" Eva said.

Sylvie knocked with her knuckles on the mirror, the name. "If this your name like you said it was, then that box for you." Again she pointed toward the distant spot where she'd witnessed this morning her present chance. "I *know* your name."

4

WHEN she'd sent Sylvie down and had stood by her bed, asking herself for a stretch of minutes "What do I want to do with this?", then she went to the top of the stairs and listened—the crack of the fire, Rena babbling to Rob. Then she spoke out. "Father."

Mr. Kendal was asleep.

"Father?" again more urgently.

Kennerly said "Eva's after you." Then louder, "Answer Eva, please sir."

The sounds that reached her were—her father waking, slowly rising, walking slowly to the foot of the stairs, his patient voice saying "Darling, what?"

She waited for him there at the landing; but when he had climbed up and stood two steps below her face, waiting, she could not speak. Her mouth refused, the muscles of her chest. So she turned—they were in all but total dark—and led the way toward her open room from which the only light crept coldly.

He hesitated in place a moment, then followed her and shut the heavy door behind them.

She had gone to her work-chair and stood beside it. The lamp was below her face and light reached it. Her work—the linen, the silk, the frame—were on the lamp-table, unconcealed. She was looking toward him.

He waited, looking; and when she stayed silent, he said, "There are not many more climbs in me—this rheumatism." He was fifty-four. "Say something to make it worth my trip." He smiled.

Eva could see it. She even tried to match it and speak at once, but her face contorted round her eyes like a fist; and her voice broke, guttural and dry in her neck.

He kept his place. "What has Sylvie told you?"

Again she worked for calm and speech, and failed though silently. So slowly she shook her head side to side—her lifelong means of restoring calm, as if some reeling or winching were done: her voice drawn gradually up from its well. "A box that came today—my name."

He nodded. "It did."

"Where is it now?"

He came as far forward as the foot of the bed, then drew out his watch, tilted it to light, read it carefully, then looked up smiling. "Twenty, thirty miles south of Bracey, Virginia if the night train's on time. The northbound train."

"You sent it back?"

"Refused it," he said.

"Tell me why. Every reason. It bore my name." She'd found her voice and, with each word, acquired firmer grip on her mettle.

Her father did not quickly alter expression. His smile survived half through her question; then it began a slow descent into gravity. When she'd finished, he was grave but utterly calm. He let the air settle; then said, "Your reasons. Entirely for you. What I do is for you. You make it plain that your life is here. Since you came back to this house that morning in August—I never asked a word of what passed that night; I know you sent him away, that's all—since that day, Eva, I determined to help you defend your own will. All I needed was one sign from you, of your purpose. You gave me that."

Again she began to shake her head, involuntarily this time; and what came was tears, full, hot and silent. She had not wept, she knew, in a year; since her opposite misery the previous Christmas in Hatt's bare house.

He came no nearer but he said "*My* reasons." He was forced to pause. When he spoke again, it was with his hands straight down at his sides, palms flat and outward.

Eva watched those, dim as they were—his gentle hands—and thought that she could not remember a time when he'd whispered before.

"I have had all the leaving I can bear this year. I am asking you, politely as I can, to stay."

His face—stroked by the light from beneath—seemed young and lifting, a hopeful boy's, long life ahead but requiring help. Entirely helpless. Eva nodded toward him, though she could not smile.

5

Hours later far into night, Eva lay awake in her bed alone, the bed she had occupied all her life except for a year from the age of four. The bed was in place in its own room—hers, empty tonight of all but her and borne cold but safe on the silent depths of the separate sleep of all her truest family beneath her. The element, her rightful harbor, the socket in which her life was made and which held it again after brief dislocation. Even Rob had been sheered away, tonight at least; when her father had taken her silent nod as answer to his plea, he had turned and gone back down to the others and seated himself and said to Rena (Eva heard it from her room), "Go see if Eva wants Robinson with her." Rena had come and knocked on the doorframe—the door was open—and then stepped forward and searched Eva's face (Eva was standing still by the lamp) and said, "I am keeping Rob downstairs with me. He is already asleep in his basket; don't worry." Eva had said "I thank you" and sat; and Rena had gone out, shutting the door. Eva had sat on, the room chilling round her, the wick in the lamp thumping drily for a while in its struggle to burn on vanishing oil. Then the light had extinguished, and she'd sat on longer through the sounds of her family working beneath her to end the day. Then when they'd quieted and seemed asleep, she'd stood in the dark and reached to the table beside her for her work and had gone to the bottom drawer of her chest and, kneeling there, had stored it deep. Then she'd risen and quickly stripped to bare skin and walked to the window and had drawn back the curtain in hopes of moonlight to show herself the nakedness she'd hardly seen since leaving Virginia—none, black night. She had not touched herself; and in all that time since her father had left, she had not had anything approaching a thought. Her mind had been, not asleep but struck or like a hand suddenly sliced by a blade, recoiling in numbness to wait till the quantity of blood that sprang would announce and measure the wound sustained, the hope of cure. And so she had entered her bed, still naked, and fallen on sleep like a plummet, depth-bound.

In her sleep she had dreamed. Dreams were uncommon to her; and when they came were mostly credible amusing stories made from the lumber of her daily life (she'd forgot the dream of her wedding night, though it also was hardly total invention). But this had been strange and entirely new, a discovery. *Light*—the main sensation was light, a clear warm sun filtered in and gentled by tall broad windows. The windows were set in a large building. The building was neither a house nor a store. *Have I ever*, she actually asked in the dream, *been in a building which is not intended for sleeping or selling?* She could not remember but went on wandering through many floors of light-washed rooms, past silent happy people at tables working or reading or looking out windows. No one spoke to her; but she did not mind, did not feel unwelcome or invisible. All that troubled her nearly perfect sense of peace was a straining forward of her whole clear mind; she felt it in the dream, probing forward to a point, straining to discover the use of this place, the purpose of all these quiet workers, the name of their work. The strain had all but brought her to grief—her steps had quickened, her face gathered tight—when she saw one man at a distant table poured over by sun, watching neither his work nor the sun but her. He was nearly her age, more nearly a boy; so it did not occur to her to ask him the meaning. And he was not smiling. Yet as she took the last step past him, he stood in place and said to her "What?" She stopped and turned and, in the effort to recognize him (he now seemed familiar, maybe kin), she also did not smile. No more name would come for him than the place, so she said "Where am I?" He said "In the school." She said "Which one?" —"The only one." —"How did I get here?" —"By needing to come." She stood and thought. Then she nodded and said "What must I learn?" He could finally smile—"You must learn that too." He put out his hands, personal bafflement; the hunt would be hers. In the instant, she accepted and was flooded with joy like the room with sun. Her smile asked it for her of its own accord—"Then tell me your name and I'll begin." His faded to gravity, his hands dropped down, his head shook twice. "That is part of what you have lost and must learn."

That woke her abruptly on her back in the dark, uncovered to the waist and cold in the frozen air of the room. But her pleasure, the joy toward the end of the dream, survived her waking and the man's last question, his own grave face. Survived too the earlier question of her dream—who was the man? Why had she felt she had known him always? That question had already sunk to oblivion through the fragile net of nocturnal memory. So she lay on awhile, having covered herself with quilts and comforts, and thought of all she remembered from the dream. Alone as she was and was likely to be, it seemed sufficient program for years to come—the learning of what she required to know. Required *in secret* apparently; for though she knew, knew above all else, that she had great needs for knowledge and understanding and help, she also knew—lying here now warming—that the question she remembered from her dream was just: she did not know the names of her needs. Did anyone else? The ones who had tried, who had offered her answers—Forrest, her mother, gloomy Hatt, the silent answer proffered by Rob, forty feet away now through plaster walls—had failed her as fully as she herself. The names then were neither *love* nor *hatred, heat* nor *cold*. And her father, pitiful in loneliness. What more did he offer than versions of love—*need* and *shelter*? She'd take the shelter. It was natural to her—his house, her room, her dark deep bed. The few things she'd learned, she'd learned in these walls, dim as they were, oiled with bad memory. They'd serve awhile longer.

She did not feel that as a sizable choice. It slid through her mind like smooth waxed thread. Behind it though it drew a question, again the man's first question from the dream but now in her own voice silently—*What do I know?*

She actually waited. Still no answer came, not even the old lies offered by others. She waited for the truth. Silence, night, cocoon of warmth in the old house cracking with bitter cold, the burden of its freight—her father, Rob, Kennerly, Rena, and Sylvie; her vanished mother, heavier still.

Then she'd wait on here. There was no other chance to learn what she must know, the name she would need to launch her own life. Simple as that. She knew she was smiling, at nothing but the ceiling lost above her. Slowly with her hand she sought herself.

DECEMBER 1904–FEBRUARY 1905

THE man was young and knew him at once. He did not smile but he said "Well, Forrest."

Forrest said "Yes sir" and knew that his own face, tilted up, was helplessly smiling. He'd have known this man in a chance encounter on the farthest star. The face was his own—as Veenie had said, his living mirror, shockingly unchanged since the one dim picture and his own clear memory. The fur on his upper lip had stiffened into mannish wire and was shot with gray, as his temples were; but the eyes, while they did not fix on Forrest, had lasted perfect in depth and sadness, clear of whatever these twenty-eight years had pressed against them. How old could he be? Forrest never had known and had not realized it till now here below him, the least of the questions that clamored for answer.

"How you coming?" his father said, not moving. He had not extended his hand for shaking, his arms for embrace, and had not stepped forward across the worn sill.

"Cold," Forrest said and shuddered, still grinning. He meant the day, the still gray morning cracking with frost even now at ten. Christmas eve.

"Where's your overcoat?—that little Prince Albert. I bought you: when was it? black with velvet piping all round. Waste. Your mother never forgave me."

"No sir. She did." Forrest shook again, all over, helpless. He was in his only suit, a worn serge, no coat or hat.

His father said, "You asking to come in?"

"I've come this far."

"How far?"

"From Bracey." Forrest pointed.

And his father looked. Then he smiled the first smile Forrest could remember on him; it came on him suddenly as if pushed at him against his will. But he kept his teeth covered and, still looking toward Bracey, said, "That's nowhere. Nowhere to speak of. Now *I've* come a distance."

"Same distance," Forrest said.

His father laughed on teeth that at once aged him twenty years—an old sick man still propped round the hole in the midst of his heart which years ago he'd asked even a five-year-old boy to fill. At the end his nose dripped. He wiped it with his hand and hacked his throat clear and said, "I took a few detours. Never travel in a line if you want an education."

"Yes sir," Forrest said. "Please let me in."

His father faced him for the first time fully, eyes on eyes. "I ain't got a penny." With both hands he patted his trouser pockets. Empty, the cloth fell in on stick legs.

Forrest said "I knew that."

"Then how come you're here, in Richmond at Christmas, a hundred miles from home on a sick old fool's doorstep in the cold?"

"To see you. Ask you a thing or two. A little help."

His father's hands stayed loose at his sides, palms outward now, bare as bread troughs. "I couldn't help a mad dog swallow his slaver. I know I've had some part in you—my eyes still work—but I don't even know I can call your name."

"You already have—Forrest," he said.

His father nodded. "I'd have guessed you was him." But he did not move to unblock the door.

Forrest reached into his own breast pocket and withdrew a small oblong package tied with string. He offered it up. "Christmas cheer."

His father thought awhile, then accepted. He turned it several times in his hands, probing with hard brown spatulate thumbs.

"Cigars," Forrest said. "I remember you smoked them."

The old man looked down, actually studied him. "You're definitely Forrest?" It was clearly put as a genuine question.

Forrest nodded. "The one thing I'm certain of."

"You can come in," he said, "but it's warmer outside. I'm by myself, not a lump of coal."

Forrest said, "I could go and find you some."

"Don't worry yourself." He stood aside and waved Forrest in.

"There's no sense freezing, with Richmond full of coal."

His father said, "Don't worry. The Lord'll provide." He gestured up, the cold hard sky, with both empty hands—Elijah and ravens. Then he looked down to Forrest. He was smiling again, the broad closed smile that pulled Forrest inward—had pulled him, he now saw, through all these years; the single question to which these years had been a set of answers offered by him in addled desperation to people who never had asked the question.

Forrest also smiled and followed his father—a final chance, though he thought of it happily with warming hope.

The hall down which they went was dim and bare as a mine. The single traces of human presence, at some past date, were wild curls of white dust which dogged their steps and stirred in their wake. Four dark doors, all shut. Mr. Mayfield stopped by the last one and said again, "This'll be freezing"; but Forrest nodded so he turned the knob and led on in. A bedroom—bright (light fell through two windows) and warmer than promised. And on the light and heat, a third surprise—the high dry smell of burnt hemp leaves, asthma cigarettes (which Forrest had smelled only once before, visiting a pupil whose father smoked them in his bouts of strangulation, slim relief). His father had gone on toward the bed; so he shut the door behind them and said "No it's warm."

Mr. Mayfield sat in the unmade covers and said "Just wait." He did not gesture to the single chair, a dark oak rocker.

But Forrest went to it and carefully sat.

Mr. Mayfield pointed to the rusty iron stove. "Woman that helps me, made a fire just before she left. Used all my coal."

Forrest saw the battered empty scuttle on its bed of black dust beside the hearth. Between it and where he sat was a woodbox. For something to do, he rocked forward and leaned to see in—more than a few scraps of dark pinebark, sufficient for a half-hour more of warmth. "Let me throw these scraps on for you," Forrest said; he moved to rise.

His father said "No" more quickly and firmly than he'd said anything else in Forrest's presence.

Forrest stopped in midair and turned back to see.

The old man was still in his stale yellow sheets, green and pink quilt Forrest smelled through the hemp. His neck, now revealed by his slumping shoulders, was dry and ropey. But his eyes had lighted again and were urgent; he'd given an order not a request.

Forrest obeyed, though with obvious puzzlement, almost fear. "I thought it was wood."

"It is. My collection," Mr. Mayfield said. "The things I make." He offered no more but was calm again.

So Forrest leaned to look. The huddle of scraps in the bottom of the crate were in fact crude figures, dim memories of human form; hacked out by one whose senses or sympathies were failing or had failed, as quick reminders of what had been lost or ceded or, worse, never known. Already knowing, Forrest said, "For what? Make them for what, sir?"

His father thought awhile; then stood with some trouble and went to the box and leaned and rummaged and came up with two figures, one in each hand. Then he went back and sat and studied them, rubbing their powdery surfaces with slow thumbs, inquiring. "Well," he said, "*time*. For time, I guess, if you want a true reason." He waited again, looked up and smiled. "How old are you?"

"Thirty-four," Forrest said.

"You know what I mean then, though years from now you'll know a lot better. The problem in life is getting through time—all the time they give you and, Jesus, they give it. I'm sixty-five my last birthday, which I'll guarantee is a good many days to wake up and walk through and stay out of harm in." He still was talking to the dolls in his hands. "So these are for that, just foolishness to paddle me on through a few more days. I'm not strong, you see—tell the truth, I never was, though till recently nobody knew it but me." He looked up at Forrest. "When did you know me?"

"Thirty-four years ago. For five years and seven months."

His father nodded. "I was sick even then. Bad rheumatism in all my joints, so sore it was like teeth aching all over me. Night after night, I'd lie on my back by whoever happened to be there beside me—them sleeping and breathing slow and rested, me alive and hurting. Nobody believed me; I was too good at loving!" For the second time, he laughed; and again the firm plain beauty of his face fell in on his mouth—ruined teeth, black holes.

Forrest looked to the dolls in his father's hands. "Who are they?" he said.

At the end of his laugh, Mr. Mayfield turned the dolls toward Forrest. "My mother and father." Then he offered them out insistently.

Forrest accepted. A savage could have made them or an idle boy. He had never known his Mayfield kin, never seen any other likeness of them; but these dolls—four, five inches long; square-necked, box-shouldered, slew-foot—were hardly more than schemes for people. Both had round eyes and slashed smiling mouths. The lady distinguished herself by a low relief of breasts; the rest of her body was finished smooth, no crease or fold. The man bore no marks but a face and a navel, a swell in the left groin. Both had been handled long and hard; the usual dust and gum of pinebark had been rubbed to smoothness. Forrest also rubbed them, found his own thumbs helplessly stroking their chests while he asked himself, "Have I come too late? Is he too far gone?" But before he could think of a public remark, his father stood again.

In place by the bed, Mr. Mayfield searched the room for something hid—stove, woodbox, scuttle, a mantel with two glass jars (one filled with buttons), a two-doored wardrobe painted apple green, a white china slopjar lidded with a rag, Forrest in the rocker, a straw floormat, the bed itself. Nothing else visible. He said, "Somewhere here I got a little dress." He reached down and took one doll from Forrest. "Little dress for Mama." He was stroking her belly again, both thumbs. "Woman that helps me made her a dress. I told her how, one I remembered. It's here somewhere. I'm arranging my things. Things are failing me."

"Where am *I*?" Forrest said.

His father understood. He took the three steps to the box of dolls and looked down at it. "No children," he said. "No children here." He smiled. "No *room*. Yet here I'm alone. Dying by myself, strangling in spit, and not a soul beside me." The smile had curiously lasted through that, though nothing in his eyes or the tone of his voice permitted any thought that he was not utterly earnest, even desperate.

Forrest said "*Me.* I've volunteered."

His father studied him; then nodded slowly, the nearest he had come to gratitude. Then he handed back the doll as though she mattered, as though she were an urgent counter in a game. Then he said, "But why come here alone, come empty-handed bringing nothing but your grin? Hell, cats can grin."

"I brought those cigars—"

"—Which I'll have to throw away. They'd ruin my chest." Mr. Mayfield rubbed at his own breastbone with the heel of his hand as though scouring it.

Forrest stood.

"Where you headed?"

"Home," Forrest said.

"You quit easy, don't you?"

"Yes," Forrest said, "whenever I'm not needed."

"Who else but me don't need you then?" Mr. Mayfield was smiling. He took a step toward Forrest.

So Forrest smiled. "That would be my life-story."

His father went quickly to the bed and sat. "Tell it," he said.

"Don't mock me, please sir."

"I'm not. I'm not. You've come this long way at Christmas to tell it. I got nothing but time. I'd be glad to hear." He motioned to the rocker.

Forrest obeyed and sat. He said "It takes a minute."

His father nodded.

"The first five years, I guess you know. Then you had gone and we watched Mother try to stand up from that. She tried oh six years and then gave up."

"Who is *we?*" his father said. "You say '*We* watched.'"

"Hatt and I. Hattie, my sister."

His father nodded.

"She is still in Bracey—a widow, two sons."

"Just tell *your* story. That's what I bargained for."

"I lived with Hattie. When Mother died I was just twelve; so Hatt got married to make us a home with old James Shorter, a whole lot older."

"Good," Mr. Mayfield said. "James is good."

"He's dead too," Forrest said. "I told you."

"Most people are," Mr. Mayfield said. "You ain't. Keep telling."

"I grew up, is all. I stayed there in Bracey in James Shorter's house and ate his food and took his orders and waited for you. I knew you were living and were somewhere near, though nobody told me. I tried to think you were hunting for me and would someday find me."

"I knew where you were. I knew very well. And I knew you were far better off without me."

"Why, please sir?" Forrest said. "We didn't agree."

"That's part of my story. You're telling yours."

Forrest waited to think. "Well, what?" he said. "I had the same trouble you just mentioned, time to endure. Stuck off up in the eaves at James Shorter's—broiling in summer, blue in winter—I had to get through my life till you'd come. It never dawned on me that children could die; so there I was in the attic, reading." Forrest raised both hands from his knees to point, whatever attic this present house possessed; and saw that he held the two dolls still, his father's parents. Pitiful faceless images of two lives whose actual blood composed his own, channeled his own, hacked out of pine by a sick man lonely as a hawk in heaven who—for all Forrest knew, by the lights he had—had never been capable of lasting love for any live object with more face than these, more vulnerable limbs, and who sat here now three feet away, reeling his own painful story from him as entertainment, an hour killed. He lowered the dolls to his lap again, then laid them in their box. Where could he go when he stood now and left, as he surely must? He had come for the first time in memory to a terminus.

His father said "What sort of reading?"

That came for Forrest like a break in the frown of some final judge, a threat of mercy. And with it came a long-postponed recognition, shaft of light thrown backward at his childhood, at all his life till now—all his aims which he now saw were single. "Anything about people getting along, stories of families, stories of friends, people older than any I'd known (give or take some Negroes). The only books children ever want to read."

His father nodded but he said, "Not so. All I read was the Bible—all we had to read except medicine labels—and nobody gets along in the Bible. Not one happy pair, not one that lasts long enough to watch and learn *how* from. So I gave up reading and took up holding onto people. You know how that lasted me." He gestured round the room, his witness, bare of love as the ocean floor. His sweep included Forrest.

So Forrest smiled. "Sir, I had no choice. Nobody to hold but Hatt or James."

"Hell, you hunt people down," his father said.

"If you've got time and strength."

"What's kept you so busy then, to be here alone?"

Forrest said, "Teaching. Teaching Latin in school."

"Good God," his father said. "*Ego amo te.* What caused that?"

Forrest laughed a little. "The reading, I guess. One book led to another book; and one or two teachers were good to me, encouraged me onward. Everything seemed to be promising what I wanted to hear—every

book, every teacher: that by working and learning I would make myself the
kind of person other people would come to, and some would love. I
couldn't go to college—" He stopped to wonder if any of this were really
true, if it were the *case* or only the plea which his voice was making for this
old man.

His father said, "Don't look like to me a man teaching school would
have much trouble drawing friendly company. You teach in the school
there in Bracey, you say?"

"I do now, yes sir."

"Boys *and* girls?"

"Yes sir."

"What age mostly?"

"Twelve up to sixteen."

Mr. Mayfield beamed and waved with both hands, a problem solved.
"There you go." But when Forrest did not join his fun, he said, "I guess
that could land you in trouble?—last train out of town?"

Forrest nodded Yes.

"You'd probably meet me on it!" he said. "I've rode it enough times
to own shares in it."

Forrest said, "Let me go now and buy you some coal, a Christmas
present."

His father said, "Say what you will, send me anywhere you want in
convict-chains; but if I was teaching roomfuls of girls that age, sooner than
later I'd be slapping one of ems little nubbin if it harelipped every Baptist
preacher in the county!"

Forrest sat in the noise of his father's laughter and planned this latest
retreat, perhaps the last. He would stand and, if urged, say he'd come back
this evening; but would go instead to the nearest coal merchant, have a
cart sent out for his father's warmth a few days longer, then make his own
way to the dark depot, find Grainger on a bench, and take the home train.
When he'd seen his way clear, he stood and worked to smile.

His father said "You're quitting me."

"I've got some quick business in town," Forrest said.

"No," his father said. "You're quitting me too." He stayed in his nest
of sour covers, hands on his knees; but his face assumed in the instant of
speech a flat finality of comprehension. This grinning gap-toothed dying
satyr knew the facts of the case and the truth they concealed and not only
knew but would speak his knowledge now.

Forrest neither wished to stop him nor had the power. He sat on and
heard.

"You let a young pretty girl slip right by you and never reached out to
grab her. You let her take your boy, that you'll never get back. You've left
your sister and her wild boys and camped out alone with a little nigger
waiter in a shack on a hill with a leaking roof. Christ Jesus, Son, who you

want to be? Be yourself, not me. If all the years you've grown up thinking I was something to copy—well, now you know. Now you know different. This is—what?—Christmas, ain't it?"

"Day before," Forrest said, "the twenty-fourth."

"That's near enough," he said. "This is Christmas eve and Robinson Mayfield—which is me if you're wondering—has washed up here in Richmond, Virginia (a place as ugly as you'd hope to find) in these old rooms as empty as his heart and far more lonesome than before he was born: he being me, you understand. You're half my age and here you sit, bad off as me and thirty years to go. Change it. Change it now if you can. I doubt you can."

From that, to his own surprise, Forrest drew the strength to say, "Who told you please? How long have you known?"

His father studied him as if for worthiness; then drew breath to speak, answer or refusal.

A distant noise far down the hall—the street door opening, entering steps, the door shut, a wait, then those same steps shuffling nearer toward them.

Forrest spoke again, "Who is it?"—as much to the door behind which the steps had stopped now, listening, as to his father.

His father was smiling past him at the door. He said clearly "Yes—" like the rising plea of a happy greedy child.

It opened on a girl wrapped tight against cold, her clear pale skin all lit to red life by whatever trek she'd made to be here. She also smiled—also past Forrest—and standing in place in the open door, set down two large canvas bags she'd brought and began to unwrap herself, her head. She was lovely and had shown her auburn hair, her tall brow, to the grim chilled room like gifts for the season to whoever was needy, whoever would take them, before she had strayed enough from her smile to catch the presence of a waiting stranger. "I'm sorry," she said but to Mr. Mayfield.

It was Forrest who stood though and said "I was leaving."

She studied him, his face, for the time it took to read his past; then a slow shock rose from deep in her chest and stilled her smile. She put a hand toward him but not in greeting—to force him back—and said, "Oh don't. I have just brought coal. Then I got to go cook his dinner; he's starving. Let me make up a fire."

So Forrest sat.

And the girl slid her bags across the sill and shut the door and then brought them forward to the stove and knelt.

Forrest said to his father, "How far did she come?" He intended by that to discover the coalyard.

But his father recalled their first exchange. "She's from here," he said. "Richmond's her home." He was staring at her.

She had set one bag of the coal aside, far back on the hearth; now she worked with quiet uncomplicated grace, with hands surprisingly white and small, to build them a fire in the ashes of the last. She wore no rings. She was twenty maybe. Maybe less, eighteen. The silent economy of her competence, the absence from her face and sturdy wrists of any trace of childish fullness or petulance—all suggested a woman well on in pain and knowledge, not the unseamed girl she appeared to be. The two men, seated and quiet as she, watched her do her task.

Through that, Forrest really only saw her. His mind was stilled. He briefly wondered one thing—"How does he pay her?"—but afterward he watched. A neighbor maybe, the landlord's daughter? He knew he was lulled, even now while the room was still stark cold; but he did not resist or question why. He was ministered to; if he'd summoned his feeling and named it aloud, he'd have said some such.

The girl turned then, still kneeling and her hands now black in midair. "You light it please," she said to Mr. Mayfield.

"It's safe," he said. "Just slow wet coal."

"Please," she said again. She was not smiling.

Forrest rocked forward slightly and said "Let me."

His father stood. "She's scared," he said. "She was burnt bad recently; lamp exploded. I try to convince her the world's half-safe; but it's early yet—early, ain't it, honey?" He paused above her a moment for balance and rested a hand on the crown of her head.

"*I* believe you," she said, "but I want you to help me." He lifted his hand and went to the mantel for a tin matchbox; and she looked to Forrest and gave a short laugh, soft but happy.

Forrest suspected he was in secret trouble, had already been damaged past hope of repair (she had not been, clearly—not the visible parts of her body at least: her face, neck, hands were free of burns; no trace of scars). He said to the girl, "I am Forrest Mayfield."

She nodded. "His son. Have to be blind not to see that much."

Forrest could not stop there with the compliment she intended. His sense of danger was growing.

The girl though was watching his father approach the stove with fire, no longer afraid, entrusted to him.

Forrest said "Who are you?"

His father stopped; a short cone of newspaper burned in his hand. He said, "My help. She's the one person helps me."

The girl said "Polly—"

Mr. Mayfield told her, "You go cook dinner."

She stood and said again firmly "Polly"—to Forrest, still smiling. Then she left apparently in glad obedience, though with no glance back.

Forrest thought that she trusted one thing at least—Robinson Mayfield, that Robinson Mayfield would wait out her absence, be here at her call or call her when needed—and he felt strongly drawn to follow her, to learn plain trust from her plain clear pattern, rarer than happiness.

But his father had lighted the fire by then; and as he stood near its cracking heart, he took quick strength—from what? simple fire?—and looked to Forrest with steady eyes. "What you come here for?"

Forrest found he had also drawn new force from his cornered state; he was battling now. He stood and took three steps back from his father and said, "I'm the one who has come this far. You answer me." Then he waited; his father's eyes never flickered. "Please sir, *you* answer. Do that much for me."

His father slowly nodded.

"Will it be the truth?"

"Far as I know it."

"I can't stay for less," Forrest said.

"What you want first?"

"—How you knew about me? My wife and boy."

Mr. Mayfield half-smiled. "My nigger kin." Then he went to the bed again and sat.

Forrest stayed on his feet, alone in the warming air.

"You better sit down." His father pointed.

Forrest accepted and went to the rocker and faced his father.

"You ain't here to harm me?" Mr. Mayfield said.

Forrest thought that through. "I don't believe so."

"And you see I'm broke, in money and health, and nobody near me?"

"Yes sir. I do."

That freed Mr. Mayfield to start. "You want to know everything. I'll tell you what counts—don't say I don't know; I've had time to think. The fourth job I had was fireman on the railroad. You don't remember but back then Bracey amounted to something—a fresh-air resort; people came from all over just to breathe the air—so of course it was something of a railroad junction. We'd change crews there; get in late at night after running ten hours, black and stinking, and go to the big old Assembly Hall and take a hot bath and eat a big supper and sleep till day. Then we'd start out again. But that's where you come in—the supper. Your mother's mother ran the dining room. They had been good people, a monied family; but the nigger war had knocked em down—killed their father, your Grandfather Goodwin, and eat up their money and (before I got to town) their land. And old Mrs. Goodwin was cooking for trash. Like me, as she never missed a chance to let me know. Hell, what did I care? I was scum and I knew it (scum is what *rises*) and didn't mind at all, enjoyed it in fact since I noticed I was grinning with my belly full while the Goodwins and all their kind were moaning. Moaning and empty. Well, one of em didn't stay empty long. Your pitiful mama. They had lost their place, that house on the hill where the Goodwins are buried; and they lived in the loft of that old Hall. One ratty room. Rats racing in the wall, gnawing hats in the cupboards. But the old lady worked half the night as I said, hollering at niggers over hot cookstoves; so I made me a number of visits to the rats. Anna Goodwin—she was eighteen years old and dying on the vine. But I brought her new life. That was in my line—don't you see?—back then. It was what I could do, though I've long since lost it. I could make people happy. Make em *want* me at least, make em think they was in Hog Heaven with me. And I never cheated. I never abused em. I was happy as they were, just offering my service, my one little gift. I'm not telling you your mother was a strumpet. I'm not saying I ever put her to bed till the night we were married. I don't think I did, don't recall I did. I'm saying that somehow I made her happy, made her think she was happy by thinking she loved me. I've wondered *how* many times through the years. How does one person—sorry as me, no education, the morals of a housefly—cause people to move? I think I know. It is some people's talent, some rare few people, to make other folks (mostly women) think this—'There's a poor ruined soul that I can help.' What most women thought I needed was *rest*, a place to lie down in and rest. Trouble is, the best place to rest is *bed*; and beds got to have roofs to keep out rain, and roofs need walls; and next thing you know, you've laid down to snooze and some woman's built a two-story house round you and stocked it with babies and is back in the kitchen frying your dinner—and you won't even hungry. Course, a further trouble with me back then was—bed was the last place I could rest, specially if some little body was beside me; but you understand what I'm driving at? I got it figured early—*Don't never stand still*, which is why I arrived in Bracey, Virginia at twenty-seven years old with no home ties. And I left it with none, as you know I guess, a little later—just cut em clean (that's the one kind way: cut clean and quick; then the wound'll stanch itself). But what you are asking me is why I lingered, why I stood still long as I did. I've asked myself; and here's the true answer—I'm a gentle soul. I saw your mother as a heart in need, saw it the first evening I ever laid eyes on her; and since pretty soon she saw me as what *she* needed, I volunteered to go on and be it for her. And whatever you may think, it never harmed her. I guess you just recall her as sad, the years between when I had to leave and she finally died. I'm sorry you can't recall her early picture. She was sweet to look at, provided you didn't dwell long on her eyes. Her eyes were scary; lot of women's are. Comes from them having to wait so much. Waiting will eat your heart plumb out. She waited very little for *me*, I'd say. The grief she'd had before I got there was caused by others, no fault of her own—her family's losses, the burdens her mother had to lay on her back when she'd been trained to expect nothing heavier than shot-silk or swan's down—and she'd borne up brave and healthy, laughed a lot. Still when I walked into that dining room on an April evening, having just scrubbed clean in a big copper tub in her mama's cellar, and laid eyes on her for the first time ever and she on me—well, she thought right away she'd been badly abused by, what do you call it?, the winds of Fate. Hell, she'd barely had a ringlet blown out of place; but have you noticed this?—when people fall in love (women, I mean), they decide on the spot that their lives to that instant have been blank torment; and *you* are the single straw on the sea, their last hope of floating? I've noticed that. I'd noticed it before your mama came along—my own, for instance. My mama looked at me from the day I was born as if I was moon and stars and hot food; but I also noticed that when I left home at fourteen to work, she took it about as hard as a fleabite. She lived and was fat till two years ago. You never saw her; pity on you. Your mama was different. She couldn't turn loose. In the ten-odd years I stayed there with her, she never blinked once from gazing at me. I was meant to be God and the angels for her—so she believed, in her honest heart—and for some damned reason, I halfway tried. Course, I still traveled; went right on working as a railroad fireman spite of your Grandmother Goodwin sneering. She wanted me to stop too and stand stock-still, not so she could love me but to better her name. I told her that the Mayfields were building good fires for the happiness of man when the Goodwins was still hauling pigshit for pennies. That shut her up. It also killed her; she passed not a year after we got married. No I went on traveling for two main reasons—to halfway wean your mother, give her strength; and for my own health, just good fresh air. I was not only trash but also a tramp, my true vocation. I always had—back then, I mean—a lot more life stored up in me than any one woman or house could use; so I spent it on the wind, spreading happiness where your mama couldn't see it to worry over, coming back to her—and you and Hatt—at the end of each turn. And I honestly think I'd be there now; I honestly think if anybody'd asked me, up to a week before I left, I'd have said 'Oh yes, I'm here for life; when I'm *here*, that is.' But then I changed all in a night, had to leave and left. You were fast asleep." The slow voice had stopped. Its certain flow had come in those minutes to seem so entirely the contents of the room that now with silence the space was shockingly empty, imperiled.

Forrest said to fill it, "I was, yes."

His father took no encouragement from that but stood and walked again to the stove—which was burning well; the ear could hear—and opened its door and bent to look. Satisfied, he rose and went to the mantel and found a piece of mirror which he held to the light; then he studied his face.

Forrest also studied. His chair was placed so that he could see all the mirror saw.

His father half-smiled.

The story is ended, Forrest thought, amazed. *He thinks that is all. He thinks I have come to hear that much, and am now fully answered. Perhaps I am?* Forrest waited to see if that last were credible. No and would never be. He said, "Sir, how? How did you change?"

His father continued to watch himself; but he said, "Like I told you, I had to go."

Forrest said "Why?"

His father looked up, hot-eyed and sudden. "I am not your pupil. Don't examine me."

"Forgive me," Forrest said but sat on, expectant.

Mr. Mayfield said, "I thought you were mine. You favor me."

Forrest said, "I am, which is why I am here."

His father's eyes had calmed but his head shook No. "Any son of mine would have stayed away—Hell, *run* to the opposite side of the world once he heard where I was. You're hers all right. She'd have tracked me down and broke me like this." With one hand he drew a half-circle round him in the empty air, the precincts of his body, the scene of damage.

Forrest said "I do not understand."

His father said, "Don't claim you forgot. You're bound to recall—how she hunted me out of that house and your lives."

Forrest nodded, a lie extended for bait. He remembered his mother as stricken prey, silent and seated.

"She built her whole long picture of me, of what she imagined I'd been at first and was now changing into under her guiding hand; and then when after ten long years some pieces of truth, of the real plain me, swum up to view, she all but lost her mind at the sight; went cutting around at crazy random like a circular saw broke loose from socket and wheeling in air. So I left—if you really want to know—for protection, for plain damn safety."

Forrest said, "What pieces? What pieces of the truth?"

His father said, "Niggering. I was niggering around. You knew that surely."

Forrest said, "I've heard Veenie, her long old tale. She's got your picture; she knew you were here."

His father nodded. "Her tale is true—or I guess it is. It ought to be. She knows it all. Or knew it once."

Forrest said "Elvira. Elvira's boy."

His father nodded, still solemn from the story Forrest forced him to give. But then, standing on in place by the stove, his face spread open and one dry laugh husked up from his chest. "Imagine being washed up here for that, being run from your home and children for that. Hell, every good boy with a pecker that worked was niggering round me—you could hardly walk on a weekday night (not to mention Saturday) without stepping smack on a bare white ass pumping joy on black—but she had to think I invented it all. She went to Veenie. Hell, went to the *preacher!*—had him praying for me. Then she came to me—at night as always; she'd wait till I was tired—and what she asked me, all she could think to ask me after thirteen years of moving in each other's shadow, was 'Rob, do you want to kill me dead?' I asked her what she meant—it was all news to me—and she talked for an hour and I said No. One word *No*. But I thought a few more and made my plans; and when I had told you and Hatt goodbye, I went on off. She killed herself, was who did the killing." He waited a little. "Now she's killing me, all this much later, these miles away."

Forrest stood but did not approach his father. He knew he had heard a sad stream of lies—a mind so confused by age and sickness or by years of flight as to be incapable of knowing the truth, the whole just truth; or else in clear full possession of the past but rigging it shamelessly for self-service, mercy—yet he also knew that when his own lips opened, he would make the farthest offer he'd considered in the weeks before coming here. He did not smile but he said, "I am willing to carry you home. Willing and glad. I've got my own house and a boy to help me. Or Hatt and her boys would be more than glad—plenty room, steady company, good steady food." Forrest looked round the room again. It seemed the merest camp that could be stowed and moved in half an hour. "We can be home for supper. Tomorrow's Christmas."

His father said "Thank you," but he shook his head slowly. He still faced Forrest though. His eyes never dropped.

"It would give me a great deal of satisfaction," Forrest said. "You are what I have got."

"It would kill her," his father said. "This is her home."

Forrest didn't speak but silence put the question.

His father said "Polly" and pointed quickly through the wall toward the kitchen. "She helps me a lot, and I'm grateful to her."

Forrest said, "You'll have all the help you can use." He was smiling now.

His father did not need to wait to think. "No," he said. He had also grown pleasant, though his firmness held. He was young again, face clear and ready, all but hopeful.

"What kin is she to you?" Forrest said.

"Not a bit in the world."

Again Forrest did not speak; but his head gave a little twist forward, incredulous—*Then you're coming with me*.

His father said "I want her."

Still silent, Forrest also pointed to the wall behind which occasional sounds of metal had ignited like distant approaching war.

His father said "Yes."

"Is she your wife?"

His father said, "No. Your mother was that. I've tried to respect her claim to that, wherever she sits in Heaven or Hell. No I've had other help—I've had to have it; so will you in time—but just one wife, one set of children: Hatt and you."

Forrest said "Elvira had a boy."

His father nodded.

Forrest said, "I'm here. Nobody else is. I'm here and I'm Forrest, and Forrest is offering to carry you home and tend you well as long as you need him. Just you. Just you."

His father looked slowly again toward the kitchen and listened as though its sounds were a steady message, unheeded till now. Then he turned back to Forrest and opened his mouth, and a rush of bright blood flooded his chin. But he stood on, calm; and when he could speak, what he said in moving blood was "Her. Call her please. Now."

2

A HALF hour later Forrest sat at a bare pine table in the kitchen and waited for the dinner which Polly was serving. She had asked him to stay. Once she had answered his call and come and quickly but calmly had helped his father to bed and had sat till the blood slowed, darkened and stopped and his father had slept, then she'd looked up to Forrest and silently nodded and beckoned him gravely to follow her. He had done so and when they were in the warm kitchen, she had not said a word but had walked to the small stove and recommenced work. Forrest had gone to the table and sat and then had said "What's wrong with him?" She had worked on awhile, then had turned and said "He calls it asthma"; then had smiled and said, "I call it the way to keep me here." Then she'd gone grave again and had said, "I'm not leaving. I promised him that. Why don't he believe me?" Forrest had said, "I can't help you there"; and then they had both stayed silent till she'd brought him a full plate of food and he'd thanked her; and then she'd said, "Can I eat now with you? Is that all right?" and he'd told her Yes.

That nearness—she sat two feet from his hand, had chosen that nearness—gave him the courage to ask her more. "You want to stay here?"

She took two mouthfuls—of turnips, yams, and boiled sidemeat—and worked and swallowed slowly and neatly; and then she looked up at Forrest. "You want me to leave?"

"I don't know," he said. "Please answer me first."

She waited again, though she did not eat. It was clear that, however hungry or cold, her throat could not now handle food. Words alone were sufficient struggle and, when they came, bore the signs of their coming, ragged and spent. But she gave them to Forrest, straight at his eyes. "Yes sir, I've thought about it a lot. I'm staying by him as long as he lets me."

"He's dying. You're young."

"That's all right," she said.

"He's leaving you. He's left everybody that ever loved him."

"I know that, yes sir. He's taking his time though, with me at least."
Polly sat and waited for an answer from Forrest, some word or move; and
when neither came, she broke into smiling, the natural product of what
she had said and was presently thinking. It lifted her small face—the smile,
her thoughts of a man who had just now hemorrhaged freely—and she
took on the color of warmth and welcome. Her high flat cheekbones were
bright with their own blood, young and durable and waiting to serve. Her
blue eyes opened, backward endless, into views of honest fidelity—the
world that existed in her head and chest, her whole easy body, quiet but
ample and incapable of lying or of truth withheld. Her hair was chestnut
and had somehow been washed in the recent cold days; and though it was
parted and drawn back tightly, it also bore the flood of her happiness,
another channel of her total life, her permanent promise. In the dim light
it burned, no threat of exhaustion.

Forrest saw all that, bore it through his own eyes helpless to refuse.
He tried to evade her by turning to his food; but after one swallow his
throat balked and closed. He was forced to look up.

She was eating now, slow but untroubled; and she watched her plate
only, her present duty, present delight.

She had staked Forrest's heart. He knew, his mouth plugged with cold
pork fat, that now this moment at an old wood table in a Richmond slum,
he was at the worst; the bottom of his life. A step from here was appallingly simple, certain as night—a self-made end or a miracle of grace; some
rope lowered to him for rescue, haulage. He thought quite clearly with the
cold and fearless abandon of despair, "I will let her choose." He set down
his fork and forced down the cud and said "What shall I do?"

"For who?" she said.

Her question with its crushing load of expectation—*to do* was to do
for *someone* simply—fell fully on him; but he also saw that, with all its
pain, it still offered rescue. He could do for her, her few plain needs. He
slowly constructed a mask of pleasantness behind his face and offered it
toward her and ate a little and then said, "Tell me please who you are. Are
we any kin?"

She genuinely laughed; the remaining corners of her beauty lighted.
"No more than usual—through Adam and Eve, I mean," she said.

"Then is this your home?" He touched the table with his index finger;
he meant this house.

"No sir. I'm a city girl." She laughed again. "Washington, D. C."

"He said you were born in Richmond, a native."

"He lies about me. No I'm capital-bred." She stopped there though.

She wants to be lured, Forrest thought; wants attention. "Then why
are you here?"

"I'm grown," she said, "and I want to be." The firmness of her
thought and speech did not have time to color her face before she had

gone on to something she felt to be gentler. "It's a story," she said. "Eighteen years long. You still want to hear it?"

Forrest nodded.

"Don't worry. The first part goes quick—seventeen years of work, hard work. I was my dad's woman. My mother had died right after I came; Dad said I killed her. She turned all septic from some blood poison; and her last cries were weaker than mine—I was five days old—so I guess I did, though I didn't intend it. Dad understood that; he was telling the truth, not blaming me; and I've always took it as truth, just the news. I've pitied her memory and dressed her grave most years on my birthday, but I never gave up growing or smiling because of her. I never *knew* her. Dad was all my kin; and with God looking on, I can say Dad tried but he didn't strain. The War had completely wore him out. He was from Virginia and fought with General Jackson on foot, and he said he had walked the equal of from here to Jerusalem and back *uphill* (they fought in the mountains). So from when I remember, he would barely move. He had walked home from up around Natural Bridge at the end, to Arlington really; and sold what little his mama still owned and moved over to Washington, saying he meant to live on the winning side. They rented some rooms and he set to thinking of things to do. He had just turned twenty and before the War had worked at tanning leather; but he said he could never do that again, smell an old hide rotting; so he settled finally on tortoiseshell. His mother, who was Irish, had somewhere learned to work tortoiseshell. So he settled on that—well, really on *her*; she of course did the work; he was just the boss—and they made combs for ladies, in tortoiseshell and ivory, which he would take out and peddle round town. A little comb factory. And you know it succeeded. At first, plain combs in various sizes; but you know what Washington is—people looking—so he got his mama to invent souvenirs: little watchfobs carved like Lincoln or Lee, little pictures on the combs (sunset at sea), helpful lines of verse ("May you never know sorrow"). And they were thriving; made enough to rent a whole house near the Capitol, small but dry, and then she died. His mother wore out. And there he was with a houseful of tusks and great turtle shells. Well, according to him, he barely missed step. A museum was what came to him at once. So he married the girl that would be my mother—a small girl named Lillian—and set her to keeping his old museum: selling tickets and guarding the junk from thieves while he went back out to the battlefields and gathered up souvenirs for his show. Guns and balls and bayonets, poor soggy boots. He even had a mummified Rebel leg that a lady sold him till some men came by a year or so later and made him burn it and bury the ashes. See, what he had set his heart to have was the first and only Confederate museum in Washington City; and you know, he got it. Or halfway got it. He could never do anything perfectly pure—he kept all his tusks and shells lying round and eventually he got an old nigger with

eczema and straightened his hair and dressed him like an Indian brave. *I*
remember that. I had come by then, laying Mother under as I just now
said; and that's how I grew up. I liked it. I really did. It mostly was
happy."

Forrest had managed to eat while listening; and he felt appreciable
strength rising in him, though he thought it came from the warm heavy
food; he gave her no credit. She herself had reached a pause and begun to
eat; so he said, "Then why are you here with him?"

"That's the rest of the story," she said. "You want it?"

"Please," he said.

"Well, it fell on me, by the time I could talk, to run the place—Dad
never remarried. It seemed like he had all of that he needed. Of course I
didn't watch him (he was gone a lot); but I have the impression I was all
he had in the female line; and I was his daughter, you understand. He
hired in a woman to get me started; but once I was up hip-high, it was
mine. And run it I did; it was run it or starve. He was drinking by then and
had lost all interest in new exhibits; and of course I was too young to travel
or buy, but every now and then some old pal of his would send us a
treasure to put in the cases (that's how we got the big finger-ring made
from Traveller's hair and the stuffed mascot of the 32nd Rifles). And
people kept coming, that's the funny part; people will pay to see a dead
dog that they wouldn't glance at in the road for free. Funnier still, it was
mostly Yankees; I guess few Rebels could afford the outing or maybe they
just didn't want to remember. No, Yankees would come with their wives
and boys and brag out-loud how they'd saved the earth for God and
progress; they'd tell the old dressed-up nigger Indian how lucky he was the
redskins had been brought civilization before Jesus came to judge their
evil. That actual thing had happened, I swear, the first day I ever saw your
father. So when he came I was more than ready for what he offered,
smiling eyes and a voice from Virginia."

Forrest said, "What words did he say to you first?"

She did not know at once but waited to think. Then she smiled.
" 'How serious is your need for a nickel?' "

Forrest said "Meaning what?"

"—Could he get in free. A nickel was what we charged for admission.
I sat at the front door and sold nickel-tickets, children two cents. It was
early fall, the first chilly day; so I was not just mad but cold. I was busy
crocheting when he walked in, and he got close on me before I saw him. I
was sitting down; he was standing over me two feet away; and that was his
plea—could he get in free? I said, 'No sir, my dad would kill me.' He said,
'What if I was to kill him first? There's sufficient means' (he meant in the
museum, the guns and knives). I said, 'Then you'd have one orphan to
raise'; and he said 'Suits me.' I said, 'Wait a minute; you don't know the
orphan.' He said 'It's you' and I nodded it was. 'I accept,' he said, 'I still
accept.' So I let him in. And was happy to."

Forrest said, "Then what did he do?"

"Started bleeding. I indicated to him how busy I was; so he'd gone on in and started looking, and it wasn't two minutes till the nigger yelled. I ran through the first two rooms before I found him. He was standing by the case full of eating equipment—tin plates and spoons, long knives and forks, leather waterbottles. Your dad was standing there staring down, and the blood was streaking his chin like now." She pointed to the bedroom, the place in time.

Forrest said "What caused it?"

Her eyes searched him thoroughly. "You really don't know? Same thing as always."

"His asthma then?"

She shook her head No and, by moving, pulled up the start of a smile—a game, another round of her happy game.

Forrest chose to play. "Tell me."

"Shame," she said. "It's always shame. I notice that every time he bleeds."

Forrest said "For what?"

"The war," she said. "The poor old war. He was twenty-one or two when it cranked up, but he has his weak chest and didn't go. All those souvenirs brought it back to him, what he'd wanted to do so long before."

Forrest said, "He has done most of what he wanted; you and I are the leavings, two of his leavings."

But she smiled, "I *will* be, after he's dead. I'm here till then. You speak for you."

So he did. He suddenly knew his intention. It seemed his final mission here, a rite that would free him to leave, walk clean away into his own life at last. He pushed back his chair and stood in place and reached deep into his lefthand pocket. He drew out a plush box the size of a small egg and offered it to Polly.

She set down her fork and wiped her right hand on the thigh of her dress and took the box, flicking one finger back and forth on its velvet—a pale rose color, worn and stained—but she showed no sign of opening it, no sign that she'd also been given permission to open it.

"It's yours," Forrest said. "For Christmas. You've won it."

She wiped her hand again and looked up smiling and opened the box. A gold ring, wide and heavy and plain. She lifted it gently from its satin socket and turned it carefully, then saw the writing. She tilted it all ways in the dim light. Then she looked back to Forrest. "This is somebody else's. I can't see whose in this poor light."

He waited awhile to see if she would see. Then he thought "She can't read." So he said it, not needing to take the ring—"*Robinson Mayfield to Anna Goodwin. My* mother's ring. She is long past needing it. My sister has her own. I've got no use for it now or likely ever. And it's mine to give. God knows you've won it."

She quickly turned serious but held the ring. "God knows very little about me," she said, "since I came here."

He ignored that, smiling. "Please wear it," he said.

She examined the ring once more, though not to read it—not the valuing eye of a jeweler or bride but the calm sad face of a judge, a mother. "No," she said. "Oh no. I couldn't."

"Why?" Forrest said.

She set it down carefully on the bare wood between them, nearer him than her. "It may be yours to give; but see, it's not mine to take while he's there alive. He explained that to me."

Forrest said "How?"

"The day he asked me to leave with him. That first day of course I led him back to our quarters and got him eased, and then I fed him; and within an hour, he knew more about me than my own dad, knew more than any other human ever had—just because he asked. Weak as he was, he asked me *questions*. Jesus in the air on Judgment Day won't dare to ask anybody half of what your father asked me, strange as we were to each other that day."

Forrest said "What?"

She looked to see if he'd use her well. "My age and weight, my health and the names of my favorite foods. The colors I liked. My full entire name—Margaret Jane Drewry. Was I happy then? *'This minute; tell me quick!'* I told him 'Yes sir' and then he asked 'Why?' "

Forrest said, "You knew. I'll bet you knew."

She nodded. "And told him. I'm as bold and truthful as he is curious; you've noticed that. It took me a minute that day to know. But he waited on the couch, Dad's old leather couch; and finally I said, 'I'm happy to have helped you.' He said 'Tell the truth'; and I said, 'That's it, though I'm naturally happy, as you'd know if you knew me.' —'When will I?' he said; and since I had seen how close he had watched me, I said, 'You *do*. You know me right now, much as you ever will. I'm the most open heart on the whole east coast as far as I know (I've barely traveled). What you see is what's *here*! So he said he'd take it, and I slapped his hand and said it wasn't for sale. He begged my pardon which I freely gave; and then he laughed and said, 'A good thing since I'm broke as Judas. Would you have me for nothing?' Well, sir, I ask you—what would you do if a total stranger walked into your house and had a small hemorrhage and then both insulted you and asked for your hand? You'd throw him out or at least call for help; I still had the nigger, two rooms away. You'd do that, I know. But I'm another story and have always been. I told him 'Yes.' Oh it took me another minute and some looking—at his eyes, just his eyes—but I knew my true answer; so I went on and said it. And here we sit in Richmond, Virginia."

"Why here?" Forrest said.

"His home," she said. "You know, his home." Her hand waved slowly round in the air.

He did not know but waited till she told him.

"This was the Mayfield place, his daddy's. His mother had lived here till just a few weeks before I saw him. He had nursed her a long time—years, I guess—and she had just died well on in her eighties, leaving this to him and all her furniture. He had sold most of that but what's in the bedroom and this cooking stuff and taken the money and given himself the trip as reward. Rest for his mind; his body was rested—he hadn't worked a day in many a year except tending her, boiling oatmeal and rice, telling her all the tales he had lived through or dreamed. Well, he got it, I think—a rested mind except for the hemorrhage—and I have to say he got it from me. I told you how quick he made his offer. I've always taken that to be the sign; he *saw* me and loved me. I understand that; I live by *my* eyes. I chose to trust him, though he told me about you and your poor mother, and here we sit. It will be yours soon." Again she waved round, the Mayfield place.

But Forrest ignored that. He said, "You're here. Where did that leave your father?"

"On his own," she said. "Where he'd just as soon be."

"Not needing you?"

"He never did; never said he did. You can see that all in the story I've told. He liked somebody around him to joke with—cooking and sewing he learned at war—and he needed one person to stand at the door and take in money; but mostly he was independent as a snake: that clean and lonely without being lonesome. He liked me though; I don't mean he didn't. He genuinely liked me. We had laughed a lot."

"He's dead?" Forrest said—she spoke in past tenses.

"Not to my knowledge, no." She waited awhile. "*I* am to him." This was painful for her, the first hard thing she had met so far. "When I went to him, nine days to the day after meeting your father, and asked his permission to leave home finally, he of course said 'With who?' and I told the truth; he had met your dad one afternoon briefly. He said, 'You are asking to marry the dead; that fellow is dead, plus he's older than me.' I said, 'There is no plan to marry nobody; he's had one wife and children that he's true to, though he hasn't seen them in thirty years.' —'Go then,' he said. 'But go for good. Take anything here that's yours or your mother's and vanish please.' He smiled all through it, but of course he was earnest so here I am. I keep saying that."

Forrest nodded. "Keep the ring." He moved it back toward her.

But she shook her head. "It's not necessary, understand. I've promised. I'm here till the end."

Forrest said "After that?"

She had thought of that also. She faced him smiling, her hands palm-up on the table before her, small for her strength. "I'm young," she said. "Nobody here knows me. I can start a life."

Forrest said "You will."

3

IN the bedroom again he took three steps toward his sleeping father, quietly, to wake him gently.

His father's eyes stayed shut, but a hand flicked up and across his face as though at a gnat.

He stopped at the foot of the bed. "It's Forrest."

"I know it is. Write down this letter." He had still not looked or raised his head.

Forrest searched round for paper. "Sir, there's nothing to write on."

His father waited. "Remember it then. Write it down when you're able."

Forrest said "All right."

Then his father lined it out on the air with a finger. "Lay in a large supply of goods." His voice was firm, the tone calm and sane.

"Yes sir," Forrest said.

"Apples," his father said, the finger still urging. "Also cheese."

Forrest said "Yes sir" but then he said "Why?"

His father looked; his head raised slightly. "You got a cook?"

Forrest nodded Yes (Grainger was learning).

His father said, "Please start her cooking for me."

Forrest wondered as always in the presence of age, "Is his mind really broken or am I being tested? And if so, how; tested for what?" He said, "You have got Polly yonder now, cooking Christmas dinner." He pointed to the kitchen, a better sanctuary than any he'd found in his own years of hunting. Cruel to tear any man from that, whatever the needs of past or future, of present duty.

His father glanced there. "Are you going to take her?"

"No sir," Forrest said. "She'll stay here with you. She wants that, has promised that just now to me. I'll send what little help I can."

"I know that," his father said—of Polly's promise. He ignored Forrest's money and laid his head back deep in the pillow. But then he said, "Is anything here that you want?"

Forrest tried to think, all this time and distance; but nothing would come. "No sir," he said.

Mr. Mayfield nodded. "It will be yours directly. You're the one that would want it. You come here and get it. You'll hear when I die. You come here and claim it."

"Yes sir," Forrest said. He did not ask what was here to claim—a bed; a cookstove; a woodbox of pine bark; a bare house no doubt burdened with taxes; remains of people he had never known (who yet steered his life), the oil and dead cast scales of their flesh in the grain of the wood, immovable. *There is nothing to claim.* He suddenly saw that. *There has never been.* He was happy at the sight, the freeing knowledge. A life seemed possible. Only one last barrier. He walked to his father's right side and, still standing, said "This is yours." He extended the small ringbox again.

Mr. Mayfield looked and knew it. "No it ain't," he said. "Who took it off her?"

Forrest said, "Hatt. Just before she was buried."

"I never took it off her; who the Hell was Hattie?"

"A girl," Forrest said. "A sixteen-year-old girl that you left the job to."

His father made a deep sound of hate in his throat. "Girls have caused four-fifths of the pain on earth."

Forrest continued to offer the ring. "I don't want this."

"Then give it to your boy. He's got the name; he is yours, ain't he?"

"His mother refused it. Here, you pawn it. Let Polly pawn it." He set it beside his father's hand on the quilt.

The hand drew back. "Polly won't touch it."

Forrest waited; then turned to go for good, the ring in his hand. His own new life, whatever that would be—at least not this, free at least of this.

He had taken three steps when his father said, "Give it to the little nigger then."

Forrest looked—the face was deathbound but smiling—then was able to laugh, the first time in months: an issue of fresh sweet blood from his own heart, the promise of more.

4

AT four in the morning—Christmas morning—Forrest dreamed this dream in a boarding-house bed (trains to Bracey had been stopped by ice, all switches frozen): he was sleeping well in his bed at home, restorative sleep through which he sank like a stone in the sea, no fear of bottom, no fear of morning or the duties of day; but then he was stopped and dredged toward light, gently, slowly but against his will. Wakened by his father who stretched above him, full weight on his body and rode there calmly as if on that deep water or a dream, a dream of his own. Yet his face seemed needful, open eyes and lips. So Forrest said, "Father, what are you after?"

But his father stayed on him, still as gall on an oak; and at last said, "I've taken it. Never you mind. I take what I need."

Forrest spoke aloud then, though still deep asleep—"All yours anyhow." He never again recalled the words; but they ended the dream, permitted his further plunge through night. He sank toward morning.

They woke Grainger though. He had slept on a pallet on the cold floor by Forrest; and despite the hard day (the blank hours of waiting on a depot bench, then Forrest's return and the long afternoon of Richmond's sights—the Capitol, the church where Patrick Henry spoke, the tomb of Poe's mother), he had slept very lightly as though set to run at some unknown signal: to run for life. Now the words had waked him, the signal at last. He heard sounds only, not their meaning; but he sat up quickly—he was fully dressed except for shoes—and looked toward the bed where Forrest was still and silent again. Grainger listened for breathing—soft but steady; he counted three breaths. *Safe*, he thought—or felt in all his chilly body. *Christmas*, he knew—by the high hard moonlight of early morning that poured through curtains of their single window. He looked to the window but could see only light, no shapes of trees or buildings yet. So he rose to his knees in the neat warm covers and looked again to Forrest. By the moon he could now see the face all surrendered to rest. The eyes seemed sunk past rising in their sockets, and the mouth that obeyed instantaneously every need of the mind (it was Grainger's vane for detecting the weather of any moment) was slack and half-open. Grainger's was smiling, broad and helpless. *I have had my Christmas*, he thought so strongly and happily as to draw him to his feet, upright but silent. He looked back again. He had not waked Forrest; so being up anyhow (however cold), he stepped to the window and parted the curtains with both dark hands and spread them in moonlight.

The left hand shone with the ring, his Christmas, which Forrest had given him six hours ago before darkening the room for their try at sleep. He had said, "You have been a good help to me, Grainger. Take this as my thanks" and extended the box. When Grainger had seen it and smiled at the shine, he said, "Mr. Forrest, this come from you?" —"It does now," Forrest said; "See if it fits." The right hand was too large; the left slipped in easily, room to grow. "Wear it," Forrest had said, "as long as you can and remember when you see it, it stands for the good help you gave me this year; and it hopes for more." Grainger had said, "I'll die in this. You count on that. I'll die thanking you." Then Forrest had simply said "Good night" and blown out the lamp; but once they had quieted, though Grainger's blood still raced with pleasure, Forrest spoke again—"Never tell a soul." Grainger had promised.

Now freezing in sockfeet by the frosted pane, he made it again, silent—his promise. He shut his lips tight to prove they were sealed, but pleasure and thanks broke them quickly open. He smiled again. *I am set for life*. He had never before imagined a life but had waited in the endless present of childhood. Now he could go back and lie in his covers, find the remains of his vanishing warmth and wait for day. His twelfth Christmas, the start of his life, three hours away.

5

February 21, 1905

Dear Mr. Forrest,

    I made you two promises—to stick by your dad and to let you know when the news got bad. I have already kept the first one, I'm proud. He died sometime this morning in his sleep so peaceful as not to disturb my own rest. I had woke up just after light and roused myself to start the fire so he could have warm air to stand up in. He had been a little under but nothing too low and the blood spells had not come no more than normal. I tried to work quiet but he heard me and looked and said "Margaret Jane Drewry." That is my full name. He was in his right mind. I said "Yes sir" but I won't say I laughed since nobody hates rising cold worse than me. So he said "Margaret Jane Drewry" again—voice strong as yours and looking young as you, all rested and clean—and then he said "I don't see how you stand this." I'm sorry to say I answered him true. I said "Rob, I won't lie and say it's easy." You knew already that I used his first name so you won't think hard and anyhow I promised to send you the news, that is part of my news. The rest of it is that I dozed back to rest for maybe half an hour while the stove was cracking and when heat woke me finally he was some while gone. Not a teaspoon of blood, no rigor nor cry, and his last word to me had been to beg pardon. Well he has it now as I hope he knows. And that is my news. Both promises kept.

    I know you are busy with your own life there and anyhow he left me his burial wishes which are simple enough for even me to follow and he has sufficient money of his mother's to cover. I could understand and would not think hard if you or your sister didn't feel drawn to come. He gave you little cause for duty I know. But this is all yours now. He kept saying that so as not to fool me and I was not fooled. The little that's here is yours and your sister's. If you send me word you can come here soon. I will wait till then and give you my keys and tell you what few little things I know that you may not. I have laid him out clean in his own cold bed and have moved myself to a cot in the kitchen. I will wait three days for instructions from you and then if none come I will do his wishes and shut up the place good and mail you the key for your convenience.

Awaiting your plan, I am
Truly,
Margaret Jane Drewry

TWO

THE HEART IN DREAMS

MAY 1921

Sylvie stood at the hot sink, straight and firm. The window to her left still let in daylight, but she'd already lit the hanging lamp; so she worked in two lights, day and oil, washing in silence.

Rob came up behind her in sockfeet, silent, and stood two feet away and said, half-whispering, "This is my night. Now. My night's coming on."

He had not surprised her and she didn't turn. She washed a gravy boat and said in her normal voice, "A whole lot of nights here lately been yours."

"But now I'm grown." He moved a step nearer—just into the edge of Sylvie's odor, clean and her own but harsh, guarding, thrown out around her in defense of a center of precious life.

She still didn't turn, though she'd finished the dishes. She kept her hands in the thick dark water and said, "Just sliding through school to the end on grinning and singing—that makes you grown?"

"No," Rob said. "But something else does." He'd kept his voice low, but now there was laughter all under it. "Look here," he said. He stepped back a little to give her room to see.

Sylvie turned. What seemed refusal and anger in her face (the blue-black skin, the yellow eye-whites) was plain exhaustion. She was thirty-three; what she'd laid out by day for this one family for twenty-odd years had not been replaced elsewhere by night. She had lived alone a good while now, since her mother's death; and her company was brief. What was offered her this evening after twelve hours' work was a white boy just past seventeen in white shirt, white trousers, white sockfeet, grinning wide—he'd pulled a starched end of his shirttail through his fly; and it stuck out, a waggling prow beneath his laughing. She had watched him prance through similar jokes all the years she'd known him, had bathed the flesh behind the cloth dummy hundreds of times. Sylvie wanted to smile but she closed her eyes and turned her back on him and sidestepped away to dry her hands.

Rob was left with no witness. "This needs pressing," he said.

Sylvie looked again and laughed. "No such thing," she said. "It need a rest." She had always liked him; he had not yet harmed a living soul; the sleeves of his clean shirt were wet to the elbow. "Fool, you don't put *on* your shirt till you finished shaving. Talking about grown! I done the last rescue I'm doing on you till you learn manners."

"Please, Sylvie," he said. They both were still smiling.

She shook her head No.

Rena called "Oh Rob" from the front of the house.

Sylvie pointed to the voice and lowered her own. "There's your presser," she said. "I'm leaving here." Still smiling, she stripped off her apron and hung it; took up her bucket of old bread and scraps and went out the backdoor before Rob could slow her.

He knew he had lightened the end of her day—she had left like a girl—and he cared enough for her to be glad of that; but he wished she had left him good luck for tonight (she had luck to give, though none of her own). He adjusted his shirttail and buttons to follow her; he'd force her to stand and confer a grudging blessing through the mocking smile that knew him as well, as long, as any.

But his aunt stood behind him. "Let me see you," she said.

Rob turned.

Rena's round face crouched. "You're not ready." She was—her one hat, her one good dress (in which, as always, she looked as offended as a dressed-up terrier, surprised and comic).

Rob said, "No but I never claimed to be. I'm ready for nothing the earth's offered yet!" He shook his bright face in smiling refusal but was serious.

Rena looked to the loud clock on the kitchen mantel. "We have to leave here in fifteen minutes." She saw his shirt. "You have ruined your shirt."

"It's water," he said. "Is Mother coming?"

She came forward to him and felt the damp sleeves. "You'll get rheumatism; this has got to be pressed. Sylvie's not gone, is she?"

"Yes ma'm," Rob said. "Is my mother coming?"

Rena's hand was still on him, the flesh of his full wrist. "You know she can't."

"You could stay with Papa." Rob had stepped back from her. The daylight had failed; he was mostly dark.

Rena tried to see him, a hunt in spring dusk for the one face she loved but had never allowed herself to trust, knowing it must leave; now she knew she'd been right. "Rob, Eva has asked me to go for her. I'll represent her. People understand."

"I don't," he said.

"You will," Rena said. "Time'll see to that." She took off her light coat and went to the cookstove and laid a hand on it. "Good," she said. "Hot. I can press that in no time. Hand it to me, quick." Hard as her hands were, she'd burned herself.

Rob obeyed and waited on the back stoop quietly, accepting her service, determined to refuse her present offer of which this was only the millionth earnest—the whole remainder of her life, time, strength. He would thank her and leave. Or endure this evening, a last hostage to her, his silly commencement—songs, speeches. Commencement truly, of flight toward his life from this dark web of feeders. Soon, soon. His whole body, beautiful and rank with the power of his father and mother, burned to go with a rising roar. He could not believe the house did not hear him—his dying grandfather, his trapped happy mother, Uncle Kennerly and his feist-wife two houses down the street, his desperate aunt ironing twelve feet behind: *I do not thank you, and I will not stay.*

2

But by half-past ten he had drunk enough lightning to ease the pressure (he had chipped in two dollars the day before, and they'd sent Bip Rollins out the Raleigh road to the best bootlegger south of Petersburg; Bip had hauled back a gallon); so his chief aim now was to fulfill the claim he had made to Sylvie—that the night was his. The object of the aim was completion of his body, use of it all; the means at hand was the girl beside him, Min Tharrington. It was not that simple to Rob now though. He imagined he loved her, that he'd plan on her when the day came to plan. Min had asked him the question for more than a year—was he serious toward her? what was his plan?—but tonight with the force of his life behind him (seventeen years and two months, lived out minute by minute), the aching needs of all his grand faculties, the freedom of drink, he felt he was ready to answer Yes: he planned on Min. "Let's breathe," he said. He meant fresh air. They were at a dance by Stallings Mill Pond, a squat little barn of a house thick with smoke and two girls' sick.

Min nodded consent, would have nodded consent to inhale torchfire; and they went out through cheerful drunks and glazed chaperones, past a few cars ringed with still harder drinkers to the edge of the pond. She knew they were young; that marriage, at best—what she thought of as *life*—was some years off, after Rob had grounded himself in money. And she also knew he had never said one word to feed her hope. All the kissing she'd yielded had been yielded to his honesty—his frank unspoken require-ment for warmth, lip on lip, which he took or accepted with laughing courtesy, stopping always at the bounds beyond which, however she wanted him, he'd have broken her trust, entered rooms within her which she still well knew were not habitable safely. He had never made her say any kind of No. All of which made her feel thanks and longing but chiefly worship. He seemed to her simply, as he'd grown all his life in her presence and sight, a piece of the one precious heart of things, the satisfied whole toward which parts yearned, requiring and utterly worthy of homage but covered and secret, easy to miss (a born Presbyterian, still Min felt that, and much of her life moved round it; but she could not have thought it out in order or said it). She thought they would stand now and mention the few stars, then move to the usual rock nearby and sit and kiss.

Rob said, "Do you want me to say I love you?"

"I never asked that."

He wanted to say, "You sing it like birdsong"; but he said "Please answer."

Min did not try to see him; she needed calm. She looked at the pond. A fish jumped once or a small comet fell—the dark was that thick. She could not see at all. She said, "Any person likes to hear that, sure. I can be set up by meeting old stinking Aunt Cat in the road and hearing her say she's loved me forever."

"I'm white," Rob said, "and I bathed this evening."

The words seemed to come through a smile so she laughed. Then she turned and touched him, her hand on his arm.

"Don't do that," he said, "till you've answered me." He pulled back from her.

"You're enjoying this, Rob—too much, I think; your own private part. "Well, I'll leave you to it." She took a step back toward the other drunks.

"You leave now, Min, and you're gone for good."

She turned and said "Yes."

"Yes what?"

"My answer. My answer is Yes."

Rob stood awhile, accepting that. Then he said "Come on."

By then Min could look. He faced the pavilion and carlights struck him. He bore, all on him, the promise of harm. He was rushing now. She could not see the reason (being younger than he, not living in his home); so she thought what, two minutes before, would have seemed beyond her power—*This is for him. I am not in this.* She also thought that drink was the cause, but she did not believe it enough to obey him. Nothing in his voice or his outline on the dark gave her anything to trust. "I'm leaving," she said.

"For good, remember."

Min gave a little laugh, immensely expensive, and said "So be it" and walked toward the lights. She believed him entirely. His only lie had been just now, the offer to say what could not be forgiven—deceit, for a purpose. All the way uphill she tried to imagine another day, this night survived; but every small hope that rose was stunned by knowledge.

3

SYLVIE's dog didn't rise, too late for that, but gave a formal display of threat from her hole in the dirt.

Rob went up to her, to the sound in darkness, and knelt and put out his hand to find her, the snarling muzzle. Then he thought of her name and said it—"Rowboat"—and ringed her mouth with his fingers tightly.

She had not smelled him for maybe twelve years (then Sylvie had been sleeping in the kitchen at the Kendals'—Mr. Kendal's first seizure—and had brought Rowboat with her, a neat year-old); but she bore him now and, when he released his grip to stroke her throat, she consumed his odor with quick old gasps but never licked him. Hot, dry.

"What you guarding?" he said.

The sound of a door, a silent wait, no trace of light. A man's voice said, "You Rowboat. Who you got?"

Rob said "Me" and stood.

"Shit on you."

Rob laughed and came forward. "Rob Mayfield, Slick."

"Well, Jesus," Slick said.

"No, Rob," he laughed. "Not even a Christian." He had reached the foot of the four steps and bumped them but waited there.

"What you after?" Slick said. "It's Friday night."

Rob said, "I was after Sylvie's place. I thought this was hers."

Slick waited. "Is."

Rob said "Where is she?"

"Right behind him," Sylvie said.

A fourth voice—behind them all: dark, a woman—laughed once.

Rob said "Hey, Sylvie."

"You done graduated?"

"Yes," he said. "Finished school forever."

"What else you finished," Sylvie said and also laughed.

"Not a goddamned thing," Rob said.

She said "Shame."

The voice that had laughed first came nearer to Sylvie. "Who you hollering at?"

Rob sat on the bottom step to hear himself named. He was suddenly tired.

Sylvie said, "My baby. My darling boy" but she laughed again.

The woman said, "Let me see him; come here, boy."

Rob could hear they were slightly less drunk than he, but he stood and waited for word from Sylvie.

Silence. Nothing but all their breathing, snoring from Rowboat, a chuckling bird they'd managed to waken.

So he said "Can I come in?"

The woman said "I told you."

"Shut up," Slick said. "None of this yours." Then he said to Sylvie, "I thought you was off work."

But Sylvie said "Sure" to Rob. No offer of a light to help him up.

Rob thought of his Uncle Kennerly's saying—"They're blind to a tumble-turd crawling cross your dinner but can see your britches swell in pitch-black night"—and began to climb, one step at a time, the thin planks swaying treacherous beneath him; the sound up ahead of bodies retreating inward to wait. His hands out, blind-man, struck the dry doorframe. He hauled himself up onto what seemed the sill; then he wished he had gone on home, safe bed, or had laughed off Min's highhorse. Failed and sick.

"Step in," Sylvie said.

There was a light, low and sooty in a corner. It showed a small table and two women standing by the table—or their dresses: there were two dresses surely; the shoulders and heads rose well into darkness. No sign of a third—Slick's voice; where was he? Rob thought, "I'm dead. I have walked into murder."

The woman said "He hungry."

Sylvie said, "Been hungry since he born. Too late now though. Stove cold as me; Rowboat eat my scraps."

Rob said "I'm fine." He still held the doorframe. "Where you hiding Slick?"

"You sick," Sylvie said. "Grown man and you sick."

Rob nodded. "Dying."

"Don't be sick in here."

"Sit down," the woman said and reached behind her, drew a straight chair to light.

"Can I, Sylvie?" he said.

"You behaving?" Sylvie said.

He extended his arms to the side, palm out as though good intentions, helplessness in fact, were visible.

"Come on," Sylvie said.

Rob thought he would never cross the twelve feet of floor; it multiplied beneath him. He wanted to find Slick or the hole at least through which Slick had vanished but needed all his vision and balance for the journey to the chair—rest, however threatened. So he chose something round on Sylvie's table, mysterious but shining enough for a beacon, and swam toward it. He was in the chair, his hands on the table; the shining thing was a glass bowl. He leaned. A fishbowl. He waited. The fish waved by—glinting, gold. *Mine*, he thought, *Money*. He looked back for Sylvie. "Is this Money?" he said (he had given her a goldfish years ago—seven? eight? for Christmas maybe?—and had named it at the time).

Sylvie seemed to nod.

He leaned still nearer. It seemed worth tears. The old fish endlessly rounding its world; a gift from his childhood when all outward gifts had been clear signals, smilingly flown, for *visits* in the midst of the busy absence of Father (gone, all questions muffled), Mother (in total service to her father). The floor of the bowl was white creek-sand from which rose various dark arms of color—shards of glass, bottlenecks; a wilderness he'd made for Money and long since forgot: a fragile gift, perfectly intact. He turned again. "Sylvie, I still give you this." He meant it as the one good deed of his day.

The woman said, "He Money but he don't buy me." Her laugh was a powerful promise of harm.

Rob searched round for Sylvie—vanished like Slick. He looked to the woman, who had come no closer but was clearer now that his eyes had settled to the light in the room. "You know me?" he said.

"All your life," she said.

He studied her for age. When he first had entered, she'd seemed as tall as Sylvie. Now she seemed a girl, small and breakable, maybe younger than he—light unlined skin that stretched on her bones like seamless cloth. At the end of one bare arm, her hand worked steadily—opening outward, then silently clamping and knocking her thigh. "How you know me?" he said.

"Your daddy," she said.

"What?"

"I seen your daddy." For an instant her hand stopped its valving and pointed vaguely toward town.

"Where is he?" Rob said.

"Your eyes," she said. Again her hand stopped and passed across her own eyes, smiling now.

"That's all you mean?"

She studied him, unanswering.

"Who are you then?"

"Sylvie's cousin. Flora."

"How come I don't know you?"

"I left this place before you could see good. Leaving it again tomorrow too. Baltimore." The name renewed her fading smile.

"Then why are you here?"

"My son. He live out with Mama in the country. Making him a visit."

"How old is he?"

"Fourteen," she said. "Bo Parker. You know him?"

"Never did," Rob said.

"He growing," she said.

"I'm grown," Rob said. "Me and Money here full-grown, ain't we, Sylvie?" He asked Sylvie, both in the bafflement of drink and the hope that he'd make her appear now to help him. He did not search round but no answer came. So he had to face Flora again. "Get Sylvie."

"She busy."

"What doing?"

"*Her* business."

"I'm sick. Please get Sylvie now."

Flora frowned and said "Don't puke in here," but she turned to the far dark corner and said "You Slick. Get Sylvie."

A dim narrow bed, a black shape rising, Slick's voice rusty with stupor and anger—"Who need her?"

"This boy."

"Shit on him," Slick said and fell back down. The bed again vanished.

But when Rob's eyes opened again, it was round him—a deep clean featherbed piled up around him. He put out slow hands and felt at his sides. Iron rails, no Slick, no Sylvie, still dark. He strained to hear—silence, eventually a weak snort filtered up from Rowboat. The rafters above him were still oiled with lamplight. He looked no farther, not from fear now or sickness (they both had passed; how long ago?) but from peace. Sad peace. He only thought of time, his familiar sadness since the age of five when he first saw clearly that he'd been left alone (or with Rena and Sylvie, the same as alone since he neither wanted nor needed them or any of their offerings, though he'd learned to thank them and laugh in their presence). *All this time I have got to get through.* His life (it would never occur to him to stop it; his gifts for joy were natural and large). He could not know he was still child enough to be desperate, no sense of the hope of change or reward, only the iron conviction of entrapment. *Here I am, and will stay. How? How?* He thought, as he'd thought for four years now, that the means of escape—or if not the means then at least an ointment—was the touch of bodies other than his own, the right to search particular bodies that swam up toward him in the barren days, bodies he'd endowed with the power to save him, should he touch them entirely, know them at their own extremes of need. He had still not tried—Min had faced him beautifully; he honored her choice but would keep his word and quit her—and now he could only think of rest. Sleep. Home. He could not sleep here; Aunt Rena would be wild with worry already. Could he rise and stand and find his grandfather's car and crank it and see it safely home, for however short a time (he remembered, and intended his promise to leave)? He made a first try. His right hand gripped the side rail again and he pulled once upward. Too weakly; he fell back. A squealing of iron.

A face bent over him—Flora's, her teeth; was she grinning or grinding them? He felt her breath before he heard words, clean and wet. The smell was from elsewhere on her, high and raw.

"You kicking?" she said.

"Still."

"But not high, huh?"

"I didn't say that."

"I needs my fare back to Baltimore then."

"You'll get it," Rob said. "Woods full of money."

It was a grin, broad. "You couldn't, could you?"

"How much?"

"Two dollars."

"Can't help you," he said. By then he was smiling, the first time in hours, since taking his diploma.

"Well," Flora said. Her hand was still working at its little chore. She took a step forward till her thighs touched the rails; then she sat beside him, not right against his body but near, by his knees. "Forget about the money; you still couldn't, could you?"

Rob thought that he couldn't but found in the long slow following time that he could, very well.

4

Eva had waited for him, nodding in a chair in the dining room, dressed; and as he came through the kitchen quietly, she opened her eyes to the pale dawn light and waited till his steps reached the door of the hall. Then she stopped him. "Son."

"Are you all right?" he said.

"Sit down a minute please." She was whispering but clearly.

"What's wrong?" he said. Her back was to him, though her head was half-turned; he did not move toward her.

"Not a thing with me. How about you?" she said.

"I'm dirty," Rob said, "and I was a little drunk and all; but otherwise fine—I'm getting tired now."

"Not yet," Eva said. "Sit down with me please." (In recent years, with the family smaller, they had made a little sitting corner by the table.)

"Yes ma'm," he said and quickly checked his clothes—only wrinkles, sweat, a little red dirt. He went to the straight chair across from his mother, eight feet away. Then he sat and looked.

She bore his looking quietly. She was perfectly well, her eyes clear of worry, only slightly drowsy. Her father had lasted one more of his spells.

In spite of his night, its hard new expenses, the full force of all the love Rob had ever felt, ever longed to offer, rushed up in him now. Could he say it, finally? Had she waited for that? He whispered "Good morning," which he meant as the start of his whole grand gift if she wanted or would take it.

She watched him awhile.

Rob thought she was weighing his offer slowly, to keep or return, when what she was doing was struggling to say no more than the truth, a truth that could neither harm this child she'd neglected (a fine man before her now, no help from her) nor be turned back by him in justice against her.

"Well," she said, "I love you."

It shocked him, the last thing he'd planned to hear, and stopped his own helpless offer in its tracks. Still he smiled and said "Thank you."

She nodded acceptance. "Have you always known that?"

Rob studied her face. Thirty-four years old (the age, though he did not know it now, at which his father had first loved her), finer in hair and lines of bone, clarity of skin, the sad depth of eyes, than on any previous day of her life—a beauty fed by time and hunger to what now shone as a lovely firm-footed needlessness: *I am mine, and happy.* Yet all Rob saw or would ever see was the simple goal of every longing he could presently remember, encased in a girl three steps away.

"Don't answer," she said. "All the time in the world." Then she reached down beside her and under the cushion and brought out an envelope and held it toward him. "All happiness, Son." She meant him to come to her and take it.

Gravely he did—money? a handkerchief?—then went back and sat and studied it: a letter. An old letter, hand-delivered, *To Eva,* unsealed but safe, kept carefully for years. "What is it?" he said.

"From your father to me after you were born."

"Why?"

"Oh it's time. It's all of him I've got, and I want you to have it."

"Why please?" he said.

She knew and could say. "Because I have thought a good deal just lately, and I see I have done two serious things. I damaged my mother, who had no shields; and I kept you and Forrest apart when you needed him."

So he said it finally, still low-voiced at dawn. "It was you I needed."

Eva laughed. "You've *had* me every day for seventeen years, give or take your few little trips with friends."

Rob saw that she simply believed herself. He could not challenge that, too late anyhow. He looked to the letter again—no feeling, though he wanted hot blood to slam through his head. Not looking up, he said, "Do I read it now?"

"Soon," she said. "When you've slept and eaten."

"Yes ma'm," Rob said. "I'll do the sleeping now." He gently shook the letter. "It's waited these years; it'll last out a nap."

"Good night then," she said.

"Have you slept any?"

She said, "Enough. I'll wait on for Sylvie, fix Papa's tray."

"Is he all right?"

She nodded. "Resting. So is Rena, praise God. Walk easy past their doors."

He moved on beyond her. "I will," he said. "So easy they'll think I'm already gone."

If Eva heard him, she did not turn. The crown of her head topped the back of the chair with the same rich brown she had always offered, lit now by morning, a memory from the literal start of his life.

5

THE door to his grandfather's room was open (no one but Rena slept behind closed doors); and he tried to reach the stairs in silence, another promise kept.

But his grandfather called out clearly—"Darling?"

"Rob, sir," he said.

A wait, then "Oh." Then "Where would Eva be?"

"In the dining room, resting."

"Oh." A sizable wait.

Rob climbed two steps.

"Robinson?"

"Yes sir."

"Step here if you would." The voice half-strangled.

"Suppose he died with me," Rob thought. "I will not call Mother. Mine, mine." He went down the steps and across to the door more quietly than he'd ever done anything. When he stopped two feet from the foot of the bed, he whispered "All right."

"Pour me some water please. My arm won't move." It had not moved for twelve years, two strokes and angina pectoris.

Rob went to the nightstand and filled a glass from the cool white pitcher, then supported the white dry head while it drank.

"Prop me up please," he said.

"Shouldn't you be resting?"

Mr. Kendal studied him; the eyes worked perfectly, a scary light blue. "Yes I should," he said. "I should be dead too. You'd do me a favor if you brought me a pistol." The left hand lifted and pointed to the mantel, the old Colt revolver yielding to rust but still fully loaded, actively waiting.

Rob smiled. "I'd have to go clean it first. It won't hurt a fly."

"It'd kill me though."

"Just sleep instead. Let me sleep too."

"Prop me up."

So Rob propped him a little roughly on pillows; then stood back and said, "What else do you want?" He was mostly fond of his grandfather, but now he was tired.

"Did you finish school?"

"Last night," Rob said. "I just got back."

Mr. Kendal checked the window for light. "From where?"

"A dance out at Stallings', some crazy drinking, telling Min Tharrington to go on off, a while at Sylvie's." Though it seemed impossible—here, now—not to tell the rest (the narrow bed, Flora—tired, vague as he was, it seemed a good memory, partial confirmation that his hopes as to others were not in vain, a rank quick flickering of what he might yet discover in the world: steady help), he stopped with that much. No lie at least. *I'm not going to lie to anybody ever, for whatever reason they ask me to.*

Mr. Kendal said, "You really ready for me to die?"

Rob smiled. "You take all the time you want."

"No, answer me."

"Ready for what, sir?"

"To grow on up in five damn seconds; you won't have much more than that, once I'm gone. Mainly to take on Eva's life."

"I'm grown," Rob said. "Everything I've got's in tip-top shape, working beautifully. And what does Mother need? She's stronger than all of us."

Mr. Kendal said, "When I pull out, she'll cave in like a shed." With his good hand he made a little show of falling; heavy fingers plunged down, splayed on the sheet.

Rob looked at the hand.

"You got to take over."

Rob suddenly nodded. "I can. Just rest." He believed himself. He suspected he was happy. The air around him—shared with a sick man, sweetish with death—the brown papered walls, the roof overhead, seemed a bearable shell that could hold his life a good while longer.

6

Rob slept without dreaming till ten o'clock. Then Rena could not wait and came in and went to his wardrobe and opened it and rummaged around on the pretense of hunting up laundry to boil. He knew she was nearing the end of her patience (having borne her dry kiss of congratulation, he had left her at nine to walk home from school with old Mrs. Bradley; she'd assured him she needed the air and the stretching, that he should go on with Min to his fun); so he said into his pillow now, "Get out of here. My clothes are clean as me. If you bang one more door, I'll go strip-naked the rest of my life."

"Who do you think that would please?" Rena said.

He waited; she worked on. "A number," he said, "A sizable number."

Rena had her bundle now, barely two handsful. She stood and walked to the edge of the bed and seized Rob's heel through the thickness of cloth (he was laid on his belly) and said "But not Min."

No answer from Rob. He was feigning and imploring sleep simultaneously.

Rena shook the hard heel. "But not Minnie Tharrington."

Rob kicked free and said from the depths of feathers, "Correct. You've seen her mother. Good work."

"Thank you," Rena said. "She all but slapped my face while I was sweeping the walk—lurked since day and once I showed a hair, came streaking right to me and lowrated you for abandoning Minnie. Left her torn all to pieces, her nerves in ribbons, to find a ride home with Sim Brasher drunk."

Rob said, "Correct. But soberer than me. Sim upchucks a lot."

"Hush," Rena said. "You are nothing but a child."

"Ask Min about that."

"Hush again," Rena said.

"Ask a number of others. Sizable number."

"Get up from there," she said.

"It would shock you to death."

Rena laughed. "Stuck-up."

"Simple fact," Rob said. "The shock would kill you."

"I'll spare myself then. Try the shock on Sylvie. She's waiting to fry your breakfast, grumbling hard."

"She's paid to," he said. His head burrowed deeper.

Rena walked to the door. "Get on up please. Everything's waiting on you."

"I'm coming," Rob said.

"Good work," Rena whispered. "She was never good for you, never fit to wash your socks."

"She wouldn't have had to, would she?" Rob said.

7

HE had half-finished shaving when he saw the old letter in his scabby mirror, across on the bureau where he'd left it unread when at dawn he'd collapsed. If Rena had seen it, she'd asked no questions (if she had, she'd be planning her questions now, careful long-term strategies to uncover every trace of motive, purpose, effect of the gift, with a minimum of realization by Rob or Eva that they'd been sacked as thoroughly as Jericho); and his mother never would. It would be her way—as he'd come to understand her—to wait all night, not sleeping, in a chair to make her strange gift doubly impressive; then proceed to pretend she'd forgot it entirely till, holding the actual thing in your hand, you wondered if it had in fact come from her or had merely been summoned from empty air by your own long need to make her act, make her reach out toward you if only in dream. The last thing you'd guess at with any assurance was her secret intent or whether she'd had one or whether she was inwardly pleased now at winning or bitter at the one more failed plea for help. Or had she ever pled? Was she ever less than happy? As he laced his shoes, Rob carefully thought, "I am nobody's fool but I do not know if my mother has asked me for anything ever."

He stood to read the letter by the bed he had slept in for fourteen years, alone and lonely.

March 18, 1904

My darling Eva,

A week ago today you met what I pray is the worst test life will ever offer you. Since the ordeal was largely of my making, I want to write down now (for your eyes only, when you're able to read) two fervent things—all the pardon my heart can beg for handing you on toward this abyss and my solemn promise to honor in the future any course your mind and body choose to follow. Your presence in my life, at whatever distance, is the cause of thanks that only deepen as I watch you grow and encounter the trials I have forced upon you.

And now this boy—fresh thanks for him. He strengthens daily as you do, only quicker (having struggled less and lost no blood at all, save in severing from you). My strong feeling is that he rushes toward a station of safe health at which he can wait for your own safe arrival. My solace in these bad days has been only that if you both live and grow together, then when I must leave, he will last and be my care for you, you for him. If you see him as clearly as you seem to do when Hatt holds him to you, you have surely registered his loving impatience, his readiness, and will come back to him as soon as your sojourn in dream and sleep relents.

Come also to me please,

Your loving,
Forrest

I write this now while I still have the force to make the necessary promise above. It will be in my Bible when you're able to read.

Rob thought, "It has never relented yet. But three of us now know it must, and soon—her, Papa, me. She is telling me she knows. She has kept me from her for sixteen years; but I grew inside her beneath her heart, and I know it better than anyone alive. She sees that finally. It's not too late." The suspicion of happiness he'd felt in his grandfather's room at daybreak was certainty now. He folded the letter and went to the drawer of his own washstand and took out the Bible that had been his Grandmother Kendal's, now his. It fell open naturally to the book of Micah as it had since long before he owned it—"Therefore night shall be unto you, that ye shall not have a vision; and it shall be dark unto you, that ye shall not divine; and the sun shall go down over the prophets, and the day shall be dark over them. Then shall the seers be ashamed, and the diviners confounded: yea, they shall all cover their lips; for there is no answer of God."

Rob hid the letter there and went toward the stairs—the kitchen, food —young again and ready.

8

SYLVIE walked from the stove to the kitchen table with his second set of pancakes on the palm of her hand—no napkin, no plate—and held them out to him.

Rob looked from her hand to her face. "Who they for?"

"For you. You ordered them." She slid them to his plate. "Now go on and eat. My hand clean as yours. Cleaner, cleaner."

He reached for the butter. "No doubt," he said, recalling his intention to take a morning shower (three summers before with full manhood on him, he had built a little stall for a shower in the yard, watered by a cistern, used only by him; Rena called it "a coffin with waterworks").

"Shame on you," Sylvie said.

"*I'm* happy," he said.

"Makes one," she said.

"What's ailing you?"

"You know good as me—fools keeping me wake."

"I'm sorry," he said. "I was bad off though."

She turned and faced him, took a sassafras-stick toothbrush from her mouth and said in a voice that reached Rob with full flat power but went no farther. "Don't never come to Sylvie's for that kind of *bad* again; plenty other folks handle that kind of *bad*."

Rob nodded. "That wasn't the trouble I meant. That was Flora's doing."

"Well, Flora long-gone so don't come looking."

"You left me," he said. "You didn't have to watch."

"Thank Jesus," she said. She turned to the sink. "My house had to watch."

"I said I was sorry." His face had composed into earnest regret.

Sylvie hissed a high stream of contempt through her teeth, but she did not look.

Rob swallowed awhile, then he said "Where'd you go?"

Silence.

"Slick find you?"

Still silence. She was standing not working.

"I asked you a question."

"I heard it," she said. "I ain't his to find. No part of me his."

Rob said, "All right. I was just being pleasant."

Sylvie faced him again. "No you won't," she said. "I'll tell you what you being—hateful. Hateful. No piece of me belong to Slick or you or old Mr. Bedford in yonder now griping." She pointed to the front of the house. She was serious.

Rob saw he, or someone, had lanced a rising in her; and he saw he had two choices—to shut her up hard (would she take that from him?) or to let it drain clean. He nodded. "All right." She had known him all his life; she had punished him before and never without cause.

Then her pointing hand moved another way. "I went in the woods down back of my place and puked up the whole fish sandwich I paid for, and then I set my tail in the dirt and drank my lightning and cried till day. Then I went home and give Rowboat some bread and woke Flora up out of my good bed and give her the train fare and told her I'd cut her if she won't gone on number eight—and gone for good till I changed my spirit— and then I walk on over to here for the twenty-ninth year. Here I'm standing, ready to wash your slops."

"She had her fare," Rob said, "but thank you." Sylvie seemed spent, eased.

But she shook her head slowly, no stage refusal. "You keep all the thanks you got, you hear? You'll need em for some of these folks you belongs to."

He could take her gaze, take it steady as she poured it like lye toward his eyes. "Who does my mother belong to?" he said.

Her eyes burned higher, then calmed into wary questioning. "You know all that."

"I don't," he said. "That's the trouble I'm in, the trouble I mentioned."

Her face closed, she shook her head. "Can't help you."

"Yes you can."

Sylvie listened to the house—no sounds but its settling: Rena was shopping, Eva asleep, Mr. Kendal silent. She reached behind her for a towel, dried her hands (that were dry as drumheads). Then she went to a corner and sat on the high stool, twelve feet from Rob. "Get this plain— I'm doing this for you."

Rob nodded acceptance.

"None of them others."

"Thank you," he said. Then he waited for her.

Considerable wait. "Ask your question," she said.

"Is Mother still married?"

"She wearing that ring."

"Widows do that. He may be dead."

"May be, may be. But Miss Eva don't know it."

"Did you ever ask her?"

"No, God," Sylvie said. "She ain't mentioned him since you lived through the whooping cough. Nobody else neither."

"He might have sent letters."

Sylvie pointed to the roof. "By pigeon-back then. I bring in the mail here for twenty-nine years."

"Who was he then?"

"You swear you don't know? She ain't never told you?"

"She nor nobody else. When I was maybe four, I asked her about him. She said, 'He is gone on a very long trip he may never finish. I'll tell you if he does. Till then he has begged us not to talk about him.'"

"Rena ain't said nothing?"

"She explained my name. I asked her who was I named *Robinson* for, and she said 'Your father's father' and I stopped there."

Sylvie said, "I never knew that much. I know what I saw eighteen years ago."

"Tell that," Rob said. "That would be news to me."

"Nothing new about people acting like dogs. Eva couldn't stand her mama, see—and good enough reason—so she took the first train ticket out of town, which was her school teacher, Mr. Mayfield, your daddy. They run to Virginia and she had you and Miss Charlotte killed herself, so Eva turned back up here. And here she sit."

"Why?" Rob said.

"What she wanted to do Miss Eva never done one thing she didn't want to. She loved Mr. Bedford and she had him all this time."

"He's going any day. He knows that himself."

"Eva know it too."

"Then what?" Rob said.

"Then if she got sense, she'll buy her a page in every newspaper between here and Hell and beg that poor man's pardon she left."

"You said she wanted to go," Rob said.

"You see for how long, don't you?"

"Is he live?" Rob said.

Sylvie nodded. "Ought to be. He won't so old. He be about fifty, wherever he at."

"Was he good?"

"Good at what?" Sylvie smiled for the first time that morning. "No I never knew him. He come here to supper a time or two before Miss Charlotte seen he sweet on Eva; even used to come here and help her with her lessons—sit yonder in the dining room and work at the table, and Miss Charlotte keep sending Rena back here to get her drinks of water just so she could spy. Rena never told nothing, to her mama nohow; told me 'Sylvie, they passing notes.' He took her from her people; that's how good he was. Not good enough to keep her though. You look some like him, got his eyes and hands."

Rob's hands were hidden on his knees. They moved together, rubbed dry palms silently. The eyes stayed on Sylvie, conscious of effort.

Sylvie stood; time to work. "How come you ain't asked all this before?—asked Eva; she know."

"Never wanted to." Rob smiled; another day ruined, killed dead in its tracks. "Never did and still don't." He stood, dropped his napkin, stooped for it, folded it. Then he went toward the door.

Sylvie said "You forgetting—"

He turned. "Many thanks."

She demanded thanks, a frugal diet. She nodded, unsmiling.

9

ROB went from the kitchen door straight through the yard, past wellhouse and woodshed to the old green stable where he'd left the car. If he'd asked himself he'd have said that he went to check it for safety; had he got it back unmarked from his night? Would it pass his grandfather's fierce inspection (if Papa ever should rise again; nobody else cared, least of all Rob himself—young as he was, he could not love *things:* a car was precisely a means toward motion). But when he had circled it and found it clean, he opened the door and raised the toolbox and took out the fruitjar still half-full of lightning and thought he must stow it in a gentler place. The ledge in his bathhouse. He unscrewed the lid and sucked two long raw mouthfuls down, thinking nothing at all, neither shame nor pride, a gesture as pure as a deep breath in sleep. Then he shut it again and held it to his chest and went out the back stable door toward the bathhouse.

His Uncle Kennerly met him, walking up through weeds at the end of the yard but in plain view and looking, apparently smiling.

Neither of them slackened but when they were near enough for audible whispering, Rob said, "Where's the best hiding place?" and stopped.

Kennerly came on to within twelve inches of Rob's bright face and said, normal voice, "What you got to hide?"

"My fun," Rob said.

His uncle said "I can handle that" and reached out quickly and took Rob's jar and, all in one move, brought it down hard on a twenty-penny nail in the top of a low cedar post beside them. The dry white wood drank all the clear liquor; not a drop reached ground.

"Much obliged," Rob said. His smile survived.

So had his uncle's. "Glad to help," he said.

"How else do you plan to help me?" Rob said. They were still no more than a foot apart. He bore the cool breath of Kennerly's cud all over his face—the second or third small chew of the day, honey-flavored tobacco.

Kennerly said, "I'll offer you work. That's the best help there is. Now I've got the freight office, I'm easing old Rooker out soon as I can—real softening of the brain. He's felt his last girl up, on my time at least. I'll make you freight agent any week you say and get him to train you. Work right here at home—free room and board, fresh well, good garden, good niggers, your people. Ought to kneel here and thank me." He smiled very slightly.

Rob nodded. "I've thought of another way. You wire me a salary once a month, and I'll stay out of your sight forever."

Kennerly thought, then offered his hand. "A *deal*," he said.

Rob put his own right hand behind him, refusal.

Kennerly said "You're bluffing. I ain't."

"I know it," Rob said. "Got jokes in my blood."

"What blood?"

"The Mayfield."

Kennerly's smile had still not faded. It burned some clearly abundant fuel, pure and secret. "The Mayfield I knew—I just knew one—was sure no comedian. More like a dried Presbyterian preacher that would steal you blind while you fed him fried chicken."

"Is that so?" Rob said. "At least you saw him, so I won't contradict you; but it looks like to me the joke was on Mother."

Kennerly thought again, then nodded. "It was. Don't tell her."

"She knows. She knows."

"Has she told you so?"

"Not in so many words."

"And she won't either," Kennerly said. "I'll bet you money. Eva knows one thing—"

"—Papa's dying," Rob said.

"That's it. That's all."

Rob said, "No she knows she will last past that, a good while past. She knows she's young. She wants me to help her."

Kennerly smiled and his head fell back, mouth silently open, his standard indication of pleasure. "What job you got for her? You firing Sylvie and niggering Eva? You planning a stroke? You planning to blow off a leg or two, little dynamite accident?"

Rob thought. "That's what you recommend?"

"You said you wanted to help my sister. I was thinking of ways."

Rob nodded. "You planning to live awhile longer too?"

"—The Lord be willing."

"Who's going to help *you*?"

Kennerly smiled again. "The old reliable—me, me, me."

"Lucky three," Rob said.

Kennerly struck him flat-handed on his left cheek, a measured blow, no pain, all threat.

Rob took a step backward. "You're breaking up things this morning, ain't you?" He worked to grin and managed it.

"Got to," his uncle said. "Need one in every family; keep the undergrowth cleared." He walked past Rob—four, five steps—then turned and said, "Son, get you a bucket and pick up that glass. Somebody'll get hurt."

"Yes sir," Rob said. "You going in to Papa?"

"Going to see can I help him, yes." Again he did his silent act of pleasure and walked on that way till Rob stopped watching and bent to collect shattered glass in his hands, saying clearly to himself, "Help him on his way."

10

God-knows-where, near Fayetteville
May 22, 1921

Dear Mother,

I hope you are well and all happy at home. This will show I am well despite the mosquitoes (the one on my forehead right now feels shod). Happy I will not claim to be. Was it you that made me go on this party or was I really fool enough to come, free-will? Anyhow I'm here and will stay, if I live, for the whole promised week; but you may not know me on my return—swollen past recognition with bites or wasted to nothing with chills and fever. Get the chill tonic out!

No, calm down now. I am really all right, just a few pounds lighter; but here's the gruesome tale. We all got here in one piece generally, although the trip took over six hours, till long past dark, since Coley's car boiled most of the way—the girls look stewed—and we had two punctures and hit a pig. More damage to the pig than the Ford anyhow. Ever hit a pig?—like a good brick wall about four feet thick. We stopped (!) and surveyed the mutual ruins—the pig was panting her last in the road—and

Christine looked up and said "Here it comes." It was the owner of the pig, slightly thinner (but only a shade) in nothing but "overhalls" and a knife. No shirt or hat. From a distance, the knife looked about a foot long. Up close, it was fourteen inches maybe; and Christine and Fanny and Niles and I—and Min, Mamie, Theo, and Coley behind us; they were still in their car—thought Time was up. Killing-Time in the Country. Well, it was—for the pig. He said not a word but went straight to the fallen and cut her throat one good swipe and then stood up and looked at Christine and said, "Thank you, lady. I been wanting to kill her ever since Mama died. She was Mama's favorite and mean as a snake." And there were we, thinking we would have to buy her at least if not fight off a crazed, armed pig-farmer. He offered us some meat!—said, "When you all head back home next week, stop by. I'll salt her down; I'll save you the chine." So get ready for that too.

Then we rolled into Fayetteville and ate some cold supper at Christine's uncle's and found out we had to drive another hour on to his fishing camp, way up the Cape Fear, eating dust all the way—his and the cook's.

That's the main hitch in the whole operation. Uncle Pepp is a bachelor. We knew that ahead but what we didn't know is he won't hire a woman for any purpose—cooking, cleaning, nothing. So the girls are tickled not to be chaperoned; and the boys are choking on cobwebs and dust—you ought to see our sheets!—and the food of course. Old Tump's fried food. He brags on it, starting at four in the morning—his good catfish, little light cornbread, little light pancakes. Light—good night!—I expect the house to sink. It is also doing that, being built on swamp.

But seriously, I am doing good and enjoying the river and most of the company and Uncle Pepp's rubs. He is one of those massagers, does a good deal of kneading on everybody. The girls are black and blue; I have got a charleyhorse. He's alone a lot so we understand and bear it—good exercise.

I wander out by myself a good bit or go fishing with Tump, who shuts up outdoors; and thus I am getting plenty of time to think about my future that Aunt Rena is always preaching about. What I think is this. I will come on back at the end of this party and take the depot job with Uncle Kennerly. Who knows, I may own the railroad eventually—all ladders have bottoms—but in any event I can live there at home and help you out any way needed. You may recall that I have thought a long time about going off for a little at least and testing myself elsewhere, anywhere away. You know too I guess that the point of that plan was hoping to force you to ask me to stay. For a while there it looked bad! But what you gave me the morning after commencement turned the tide.

Now Mother, you can rest assured that whatever the next months and years hold for any of us in the way of trouble and loss, Rob will be on hand to offer his service for what it's worth.

Maybe it will not just be worth nothing *as it's been up to now. As years go by, I will show you I love you and ease your way.*

Thank you for asking,

Your own son,
Rob

Love also to all.

APRIL 1925

Dear Rob,

I have given myself a month since the morning you left. I am not, as you well know, a powerful thinker; so I have given myself that time to think over all you laid in my path before taking your own way out of here. I have needed almost all those days, but I think I have some answers for you now. What will take a great deal longer will be to forget both your questions and my answers, both our awful voices—and above all for me, the shock of coming in to wish you "Happy Birthday" on your day of manhood and finding you ready to go with no warning. I know that people leave, both willing and forced, and you must surely know I have made my own share of sudden departures; but admission of guilt permits me to say one thing I know that you didn't ask for—abandonment of any soul that loves or trusts you is never pardoned, in Heaven or here. (I have also been left, by my own mother, once; and though I choose to believe you in saying that you would have come in to tell me "Goodbye," I still need to say: you should thank God above that I found you and spoke, that you could not be even so much as tempted to flee and then spend a lifetime paying on a debt impossible for you to pay or me to cancel.)

Enough of that though. I am not here to blame; and I trust you will not, when you hear my answers. They are explanations and I think they are true.

That I have not loved you. I have, I think. I have always enjoyed and honored your presence; and more than a few of my grateful memories were gifts from you—the day you looked up from your book on the sea, that Rena gave you (you were four years old), and told me your plan for making friends with a shark (you had had sharks very much in mind for days, had drawn pictures of them with men in their jaws): "First, you catch him. Then you don't cook him." —The time you hid my luggage *strap in hopes I would cancel my outing to Richmond. There are also however, as you're old enough to know, a few dark spots that have never bleached out—the simple fact that your birth tried to kill me; and though I fought for and won new life, I still and will always suffer that damage in mind and organs. I was torn for you. There is also the fact of your father in you. But no, I repeat I have honored you, liked you, and taken much pleasure from the years you were here. If I spent less time on your daily care than some mothers would have, you need to recall that I had prior claims—Father's sadness and need, the pain I had caused him—and that there was ample care at hand, your aunt, Mag, Sylvie, a whole loving house of which you were one of the actual centers. To say you were not loved here, and by me among the others, is only to say you have small notion of what love is or entails and exacts. Never say it again.*

That I held you back from your father and his people. *I did; I agree. For these two reasons—first, I thought I had harmed you enough in advance by bringing you into the life I could offer, without splitting you into further pieces. My own life has taught me the Kendals are very poor at trouble; we generally run. So were the Watsons, my mother's people, and so—to my certain knowledge—were the Mayfields, all except Hattie your father's sister. Why would I flag you onward then into trouble I knew you would surely not face but flee and thus deepen? Second, your father has not asked for you since Christmas of 1904. Not a word nor a cent.*

That I kept you in ignorance of half your family. *Again I did—and again I did it out of what I intended as kindness to us both. I never knew the past to be of help to anybody. Far from it. I have seen it ruin my own mother and paralyze your father as surely as a stroke, though young and strong and with much to lose—namely you and me. My aim is generally to live for the day, or the day after; but all around me I have always had, and felt smothered by, people who live for a past as dead as Didymus. Please don't you, which brings me to the most hurtful question of all—that I* want your care, demand your presence as a means of protection for my own future life.

I honestly do not. *Again two reasons—I am permanently cared for (you well know) by Father; he has seen to that and explained all the business to Kennerly and me. When he goes there will be no trouble at least; not riches but life as always, I guess. Even if he hadn't though and I were alone, I am sure I could live. I am strong enough to work. I could teach school, nurse, sew for people, paint flowers, bake, scrub if need be, pick cotton, hoe corn. What pride I possess is not the lady kind. I know ways to fight, and some ways to win. You are witness to that, one of the chief.*

Those are the answers which, again, I obviously think are true. I offer them anyhow, this serious and full, because you asked so seriously. You will

use them your way but—however, wherever, need it or not—always with
my love.

My love then,
Mother

Everyone else here would send love too if they knew I was writing.
Father asks after you several times a day. Rena has no doubt written you
that, and all the other news. Sylvie may miss you worst of all. She is poorly
and cross but keeps your room like a bandbox, ready. Come when you will
and know you are wanted. I trust this will find you, since I do not think I
could write it out again. I will use the only address you gave and hope that
the Shenandoah Valley knows your name.

Again,
E.K.M.

2

THE letter reached Rob in Bracey, Virginia—his Aunt Hatt's kitchen—in
the hand of Grainger, a clear Saturday noon in the middle of April. He had
wandered a month after leaving home in the third-hand Chevrolet bought
with the four-year savings of his job at the depot under Kennerly. He had
left accompanied by Niles Fitzhugh, his oldest friend. They'd intended to
sightsee awhile at first—Petersburg, Richmond, Lynchburg, Lexington—
then on up the Valley to Staunton where Niles had an older half-brother
in hardware who had offered them jobs and room-and-board till they got
on their feet. The trip went well in spite of the roads, fourteen punctures
in the first three days. They saw any number of battlefields, pocketed a
good many scrap souvenirs (bullets, balls), talked with two fairly addled
retired Confederates, seen the tomb of Lee (and Traveller's bones) and
gone to a whorehouse in Buena Vista called Roller's Retreat (they'd retreated more than once with girls much older than they'd hoped to find yet
grinning and ready, cheap and restful). But Staunton was a washout—ugly
and all brick, tall pointed houses hung on the sides of hills like red shirts
on pegs—and Niles's brother had the jobs all right but also a wife like a
bandsaw spinning and three children under the age of five. So Rob worked
there a week in misery till a mountain farmer built like a wharf rat accused
him of cheating (a subtraction error), and he packed and left. The one
week's wages and the rest of his savings would fuel a little more looking
round.

So he drove across with some difficulty to Warm Springs Baths; and
finding it much too rich for his blood (girls dying for husbands, mothers
hoarse with urging), he slipped on down to Goshen Pass and stayed in a

wild old widow's boarding house and drank the strong waters (more for fun than in hope; he had drunk no liquor since leaving home with the single exception of some beer while retreating, to ease the sights) and learned that a foreman was due there soon to hire on a crew to widen a road through the pass by the river once the spring weather settled. He would wait for that.

In all those days he had thought very little of home or his mother, their hard last meeting. He had not left in quite as much anger as she'd thought—more restlessness than anger, so he honestly believed; she had forced their farewell to its cruel pitch—and the trip itself (he had traveled so little) had been specific to whatever sadness lingered. But once his chances of work seemed good (his landlady said, "They'll have to hire you; not two other men in this whole county would know a road by sight if it ran in their front door and out the back and killed their wife, much less how to lay one"), he could take time to stop long mornings in bed, long evenings on porches; and then he began to think of his life—all he did not know, had been denied. Three days of that, and the rusty alum water he drank from the springs, and he'd sunk himself back dangerously near to the paralyzed misery he fled at home; the four years of thankless loveless work in the thick immortal shadows of his family. Half his family.

He dreamed of the other half one Thursday night, having eaten his landlady's leaden supper and answered her questions for an hour on the porch ("You told me you're saved? Do I recollect that?" —"You do, yes ma'm. I was barely lost") and taken a lonely walk to the river with the town all asleep. Then oddly he dreamed not of his father but his father's sister. He'd had a face for her for some years now. Shortly after commencement, he had asked his Aunt Rena a single question one morning early while his mother was asleep—"Can you put your hands on a picture of my father?" She had waited awhile—they were in the kitchen and Sylvie was present—then she'd said flat "No." But Sylvie had said, "Step yonder to the mirror" and pointed to her own piece of glass on the mantel. He had kept his seat, would not walk an inch to see his own face; and Rena had gone out and come back soon and walked straight to him and held out a picture, a good-faced woman plain as a board, two plain boys beside her. Rob had said, "Which one is he, then?" —"Neither," Rena had said. "They're your cousins. She's your aunt—Hattie Mayfield, married a Shorter, who died." —"Does she favor my father?" —"'Not a bit, thank God, and neither do you. You're a Watson to the ground; Mother's all over you." Sylvie had shaken her head No, smiling. Rob had said to Rena, "Why do you have this?" She had gently taken it from him then. "Because she sent it to me. When Mother died I wrote to her a time or two, knowing Eva was so weak from having you but wanting all the same to pass on the news, to punish everybody. I was great on punishment then; girls are. But Hattie took it all with kindness and pity and wrote me long letters about the good weather and spring in the hills and of how you were strengthening, so I asked her for this and she sent it down. When Eva came back, I broke off writing." Rob had asked one other thing, "Where is she now?" —"In Heaven maybe. Or Bracey, Virginia. She lived near there."

Alone in the mountains then, Rob dreamed of Hatt, a simple dream with no clear demands—she was doing man's work, shoveling a stable clean. The stable was dim, lit by the open door toward which she worked and a far clouded window. Beneath the window on their haunches and hunkers were numbers of children, all boys, pale, their heads shaved. Their eyes were brighter than either source of light, and they watched the open door. They were waiting to run, past her and gone.

The next morning Rob inquired again in town about the road-man— due in five days, a week if it rained—so he asked his landlady if she'd hold his room through a long weekend while he visited family (there was no other guest, slim chance of one till summer deepened; he asked to be kind). She said "Not a chance"—alone as a rock—which forced him to pay her and leave with her grudge, one more set of eyes aimed cursing at his back (he asked her to forward any letter that came in the next two days— *Bracey, General Delivery*—and, going out the door, he tried to say "See you Tuesday maybe"; but she said "Don't never try again").

He drove the whole rough seventy miles under heavy clouds, a piss-ant drizzle, occasional fog; and when he'd reached Bracey, he was so low and fearful as to make him think he would pass through toward anywhere— home even, any company. But he stopped of necessity at the one gas pump; and when the storekeeper had filled the tank and was bringing his change—it was past six o'clock, little daylight left—he stared up at Rob and said, "You a Mayfield, ain't you?" Rob said "What told you?" The man kept staring, searching Rob's face as though for some sort of goods that could be converted to use, quick cash. "Know all the Mayfields," he said, "or knew them. You got to watch close to see a Mayfield at all—big runners. Whose are you?" Rob said, "Hattie's" for no clear reason; "Where is she living?" The man said, "You the oldest or what?" Rob said, "The youngest, by a long shot the youngest"—a game by then, more dangerous than most he had ever played. The man's whole face and body said *fool* or *simpleton* or *scoundrel*; but finally he pointed, "She's out there in that same old piece of house where you boys left her, lonesome as an angel." —"I heard they came in choirs," Rob said and tipped his cap and drove on in the general direction.

Two miles by the gauge till he saw a dark solitary house to the right and turned in there. He drove to the empty backyard, searching for lights; and when he saw none, he still got down and headed toward the back steps. If anyone was there, they would be in the kitchen.

She was on the steps though, waiting for him trustingly—Hatt alone in darkness, saying "Yes" as he touched the bottom step. Startled, really scared, Rob jumped back down but quickly recovered and laughed and said "Yes to *what?*" She also laughed—did she have a gun, an axe?—and said "Yes who are you?" He paused over that and then said politely, "Excuse me asking but if you'll go first, I'll know if I'm wasting your time or not." —"Hatt Shorter," she said. "The widow Shorter. Helpless as a girl." She laughed again, a deep-fed laugh—"Which I'm far from being." —"Then I'm Robinson," he said. "Forrest's boy." They both waited then; she must say the next. "Oh Jesus," she said but it came through a smile, the sounds of welcome.

She rushed him indoors to her strongest lamp and fed him enormously and asked him only the gentlest questions before suggesting he was tired and should sleep and leading him up to the small high room that had been his father's when his father was a boy, though she didn't mention that till the following morning after heavy breakfast in clear spring light—late: he had slept past ten, deep, untroubled.

3

HATT cleared the last dishes—the platter of steak and gravy, the last fresh biscuits—poured him more coffee; then sat for the first time and said "You slept."

"I did, yes ma'm. Like the peaceful dead."

"They don't sleep," she said.

Rob looked up slowly to check her fervor. Was he stuck with a Christer?

She was smiling though, no zealot's rictus. "I meant they were happy and never tired. Their search is ended."

He took a long draft of the strong tinny coffee. "So is mine," he said. "Let me just say this—I'm here out of nothing but polite curiosity. I don't bear a grudge or a past-due bill for money or service, or a writ or nothing. I was just up in Goshen, waiting as I said for a job to start; and dumb as it sounds, I dreamed about you, knowing your face from my Aunt Rena's picture."

"Nothing dumb in that. I've wondered if she ever showed you that picture, only good one ever made of me. And I've dreamed about you for twenty-one years."

"Thank you," Rob said. "I hope they were fun. No I'm here on a visit, not a hunt or a raid."

Hatt said, "I knew that. Your name's Mayfield. All the Mayfields but me are short-term guests—travel light, take no toll but gray hair and wrinkles on their poor fool hosts. I've got them already so I'm safe at last."

She stroked at her clean bare face with her hands, combed back through her hair—seamy skin, gray hair. But the large eyes were happy, more nearly at rest. "You were in your father's bed," she said.

Rob said "Is he dead?"

Hatt studied him closely. "You really don't know?"

"No ma'm. Not a word."

"Doesn't Eva?"

"She claims not. I have to believe her."

"He's alive," Hatt said. "Fifty-four years old." She stopped and knocked her front teeth with a knuckle, then bit herself hard. Her wrists and shoulders, her hair, neck, face were a legible receipt of the tolls she had mentioned, all taken on her and no return (her father, James Shorter, Forrest, her sons; this nephew fresh-burgeoned at her table, demanding). The same knuckle knocked the table twice gently; her eyes had never let go of Rob's. "Will you use this right?"

He nodded. "Yes ma'm."

"Won't hurt nobody with it?"

"No ma'm, I'm kindly." He smiled at her broadly, a bid to break the tone.

"You're a Mayfield," she said, "—*Robinson* at that. My father's all in you. He'd have hurt Baby Jesus if he needed to."

"Not me," Rob said. "I promise, not me."

Hatt knew he was wrong—not that he lied, only spoke in young ignorance—but she said anyhow, 'He is living in Richmond in our grandparents' house."

Rob said "They're dead?"

"Yes God," she said. "Before you were born. Our own father too, Robinson your namesake."

"Is Father alone?"

"No," she said. "He could never stand that. I'm the hermit in the family. So it's turned out at least—the best-natured one of all, the one that loves noise: here you see me on a windy hill, an old crow-roost!" She had made herself smile; it drained off slowly. "No he has a housekeeper; been with him some years, ever since he moved there. She's made him a home. I can thank her for that."

Rob waited to see if she'd come to an end. Then he said "So can I." It cost him nothing.

"You won't be needing to see him though." Hatt did not stay for an answer to that—it was not a question—but stood and went to the stove for the kettle which had boiled through their talk (she would wash his dishes). It held a gallon and was heavy even for her strong arms; but she stopped halfway between stove and sink and said, "You don't hate him, do you?"

Rob laughed at once, the oddity of it. Did he hate squirrels in trees, grapes on vines? They pertained more nearly. Yet he wanted to answer both truly and quickly; she would hold the hot kettle there suspended till she heard. So he said "No surely," which freed her to go on at least and pour the water.

She poured it slowly and refilled the kettle from the bucket he'd drawn her and set it on the stove and came back to sit again, a different chair, farther from him, opposite. She was waiting for more.

"I'm speaking only for me," Rob said. "Nobody at home ever mentioned him."

"I'd have guessed that," Hatt said. "I always liked Eva. She had a hard time here. I knew she'd never abuse your father's name, whyever she left him."

He said "Why did she?"

Again Hatt waited; she had not thought of this for a number of years. "I never thought she did. Of course about some things I know less than you—they were neither one *talkers*—but unless you convince me different today, I'll go to my grave (which won't be long) claiming Eva Mayfield is waiting on him still."

"No ma'm, she's not."

"How come?" Hatt said. "What else has she got?" She answered herself—"You, to be sure."

"No ma'm," Rob said.

Hatt thought and decided to let that stand. "Me either," she said. "I repeat, here I am. I have raised a brother, kept a husband clean and fed, brought his two sons to life and trained them. And here I am—I am fifty-seven years old; I'm not even tired and all that's left me is to scrub this old house that I still hate (it was never mine: the Shorter place)." She waited, solemn awhile; then she said "Well, I'm naturally happy."

"Where are your boys?"

"Not here, God knows. The baby is buried in Flanders, I think—gassed, twenty-five, *Whitby Shorter*. Gid's in Danville selling silk stockings, married to a woman that can't stand the country. I don't much blame her; she was raised on a hog farm a mile from here. I see them at Christmas when they ask me down, no pride at all." Her whole face smiled, raw as a flayed dog.

Rob said "You'll live."

"I'm *living*, thank you." She nodded and stood and went to the sink. She turned her back and began to wash. "When have you seen your mother?" she said.

"A month or so."

"You don't know exactly?"

"Yes. Thirty-four days."

"How was she doing then?"

"The same," Rob said. "She is always the same."

"That don't tell me much," Hatt said. "It's been some time."

"You'd know her."

"Is she pretty? She was pretty as a girl."

Rob stood, reached into the pocket of his coat and found an oval velvet case. He opened it, looked a moment, then stepped toward Hatt and offered it to her.

"I'd ruin it; I'm wet."

So he held it for her—Eva, a girl, the miniature made from a picture taken just before her commencement, ordered by her father before the marriage but kept through the bad times and given by him to Rob on his twenty-first a month ago. She was turned to her right and showed only one eye; but all her hair was drawn round and fell down her visible shoulder, bare and full for her age. She wore a gold chain that had been her mother's (never worn since by anyone). Rob studied it again as carefully as Hatt. Despite his life, what he felt was pride—in the chance to carry and show such a likeness of what had once been alive and available, even in this house, for actual witness; what was still (only hours from here) as grand in its darker less promising way.

"That's her," Hatt said. "And she's lasted, you say?"

"Very well," he said. "If you'd never seen her, you'd know her from this. It was given to me just recently."

Still looking, Hatt said, "She would last, wouldn't she? She wouldn't take wear; she would not *take* it. You can choose that, you know—oh up to a point. I'm worn to the socket; and still I'll live, maybe thirty more years." Hatt turned back to work. "Is she happy at all?"

"Yes ma'm. Quite a lot."

"Doing what?" Hatt said.

"Her father, tending him. He takes a lot of care."

"He's still alive? Lord God, he's a hundred."

"Oh no," Rob said. "It just seems long. He has strokes regularly; spells with his heart."

Hatt said, "Well, a job's a job."

"I don't know," Rob said. "There's all grades of jobs."

"What's yours?" Hatt said. "You told me; I forgot." She was almost finished; she was scouring the pans.

"No ma'm, I didn't. I've made two or three little messes since school, but I'm out of work now. Plan to be back Monday; money's running out!"

"Down at home?"

"No in Goshen."

"Dipping water? Bathing ladies?" She glanced back, laughing. "They like good rubs, the old ones specially. You'd be just the ticket, strong hands and back!"

"I would," he said, "if my heart didn't fail. The Kendals have bad hearts."

"Don't worry," Hatt said. "You're pure Mayfield, to look at at least—my father, God help you." She had not stopped smiling. "But you were talking jobs."

"Road-building," he said. "Through Goshen Pass soon as spring really settles. Dynamite and rockslides; I may not live! I'm signing-on Monday."

Her smile didn't vanish but underwent a stiffening, the flush of pain behind it; her teeth looked dry. "You're leaving me then?"

Rob thought it was banter, mock family-pleading. "Afraid so," he said. "I never promised more."

"And you're not going home to Eva either?"

He saw she was earnest; had she broken a little, out here scot-alone? "No ma'm, least of all. I'm not needed there."

"Who are you trying to kill?" Hatt said. Her skin had tightened with the force of her anger.

He tried smiling; felt its uselessness and took two steps back, pocketing the picture. "Maybe me," he said. It seemed fresh knowledge but undoubtable.

Hatt said "I could help you."

"By keeping me?"

"Yes."

"Here on this hill?"

"I'll close this tomorrow and bury the key if you'll say the word. Goshen or Lynchburg, Fontaine even. I'm a well-known cook and I'm neat as a bird, eat practically nothing, sew like a spider." Flat in abjection, she was cheering herself. It all was true but she offered it as fun.

Rob smiled to help her, but he also weighed her offer. To his conscious surprise, he felt himself standing at the edge of a choice he had not made before—to ask for a life or to take the life offered (they'd been offered before).

"I mean it," Hatt said.

"I know you do."

"What have you got better?"

He tried to think.

"I knew the minute you drove up last night, you were bad off as me—once I seen your face."

"I am," he said.

"Do something about it."

"I want to," he said.

"Eva won't—"

He raised a hand; his eyes crouched inward. He intended to stop her. And she saw her mistake, flushed hot with regret. But his gesture held on, a warning, *listen*.

Steps on the backporch, the door, the hall. "Miss Hattie?" A boy's voice.

She said "All right."

A young Negro man—light-skinned, tall, lean—opened slowly, took a step toward them and stopped. "I saw you had company, car out yonder." He pointed through the wall.

"I do," she said. "It's Forrest's boy."

The man nodded to her; he had not looked to Rob. "I knew that," he said. He brought his hand up, a clean letter in it, and crossed the space between him and Rob. "This just come for you. They ask me to bring it." He pointed again—toward town, the mail.

Hatt said, "This is Grainger, Rob. He helps me on Saturdays."

Rob nodded half-smiling and took the letter—his mother's script, forwarded from Goshen. Grainger's empty hand stayed out so he shook it.

"They didn't know who you was at the Mail; thought you was your granddaddy. I told them better. I figured you was here."

Rob said "A little visit," but his eyes and attention were all on the letter.

"Yes sir," Grainger said. "We been waiting on you." He saw he was ignored and understood the reason; but he said to Hatt, "Ain't we waiting, Miss Hatt?" He was not ready yet to leave for the yard.

"We were," she said. "Fools forever! He's leaving any minute. Look at him while you can."

Grainger looked, frankly, gravely.

But Rob said to Hatt, "I can stay through Monday if you've got room for me."

"*Room?*" she said. "I could put up the veterans of the Rainbow Division, no two in a bed; and Grainger could cook—he's a good *egg* cook."

"Yes ma'm," Grainger said.

"Then I'll go shave," Rob said. "The day looks bright. Maybe I can help Grainger some, outdoors." He was smiling but the sealed letter chilled his hand.

Grainger said "Yes sir."

Hatt said "Take your water." She moved toward the steaming spitting kettle, a service planned in advance, now rendered.

4

WHEN he'd read the letter a single time, standing by his bed, he carefully returned it to its envelope and opened his small grip and buried it carefully—its edges straight, right angles to the grip—beneath his clean linen (washed in Goshen by his landlady, free). Then he went to the washstand

and felt the kettle with the palms of both hands, not gingerly but reckless.
It still was scalding so he poured it out, threw off his coat, fished out his
razor, his badger-brush, the bar of castile soap worn to a coin, and lathered
as best he could and shaved. An action as unpleasant as any in his life,
though it gave him the silent minutes of thought in which he considered
his mother's refusals and generated his own reply. Finished, wiped clean,
he slapped on cold raw alcohol and, every pore howling, emptied the water
in the china slopjar.

Then he wiped the basin entirely clean of stubble and poured in the
last two inches of water, smoking still, and went to his coat and found the
velvet picture case, opened it and carefully slipped out the porcelain on
which the image lay, had lain these years. Eva as he all but remembered
her—she'd been this nearly, in his earliest memories; this grand at least.

He took it to the basin and with both hands gently laid it in the
water; let it rest for a minute—the face survived. Then he reached in again
and scrubbed it with his thumbs till the water was pale brown, the porcelain white. He emptied that water too and dried the plate thoroughly,
returned it to its case—a picture of nothing, a sheet of white china
polished and ready—and put it into his pocket.

Then he hooked on his collar and knotted his tie and went to the
window and searched the view, a far round hill crowned with trees that
were starting the annual revival. New yellow leaves hung like fume on
black limbs; some scrubby pasture with a scrubby cow, udder shrunk and
slack as an empty glove; a single dead tree at the edge of the yard, long
dead, stripped of bark by years of weather till it stood in naked simplicity
more nearly like a manmade thing than a former life (a giant machine for
lifting loads, a multiple gallows); a few outbuildings all standing by little
more than faith and grace, rotten at the ground, rotted halfway up; and
Grainger in a small patch of garden, plowing with an old one-wheeled push-
plow whose squeak Rob could hear, even high as he was and protected by
glass. The sight of Grainger's strength—in wrists, neck, shoulders—the
speed of his gait as he scored hard dirt produced in Rob the one plain fact
he had known all day, the one thing known which brought him hope, a
chance of pleasure, rest: "That nigger can show me where to buy cheap
liquor."

Among the many facts which this room offered for use and help,
unknown to Rob, was the glass he looked through, the bubbled pane. His
mother had held him to that same glass a thousand times in three long
months as she waited for strength after his hard assault, strength to bear
him away (or draw him behind her in her own fast wake). His father had
seen him through that same glass on the day Eva left this house for good
and changed many lives.

Rob repeated what he knew, a saving kernel in general famine—"Hatt's
man will help me."

5

April 22, 1925

Dear Mother,

    I would thank you for your careful letter except that I don't feel thanks are in order. I know that I asked—and hurt you by leaving (why else would I leave?)—and I know you took pains to speak your full mind. But also you gave pain and gave it so strong that I'm just now coming up for breath and light, to see can I breathe and is it still day. You should be more careful—I speak from respect and long years' experience—because you are fitted with terrible weapons; and as I should have known, the worst is your voice: the things you know and can say, and will. Well, the worst is your face—my memories of hard times I've caused your face—but your voice, on paper, can still cut rock. Not that I'm any rock—fewer words would have worked to silence me, very nicely too—but I split anyhow into numerous pieces for several days. I want you to know.

    The letter found me in Bracey at Aunt Hatt's. I had driven down there, not to harm anybody, least of all you (barring your letter, I never would have told you I went at all), but out of curiosity and time on my hands. Was anybody still there? Had anybody ever been? Would any of them know me?

    Two of them did—Aunt Hatt, who said I was pure Mayfield (old Robinson my namesake), and a colored boy who helps her out (Grainger, who said he never saw you but worked for my father and so knew me on sight at once). And I was hoping to have a day or two to talk to them about various things—they were welcoming me; the weather was dry— when your letter came, in Grainger's hand, sent up the hill to that house by him, the house you knew, where I was born; you are still all in it, especially upstairs; you didn't need to speak, not while I was there anyhow. I was in the process of coming to understand a thing or two—one of them was you as a girl—and I hadn't intended to stay long; but you took care of that.

    The letter got to me about noon; and by six I was well on my way to forgetting it, and you. I had to wait till then because Grainger was plowing and couldn't stop to lead me to the nigger bootlegger; and since I had to fill that time somehow—I was already hurting—I called Aunt Hatt to come upstairs and said would she kindly help me out? She had already offered help numerous times—she is all alone—though surely she never planned to have her seriousness tested so soon and in such a hard way, but anyhow she said "Yes" of course; so I said, "Whether you know it or not, two of my ancestors killed themselves; and I'm wondering—what's your advice for me?" I handed her your letter. She took it and saw your hand

and put her big hand across my lips and said "God shut him up" with a broad deep smile. Did she smile all the time when you lived there? Is she maybe a little simple by now? Simple or not, she sat down by me on the edge of the bed where she said I was born and read it through slowly, tracing lines with her finger; and then when she finished, she couldn't look up—just would not face me—but stared on down at your signature and finally said "That's your decision, Son."

I decided to live, not that minute though. I don't think she meant to scare me but she did. She meant to tell the truth like you; and she did (will I ever have the luck to meet a lady that can lie; tell me just what I need, not what I ask?). No it took a little while to make up my mind; and I spent the time hearing Aunt Hatt tell all she thought I should know. She said at the end it was all she knew. It may not have been. But it surely was enough to help me around some of what has lain across my path since I heard there was a path and that I must take it. I mean you mostly, and Father (though he has not been a sizable worry, ever for me—anyhow now I know a lot more about him; Hatt says he is happy and, as I've said before, I don't think she knows any ways to lie. Of course she hasn't seen him for several years now since her younger boy Whitby was killed in Belgium and Father came down to stay a few days and see her through or so she says). She helped me to recognize you both as children; and since I am likely to stay one myself, I can greet both of you—as you were then, before me—and wish you the luck you will not have. The luck that would have left you safe enough, free enough, to allow you to love not honor me—your freezing offer, honor. I never was honorable and never want to be.

So the child got drunk by dark as I said and did a good deal of raving around in the local hills—some dangerous driving, mechanical damage (cost me fourteen dollars); and I cut myself, not in very much earnest as I already hinted but enough to scare Grainger who was with me (sober) and made him half-haul and half-persuade me to go home to Hatt's and try to sleep. So he drove me there after mending a puncture in night thick as grease; and what I discovered in no time at all was that whatever Aunt Hatt is good at, and she claims wide skills, she is what I would call a piss-poor nurse for a drunk. Pardon French.

This is all meant to be fairly painful, you see—just a boy, make allowance.

The first thing she did was to start warming milk—I should drink hot milk; you know you're in trouble when they start heating milk—so I waited for that, laid down on the old leather couch in the hall outside the kitchen and waited in peace (peaceful to onlookers; different within, though easier by then); and what did I hear in the next five minutes?—her whispering to Grainger, him going outside and coming back in, then some more low talking, then the awful sound of pouring. She had given Grainger orders to bring her my liquor and was pouring it out in her old slop-pail. Her idea of

*help. Poured the last pure drop, and I lay there and listened. I didn't say a
thing. I waited till she said, "Can you come drink your milk?" Then I kind
of walked in and sat at her table. She had made a bowl of milktoast; and
someway, I ate it. She and Grainger watched me awhile; then she told him
to bring her some wood—to get him out. When she had us alone she of
course said "Why?" and I think I told her. You already know and I
thought she did, though another thing I'm coming to know about women
is that none of them understands forgetfulness, that a sane strong man
might need to forget a thing or two (temporarily of course)—no women
I've met. Why is that, do you think? Are they scared the thing you'll forget
is them, and permanently? Why have they ever doubted their strength?*

    *Then she and Grainger got me upstairs and put me to bed—I was able
by then; but I let them do it: most fun they'd had since the big ice
storm—and scared as I was being there on that hill just started on my
comfort and it all wasted in with Hatt's hogslops, I went on to sleep and
slept like a great long trip to whatever's in the heart of the ground: not a
sound, not a sight, not a soul trying either to harm or help.*

    *Of course I came-to around four o'clock. She'd left a lamp lighted in
the corner of my room, dark as Hell outside; and I looked at the little
flame and prayed a good while. I just kept praying all you told me to
pray—"Thy will be done"—oh for maybe half an hour. So apparently what
happened next was God's perfect will. I got out and dressed and made it
downstairs without waking Hatt up; and what I figured was—I thought I
was sober—I could get out the back way and crank my car and find that
bootlegger one more time. Hatt sleeps like a chain on the ocean floor. But
Grainger was awake. What hadn't dawned on me was that I'd been so bad
off that evening that Grainger volunteered to sleep in the downstairs hall
on the couch. Do you recall the couch? It must have been there (must
have been at the circumcision of Moses, the making of the hills). A rock
couldn't rest on it, much less Grainger; so when I tipped past him, he just
said "What?" and I said, "You know. You let her ruin me." He said, "I
did. I asked her to stop. I knew what you felt." —"No you don't," I said;
"I'm going back for more." —"And I'm coming," he said. Someway we got
out without waking Hatt—maybe she has gone a· little deaf too with
years—and Grainger did the driving plus saving my life.*

    *He's here with me now. How that worked out was that after we had
waked up the poor bootlegger and bought what he had left (he'd had a big
Saturday)—a quart of brandy buried out in a shed—Grainger drove me on
to his place. I've been in worse, been drunk in worse; so we sat down there
and before day broke or I got scared again, Grainger talked to me about his
life and I truly listened. We are half first-cousins according to him—old
Robinson grandfathered both him and me. Said he never did know it till
my father told him. He worked for my father from the time we left for a
year or so; had grown up in Maine but came down to Bracey to visit some*

ancestor named Aunt Veenie and met his Uncle Forrest Mayfield, your
husband, and lived with Forrest as long as he could; then lived with his
Bracey ancestor till she died at past a hundred, plus serving a year in the
army in France—"Digging trenches for white boys to climb out of into
sheets of fire; I stayed low, digging, and here I sit alive as you"—then came
back here and had a dark wife (who is now long-gone up north somewhere,
though he says he expects her eventually) and worked as janitor in the
school and some churches. He also reported that my father is happy,
though he has not seen him for some years either and only speaks of him
in the distant past. He has a few books that belonged to Father, just
children's books. He can still read in them. He read me the story of
Pocahontas when he'd finished with his own—"She died of a broken
heart beneath foreign skies with memories of the green woods of east
Virginia, the swarming streams, from whose sweet shallows she is still
divided by the thousands of leagues of rolling salt deep by which she sleeps
her longing sleep." I think he recited, though he looked at the pages and
turned them at times. At the end he offered the book to me, saying I
might want some part of my father, that he knew it by now; but I left it
with him since he seemed to care, and anyhow he has been on that rolling
deep which I never have.

By then it was light and, all things together (the brandy half-gone), I
was feeling pretty firm on my feet again—well, able to stand—so I said
would he drive me to Aunt Hatt's again and I'd eat and rest and then head
for Goshen? He said was I ready to face her yet? I said "Meaning what?"
and he said, "She'll have to abuse you some before she lets go." I said that
I had to get my grip someway—it contained a few objects of sentimental
value not to mention my drawers—and he said if I'd just wait a little while
longer, she'd be at Sunday school and I could get in safe and out unseen. I
said "Fair enough" but that I needed something to eat and some air. The
house we were in was his old ancestor's and still smelled like her, though it
looked clean as Sylvie's or ours for that matter. I ought to have known
there was no cafe for twenty miles round, that he'd offer to cook. He
did—"Miss Hatt say I cook good eggs"—and I didn't want to harm one
more damned soul; so I said I'd be grateful, and he went out and squeezed
his old Dominecker hen and cooked me up a breakfast as good as I've seen.
I couldn't eat much so I told him to finish, but he said he was not a big
eater and didn't. Then he said did I still want to take a walk? I had
mentioned air—I was thinking of a ride—but I said "All right," thinking
he might have some famed local beautyspot he wanted to show. (Nature
has never done much for me. Of course I've never done much for her.)

It was nothing but a little house—one-story, three rooms, painted
yellow once, a front porch, a johnny—where he and Father had lived for a
while after you and I vanished. He said it had been empty more than a
year. Some local boy came home from teaching piano at Johns Hopkins,

Baltimore, and moved in to spend a summer for his nerves and wound up shooting himself on the porch in sight of his mother's house across the valley early one morning. She may not have watched—Grainger didn't know that—but he lay there with what was left of his head till way after noon when some passer found him. No takers since then. We walked right in and Grainger took me round it, telling where things had stood, where little things happened. He had been twelve, thirteen years old and had slept on a little cot back in the kitchen. Father taught him to cook. He was naturally neat. He would stay home and clean while Father taught school, go to see his ancestor, help her get around, come back and study in the afternoon (Father made him recite a lesson every night—reading and simple figures, household management, a little agriculture, mythology: "Ladies changing to trees; being stole by bulls, great birds, swans, eagles!"); then he'd start their dinner and Father would come. He showed me father's room. The bed was still there—they had got it all furnished—a narrow child's bed with side-rails Grainger had lengthened for Father so his legs could stretch.

It was Grainger's site, see? He wanted to show it. He was still proud of it. So I let him talk on and listened politely but didn't really calculate where he would end. He said, "Listen, you've left the only home you got. You hurting all over. You could rent this place, get a job around here—teach school, clerk store—and I'd move in here and keep it nice for you. Or I could still stay at Miss Veenie's where I am and walk over here—it ain't any ways. That'd help you a lot."

I am in demand. Mother, understand this—there are numerous people by now, none crazy, who have asked to spend full time with me. I am not bragging now; I am hoping to show you—they recognize something, and in me. I've asked myself what in God's name it is—Aunt Rena, Min, Hatt, even Sylvie, now Grainger—and I think I know: they see me in need and they see I am loyal which means to them that I've got gold to give. I have. They are right. But not for them. I must choose my own and already have.

I thanked him and said someday I might need a set-up like that and would call on him then. He said "You need it now," a little harder than he should have; so I thought it was time to conclude the tour and dodge Aunt Hatt and head for Goshen. I could drive by then—I was clear as the day, which was already perfect—but I let Grainger do it so as not to hurt him too far; and since my hands were idle awhile, they occupied themselves with the rest of the brandy. Grainger never said "No"—a true drunkard's friend—and by the time we pulled up in Hatt's poor yard, I had fallen into something like the Sleep of the Just (Just couldn't stand up!).

When I knew myself again, we were three-fourths to Goshen. It was midafternoon and Grainger was driving like he had good sense and knew my will. Maybe he does. I sat up as best I could and looked out (try that

*after sleeping several hours in a Chevrolet on mountain roads and you full
of homemade-brandy and eggs). I said "What's this?" and Grainger said,
"It's help. Going where you said." So I laid back and he got us on in to the
edge of Goshen and then stopped and said, "Can you drive on from here?"
I could but I said "What about you?" of course. He said, "I'll head on
back if you're ready." —"How?" I said; "It'll be dark soon. These are
mountains, boy. You fall and you're gone." He said that was all right; so I
had to say, "No, come on with me and stay till tomorrow; and I'll get you
over to the downhill train." He nodded to that and rolled ahead and left
me with something like half a mile to decide two things—a place that
would take a man looking and smelling like me, plus a bed for a Negro in a
county where Negroes are scarce as smiles. I knew my old widow had
meant what she said; and at first I thought we should just move on to the
country beyond and sleep on the ground (I had that afghan you gave me
years ago); but then I remembered a place I'd passed on the far side of
town, rundown but big, an old-time resort. I'd seen a Negro girl out
sweeping the yard there, so at least I knew Grainger wouldn't scare them
dead. I guided him to it; and when we pulled up in front he said, "You
don't care nothing about yourself. You ain't staying here." —"We got to,"
I said.*

*And three days later, we're still staying here—me in the main build-
ing, him in some old quarters left out back. I'm waiting on the foreman of
the roadbuilding gang and so now is Grainger. A true Mayfield. He has got
a job already and decided to stay. A number of reasons, all of them simple.*

*This whole thing is simple. What I'm saying in all the above is this—
all this is very simple: what is wrong with me. I am just twenty-one. I have
just started this. I can be turned around. It could easily be helped.*

> *Help then,*
> *Love,*
> *Rob*

6

Rob mailed his letter in the late afternoon; then walked awhile to clear his
head and hands; then ate a light supper in the hotel dining room, empty
but for him and the owner Mr. Hutchins and Grainger who, as one of his
jobs, helped Della serve what little there was (Della being the girl Rob had
seen in the yard, the cook and maid). Then he sat on the porch and
listened again to Mr. Hutchins' plans to rejuvenate his property in hopes
of a new influx of guests provided by the road that was coming through—
"There are people right now all over Virginia just as sick as dogs and no
way to get here for this good air and this stinking water but that mountain

track that's killed more dozens than I'd care to admit. Not even counting Maryland and Washington and your poor state. You build that road and I'll be here ready."

Rob said, "Will you have a doctor by then? You'll need a doctor." He referred to the fact that Mr. Hutchins' wife had been in Lynchburg six weeks apparently to keep a sick daughter under doctor's care.

Mr. Hutchins said, *"They'll* be here, have to beat them back with sticks when they see that traffic all green with money. They follow the color *green* if you notice. That's been my experience. You may have doctors in your family that are saints."

Rob said, "No sir, we are sick as dogs too. Why you think I'm here?"

Mr. Hutchins said, *"Smart* but you're several months early."

Rob said "Do or die" and excused himself and went to his room. There he lit his lamp and tried to write again—a note to his Aunt Hatt: apology and an explanation of Grainger's disappearance, a promise to come back later that summer in perfect shape and make it up to her and be a loyal nephew—but after two starts, there seemed no need. She would either forgive him in the weeks of silence or add him to the roll of those who'd left her and could never earn pardon. Then he stood to undress and was down to his skin when a voice said "Rob?" beyond his door— Grainger, whispering. Rob half-opened on him and saw he was alone and said, "Step in. Make yourself at home. I'm bound for the arms of Morpheus" (Grainger had been coming to his room each night with the stated intent of discussing the day, their chances for life here, but really— Rob knew—to check on his health, the state of his mind). Rob went to the bed and entered it deftly as though this were winter, not warming April.

Grainger came in and shut the heavy door behind him and sat in the one straight chair by the lamp and said, "I have got something serious to ask you. I'm older than you and have wasted enough of my time on liars; so please tell me true—you honest in saying you mean to stay here?"

"All depends," Rob said.

"On what please?"

"On whether I get a decent job tomorrow, whether I can do the work once it begins (I've never built nothing), whether anybody back home should need me. Hell, Grainger, I could die in my sleep tonight."

Grainger studied him hard by the warm steady light—the wide chest propped dark against the dark walnut, muscled as though he had hauled great burdens in heavy harness since the day he could walk, not swum through a life like warm bathwater; the face with its calm breadths on which you could lay your whole flat hand if the skin itself didn't threaten to burn with a fierce life flickering out from the eyes which could watch you as steady as a picture of Jesus, as full as Jesus of the promise to speak and stay at hand till all wounds healed, perfect peace arrived. Grainger smiled. "You not dying no night soon, less some girl kill you."

"Then I'm safe," Rob said. "Don't know but one girl from here to Buena Vista and she works nights."

"Mine too," Grainger said.

"You getting into Della? You're moving, boy."

Grainger laughed a little, nodding; but then he said, "Listen, I'm lying again. Della's nice to me but I ain't touched her once and may not never."

"You've got *my* permission," Rob said. "Go to it."

Grainger nodded again. "If I need to go."

"You'll need to," Rob said, "in this good air."

Grainger thought; then said, "It puts the stiffening in you all right; but I'm waiting, I guess."

"What on?" Rob said. "Della's hot as a pistol. I had to just leave this room this morning—she was spreading my bed and giving off power."

Grainger said "On Gracie."

"If she's ever coming back, you taking a little fun here won't stop her."

"Yes it would," Grainger said. "I feel like it would."

Rob said "Is she worth it?"

Grainger said, "Nobody asked me that before."

Rob wanted to ask his pardon but couldn't.

"She used to be anyhow—to me, just me. Everybody else but me called her trash—Miss Veenie, your daddy."

"What did you call her?"

Grainger visibly retired into memory, pictures. Then he said, "Nice. She was just the nicest somebody I ever knew." He seemed prepared to stop.

"What way?" Rob said.

"Every way you can mention—at the stove, in the bed, at church; she could sing. Lot of other women got Gracie beat for looks but she suited me. I could watch her all evening. I could sit here right now and watch her till morning, if she was where you are, just to see her wake up and take first light—an easy riser; she can speak right off, don't have to go dragging around till noon. First time she pass a whole night by me, after Miss Veenie die, I'm lying there watching her and day creeping in; and she breathe deep once (her eyes still shut) and say out loud, 'I am certainly pleased.'" Grainger stopped again. "So I'm waiting on her."

Rob said, "Go to it. But my father—what did he have against her?"

"Same thing everybody did. *'She after your money.'* So what if she is? Ain't nothing but money. Nobody but me dug trenches to get it; let me give it where I please. No, money scares people. Scared em terrible in 1919, I tell you—colored boys coming home from the U.S. Army, shovels in one hand and money in the other. Scared people to death; thought we'd buy up land, you see, and own the damn world. Two or three did, little poor piece of dirt; but you want to know the truth?"

"Yes."

"You want to know who saved the world from niggerboys?"

"Sure."

"Mr. Henry Ford."

"How?"

"Model T. Every nigger had to have one, poured his money down it, saved the land for white folks." Grainger ended smiling.

"Good thing," Rob said, smiling also. But tired as he was, he would not be derailed by a joke, even true. "Why did my father care either way?" he said. "You had left him by then."

"He wanted me to get some more education. Wanted me to buy it with my army pay. I was twenty-seven years old and hadn't been to school since I left home in Maine—1904—except what he taught me when I lived with him and those little children's books I read through the years. When the Armistice was over, he got my address in France from Miss Veenie; hadn't heard from him once in all that digging, and him about the only one I knew that could write. He wrote to me then and said was I still alive and, if so, take my money and come to this school he was teaching at in Richmond; said I wasn't too old and could better myself for the time Miss Veenie died and I was alone; said he would help me again, all he could. He was teaching niggers how to write their name, read about old gods."

"You turned him down."

Grainger nodded. "Right flat. I didn't tell myself I was going to though. I got home that April on a boat to Norfolk; and I headed straight to Bracey to know was she dead—Miss Veenie, a hundred and four years old. She was picking cotton! Or claimed she was; her mind came and went. She could walk in the yard, kick the chickens some; but she hadn't picked cotton in eight or ten years. Picked *me* was what—picked on me terrible: buy her this or that, warm her up, knock her up (said she wanted a baby). I knew it was age and wouldn't last long; and I knew she had been good to me as anybody—three times better—but she wore me down those first weeks at home (I was long out of practice); so I was half-thinking about your daddy's suggestion. Hadn't written to him though. Then I come on Gracie, at the church, spring meeting. Hadn't told Miss Veenie I was going even or I'd have had to tote her, and she couldn't hear a cannon (just gave her a big drink of liquor with her supper and laid her in bed); but I headed on down there to listen to some noise. Missed the biggest noise though; she had finally shouted just before I got in, Gracie had. Been on the mourner's bench two whole days, not eating once, just to get religion. See, she was seventeen and time was getting late—you want to get religion as soon as you can, get your habits all set. Well, Gracie got it late (and I never got it); but they said she made up for lost time, shouting. Said she climbed over six rows of heart-pine benches yelling 'Safe, Jesus, safe!' When I walked up though, they had her in the yard—her auntie, old Sandra (her folks were gone, turned out to be dead)—and were giving her little drinks of water from the well. I didn't know what she'd been

through, you see; so I stopped right beside her and said 'Where you been?'
Back then I thought I was nigger-number-one that had *been* somewhere (I
had known her since a baby; she had stayed right in Bracey), and I meant
it just for fun; but she looked me dead-straight and said 'Near to Heaven'
and I said 'I believe you'—her expression, I mean: she was light as a blaze.
I had known her forever; but I hadn't never seen her lit-up like that—
nobody else had—so what I told myself (in my head, standing there) was,
love at first sight."

"And believed it," Rob said.

"Had to," Grainger said. "Never felt it before, first sight or fiftieth."

"What?" Rob said.

"—That I wanted her company from then on out everywhere I would
go."

"Did you tell her that night?"

"No, God," Grainger said. "My first mistake. I ought to said, 'Sandra,
I'm taking her now' and carried her with me back to Miss Veenie's then
and next morning said to Miss Veenie, 'Here she *is*. She is something I
want, first thing in years; so don't say one word that sounds like No.' "

"But you did what?" Rob said.

"Tried to be nice like everybody taught me. See, I hadn't never
wanted nobody before—little fun now and then but fun is easy—so I
thought you went after people you wanted the same way you went after
money or dinner: smiling and asking. It worked for a while; she had never
been asked, just told, and she answered."

"What did she say?"

"Various things; we had three years. At first it was mostly just 'Lead
and I'll follow.' And since I was fresh from the U.S. Army, I knew how to
lead!—straight into the woods. We didn't come out but to eat and sleep.
What I'm telling you is, it was new to me. I had been kept back by
different ones—your daddy, Miss Veenie. Not all the way back but far
enough so what she was offering was new ground to me. I felt like the
white men seeing Pocahontas, first time of all. I don't think she minded—
she knew more than me; several ways to Heaven and she'd tried them all.
So it wasn't too long till the tune started changing to 'Come here to me;
eat out of my hand.' I heard her changing and I came right on. What I
am—you know it—is obedient. To people I love. No other way to thank
em."

Rob nodded and said, "Please blow out the lamp—mosquitoes, I
think." When Grainger had done that and sat back down and they were
dark, Rob said, "Her hand, the one she was holding out—what was she
offering in it to eat?"

Grainger thought awhile. "That was just my way of putting it," he
said.

"Putting what though?"

It took him even longer. "I have already told you. You already know.

Every member of your family know it by now—Grainger got a good heart.
He like to help."

"Thank you," Rob said. "But why is that?"

"That's something I know, worked it out in France. See, all the army
gives you is time to think (last thing *you* need to be is a soldier). Reason
is, I had such a happy life. Till I got down in them trenches and mud,
hadn't nobody done one mean thing to me that I could remember. Good
mama and daddy, Miss Veenie good as gold till she got crazy, your daddy,
Miss Hatt. Not to say I hadn't heard some hard words now; I'd learned
trench-digging in Camp Dix, New Jersey. I'm speaking of deeds; they'd all
been kind. And even the Germans weren't aiming at *me*. Nothing personal, you see. So I been good myself, tried to please. Simple as that.
Niggers been telling me all my life—you a sapsucking *fool*. I'm the nigger
that's warm though, good roof on my head."

"But you didn't please Gracie? Is that why you're waiting?"

In the dark Grainger couldn't test Rob's face for cruelty. The voice
seemed only curious though, a further need. "I wouldn't say that. And I
don't think if you could find Gracie, she'd say that either. She'd say
Grainger done a lot better by her than any other man before him or since.
She say that in every message she send me (I taught her to write a few
words and she writes em—*Needing to see you, Coming home soon, Cold
up here*; I didn't never show her how to spell *cash money*, but I send it to
her anyhow; it might be her fare). No I've worked on that a whole lot too,
her going to Newark. *Curiosity.* Curiosity is all. I'd lived in Maine and
traveled back and forth on Seaboard trains and been to France, been to
east New Jersey; so I know what she don't yet—it's all one place; there are
just different people. She learning that in Newark, put it in her last
message—*Nobody nice as you north of you.*"

"When is she coming then?"

"When she get ready."

"How will she find you, off in the mountains?"

"I already wrote her my new address. Told her my plans."

"What are they?" Rob said.

"To stay by you long as I'm helping out or till she need me worse."
Grainger said it as fact, expecting no reward now or ever, only the chance
to pass what time still stretched before him in ways he understood and had
been good at.

And no reward came from Rob. Silence. Then the sound of him
sliding down flat on the bed, a deep sigh addressed to sleep, hopeful
greeting.

The dry sound of skin on cloth, all dark, came over Grainger like word
of refusal, a bad long minute of possible death. He worked to survive. In a
low voice, low enough to leave Rob asleep if he'd already gone, he said
"You believe me?"

Considerable silence; then Rob's voice, normal. "I believe you," he said. Exhausted as he was from his own hard day, his effort to tell a whole truth to his mother and endure the tale, Rob thought he believed what Grainger had offered, a pitiful fool's life story to now, and thought he could bear Grainger's gamble on him. Even fully awake and his mind at ease, Rob would not have thought to search farther in, would not have believed that a search through Grainger's omissions and lies would have yielded the real help Grainger could give, the lifelines extending toward a center of rest in the scattered heart of his hurtful family—the dream Grainger dreamt that night for instance.

7

A BOY again, Grainger was seated on a train that moved through successions of day and night as he stared out the window at fields and towns in the gradual process of undergoing spring—leaves, blossoms, grass. There were several more passengers; but he was alone, a small wicker satchel in the rack overhead (his father's, containing his change of clothes). He thought as he rode through the various days that he had no baggage or worry but the satchel—young as he was he could handle that—and he thought he was headed to his great-great-great grandmother's, Veenie's in Virginia. Simple destination. She would be there to meet him, give him all he lacked. So he thought he was happy and smiled at himself in the window-pane whenever they passed through tunnels or darkness. He thought that he only needed to wait; his trip would *happen* like spring to the land. Then the train stopped awhile—no town, open country—and the whitehaired Seaboard conductor came to him and smiled and said, "I have got you a new place to sit. Good place. You follow me." The conductor reached up and brought down the satchel and said "Is that all?" When Grainger said "Yes sir," then he led the way on back through cars—white cars, black cars—to a final car with a single seat. He pointed Grainger to it and stowed the satchel gently in the single rack and then, still smiling, the conductor said, "Now you're sure you've got your message?" Grainger said "Yes sir" and the old man left. Alone, he was miserable. He did not have a message and did not understand, could not even think what a *message* was or who one would be for if it blossomed now in the palm of his hand (Miss Veenie needed nothing; she was well-off in life as his father said). He stood on the plush seat and searched through his satchel—two union-suits, two pants, two shirts, a pocketknife, and a bar of soap. Nothing new or useful to anyone but him. So he rode on in misery another long while till the old man came back and said "You're there" and took down the satchel and said again "You've got it?" and led him to the steps down. The train was in Bracey, stopping at the station. The old man said, "You've been a good rider" and went down first with his satchel; then lifted him slowly through warm air to the ground and said "Goodbye" and climbed back and vanished. No Veenie in sight, no other soul. *They know I have let them down and are gone. I am left here forever, nobody but me.* Then a man stood above him—white, the age of a father—and promised kindness, though he did not smile. He held out a big hand and said, "Please. You've brought it. It's meant for me." Grainger said, "No sir. I am just what you see." The man's face clouded, sadness not meanness; and he said, "You're sure? Try hard to recall." Then Grainger knew, sudden and whole, and said it out quickly, "Forget all that please. All that's over. They say tend to me." The man, whom he saw then as Forrest, smiled and reached for his hand. No thought of Veenie or the long trip behind him.

In his sleep on his back in cold mountain air, Grainger also smiled, though alone and dark, stretched his long legs and rolled to his belly. Long hours of rest.

8

Rob also dreamt—after Grainger, toward morning—a dream which brought him no news or rest, only further pictures of a knowledge he was powerless to use or abandon. He stood in the door of an army barracks—French, in Flanders. He thought he was searching for his Cousin Whitby Shorter, had been sent by his Aunt Hatt to rescue Whitby. The room was huge—a low room of rough dark lumber, unpainted—and seemed entirely empty of all but its furniture: many rows of beds. So his search must consist of walking down the rows, each separate bed. They were oddly built; same wood as the walls, crudely nailed into long deep flatbottomed boxes like coffins or mangers. One by one they were empty of all but bedding. Each contained an identical wad of bedding, a brown cocoon of quilted cloth thrown back by the rudely awakened sleeper to show his leavings, dried plaques of stain—some colorless, some bloody, some excremental. No single exception; all were fouled, though none gave clues to the occupant's name or whether he meant to return here at night—whether rest were possible in this dry filth—or had left in revulsion or spilled all his wastes through a wound on the field. So why was he hunting a cousin here? No hope of his presence. He would be underground, returning to dirt, or fighting above it. Rob thought he would give up and turned to leave, head back out the door. The last row he walked down was like all the others except that on one bed midway down its length a person was seated, lap covered by quilting, toward whom Rob walked—his mother, a girl, longhaired, in tears. She did not see him. The search was for her.

MAY–SEPTEMBER 1925

May 27, 1925

Dear Alice,

I feel awful not to have written you till now. But since it is really the only thing I feel awful about at present and since I am devoting an hour of my twentieth birthday to you—today: you forgot but how could you remember? I never told you—I trust you will forgive me and reply very soon and set a firm date for your promised visit here. Set it late in June though or early July—come for the Fourth and maybe I will explode— since Father said, when Mother showed him Dr. Matthews' letter, that I must rest on for at least two months, just sitting and staring. Two months will be over on June 29th if I live till then. Oh my chest is strong—I doubt it was ever weak—but my nerves may be hanging in strips by then from all this stillness. It has always just been nerves from the start.

No actually, they are strong now too; and when I have told you the news that follows, I think you will guess the remedy that's worked when nothing else seemed to—your father's medicines, your mother's good food, even your own high spirits and jokes.

You remember that a strange Negro turned up to get us in a strange Chevrolet? That was only the first two surprising links in a chain that ends, I think, in a heart—a large heart containing a wonderful face, strange to me till now but likely to heal, I fervently hope. You remember also that Father never wrote us more than duty demanded, so how could we know that he'd done a good deal of moving in our absence? The Negro again was just the first hint. He'd been hired in April to help Father put the old place here in shape for what Father guesses is a golden wave of guests heading toward us on a new east-west road running through the mountains which is just now beginning to be widened from this end (the previous quick way to get here from eastward was to make prior plans to be born on the spot).

One of the builders is Robinson Mayfield. He is the face contained in the heart toward which all the recent surprises lead. Twenty-one years old and not well himself; with him also it is nothing but nerves.

From the start of it though. The trip home was rough. I was weak from all the resting; and the new Negro—Grainger—told us nothing substantial of the changes at home, only that he'd been hired shortly before and that the Chevrolet belonged to a man who was boarding with us while he worked on the road. Father's old car was laid up as usual, so he'd offered the man a bargain on a week's rent if we could use the Chevy. It got us here at least; but I won't be needing Grainger to drive me again— Donner and Blitzen! And what was waiting at first was just Father. He may not have written much; but he has been worried (I told you he lost his own mother and a sister with galloping consumption, though long years ago). The signs of that were that he met us in the yard, kissed Mother and me (he is not a big kisser), tipped Grainger a dollar in the presence of us all (my father and dollars are magnet-and-iron), and then said Della would show me my room. I told him I remembered quite well where it was—it had been mine forever—but he said "No you don't"; and he and Della led me (Della is the maid). He had changed my room—every stick, every picture—and set me up in what used to be the old Bridal Suite on the southeast corner: not a suite, to be sure, and no bridal couple ever crossed the doorsill in my recollection, but a big high room with good exposure to cross-ventilation. All for my chest, when all my chest needs is just a little padding! Well, it was very thoughtful and I did appreciate it, even if I noticed he'd neglected to paint the old walls (the chest may fail; no need to splurge yet!). But when they all went out and left me to rest for the hour before supper, I was low as a mole. And because of Father. In spite of your father's long letter explaining that now I was largely out of danger and could live my life, here he was intending to shore me up in a run-down resort that if he poured thousands of dollars into would not draw flies, much less rich Virginians if he offered to bring them here in his arms over that new road (and all he intends to pour is a trickle—ten dollars here, thirty-five dollars there). And if I am rushing toward death, what a place to die!—a hotel swarming with loud old ladies.

I am not going to die, but I prayed to then. I'll admit it to you. I lay on my bed on April 30th and prayed to God to strike me with everything they thought I had—failed lungs, failed mind—but make it quick please. I meant it so much that I said it out loud, some part of it anyhow—I was in the Bridal Suite; nobody was near.

Or so I thought (my mind is weak).

Somebody knocked in the midst of a groan. I thought it was Father or Mother at least; so I had to say "All right," still lying down. And there stood this strange man looking concerned. I sat straight up and said "You're in the wrong pew" (I was fully dressed). He said, "I was hoping

*to save a life—heard a soul in distress." I said "Not me." He said, "Give a
groan; let me hear you groan." I gave a little groan and he said, "You're
lying; that was you just now." Well, in spite of his looks, he was dirty as a
clam (he had just come from work—blasting rock since dawn—but I
didn't know that); so I said, "So what please? And who are you?" He said
"I'm the groom." I must have looked baffled; so he said, "The bridegroom.
I live in the other half of the Bridal Suite." (It turned out he did—our
new paying guest; Father had given him the other room; mine was second-
best.) I said, "What's the groom's name then, please sir?"; and he said,
"Rob Mayfield the Second, and willing." I decided not to go a step farther
that way but said, "I am Rachel Hutchins, just back." He said, "I know.
Know all about that." —"Tell me then," I said; "I sure God don't." He
waited a whole minute, staring hard at me. "You're better," he said. "In
fact, you're well." I said "Who says?" He said "My eyes" and touched his
eyes. —"Are they truthful?" I said. He said "You decide" and walked
forward to me. So I sat to the edge of the bed for that, my feet on the floor
in case Father came—he'd have shot Rob dead. They were brown. I can
never tell about brown eyes. "What's the verdict?" he said. I said, "They
go very well with your hair; that's as much as I know." —"Or ever will," he
said.*

*I was ready to get mad, but Della walked up to the open door and
asked did I want a tray or would I come down? I found I'd decided to trust
the eyes. I said I'd join everybody downstairs as soon as I'd washed; and
since everybody was nothing but my parents plus Rob Mayfield, I've hardly
been back upstairs since then. That was almost a month ago; and more
things have grown than just the flowers, mainly my care for Rob.*

*To tell the pure truth, I will have to say that my care has grown both
higher and deeper than Rob's for me. Apparently at least. He often doesn't
get back till long past dark and then is tired and eats in the kitchen and is
something of a night walker (easing his nerves), and Father watches me
like a hawk; so until last weekend I knew little more than the thing I felt,
which was happiness to know he was in the world or that I was in a world
which offered him—when these recent months I've suspected much worse.*

*He came in on Saturday evening from work and washed in his room
and stretched out to rest on his bed before supper; I knew because I've
learned to read his life through walls. I was also "resting," as per Father's
orders, though what I was actually doing was straining in every nerve to
hear when he'd rise and which way he'd walk. I was testing my strength;
could I cause him to come to my door and knock and say something
hopeful (the previous two nights he had either been exhausted and had
barely spoken or had gone out riding with some boys on his crew). I was
thinking, "Now get up and help me please. Nobody else can need you like
me." I was also working against the clock—the dinner bell. Della would be
ringing it at six.*

Then with four minutes left, he stood to the floor and waited a little on the rug by his bed and opened his door and walked down to mine and knocked once so lightly as to be heard only by the nearest hound or by Rachel waiting.

To stay still myself, I went to the door and opened it on him; and he said—no greeting, never calling my name—"I know you've got a birthday coming next week. I'll be working of course, and you've got your family; but I'd like to help you celebrate tomorrow afternoon. A picnic maybe."

I said the next three things in backward order—Yes; who had told him?; I would have to ask Father. He said he did not remember, maybe Grainger, and that if I wanted he would speak to Father and assure him of his wish not to tire me out. I thanked him and said No, I'd better handle that; and he said again, "I just want to help you celebrate."

It came true. Nobody ever helped me more. After supper that night— nobody left at table but Father and me, and Della clearing—I said, "Could I ride out with Rob tomorrow and breathe a little hill air and eat a good lunch?" He stared down awhile and then just said "Whose idea is it?" —"Rob's," I said. "He is trying to help me." He stared awhile longer and gave no sign of answering; so I said, "Do you want me to go on and die?" He looked up and checked me for seriousness and said, "That is not my intention, no." Then he said he'd speak to Rob and, whatever got said, it all came true.

And no lies told. It was just what Rob promised and what I told Father—a smooth ride and fresh air down by the river and Della's cold chicken, a helpful celebration (I did leave out the celebration part in all my descriptions, before and after, since excitement is supposed to be rat-bane for me). But it was a celebration and as calm as the day. I was weaker than I knew from being cooped-up; and though Rob never once asked was I tired, he used me all day as if he knew what there was to know about my condition and was gauging every movement, every question he asked, to strengthen not abuse. In fact there were very few questions at all and none about my life. My guess is he'd heard from Della, through Grainger, some version of the past—Della knows all you know, likely more—and I hope that he has. The last thing I'd want is to be deceitful about my life or the little meager offerings I can make to his needs.

That's what we talked about finally, his life. He thinks it has been poor; it sounds good to me—a father that left them when he was a baby, a mother who watched him as little as possible. When he finished his story (longer than Leviticus and he's just twenty-one) and turned to me, expecting an answer, I said, "Is that a complaint or what?" He thought it over by looking at the mountain (when you come here I'll ask you to draw that mountain; I want it framed near me for the rest of my life); and that gave me a close chance to study him—a long oval face with a high clear forehead, great wide cheekbones like wings laid back from a firm inquisitive

nose, a broad mouth that flares (almost shocking in a man). Brown eyes
as I said—beautiful but shut to me; by his choice, I think. Strong coarse
brown hair, lightening with the long days of work in the sun—his skin of
course darkening. (What good is all that to you, you wonder?—none, I
guess. You could not construct him from a ream of words; but I have no
other likeness to send you except all this letter which is testimony to him.
You might well find him an ordinary sight. Mother does.) Anyhow when he
had thought, he said, "No I figured you would see. It's an invitation." I
had to ask "To what?" though I feared the whole day would collapse right
there, and he nearly died laughing. I joined him, confused, but stopped
before he did; and when he recovered he said, "You are cured. Nothing
wrong with you." I said, "I agree. Now answer my question." —"To be
good to me," he said.

I'd been doing that!—though it was a relief to have his permission—
but being me, I just said "Thank you" (I am bad under pressure as you
well know). And he left it there. He didn't say "Thank you Yes or No,"
but nodded and smiled and ate the last shortleg. So I relaxed too—as far as
I could with a satisfied heart!—and after we had talked on some about his
road job (which he's flabbergasted to find he enjoys) and Father's grand
plans for a tourist magnet (which we both think are crazy), he calmly said,
"It's time you were home. That was part of my promise."

So home we went and happy it's been. We have not been off the
premises since—together, I mean. Rob's worked, to be sure; but two of the
last four evenings we have sat by ourselves on the sideporch and talked. He
has still not asked me an unkind question, and I don't think he will. With
me he seems determined to live in the present, and you'll know how grand
I think that is.

It does of course raise thoughts of the future; but all I can do is hope
and be calm, try to get myself into good working-order and accept his
simple invitation to be good (to keep you calm let me just explain that the
most touching we've done so far is his hand now and then to help me
through a door). He plans to board here another few months, at least till
the road pushes so far away that the crew can't make it back here in the
evening (two more of them are staying here now—young boys and quiet—
on Rob's recommendation, which greatly pleases Father and feeds his
hopes). Beyond that he says he won't think. But you'll know I do. All I
know about love—all I know about simply being good to the needy—is
that such contracts are sworn forever. I'm nothing if not lasting.

Certainly this letter has lasted forever. I beg your pardon. But you
helped me so much in those weeks at your home; and now I've been silent
so long, and apparently ungrateful, that I had to tell you at some full
length of the new help, the new chance, that's been offered to me. I am
trying to take it this time, for good. But calmly as I said. Another month of
calm enforced by Father—another good thing, I begin to suspect.

So make your plans now to come in late June and really visit. By then I hope to be unrecognizable—stronger, a better friend; by then someone you can confide to, not just listen to day after day.

Write me all your news. Warm regards to your parents—don't show this to your Father (in fact burn it), but tell him I am better! Thanks and love to you,

Happy birthday to me,
As always,
Rachel

June 14, 1925

Dear Niles,

Aunt Rena has forwarded your letter; and I take this first chance, my one day off, to tell you that Yes I'm alive and all right. Matter of fact, I am also close by. After leaving you in Staunton with the cowchain and slopjars, I wandered a little and drank a lot and wound up begging a job with Lassiter Construction Company. We are building a road going east through the mountains from Goshen to Roller's Retreat (remember?), and I'm not sure if I can wait to get there.

I am sure, to tell you the pure-God truth. I can wait here forever, the way it feels now. I'm well taken care of on all sides here and the job—third foreman in charge of moving rock (with dynamite; I learned blasting quick)—pays better than I've ever got before and has the added virtue of wearing me down to a nub every evening.

Unfortunately, as various Baptist deacons might say, the nub still works. And the nub is what's getting all the good care (not all, but a good part; one joy at a time though). The nub's care is coming, on the strict Q.T., from a girl that works at the place I'm boarding. Snuff-brown, age nineteen (she thinks), the cook and general-help at this place. I'm whipped a good many nights as I said; but when I'm not and can creep out back where she has her room without being seen by the various watches, then it's all I need; then it's perfect proof of what I have told you these past five years—there are remedies, boy. The world is a doctor if you know who to ask.

Otherwise I spend what hours are left—oh precious few!—being good to another girl. White this time, daughter to the manager of this old dump of a watering hole. Good in her case mainly means listening. She has just turned twenty, been in poor health for years (just home in fact from a stay at a chest place over near Lynchburg, apparently safe now but weak on her pins) and talks a good deal; but tired as I am by the time she gets to me, she does have the power to command attention. My attention anyhow. Partly her looks—she is almost as tall as me and thin, but the main thing about her is hair and eyes. Black horse hair that, old as she is, she still

*wears long so that, when she starts talking to me at night, it swags round
her face and hides her neck like two dense stranglers; and then her face
(pale from the months indoors) just hangs on the dark and carries her
eyes—the steady thing. They are dark as her hair and hold dead on me. I
am the rescue; I know that clearly. She has made me that; chose me from
thin air—her name is Rachel Hutchins—and so far I've let her and listened
as I said.*

*Certainly I'm flattered and since the "staples," so to speak, are coming
from another quarter (and no questions asked, no answers expected), I
seem to be liking her and looking forward to her. She is by the way no
fool at all—no show-off either but a good tough wit, a hard little scrapper
(if she's stronger now, it's her own mind that's done it—her parents would
make General Pershing nervous, and her Lynchburg doctor sounds like a
loud quack); and most of the talk anyhow concerns your old friend and
mine, Rob Mayfield the Second.*

*—Who is as I say doing tolerably well, though sinking right now
toward the bed (alone). If the work eases up in a month or so, maybe I
can take a Saturday afternoon off and drive down to meet you in the feed-
and-seed; and we could tour the churches of Staunton on Sunday. Will I
know you at all? Do you wear sleeve garters yet? An isinglass eyeshade?*

*You won't know me. I am handsome again. Keep me posted please
(assuming, that is, that you know something more than the current price
of nails; how's your own nub, for instance?). Have you been home yet? Any
real news from there?*

Ever,
Rob

June 23, 1925

Dearest Rob,
*You know me. Others may keep an infinite silence, and God knows I
try at appropriate times but finally I burst. So here are the burstings.*

*Very little has changed. You'd recognize us all if you walked in
tonight which of course I frequently pray that you will. Three and a half
months is one hundred days, a very hard diet to ask us to eat after twenty-
one years.*

*Well, we eat it is all and are grateful, I guess, to be all healthy and
shambling along day to day. You'll know what the news has been since you
left—barring deaths or the sudden descent of Jesus, you'll know the news
here wherever you go, however long you stay. We are dedicated to the way
things are, which you also know.*

*For something to say though, here's how they are. Father has been
stronger with the good warm weather. No hot sieges yet so Sylvie and Eva
have managed to get him out in the yard several bright mornings. He can
stump along between them and sit in the shade in the old wicker rocker*

(but still as a stone; rocking just sets him wild). What most concerns him now is the palm tree. Slick got it back outdoors the same time as Father; and he likes to watch it and call passers over and tell them its age, which is going on forty, and the whole thrilling story of how Uncle Deward brought it up in his lap *(a six-inch seedling)* from Gainesville, Florida; a Christmas gift to Eva just after she was born, well before me! It is eight feet tall now—was when you left—and gives every sign of being in the best health of any creature present. Father runs it a close second.

Not that anybody else is really down. I have had the eczema all over my hands since right after you left. Has driven me all but crazy this time—in fact I can't imagine why I haven't gone. Dr. Turner has me wearing thick mittens at night so I won't gouge myself all raw in my sleep. Sleep!—slim chance. If I've slept a solid hour in the last four months, it has gone undetected by me at least. Still I trust to recover. When or how is a secret *(can you shed any light?)*.

Eva's all right—busy of course. I saw the letter you wrote her, Son, unbeknownst to her. I trust you'll excuse me when I tell you why. Sylvie told me you'd written, right after she delivered it (she had been waiting as worried as I); so I didn't say a word but watched Eva closely, from desperate curiosity to hear about you and also because, as you may not know, letters have been the cause of disaster in this house before. I watched but there was nothing to see, nothing I hadn't seen every day of the years since she came back. By suppertime, I was quite upset but held my tongue; and when Eva came in to get Father's tray, Sylvie said, "How is Mister Rob getting on?" Eva turned, as calm as sunrise at sea, and said, "Everybody can rest in peace. He is safe and sound in Goshen, Virginia; has a job all but promised and sends his love." Well, I haven't known her all this time for nothing (Sylvie either). Both of us just said "Good, good" and let her go on. When she got out of earshot, Sylvie said, "Miss Rena, she lying. That was the biggest letter I ever brought here." I told her to hush, but I went on watching. Eva sat with Father extra late that night and to my surprise read to him from the Bible—Mother's Bible that she took from your room (you know roughly how much the Bible means to Eva), gentle parts from the prophets, those promises of help that have been inexplicably delayed. When she left him though, I gave her a while; then went in to her and said, "Is there anything you need me for?" She smiled and tried to say "Such as what?" but her tongue seized on her. I had not seen Eva at a loss in something like twenty years; so I went and touched her, just took her by the wrists and offered to kiss them. She didn't draw back but she shook her head. I walked her to the bed and sat down beside her, still holding one hand. I didn't speak again. If I've learned anything in my life it's to wait. Eva also waited, dry and cold, and finally she looked square at me and said, "He is trying to finish me. Maybe I should let him." I just said "Rob?" She nodded Yes but then said, "Please don't ask any more. I'll talk when I can." I said, "Just this—were you truthful? Is he safe?" She *said, "For now. Yes you can sleep easy." I said, "Would you like me to sleep in here? I could make a pallet." She smiled—"No thank you. I am not Mother anyhow. You get your sleep."*

Curiously I did. I could barely get through my prayers awake, worn out from waiting; but I got my mittens on and plunged to the depths where I dreamt for what I honestly believe is the first time since Mother died. It concerned you and me being chased through snowy woods by men. I was happy all through it and happiest at the end, that I crawled through to safety for both of us. I was bearing you. You were going to be free. So the next morning I was unusually rested, and Eva had managed to seal herself over. She gave no sign of even remembering our previous words; and I didn't press, warned Sylvie not to. But when more days passéd with nothing else from you and Eva never offered me a chance to ask what had struck her so hard, I was forced to act and went for the letter. I have since read it twice (she keeps it on her bureau, plain to all).

I can't say that much of it was news exactly (except your movements and the tales of drinking; you can stop that tomorrow as you say and you must—there have been all sorts of weak minds among the Kendals but never a drunk, so don't be the first one; and even if the Mayfields are sots back to Noah, you break the chain); so it didn't affect me as heavily as Eva. I also know it wasn't meant for me. You are one of the few occasions in my life which I do not regret. I would stand before God Almighty tonight and dare him to name one sin I did you; one time I failed in the work I saw laid down for me the moment you entered this house, a helpless babe. I confess a billion other grave faults, but in you I succeeded.

What failed, Son, was you. Eva won't tell you that because she does not see it and because, above all, you love her so and she can't risk losing that, however she's ignored it—especially now when the years have left her all but alone and will leave her that soon. But I know it with the knowledge of a loving witness who has gone unloved (this is no plea now; you are too far gone; there is nothing you could give me now which I could use; nothing which I could believe in, even). I can and will tell you—you accept gifts badly. You abuse the generous. Children do that and are pardoned for their youth. You are fully a man now and are not forgiven— and will not be, not by me or Father (whose money you've eaten since before you could stand) or your own strange mother (who has loved you, I see now, as best she could in view of her life—and of your cold nature), not even by Sylvie who has told me more than I wanted to hear. People like you who have won heaven's grace bear the largest burden of all, I believe; and bear it you must—learn to take the world's praise, its helpless thanks—or spoil in the way you're spoiling now. You complain of lacks, of long neglect. I cannot in all my admittedly narrow experience recall another human who has been so continuously attended. Most men are solitary marchers, by you; not to speak of women.

Leave us then. By all means, go. And for the sake of mercy, stop begging your mother for what she does not have to give. For your strange reasons, some of which I grant are no fault of yours, you have made us your poison. Have the sense—and simple dignity, Rob—to stop licking at us. Find something that is actually food you can eat, that will offer itself; then eat till it's gone.

Will it seem crazy of me at the end here to reaffirm what you've known for years—you're the love of my life? Simple as that. And I could not be turned around tomorrow—too old, too accustomed, nowhere else to go. So you know you are always welcome here. Anything I have said elsewhere above should not be construed as "banishment," only as the long-thought-out advice, painful for me as you, of one who has at least watched you more steadily these twenty-odd years than any other human breathing air at present.

Everybody sends love or would if I asked them. Don't mention me or any of this in your next to us; but do write soon with calmer news—and remember to include a greeting for Sylvie. She literally pines. She said this week, "This place like a engine without no gas." I told her, "I didn't know you could drive." —"Can't," she said, "but I sure can ride."

So can I,
Rena Kendal

July 4, 1925

Dear Mr. Forrest,

Here is Grainger finally. I guess you think it has been a long time but I have kept busy since I come from the war and have not had other reason to write. Thank you for your letter that got to me in France with promise of help. I planned to accept but went home awhile and found duty there. Also decided I better not try a second time and put everybody in misery again like I did before. I was still young then and had high notions. Miss Polly knew that so I guess she excused me in her heart by now. Tell her please that I feel different now and am truly sorry if she is still there nearby to hear you. I learned right much in my own dealings in these past twenty years trying to keep Miss Veenie and fight the war and live with a wife who has gone off now.

What I am writing you about though is not me but Rob your boy. He turned up in Bracey three months ago to see Miss Hatt. I guess she told you. Curiosity mostly. He got upset and she asked me to watch him. Wasn't much left for me around there and he seem to want me so that landed me with him up here in the high mountains, Goshen. He is building a road and I am helping out at the same hotel where he stay and eat. He has been fair to me, don't notice me much as you did at first, and you know how young he is but here just lately he gone off the track more times than one, drinking heavy and leaning on women, one colored.

Much as I watch him I can't do all, trying to save a little money for my own family all scattered, and you know how much he listen to me, just laugh and leave and do his next wish. Already been in a wreck and a fight, that much known to me, and somebody else bound to get hurt soon, mostly one of his women.

What I'm asking is, you speak to him and find out his trouble and see can you stop him while he still in safety and nobody ruined.

Just thought you would want to know this in time, after all this time. Wishing you the best and to see your face,

                                        Your old friend,
                                          Grainger

Write Rob Mayfield, Hutchins Hotel, Goshen.

                                              July 21, 1925

My dear Robinson,

I am or was your father. Though you can surely have no memories of me, my images of you are clear and correct despite these years; and though you will have grown past knowing, I still hope strongly to see you soon and match valued thoughts against the reality worked by time.

What this constitutes then is an invitation. Will you come here soon and visit me freely for as long as you wish or your job permits? I am myself in vacation now, so am mostly open as to time and duty but have learned from my sister of your whereabouts and work.

I could come there to you if you wish it at all (the mountains have always been good to me, and I have not seen them for many years); but my own hope is that you could find time to come here long enough to meet and talk. There's a great deal to say, which you might care to hear or need to know; and the house I have is my dead father's house, the Mayfield place. It would be part yours, if I ever die.

You have some cause to blame me, Son—may I call you that? It at least is simple fact, never challenged by any. There are also long due debts to me, never paid or acknowledged—which I've long since canceled. If you find it in your heart to discard a past so long and heavy, the lies and failures made mostly by others (who, whatever their errors, meant you no harm), you will find me ready—even eager now—to begin a friendship, an explanation, a try at amends. Please speak up soon.

                                        Yours ever,
                                        Forrest Mayfield

care of The James Normal Institute
Richmond, Virginia
P.S. You would have a private room here. No lack of space.

July 29, 1925

My dear Rob,

    Again I have waited a long time to answer word from you. Waited and listened in the hope I would hear somehow in my empty head a useful answer that would ease my failure and fill your need, punish you and help you. I have even called on God for the words, a course which you know I seldom take, feeling He has enough to trouble His depths without the annoyance of what little gravel you or I pitch in to stir His shallows.

    I'm sorry to say though, nothing has come. You picked the wrong mother.

    Is that the answer? Could well be, it strikes me now. In which case, in any case, the next thing to do is have your life. I've had mine, you see—am having it daily and for years to come, I trust—and whatever others think about my accidents and choices, I can say in full truth—here in roughly midstream—that I do not, cannot, regret or condemn it. I accuse myself of hurting some feelings, through the ignorance of youth or the need to preserve my sanity and health in the face of another person's claims on me—my mother, your father—but the acts of others were theirs not mine; and I have not tortured myself for them and never intend to. I have paid however. But I've had much pleasure, some deep satisfactions—I've given some—and hope to have more. The surest blight I could fall to now would be the belief that love was the best thing life could give. After years, and the sights I've seen and lived, such a fall is unlikely.

    You suffer that blight though, I honestly believe—in relation to me— and now Rena tells me you have written to say there's a girl up there who has cheered you up in recent weeks and that you are considering a life in harness. Consider it hard; let me urge that on you. You have numerous blessings. I can see them all on you—a man, young, bound to no parent (never likely to be; I've told you I'm safe), graced with the open face and manner which the world seeks out and gladly rewards, with a keen able mind (if you'll keep it clear and straight) and a body which can be its own solace alone far more than you'll guess till you've yoked it to the mercy of another body's needs. Forgive me but I'm telling you the little I know.

    I'm not asking here that you care for no one or hoard your gifts so they wither and choke you, just that you give much thought to two things—your family history (mine and your father's; every day I breathe I believe more strongly that your home is your fate, all laid down and waiting) and your own long future with the few little scraps of freedom you possess. I also suggest that your home is here. I cannot guess where else it might be.

    So bait hook and fish for your own life, by all means. But be sure you cast into water not air and that what you catch will be what you can use.

    We are all right here, blessed by lovely weather—bright days but bearable and short cool nights. Father sits out a good deal as Rena may

have told you and profits by the passers who stop to talk. A day or two ago
I left him for a minute (I mostly sit with him and work at the mending;
I'm brown as a field hand, which maybe I'll become); and when I rejoined
him, he was entertaining Min Tharrington. She's back with her diploma.
Plans to spend the summer here, then has a job teaching in the country
near Raleigh. God help her in that; she still seems a good deal too gentle
for the world, especially children. But then she's got Tharringtons and
Spencers behind her, stretching to Adam (a lot of grit!); and maybe they
will gather in her craw soon now and toughen her more. Her looks are
already settling down—a good calm face; her eyes are relaxing. She was
hoping for you though. I knew that at once so spared her the shame of
having to ask by telling her you had a laborer's job, were making good
money, and keeping your own close counsel as to news or the promise of a
visit. She said "Good, good," though I saw that her view of the summer
was marred; but Father broke in and said "Fool, fool." No more nor less.
Min or I neither one asked Who? I gave her your address; she never would
have asked.

Nobody wants to see you more than I. But that in no way cancels
what I've said all above here about your own life. Trouble with me always
is that I mean everything I say—and I say so much in various directions.
I'm not to be trusted, I guess is the moral. But I know I am. Believe me
and keep me posted.

Love,
Mother

August 15, 1925

Dear Alice,
We all got your kind letters of thanks earlier this week. I will let
Father and Mother speak for themselves (Mother anyhow; Father
wouldn't answer an autographed letter from Jesus, in English); but all I
can say now—a worn out record!—is thank you, my dear. For your own
good company, a tonic in itself (you're the only female I have ever really
liked, not to mention trusted—you're the only one worthy who's crossed
my path) but maybe most of all for your understanding Rob or my view of
Rob. The trick about friends, my few friends at least, is to like their
friends; not to finally decide they are fools or crazy to fall for some crook or
crank that they cherish. Not to mention require.

I think it is now safe to call it that, on both sides. Despite the fact
that Rob took to you and arranged those outings, he seemed to me more
than a little set back the whole time you were here and, as you noticed,
practically invisible the last few days. So much so that, once you were gone,
I asked him about it and he said, grinning widely as he always does when
serious, "I know it is wrong but what I believe is, I am the only person
alive who can love two people or more at once. Anybody else who tries is a

cheat; and I have to leave them, can't stand to watch." I thought and said, "Oh no you are right. Alice is a friend, the first I've had; but Alice would be the first to know I would leave her for you if you said the word." He waited a good while—dark on the porch, Mother ten steps away, Della clearing off supper through the window behind us—and then he said, "What word would it be?" I said, "That's unfortunately for you to discover. I'll know if I hear it." He nodded then—"All right. Give me time. I'll rummage around. You may hear it yet." I said "Please hurry." He said, "I will. I'm ready as you." I asked him "For what?" and he said, "That's more of what I got to find." So I sat on and then said "Hurry" again. He said "What's your rush?" and I laughed and said, "The little time left; I may not last!" He said, "You'll be living ninety years from now." I said, "Not long enough by far." He sat a few minutes more, pleasant quiet; then got up and whispered he needed a walk. I'd walk to Asia of course with him, but Mother was still on duty nearby, and I'm not supposed to breathe deep at night; so I kept my place and have hardly seen him since; he has been so busy, day and dark.

But late last night he knocked on my door. I was nine-tenths dressed and brushing my hair. I went as I was, barefoot for silence, and opened on him, not certain it was him. I have not seen more than two or three drunks (Father won't let them stay); but I think he was drunk—all oily with sweat, his face unstrung, his eyes skimmed over. He stood straight though and kept his hands down. I said "Good evening." He said "No, bad." I said "I'm sorry" but he said, "Don't be. Just answer one thing; are you still waiting?" I said I was; for a number of things—a place in glory chiefly. I honestly thought he was going to strike me. I still think he was. But I quickly said, "Don't. Please what do you mean?" He said, "For the word that would bring you to me." I said, "Oh that. Lord God, I am there." He said, "No you're not. But wait till Monday. I may know then." I was whispering; he was not—I expected Father's presence momentarily—so I didn't risk asking why Monday was special but just said, "Rob, are you sure you're all right?" He said, "Hell no. Are you waiting or not?" I said I was and he left again.

That was Friday night. This is Saturday noon. Somehow I haven't worried but have been mostly calm—the surest sign yet that, for whatever reason, I am more nearly back to my best true self than in many dark years. Alice, you bear a part of the blame for that rescue! (you and your parents); and whoever commands me in whatever words, whoever I follow or if I stay here and wither alone, I'll remember that always as a gift barely second to any I've received (whatever Rob offers will not be a gift but a serious burden). I hope I have given you more than just care. You laughed a lot here; so I'll treasure that at least—that I caused kind laughter for two good weeks toward the end of a summer which I'd neither hoped nor intended to survive.

Let me hear by return please more news of your return and, if you will, your considered opinion of all you saw here. I need it in writing, so to speak. Renew my grateful greetings to your parents and to anyone left in the Weak-Chest Wards who remembers

Your
Rachel

P.S. I had just closed this and was washing my face to walk down to mail it when a knock at my door, which was Grainger, standing. Did I know where Mr. Rob was today? I said "No why?" He said, "That's all right. I just needed to find him" and thanked me and left before I thought to quiz him further. So now I'm afraid I'm a little shaken. What Grainger doesn't know about Rob will be strange. What Grainger doesn't know about anything— Well, Rob said to wait. Monday's two days off. I wait, I wait. Ever, R.H.

2

THE woman who answered Rob's single knock stood silent, carefully looking, and then said "Morning" in a voice with no trace of question or fear, more nearly the calm spontaneous answer to a question posed long years before, considered ever since. She smiled very slightly and looked maybe thirty—Rob judged age poorly like all young men: there were two stripes of gray in auburn hair that seemed fluid with satisfied life of its own, one at each temple. She was middle-sized and met Rob's eyes dead-level (he was one step down).

"Forrest Mayfield," he said. "Is he living here?"

"He's been here twenty-one years," she said. "But right this minute he has stepped out to buy him a black shoelace." She touched the back of her own neck gently; she liked herself.

Rob scrubbed his chin with the heel of his left hand. He said, "I'm sorry to look so scrappy." He pointed to his muddy car at the curb. "But I drove through the night from back in the mountains."

She nodded. "That's easy to mend. You can wash. You can use his razor." But she stood in the door still, not waving him in.

"I'm Rob Mayfield."

"The Second," she said. "I was figuring that." She touched both eyes. "I'm not a big reader, but I've trained my eyes fairly well through the years." She looked on, still standing, as if there were more than a name to figure, a face to see. "I'm your father's help."

"I heard that," he said.

"Who from?"

"Aunt Hatt."

"What word did she use?"

Rob thought. "*Help*, I think—that you'd helped him a lot."

She nodded. "That was kind. It's been my wish anyhow, God knows. He needed it. I am Margaret Jane Drewry." She stepped back, smiling again. "Come in."

Rob thanked her and entered the long hall behind her. The back of the hall, a wide door, was open; and the clear sun of early afternoon boiled slowly in the space, on clean cream walls hung with wide brown photos of ancient Rome in dark oak frames—*The Temple of Virile Fortune, of the Magna Mater, of Venus Genetrix*. Rob passed them, not looking, aiming only toward the woman who waited near the end by another open door (every school he had known owned similar sets, supremely unnoticed except by the spinsters who now and then pointed to one with startling passion).

But she said, "Those were left to your father last year by an old-maid teacher that believed in him. I think she was hoping to drive him back to Latin."

So Rob paused and stared at the *Virile Fortune*, glum tan rubble. "I see why he left." Then he faced her. "*Did* he leave?"

"No," she said quickly. "Oh no he was left." Even finished and silent, she rang like a bell with the force of her peal.

He smiled. "I just meant Latin," he said and gestured to the pictures.

She nodded, relieved. "He had to leave that. It's a colored school—teaching them how to live: machine work and all. He teaches just reading and a few little poems—John Greenleaf Whittier, all they can take."

"Well, I'm sorry," Rob said.

Quick and urgent again, she said "Don't be"; then stopped herself and deeply blushed—embarrassed revelation—then recovered conviction. "He's happy, I mean."

Rob said, "I'm glad. Hatt said to thank you."

She stood still and looked down, listening to that, cradling it side to side in her mind, one spoon of water on a parching tongue. Then she swallowed it slowly; and when she looked up, she said, "Wait for him in here. This is where he works."

Rob moved to obey—he'd made her forget that he needed to wash; he would not tell her now—but before he had walked three steps toward the light, she said, "If you sit in that black leather chair and lie back and rest, I'll come in and give you a painless shave and never even interrupt your pleasant dreams." Rob nodded and went on, accepting her offer, and not only rested but slept—no dreams. Too tired for dreams.

He had driven all night and half of today, starting in bad shape and worsening steadily. The sights and messages of recent days had mounted and pressed; and he'd started drinking at work on Friday—his first turn to drink, with serious intent, since the bout in Bracey with his Aunt Hatt and Grainger (the other times had served the purpose of fun, nights with his work-mates; so he told himself). He thought he had got through till quitting time without his boss's notice; but when he'd stepped up to collect his pay, Mr. Lassiter had said, "Mayfield, are you coming down sick?" There was nobody near and Mr. Lassiter had seemed to like him since the day he'd started; so Rob said, "Could be. I've been under pressure." Mr. Lassiter said "The Hutchins girl?" Rob had said "No sir, home"; and Mr. Lassiter said, "Take till Monday morning and get the pressure off. If you aren't here Monday morning fit to work at six, I'll hire a new man." Rob had thanked him and passed up a ride back to town on the little gang-truck, saying honestly he felt like taking a walk. There had been a lot of laughter—who was waiting for him where? would she take him all dusty as he was, unshaved? But they'd gone off without him, and he'd walked on behind.

The walk was five miles, some three hours long since he stopped several times to suck on his bottle and mull on his worries in various spots by the loud white river in shades of dying light. When he'd got near the hotel, it was well past nine—supper over and cleared—so he'd walked a long arc and approached from the back in hopes of finding either Grainger or Della off-duty in their quarters.

Grainger had gone off with Mr. Hutchins to talk to a carpenter back on the mountain about rebuilding the springhouse cheap; but Della was sitting barefoot in the dark at the end of her cot, singing hymns to herself. He had walked in on her in total silence and waited till she said, "You early. What you mean?" He had said, "I mean I am in bad trouble." —"What you want me to do?" (she had said it gently, an offer not a spurning); so to give her a task, to give himself a little more quiet time, he asked her to go back and pack his dinner pail—he was taking a trip. She had asked him to where and was he coming back? He had said, "I'm thinking. Just get me some dinner" (no trip had crossed his mind till then). She had smelled his harsh breath, known food was the last thing he really wanted but had gone on and rummaged by a single candle to find him enough food to keep him alive; then had come back and, finding him waiting in her chair, had said, "Here it is but you leaving here stinking." Rob had said, "I'll be crossing a number of rivers. I can wash—Hell, drown." She had said, "I got all your pressing right here" (she washed his work clothes), so he'd let her find him a clean shirt and pants; and then he'd turned and left without another word, though he'd laid a silver dollar on her bureau as he passed. He'd stowed the food and clothes on the seat of the car, checked the tool box for the pint of whisky wedged there, then had felt his dark way round to crank the engine. He'd seen Rachel's light and, not really waiting a moment to think, had climbed the stairs to her—unheard by anyone—and made his vague promise with no conscious prior intention behind him, no serious pledge. Then he'd driven away and run all night over miserable roads—down the mountains, fording creeks that were swollen to torrents, stopping twice for punctures, and one time to contemplate his death.

He had brought himself to that, let himself be brought. He was in grave earnest fifty miles west of Richmond, the last of the hills above the James River, eight in the morning. He had seen from the road that the hill made a clean hundred-foot drop to water, sufficient wet rocks; so he'd pulled over there and stopped the car, thinking, "Rest your eyes for a little anyhow and maybe end it now—the whole damn relay race you've been in for twenty-one years, no choice of your own, running hell-for-leather with a baton passed by the dead or the useless and no one to take it." He had sat on a flat rock the size of a pillow and watched the moiling water for ten full minutes, not thinking especially but listening in calm pain to all that his body or mind volunteered, neither news nor hope. And his head was clear, his body cleaned out. He had not had a drink since leaving Goshen or eaten the dinner. His access to liquor was still in his own grip. What he'd told his mother in the spring held true—he could stop it at will; it was not yet a necessary substance of his blood but an easy comfort. By the river, in slant early Saturday light, the question had come to: *what thing to stop, of the stoppable things?*

Then he'd heard from far down young high voices and hunted till he saw two boys, ten or twelve, on the opposite bank with a single rifle. They quieted soon and studied the water as if it withheld some urgent unit of their own further lives. Rob had strained to find it with them; feared he'd found it before them—a snapping turtle the size of a galvanized tub treading calmly in a still center pool, a great floating melon, a gray precursor who fiercely promised to survive brief man if granted this space (Rob felt that, never brought it to conscious thought; like men of any age, much less of his youth and degree of training, Rob thought very little). Then the younger boy had seen it and yelled "Yonder, yonder!" and the older boy had shot, reloaded, shot—four quick times. His aim had seemed fine; the turtle had sunk (dead, hurt, or fleeing); both boys had sat down then and waited for the river to offer up news of death or another escape.

Rob had said to himself with no further waiting, "I will give them something"—the sight of his body in air, a sure end. That became his huge wish, the one known feeling subduing all others, the job at hand—"I can show them what they've done" (intending by *them*, at first, ranks of people from his parents forward but finally these boys). "*They* need me at least, my message to them."

He had stood up slowly so as not to draw their gaze too soon and had gone to the car to unload his pockets of his wages and the case with the porcelain which had borne the picture of his mother, now canceled. As he'd bent above the seat, he had smelled the food ripening in the dinner pail and had known he was hungry, not a solid bite swallowed in twenty hours. He would eat something first, fall better for the breakfast, leave the empty pail. The boys below would wait, showed no sign of leaving; and word would reach Della that at least he'd finished what she'd bothered to fix: that much of a message to one person likely to regret his leaving. Nothing to Rachel, which he briefly regretted; but she'd given him nothing. Nothing to Grainger.

So he'd gone to the rock again and sat and eaten two pieces of chicken and two cold biscuits; and when he'd reached again for maybe something sweet, had found not a layer of slick waxed paper but a folded page from a cheap school tablet. He'd opened it and seen, sprawled in dim pencil letters, *"Rob, hoping you like this stuff from Della, think about Della in the city, keep smiling, so long for now."* Rob had wadded it tightly and flung it toward the river and had noticed then that the boys were gone, no word from the snapper. Then he'd eaten the remains of the food—wilted celery, good pound cake—and gone to the car and in broad daylight changed his filthy clothes; then had driven on to Richmond, an arbitrary goal.

3

WHEN Polly had shaved him and dried his face, she saw he was dozing; so she tried to go silently and leave him unshaken. He spoke though, eyes closed, "You going far?"

"The cookstove," she said, half-whispering, "—twenty feet from here. Dinner's at one. Speak if you need me."

Rob said "Thank you, ma'm."

She stood and waited; then she said it full voice—"I'm just Polly Drewry. Call me Polly please."

Rob still did not look but he nodded. "All right."

Then a force in her—held twenty years by locks of gratitude, safety, steady reward—rocked; then spilled. She came back a step toward Rob and said, "You've come for yourself, just yourself? Is that it?"

Rob looked. She was older by ten years or so. Her skin had thinned down and paled in these minutes. She was on some cliff of her own, alone. He smiled and whispered as if she were the sleeper, "Oh yes ma'm, for me. I'm a free-will agent. You can cook in peace."

She also smiled but could not rush the fullness and calm to her face. Her top teeth showed through the paper of her lip, and she did not risk another speech till the door. There she stopped and said it again, not turning, "Say Polly please." Then she left and shut the door firmly behind her.

Rob said "Polly" once aloud and tried to settle back to rest, his exhaustion so great that he did not object to the thought of being found asleep and helpless by a father he had not seen for twenty years, of whom he had no physical picture or knowledge of intent. He slept for an hour in the room that offered no threat to his peace, though after forty minutes the door opened quietly and Forrest stood silent on the sill looking in. When Rob slept on, Forrest stepped forward to him and waited four feet from the chair, looking down; then when that didn't stir him, Forrest went to his own desk, bright by the windows; and turned one picture face-down and went out.

4

It was Polly who woke him. She softly whistled a two-note phrase as introduction, more wind than music; then she said "Dinner please."

Rob had gone deeper down than a casual nap, and he came up slowly against his mind's will. When his eyes broke open, they were fixed on the room not on Polly at the door; and since he did not know either at first, he studied the room before facing her—one wall of books, lined square and neat, faded and used; three bare cream walls (a fireplace in one with a plain brown mantel, its shelf populated with souvenirs; in another, two windows and between them a desk, papers laid on its top at strict right angles). Rob was still unconfirmed in his whereabouts, still half-asleep. He turned to the woman.

"I know you are tired," she said, "but it's ready."

Rob stood. She stepped aside in the door and waved him through. In the light hall again, he looked back to her, awaiting guidance.

So she said "Just here," and walked on before him through an opposite door by the picture of *The Altar of Augustan Peace.*

Rob touched his uncombed head with both flat palms; then followed her in—another light room, a small round table set plentifully. A man on the far side, standing, turned to Rob. A sizable wait.

She said, "Take the seat by Mr. Mayfield. There."

The man said "Robinson. Please" and bowed slightly.

There were three places laid. Forrest stood by the farthest one, near the window; and though his face and voice were pleasant, he did not move forward to greet Rob directly. So Rob said "Thank you, sir" and aimed for the middle chair, four feet from his father's. After two steps he thought, "I am on the bottom of the James after all"; he seemed to be struggling upright to walk through millions of tons of fast dark water. He stopped short of goal and said, "Excuse me. I'm dirty from work. I came here from work." He looked round for Polly to mention the shave. She was gone, just his father.

Forrest said, "I'll take that as a compliment then."

"How so?" Rob said.

Forrest smiled. "That you hurried."

It seemed necessary here to tell pure truth—new room, new chance. Rob also smiled, a hard expense. "*Ran*," he said, "—more *from* than *to*."

Forrest waited as if he were also submerged and must turn dim echoes into usable words; then he actually laughed. "That's the purpose of legs." He stepped to the middle chair and offered it to Rob. "They've run you to this." Then he turned to the open door on his right. "Polly, *food*. We're sinking."

"Rescue," she said, appearing at once, both hands full and steaming. Rob found he could cross the rest of the space.

5

THEY had eaten calmly with sparse but easy talk—Rob's trip, his job, the quality of the day after undue rains. Any silence that had threatened had been promptly filled by Polly, not with chatter but funny memories—a recent letter from her aging father on his year-long attempt to sell his museum to the federal government, then the state of Virginia, then (rejected by those) to the other Confederate States in order of secession till finally he had given it to a Baptist boy's school in north Alabama and wound up paying for the crating and freight, and no invitation to come and caretake it—which had been half his plan. When she'd brought them the hot rice pudding though, she'd left—pleading work upstairs—and Forrest had said in the first moment's quiet, "One thing first: will you spend the night?"

Rob had said "Yes" at once, mildly pleased to say it.

"Then you'll want to continue your nap now, won't you? We'll have all evening to talk, when you're rested."

Rob had thought, "Maybe my main trouble is I'm tired." He had said, "Yes sir. I am no good now, the shape I'm in."

So Forrest had led him to the study again, a cot draped fully in a paisley shawl; and said, "I have got to go to school for a while. Polly will be here if you need help. Meanwhile you can die-to-the-world in peace." Then he'd shut him in; and for a second time, the room gave Rob an oblivion as simple as any in a cradle, as bare of demanding memory or image, as untouched by knives of past or present, the future blank.

He woke in the light of late afternoon on his back, eyes open on the high wide ceiling. Its unbroken stretch seemed an emblem, an earnest, of plainer life; a field on which he might outline now—with no threat of veto or external change—a life he could walk through with pleasure and generosity, not only having skills and gifts to give but easily finding the hands to receive them, hands behind which would lie faces he could honor, faces he would need. He began, as he had so often when a boy on summer mornings before the house woke, to write with his mind on the patient plaster surface—imaginary words inscribed by his eyes but clear and straight in his customary script: *Robinson Mayfield, twenty-one years old; a one-story home under old oak trees never struck by lightning, Sylvie in the kitchen, three miles in the country from a crossroads town where his two parents live in their own large house which he and his older brother and sister visit on Sundays and holidays for dinner; a wife two years his junior, dark-haired and a whole head shorter when standing before him, though her eyes greet his eyes four inches away as she turns each morning in early light and wakes him slowly to welcome his body in the secret leisure of their own house and time, no further drafts on his energy except some job that will yield to the arcs his body must make as it swings toward happiness and finally rest.* Rob saw it, as legible as Moses' law; held it for long healing moments there above him. No visible reason why he couldn't enact it, obey its claims. He heard a dry rustling; his eyes cut left.

His father was seated at the desk also writing (having come back from school at four o'clock and waited awhile for sounds from Rob, then entered to work beside him in silence). He had not seen that the boy was now conscious.

So Rob watched him secretly—at first as an image, a proximate stranger, a man maybe fifty whose skull had refused to acknowledge time. No skin-slides or ruts at the jaw or neck, not a cell of fat to conspire with the downward haul of the earth. The one dark eye which was visible to Rob seemed never to have rested but always studied and not been dimmed by the sights but fueled, made hungrier minute by minute yet *fed*. There was none of the low wail of vacancy in him—the woman's assertion of grievance, desertion, offense endured, deliverance begged.

Rob then looked in the effort to settle some blame on the man for his own stagnant misery, encirclement. He was not by nature an accuser or a judge; but here in this room after so much time, he saw that his life had been *made* after all; that one of the makers was near him now, revealed in the total shape of his guilt—a young girl abandoned, an infant boy, thrust back to a nest which had proved a cage, a magnet attracting to its famished self all human impulse before it could rush to other poles. Rob actually narrowed his eyes, crouched them inward to draw from the face ten feet away a silent acknowledgment of damage done, penalties owed, fines offered (the man had spoken first and had mentioned amends). But nothing would come either out of Forrest or from Rob toward him. No charge, no conviction.

Then he tried affection. Would it have been good as a young boy to wake from hot summer naps on musty sofas to find this man in the same room working, light on this same face (but younger, gentler, still useful for years)? Rob relaxed his eyes, the cords of his own face, and waited whole minutes. Nothing again. He had never wanted this man, could not now, would not ever. He spoke to be speaking, no intent but sound. "This is a pretty good house you've got" (he'd forgot Forrest saying it would be his in time).

If Forrest was startled, he gave no sign. He answered while writing a final phrase—"For ninety years old, it's doing all right. Your great-grand-father, who was Forrest before me, built it hand-over-hand—just himself and two slaves—in 1835. A gift for his bride, whatever bride he'd get. And with such a dry house, he found one quick—Amelia Collins, somewhat his inferior. They moved in in '36—sold one slave, both were single men—and had my father (your grandfather Rob) in March '39. Then old Forrest fell dead—a master carpenter, on a roof—and she lived on here, a seamstress and candy-maker, sixty some years: most of them alone. Kept the Yankees out though, kept the roof and walls standing when most of Richmond fell. Just pure force of will; she wouldn't be buried."

Rob said "Did you know her?"

"I didn't, no, I'm sorry to say. In the years my own father lived with us, she wouldn't speak to him, wouldn't meet his wife, wouldn't even so much as acknowledge our births—mine and Hatt's."

Rob said "He had left her." It was not a question.

"That may have been. He never spoke a word about it to me. I thought she was dead. But then I was five years old when he vanished, just saw him one more day before he died. He explained it to Polly. He came back and lived here with her, you see—his mother Amelia till she died in her eighties. He went shortly after."

Rob passed up the questions of what explanation and why to Polly. He looked round the space again. "Whose room was this?"

Forrest thought awhile. "Grainger's," he said. "That's where I come in. Before that, I think it was some kind of pantry. When my father died it was cram-full of junk. Then when I moved here, we cleared it for Grainger. He slept where you are—why the cot's so small: he left at thirteen."

Rob nodded but had no question to ask.

His father said "How is he?"

"Waiting," Rob said.

"For what?"

"He says *Gracie*; she's still in Philadelphia, sucking money like a funnel."

Forrest said, "Oh no; on us, on us. He is waiting on us, the Mayfields, his people. You know who he is?"

Rob said, "He told me; old Rob's grandson."

Forrest said, "Apparently. No reason to doubt it. No doubt we've got kin, all shades and grades, scattered broadcast all along the eastern seaboard; my father needed frequent company." He smiled.

Rob responded. "I suspected that; may run in the family."

Still smiling, Forrest said "It skipped a generation."

Rob showed pleasant doubt.

Forrest shrugged. "Not entirely." He paused long enough to reassume seriousness. "What else has he told you?—Grainger, I mean."

"That you taught him a lot; that he lived with you as long as he could; that then he went back to Bracey, kept his old grandmother; went to war in France; that you asked him to come on here to school but he found a girl, the Gracie I mentioned."

Forrest said, "Go back. Did he say why he left me?" His face showed the matter was calmly urgent.

Rob worked to recall. "No sir, he didn't; just why he didn't come here to school from the war."

Forrest said "The girl."

Rob said, "Well, her and the fact you didn't write to him till the war was over. He had missed hearing from you."

Forrest shook his head once. "He hadn't heard from me in thirteen years. He left *me*, you see. Most people have. I had offered him a life well past his own hopes. But he ran back to Bracey; should have gone to Maine at least."

Rob saw he was in the presence of a pain which had not yet decided it could bear exploration. He said to himself "For once I'll wait"; so he didn't speak but sat upright to the edge of the cot, then leaned against the wall.

Forrest said "You've seen Bracey."

"Through something of a haze as you probably heard; but yes sir, I have."

"How was my sister?"

Rob said, "Friendly but baffled a little"; he meant by his visit, his own behavior.

His father said "Crazy. Solitary desolation."

"You left her," Rob said.

"Everybody did. It was leave her or *be* her, turn into her ghost. She was far too kind, our mother's child. I had to work, you see—work or strangle in misery—and the work was here."

Rob said, "I thought you were teaching in Bracey. Grainger showed me your little private house on the hill, where the man shot himself."

Forrest studied the boy for malice, found none—if anything, a courteous puzzlement: *He's accepted my dinner, my cot for tonight; he thinks he owes me attention now.* Forrest said, "Awhile back, you spoke of running." He stopped at that.

Rob nodded. "Yes sir, running *from* not *to*."

Forrest smiled. "I was doing both," he said, "twice as hard as you and some years older."

"The *to* part was just teaching poems to Negroes?"

Anger stood up in Forrest's throat—he thought it was anger and felt he must down it; but waiting, he knew it was memory. "I forgot your mother was a Kendal," he said, "—Kendal and Watson, mean streaks on both sides." Then he felt he had no right to blame, having passed on the Mayfield and Goodwin hungers (the victim's eyes) but not stayed around to help forge the polar strains into one working man, both true and merciful. Yet he begged no pardon. He said in his normal voice, "The *to* part was Margaret Jane Drewry, called Polly. I thought you'd seen that and would understand, thought you were old enough to honor that."

"I am," Rob said.

But Forrest had more. "I've had two accounts of your own recent troubles—troubles or mischief: please help me distinguish. Hatt sent a rather high-strung tale of your visit; and Grainger broke a fifteen-year-long silence and swallowed much pride to write me that you had gone past him and his power to help. Don't tell him I told you; he's a generous heart and acts by his lights, no easy lights to follow; but he's why I spoke up and asked you here. Nobody's said what your trouble is. I thought I would show you what I had to give though and hope that would help."

Rob thought and then smiled. "The dinner was good; the nap was needed."

Forrest said, "I meant a good deal more than that."

"I'm sorry," Rob said, "and I'm here to watch."

Forrest said, "You've seen it, the best part anyhow—she shaved you and fed you. The other parts are this house, a good still place, and the work I do both here and at school."

Rob said, "Sir, pardon me. I *am* half-Kendal (you chose a Kendal, no fault of mine); and I can be hard—you're not the first human to tell me that—but I don't mean to be one thing more than honest in saying: how on God's earth can you help me by showing me pictures from your life here when you barely know more of me than my name? You don't even know what's troubling me, what one damned day of my life is like."

Forrest nodded. "I'm free. I'm ready to hear."

Rob waited in silence for a reason to tell it, a reason for being here at all. It came—*There is nobody else to listen; nobody with the patience to hear it out or the calm not to panic, not to use it against me, or the good sense to guess what festers all in it, the guts to pick it out*—so he said, "I wake up at six in the morning to a bell that sounds like Jesus at Judgment. I go to my wash bowl and clear up my eyes and brush my teeth. Then I lie back down and say my prayers; I like to be halfway clean for that. I just say the names of the ones I love or am worried about and 'Thy will be done.' Then I may have a little quick fun with my body: you asked for this now;

and you're getting it straight (not every morning certainly—sometimes I've had that seen to otherwise the previous night—but morning is of course when I'm not worn out). Then I put on my trousers and my undershirt and go downstairs to the hotel kitchen—I live in a rundown springs hotel—and get some hot water from the cook and shave on the backporch and look at the mountain standing up there before me. I'm not that much of a nature lover, but a full-sized mountain with a falls and laurel does help me get started if I wake up low. Then I put on my shirt which I bring down with me and sit at a table on the same long porch and eat a big breakfast cooked by that same girl. There are other people present—other men on the crew, the hotel owner (checking up on the portions, though he never says 'Stop'), and Grainger waiting table—but I say very little that early in the day: my head's still frozen. And nobody there's got a claim on me anyhow. Grainger maybe; I'm friendly to him. By the time we are finished, Grainger's brought out our dinners all packed in buckets by the cook (ten cents); and we head out to the crossroads and wait a few minutes for the crew truck. That's half of my day. The other half is evening. The eleven hours in between, I widen the old road down through the pass, eastward toward money—slowest work known and dangerous and dirty but it pays fairly well, and I've learned it fast. Then evening as I said. It generally comes."

Forrest said, "Wait. Do you like the work?"

Rob thought it half-through and laughed. "Wouldn't everybody like to blow up rocks? Of course the novelty wears off." He waited. "No sir, *like* is not part of it. It's what I'm doing to wear me out till something harder comes; and you see, I'm young with a good deal of strength; so it doesn't even tire me more than half of the time." He laughed again; he had talked himself through another narrow passage—his father's face agreed. "I get to the hotel and wash off the dust and go downstairs at just about dark and eat my supper in the dining room, whatever time it is. Me and two Roberts boys from Jennings' Ordinary who work on the crew are the only three regular paying guests, plus a dogeared drummer every week or so; so they hold supper for us, and we all eat together—Mr. and Mrs. Hutchins and Rachel their daughter, the Roberts boys, me, and Grainger serving every good thing Della cooks (she's the girl I mentioned—till Grainger came, the only black face in sight around there). That's generally pleasant. Mr. Hutchins has some pretty grand ideas about the amount of money that's going to stream toward him down our new road—he's sixty-some and remembers the time when his mother had twenty guests a night from May through August—so he's got Grainger also working on repairs: some whitewashing, changing a board here and there. His main aim now is to get the spring covered, new shingles on the springhouse, lattice on the sides. But far as I'm concerned, he's been decent to me. He trusts me with Rachel, who has not been well; but he's right to trust me. I've been decent to her, clean as a pin. Most evenings after supper I sit down with Rachel on the dark sideporch. It helps her to talk—she talks, I listen. She's been a nervous girl all her life it seems, which is twenty years; but her father decided after this past Christmas that she had T. B. or the warning signs and sent her off to some little chest place in Lynchburg, her mother in tow. She's strengthening now and talks a lot about her future which I'm afraid she thinks means me; she counts on me, I think. I've tried not to fail her so far as I'm able—which hasn't been easy, considering that two or three nights a week, once Rachel has gone upstairs to bed (at ten, Father's orders), I get to stroll out and visit the colored: Grainger if he's up, which usually he isn't since he turns in soon as he's finished supper dishes, but mostly Della. She's younger than Grainger, younger than me, and a restless sleeper; so I pay her little calls, and she lets me in."

Forrest said, "That's being friendly to Grainger?" He smiled slightly, falsely, so as not to stop Rob.

Rob nodded at once. "No doubt about it. I waited till I saw he had passed up the chance, even asked him about it before I moved. I'm keeping her out of his way, you see, so he can go on waiting Gracie in peace."

Forrest said, "I told you what he's waiting for"; but he motioned Rob on.

"If Grainger is waiting on me, you mean, to bring him happiness from God on a tray, he's simpler than he looks. I let him trail me, I listen to him talk (he'll talk you dead if you just sit still), I waited till I saw he had no intention of visiting Della in the same building with him; then I lived my life. I enjoy human company; I take it when offered if it warms my eye and comes bearing no due-bills or claims." Rob had stumbled, in that, on a door he had really not known to exist; a door concealed near the pit of his throat—he felt it now as keenly as though it had locus and heft and hinges. It opened inward on a small low room, white, utterly bare. He stared at the sight and said, "Father, please listen. I was twenty-one years old five months ago. That may seem the wink of an eye to you; it has been my life. And if you've sat here those twenty-one years, eating good hot meals from a white housekeeper and thinking your son down in Fontaine, N. C. was laughing non-stop at his little happy life, I can tell you he wasn't. Right now, today, let me guarantee it to you—Hell, look at me, sir. I was raised in her spare time by my Aunt Rena and black lonesome Sylvie while my own mother, that I loved like the world, was tending her father who was due to die but is still to my knowledge as healthy as most fieldhands at harvest, barring strokes and pain (I mean he won't die)."

Forrest said, "Most mothers have to nurse somebody—you never had to fight a brother or sister—but a day's a long time, lot of chances in a day. I'm sure Eva gave you more than you grant."

"She didn't," Rob said.

"What did you want?"

"What you wanted, I guess."

"But she married me."

"And bore me all bloody." Rob had said that quietly, no trace of pride or pity. Then he stared at the small green rug at his feet and scuffed it slowly. When he looked up again, his face (his whole body) wore the silent still radiance which he'd previously shown to only three people— Rena, Min Tharrington, Rachel Hutchins. Helpless he turned to his father with it now, not knowing it had passed through his father to him from vanished ranks of Mayfields.

Forrest failed at first to see it. He said, "She never wanted either one of us—me because I was me, you because you were mine. You are dreadfully mine, my father's and mine—the way we were at least. Now you have come this long way to show me. I'm grateful." Forrest stopped as if at an end. He thought he had finished, seen the sight to be seen. But the boy held still; so he looked on at him and saw him at last, grand in his face as the young Alexander horned like Ammon, in all his form like Aeneas at Carthage (*ante alios pulcherrimus omnis*, before all others most beautiful); and made by Forrest, the sole remains of his old unhappiness—those famished dreams of an aging boy, corrosive hungers but potent and eating at this boy now. Forrest leaned out and pled in a gentle whisper, "Oh Jesus, Son, change. Change now while you can. Find someone to help you and start your life."

"Yes sir," Rob said and intended to obey, ignoring the live working presence of Eva in all his fibers (as Forrest had forgot it through happiness and years).

6

THAT evening when she'd fed them a second time and seen them rush off in Rob's car so Forrest could show him the school while daylight lasted and then to the last night of Pola Negri in *Shadows of Paris*, Polly put fresh sheets on the study cot and turned in early, puzzled by tiredness (she was seldom tired), and slept at once. No fear or grudge of which she would have spoken or privately thought—awake by day.

In her sleep she walked through a large busy town, strange from the first and increasingly frightening as she lost her way, whatever way she'd had, and was finally forced to stop one stranger after another and ask directions to the Drewrys', her father's. She was clearly herself, a full-grown woman with her present skills and knowledge, not a child or senile; but the strangers all treated her as shameful, repulsive. All of them were men, no woman in sight, and would either turn from her in scorning silence or give her some scrap of direction so brief as to lead her farther into loss and confusion. She knew less of where she was with every step till she'd come to the gloomy heart of the town where dark old houses of the poor leaned together, propping one another in a useless struggle against decay. She stood at the junction of two narrow streets in stinking mud and was desperate. A Negro boy came from an opposite alley, walked too close on her, and stopped and said, "You never going to find it. You want me to show you?" She could not speak but nodded, and he took her hand. She thought, "At least he is not shamed by me," though her own hot wrist (which he ringed with dry fingers) was pained by his touch. He led her a long way till she understood that where she had met him had been no heart of misery but a limb, a pale extremity. They walked through streets past houses so poor she could feel their odor, the scent of offense, like a scalding poultice across her mouth and eyes. Then she realized that the boy had left her, vanished in silence; but she found that she now knew her way somehow—the Negro's grip had conveyed it like grease through her skin. She went another fifty feet and stopped at a house right down in the street, no sidewalk or steps. She knew she was there. Dry curls of the dark brown paint on the door fell at her knock, and more as it opened. An old woman—white, straight, clean for the place, stiff white hair like foam round her head, a long face strong as a flagstone slab, as blank and un-knowing. Polly said, "Where is Mr. Drewry please?" The old woman dried both hands on her worn skirt, working to recall. At last her voice was older than her face—"With Jesus in Glory, I hope, but dead." Polly said, "I have come here to stay with him." The old woman stood on, now blocking the door. Polly said, "I'm his daughter. He expected me." The old woman nodded. "No he didn't," she said, "and I know who you are. You are Margaret Jane. But you can't stay here; the young man is here." Polly looked past the woman and could see in the dark room a single man, dark-haired, seated at a table examining his hands as if they were one thing in all this filth that bore close study, might yet prove precious. He did not look up, so he had no face; but the old woman said, "You can stand in this room a minute and rest"; and Polly saw that the woman was her mother, secretly survived but ancient and ruined. Undoubtedly her. Polly took the offer, entered and stood one stifling minute in the room crammed with heat, the odor of rancid lard in the walls; then was led out silently and shut in the street.

She was wakened by the front door opening downstairs. She half-sat up and—stunned, pulling for breath—listened for voices: Forrest's first, low, "I'll see you to bed and leave you to sleep; I know you're exhausted"; then Rob's young and clear, "No sir. I could talk if you want to talk." Their steps down the hall to Grainger's old room, its door shut behind them, their laughter and talk stripped of words by the thick walls, the oak door, but not of their meaning. Their glad relay of muffled exchanges came at her like the lucid sentences of blame, announcement of desertion. Her life discarded.

She lay back and waited in thick hot darkness for the sound of Forrest leaving, coming upstairs to bed. After nearly two hours by the chime of the station clock, a half-mile away, she heard him on the stairs—quiet not to wake her. He passed her open door (no pause, no audible thought); went on to his own room, poured a glass of stale water, drank it, undressed, breathed the regular rhythms of sleep at once. The downstairs was silent.

Polly said to herself, "Sleep, goose. Just a dream." And later she slept, though a wading in shallows, no cleansing fall. She had had no previous such dream or threat in the thirty-nine years since killing her mother.

7

WHEN Forrest had left him, Rob did not try to sleep. His afternoon nap and the unexpected curious excitements of the trip, transfusions of life, had him wide awake and more nearly on the edge of the sense of a *turn* than at any time since March—the chance at least of continuance and change, departure from childhood. So he stripped to his underpants and studied the room, books first since books were the main thing in sight. He passed them quickly. Almost half were in Latin or Greek, and the half in English was mostly verse. Few stories, no accounts of animals or travels, no life of Jesus telling more than the Gospels, no medical texts of the sort he had always hoped to find and knew to exist—his body's resources all clearly explained, his needs both acknowledged and briskly forgiven, calm guidance given to chances he had never yet taken (or heard of) for sanity and pleasure. Then he went to the mantel where he'd seen what he took to be souvenirs—the cast dried skin of a red rat snake, which Rob could not touch; a small polished disc of petrified wood; the skull of a bird (the size of a bird egg and paper-thin but intricate as gears, also untouchable); an old bronze coin (some fat man's profile—a Caesar, Rob guessed); a small gold medal on a faded ribbon (*The Orator's Medal to Forrest Mayfield, April 1887—Vox Humana, Vox Divina*); and two rough carvings the size of a hand in soft pinebark, old and polished by touch.

Rob reached for one and remembered at once his own crude carvings at six or eight, when a whole afternoon spent carving some horse or bird or girl was not so much an effort at skill as at simple courage, the struggle to fight down the scary feel of pinebark; the dry rind of trees whose hearts were streaming rosin, skin scaly as a lizard's and slightly feverish. A little square man—bullet head, gouged eyes, club-footed, legs wide. Down the man's right leg hung the equally rough indication of genitals. For no reason known to him, other than the need to conquer fear, Rob cradled the man in his large right hand and stroked the bark. Safe, no fear—the bark's own polish, the hardness of his hands after months on the road. He put him down gently beside his mate, a breasted woman, and stood a moment thinking.

He would write his postcards (they had stopped at a drugstore before the picture, and he'd bought three cards of the Richmond sights)—to Della and Sylvie, no thought of consequences for them or himself, only of their pleasure in a distant thought. He would see Della well before the card could reach her, but he owed her that much. Sylvie would use hers as she saw fit, secret or public; there was no predicting (she would sometimes keep letters days or weeks till she found some person she could trust to read them to her).

He went to the desk where he'd laid them and sat, expecting to find a pen or indelible pencil at least. None in sight, only mail of his father's and the stack of school papers on which his father had worked that afternoon. Rob reached for the top one—*Jonathan Simpkin, Last Composition, My Thought Upon 'Laus Deo' by Whittier*, "This poem says Mr. Whittier is glad to hear about the freedom. He is living up north and word come to him. He think about God first thing in Latin." Rob put it back thinking that, so far at least, it matched his own Last Composition except for the errors which his father had patiently corrected in red (Aunt Rena'd checked all Rob's work and saved him often); but who could spend a life knocking s's off the verbs of future masons, farmers; stuffing words into mouths incapable of holding them? (hungry for a damned sight more than words).

Rob remembered what his father had said of Aunt Hatt—"Crazy: loss and loneliness." Was it also the verdict on all known Mayfields?—his father, Grainger, his own moaning self? He would not think that through —thought had done enough already to ruin his trip—but it did cross his mind that, whatever Forrest Mayfield's past or present pains, he had given a first-rate imitation of contentment today: a life in harness to round greased wheels, the wheels rolling quiet and smooth, level ground.

No pen in sight though. Rob opened the one long drawer to hunt, silently; he knew he was now out of bounds (drawers of the Kendal house were private as toilets). Two cheap steel pens, a bottle of red ink, a neat further lot of school work, gradebooks, a small picture-frame face down toward the back. Rob naturally took it, raised it out to the dim hot gooseneck lamp, and looked. His mother and himself, no question of either, though he'd never seen the picture and (despite his age in it—four, maybe five) did not remember the day or the sitting. His mother was gazing dead-level at the camera, her dark hair lustrous and straight as an Indian's rising from a high smooth forehead to a height half that of her face, her full lips pale and entirely closed, though drawn slightly back as if ready to answer or to tell the man No, the darks of her eyes enormously deep and lit by real light, her right brow raised not in anger or question but as if to throw one single line askew. Her right hand was hid in the lap of a fine light summer dress; her left lay free on the arm of the chair. Rob himself stood by that, his own eyes down, as grave as some leader at the end of a life—a white sailor suit, blue-trimmed; a wood whistle on an oddly knotted cord round his neck, untouched. Eva seemed to have borne all the weight of the world, to be bearing it *then* with unquestioned competence, no hint of complaint, only the firm reservation of her eyes as they spoke their sentence, *I am bearing it. I can. I cannot stop you watching.*

Rob touched his dry lips to the cool glass above her. Then he carefully returned the frame to its place and wrote his two cards.

Dear Sylvie, Rob thought about you in Richmond.

Dear Della, Safe trip, much obliged for help, I trust to see you before you see this.

R.M.

Then he wiped the pen clean with paper from the grate, turned out the one light, raised the two windows higher, stripped himself entirely, and lay down to sleep on top of the cover. His troubles though real were as old as he, as natural as his hair or the eggs of his groin and older in power and need than they. His body had learned to live in their presence if he'd only trust his body, surrender his mind. He trusted it now, made a quick sweet resort to its offer of pleasure (no image before him of any living creature: himself a closed engine, adequate and lovely); then he slept. Plain rest.

8

HE woke in clear light to a cool house, still silent. For the fifteen minutes that he lay slowly surfacing, he thought it was only a little past dawn and that he had waked first and must wait for the others. He had started another experiment—that this was his home, this room his room; that his parents were overhead sleeping still or silently conducting the secret rites which parents require, rites which did not exclude him but in fact had summoned his existence and now by repetition insured his continuance, his own eventual manhood. He could bear the thought easily and began to expand it to include the pictured bodies of his father and Polly, their faces in the spreading rictus of joy, both younger than now, unmarked by their lives. Rob had had no prior occasion in his life for such a soothing game and would have run on to the vivid end of his present vision; but through windows the station clock started its chime. He counted ten strokes and thought it was wrong (outside the town was as still as the house); but he jumped up and went to his watch on the desk and found it was ten. Naked, he stood by the windows in dry sun and listened to the house again, straining for news. A child's blank fears—*They are gone or dead.* There seemed to be rare muffled knocks from the kitchen.

Unwashed, Rob scrambled into his clothes; opened the door; stepped into the hall and listened. He was barefoot. The kitchen door was shut. No speaking voices but there were sounds of work with water and metal, so he went there and knocked. A considerable wait.

Polly said "Is it you?"

"—Rob if that's who you mean."

"I did," she said.

He opened. She turned from the sink, not smiling. He saw his bare toes, ugly as most. "Excuse me," he said and pointed to his feet, "I was scared."

"What of?"

"The house sounded empty."

"Your father has gone." She had not yet smiled, and she turned back to scouring a deep black pan.

Rob suddenly laughed. In place on the doorsill, he laughed so long that Polly turned to watch him and, despite her seriousness, was forced to join.

She stopped before him though and said "What's the joke?"

"That he's gone," Rob said. "Lady, he was never here."

She smiled but she said, "I am Polly, again; and yes he was here. He's been here twenty years, wherever else he hadn't been, and will be back by two p.m., I know, if he lives that long." She paused till it reached him. "Are you ready for breakfast?"

Rob remembered. His father had told him last night—he must leave at eight-thirty to teach Bible-class at school, then be monitor at chapel; then preside at dinner for the hundred summer students, his duty once a month. Rob nodded he was ready. "I'll put on my shoes."

"Not for me," Polly said. "Stay cool while you can. Sit down and start your coffee." She went to the icebox and took out four eggs; and Rob moved on to the table by the window, a long narrow table painted red. Polly set the brown eggs in a bowl by the sink, took a thick white mug, and filled it with coffee from a blue enamel pot. She brought it to the table, set it by Rob's hand.

He noticed again her youth in her hands; and when she returned to the stove to cook, he fixed on them in their quick neat work—frying bacon slowly with the gravest care; cracking eggs, whipping, scrambling. Bare of rings, her hands were also unmarked by age or damage, only the intricate cords of her strength obeying her will which was also her wish. Rob's throat was rushed by a hot contentment he had not felt for years, since childhood surely (he recognized the flood but could not remember or pause to recover the rare occasions; they would all involve Eva). He sat and welcomed it, not even so much as worrying to name its cause or end. Polly never looked toward him. His first clear thought was "She likes this work"; then its valid extension, "She is working for me." He had seldom been served in a safe calm room by a young white woman who was not simultaneously pleading for rescue, the chance to accompany his life from that moment. He took a long draft of the hot black coffee and said, "You're a very happy lady; am I right?"

She was spooning the eggs from the pan to a platter. She did not look round; but she said "Well—"; then stopped, clearly searching for an answer. Rob waited and she brought the food over to him—the eggs and meat, then a plate of fresh biscuits. He thanked her and she went to the opposite chair and stood straight behind it, her hands holding firm on the thick side-rails. Her face was serious though not deeply troubled. She said again "Well" and smiled. "Half-yes, I guess. I don't have to answer to 'Lady' every day. Many don't think I'm that, but many are meaner than mad dogs in August. I think I've been happy though—by nature, I mean. I have to be, don't I?"

Rob said "Why?"

Polly studied him carefully; then pulled out the chair and sat upright, not leaning toward the table. "Your eyes look strong. You can see good, can't you?"

Rob nodded (he was eating).

"And you're twenty-one years old?"

"Yes ma'm," he said.

"Then you ought not to ask." With one hand she stirred a large circle of air before her chest, by which she meant her life, her surroundings.

Rob said, "I'm sorry. I'm not the brightest Mayfield."

Polly studied again. "You may be," she said, "and don't all the time be begging for pardon that you don't need. You haven't harmed me but someday you might, so you don't want to wear out my pardons now." She had brought herself to smile.

Rob nodded. "Sure. *Damn* me."

"That's not called for either yet," she said. They both paused then— Rob eating, Polly watching. At last she leaned forward and offered him a glass dish of fig preserves; she stayed that much closer (just her hands on the table edge) and said, "Could you tell me why he asked you to come? I mean, I'm glad to meet you—"

"He didn't," Rob said. "It was my idea. He heard from Grainger that I was in trouble and wrote me to offer what help he could; but coming after twenty-one years of silence, it didn't exactly thrill me, you know. I figured I had got by that long without him."

"Your mother left *him*."

"So they tell me," Rob said, "so he told me last night. But why does he have that picture of Mother and me as a boy?"

Polly said, "It appeared on his birthday one year. I think he asked for it. You better ask him."

"No matter," Rob said.

"Oh it may be," she said, "to you and him." She paused. "You were telling me about your visit."

Rob faced her, eye-level. "You want me to leave. I'm leaving once I eat." His face could have been read as angry or joking.

She worked at reading him, decided on anger. Her own eyes suddenly filled with tears. She struck the table gently with both flat palms. "*Yes,*" she said.

Rob laid down his fork. "How have I harmed you please?" he said.

It took her awhile before she could speak; but she never looked down or hid her face, never loosened the grip of her hands on the table. Finally she could say, "I am not sure it's harm. All I know is I'm scared. I had the worst night of my life last night, saw things I never really hoped to see. I take what is offered to me in sleep as serious, maybe more so than what comes in daylight, but that's just me. You surprised me, you see—whyever you're here. I have answered that same door for more than twenty years; and I don't remember ever letting in one soul that meant me harm—ever answering to one (Grainger came in the back door and left that way). I was brought here by your Granddad Rob; and I tended to him till he died in his sleep—sleep is just as real as day. I was left just a young woman, nowhere to go but back to my funny old dad I mentioned. Then your father came here to see to the funeral; and since he was also at the end of his rope, he asked me would I stay on here and cook; take care of the place. It turned out he'd already got his present job and needed a home. The house of course was his (and his sister's, I guess); and he treated me as decently as anybody ever had in nineteen years. Much more so really; he's a gentleman of God, whatever else he is. If you don't think a nineteen-year-old girl who has grown up in cities and kept a museum of Confederate junk has met a lot of treatment that was far less than decent, then you don't know girls or cities either. Not to mention museums. But you probably do. Anyhow I accepted. He had his job in Bracey till the end of April; so I cleaned around here good and then locked up and went to Washington till May—on the train, one bag. I'm a Washington girl. I had left my dad there a good while before with his museum to tend, when I came down here. He had said to me then, very pleasant but firm, that if I left him not to ever come back. And I nine-tenths believed him (he will change his mind thirty times an hour about himself, but he's set like lockjaw in what he thinks of others); so when I walked up to his Washington door, I didn't know whether he would spit or kiss me. He managed both. At first he pretended he didn't recognize me. I stepped in the open door, bag in hand, and went to the table where he sat selling tickets. He glanced up briefly and then back down and said 'Ladies five cents.' I went along with him. I fished out a nickel, of which there were few, and pushed it toward him. He actually took it, put it in his tin box, pointed to the rooms where his old stuff was and said 'Take your time.' I had to stop it there—I am happy by nature but bad at jokes; they always scare me. I said 'Dad, it's Margaret Jane.' —'I know that,' he said. He was reading the memoirs of P. T. Barnum for the eight-hundredth time and went back to them, really read on awhile; I could see his eyes flicking. I was young enough to figure he was asking me to beg. Well, I've never minded begging; that's all prayer is, except for the few little compliments to God which I'm sure He ignores. I said, 'I have got a two-month vacation till my next job starts; and I've come home to help you.' He still looked down— 'What help would that be?' I said, 'I doubt it'll be any help, now you mention it (I'll cook you some meals); but it might be fun. I'm good-natured, remember?' He thought that over and apparently remembered and pointed to the stairs and said, 'Your bed's where it was, not used since you left.' So I took my satchel and climbed upstairs and found my cubby-hole the way I had left it. The sheets I had slept in my last night at home were still on the bed with my wrinkles in them, my hair on the pillow (I hemstitched the pillowslip at age eleven; I'd know it on the moon). Strangest old bear in the woods, my dad; but from that minute on, he acted like I'd never been gone ten minutes; and we did have fun. We always had, nothing out of the ordinary—talking and teasing. I stayed two months and cooked and cleaned and sold people tickets to see his poor show (by then he had bought a little railroad stock and was halfway solvent); and then your dad wrote me toward the end of April and said everything was straight on the rails and would I beat him there and air-out the house? I washed my few duds and, that night at supper, said 'Tomorrow's the day'; and Dad said 'About time.' I cooked his next breakfast and packed and combed my hair. He was not downstairs when I went to say goodbye, so I caught the streetcar to the 12:20 train and have not been back. I've written of course and he answers now and then if he's got some funny news. I've been right here in the Mayfield house; and excepting the last few weeks of Grainger's stay, I have generally been happy." Polly stopped and sat a moment; then again touched the table with her beautiful hands, this time more nearly caressing than striking. She was smiling mildly.

Rob had eaten throughout her story. Now he set down his fork and said, "Why did you tell me all that please?" His tone and face were pleasant.

She had not lost her way. She knew at once. "To show why I wanted you to leave," she said.

"Then you failed, I'm afraid; or maybe I just failed to understand."

"That's it," she said, still smiling. "I was clear as a bell. *This is all I've got, and I hate for you to take it.*"

"This house, you mean? You can have my share when the great day comes; of course I don't know who else has claims. Maybe Mayfields abound; I suspect they do."

She was grave again and, firm in her purpose, she neglected to offer Rob fresh hot coffee. "Not the house," she said, "though it is a good house; and I'm rightly grateful to it. No you're making me say it when I hoped you would *see*. I mean Forrest Mayfield. He is what I have."

Hearing that, Rob discovered in himself a hardness he had not used in months, more likely in years. He actually thought of Min Tharrington's face as she turned from his meanness four years ago. But again he accepted its demands and said, "Could you live without him?"

"Of course I could; people live blind and dumb with no arms or legs and their backs raw with sores. But I wouldn't want to; I would pray not to—and I'm not a church-goer."

"Me either," Rob said.

Polly thrust to the rank tender center of her fear. "Didn't Eva send you here?" She stopped and flushed deeply, from embarrassment not pain. "Your mother, I mean. He still calls her Eva when he mentions her at all; I've never seen her face."

Rob said "Yes she did," the coldness still in him, though he knew he hadn't lied.

Polly said, "I knew that. I knew she'd try again."

Rob nodded but was silent.

"That picture you saw on Forrest's desk?"

"In his drawer," Rob said.

"Then he hid it from you; it's always been out. She sent him that picture from a clear blue sky on his birthday five years after she'd left him, five years without one word or sign when he'd walked through coals of white fire just to live and forget you both."

Rob said "With you helping."

"So *right*," Polly said. "I was helping like fury. I had met the postman that day, like I said; and here was a little square package for Forrest. I didn't know the writing; but I knew the postmark and knew anything sent from Fontaine, N. C. was bound to harm him. So I hid it at first in the hall-table drawer; he was here eating breakfast, set to leave for school. I didn't know whether I would open it first or burn it; but I lied to him then, just gave him a bill and a card from his sister and said that was all. Then once he was gone, I tried to work and think. The Christian thing was to wait till evening and say it had come in the afternoon mail; he'd at least have evening and night to recover in, whatever the damage. But by noon I was wild and mad and scared; and I brought it back here and opened it as secret as if I was some hateful enemy at night, not his help at noon. I was sick as I did it—the knots in the string—but nothing like as sick as I got to be when I saw those faces: Eva Mayfield and Rob. I stood up to burn it. Who on earth would know? Strings of *pearls* are lost in the mail every day, not to mention pictures of people who left you to struggle alone."

Rob said "What stopped you?"

"The fact I wasn't *sure*. I was nine-tenths certain—I had the post-mark—but, see, I had never seen Eva or you. He'd denied to me that he owned any pictures—said he had her living presence so why take pictures?—and I don't think he lied. You were too young to resemble him yet; he hadn't taken charge of your eyes and mouth the way he has since. I stood at the stove and told myself there was one slim chance that woman and child were somebody else and were safe to us both (there was no note or card in the package, just faces; the letter came the next day, delayed somehow); so I wrapped it back up and put it on his desk with the afternoon mail, and he never gave me one hint of getting it. He was a little quiet at supper, I thought; but that could have just been tiredness from school. Then the next day, the letter in the morning mail. He took it off with him unopened on the streetcar; and still not a word to me, not a flicker. I was sick all through it; but again if he noticed, he kept his own counsel. I knew he was thinking. And I knew very well my life was before him in some kind of balance with you and your mother. Every day when he'd leave, I'd hunt for the letter; I guess it was at school. I am telling you this, though it's my hot shame after sixteen years."

Rob said, "You could leave. You are not chained down."

But she nodded. "I was."

"A baby?" he said.

She shut her eyes, shook her head. "Never. No." She waited and swallowed as if at a knot of dry cloth in her throat. Then she looked again. "I understand a lot from you being here—his past, I mean; what your mother put him through. You are hers all right."

"I am," Rob said. "I'm sorry to be."

"Too late now," she said.

Rob said, "Maybe not. She left me as sure as she left Forrest Mayfield."

Polly shook her head again. "She never left Forrest, not for good, still hasn't. I found the letter. After nearly three weeks, I went in to clean his study one morning; and there stood the picture on his desk. He had framed it. I sat down and tried to study it calmly. I was cold as Christmas. You've seen it yourself; you know what it says even now after years—*Is there some way back?*"

Rob said "I doubt that," though he didn't doubt it.

Polly said, "You wouldn't if you'd read the letter. I found it in his desk drawer; he'd brought it home the same day. It disappeared later and I guess he may have burned it or I'd show it to you now. But I sure God read it three times that day. She started out by asking how he liked his work (she had got some news from Hattie and his Richmond address); then she went on with news from you and her (funny things you were saying, little jobs she was doing—hooking rugs, crocheting for various friends); then she said everything there was going on as ever except that her brother had got married recently and come home to stay with his new little wife till their own house was built some while in the future and that seams were bursting, not to mention people's patience."

"They were," Rob said. "I was sleeping in her room. That was just the true news she was telling him, no begging in that."

"Oh there was," Polly said. "Forrest knew it well. The picture was the begging, and it shook him to the sockets."

"You said he never spoke."

"I can *see*," she said, "and I watched him for days as close as I could; he kept shy of me. In his study always writing, little notebooks he'd take back to school every morning. Then he gradually eased and talked to me more; and one night I went in to where he was working to tell him good night and found him so calm that I got nerve to say 'Is that Eva and Rob?' —'Aren't they lovely?' he said; and I had to agree, looking through his eyes, though for all those weeks (looking just through my own) I had felt like wiping you both off the earth and had prayed for the power." She managed to smile at the end of that; it was clearly an end, a fistula drained.

Rob touched his white cup. "I would give a good deal for some coffee," he said.

"Such as what?" She was playing.

Rob was thoroughly grave. "This much for certain, which I won't take back—I came here purely on my own. I was hurting. He can tell you how. It is not to do with him, not directly. I have not blamed him for anything ever; and I didn't come here with messages or claims from me or anybody. I was down, far down; he asked me to come here, and here I've been. I'm leaving as I said." He began to fold his napkin.

"Your coffee," Polly said and moved toward the stove where the blue pot was steaming. She touched it with the flat of her hand, satisfaction; and brought it to his cup, poured it carefully. On her way to the stove again (her face turned from him), she said, "You've been sick lately, you mean?"

Rob laughed a dry chuff. "—As a dog," he said. "Maybe past curing."

Polly turned to face him and touched her own breastbone with her strong right thumb. "Your chest? Is it that?"

Rob mimicked her gesture in the center of his forehead. "My empty head."

Polly came back and sat while he sweetened his coffee. "Empty of what?"

"Don't make me," Rob said. "He made me last night, and it didn't help at all."

She nodded. "I'm sorry." She waited, Rob drank. Then tracing a delicate curve on the table (over and over, precise and perfect; her eyes on the curve), she said, "I am going to tell you the truth. I am thirty-nine years old so no need to lie. I have loved three people in all that time. My mother died when I was born, so Dad was the first. He never needed me; I've shown you that. The second was Rob Mayfield, long dead. I came here with him and eased his death; he died right beside me, and I never even stirred (and I as light a sleeper as a bird on a bough). The third was your dad—and I trust will be the last." Her tracing finger lifted and her eyes met Rob's. Again she had reached some end of her own.

Rob waited till he saw she had finished her message. It had not reached him, but he first said "Thank you."

Polly nodded. "Very welcome."

Then he said, "How is that meant to help me please?"

She knew he was earnest. "It means I have told you all I know."

"Did you marry my grandfather?"

"No. We spoke about it but he didn't want that. He had run from his children; he had to save them something."

"This house?"

"This house and the few things in it."

"One of which was you?" Rob intended it kindly as plain description.

Polly read his intent. "You could say that." She smiled. "You wouldn't be the first. I was part of his leavings, but I wanted to be."

"Did you marry my father?"

She shook her head slowly. "He is married," she said. "He's also married. You know, your mother. He won't change that, wouldn't change it if he could; and I don't know the law, haven't tried to learn. He has not ever spoken about it to me except that one day I mentioned your picture and he asked weren't you lovely? That broke me from questions." She was smiling still.

"You said a few minutes ago you were happy."

"By nature, I said." She paused, thought it through. "And also by *luck*. They were three kind men, Rob and Forrest especially. I call that luck."

"—That they kept you a servant?"

Again she tested his face for malice, the edge of his voice. "That they cherished me." She had said it gently; but the words drew behind them a flock of feelings—pride, secret joy, continuing hope (however assailed)—that decked her face and shoulders all fresh with a greater beauty of light and depth, victory and promise, than Rob had witnessed on any other form except his own mother's the dawn he had crept home stinking from Flora after high-school commencement and found his mother awake and extending what she never meant to give. Lacked the will to give, lacked the knowledge of how.

"They love you," he said.

"Thank you," Polly said. "That is all my hope. I love them surely. And I've told them, many ways. I can beg for you that you'll have such a life." She waved round her slightly with one slow hand as if all her time and luck were gathered in this warm room and were visible—witness and proof.

Half-smiling, Rob looked. Then he said "Beg who?"

"Well, I pray some," she said. "I mentioned that."

Rob said "Wait please," even held out a staying hand. "I doubt I could bear it."

"Me praying?"

"—Such a life."

"Then you'll die young," she said, "or dry at the heart before your time. No Mayfield has, not in my sight at least."

He waited a good while; his question wasn't idle. "Say what I must do."

"Do you love anybody?"

"My mother," he said.

"Anybody with a chance of lasting you for life?"

"No ma'm," Rob said. "One or two love me."

"Pick the strong one," Polly said.

9

WHEN Rob drove up by the dark hotel, his own frail headlamps were the only light. He cut them; cut the harassed engine; and hands on the wheel still, slumped round a sudden hole in his chest through which the gains of the past two days, gains that had fueled him in calm elation through the long trip back, seemed unstanchably flowing. For the past three hours, he had only thought of sleep (he had no watch but the fact of darkness in Mr. Hutchins' room meant eleven at least, maybe twelve or one); and as he was now, sleep seemed not only desirable but urgent. His strength had measured itself with utter economy, had lasted him to this dark yard precisely.

Yet when he moved, it was not toward the side stairs (the second-floor porch, the hall, his room) but back toward Grainger's and Della's rooms. The end of his strength was taking him there in no light at all; there was no moon or stars.

He opened their front door and entered the trapped warm air of their hall. The door on the left was Grainger's. Rob stroked it twice with his knuckles. No answer. More firmly, two knocks. No voice or move. He felt down the ribbed pine of the door to the china knob and turned it and pushed.

Grainger's close black air—every window chinked shut—stood to meet him, a solid element neither foul nor harsh but such as no white man could lay down around him or breathe for long, a separate diet. Rob took a step inward and said once "Grainger—" Nothing, though Grainger slept lightly as a rule. He took a second step, raised his voice and called again. When only silence answered, Rob felt so strongly that he needed Grainger now that he walked all the way through the foreign air till his hands found the edge of Grainger's bed, then blindly searched it. The covers were thrown back, the thin pillow crumpled; and though they were hotter than the room—freshly used—they were empty of Grainger. Rob stood and tried once more, whispering "Grainger?"

Then he went out quickly to the hall—Della's door, stood and strained to hear. Nothing again. Or was there a single whimper, smothered? Rob did not knock but found the knob easily and opened full. The same thick element; the dry sounds of movement, skin on cloth.

"Something wrong?"

"Della?"

A stupified wait, more movement. "Something wrong?"

"May be. Della?"

"You back," Della said.

Rob could not speak, for gratitude.

"You hungry?" she said.

He knew that he was, that likely she had some cold bread on her bureau, that what he wanted first was to ask after Grainger; but he said "You alone?"

Della laughed. "Is a rock?"

He said "Yes" as if she'd intended an answer, then began at the buttons of his shirt and was naked in fifteen seconds. He stood in the pile of shed clothes and said "Where is Grainger now?"

"In Heaven if the Lord be merciful to *me*."

"He's not in his room, but his bed is warm."

"You go on back and wait for him then and keep it warm, not waking me up when I need rest to talk about a fool that I hadn't seen since dark tonight."

Rob regretted his bareness, however concealed, and knew he should quietly dress and leave—Della to the few hours' sleep before dawn when she'd rise to cook; himself to ruinous solitary night, his heart still draining.

"You going or staying?" Her voice was as harsh as in dealing with Grainger and bore to his nose a pure raw gust of the metal deep in her, the actual high smell of fingered brass, the shock of tin on his own back teeth.

But he went on toward her and met her silent welcome—her thin white gown shucked quickly; her short close bones and hot dense skin extended as an unseen harbor, a bed, in which he could hunt again the consolation of permitted triumph. Hunt and, as always, find. Even as he hooked his bristling chin on the hinge of Della's shoulder (he had never touched her mouth) and felt for her hipbones to haul her upward (she never moved at first of her own accord, only toward the end), he knew he would win this time as always. One good thing which had never yet refused him. It didn't now.

Exhausted as he was from the trip, the real *journey*, the whole elaborate net of his senses poised itself slowly (no haste, no fear); cast itself surely and caught its small prey—a spot on his forebrain the size of a child's hand in which his total body met a rest so perfect, reward so sufficient, that he did not resent Della's own private seizure, her hoarse employment of what seemed now a distant county of a country at peace. Nor the cries she stifled in the heel of her hand, a blind fed puppy.

"You all right?" she said.

"Now," he said.

"Well, you back like I said." She touched the knob at the back of his neck, the crest of his spine beneath which his powers of movement lay bound in a simple cord.

"Not for long" Rob said.

"Where you headed?"

"Out of *here*."

"When you leaving?"

"Not sure."

"Who you taking?"

Rob paused, uncertain of her meaning.

"You come here with Grainger. Who you taking when you leave?"

Rob thought that he knew. For the first time today, in all his life, he thought that he knew who would leave with him; go with him toward a life he could live. He could not tell Della, not now in her arms—rank, wet with her gift.

10

TEN minutes later, threading rocks and roots in the yard, he passed his car on the way to sleep; and Grainger's voice whispered "You all right, Rob?"

Rob was too tired for fear, but he stopped and searched the dark before answering. He thought he detected some signs that Grainger was sitting on the nearside runningboard, so he said "Where you been?"

Grainger said "You the traveler."

Rob came closer to him, stopped five feet away. It was Grainger; Grainger's heat reached him even through the cool air of mountain night. He could not now remember why he'd sought Grainger first half an hour ago or what he might have said if Grainger had been waiting; but he knew he must not cheat him now and leave without some greeting. Rob went to the car and sat beside him on the hard runningboard and finally said, "You have been to New Jersey and Maine and France."

Grainger waited awhile. "You been to Richmond?"

Rob also waited. "Yes thank you," he said.

"See your daddy?"

"Yes."

"Miss Polly?"

"Yes."

"They doing all right?"

"Good as anybody else," Rob said.

"They treat you nice?"

"Very nice," Rob said. "Good food, good bed."

"You like your daddy?"

"All right," Rob said. "Too early to know."

"He going to help you?"

Rob said "He tried."

"Talked to you a lot?"

Rob laughed. "He's a talker. Nothing wrong with that Polly's public-speaking either."

"Never was," Grainger said. He laughed, then waited. "He get you a job?"

"He said he would try. I didn't promise nothing."

"If you were a nigger, he could send you to school."

Rob said, "That might be a good idea."

"—Being nigger or smart?"

"Some of both, I guess."

"Too late," Grainger said.

"Could be," Rob said, "but I may keep trying. I just now came from rubbing on black." He pointed toward the quarters, dark as it was.

Grainger said "I seen you."

"Where were you then?"

"Out here. I mean I heard you coming out."

Rob said, "Where were you before that? I went to your room."

"I been looking for you."

"You'll get yourself shot, poking round at night. These mountaineers don't give you time to explain, specially if you're dark."

Grainger said, "You the one been poking, not me. More people shot for poking than looking."

"Where the Hell you think I was hiding round here? Didn't Della tell you I had gone on a trip?"

"Wouldn't ask Della for moisture in a drouth. I knew where you were. I was waiting not looking. I couldn't get to sleep. I was down by the spring—worked there all day; got the new shingles on. Start cleaning it tomorrow."

Rob hauled himself to his numbing feet and walked a step. "Stop waiting," he said. "For God's sake, stop. I'm back. Day's coming."

"I'll see," Grainger said. He also stood, came toward Rob, and easily found Rob's wrist with his fingers. He ringed the wrist tightly and twisted three times before Rob pulled free. "If day come," he said (he was whispering again) "you look at that good; see did dark rub off. Did—it come off Grainger. Grainger give you your wish."

11

At the hint of day five hours later, in Richmond not Goshen, Forrest Mayfield's eyes opened fully from sleep, awake in the instant, though he'd slept only five hours since turning in at one after finishing a letter to Rob in the study. He had stayed on at school till three on Sunday; then had come home to find Polly gone, no note. He had read until five—a search in Vergil—when he'd heard her come in, climb straight to her room, and shut her door quietly. She often took walks; he knew she was low from Robinson's visit, a state which he counted on time to repair; so he'd read on till six; then despite their having late supper on Sundays, he wondered at her silence and went to the foot of the steps and listened. Nothing at all. He'd called out mildly, "Are you starving me from home?" and after a while, she opened her door (her face webbed with sleep) and said "No it's yours." —"Please feed me then," he'd said and waited smiling as she went back to wash her face. He helped her in the kitchen; and they ate with few words on the smallest subjects (Polly ate very little). He had tried to crystallize in his mind one thing he could say to satisfy her, to acknowledge his thanks and the size of her care, to honor her fears but belittle them gently. Nothing useful would come, only lines with multiple edges, all keen— "Did you take to him?" "Can we help him at all?" "Should we try now or have we already done enough?" So while she cleared the table, Forrest sat and watched her face till at last he could say, "Is there anything you need to ask me, Polly?" She had drawn a pan of water and begun to wash dishes before she said (her face still to Forrest), "I need to know how much is changed." —"Nothing" rushed to his lips; but he'd held it in, suspecting a lie; and when he'd stood to go do Monday's preparations, he'd said, "I will tell you as soon as I know." She had nodded, not turning; and he'd worked on his lessons till he heard her turn in, then had started the necessary letter to Rob. When he'd finished and climbed to bed at one, he had not paused at Polly's open door, though he'd noticed the darkness and silence beyond it and felt the intensity of baffled waiting.

Now at dawn, a little startled to be thoroughly rested by so little sleep, Forrest lay in cool sheets on his narrow bed and consulted his body with the flats of his own broad hands under cloth. He did not often touch himself at leisure and, though he had never despised the offers of pleasure (even transport), he lacked the voluptuary's constant wonder in the constant resources of self, simple meat. But what pleased his hands now was

firm lean health—the fact that, with no conscious effort by him of exercise
or diet, he had withstood years; his body had ignored these fifty-four years
(or, say, the past fifteen: he looked a man of thirty-eight and felt it),
though he knew there were millions of ambushes gathering, suicides
planned in every cell. With his hands on the hot dry stripes of his groin,
where his long legs became his high full balls (the balls of a boy in the first
rush of power, the embarrassed crest of male generosity), Forrest said to
himself what he suddenly knew and had not known before, "I have chosen
this." It was something that he might have guessed long before—twenty-
one years before, naked in a stream near Panacea Springs, having seen Eva
leave him the final time. He had waited till now—a gift from Rob? his
letter to Rob? Polly's separate fear one room away? He was roused as
always by real news, by knowledge—roused in spirit.

So he rose, poured water in his china bowl (running water was piped
no higher than the kitchen), washed his mouth and eyes, and walked to
Polly's doorway.

Her eyes were open; she was facing him. She lay on her right side and
faced him unsmiling; her left arm splayed back behind her grotesquely,
boneless or wrenched.

Forrest wanted to speak. If he'd been fully dressed or covered by
darkness, he could have stood ground on the sill and said, "Very little is
changed. Maybe nothing at all. Whatever may flow from these two days
will not move you." But he stood in pale daylight in the crumpled absurd-
ity of underwear at the end of her gaze; so he did what he seldom did at
all, maybe ten times a year, and never till now without her permission. He
walked quickly in and sat at the foot of Polly's bed. They were silent
awhile; then he said "Have you slept?"

"I think so," she said. She looked to her window; the green shade was
down. "What time is it now?"

With his hand Forrest sought her shin through cloth, a muffled blade.
"Five-thirty," he said.

Polly did not move her leg from his grip.

He took that to be her latest permission; and waiting a moment to
allow her denial, he touched the sheet on the crest of her shoulder and
drew it down enough to allow his entry into space that was neat as if she'd
made it freshly to greet his arrival and cool as the coolest hour of the night
which had left him so ready—the night through which, he now understood, she could not have slept. He stayed on his back in the narrow place,
touching Polly nowhere, and fixed on the single black light-cord that hung
from the spotted ceiling like a plumb. It seemed to promise that the
answer he would give—must give in a moment—would be true and just,
merciful and grateful. He waited for words.

Polly touched his arm, with one left finger. Then she raised herself
very slightly from the waist and removed her gown—drew it over her head;
her hair was loose—then dropped it on the clean floor and lay flat herself.

Forrest took that as his best hope of answer. Years of contiguous restraint had given their bodies a gift of speech more lucid than words; their rare full meetings had therefore preserved the power to delight, deepen mystery, appall, but chiefly to confirm in plain detail with a logic as bare as the figures of Euclid their mutual love. They confirmed it now in mutual silence. The sounds around them were the sounds of objects—cloth, wood, iron, the approving air.

Done and rested and the room filling quickly with Monday through gaps at the edge of the shade, Forrest only said, "I must leave in an hour."

"All right," Polly said. "You dress; I'll cook." She raised herself again and fished for her gown. "What you teaching them today?"

"The names of God in fourteen tongues."

She laughed and he joined her.

12

By six-thirty, Rachel in her bed in Goshen had sunk to the lowest shelf of sleep. She had gone to bed early in search of refuge from the speculations of her mother and the Roberts boys, the dumb pain of Grainger, her own fear and hope; and of course she'd pitched restless through the next three hours till the whole house was quiet. Then she'd paddled through a long stretch of what seemed no more than harassed darkness (a cruel taunting) but was actually sleep, hectic and frail yet deep enough to shield her from the various sounds of Rob's return. Some ear in her mind perceived that though—his arrival in his room, his quiet undressing, not his visit with Della or talk with Grainger—and freed her then to begin the oblivion she'd wanted since Friday when he'd left with his curious promise to come back bearing the word that would win her or to hunt it at least. So she'd roamed through a number of levels of rest on her slow descent—the quick bright chatter that she often so easily delivered in sleep (little poems, long volleys of witty exchange, neat but lethal retorts: all gone before day), a tale in which she was learning from Lucy (Della's long-dead mother) how to carve up dirt into squares like candy that would please her father who did not like sweets, a perfect list of the names of the children she had known in school from the age of seven till nine years later when she'd finished with honors—but no trace of Rob. Her mind thought of that, the peculiar omission, tried to force itself to imagine his face and rig a tale round it, to sort through the language in search of a word which by day she could give him, the necessary word.

No use. She was flat on the bottom of rest, all voices appeased, when at six-thirty Monday, a hand on her door. Or a long warning maybe. She wrenched herself conscious with the thought that the hotel was far-gone in flames, one hand struggling to wake her. She sat up, said "Yes?", checked the windows for safety—clear morning, no smoke. But no voice answered. Then again gentle knocking. "Father?"

"No. Rob."

She reached for her robe and was almost at the door when he opened it a little. "Good morning," she said.

He nodded. "I'm back."

"You are; I see. I've thought about you."

"I've thought some myself."

"About what?" she said.

"Living my life or not."

Against her will, she smiled. "You're white and twenty-one. Did you reach a conclusion?"

"I hope so," he said, "but first, have you?"

Even torn from sleep, Rachel could not hedge or lie. "Not yet," she said.

Rob said, "Then listen. If I was planning to live out a life, some decent sort of life, would you live it with me?"

Rachel thought, "If someone had said to me 'Compose the speech you would most need to hear from a person you love,' could I have guessed this?—guessed anything half as close as this?"

"You don't have to answer this minute," he said. He must leave for work or forfeit the job.

"Are you *planning* that?" she said.

"It depends, I guess." Rob had not smiled yet.

"On me?"

"Yes ma'm." He smiled and ducked a little bow. As his head reached its low point and saw her bare feet, white as tallow and dry, he knew he had lied, though he did not know he'd forget that knowledge, remember it only long months from now.

"Then thank you," she said.

"You will?"

"Yes thank you."

Smiling still, Rob clamped his eyes shut and nodded. Then he looked again and said, "I'll see you this evening."

"See Father," Rachel said. "He has got some say."

13

Rob had worked late on Monday, been exhausted and gone to bed once he'd eaten, barely speaking to Rachel and not even seeing her father or mother. On Tuesday when he reached the hotel at seven, this letter was waiting on the dark hall-table. He went to his room and read it before washing.

August 16, 1925

Dear Robinson,

I had hoped that somehow you could hold off leaving till I got back from school, but I well understand how you had to leave. What a cruel distance, and twice in two days. I only hope you are safely there and will rest tonight for your new week tomorrow. It is strange for me that after long years of having you out of my cares entirely (though not from my griefs, however buried), I now find I've worried all evening about you; guessed at your whereabouts, pictured your condition.

I suppose you have felt, if you've felt at all, that I let your mother leave with very little struggle, which would also mean little struggle for you. That is less than half-true. I wrote strong letters, sent valuable gifts returned by Mr. Kendal, and made a last trip to Fontaine in August (you were five months old; I was not allowed to see you). Then I pled on by mail till I saw, was profoundly made to know, two related facts—Eva and me. We were separate and strange to one another as a cat and a dog, though without that enmity. We never once fought, however hard we spoke in the effort not to lie. A cat can be made to adopt a puppy if his mother dies; she will even nurse him if she has milk to give; but however grateful and needful he becomes, she will walk off and leave him when he's big enough to wean. Claw him blind if need be; I've seen it happen. And the puppy will imagine desperation and death. But he'll live of course and find he enjoys it and seek his own kind. You know all that. What a puppy cannot do or a full-grown dog is imagine and feel the weight and value of a fellow creature as I've imagined yours this afternoon and evening (it is past midnight), to my deep surprise. It has been my observation in fifty years of watching that few men are capable of close attention over long spans of time to another human being. That is woman's great gift and her steadiest pain, to gaze at another for years on years and care each moment as much as for herself, occasionally more. My sister Hattie, Rena Kendal (from what you tell me), Polly Drewry, maybe Grainger. Of the men I have watched—maybe Grainger, now me (or me again: I felt this with Eva, but it had to fade).

Is it also your burden?—too great an attention? From the two talks we had, I suspect it may be; and because I have spent a large part of my life in the company of books (by no means the safe flight or warm consolation so often charged) and because I believe from my own experience and that of men far my superiors in life that the wisdom of a few books carefully studied will prove more useful and slightly less wearing than the raw fray of life—because of those things, I have searched this evening for a passage in Vergil which began to pull at the edge of my mind through all you told me of your own life and worries. You said that you read Book Four of the Aeneid under Thorne Bradley in school; I do not know that you read other parts or encountered this passage, so I write it out for you. (I'll confess that my own work has kept me from Vergil so long that I did indeed have to hunt for the lines.) But first will you grant me, a lifelong teacher, a little preamble to set the stage?

Aeneas has fled the ruins of Troy and is borne on a storm of Juno's hatred to the shores of Africa, confused and despairing, having lost his wife, his father and home. There on Libyan sands his mother comes to him. She is Venus but disguised from his recognition as a huntress, armed. He sees her divinity, though not her name, and tells her his plight. She urges him onward to the palace in Carthage, the seat of Dido. Her parting words are,

> Perge modo et, qua te ducit via, derige gressum.
> *Only proceed and walk with the road.*

From there, in light of your claim to bad Latin, may I translate for you?

> *She spoke and, turning, her rose neck shone.*
> *From the crown ambrosial hair breathed fragrance;*
> *Raiment fell round her feet and in gait she was shown*
> *An actual god. He knew her as mother*
> *And chased her vanishing with words—*
> *"You cruel too? Why tempt your son*
> *So often with false games? Why may*
> *My right hand not greet yours and why*
> *Not hear true words and answer truthfully?"*

—Well, I offer you those for whatever good they hold, restraining myself from comment but for this: remember her last words,

> *Only proceed and walk with the road,*

and that, despite the cries of Aeneas, it is she who is godly and sees his fate, not miserable he. His fate is not her.

I certainly don't claim special powers of foresight or wisdom as to where your road must lead or what the road is; but I can say this much now with some assurance. You can have a job here on January 1st in the business office. As I told you last night, the bursar's clerk is retiring at seventy (and none too soon; no two columns of figures have balanced in the past five years). I went in to see the superintendent this afternoon and mentioned that you were in hopes of bettering your outlook, and could he help out? He thought awhile and said he'd intended to put a young Negro in the job, a graduate if possible; but had recently had second thoughts on the subject (the job calls for some little traveling in the state and into

*Carolina, some meeting the public—bankers, preachers, etc.). So in short if
you are inclined to take it, he would lean your way, I am virtually certain.
He hinted as much, being heavy on hints and light on decisions; but you
must act fairly soon. First, tell me if you are interested. Then I'll send you
the outline of what he would want by way of application and references
(would Thorne recommend you? who else in Fontaine? would your
present boss?).*

*Please give this good, but not slow, thought. You need to act soon.
And if you should ask, as you very well may, why Forrest Mayfield comes
now after twenty years of silence and absence, seeking company, I would
answer you or Eva or anyone else something close to this. It is not for
personal gain or even pleasure (though I'd hope to take pleasure in your
nearness, to be sure) but in the strong and natural hope of recompense; of
showing you something, after years with the Kendals, which one Mayfield
at least has learned—in fact all the Mayfields I've known before you: how
simply to proceed. Any of the others could show you as well as I, I'm
sure—my father, were he here, or Hattie or Grainger—but I at least am
willing and probably have less desperation of heart than they, which is my
commendation.*

*Thank you for coming here and hearing me out—well, hardly out. I
have nothing if not a long stream of words, but we are after all amending
the faults and omissions of decades. Many still yawn; some will never bear
filling. If you come back and stay—this home is ready for you; it is yours as
much as mine—I will work more quietly at a stronger repairing: by act, by
deed.*

In any case, proceed, Son, and answer me please.

> *Your hopeful,*
> *Father*

14

WHEN Rob had washed and eaten and sat on the sideporch with Rachel
till dark, talking only of what didn't matter a hair to anyone alive (they
were both a little rigid with the effort to avoid spoken recollection of
yesterday's promise; and they separately wondered if they'd dreamt the
meeting, the contract made) and when Mrs. Hutchins had said her good
nights and gone indoors, pulling Rachel in her wake, Rob went to the
corner where Mr. Hutchins sat every night till eleven and said, "May I sit
here awhile, Mr. Hutchins?"

Mr. Hutchins said, "You've paid for it. Sit anywhere."

Rob sat on the railing, his back to the night, feet hooked in the posts.
He was six feet from Mr. Hutchins but eye-level to him. Rob sat awhile in

silence (Mr. Hutchins had started his final cigar). Then he said, "Have you known me long enough?" He was smiling, though at air; Mr. Hutchins wasn't looking.

"Long enough for what?"

"To judge my nature."

A sizable wait. "I think so, yes."

"Then tell me please."

Mr. Hutchins laughed. "Haven't known you that long."

Rob said "How's that?"

"I mean I have my own clear opinion, but I don't know you well enough to say if you could take it."

Rob said "It's that bad?"

"It has some rough edges." He did not laugh again, but his words were colored by the smile they slid through. He sucked at his cigar; then he said, "Which one are you after?"

Rob said "Sir?"—caught and chilled.

"There are two women roughly your age around here."

Rob had honestly assumed himself to be invisible to the man. His plan, the speech he'd relied on to come, was paralyzed.

Mr. Hutchins said, "Have you been down to the spring since Grainger fixed the roof?"

Rob said, "He told me but, no sir, I haven't."

"You're thirsty, I trust?"

"Yes sir," Rob said with no conception of what would follow (he had not passed a hundred words alone with Mr. Hutchins since moving here).

Mr. Hutchins stood—"I'll show you"—and was half-down the steps to the yard when Rob joined him. They had gone ten yards in the cooling thick darkness before Mr. Hutchins said, "I've killed two rattlers right here since spring" and proceeded from there with slow high steps.

Rob said "Grainger told me" and also stepped higher.

Mr. Hutchins said, "Yes but Grainger didn't *kill* them, came calling for me"; and neither spoke again (they were flanking the quarters) till they reached the springhouse, an open-sided octagon twelve feet across, lattice work all round maybe three feet high. Mr. Hutchins paused at the entrance side and reached up to touch the edge of the sloping roof, stroked it like the neck of a dog three times. Without looking back, in a studious voice, he said, "Now this is one thing will outlast you, a red cedar roof."

Rob came up beside him and also reached. He was shorter by a head, so only the tips of his fingers could touch the dry fragrant verge of Grainger's work. Yet it seemed important to touch what he could of the substance which would silver through the next ten years, then begin to moss over but still turn water maybe fifty years from now when Rob Mayfield would be sodden or vanished; to touch it not only to please Mr. Hutchins who was watching but to search in himself for the small coal of serious hope uncovered by Polly and his father or put there by them. Rob found the coal and warmed it; he would not lose it now. He lowered his arm and entered the springhouse before Mr. Hutchins, passed the round central font, and sat on the railing of the dark far side.

Mr. Hutchins stayed out.

Rob said, "I am after Rachel, Mr. Hutchins. It's Rachel I want."

Mr. Hutchins reached up again and patted his roof. Then he stepped inside and came on as far as the spring itself and stood behind that. "The roof before this one was put on in eighteen and seventy-three by my grandfather once he'd figured the war was actually over and that people might start getting sick again. My mother was the main one he had in mind. She was his youngest daughter and had married my father, young Raven Hutchins, the previous year; and they'd moved here to live and help with what few guests still came. The worst guest was me. I came in the late fall of '72—November rains—and just about tore my mother to pieces. She was short and narrow. I was big from the start like my father's people, and she stayed down in bed the rest of that winter. Then in spring when it looked like she still couldn't strengthen (and all my father could do was grieve—sweet man, helpless fool), my grandfather thought this water might help her, make her think she'd live. It had been boarded up since during the war when a young girl that refugeed here from Richmond caught the typhoid and died and her mother blamed the water; she may have been right. I've never claimed that it had anything to recommend it but wetness and sulphur; if you're dry or have got the itch or mange, it may help you some. Otherwise you're better off drinking whatever you were drinking the Sunday you came here. Anyhow my grandfather had it cleaned out and tore down the old shed and built this new one, twice the size. And she did improve—my mother, strange to say. In a matter of weeks, she was out on the porch; and by the time my clear memories begin, she was strong as you or me and stronger than my father. They worked on here to run the hotel. I grew up here; only place I know, only place I'd ask the Lord to spare. It was always a one-horse operation, never more than ten rooms. We never doubted that—Warm Springs and Rockbridge Baths were right down the road—but we had a small number of elderly people who came every summer and rocked and talked, even drank a dipperful of this stinking water once or twice a day. Good for their bowels; we had four johnnies. What they mainly came for was Mother's good meals three times a day. Cooked and served by Mother—great *tubs* of fresh food, fresh bread and cakes—with nothing to help her but my sister Lou, and me to chop wood, and Della's black mother (the mountains were not strong on Negroes then). But they did have to struggle to get here like I said—catch the train to Hot Springs; I'd meet them in the wagon and haul them to here on that little road: it has stopped several hearts and no water would start them—and people these days aren't looking for struggles; so gradually the business thinned out to nothing. A widow or two, some mean old maids. I was grown by then and clerking dry goods for Wilson Hamlett. Grandpa had died. My own sorry father just sat on the porch and prayed for money; what little we had was squeezed by Mother and me from odd drummers and the few summer guests. (I helped her at night when I got home from work. We'd sometimes scramble till one in the morning, turning mattresses or cooking. I'd help her put up great bushels of food; we worked smooth together.) This spring here had come down to nothing but spiders, lizards all in it, big healthy snakes. And then I got married; you know to who. She had grown up in Goshen way out by the river (her people had come here to teach from east Virginia—Isle of Wight, near Suffolk; good stock, big readers); but we planned to move out of here when we could. I was planning to take any job God offered just to leave this hole. Well, God wasn't offering—not in 1894, not through the mails (which is what I was trying: writing off for jobs)—so finally I decided to hunt in person. That meant telling Mother. I came down early one Saturday morning (I had begged the day off), and she fixed my breakfast (my wife was upstairs). She thought I was just going off to Hamlett's, and I had decided to let her think it; I told my wife, 'If you come down and tell Mother where I've gone, I'll leave you flat.' But then she touched me—my mother, I mean. She was not a great toucher; I don't think she'd touched me in oh nine years; but she came up behind me that Saturday morning— nobody was with us—and carefully touched my head with her hands, parted my hair with her long tough fingers. It almost killed me; food seized in my throat. I thought, 'I am Peter and the cock's crowed thrice.' But I kept my own counsel and prayed she would just go on with her cooking. Well, she finished my hair and moved her hands down to rest on my shoulders; then still there behind me which didn't help a bit, she said, 'You feel like you're leaving me.' —'I'm warm,' I said; 'Is that what you mean?' (it was early June). 'No it's not,' she said. Then we both were quiet and still as old logs. Then somebody's feet started coming downstairs—a lady named Simpson from South Carolina; from Mullins, I think. Mother said "Tell me quick." So I swallowed my cold cud and told her, not looking, 'Yes ma'm. We are hoping to move to Lynchburg.' And back quick as voltage, she said 'Then damn you.' But I went to Lynchburg."

Rob, in the dark behind the spring, thought Mr. Hutchins had only paused for breath; so he did not speak through a sizable wait, though he saw Mr. Hutchins was looking to him. Finally Rob said, "You went and she died?"

Mr. Hutchins stepped up and under the roof and came as far forward as the edge of the spring. "You figured that out or did Della tell you?"

"Rachel," Rob said.

"It's true anyhow."

"Right away?" Rob said.

"No a year and a half. She waited that long. I got a job in Lynchburg, clerking again; and we moved there in August. She never tried to stop me after that first time—wrote me letters every Sunday, sent me little gifts of food—and we came back here to visit at Christmas. Everything seemed the same. It wasn't; she was hiding, not her sickness maybe (it may not have started) but her misery surely. She was left alone. Father was there and Lou and the help, but it turned out they didn't matter to her. I had almost killed her one time before; so she gave me the power to do it again, to finish what I started twenty-five years before. I finished it. We went back to Lynchburg, my wife and I; and the following November when I came up here one Sunday for my birthday, I found her just about dead. No warning except that one little time like I said when she damned me. Advanced T.B.—really galloping consumption as the old people called it. Everybody knows, or knew back then before doctors ruled the world, that consumption was something you wished on yourself or at least welcomed-in. She had made everybody else promise not to tell me; so I walked in cold on the sight of her wasting. What it did was make me mad, at her and the others. I think I kept it from her; but I felt it like gall in my mouth all that day, just pure damned mad that she'd used me like that when all I'd done was start my life: she pretended I'd loved her and had gone back on that; it was her loved me. And I left again to prove it. It killed her by Christmas, six days before. The last thing she told me when I left that Sunday (my birthday visit) was 'You can come back now, just a few more days.' I told myself I never would; but after the funeral I could see my father was all caved in and would follow her soon. He had not known he loved her. He was left like a pissed-out bladder, that empty. I thought I would move back long enough to close this dump down and see Father through to his end—he was older than Mother, well on in his fifties and had a bad heart—and then sell all this and strike out again on my own plans. So back we came and here we are. It was Lou that died; she had caught it from Mother. Father lived on till just before Rachel got sick, two years ago; and sometime in there after those two deaths, I just gave up. You've seen me here." Mr. Hutchins waved round himself with both hands mildly. "I guess I stayed for Rachel. It is all she knew, she was always frail, I hated to move her. Now it's harming her."

Rob said, "Then I offer to take her away."

"To where?"

"Maybe Richmond. I can get a job there much better than this one. My father will help me."

"—Teaching Negroes *what?* What else do you know that Negroes can use?" Mr. Hutchins was calm but his voice meant to damage.

Rob laughed. "I thought you slept better than that."

"No I don't. I've heard every time—you creeping back here. Thank Jesus I haven't heard more than the creeping."

"Yes sir," Rob said. Silence extended. Then he said, "I never heard you tell me to stop."

Mr. Hutchins said, "And won't. I offered her to you, still offer her now."

"To keep me off Rachel? I have not touched Rachel."

"I know that too."

"How please sir?" Rob said.

"Because Rachel's happy. Rachel's stronger every day."

Rob waited again, then was forced to say "I don't understand you."

Mr. Hutchins said, "She really hasn't told you?"

"No sir. I mean, she has mentioned Lynchburg, that doctor's place. She says it was never her chest, just nerves."

"She was sick all over," Mr. Hutchins said. "See, nobody claimed that place in Lynchburg was just for T.B. It's a real hospital. I thought she had it; and Dr. James here did, for what he's worth—which is less than he charges (he tended my mother and also Lou, watched them strangle). But everybody knew her nerves were involved."

Rob said, "I'm no doctor but, as women's health goes, she seems well to me."

Mr. Hutchins waited, then bent where he stood and lifted the round wood lid that covered the mouth of the spring. He reached above in the peak of the ceiling and found the great dipper—a yard long, copper—and stooped and carefully filled it with water. Then he walked to Rob and, still holding the handle, offered the drink.

Rob accepted, set lips to the strong-tasting metal, and held the first draft from this spring on his tongue. A frightening presence within his own gates, old with minerals and rank with gas—poison or balm? He could still spit it out and refuse its effects.

But Mr. Hutchins stood above him, watching as keenly as if it were day and Rob were a message he could read with effort.

Rob swallowed twice.

Mr. Hutchins raised the dipper to his own face but stopped. He turned slightly sideward and threw out the few drinks Rob had left. Then he hung the dipper in the dark again and said, "I can thank you for saving her life."

Rob said, "Not I. I have just cheered her some. She has helped me as much."

Mr. Hutchins said, "And you swear Della hasn't told you?"

"Della's never said her name."

Mr. Hutchins sat on the edge of the spring. "Rachel lost her mind. Two years ago. She got the idea she was having a baby. Don't ask me how. The doctors that looked said no man had gone near her; she swore so herself. But she showed many signs of carrying a child for more than six months—the curse stopped in her; she was violently sick but gained flesh steadily. To see her, you would think you had met a soul in torment, though she never claimed that. She would barely speak, and then just a word to Della or her mother. I went in one morning after maybe four months and tried to be pleasant, tried to pass a little time (which hung heavy on her—she had finished school; she didn't have friends). I said did she have all the clothes she needed, meaning we could order her something nice. She nodded Yes three times and walked to the mantel and took up a tape measure, measured her waist right in front of me. Then she came close on me and said—fierce as you would say '*Die!*' or '*Kneel!*'—'This baby is coming here day by day and not one stitch in the whole house for it. It will perish bare.' I said to her, 'Rachel, there is not any baby. You are tired and confused. But you're also young—just relax now and rest; don't press on your mind. Then you'll be yourself again and can get on with starting your life with those you love.' "

Rob said "Who were they?"

"Her mother and me, the whole place here. She was partial to Della's mother, Lucy."

Rob said, "She was bound to be in love with somebody."

Mr. Hutchins thought it through. "She had had some school friends, a boy or two that came to see her, take her up on the mountain with a big crowd—picnics. But no love, no. I'd have been the first to know. She's a mystery to her mother, but to me she's plain as print. We are hopeless close-kindred."

Rob said, smiling slightly, "Then she knew I was coming."

Mr. Hutchins said, "She may have. I sure to God did." He stopped as if regretting it, then bowed to explaining. "I knew the night you got here she would love you soon."

Rob said, "She was still in Lynchburg then."

"She was. But I knew."

"How please?"

"I've told you. She and me are close-kindred. She's all I've cared about in all my life and I'm fifty-two. My mother worshipped me and I killed her for it, but I can't say I loved her. I had hurt her too much, from right at the first when I tore her so badly—you can't forgive that: that you tried to kill a woman and she lasted and loves you. My wife—well, you've seen her; she does what's needed, does it quietly and well. But Rachel is a daughter. You can understand the rest—you were born, I trust; and I know you've had women—but you've never had a daughter; so you can't know till then. She is something you make in absolute pleasure with no work at all; and she comes into life bearing half your nature—in some cases, more. Treat her gently and decently, she'll turn to you like leaves to light before she can talk and tell you her care. By the time she's a child—say, seven or eight— you will find, if you're lucky (though I wonder is it luck or one more burden?), she has turned *into* you. You and her are one thing. So back last

April, I saw you coming up my yard with Grainger; and I knew you were hers."

Rob said "Can she have me?"

"When?"

"Oh end of summer."

Mr. Hutchins stood and closed down the lid of the spring. "Might as well," he said. He turned, walked three steps toward the entrance; then said, not looking back, "But kill her and I'll find you wherever you are, make you pray to die."

Rob said "Yes sir."

15

August 23, 1925

Dear Father,

    Yes, Mr. Bradley did take us through that part of the Aeneid. *I could have told you about the meeting with Venus; but as you suspected, I'd mislaid the advice or never really heard it (the way we were hauled through Vergil—kicking, bleeding—would have deafened a deer). Walk with the road—I'm doing that, I guess, since I'm building the road; and it seems to aim at Richmond, eastward at least.*

    I didn't plan on that. It was planned by the Commonwealth of Virginia. Looking back over my twenty-one years, I can't see that I have planned anything much. I hoped some things would happen—a life of long content—but until I was forced to pull up stakes in Fontaine this spring, I don't think I did much to help them happen, unless it was to reach out and take somebody (nobody I had hoped for anyhow). Even that pull-up was forced by Mother, as I tried to explain, and by Kennerly Kendal's meanness of heart. Even my visit to you and Polly was planned by Grainger and urged by you which is not to say that I didn't enjoy it (I did and am grateful; please pass that to her).

    But now after five little months of misery—three of them spent pulverizing hills that God intended to last till Judgment—in a job just two notches better than what any barebacked rockheaded fieldhand black as a stove could ask for and get (and better me at): now I have done one thing on my own, Rob Mayfield has. I plan to be married. Nobody but me and the girl involved; and the idea was mine, though I know it had crossed her mind once or twice.

    She is who I mentioned to you last Saturday when we had got back from the show and you'd said, "Then who on earth will accompany you?" Remember I named Aunt Rena and Sylvie and Grainger maybe. I was smiling, I think, to show I was joking; but you didn't see that. You said,

"Think, Robinson. They are all your seniors; they will die and leave you";
and I'd said "All right." But once you'd asked who would go with me, this
name came to mind—Rachel Hutchins, remember? I'd known her three
months and had felt drawn to her by needs of her own; I had even made
some curious promises to her. So she didn't rise up from the blue that
night just to answer you. But I did come straight back here Sunday evening, my mind made up, and asked her Monday morning and her father
Tuesday night.

We plan on being married here this coming Thanksgiving. My job
lasts till then and Rachel needs the time (she has been a little sick but is
much improved; three more months should do the trick). I invite you
herewith to be present then. I also mean to ask Mother and Rena. I hope
you will come.

Then after that I hope to accept the job you mention in Richmond.
You say it would be in the business office. I am pretty good at figures as I
think I told you, so I guess I can do it or learn quick enough. Would you
please let me know what letter I should write to whom saying what? And
will you make any deeper search you can into whether I will really get the
job or not?

If I don't maybe Grainger can. He would be the right shade and is no
doubt as good at figures as me. In fact now I mention it, I spoke to
Grainger on all these developments this afternoon, the November wedding
and the Richmond job. He listened at first and wished me well; but later
on when I was asleep (Sunday nap), he came to my room and let himself
in when I didn't answer and woke me up and said would I need him once
I'd made those changes? As I told you, he came here with me last April on
the spur of the moment when I was bad off and in need of help: just shut
up his house and came, clean and bare (once he got the job here, he went
back for two days and got a few belongings—the books you gave him—and
moved some old woman cousin of his in to hold down his floor till he came
home, if ever). So in short I said I would. Need him, I mean. He said,
"Then you're asking me to come with you?" I said I was, providing I went;
and he said "Does Mr. Forrest know?" I said no you didn't but that I
planned to write you a letter tonight. "Then ask him," he said; "ask him
can I come." My own quick plan was that we could use him—that is,
Rachel and I. He is good in the house, and she will need help. So I told
him that though you had kindly said that I could move in at the Mayfield
place, I had tripled my numbers without warning you and thus would
intend to find a small place of my own, room for him. He thought about
that but still said again, "You ask Mr. Forrest does he want me to come.
Then show me his answer." I promised I would—and I have, so please
answer. I thought I noticed some reservation on Polly's part when I spoke
of Grainger; if there is, tell me now. And kindly answer soon.

I am trying—do you see?—just to proceed. I am making these plans
now entirely on my own. If others can't bless them, then I'll go on alone;

or Rachel and I will. *Clearly I hope you can bless and welcome this latest Mayfield who has only now started to learn what you promise my elders know.*

Thanks again to Miss Polly. I'm waiting to hear.

> *Your loving son,*
> *Rob*

August 23, 1925

Dear Mother,

No word from down there for ten days now. Has the heat laid you out or has Rena's hand withered? I trust you are all there and upright and breathing or someone would have wired me.

I think I am better than I've been for some time; and I hope that an explanation of why will give you maternal satisfaction if not joy.

I invite you to my wedding in Goshen, Virginia sometime in late fall, most likely Thanksgiving. You can get here by train in under eight hours; the days will be cool and the mountains in their beauty; so I'd like to see you here if your work at home permits. It goes without saying that the rest are invited if they all care to come—Kennerly and Blunt, Sylvie of course. I will write a special note to Rena after this. You would have a good seat, the clearest view available of Rob starting life—his life as you've urged.

The bride is Rachel Hutchins. I have mentioned her in past letters to you, I think. I know I have to Rena; she expressed her pleasure and her usual warnings.

In any case, her family own the hotel in Goshen where I have lived since April. They are people you could honor, have held this spot for years (there's a little mineral spring, not famous, not healing; but it won't stop running, so they built next to it some hundred years ago and have stayed right on). Rachel is in certain ways a likeness of you—not in looks or size but in having, like you, a death-grip on one single vision of life and of what she wants in it, and the courage and strength to seize out and hold it. Like you too she's strained herself in the effort; but she's young, just twenty, and is in careful hands (her parents' lavish care); and she thinks I am what life intends for her. I want to agree. She may be right.

Once the wedding is over, my job here will end. After that I am planning to move to Richmond. I have hopes of bettering my outlook there—more money, cleaner work. It would be at the school where Father teaches. I have now met him, and he has offered to help me onto my feet. Of course I asked him to be at the wedding. There is no other way. That doesn't harm you, anything you have meant to me in the past or will go on meaning. Please understand that. You, if anybody, can. You are back of this.

I had hoped to be able to beg a day off and get down to spend a weekend with you all; but now with these plans, I will need to stay here.

We are also pushing the road extra hours to get our stretch finished before the fall rains.

Please write to me soon, give me news of all, give love from me to all that would want it.

> *Your effortful son,*
> *Rob Mayfield II*

16

Two mornings later when they'd finished breakfast and Eva had washed her father and shaved him, Sylvie helped her to walk him out into the yard and seat him in the shade; then she went for the mail. Eva asked him a question or two about his comfort. Then he nodded off and she got to work on the last of the cutwork napkins she was making for a distant cousin who had finished school in May. She was months late as always; but the girl should be grateful to get, any time, eight handmade napkins from kin she barely knew and cared less about. She was thinking that through—had almost decided to put them in a drawer and save them till someone she actually liked graduated or married: they would keep forever; the cousin was ugly and would never use them—when her father spoke clearly.

"I wonder where she went."

He frequently talked in half-dreams or stupors, and Eva seldom answered unless it was plain that he'd asked her to. She worked on in silence, and he lapsed into what seemed certain sleep.

But in less than a minute his chin kicked the air; he fixed his eyes on her—she still had not noticed—and watched with a fierce intensity of waiting. His blue eyes never blinked. When she did not look, he said, "I begged you to tell me."

Eva turned and was startled but pretended calm and said, "Please ask me again. The heat's blocked my hearing."

He worked to remember, then said with slow pain and the urgency of morning, "I asked you to tell me where she went. An easy question. You did not answer."

"Who, Father?—Sylvie? She's gone for the mail and will no doubt take her time coming back. Rena's indoors waxing the dining-room floor."

He sat awhile, eyes shut, as though that were his answer; as though his need were as simple as that—had been purified by age and apoplexy to a dog's need, a baby's. Then he begged again. "Charlotte Kendal, my wife. Charlotte Watson, she was." He had turned again on Eva.

Eva felt she should touch his hand that was gripped to the arm of the chair, but his eyes refused her. She looked at her work and said "In Heaven, I trust."

He said, "You don't believe a word of that."

"I do, yes sir."

"Did you ever know her?—a Watson child, an orphan?"

Eva said, "Years later, well after she was grown."

"Too late," he said, "long years too late."

"How is that?"

"I ruined her. I got to her early."

Eva said, "You loved her. Everybody knew that."

"*She* knew it," he said. "All Hell knows she knew it; if she's anywhere, she's there. But she also knows I harmed her."

"Her mother and father did that, Thad and Katherine."

Mr. Kendal's face could no longer show feelings more various than rage, exhaustion or boredom; so he watched her with what seemed sustained fury still, though in fact it was honest surprise. "You knew them, did you?"

"No, Father, they were dead. You told us the story."

"Never," he said. "I never told a soul."

It had been Eva's observation since her father had suffered two strokes that no good came of humoring his confusions—he would fly too far afield—so she said, "Sir, you did. I remember distinctly. You told it to Rena and Kennerly and me the night I went off with Forrest to Virginia." Her voice had stayed calm; she'd worked at the napkin. She had not mentioned Forrest's name to her father for maybe twenty years, eighteen at least. He had made it easy for her.

"You are lying again."

"No sir. I haven't lied to you since that same night."

Two mentions of the night, blunt shocks to his chest, set him back on whatever narrow rails he possessed. He waited awhile. Then he said, "Well, thank you. I can thank you at least."

She was able to touch him, her right hand on his wrist, though she did not meet his eyes.

With great difficulty he turned his stiff hand palm-up on the chair.

The move left her fingers on the crest of his pulse—a strong life, regular and harsh as cries. She bore it long moments; then she reached farther down, and his fingers gripped hers. They sat like that all the time it took Sylvie to come from her laughing meeting at the corner, with Nan the Bradley's cook, up the walk to them. Eva took back her hand to accept the mail.

Sylvie stood beyond her reach and said, "You got you one from Rob."

Eva said, "I am glad you're not all that he remembers." She was smiling but, as Sylvie knew, the card that came from Richmond a few days before (first word from Rob in August) had gone down badly—intended for Sylvie.

Sylvie stepped a little forward and surrendered the letter, then stood as Eva opened it. "Did he get back from Richmond?"

Eva read a few lines, then folded the sheets. "Thank you, Sylvie. You'll want to get those squash on for dinner."

Sylvie stood on awhile to show that she could (Eva straightened the neck of her father's robe). Then she said, "He telling you he ain't coming back" and headed for the kitchen, muttering as she went—"Some people got sense."

Eva opened the letter and read it through quickly in the late morning sun that was finding its way through their thin screen of leaves.

Her father didn't watch her, clamped his eyes and suffered the creeping glare; but when he heard paper folding again, he said "When's he coming?"

"Sylvie's right; he's not."

"Need money?"

"No, Father. He is paid every week. He needs a wife apparently. This says he's getting married."

Mr. Kendal didn't turn. Eyes shut, bare crown of his head assaulted by glare, he said "Read it to me."

Eva read it through clearly in a low voice which many good ears could not have understood; she knew her father could. When she finished, they sat in silence a moment; then she said, "You are broiling, Father. Let me go call Rena and help you in."

He shook his head. "Sit still." She sat and they waited another little while till he turned his eyes and slowly looked toward her.

She bore his gaze as he searched her, merciless.

Finally he turned back and faced the street again and said, "You were who I meant."

Eva needed to stop him now; she couldn't let him wander. She said "I'm grateful" and moved to stand.

"Sit still please," he said. "Just obey me once more. I have meant to say this for some years; but it slips my mind—you know my mind." He paused, staring out as though the street held his message. "You were who I meant." He looked to Eva, smiling the disastrous smile which his age would permit.

"Sir, I don't understand."

He scratched at the air with one long finger, writing it for her. "—Who I meant just now. The one I ruined."

Eva smiled but did not speak, still plainly puzzled.

"Your mother was responsible for all she did. She killed two people before herself. I loved her just the same. It was you I harmed."

Eva shook her head slowly.

"I am begging your pardon."

She said, "Father, Mother was nothing but a child; a baby just born."

"But she paid. Don't you see?"

"She was unhappy, yes; through no fault of yours. She explained that to me. Put her out of your mind."

"She's out," he said. "It's you I'm begging."

"I've been happy," Eva said. "I've had a good life, and I hope to have more."

Her father said "Liar."

Eva said "Please don't."

"All right," he said.

She stood and laid her work on the chair and called loudly, "Rena—"

Quick, strong as a boy, Mr. Kendal reached out, ringed her wrist, pulled her toward him (she managed not to stumble, to stand straight before him). He whispered now—"But you know my meaning?"

Eva said "I do" and knew that she did, saw clearly for the first time that he'd given her her due and would leave now soon. She called again for Rena, pleading.

17

FIVE hours later Eva sat on the porch alone, slowly swinging. Her father was asleep; Rena had gone in search of a load of manure for her fall garden; Sylvie was at home for her own short rest before cooking supper. At such a time Eva would normally have gone to her quiet room and shut the door—at her Father's first stroke, she had moved downstairs to the room behind his; Rob had taken her room—but two things had forced her out to the porch: the heat indoors, stifling by four, and the need for a space between her and her father. Breathing space, to settle her mind and prepare her answers for the questions that would rush her from every side by tomorrow at the latest when Rena would get her own announcing letter from Rob (she had so far told no one except her father and had managed, last moment, in the yard to warn him—"Don't mention Rob's marriage. It would ruin Rena's day").

But alone and quiet in the hot little wind she could raise by swinging, she found that her old devices for calm had also left her—she could not shut her eyes and by force of will flush her mind clean and blank, she could not pray that Jesus stand by her with strength, could not say a poem to herself, hum a song. She could think one thing. It seemed total knowledge, the sum of her life, both pitifully meager and pressingly huge, crowding all else aside—*You are being abandoned.* Father miserable and dying; Rob gone in condemnation but heaping coals of kind fire now on her head; Forrest barely present in her memory even, much less in her hope (she had no picture of him, had never had; only Rob's growing image, an innocent mimic). She was left with Rena and Sylvie, coal-black. It seemed to her— for the first time now (she had never considered the blame till now, having never been alone)—entirely her fault.

What the present weight of omen saved her thinking or recalling (she'd dreamt it clearly twenty years before) was the fact that she'd willed the choices of her life, the company she'd had, and had lived in what any sober witness might have called unusual happiness. The life she had wanted. It was quitting her now with the suddenness of death, of all catastrophe.

She stood and went down the steps, down the stone walk, aware that for the first time in sixteen years she had left her father entirely unattended. A cry would reach her though; she was walking nowhere, only stirring the heat. She stopped at the end of the walk, at the road, and crouched and began to weed Rena's bed of zinnias. It had been a wet August, and Rena had been busy in the back with her vegetables. As Eva worked she knew that Rena would notice ("Some rabbit was down at my flowers today"); but she worked on delicately, harming nothing. When she finished she had a little stack of hay beside her. She'd walk to the sideyard and put it round the roses; but rising quickly in the heavy sun, she tottered. Dizzy blood flooded her sight. She sat backward hard, to keep from falling. She was in plain view of the road—any passer—with her dress caught high on her folded calves, her hair matted wet on her forehead, mouth gasping; but she did not look out to check for passers: she did not care. She cared for herself, the small dry room in the front of her skull where her bare self lived; had happily lived these thirty-eight years, give or take a bad hour and the year with Forrest. The room had been light; and though the one door opened outward only, it had let her move freely to the few destinations she required and loved. *Vanishing* and no substitutes in sight. The room itself darkened, the air brown and close, the one door sealed.

Eva thought she would weep; tears were all in her throat, at the backs of her eyes. While she waited for tears, she searched for when she had really wept last. Mag's funeral maybe, six years before?—not that Mag had ever quite welcomed her back when she'd come home with Rob or in all the years after; but she couldn't remember a later time. And she didn't weep now. No pressure relented but no release came. Still unsure of standing, she looked down and saw she had landed on the name-stone, a small granite wheel from a disused mill on her father's river place. He had hauled it here when Eva was seven or eight and sunk it in the walk among smaller stones. It had been late summer—school had still not begun—and Kennerly had come out next morning with a chisel and hammered K.K. very neatly in the granite, on the edge of the hole. It had taken him till noon; she and Rena had watched him. When he'd shaped the last serif, he'd moved round and started on an R for Rena, who was youngest and could barely make her letters on paper, much less in stone. Eva had watched till he started on the curve that proved it an R, not an E. Then she'd said, "I am going in the back to play with Sylvie. When you finish with Rena, I want to do my own." Kennerly had laughed, "Good luck!

This is granite." Still he'd called when he finished; and once they'd eaten dinner, she had chiseled at her own *E.K.* for hours. Smaller than the others and listing to the right but there in its proper place beside the great socket.

And there still. She traced it with a finger now. The simple touch, rough and dry, proved the channel she'd needed. But no tears came; only a retching in her throat which she did not try to strangle. She yielded to all its awfulness. A shameful release in August glare not three yards short of the public road. She did not hear the steps behind her, would still not have cared.

"Mrs. Mayfield?"

Eva turned—Min Tharrington, frightened above her.

Eva nodded. "You caught me."

"Not soon enough. Are you hurt anywhere?"

"Yes," Eva said. "But nothing you can help." Her vertigo had calmed; she stood up easily and smiled at Min. "Can I help *you?*"

"I just came to say goodbye."

"That's no help at all. Anybody can leave." Eva stroked back her hair with both hands blindly. "Your school hasn't started. Why leave so early?"

"Brother's taking me to Raleigh this Saturday. My principal has found me a room near the school with a satisfactory widow; but Mother has insisted that Brother go and check so Saturday's the day."

"Luck to you, Min. You've earned it at least." Stronger each moment, Eva made no move toward the house or porch.

Min waited a moment for an invitation; then said, "Could we sit down a minute, if you have a minute?"

"To be sure," Eva said. "Just let me check on Father."

They climbed up and Min sat while Eva went in (her father still asleep) and combed her hair. When she came back, she brought two glasses of water which they drank in silence before they spoke.

At last Eva said, "This has been hard on you. I can see it has." She looked to the brown-haired girl beside her, calm in a yellow dress—a grown woman leaving.

"Not really," Min said. "I was scared you had fallen."

"Oh that," Eva said. "I sat to *keep* from falling, sun on my brain. No I meant your plans."

"Well, I've got this degree, four years in the galleys. I might as well use it."

Eva nodded. "So right." Then she finished her water. "But you had to fight your mother. I meant that part."

"Did Mother tell you that?"

Eva smiled. "Several times. I was on your side and I told Kate so."

"Thank you," Min said. "I suspected as much. She never said a word to me against it—didn't dare after Father's deathbed wish that I *train* for something—but of course I felt her grudging every step of the way."

"She's a mother," Eva said. "Don't blame her too much. You've made little things in your life too, all those good grades, your clothes, your pictures. Someday you'll make a child."

"Maybe not," Min said.

"With that hair of yours and deep green eyes? Try to stop it," Eva said. "And when you've made it and seen it through the years, not days or weeks, when you honestly wanted to push it out the window or prayed it would melt like a salted snail, then you'll understand."

"I understand now; I've loved somebody."

"I know you have, know it very well. But it's not love I mean, though it may include love. It's ownership. You want what you've made; it's familiar easy company."

Min waited awhile. "How is Rob? Have you heard?"

"This morning," Eva said. She decided that instant—she would keep her own counsel; she would not risk telling. "He is doing very well, working hard, sounds healthy."

"Will they work up there in the mountains through winter?"

"I doubt it," Eva said.

"Will he come back here?"

"To visit at least. He misses Sylvie!"

"But he'll keep the road job?"

Eva searched Min's face; then laughed, "You ask him. *You're* his friend. I'm his mother; boys tell their mothers very little."

Min said, "In that case we'll neither one know."

"I thought you two were in regular touch."

"No ma'm. I have not touched Rob in four years."

Eva laughed. "He wouldn't mind."

Min nodded firmly. "He would. He knows I want him."

Eva waited. "For what?"

"For life."

"How do you know, Min?" Any edge on Eva's voice, of harm or raillery, had yielded now to real curiosity.

Min heard that, agreed to answer the truth. "I've thought about very little else for four years. He's all I want."

"Did you ever tell him?"

"He knew," Min said.

With a quick flood of pleasure, Eva thought *Me in him.* But she held back the smile that would naturally have followed. "God help you," she said.

Min waited. "I don't understand, Mrs. Mayfield."

Eva said, "I'm not sure I do myself. Maybe something like this—it is built into him, in the *mortar* joints, to run from being held. He came by it rightly."

"How so?"

"From his mother." Eva did smile now. "I'm a runner. I have run all my life. No doubt you've heard."

"No ma'm, I haven't."

"My marriage, Min. I'm sure you've heard. It was quite the topic."

"But before I was born. I've heard a few stories. I didn't pay attention."

"*Do,*" Eva said. "They are worth your time, I honestly believe."

Min waited as though the stories would follow.

Eva said, "When I was sixteen and had just finished school, the night before commencement, I got up off that stoop right there and walked through this house and out the back door to marry in secret a man almost twenty years older than me, who had been my teacher. For two reasons only, as far as I can see, and I've looked for reasons—I thought I was unhappy living with my mother (I was far from her favorite; we were too much alike); and I thought that no honor would ever come to me like the honor of that kind gentle man asking me to be his: for life as you say." Eva stopped as if that were the story, told.

Min said "Were you right?"

Eva looked to her, baffled.

"Did a better honor come?"

She had never thought it out. She did, quickly now. Then she shook her head. "Never." It made her smile. "Of course I have only lived half my life. I've barely begun. Earth lies all before me!"

"But you're sorry for the past?"

Eva saw that Min pressed her from need not malice; so she said, "What part? There are terrible parts—my mother, Rob's birth."

"—That you came home here. Never saw your husband. Mother said you have never seen him again."

Eva nodded. "Never. August the third, nineteen hundred and four. The length of your life, and a little more." She paused to think. "What did you ask me?"

"Are you sorry?" Min said.

"What right do you have?" Eva said it as calmly as "Another glass of water?"

"—That you started to tell me, that you've known me all my life, that you see as clear as anybody why I need to know."

Eva shut her eyes. "All right." She leaned her head back on the chair's white wicker and spoke from there as if from a distance or the wisdom of sleep. "I was not sorry then; there was too much to do, the turmoil here after Mother's death, Rob's case of whooping cough, Father's pitiful state. Then when they began to ease, I found I believed one thing above all— Mr. Mayfield had picked me for reasons of his own which he didn't understand (and God knew I didn't). He thought of my reasons no more than you'd think of the wishes of a warm egg you take from the nest. Does a thing have wishes? Very likely it does. So sitting here in that first year or two, I thought that at least my wish was not *him*, not Forrest Mayfield. I thought that I just wanted something to do—the kitchen was held down by Mag and Sylvie, the house (and more than half of Rob) by Rena; Father was active at his farms and in timber. So I gave voice lessons. I had a sweet voice and knew how to use it. I thought I could pass time in that useful way—please God, make some money, and beautify the air; but the pupils didn't care. Nothing on earth is worse than bad singing; I'd rather hear tin scrape tin any day. I stopped in a year and sat here awhile. Then I wrote to my husband—or sent him our picture, Rob's and mine. A stone would have wept. Not a word of reply. He was living in Richmond by then, teaching Negroes. I had ruined his reputation. His sister had told me; we exchanged Christmas greetings for several years, the sister and I. He had a housekeeper that had worked for his father. Their family home. That was eighteen years ago. He's still there, I think. I have been to Richmond twice in that time—once with your mother shopping (up at dawn, back at dark); once with Sylvie to look into me taking courses from a correspondence college to teach grade school—but he never crossed my path, and I wasn't out to hunt him. I was leaving it to fate, and fate left me here!" Eva waited, smiling. She had seen Sylvie far down the road; coming onward in the heat, no hat, no shade. She would grumble all evening.

Min said, "What happened to your plan to teach school?"

Eva turned. "—Father. He had his first stroke. He was all I could do. Has been ever since." She stopped again; she had told the story.

But Min said, "The answer is, you're sorry for it all?"

"I wasn't, no. But I may be soon."

"Then please," Min said—she leaned to say it—"Please tell me why you thought I should hear that."

Eva said, "I suspected it was not in your books, not taught in college. Postgraduate instruction. No charge at all." She smiled and waved to Sylvie, who did not wave back.

"Do you think I'm a fool?"

"In what?" Eva said.

"Leaving home. That job."

"No," Eva said. "You have got to pass time. Your family live forever; you're a babe in the womb."

Min said "Forget Rob."

Eva laughed. "Please explain."

"You are telling me, 'Forget about Rob; go your way.'"

Knowing all she knew, with no intent to harm, Eva said, "No never. Hold him any way you can." Her left hand had reached through the heat toward Min; Min had not reached to take it.

Sylvie called from the end of the porch by the palm, "What Rob say today?—that letter I brought you."

"Said he's happy," Eva said. "Sent his love to you."

18

September 13, 1925

Dear Alice,

I've held off answering till I knew what I felt and if that was what I meant and then whether I would be able to say it.

What I mainly feel is puzzlement that you step forward now with objections to Rob—you say reservations but objections is the word—when you liked him here and wrote me to say so. I trusted that you had been telling the truth, and I really continue to think that you were. I can only explain your turn in this way—in your first letter after your visit here, you were praising a surface. He was making it lovely; he wanted you to like him. And I think that's a natural thing to praise. I surely don't deny that he has lures and snares all over him. The first time I mentioned him to you, I seem to recall waxing big on his face. He still has the face; and now you warn me against it—"Those eyes will go on inviting people in, and the people will come . . . He is not looking outward any farther than his lashes . . . He is built for harm."

No doubt he is (I know I am. I have kept two people in misery for years, and I may not stop; I may add more); but if what I honestly believe I know about why human beings choose to follow each other is true at all, then whether he is hateful as a Hun on horseback or gentle as a pastry cook is no concern of yours or even of mine and his.

This is what I believe, seems all I believe these recent weeks; and it's what I have to tell you. Two people who are grown in good control of their bodies and minds, who are not being forced by parents or a baby or either party's money or anything other than their own heart's speaking, will contemplate spending the whole of their two lives beneath one roof (whatever time holds for them and the roof) for one reason only—they want each other. They also suspect and may even believe that want is need and will always be, but here as in other ways the mercy of time is their only hope.

Rob thinks he needs me. He has said so directly on numbers of occasions to me and to others—my father for instance (my father trusts him). I have every reason to believe he is in fair control of his faculties (Jesus drank at times).

I deeply believe I am in control of mine—partly through your help, your father's, partly Rob's. I also believe, and I've thought it through as sternly as a judge thinks a sentence, that the troubles I've had and have visited on others were not true diseases but symptoms of an illness in no book known to me or your father—some strange starvation in the core of the heart for which no one but time can prescribe, if time ever does. I believe it has for me. I would be the one to know, the heart being mine.

Of course he has faults. I know them better than you, better than any other woman in Virginia. I know he's needed pieces off of other human beings (with him, needing is taking)—I know more there than he thinks I know, having good night-vision—but I'm the only person that he's asked for all of; and I'm giving it all two months from now. He knows my faults in honest detail; Father told him in advance. I'm giving it for three very simple reasons that are both entirely scary and the sole consolation I have found to date—he's asked, I wanted him to ask, and I've answered. It may ruin us both—or him or me or some unborn, unthought-of, consequence— but so might the beefsteak we ate for supper, the breath I'm drawing as I write this line.

I asked you to bless us as my Maid of Honor, and I ask you again. If you wish us well, can stand there behind us and watch the joining and wish it well, come. I say well in every sense—good luck, good healing, fresh water in our deeps. If you don't, if anything in you says stay, then for God's sake stay. Whichever you choose, be always certain that my present hard feelings will in no way cancel my grateful memory of the strong warm care you offered me before when I was prone to die. My memory has always been my perfect trait.

Till I hear then,
Love from
Rachel

NOVEMBER 1925

MR. Hutchins rose at the head of the table, leaned far forward, and turned up the wick of the hanging brass lamp. Lamps burned on the sideboard, the mantel behind him; so now the whole room was brighter than warm (the iron stove beside him was stoked but barely drawing, and the evening was cold). Then he stood in his own place and thumped his waterglass for attention. It rang, high and pure, and everyone turned. He said, "As the proud host of all of this, I get the first word. But since I'm a mountaineer and paying for the oil"—he gestured to the five lamps—"I'll make it just a word; everybody please copy. The word is *glad*. I am yielding a daughter that I love like myself to a boy that I trust will know her needs and struggle to tend them. He's a worker; the Robertses can swear to that, their job being finished here a week ahead of schedule—"

The two Roberts boys, twelve feet away toward the foot of the table, nodded smiling. They were too dark to see.

"—She also, even if she is my child (mine and her mother's and all her strong ancestors'), has big gifts to give. A feeling heart. Miss Kendal, Mr. Mayfield, I think I can say with no fear of lying, and no intention surely, that all our families have made a good swap and stand to show a profit from what we're here to do." Mr. Hutchins stopped, thought a moment, had said his full say. "Mr. Mayfield," he said, "the boy's proud father—I take it you're proud—your good word please."

Also dark at the far end, at Rachel's mother's right, Forrest half-rose long enough to say, "Mr. Chairman, yes, *proud*. I defer to Miss Rena. She has done all the work." He looked up to Rena, met her firm clear eyes. Neither of them smiled but they both nodded grave and mutual acknowledgment of parts played, honors earned.

Rena kept her seat but took a long drink of the water before her; and when she spoke, she spoke of course to Rob. "*Thank* you," she said.

Rob was opposite her, four feet away. He kissed the back of his own right hand and turned it to her slowly. Another gift. Everyone sat in silence till she took it—the gift not his hand. She threw her head back and laughed a high short cry; it came down smiling and everybody clapped.

Mr. Hutchins said, "Are you done, Miss Kendal?"

"I've said my word."

"You can have several more since you've come such a way."

Rena shook her head, then thought, then looked to Mr. Hutchins. "I'll speak for his mother."

"Please do."

She looked to Rob. "Eva sends you a world of luck and her love."

Rob said, "She could have brought it." His voice sounded happy but he'd said it all the same.

"But she didn't," Rena said. She looked at once to Forrest. "Please say a little more."

Rachel sat in front of Forrest, so he said it to Rachel. "You know this boy at least as well as I do—this man, he is. You've really known him longer, though I saw him for a while at the very beginning of his life. *Yesterday!* It has brought me tremendous happiness since summer, that he hunted me down and offered me a bond where I had no right to expect anything but continuous parting. He has also found you. From your eyes and joy, I can guess you believe you have found him too. I am trusting you have, and I'll offer such prayers as I pray to that end. It would be a great victory, for our family at least and—and if I might have your permission, Miss Rena—for his mother's as well."

Rena's eyes never flickered off Forrest's face, however far away; but she gave no sign of permission or refusal.

Forrest went on, to Rachel. "You will have the harder job. He's half-Mayfield and will not like pain. But he's also half-Kendal; and as all here can see at this table tonight in good lamplight, the Kendals are lovely and invite us to follow." He nodded toward Rena.

"The *Watsons*," Rena said. She smiled at Rob, then returned to Forrest. "My mother was a Watson; it was them that people followed—my father, you. I'm a Kendal. Kendals *follow*; here I am today."

Forrest laughed—all did—and concluded for Rachel, "There's part of your job—sort out who he is. And you'll likely find he's many. Then love all you find." He found his eyes were filling and turned to Rachel's father. "If this were drinking country, we could drink to their health."

Mr. Hutchins said "We can." He looked to his wife. "We are all friends here." He turned to Rena. "Miss Kendal, would you drink a glass of old mountain brandy?"

"Very gladly," Rena said.

Mr. Hutchins nodded to his wife, who rang a bell. Everybody sat silently as if on a train and heard steps come quickly toward them from the kitchen—Grainger at the door, smiling like a guest. Mr. Hutchins said,

"Go down in the cellar past all the preserves. You'll find a gray jug that says *Raven* in blue—my given name, my father's before me" (that was offered to Rena). "Bring me that and ten glasses."

Grainger said "Yes sir. Everything else fine?"

"Very nice, yes thank you."

"Mr. Rob, you holding up?" Grainger pointed to Rob.

"Sinking fast," Rob laughed. "Bring the jug here quick."

Grainger said "On the way" and turned to go.

Mrs. Hutchins said, "Grainger, while you do that ask Gracie to pass the ham and the rolls."

"And a pitcher of water," Rob said. "From the spring. Could we please have that?"

Grainger looked to Mr. Hutchins.

Mr. Hutchins laughed and nodded.

But Rachel said, "Don't. Well-water please. You'd kill the guests."

Mr. Hutchins said, "Well-water then for all, but do your errand first."

Grainger said "A gray jug" and went to find it.

Forrest watched him out of sight and listened to his steps; then he turned to Alice by him and said, "I believe you have known Rob awhile?"

Alice said, "Since summer. Just three, four months."

Forrest said, "As I told you, that's longer than I."

Alice said, "Then you have a lot to look forward to."

Forrest said, "I hope I do. You really think I do?" Alice sat on his right; he had spoken to her softly, requesting an answer.

She looked to Rob quickly, six feet past her beyond Wirt Roberts, who was still eating loudly. "They'll be living near you. I meant you'd be close and would have time to know him."

"Would you trust him?" Forrest said.

"With what?"

"Your life, something serious as that."

Alice said, "I am trusting him with Rachel's at least."

"That's easy," Forrest said.

Alice said, "I doubt that. I'm her Maid of Honor. I will march down tomorrow in the presence of the Lord and say I approve what the Lord is asked to bless."

Forrest shook his head. "You won't have to speak a word."

"I will *be* there though; speech enough for me."

A tall dark girl had entered during that and came first to Forrest's left and stood—the plate of ham. All the previous serving had been done by Grainger; and since Forrest had got here only an hour before supper (the last train from Richmond), he had not had a chance to visit the kitchen. He looked up at the girl now and said "You're Grainger's Gracie."

"*Gracie*," she said and shook the dish slightly, a final offer.

He served himself a slice. "We'll be seeing you in Richmond."

"If you seeing quick," she said.

Forrest tried to search her face, as fine as a hand in its power and concealment, the eyes huge but narrowed, the mouth smiling inward.

"Serve Miss Alice, Gracie." Mrs. Hutchins moved her on.

Then Grainger was back with a large round tray, the jug and the glasses. He set it on the sideboard behind Mr. Hutchins and said, "You going to pour it or me?"

Mr. Hutchins said "You" and went on talking to Rena and Rob. Only the two Roberts boys were silent and Forrest who had pushed his chair back a little to watch Grainger work, five yards away, pouring thick amber brandy into small waterglasses as carefully as if he had transmuted water itself for these guests (empowered by the day, his part in its slow and happy unfolding), these few strangers held by a brief common purpose in their contrary lives, and would offer it now with grace sufficient to the night, the coming day.

Mrs. Hutchins asked a question. But Grainger held Forrest; he did not even face her.

Then half his job done, Grainger lifted his tray again and went straight to Rena, who accepted her glass and smiled and told him "Thank you," her only words to Grainger.

Grainger chose to answer, whispered in the midst of six conversations; but Forrest heard him clearly. He said "I'm glad" and moved on to Niles Fitzhugh beyond Rena, Rob's best man tomorrow.

Forrest stood where he was and said, "My heart is very full. Mr. Hutchins, before I drink your brandy, may I say a word more while my head is still clear?"

Rob said, "Yes sir, you'd better. This stuff looks mighty."

Rachel said, "Very mighty. Mr. Mayfield, speak."

Mr. Hutchins said "Quick."

Rena clapped; the others followed.

Grainger rounded the table.

Forrest said, "I am fifty-five years old this month. Never say 'Time flies'; it has seemed like forever. But things have come at intervals to lure me on, make me still yearn to last; things I now trust were *sent*, not accidents of time. This evening and the morning that awaits us are such things—of a beauty and hope which nobody present (this is bald presumption but I'll wager its truth) had any right to plan for, dream for, expect. Not Miss Rena, if I may, whose own good home has been troubled for decades by onslaughts of anguish as hard as any on mine or me. Not Robinson my son or Rachel his bride, whose beauty of form and spirit and laughter were no guarantee that life would prove yielding—the opposite, in fact: grace has often drawn nothing but the envy of fate, its sour grim grin. If I were the genius I once pined to be, I could paint you in words the face of my father, of Miss Rena's mother (Rob's Kendal grandmother), both lovely as daylight, both wrecked by time—"

Through that, Grainger quietly served all the others; then came back and stood five feet behind Forrest with the one last glass. In the pause he offered the tray, not looking at Forrest's eyes (because of Forrest's lateness, they had still said no more than ten words of greeting over platters of food; their first real meeting in twenty whole years was before them, if ever—the drawn scars of love and rupture untested).

Forrest reached for the full glass, let Grainger step back and turn toward the door; then continued, "—Not Grainger who has been with my people, been one of my people, since his early boyhood: since before his birth."

Grainger waited and looked.

Forrest faced him at last. "You did not plan this, did not even dream it, that first day in June twenty-one years ago when you brought me good news of Rob and his mother that proved bitter lies—surely not. Am I right?"

Grainger said, "No sir. I thought it would end some way like this."

"You were twelve years old—"

Grainger laughed. "N'mind. I still wanted things. Course, I doubted them since. No more. Not tonight." He stood quiet a moment, then knew he must go. He reached for the gray jug and set it on the floor by Mr. Hutchins' feet.

Mr. Hutchins said, "Go back, get three more glasses, and come in here with Della and Gracie."

Grainger said "Yes sir."

As he went, Forrest sat and, after brief silence, talk began again—the hum of waiting.

Rachel leaned toward Forrest. "I'm on Grainger's side. He knew, he said. God knows, I didn't; didn't know day from night for weeks on end. But I always hoped. I've thought just lately that hope was my trouble. I wanted all this, all Rob is giving; and I strained so hard to hope it into being that I almost ruined it. I thought I couldn't wait. Most children are hopeless; they think they are trapped and will always live in whatever misery they feel that instant. I was living for this." She smiled a little fiercely and looked to Alice. "Tell Mr. Mayfield I'm really not lying."

Alice said "No she's not."

Forrest said, "I believe you. The failure was mine."

Mrs. Hutchins touched Rachel on the back of her long hand. "Eat your supper, darling. What you still need is strength."

Rachel said, "I am stronger than anybody here. I've lived through my life."

"It's not over yet," Mrs. Hutchins said and tapped Rachel's plate—chicken, ham, corn pudding, green beans, stewed tomatoes, chow-chow, a buttered roll.

Grainger entered again with the same large tray—three glasses, the same kind—and Della and Gracie. Della still gave off the heat of cooking;

her brick-red dress was wet in great splotches shaped like countries on maps or the organs of animals, dark livers, lungs.

Mr. Hutchins bent down and brought up the jug and looked to Grainger. All the talking stopped, though Wirt Roberts ate.

Grainger offered the tray and Mr. Hutchins poured three-quarters of an inch of brandy for the Negroes. Grainger passed it to the women— Gracie first, then Della.

Mr. Hutchins took his own glass and warmed it in his hand, looking down toward his wife and Rachel and Forrest. Then he said, "Who's the one to pronounce this blessing? I'm about talked-out."

"So is Father," Rob said.

Forrest laughed with the others and nodded and said, "Since Grainger has planned this whole happy evening for twenty-some years now, I nomi-nate him." He took his own glass.

Gracie's eyes turned on Grainger, the side of his face, like a pair of matched hunters who had never yet failed to rout and cover any chosen quarry.

Della tried to see Rachel.

Rachel only watched Rob.

Rob was rocking his glass.

Grainger waited, not smiling.

Mr. Hutchins said "Grainger."

Grainger said "Yes sir."

Mr. Hutchins said "Bless it."

"Bless what, sir?"

"This crowd, everybody present here. This union tomorrow."

Grainger said, "I have said what I know to say."

Rob said "Say it again."

Grainger smiled toward Rob. "I knew this was coming. I knew you people would end up happy and doing me right. Me and Gracie look forward to helping you in Richmond. Mr. Forrest, I told you long years ago it would end up like this if you be patient."

Forrest nodded. "You did."

Rena led the others.

Gracie wiped her wet mouth with the back of her wrist and turned back to Della, who was two steps behind her. "Nothing finished, is it, Della?"

Only Della could hear her, and Della bent to laugh.

Gracie rolled her head back and licked the sweet hot rim of her glass.

Only Forrest saw the broad gold ring on Gracie's left hand—his mother's, waiting there in dull lamplight on its permanent journey through a melting world. "Content there," he thought. He smiled and, seated though he was, bowed deeply to Rachel (lit with surety, her eyes bright as any two lamps around her).

2

At ten-thirty Rob left Niles and the Robertses laughing in the parlor and climbed upstairs in the chilling dark to his Aunt Rena's door (her room flanked Rachel's on the other side from his). She had come to him shortly after supper and asked if he'd find a good lamp and lead her to her room; she was tired from her trip and had mending to do. He had led her and seen her in and fed her stove; and when she had thanked him and offered, like her best gift, a simple goodnight (a quick kiss, no speeches), Rob had said, "I will come back up in an hour and see that you're safe." She had said, "I'm safe. I will not let you down. Unlike some people, I have not come all this way by train to show-off such wounds as I have to a houseful of strange mountaineers. I'm a house-broken guest." Then she'd laughed to prevent his reading her too closely and had pushed him toward the door.

He leaned to it now and listened. Silence from Rena, though the voices of Rachel and her mother, muffled, leaked from Rachel's room. He stepped back and crouched and strained to see beneath. A frail warm draft blew against his mouth, but he saw no sign of light or glow. He had waited too long; Rena was dead asleep. Though he'd borne the weight of her love all his life, it did not occur to him that pure morphine could not have made her sleep while she waited for him to keep another promise or break another. Kneeling in the dark hall, he felt he must keep it—this last time at least—and felt he must keep it for Rena's sake, not permitting himself to see his own need: obeisance to the actual servant of his life. He stood and brushed the knees of his suit, rubbed his palms. Then he turned the cold doorknob and gently pressed—open. Dark and heat. He opened it another few inches and listened—nothing but the stove. He could not speak; he was dumb with sudden shame. *She is tired as a dog, and from nothing but me, her only work (my childish show); and here I stand to wake her, to pull more from her when the whole house and yard are live with other offers—awake and ready, more usable to me.* He was more than half-sober too (they'd finished the gray jug among the six men and a second glass for Grainger, a harmless division); but still he stood waiting. Long moments that seemed as empty as childhood of purpose or hope or even impatience. Given cover of dark, he could stand so forever.

At last Rena said, "I am trying to see." Her voice seemed to come from the chair not the bed.

"It's me," Rob said.

"I was trusting that."

"You were right again."

"You can come in," she said. "You're wasting the heat."

Rob stepped fully in and shut the door behind him. "How come it's so dark?"

"I had given up," she said. "I am in my nightgown. I figured those boys had you tied up till dawn."

"Oh no ma'm," he said. "They are just telling tales. I could leave them easy. They were trying to scare me."

"How was that?" Rena said.

"You know," Rob said, "—all the terrors of a wife, the sweetness of freedom."

Rena made a short sound in the pit of her mouth which Rob knew at once she had learned from her brother—Kennerly's glee at the gall of life. "Was your father joining in?" She was tense with power.

"Oh no ma'm," Rob said. "He is visiting Grainger."

"That's something then," she said. Her force was still gathering.

Rob heard but couldn't name it.

Then she launched it calmly. "I didn't mean to offer you a word of advice. I have gritted my teeth for long months now since that letter I sent you in—what was it?—June. But let me say this much and shut up forever. I have worshipped you, you know. You gave me nine-tenths of the pleasure I've had in the past twenty years, in all my life to now—you and flowers. But I never once doubted that a far greater thing for me as for most would have been a good marriage. From the depths and the heights of my spinster state, I can still see that—the greatest good. I've known what there is to know about solitude, for all that busy house. It has handled me kindly on balance, I guess. I am in strong health, I've kept my mind clear, I am not an old crank, I wish the world well. I've also known, through the kindness of my kin—my own parents, yours—how most sets of two people scrape themselves raw or, worse still, *smooth* through blindness or mean-ness or maybe just idleness: time enough to kill in; chickens in a coop pecking each other bald, then bloody, then dead. I've witnessed that closely. But I still swear to you on my gravest honor that the thing I know most surely of all, the thing *Jesus* knew (and knows this night, wherever He sits) is nothing but this—a single journey is a dry rag to suck. A single life. It was my given lot. I've often asked why but I never blamed a soul, just gnawed at the rag till it turned into food, a thin steady diet. But never say again that you spit on marriage, never laugh with any fool who peddles freedom to you. Son, *spiders* are free. Freedom's one more rag."

Rob waited till he knew she'd poured it all. Then he said, "I knew that and I haven't been laughing. Those boys are my guests; I was just being friendly."

Rena also waited. "Are you serious?" she said.

"Yes ma'm."

"About Rachel?"

"About what I'm doing."

"Which is what?" Rena said.

"Taking something life has thrown me."

Rena waited. "God help you. God help Rachel Hutchins." She did not sound desperate, was not imprecating or begging for help but calmly praying.

Rob said "Where is your lamp?" He needed now to see her, confirmation through his eyes that the flood of thanks he felt should run toward her.

"Please don't," Rena said.

"Why?"

"You need to leave."

Rob said "Why?"

Rena laughed. "You need your strength."

"I've got it," he said. "I'll have it tomorrow."

"No doubt," she said. "No doubt about that." She waited awhile; he did not move to go. So she stood in place. "I'll need *mine*," she said. "Son, I'll need all of mine."

"Yes ma'm," he said at last. Then he felt his way forward through air that grew hotter as he neared the stove till he found her cool face, her cold left hand. With his own right hand—warm, soft as he could make it—he felt for her brow and bent and kissed her once. Then he turned and quickly left.

3

Yet he paused at the foot of the stairs and listened for sounds of his friends; they had quieted but were there. Niles' voice had dropped to give them the story of his and Rob's visit to Roller's Retreat, a lengthy triumph (mainly for Niles). Rob hoped his father was still out with Grainger; he knew Mr. Hutchins had gone to his own room an hour before to give them this freedom, part of his welcome.

There was nowhere else Rob wanted to go and nowhere he needed, not reachable from here anyhow, not by morning (he felt morning coming). There was no human being he wanted to see. In fact, now he stood and plotted a course, there were several he dreaded to meet at all. A word in their voices, a thrust of their hands might rupture the paper walls he'd propped round the cube of space at the core of his chest, walls he'd shown to Rachel as permanent ramparts, worthy of trust, offered for life. Grainger and Della—powerful enemies, terrible friends. He'd go to them (he had not thought of bed; bed was hours from now, with Rachel twenty feet away merely hidden by lathing and plaster, merely postponed).

There was no light from Grainger's window or Della's; but he went on anyhow, strengthened by the cold (it had already frosted; his feet bit drily into brittle icing, parchment leaves); and as he passed the springhouse, Forrest said "Rob?" He turned and went there, stopping in the entrance, and saw by the starlight that his father was seated on the far-side railing, no overcoat or hat. Rob said "This'll kill you."

"It's advertised to *heal*."

Rob said, "I meant the night air."

"It won't," Forrest said, "and if it does, I die happy. I need to cool off. Been with Grainger and Gracie; they've got it hot as August, hot enough to cure tobacco."

"Old as they are?" Rob laughed.

"With their woodstove, I meant. They were just sitting talking, when I left anyhow."

Rob said, "What did Grainger tell you?"

"Nothing," Forrest said, "Did he have a thing to tell me?"

Rob said, "So I thought. He's been worried about you, that you'd come here and shun him."

Forrest said, "That was useless. I wrote him a letter oh a month ago to say any feelings that had backed up between us in the past twenty years could scatter now in peace; that as far as I intended, he was welcome back in Richmond as a help to you and Rachel—I would help him how I could."

Rob said "Maybe I should know—"

"What?"

"The cause of hard feelings, why you sent him home to Bracey."

Forrest paused. "That's over. Don't worry. That's past; he told me just now."

Rob said "All right" and stepped into the springhouse; went and sat on the railing, two feet from his father. He had no intention but patience, time to pass.

But Forrest said "Maybe you should," then stopped. "—If you're going to live with him. You may have him forever—Gracie won't stay long; I can see that even by oil-light in darkness." Then he stopped again and felt he was too near Rob, the presence like a live field of steady repulsion. Forrest stood and went over to the lid of the spring and sat down there. "He's told you who he is; you said that, didn't you?"

"Yes sir, he did."

"I told him that, my worst mistake."

Rob said "You sure it's true?"

Forrest said, "Father said so, the last time I saw him. It was right after Eva had taken you and gone. I had begged her back by sending her a Christmas box—a wagon for you and my mother's ring for Eva, Mother's wedding ring. Mr. Kendal sent it all back to me, next train; and when I found Father a little while later, I offered him the ring. He was with Polly

in the Mayfield house in Richmond—Polly'd come there to nurse him—
and I thought he might want to give the ring to Polly then. It was rightfully his since Mother was dead; he'd bought it years before. But he
wouldn't hear of taking it or letting Polly wear it; she also refused. I was
near-desperate then; and Grainger was with me (though he hadn't come to
Father's, waited at the boarding house). It seemed like I couldn't give
anything away. It was drowning my heart—my hands were full; nobody
would take me. So I gave it to Grainger; Father told me to. Grainger's
Christmas present—Gracie's wearing it tonight; says she's never had it off
since Grainger gave it to her. The sights it's seen. And some months later
just before we packed up and moved to Richmond, Grainger asked me why
I had given him the ring (Hatt never forgave me, though she didn't blame
Grainger); and I told him what I knew, what Aunt Veenie had told me
and sworn me to keep. She knew it would ruin him. I thought she was
wrong. I had lived with your mother for the previous year; and I thought I
had learned one good thing from her, that telling every scrap of truth your
mind might hold was the answer to trouble. So I told it to Grainger; and it
ruined him slowly, heightened his hopes far beyond my power to satisfy.
(Eva went on winning in my life, you see, long after she left.) If I'd just
held my tongue, he'd have loved me anyhow. He was well on the way. And
I treasured him."

Rob said "Where'd he go?"

"Not a single step. I mean, he came to Richmond and helped me
settle there. I didn't go till May when my teaching had finished—except in
February, two days to bury Father and to do right by Polly. I thought he
would like to live in Richmond—he had grown up in Maine with people
teeming round him; Bracey must have been a desert—and he did pitch in
like he meant to help. We stripped that house from attic to cellar, he and I
alone with Polly watching; took every stick of furniture out in the yard to
let the sun clean it. Then we scrubbed every inch of the inside with
brushes and carbolic acid; then we painted it white and varnished the
floors. I sold some furniture, gave some away—it had Father all in it—and
then we moved in. A little bare at first. I got a few pieces we needed later
on, but it looked then very much the way it looks now."

"Grainger slept in your study."

"It was his room then, entirely his. I had promised him that too."

"You sent him to school?"

"No I trained him at home. I hadn't gone to work at the Institute
then; that was two years later. I was still dragging white children downward
through Latin till my past caught up, as pasts will do—a cradle-robber was
the general impression. Not easy to deny, being more than half-true.
Anyhow I trained him in the evenings as I said. In the days he went on
fixing up the house—he knew a lot of carpentry; his father built boats in
Augusta, Maine—and he'd try to help Polly, with the cooking especially."

Rob said "Polly was the trouble."

"Did she tell you that? I know she talked to you."

"No sir, but she let me know she lost no love on Grainger."

Dark as it was, Forrest tried to see Rob. He wanted to see that his meanings were clear; that they registered clearly in the one living person for whom they now had urgency, a possible use in the matters of life— simple peace and continuance—which Rob was now volunteering to master: four sizable lives. But against the sky, Rob was dark, a shape. So rather than stand and go to him again, Forrest said, "Let me say this now once for all; and you please use it like the burdened man you are—Polly's never had love to lose anywhere. She has always been *at mercy*—of her father, then my father."

Rob said, "Polly chose that. She told me she was happy just three months ago." He pointed as if Polly's heart were a place, however far off.

Forrest said, "Only partly. No woman I've known, except your own mother, chose all of her life. They are dreadful to watch—women, I mean. I say that with knowledge; I have watched two of them living minute by minute through the life I gave them."

Rob said "Mother and who?"

"You know already. But I mean to confirm it so there'll never be a doubt once you've come to Richmond, so you'll know above all whenever I die—Margaret Jane Drewry has made my life. If you value me at all, help me repay her for it."

Rob nodded. "I knew. She told me that morning; but the other way around—she said her life there with you had been good."

"She was mainly being brave. She was scaring you off. It has been hard for her. She lives in a private cupboard of my life. She knows the space is, small (because I am *me*) and always in danger, from me and the world; so she fights for her corner."

"She fought-off Grainger?"

"He tried to fight her."

"How?"

"By worshipping me."

Rob laughed.

"No I mean it; not that I was any statue of God. Don't forget he was a child six hundred miles from home; his father turned him loose as easy as a pet. And he thought we were kin. That again was the worst. He'd lived in Maine—Negroes scarce as palm trees till Rover at least (now I guess there are Mayfields all over New England in shades of beige, called Walters for their grandmother Elvira Jane—my father's strong life still pumping through faces you and I will never see, the most of our kin. And he'd been treated well by his own people there; so he got it in his head he was nearly my son. I'm responsible for that. He was what I had in the awful months after Eva had gone—he and some little poems I was trying to write, pitiful trash. Hatt was no good to me (for all her kindness, she was nothing I needed); but Grainger filled in for a good many things that were suddenly absent or had always been—a son, a brother, another kind animal weaker than me and therefore safe and (while kin) strange enough to be always of interest, a little scary but invariably gentle to me. For me."

"It was Polly he fought?"

"Yes."

"She sent him away?"

"No she had no right to. I sent him away."

Rob waited awhile, then said, "Better tell me. You said yourself that I might need to know."

Forrest said, "He and I moved to Richmond in June. The next November—Thanksgiving in fact, eleven months exactly since I laid eyes on her—I went in to Polly and asked her to take me: as a wife would, I mean. I promised her nothing but the care she'd need while she chose to stay. She seemed to understand and has never asked for more, though she's had much more—twenty years' faith from me if that matters to her."

"She said it did."

"I'll choose to believe you. She's a very poor liar. Anyhow by Christmas, Grainger understood. I've never known how."

Rob said, "I knew the minute I saw her, when she answered the door."

"That was after long years; it had marked her face. Grainger knew in a week."

Rob said, "It's not a mansion and he's got good ears."

"But I tried to protect him."

Rob laughed again. "From what, please tell me?—a Negro boy with his own nature growing?"

"Oh the news," Forrest said, "—that I'd used him, compelled his love by claiming kinship, then discarded him already. Understand, I didn't think I had discarded him. I thought he could live there the rest of his life—it was fine by me; there was work to do. But he knew I'd ruined it; and the one thing he is is purer than Christ, in his purpose, his meaning. He means what he says—every word, every move—and will act it all out in the face of white coals of blinding fire."

"He will," Rob said. At last he yielded to the cold and shuddered from his belly upward to his chest, throat, teeth. He could not stop himself; what had started as a chill surrendered to some other force within him, a deeper fever that must have its way.

Forrest saw through the dark and patiently watched.

In a minute it had passed or shrunk into hiding again, pleased for now. Rob bound his coat tighter about him, hugged himself. "So will I," he said.

Forrest waited. "What, Son?"

Rob quietly drew all the breath he would need, seamless through his teeth. "I will do what I promise. I have always said I would, all my life. No person has asked me, not till now. Now I will."

Forrest said "God help you" and stood and came forward. With Rob still seated, Forrest was taller by a head; so he leaned and carefully kissed his son at the crest of the brow where cold flesh rose into colder hair.

4

In the little hall between Grainger's door and Della's, Rob stood to listen. He had come to see Grainger, delayed by his father but strengthened in the need; and he silently tilted his head toward the door for signs of life. At first he heard none. Then because he was urgent enough to consider waking a man who had just finished seventeen hours of work and must start again in five more hours (and whose long-gone wife was with him again after nearly four years), Rob went on listening till finally he could hear what at first seemed the life of the pine door itself, some peaceful exchange of life in its heart. Tired as he was and the brandy still in him like a soft bass line, Rob was primed for comfort in any shape; so his left ear pressed to the ribbed wood, his eyes shut. The life continued. Their struggling of course—Grainger's and Gracie's, their bodies joining, their wordless swapping of welcome and hate, thanks and blame, in the voices of children: helpless but accurate, utterly precise as they dug and worked in one another to find that childhood of perfect assurance one step beyond which lay endless peril, a lifetime of danger, abandonment. More silent then ever, Rob begged them not to stop, yearned somehow to join them.

But Gracie stopped—four cries of loss, maybe also of gain (some private gain of strength or knowledge she could take away with her).

Grainger dug awhile longer—Gracie's voice clearly said "You getting anywhere?"—then his own stop came: blunt stop, no sound. Then long silence from them both. No noise from the bed or the dry floor beneath them or the stove that would surely be roaring high—as if they had spent not only their little savings of force and want but their lives as well, total being, and had left the bed empty, the room, the house.

Rob turned toward Della's, first time in three months, the last intention he had had for tonight. He did not listen but quietly knocked and stood back to hope. He could not hear steps or Della listening or her hand on the knob, but after a minute the door slowly opened.

Her one lamp was lit, not bright enough to show through her window shade but enough for her work (a collar for the dress she would wear to the wedding) and to outline her now as she stood, looking out.

Rob said, "You ought to been asleep long ago."

Della said, "I ought to been an angel with wings and long yellow curls."

"Well, you weren't."

"What you doing about it?"

"Praying," Rob said. He could smile by then.

Della stood on in the door, the heat running past her like a breath against Rob.

"Can I step in?" he said.

She thought it through slowly. Then she stepped back a step. "You used to know the way."

"Still do," he said. He entered in one move and shut the door behind him, then looked first to see that her shade was truly down. It was—he was instantly safer, calm: a ship, a sealed ship plowing the night, unsuspected, unseen.

Della went to her bed again and sat where she'd been, in a narrow nest by her pineboard table where the lamp burned steady. She reached to turn it up.

Rob said "Leave it please."

She studied him a good while. "You hiding again?"

He smiled and nodded and started toward her one chair.

"You come to the wrong place then," Della said. She picked up her sewing.

Rob stopped at the chair, held the tops of its back. "Why is that?"

"You know." She did not look up but took three stitches, small and neat as a nun's.

"I don't," he said. "You have been good to me."

"I done finished that."

"How come?"

Della looked. She could hardly see him for the dark, but her mind supplied what her eyes were denied. "You know; that's all." She stared on a moment. "Anyhow I'm busy."

"What at?"

"My plans."

Rob laughed once. "What are they?"

"*My* business," she said.

At that he sat down. Della showed no response. "You planning to die?" he said (the dress on her lap was a dark shade of green and seemed nearly black in the dark).

"Be good to me," she said.

"I was joking," Rob said. "I'm tired and crazy. Are you going somewhere?"

"Yes sir," Della said. "Tomorrow morning I'm going in the front room to see you and Rachel get married together. Then I'm running out here to this little piece of house to get out of this good dress in a hurry. Then I'm going to the kitchen and cook my black titties off all day so Grainger and Gracie can put on aprons and serve all the company."

Rob said "You're paid." He offered it gently, a mild reminder of a fact forgotten (he intended to leave her ten dollars tomorrow, had saved it for the purpose; but he didn't tell her now, a final surprise).

Della nodded. "So right. And I saved four pennies out of every five."

"For me?" Rob said. "You making me a present?"

"You got the last present you getting out of me." Her face was calm as wood. But her voice was earnest; she would not be mistaken.

"—And I came here to thank you. You've helped me keep going."

"I'll carry that with me then."

"Not tomorrow," Rob said. "Just enjoy tomorrow. But after I'm gone, you remember I'm grateful."

She turned up her lamp to the edge of smoking. Rob was clear to her now. "Shit *on* you," she said.

Rob said, "Don't, Della. I need a lot of goodness."

"More than goodness," she said.

"What?"

"You marrying Rachel?—Rachel's your bride, ain't she?"

"Tomorrow morning."

"Well, it be morning soon if it ain't already; and when you get Rachel, you got you a job make road-building look like stuffing feather beds."

"You sure?" Rob said. He had not spoken Rachel's name in this room before.

"Rachel always been a job."

"How long have you known her?"

"Lot longer than you. But you the one getting her."

"How long?" Rob said.

"Born with Rachel." Della stopped again. She genuinely did not want to speak of Rachel—delicacy, hatred.

Rob said, "Please tell me what you know. I may need to use it."

"My life or Rachel's?"

"'Rachel.'"

"Too late. You *in* her."

"Tomorrow," Rob said.

"And from then on out."

It was part of the slender power Rob possessed, that he did not guess the cause of Della's edge. He suspected it came from her being a servant with years of time to witness Rachel's case and now a final judgment of despisal. He did not think in any part of his mind that he himself—in all his different shapes, the air he bore around him—had poisoned one more thing by his presence. He saw Della now as a generous friend who had helped him in need—the morning when he'd stood above the river and intended to die, the nights on her body—and of whom he knew more than of any other human besides perhaps his mother (he had shared their bodies in various ways; lived in his mother's, visited Della's). He thought she could help him again, and should. He tried to persuade her. "You were born around here?"

"This room," Della said.

"Your people lived here?"

"Worked here—my mama did; my papa was gone."

"How did she get here?"

"Her mama worked here—my grandmama Julia. *Her* mama belonged to Mr. Raven's people; and my great-grandaddy was a man that come through after the freedom—so few niggers round here, he settled on her; but he passed on off when Julia come. Same as my daddy. Nothing round here for men to do less they want to turn woman and wait on people. No land to farm. So anyhow I was born right in this bed; some hot summer nights I can still smell blood. I come after Rachel, just ten months later; but she use that to try bossing me. She want me to dress her up and plait her hair and pull her round the yard in a old goat cart. I won't studying Rachel. I played by myself when I won't helping Mama; and sometime some little white children would come to stay in the rooms, and Mr. Raven pay me a nickel a week to tend to em. Then Rachel got to like me. I didn't change a bit, but she grew up enough to stop being mean or to see it won't getting her nowhere but ugly. And for five or six years we was close as two sisters. I would sleep in her room when Mama would let me—little cot she had—and we used to teach each other what we knew." Della stopped at that and rethreaded her needle as quickly as in daylight and worked on in silence.

Rob said "What did she know?"

"School stuff. How to read. She was funny then too, knew a lot of funny stuff. She could take-off people till you fell down laughing or were scared to death—sometimes she would change into some other person, some girl that had spent the summer here or a boy that was dead, and stay that way for an hour, all night. I slept right with her, more nights than one, when I couldn't swear I knew who she be in the morning when daylight strike her. It was just fun then."

"What did you teach her?"

Della waited awhile. "Nothing dirty if that's what you aiming at. She knew all that; she the one went to school and saw other children. No I guess I didn't show her nothing but care. I liked her by then—she was bigger than me—and I always told her. I never held back; didn't lay down my head in her room *one* night till I ask her, 'Rachel, you still staying here, ain't you?' or 'Rachel, you want me to call you in the morning?' (she outslept me; I was up with the roosters and would lay down beside her on top of the cover till she finished her dream, then I'd tell her 'You late'). Nobody love her but me and Mr. Raven, back then anyhow. And she loved us, acted like she did—us and my mama."

"Where is your mother?"

"In Heaven."

"How long ago?"

"Two years this Christmas. While Rachel was sick."

"Tell me what that was like."

"Mama dying or Rachel?"

"Rachel please."

Della smiled for the first time, long, straight at him. "You going to have a whole life to hear about Rachel in."

"I know it," Rob said.

"I'm the one that *know* though."

"What?" Rob said.

"Her dream that caused it." Della pointed to her table. "I got my book."

Rob stood to see. In all his visits here, he'd never had light; so the things he knew, he knew by touch. He had thought it was a Bible—*Thompson's Egyptian Secrets Unveiled: The Book of Dreams*, bound in something like blue oilcloth, heavily used. He did not want to touch it but sat down again and said "Tell me then," no request, an order.

Della went on as calmly as if it were her wish—by now it was; it would show her power, the rest of the story. "One morning I woke up and was lying down by Rachel; and she started shivering in fast little snatches, hard as pneumonia. I thought she was teasing—she was out on her back—so I leaned over close to study her eyes. They were shut down tight but shivering like her. She was suffering something, so I let her do it. Then finally she slowed down and rested too deep—too much like her corpse—so I woke her up; and she said to me 'Thank you.' I told her, 'You been somewhere; where was it?' She say, 'I been hunting my boy that was drowning.' I say, 'I saw you. Look like you found him.' —'Did,' she say, 'but I couldn't get him out.' I ask her 'Where is he?' So she lie there—it's early; nobody up but us, not even Mr. Raven—and tell me, 'Della, I had this boy that was close to me as skin; but I woke up one night, and he won't there with me. I stripped down the bed to see where he hiding, right down to the slats, or maybe in my sleep I had smothered his face. I was having to feel; the whole thing was dark. But I still couldn't find him; so I ran outside in my thin nightgown—it was summer and hot—and went to some woods and called round there till he answered his name, way off, real weak. Then I kept on calling, and he answer his name, and I finally get to him. I still can't see him, but I hear him speak his name, and he's struggling to float. It seem like a pond and him at the edge. I try to reach out; fall down on my stomach and stretch way toward him. And I do get to touch him—brush his fingers: so weak they can't hold me now—but he go on sinking, and I run back home.' That was when she could rest again, when I saw her resting."

Rob said "What was his name?"

"She never said that."

"Then what did it mean?"

Della said, "It *still* mean. Dreams always true, true all your life; that's the trouble with dreams. But I hadn't paid all that much mind to dreams, not up till then. The book belonged to Mama; she kept it for years, all she could read. So that morning, laying there, I thought it meant a sweetheart, some boy Rachel was loving and couldn't get to. She had quit school by then; but some boys hung around—she won't that shy. I told her right then, 'It mean you getting married.' Rachel stare back at me like she planning to cut me. She say, 'My baby. That boy was my baby.' "

"Who was right?" Rob said.

"Rachel, part right."

"What part?"

"The baby. Later on that morning after I cooked breakfast and helped Mama sweep (I was cook by then; Mama had what killed her), I come out here and read in the book. Trouble is, you got to know what to look for, where the seed of the dream is really at. So I picked *drowning*; it was what Rachel said when she first woke up. And *drowning* in the book mean 'A healthy baby coming.' "

"Did you tell Rachel that?"

"I told Mama first and she say 'Don't.' "

"Then what did it cause? You said the dream caused something."

"You bound to know that." She had finished her work and began to fold the dress as carefully as though for perpetual storage, no hope of use.

"I talked to Mr. Hutchins. I know what he told me."

"He tell you she spent the best part of a year working on a baby?"

Rob said, "He told me she imagined a baby."

Della looked up and nodded. "Imagined it, started it growing inside her, and nearly let it kill her. She not well yet."

"But she didn't have a sweetheart?"

Della smiled. "You."

"—Before her sickness."

"Nobody ever touched her deep, I know, if that's what you asking."

"So why did it happen?"

Della said, "Ask Miss Alice; her daddy was the doctor."

"I'm asking you."

Della searched his face slowly for seriousness. "Punishment," she said.

Rob could not ask *for what?* He knew enough answers.

"Mama thought so too."

"Where is she?"

"In the ground; I already told you. While Rachel was crazy. Mama knew Rachel even better than me; so when Rachel got bad, couldn't nobody else but Mama make her eat—couldn't nobody else get near her half the time. She hated her daddy, turned against him like he was dog turds. Things I heard her say to Mr. Raven would stop most hearts: '*You asking me to kill this baby I love. I'll kill you first.*' And he never done nothing on earth to Rachel but cherish her, give her all she need. But she stayed good to Mama—and me too really; still I couldn't make her eat. She was trying to starve that baby out; but Mama would sit with her hour on end and talk to her gentle and get her to swallow three mouthfuls of something, then take out her slops. Mama never told her once that she didn't believe her, that the baby won't there. She just say, 'Let him go on and *come*, Rachel. We ready to love him.' And Rachel got better."

"At the clinic?" Rob said, "—Alice's father's?"

"Right here," Della said. "My mama talked her round in under a year. Got her out and talking sense and facing people; and then died herself, Mama did. Fell dead out yonder on the way to the spring. I saw her out the window and flew straight to her, but by then she didn't know me. Doctor say her brain split right down to the core like a twisted apple; say it pressed her to death, just drowned her in blood. And Rachel ain't mentioned her since to this day, hurt her too much when she still so weak. That hospital business in Lynchburg was something else, just resting up and eating and making new friends after Lucy my mama worked herself dead to bring her back to life." Della put both hands in the cover at her sides, buried them deep as if protecting some precious part from what might come. Then she said, "Rob, how come you taking her on?"

He was not offended. He knew an answer which he thought was true, and he knew nobody who deserved it more than Della. "She's the person who has asked me."

Della smiled a little and looked at the floor. "More ways than one to ask somebody. More than one thing to ask him."

Rob studied her then—what little he could see, folded on herself in the dark as she was. He had never seen all of her, however much he'd held or delved in for solace. It seemed to him now a necessity to see her; to honor her entirely by a grateful searching of her only gift, this small strong body that would last a few years at the rate it was burning (less than years if she went now to Philly or Richmond even), an image of help. It was nothing he had planned; it would not be for him—for Della finally, a clean farewell they could both understand. He felt no constraint from the idea of Rachel or his duties tomorrow but stood and stepped forward quietly, no hurry.

She did not look up.

He reached for her chin—his hands had not touched her face before—and tilted her skull (a bird's skull) upward.

She was managing to smile.

Rob said, "More ways than one to answer too."

She did not understand but, still in his hand as a polished stone, she took time to think. "N'mind about that. I was thinking to myself." She lifted her face very neatly from his hold and stared toward a ceiling which, for all they could see, might have been the bare sky—a night to fly through, in dream, from here. "You go," Della said. Her face never looked back down to watch him—his quick obedience, his simple "Thank you"— and long after he had gone out the door and shut her behind him with no sound at all, she was still looking up, recalling the sight of her mother struck dumb in wet cold dirt, not knowing her, not caring, refusing even to clasp Della's finger which was all that was left her as she rushed toward whatever peace she had won, what secret reward.

5

In his own room once he had lighted the lamp, Rob found two things, both waiting on his bed, both in white envelopes, one on the other. He turned the lamp higher and examined them. The top one said *Rob* in a strange script elaborate with flourishes. The other said *Robinson* with Rena's manly economy. Hers was the thicker so he sat on the bed by the light and opened it—a picture and a note. The picture was clearly Rena but a girl, no Rena he remembered, just the bud of her present face behind a wild laugh. A girl at the stable door, fifteen or sixteen, a heavy wood rake like a banner in one hand, a child in her other hand (its fingers held loosely). Rena faced the camera and was laughing for that; the child faced her—a long look up; the child was maybe three—and laughed for her so gladly that its face was a fading ghost. The note said,

Rob,

This is you and I nineteen years ago. I was cleaning out the stable, much against Eva's will. She had tried to argue me out of it all morning, saying if I couldn't stand a little manure underfoot, Father had good strapping men for the job. I told her "None better than me" and went. So she had the grace to leave me alone two hours, when I'd almost finished. Then she woke you up from your nap and dressed you—Eva made the sailor-suit—and taught you a sentence to say to me. Then you both came to get me. Eva brought her Kodak. You were meant to stay with her, well back from the stable, and call out to me "Your beau is here." Then Eva would snap my picture as I came to the door all embarrassed (I never knew at what; there was surely no beau, in the yard or on the moon). She had

*just got her camera as a gift from Father; took her five years to stop
catching people off balance. Anyhow you said your piece and I heard you;
but I thought you said "Your boy is here," and I still think you did (what
did you know of beaux?). So I trudged to the door with my dirty rake to
see you—me dirty as the rake—and you ran toward me while Eva was
sighting. Sylvie was behind her, laughing too. You were meant to stay clean
and save your little suit.*

*Well, I thought you were mine from then on out. I had prized you
before, since the day she brought you home after Mother's death. But I
took this as proof, and you never let me doubt it in all the years since. It is
one of the few things I'm glad have lasted; and I hope you will take it now
this night as not just the record of a child's laughing choice (in the picture
I am looking at Eva to see if she knows it yet—she does, she does) or even
as my cheap wedding present to you but as further proof of my outburst
tonight: that two of anything are better than one, dirtier no doubt but
likelier to laugh.*

Sleep well, dear boy. I will watch you tomorrow.

> *Your satisfied,*
> *Rena*

He laid those two things carefully on the table—he would put them in
his bag, take them with him tomorrow—and studied the other envelope.
Still strange, and he knew every script in the house except Gracie's. It was
firmly sealed so he tore it open. *Dear Rob . . .* signed *Rachel* but not in
Rachel's hand. Dictated—to whom? Suddenly colder than the unheated
room, Rob strained to read it.

Dear Rob,

*Before I can go to sleep, I want to give you one real chance to
stop—to think it through again now, with hours still left, and see if you
thoroughly want to do what you'll promise tomorrow. If not, I can swear
to you now and for always that I will understand and will not blame you
long.*

*You are packed. You can take your grip now and go, letting absence
be your answer.*

*Or else you can come to my room and tell me. I will not be asleep;
that's the one sure thing.*

*If I see you tomorrow I will take that as sign that you mean all we do
and will always mean it.*

> *In grateful honesty,*
> *Rachel Hutchins*

The hand was Niles'—Rob was almost certain (Niles disguised by a powerful effort that caught Rachel's voice but missed her plain headlong script). Almost certainly Niles. Rob had waited two days for the wedding jokes to start—from Niles, the Robertses, even Grainger—but nothing till this. He tried to summon anger—they were still awake downstairs in the parlor; an occasional laugh filtered up, a happy word: all smeared with ignorance, ignorant fear, of the simple pains and duties of love which Rob had yearned since childhood to shoulder and was shouldering now.

Yet he read it again; and despite the fraud, was shaken deeply by Niles' understanding of the life at stake; more deeply than at any time since August when he'd run toward his father, a random goal almost not reached, and settled the course he'd begin tomorrow. He did not doubt what the fake letter doubted—his own strength of purpose, the durability of present intentions. He doubted, feared, Rachel's own capacity to bear his purpose, his loyalty. In his whole life till now, only Rena had borne him; and he'd chosen her early, a laughing girl cleaning out a stable. Maybe Sylvie. Maybe Grainger—though with Gracie back, Rob hoped that Grainger could stare at her awhile, spare the Mayfields a little of his expectations. But Rachel. What had Rachel ever borne but herself?—her own fears, the murderous wildness of her heart. Why had he thought she could ever support a thing as crushing as constancy?

He listened to the house. Sounds still came up from Niles in the parlor, and oddly still caused no anger in Rob. He had spent his whole life being understood. What he gambled on now, or would tomorrow, was blind and dumb—permanent welcome, permanent thanks. He was listening for Rachel. He sat in the thickening cold of his room, having doused his lamp, and listened in total stillness for minutes. No creak or breath. When he knew she was sleeping or gone or dead, he rose and groped through the dark to find her.

6

RACHEL was sleeping lightly and so heard his one knock as merely an innocent noise of the old house yielding to frost. He was at her bed and sitting on the edge before she knew she was not alone. The room was black but she felt no alarm—Rob, by his smell: the thread of brandy on the broad deep mass of his nature, clean, dry. She lay in place and looked toward his presence. "Everybody else asleep?" she said.

"I don't think so."

"Who saw you come in?"

"How much does it matter?" Rob spoke normally, not whispering.

"It all depends."

"On what?"

Rachel waited in the hope that day would break or her eyes adjust to see his face and test it for gravity, cruelty, drunkenness maybe (no, he smelled too sane). Then she said, "It depends on how many people you want to hurt before tomorrow comes."

"None of them," Rob said. "If me coming in here to talk to you hurts a living soul, then it's that soul's problem. This is not their business."

"Is it mine?" Rachel said.

"You are Rachel, aren't you?"

"Yes."

"You plan to marry me?"

"At eleven o'clock tomorrow."

"Then it's sure *God* your business." His voice stayed steady as a glove reaching toward her with a still hand inside it, powerful, cold, and urgent to seize or harm or save.

Rachel waited again in hopes Rob would offer more explanation, but after a while she said "Don't scare me."

"Why not?"

"I think you know. I've been scared too long."

"No I don't know," he said.

"You talked to Father. He told me he talked to you very fully. Rob, they know everything I know," Rachel said, "—everything but the terrible ways I felt. And I thought you knew that. You promised you did; your kindness promised you knew my feelings."

"I do," Rob said. "I've thought I did. But I wonder now."

"What?"

He lay down beside her, his head on the vacant pillow but his body outside the cover, fully clothed. "I wonder what the story of all this is."

Rachel turned toward his nearness, but they did not touch. "What if I told you the truth?" she said.

"I'd marry you tomorrow."

"What if I lied?"

"I'd marry you still."

"Tomorrow?"

"Yes."

Rachel stayed on her back but raised both arms toward the distant ceiling. "Then I'll tell you the truth. It's just a story; there's no explanation. But the story happened, and happened to me." Her hands came down and, with perfect accuracy, her left hand lighted on Rob's own right—her hand, herself, the survivor of her story. Rob turned his palm toward her, and her fingers stayed there. "I lived in misery all of my life till you came here—the honest truth. I had what I needed of clothes and food and Father's goodness, constant care. I know that the world is mostly people who are naked and starved and crusty with sores and alone as mules, but I also know my misery was real and strong enough to wrench up a mind like a tree. Not that I was any white oak, but anyhow I went."

"What was wrong? What misery?"

"That's the hard part," she said, "—where I sound spoiled and whining. But I think the fact is this—by the time I was four or five years old, I had looked around enough (at Father and Mother, my poor grandfather, the few guests here, Della and Lucy) to figure out that what waited for me was *time*. Not punishment or age but simple time. Tens of thousands of days, all waiting ahead, requiring me to live them."

Rob said "You could have quit."

"I didn't know that. Children don't kill themselves; they don't know they can."

"I did," Rob said. "I knew the very gun on my grandfather's mantel that would do the trick. I used to get a footstool and climb up and watch it, watch it for signs that it wanted to serve."

"But watching was all?"

"I stroked it occasionally," he said, "—never gripped it though. I was in love; I had some hope."

"Who with?" Rachel said.

"I told you. I loved my mother. She kept dropping promises like notes in my path that she'd turn to me soon and let me tell her, stand still and let me show her."

Rachel said "You were lucky."

"I was miserable as you."

She pressed his palm hard. "You were so deeply lucky you should fall on this cold floor now and thank Jesus. I was bare as a bone."

Rob said "What was the difference?"

"I've already told you."

"Again please," he said. "It's late and I'm worried."

"Several people loved me but I couldn't love them."

"Boys?" Rob said.

"Oh no, just my family. You had your mother which taught you a lot, proved to you anyhow that people existed—one person at least—who could pull you through all the time ahead."

"Your father told me he worshipped you."

"That was just what he did; it was part of my trouble—he worshipped the likeness of his mother in me. I'm her likeness, they say (I've startled old ladies that have stayed here for years by walking out onto the porch in the morning, and they'd think it was Grandmother fifty years ago). He had hurt her, you see, by trying to leave here and then she died; so all my life, he's been recompensing me."

"He said he understood you."

Rachel said, "I think he did. I still think he does. I think most men understand most women if they just stop to think—men were made by women; every man ever born lived inside a woman's body, the whole safe world, for almost a year before she turned him out. What my father knew though was mainly this—there was nobody near me, nor any sure hope of anybody ever, that my heart could move toward. He'd known his mother and he'd been himself. He knew there were people who must live their lives with not one object they can sacrifice to, no room they can dress with the gifts they have." She turned her head to Rob, to try again to see him. Nothing still. So she lay on in silence.

He said, "That's the story? That's all the story?"

"It's the part I'm sure I can bear to tell tonight."

He took his hands from her and said "Tell the rest."

Rachel waited till she knew he was serious—he did not return his hand. Then she waited till she knew she would not refuse him. Then she searched for his hand and found it on his thigh.

He accepted her touch, returned a slight pressure.

She said, "By the time I had finished school, I still knew my one thing—the world was empty for me. I could read and cook, I could make people listen when I talked in a room, I could even make them watch me and smile when I passed (I had strong teeth that are naturally white); but I hadn't found a soul that made me want to draw the next two breaths."

"Was it simple as that?"

"That simple," she said. "I've had a simple life like everybody else."

"So then you lost hold." Rob gave it as a fact to ease her onward.

"I tried to *take* hold. The whole thing that got everybody so scared just started by me trying to change my luck."

"How was that?"

"That child; you knew about that?"

"The one you dreamed about?"

"Della told you?"

"I asked her," Rob said.

Rachel weighed that a little—a bearable burden? Then she said, "All right. Della knows as much as any other body, excepting Father. She was in at the first; she was cut off like me, only she never cared."

"She does," Rob said.

"You asked her that too?"

"Yes." He pressed her hand again.

It was not enough to go on. She was suddenly famished of fuel to continue. She took back her hand and rolled slowly toward him, to her own left side, stopping so near him that the breath from her nostrils was still damp and warm when it struck his right cheek and returned to her.

Rob turned also and accepted her nearness. They swapped breath silently but did not touch.

Then Rachel could say, "Della thought I was actually carrying a child that would grow and be born. So did Lucy her mother. I'd given all the

signs; they had every right. I believed it myself, eventually at least, once
Mother and the doctors had said I was crazy. It was Father that knew and
never really doubted. When I had got bad and turned on them all and
stayed in my room, trying hard to live in the face of them saying I was sick
and must die—when I was like that, Father came in one morning and I
wouldn't speak (he had tried a few days before to say I was only imagining
and should face plain truth; I was Rachel, alone). I was lying full-dressed
on my bed—not this one; then I lived downstairs—and he said 'Can I sit?'
I said, 'You can sit or jump or swim; I will not listen to you.' So he sat
there awhile quite a way from the bed in a white cane rocker; and then he
started in just easy and quiet, that good voice of his I could no more
refuse than a crown from angels. He said, 'Rachel, I have come to beg your
pardon for yesterday, for doubting you. I have thought all night, and I
know I was wrong. I not only doubted you but also myself, my own heart's
knowledge, the one kind that matters. I know what I've known since
before you could talk—you are trying to make yourself a life you can bear
to live; you are craving this child. If you'll come back to us, if you'll live
here with us again and wait awhile longer, I will promise you this; I can
give it like a gift—the world will open and let you in; there will be somebody to meet you when you enter.' I decided to believe him. There was
nothing else to do but rot here in hatred or bafflement. So I said to him,
'Tell me how to come back'; and he said 'Let me think'—I had caught him
off guard; he had just not expected me to answer him then. He didn't
know the powers he had earned through the years, to calm me and ease
me. He sat on awhile. We didn't speak again but late that evening he came
back in and said he had thought and would I make a short visit to Lynchburg for strength and rest? I knew what he meant, but I said yes I would
(he had already wired to see if they'd take me); and two days later
Mother, Della, and I went down on the train—Della just for the trip, to
help Mother out if I broke my promise. I never did, though I had some
bad days, and Father didn't either. After all those weeks with Alice's
father, I came back home; and you know it from there. I was helped
several ways." Her face was still toward him. They still had not touched.

Rob said "That's the story?"

"Till now," Rachel said.

"And it's true?"

"I swear."

"You know mine," he said, "—why I'm here, why we're going."

She found his face, his jaw, with her fingers. "One question," she said.
"Why am I going with you?"

"You just told me that."

"No. Why have you asked *me?* Why do you want me?"

Rob knew that he didn't. For the first time clearly he saw, as a picture,
the enduring future of this small choice—years of days with a poor child he

knew he was bound to harm, as he had been harmed by his own mother's choice so soon regretted. A future to which he was bound now by honor, natural courtesy, because this thin girl stretched here beside him, stroking his face, had asked for his life; no one else had. But they *had*—Rena, Grainger, his wild Aunt Hatt. He also saw them now; they seemed welcome refuge compared with this—generous calmers whom he'd cruelly abandoned tonight, tomorrow, in a quick resort to remedies as harsh as any his mother had seized as a girl, his mother's mother self-poisoned on the floor. Della, Sylvie, his father, Polly—he was generally loved: Min Tharrington. But he'd now chosen something lonelier than solitude despite the plain fact that, all his life, he had liked laughing company, the nearness of others. The thing he did not consider at all was refusal, this moment—clean quick flight, the lesson of old Robinson his father's father. He did not take the fingers that warmed his cheek, but he yielded to the gentle endless plea. By slow degrees his face pressed forward—the growing of a vine, the progress of a hand on the face of a clock—till his mouth met hers.

She welcomed him fiercely with both her hands.

Rob gave what he could with mouth and head. Nothing else of his body wanted to serve or offered to. It had not reneged, for four years now, such a fervent chance. After two long minutes he drew back and lay staring up, not breathing. Then he breathed out in one long silent flushing.

Rachel said, "Everything I have told you is true. It is all I know."

Rob laughed, the loudest sound either had made. "Well, I thank you," he said. "It's more than *I* know, more than anybody else ever told me before. I believe you though and I swear to use it every way I can." He stood and left quietly; not touching her again. He would trust time for that; tired as he was, he was young and learning. Time would teach him to take her.

7

November 28, 1925

Dear Mother,

It is just about three in the morning. My clock has run down; so I'm guessing by the state of my brain and eyes—very poor but I'll live till tomorrow, I guess. It is tomorrow. Rob's wedding day and Forrest Mayfield's birthday (had you remembered that? Of course I never knew it; but Grainger said at supper, "Mr. Forrest, you're celebrating two things tomorrow," and I asked what he meant—fifty-five years old). He looks very strong and well—Father, I mean—and is here by himself and has asked after you. He has never said one word against you ever. So you could have come, you see; I told you you could. Even if he'd stood here with Polly his help on the steps to meet you, pouring out contempt; even if I'd let him, you still could have come. You have faced worse than that. I am your only child, all on earth that will love you once Papa dies. Sylvie could have nursed him there as well as you, for one day and night. Anyhow you aren't here for the curious to watch (they all need to see you, having heard me for months); but you're here for me. Very much here and running the whole strange show, driving it—the engine.

All's quiet right now. Even the groomsmen are long since asleep or dead or in comas (Mr. Hutchins broached a jug of mountain brandy; we may all die by dawn or be blind for the service, an all-blind wedding! It's that anyhow). No one but me seems to be awake, and I won't be any longer than it takes me to tell you this. What I mean by calling you the engine of this is—I do it for you, as a gift and as obedience. The gift is that now I take my weight off you. The obedience is that you urged me toward life, and this looks like life. You of all living creatures should be here to bless me.

I will just have to guess what you mean when you say in the note with the gift (we thank you for that; Rachel will write you)—Long lives together. That will occupy my mind quite sufficiently, I think, through a whole wedding day. I am scared you are right; all your wishes are granted or have been till now.

So you'll know where to reach me in case of trouble, we are going to Washington tomorrow evening and will be at the Hotel Hamilton there for four or five days till we run out of monuments, museums, and money. Then we'll be at the Richmond address, which you have. Grainger and his wife (who is back for now) will go on ahead and get the house open and well dried out. It should be in good running order by Christmas, and you are invited to spend that with us. There is plenty of room, and I won't go to work before January second. You would do Rachel Mayfield an honor and a favor if you make the trip. She may well be shaky on her pins for a while, having never left home except for treatment; and you, I know, could show her a lot about steadiness. It's what you've shown me.

> Thanks for it,
> Love,
> Rob

8

Two hours after that, just before she must wake in the cold damp dark and head for the kitchen, well before day, Della made this dream from the trapped reservoirs of her mind, heart, body, and not only watched it in sleep like a hemorrhage streaming up from her but wished it on all the sleepers around her in quarters and house, a permanent hurt.

She had gone in and started the stoves and was baking six brown-sugar pies for the wedding dinner (Grainger puttered behind her but she took no notice) when the door from the dining room opened and through it her mother walked, young as when Della could first remember her and strong, though not smiling. Della thought to herself, "Mama dead and gone; why she coming here?" and she went cold with fright; but she could not speak or move for joy. She was still young herself—young as her mother, well and strong—and now the one deep grief of her life was canceled, healing. Her mother spoke quietly to Grainger; then laughed and said, "Della, get busy. They coming." Then the house was full for the rest of the dream—loud rooms of people all eating food as if food were new, not simply free. Della cooked it, not stopping—deep skillets of chicken, two turkeys, a beef roast, hot biscuits and rolls, whole tubs of corn pudding, a fresh set of pies—and her young mother served it with Grainger ducking round her like a pigeon in heat. But Della was happy, did not mind the work—no sign of the Hutchins—because of this luck, this piece of repair. She said to herself, "I could cook night and day—no rest, no water—for a yard of hounddogs and still be glad." But she had not yet said a word to her mother and seldom dared to look, though her mother went on throwing jokes at Della (little peaceful flowers that Della took, smiling, and strained to remember like prayers for help or the meanings of dreams). Then the day was dark but the house was still full, and Della began to know she was tired. Yet her mother came at her every minute or two with hands extended for fresh plates of food till finally she knew that her mother was real, had strengthened in death and was really come back and was planning to stay here, their home again; so Della said finally "Mama, let's *breathe*," meaning pause and rest. Her mother thought quickly and said, "Sit down. Every mouth fed now and the bellies can wait." Della sat by a table at the side of the room and leaned on her hand. Her mother stood on in the empty middle beneath the hanging lamp; and Della could watch her now steadily, no fear of her wasting. She even said, "Mama, come sit down here" (there was just one chair; the place was her lap). Her mother gave a laugh and said "*I'm* staying; n'mind me." Then the hall door opened—Mr. Hutchins, one arm stretched down, leading something. A pale naked baby all arms and legs, too young to walk but standing anyhow on shriveled white feet and pulling at Mr. Hutchins' hand like the tits of an udder. Della's mother didn't look; she was still facing Della. Mr. Hutchins said, "This thing has got to be fed." Della looked round for Grainger—nowhere, gone. She knew that she had nothing to give it. She was tired and resting. Again she didn't speak. The baby came forward; left Mr. Hutchins and lurched forward fast on its spidery toes and went to Della's mother and (with no help from her, no notice even) began to clutch and climb her, fist over fist, as if she were a rope. She never touched it, never reached out to help it climb; but when it reached her waist she opened her dress and gave it her breast, the full left breast which Della still knew as well as her own: the dry purple nipple pleated once through the middle to give warm milk, all a child could need. This child climbed to it and reached well round her and gripped her loose dress tightly at the sides and ate her slowly, small quiet mouthfuls like the chews of a cat, which gave it new life and color and strength while beneath it Della's mother shrank slowly and was gone.

When she woke it was too dark to hunt in her book for wisdom or warning. She thought but decided not to light her lamp; she knew all she wanted to know now or ever. Quickly she dressed to beat Grainger there (she could hear Gracie stirring) and walked out silent toward the high black house. She slowed only once at the spring a minute to rinse her mouth three times with water, foul with sulphur but sweeter than her own taste, the rags of the dream still strewn in her mind. Then she went on to work.

DECEMBER 1925—MARCH 1927

December 3, 1925

Dear Rachel and Robinson,

You were good to let me know about your wedding and job and plans. I am trusting that a new bride and groom could use some help in the cooking department so have packed you a case of the vegetables and fruits I put up this summer and will ship it on to you soon as somebody passes that can haul it to the depot. Or you could come get it. Rob, you know the way and remember you promised you would come back and sit for a better visit when you got on your feet. That last one was nothing; didn't get my eyes focused before you were gone. I know you will have your hands full getting settled in the next week or two but how about Christmas? Gid has asked me to come to Danville and celebrate with them; but after last year I made up my mind it was more celebration in my house alone—just me and the wind—than down there with him and his wife, an ill-wisher. So I will be here. I will be here so far as I know till I die and a good while after if nobody finds me. You are welcome both, Christmas or anytime. No need to warn me, though it might help an old heart to weather the shock if you drop me a postal card and say you are coming. I am always ready, nothing else to be. House clean as your hand, pantry sagging with food.

Is Grainger still with you? I saw old Elba who is living in his house about two weeks ago; and she said he sent her a message to say he was happy again and for her to stay put, he was not coming back. Elba took it to mean that Gracie was back or had promised one more time to be back soon. If he's there and Gracie with him—Rob, I hope you will watch her. She has never been no use to anybody—well, you know the one use. She pulled the wool over poor Grainger's eyes the first time he saw her, and he's never seen clearly from that day to this. He is yours to guide now as I guess your daddy told you. I took him from Forrest when Forrest let him go, you took him from me. God's watching it all so do right by him. He's a gentle soul. I would welcome him tomorrow if Gracie would vanish. Tell him anyhow that Elba said the stove has cracked and draws very poorly but otherwise things are still waiting safely for him. (*If stoves were just the only things cracked!*)

And how is Forrest? I have not had a word from him in over a month. Tell him if Miss Drewry is going home for Christmas, he should come on and join us. This house knows him well; he could still breathe in it.

Let me hear you are coming. I need to know you both, and the day may come when you need to know me (Rachel, I'm a far better cook than Grainger, much neater than Gracie)—don't wait too late! I am fifty-eight now and will need glasses soon.

> *Your hopeful,*
> *Aunt Hatt*

> *February 12, 1926*

Dear Mother,

Happy birthday. I'm sorry to be a little late; but as you can imagine, since I tend so many fires now, I sometimes leave one awhile too long. No smoke, I trust? There is smoke enough elsewhere. I hope you had a good day; it was bright here and warmer after all the recent ice. I thought about you that night and wished you—backward (and forward of course)—more years of happy time.

Things are pretty happy here as a matter of fact. Rachel has stood up to all the newness and, with Gracie and Grainger, has made this house a good place already. She says she has told you the household details, so I won't repeat them; but all we really lack is a little more room. When Father got it for us, we planned on being three—two Mayfields and Grainger—but then he told Gracie he was moving to Richmond, and she volunteered to join him after years of empty promising (or so Grainger says; I suspect he begged her). We've got enough beds at least and doors to hide behind, though sometimes the moving space gets a little full—not too full to fit you comfortably in when you make your first visit that I still count on.

My job is all right. For now I mostly just sit in my office and try to learn to bookkeep by checking back through my old predecessor's records. Highway robbery! To my certain knowledge, he made off with well over four thousand dollars in his thirty years here. They vanished anyhow and his books admit it as bald as day. Nobody's looked before so I guess they didn't miss it, and I don't plan to tell them. He's retired to a nice little house near Jamestown with wife and new Plymouth (his first car ever—he is seventy-five); I'll try to keep his secret.

My secret is simple and I'll tell it to you. I think I am finally learning to take what the world provides and call it my need and believe it will nourish me adequately. You can learn to live on air; you've been telling me that for some years, I see now, but trying is believing. Why couldn't I see it? Why couldn't I just look at you in your health and understand? Well, I guess you know; I was looking steadily but for the wrong message. Belated thanks.

This is not to say, Mother, that I'm living on nothing or just on the pleasures, however tremendous, of light bookkeeping for a Negro trade school—no, on the contrary. I find little pieces of food everyday, little pieces of life that (a month ago even) I'd have stepped on or over but which stop me now and hold me and make a contribution to the deep empty coffer I've been for so long. I was talking today to William, the Negro that sweeps our building. He was stirring round behind me; but I kept working—if he speaks and you answer, he's got you for a talk or a very lengthy listen. Anyhow I worked and he finished his dusting and was at the door to leave when something pressed him harder than he knew how to bear. He said, "Mr. Mayfield, did you fight in the war?" I told him I was fourteen at the Armistice, but yes I did my duty and manned the Belgian trenches and killed twelve men. He was thinking that over, so I said "Didn't you?" (he is in his late fifties best I can tell). He said no he didn't. So I said, "Why not? Don't you love your country?" and he said, "Mr. Rob, I'll tell you a fact; I've lived in town so many years now that I don't care nothing bout the country no more." I told him neither did I, and I almost meant it. —That's a contribution (he knew it was and meant it to be; he's laughing still), and Rachel makes her share. Last Sunday morning she told me she hadn't known the world had doors, real doors you could enter and, just as important, walk back through. I said I hadn't either. Grainger came out the other night to where I was buffing up a scratch on the car and said he thanked me. I said he was welcome and then said "For what?" He said, "You getting Gracie back here with me"; and I saw later on that I had got her back—that I give them the room and the chance to last—but also that Grainger has saved me twice and may do so again. I owe him more than room. And I mean to try to give it.

Rachel's gone on to bed. I am mighty tired myself and badly need to join her. Wish me sleep and rest. Come to see us.

Love,
Rob

P.S. Remember me also to Rena and Papa and Sylvie. Tell Uncle Kennerly that even he could pass on my neatness at work. My books are clean as saucers and I steal not a penny—not needing to, now.

April 11, 1926

Dear Miss Hattie,

I got what you sent me for my birthday. I sat here tonight and thought you never had forgot me in all this time, twenty-one years. I will *remember you. I am going to save it and once I get a chance, I am going to buy me a good Sunday shirt. You can get real nice ones for two dollars here and I need something nice when I go to the school some days with Mr. Forrest. I sit in his classroom and listen to him talk about stories and poems and how to write letters. He has come a long way like all the rest of us and I hope he is helping these boys and girls like he thinks he is. They all dress up anyhow and be quiet so I guess they are listening. I haven't gone but four times since Miss Rachel needs a lot of help in the house and Gracie can't do it all and I am trying to get the outside going, planting grass and some bushes. But that's all right. Grainger knows most of what Grainger going to know. One big thing is, you wrong about Gracie, Miss Hatt. I'm sorry. She was young when she left but she got good eyes and she learned a whole lot. She like living here and I think she like me. Think she always did, just needed to travel. I had been to France, see.*

Rob says he going to bring all of us down to Bracey soon to spend a few days. I can see to my house and visit you then. Then see do you think I been lying to you all along about Gracie. See don't you believe me.

Your friend,
Grainger

June 17, 1926

Dear Rob,

Thank you for being so loyal with letters. Your latest cheerful word arrived this morning; and I'm glad for you that, after only six months at the job, you are getting a week's vacation now and the hope of another in August. You are obviously pleasing someone in power! (I trust though that you haven't had to expose your predecessor's sins in your own march to virtue; let him die in that new Plymouth, cooling-off.)

And thank you warmly for the new invitation to visit you there. I really never thought that sixteen months of my life would pass with no sight of you—none of us here ever dreamt such an absence and are saddened as it lengthens—but I've thought this out, Son, and have to say it now since I gather you do not understand my repeated declining to come. A good many of my reasons do pertain to Father as you always suggest. After all these years of his kindness to me—after he fed and clothed and fostered you and me both when Forrest had taken up another life that prevented his sending us an ounce of help—after such devotion, I am hardly going to risk leaving here now he's weak and may go anytime. I've managed to forgive myself several things; but I couldn't face that down, however long I lasted—having him die in pain and calling for Eva, and Eva not there. You understand that, I am almost certain; that is love, pure and simple, and gratitude. What I've known for almost a year is this (since

*you first went to Forrest)—you don't understand much of self-respect or
fear, not as they pertain to me at least. I won't speak for you. For me
though the main impediments to coming are those two things.*

*You deserve an explanation and as I have thought a great deal since
you left here and warned me of your marriage, I think I can explain. I have
not tried before because it's still painful, and I didn't think you cared; but
I guess by now you'll have had other versions from other onlookers, so
you'd better have the truth from the one who bore it.*

*Despite what you think, you didn't have the first unhappy childhood.
I was paralyzed in woe from twelve years old, when I turned into a woman,
through all the years of school. No very strong reasons now I look back on
it, except that I thought Mother had it in for me (she did love Kennerly
but Father loved me). It turned out later in her awful death that she cared
a good deal about me and my life. I had never really known it. She had
never tried to tell me, yet I pressed her to death; and she let me do it in
absolute silence, though she left me a message that made a lot plain. Your
father walked into that misery of mine; and because I was honestly a lovely
girl and smart in school and because he had had short rations himself (for
longer than I), he saw me as what life was offering him—as food, as
reward—and he reached out to seize me. Very gently at first so that I
quickly came to believe what he said, that I would be simply obeying
time's will in joining with him and nursing his need. I also saw him in my
smart little head as a gate that would lead me out of a place which I
blamed for my misery. What he led to though was deeper trouble. He
turned out to need much more than I could give—to him anyhow and at
my age then. He was full-grown, a man; and I think he loved me—wanted
me there at hand forever. We were in a place he had always known (his
sister's house in Bracey); he could show his happiness to onlookers daily,
his old friends and family. I was a child as I soon came to know who had
never left home and who now realized that, of the places offered, I pre-
ferred Father's house and that, of the offered people, I most wanted
family—Rena, Father, Mag and Sylvie, even Mother finally. Simple as
that, I honestly believe—a homesick girl. And if Forrest had sent me home
that Christmas and let me make my peace with the family, I still think I'd
be living with him today. But from hunger and fear, he held on to me; and
then you came—and that was too late. Too late to save our life. I was so
weakened then that it forced Mother's hand—she felt she was responsible,
had driven me from home, and had kept them from forgiving me. So once
you and I were strong enough to travel in early spring, we came here to
make a solemn visit of grief and reconciliation. You got sick with whooping cough (brought to you by Sylvie); and during those hard weeks, I
settled far back into my old life—a daughter, home. Too far—your father
came to get us that August, and I turned on him badly. He was easy to
turn on, easy to punish for all his deep hungers with my bright eyes and*

tongue. Right tonight I remember most of what I said to him, much of it true but crueler still. God may have excused me—I've asked Him to—but I blame myself and will die in regret. Anyhow by November I understood my failures, and I wrote and asked him to send for us by Christmas. What I knew I felt then was unhappiness at home—my old deep sense that this house loathed me and was forcing me out. Again I was thinking of Forrest as a gate. But by then I was wrong. Through my love of you—a little hot creature with no speech or gifts to give—I understood in secret what I only now begin to see in broad day: I can go many places. My heart can, I mean—or could have gone then. If anyone had showed me, I would gladly have believed that love is by no means a hard thing to get and surely not to give. Forrest learned that soon enough, I gather, once I'd turned him back again—well, not I but Father. I wrote him as I said and told him we were ready to join him for Christmas. He didn't come to get us or send any word; but he sent a large box—gifts, I've always supposed—and Father refused it, never let it be delivered. When Sylvie let me know (she had seen it at the depot), I broke and blamed Father; and that night in this room, he asked my pardon and begged us to stay. Mother's wounds were very fresh in all our breasts, and I'd loved Father longer than any other human; so for then I stayed—we stayed, you with me—and the time slid by.

You may know all that, as I've said, in some form—my form is honest to memories as hard as the days I bore them. What you may not know (Forrest may not have told you; it may be his shame) is that four years later, I broke long silence. There had been not a word, a check or a coin, passed between us those years. Silence feeds on silence. Then I sent him our picture, a sudden decision. I had not planned to do it; but a man named Nepper from Raleigh came through, and people around us were going to pose. All I had of you were little blurred snapshots I'd taken myself—just you and Rena, you and Sylvie. So I asked Father could I; and he put up the money. It was very expensive. We looked our best, both of us, if I do say; and when the finished product came, it almost broke my heart. We looked so lovely and so deeply unloved, dreadfully wasted hanging there in brown air like unreachable ghosts not knowing we were dead. I had ordered four prints—for Father, Rena, Sylvie, and me. Rena didn't like hers (you can surely guess why—I was in it beside you); and two mornings later I wrapped it myself and walked down the street and mailed it to Forrest. The end, the end. I'm certain he got it; Hattie had kept me posted on his whereabouts. He just never answered. I had to assume it arrived too late, that he'd already learned what I secretly knew—you can eat anything; you can live anywhere. I waited the best part of two months for an answer. Then I sat back and started my life again, this girl's life I've led and will no doubt lead to my nearly-virgin grave. It was also your life. I apologize for that but I had little choice as I hope you see now. Where could we have gone? We were honored here at least.

Please visit here then. I would meet you in some third place except for Father and the silly expense of renting "neutral ground." You have seen Rachel's home. She needs to see yours. It is different from hers, by Rena's account, and will tell her things she may need to know in the long years I hope she has with you.

So I'll turn the tables on you and ask you here for that second week of vacation coming in August. It will be no hotter in Fontaine, I'm sure, than the pavements of Richmond. We will keep the trees standing to shade your brows; and anyhow Father, as I know you remember, always strengthens in heat (being tempered he says) and can welcome you better. If you want to bring Gracie and Grainger for the ride, Sylvie knows several places where they could stay. She'd be glad of the help since (like others I know, including myself) all her old good faculties are slowing down now— all, that is, but the grumbling: that's picking up speed.

Two months to wait then. I'll possess my soul in patience and start airing beds. Say yes.

Love,
Mother

August 27, 1926

Dear Alice,

Please excuse me. This is the first time in six weeks that I've had a truly sustained free moment to sit down and undertake answering your last. I am in Carolina, Rob's home, Fontaine. We are spending the last week of his vacation with his mother's family. I had not met her of course so dreaded the trip, though her few letters to me were funny and kind; but this is the fifth day, and all has gone well. They are just a family very much like all in their loyal jostling and scraping, thicker than hops could ever grow (no crowbar could part them much less a new inlaw if she had the mind, which you know I don't). They appear to have liked me, even Rob's Aunt Rena who as you remember from the wedding party had rights of resentment against me but refused them. What puzzles me is only what must puzzle any bystander lonely in the midst of people holding hands— the question Why? Why do they choose each other so steadily? Why can they bear it?—these unbroken gazes through whole lives of years, these permanent burdens of weight and demand. Why don't they see they are just simple humans?—replaceable at any moment's notice by thousands more worthy than they of such love and more needy. I confide those to you, no need to answer; rest assured I will not be asking them here, though I really think the Kendals are a family that might answer. They strike me as people who know what they mean—every word, every hand moved from here to there. Even Sylvie their cook has the dark heavy air of intending her actions and silences (she is silent to me; but knows me by heart, every pore of my skin—she watches me).

The real news for me of course is Mrs. Mayfield. Rob had told me last spring of her part in his then unhappiness; and while I never said it, I thought more than once of the oddness of a young man's still volunteering his peace and his plans to the mercies of a figure so far in his past, so safely survived (my own desperations were caused by the future as you well know—a fear that the present would simply endure). But after four days in her presence and shadow, I understand more. She has genuine size, not of form (though she's tall and bears a grand head on a round firm neck not yielded to age) but, well, of merit. She has done what I beg God I'll some-day do, earned her space and the air she drinks. She has earned it by keeping her face intact through decades that must have been all but bone-dry (she left Mr. Mayfield when Rob was just born). Miss Rena looks hungry as a stoat, hot-eyed; Mrs. Mayfield is fed, though on what is her secret. She is straight as a maple and smiles like one; she is funny and leaves rooms laughing behind her; she quietly tends to a crippled old father (bedpans, bedsores, the stench of dry skin) as if that were a privilege and pleasure to do. She makes me welcome with the ease she'd have shown some school friend Rob had brought home for supper, though she doesn't look down. She sees my needs and lets me fill them; never hoards back from me or shames my little graspings (of Rob, just Rob). I think I may hate her, but there's time till then. Rob is freer than he was. I think I can free him entirely and soon, give him better refuge.

I am happy, you see. The literal truth. You can tell your father. My father said I would be if I could hold out and lo!—I am. The thanks go to Rob. He has quietly borne all I needed to give; and since he bears it with such pleasant patience, I think he is finding me more than a burden. I work at that all the time anyhow—to be a help, an answer, not a set of heavy questions when he's had a life of those. I think I am winning; there are no bad times, not for me, not yet, though I'm told they will come. Rob has these burdens—his father and Polly, his mother, his job at the school— and it's part of his nature, I know, to plunge low about every fourth day when some fool sets a small rock in his path—Grainger's feelings get hurt, Gracie goes for a night (she did that the first time a month ago; but he stayed out till morning driving Grainger, and they found her—a natural cat; they'd better let her be, though she works like a sawmill hand when she's there and not pouting and I value her spirit). I seem to have no burdens whatsoever. Euphoria you'll say and no doubt it is, but give me my head for a while. I'll slow. I only hope I can stand it when I do.

The house here is roughly the size of ours, with more people in it; so we whisper a lot. But Rob is clearly enjoying the rest and is showing me sides of himself hid till now. He is better than I knew—plain kindness, I mean. He likes to please people. His idea of rest yesterday was to strike out in the broiling heat and drive Mrs. Tharrington, a lifelong neighbor, to a dentist thirty miles away. Miss Rena managed to tell me in the middle of his absence—I stayed here in the shade—that Mrs. Tharrington's daughter

*was along for the ride (and with perfect teeth). In any case he was back
here before dark which at present is as much as my mind seems to ask. If
his need is bigger than mine, so's his gift.*

You'll snort at that, to which the true *answer is also cruel. You do not
yet know what strangeness is involved. You will not till you live day and
night in small rooms with someone you cherish, and with no thought of
living otherwise now or ever. I say that not to hurt but in explanation of
the distance between us which I hope you can close soon by sharing your
life with something more yielding than a houseful of pale and querulous
sick, your mother and father however good and grateful. You are lovelier
than I, and I've seen men see it—Niles Fitzhugh for one, at the wedding
parties. Let your heart face the purpose of all that beauty and open doors
other than the one marked* Friend. *There are several other doors as you
must know by now. Anyone who has stared at the world as intently as you
with pencil in hand has seen that, Alice, and long before me. I've seen it in
drawings that you threw aside, of just my face when I was near bottom.
You could see I was hunting to live and would find, see it and set it down
in lines. See yourself now and notice the doors all opening out.*

I am hoping to open the one marked Mother. *I have asked for a child.
Please do not tell your father or either of my parents if you're in touch
with them. I have just told Rob, just now this week. Till now he has not
raised the question but has gone on and done what was needed to protect
me. Now I've asked him to stop, to let me truly risk what I played at
before—simple creation. He has asked me to give him a few days to think;
he says he may really not be willing yet. His* mind *may not but the rest of
him is. His body yearns toward me.*

Pray for us.

*Love,
Rachel*

December 22, 1926

Dear Eva,

*Robinson has asked me to send you a wire; but since years ago I
conveyed one quick mortal shock to your home and since he tells me your
father is low, I take it on myself to tell you in a letter what cannot be
gently told. Rachel and Rob are alive and in hope. Threats have retreated,
though not yet gone.*

*At five this morning Rachel lost her child. She had had a good night
of untroubled sleep, it seems; and was only wakened by a painless rush of
blood. She lay in dark awhile to be sure she wasn't dreaming and even then
made no real try at waking Rob. He told me he was wakened by the quiet
sound of grief; again her only pain has been mental, wounded hopes. He
turned on their light and was badly frightened but called the doctor*

*quickly, who came at once. He was there in twenty minutes, and the issue
had stopped. Still he recommended taking her to Barnes Hospital; and on
the way, with Grainger at the wheel and Rob in back beside her, Rachel
quietly delivered a well-formed son—a boy it would have been, the doctor
told Rob, four months underway; never drew breath or moved. The doctor
told me when I saw him this evening that, barring infection, Rachel's
chances are good. Rob of course is with her and will sleep there tonight,
which is why I write this.*

*It is ten-fifteen and now I must hurry to post this on the last train so
you will know tomorrow. I can't resist saying though that part of my
sadness, and no small part, in today's mischance is the fact that again, after
all this waiting, you and I are foiled. At a distance to be sure and in a first
try at a living "posterity" which may yet live in a later child (doctor sees no
reason that she could not try again); but still I feel saddened more deeply
than I planned, and I wanted you to know.*

*Rob will no doubt write tomorrow. We have him at least, proud man
and strengthening daily. Tonight when I left him—grieved as he was,
transparent with fatigue—he was lit with the firm light of your own early
strength. I told him that I hoped this would not set them back or lock
them in the fears of life that halted his parents in their tracks too early. He
thought it out slowly and faced me and said, not a trace of a smile, "I don't
think the suit of clothes has been invented yet that will hold my body back
from doing its will if she lives and still wants me"—the voice of my father,
old Robinson. He is in better hands then than yours and mine.*

*In haste with Christmas hopes for Eva
from Forrest*

February 23, 1927

Dear Miss Hattie,

*I'm sorry you haven't heard from us in so long. Everybody got your
good Christmas box and Rob and Miss Rachel got your last two letters but
couldn't answer right then so I'll tell you now. Things here have been
going downhill since Christmas, three days before Christmas. Miss Rachel
woke up bleeding in the night and lost her baby she was expecting in May,
a little boy she named Raven for her daddy, saying he never wanted her to
have any that lived. She told Rob that and he told Gracie. Told Gracie if
Miss Rachel feel like that he won't going to help her with no second
chance at a live one. So since then he has been very gentle with Miss
Rachel but that's all. Her mother was here to nurse her till a week ago and
almost half the time then Rob was out late, coming home drinking sometime but always gentle and laying down in their bed the same as before but
not helping Rachel. She told Gracie that.*

We been having bad weather which has not helped either. Everybody low and damp. I spend so much time downstairs stoking coal that I don't get to watch Rob as much as he need me and if I leave at night to find where he's roaming then Gracie's here by herself with Miss Rachel, a bad idea. You'd be proud of Gracie now, Miss Hatt. She's holding ground and helping. I'd be bad off without her. Don't wish me that again.

I hope you got better news in Bracey than us. Maybe if spring ever come Miss Rachel can go to her home in the mountains and rest some there and Gracie and me could come up to Bracey and see everybody. Rob say he would like to come when I mentioned it to him. He took to you. Don't worry too much. I have seen him worse than this and so have you and he say Miss Rachel been a lot worse than this. Everybody just down like I say and damp, just waiting for some sunshine. Keep well and I'll tell you when the news here change.

Your friend,
Grainger

February 28, 1927

Dear Father,

Your letter came in the first mail this morning; and I hasten to say how sorry I am that Mother told you as much as she did or in the way that she did. I can see she has misunderstood and misled you. I am a good bit stronger than she thinks. She has never believed in my fiber—I guess I've given her reasons not to—but you know it's there, woven strong right through me (I mean to live and like it); and since you have promised me a better time, I plan just to hang on and have it when it comes. It is already better than it's been before—my days, I mean—and the doctor here says I am not badly damaged but can hope for more chances once I rest my resources and heal the ripped edges of various things.

So I read a lot and help what I can with the house; and three bright days in a row this week, I went to work with Rob and attended English class under Mr. Mayfield. He taught me and twenty-eight Negro boys something I at least had never heard before (the dark ones seemed to know it; at least they didn't flinch)—God wants us to understand life as a comedy. He thinks it is funny since He knows the outcome, has planned it fully and knows we'll enjoy it when we get there at least (the trip seems longer to us than to Him but that's not important). Mr. Mayfield has got them studying Milton!—Paradise Lost—and they sit there like ebony angels (in their twenties, some of them men with families) and listen to him lecture on and on. God's plan and man's pranks—what on earth can they think? Well, nobody cracks a smile as I said. I come home and ponder. I can't speak for them; but maybe they are learning as much as I, in and out of class.

Rob is all right, Father. Calm down about him please. In a way what has happened was hardest on him. I mean, I could have died and all; but stay or go, he feels he's responsible for aiding me in this, that he volunteered too quickly to help me forward on a dangerous path. So he's had some bad nights, two of which Mother witnessed. Bad only to himself though; I trust she told you that. To me he is nothing but kind and caring, quietly needful. That helps me, Father—some real work to do. You will understand that, as Mother never will, if you just think back to the poisonous idleness of all my years till now.

Not entirely idle. I loved you in them and have every plan to persist in that. So uncrease your brow now, clean up the place, get the spring dredged out; in the second half of March, I hope to come visit. Rob will be on the road awhile, scaring up scholars for the Milton classes. Keep laughing. It's a play!

Love for now,
Rachel

March 10, 1927

Dear Robinson,

I mean this to reach you on your twenty-third birthday. I have never spent any of your birthdays with you; but I watched your birth and helped what I could to save your life and your mother's, that were doubtful. Several of us helped hard, so I guess you owe us a really good job of it—live on proudly.

Grainger wrote me your news two weeks ago. He is not my spy so don't turn on him, but I hadn't heard from you or Rachel either one since awhile before Christmas and nothing from Grainger, and I was brooding on you—I have lots of worry-time. You know I'm deeply saddened. I've had fair experience with loss myself—Father, Mother, James, Whitby in Flanders, even Forrest (he's gone just as far as if he'd died, to me anyhow)—so I hope you won't take it hard of me when I say there are worse things than losing another. I say this to you; never tell Rachel however strong she gets.

One worse thing, I know, is losing yourself—losing that place inside your own chest where you honor yourself and can bear your own company in the face of pure solitude. I'm lonely as a chicken hawk—you saw that in person—but I'm pretty good company too, for myself. I enjoy myself, though of course I welcome the faces I love, a very rare welcome as the years run on. Worse still is losing your courtesy to others if there are any others, just bathing in yourself as if you were single on the whole blank earth and could rear and pitch at will.

Our father did that. Forrest doesn't remember—he was far too young—and since he just saw Father at the end, all weak in Richmond with Miss Drewry there to tame him, he may have told you things that are not really so. If Robinson Mayfield ever thought once, not to mention twice, of his wife and children's feelings—the sights they must carry in their memory to the grave—well, he never told me or gave me any sign. I liked him a lot. Everybody likes a good-looking tall laugher that smells as good as he did after he had scrubbed. But I watched him ruin several and never ask pardon, never know what he'd ruined. I was not one of them—I decided not to be, the week Mama died; I would not be her—but behind me, Forrest was. He surrendered to Father at the age of five and is still in defeat, hauling poor Miss Drewry like Father's old washing and teaching poor Negroes useless poems all because Rob Mayfield had a few mulatto children. One for certain.

Son, please don't you be another meal for him, his strong empty cravings—my sweet killing dreadful father. Don't be him either. One was more than a plenty. Grainger says you are worried. I guess you have been; you've had real cause. But I trust that the causes are fading out now and that any need for running toward doors (that are never really there) is gone. I hope to see a man in this family just once stand and take what he's chosen, take it and all its secrets and hang on till Judgment. Several women have already.

Give Rachel my greetings and best prayers please. I'd send her my love; but since she hadn't seen me yet, she might not want raw love from a stranger. You've seen me though so whether you want it or not,

> Love from
> Hattie

You are still wanted here whenever you can come. And I'll go anywhere you say if you need me. Aging but ready,

> Ever,
> H.S.

JULY 1929

Rob woke at a loud long shudder of the axles and looked out quickly—safe, a deep hole behind them in the road.

Grainger said, "Didn't see it. You can go back to sleep."

Rob put his head back to try again, thinking, "I will need every minute I can get"; but the heat and light pressed steadily at him, so he rolled his eyes right and watched the sliding country. At first he was lost; this could be any one of a hundred roads he'd traveled before—narrow through scrub pine and parched wastes of corn, cotton, weeds, and rough as a cob. Not a human in sight—three starved black cows posted out in an open furnace of a field, still and bony as a doctor's office furniture. Then as Grainger slowed for another rut, a shack swam by and an old man before it, black as any cow they'd passed and dressed to the neck in a snow-white Spanish-American Navy uniform—Deepwater Pritchard, drunk at nine in the morning. Rob looked back and waved.

They were twelve miles from home, his home at least. Fontaine, the Kendals, his grandfather maybe dying at last, maybe already dead (the call had come at three in the night—his worst stroke yet; he was speechless, still and staring—they had dressed and eaten and left by four, leaving Rachel alone for the hour till dawn). Rob had seen none of it since the previous Christmas when they'd come down from Richmond for three fair days; so he felt its power now, not a power to hurt (that was long since dead, he could tell himself) nor even a power to rake old memory (he thought of nothing older than this morning as they rode) but the force of attraction. Rob was held on this road as on magnetic rails by the place's desire that he rush on through it to its waiting heart—a deathbed postponed for twenty wasteful years, the lodestone (still potent) of his grandfather's life, still arranging, requiring the lives of others. He turned left to Grainger. "You tired as me?"

Grainger looked over quickly. "Tireder," he said.

"I apologize."

"For what?" Grainger said, not looking again.

"Taking you away now."

"What's wrong with now?"

"You were waiting for Gracie."

No answer from Grainger.

"She'll be back," Rob said, "and Rachel can hold her."

Grainger watched the narrow road. "I thought myself I was waiting on Gracie, waiting all this week; but just last night I was sitting in the room still dressed in the dark, and I knew to my soul two things quick as lightning—one, Gracie was gone; and two, I was glad. I won't even studying waiting on Gracie."

Rob waited and then said, "You don't still want her?"

Grainger knew at once. "No sir, I don't."

Rob was genuinely startled—the nights he had spent hearing Grainger extol her, implore her return; the nights of hunting her down when she'd run (Rob waiting at the wheel of the car by some cafe, miserable as pigshit, in deep Niggertown while Grainger went in and, finding her, begged). He studied the right half of Grainger's face, blank as new calfskin and age thirty-six. What had ever moved him, ever hooked deep enough in that fine hide to hold or hurt?

Grainger bore the gaze awhile; then turned, smiling fully, and said in a rich mock-Rastus voice, "I tell you what's a fact. I lived in town so long, Mr. Rob, I don't care nothing bout country girls now."

Rob smiled but said "Why not?"

"I meant just Gracie. I don't want Gracie." Grainger stopped with that—what seemed a full reply. Then something more rose, more knowledge than Grainger had known he'd earned and could face and describe. "Not so," he said. "I mean everybody. Don't need any of em."

"I doubt you know everybody," Rob said. They rode a mile in silence.

Then Grainger said, "Maybe I just know Grainger. I thought I knew you."

Rob said "Lucky if you do" and faced Grainger, grinning.

"How's that?" Grainger said.

"—You know a happy man. Anybody knows me today knows a happy man." Rob touched his wet breastbone with the pad of his thumb through the damp white cloth.

Grainger said, "We headed to a funeral, I thought."

"Most likely, yes. I didn't mean that, though I'm not the only soul that's waited for the day."

Grainger nodded, not looking, and asked no more. Tired and possessed by his own new knowledge, he did not want more.

Rob went on and gave it. "I mean I'm lucky too. It's nothing I've won for being sweet-me; but just these last few months, few weeks—Hell, just last night—I've noticed I'm happy."

Grainger said "All right."

"And it's her. Rachel."

Grainger turned full to Rob. "She giving you all the stuff you can use?" He held his eyes off the road, unblinking as if he had no further intention of guarding their lives, reaching their goal.

Rob bore the whole moment—the speech, the eyes—like a lash on his mouth. Stunned, scared, angered, he said "You drive."

Grainger looked back, a smooth empty stretch of road; and drove a little faster, his face all clear and blank as the tan dirt that drew them on.

Rob waited till he found a tolerable answer—he had misunderstood; no harm had been meant. Grainger only meant love, Rachel's patient gifts. Then he could go on, calm again, to explain his new life. "You saw me marry her. You know why I did it—misery and meanness, and she asked for help. Nobody else asked."

"Not so," Grainger said.

"Who else?"

"You think."

"—You *got* it," Rob said. "Didn't you get help?"

Grainger said "All right."

Rob said, "You have worked every day since you knew me."

Grainger said "I have."

"And you're guaranteed." With his gentle fist, Rob stamped Grainger's knee. "Long as I'm able, and I *mean* to be, you are guaranteed."

Grainger said, "I thank you and I hope you last."

Rob said, "I said I mean to. I have to now—you, Rachel, Mother soon as this old man dies, Aunt Rena, all them. And like I said, I want to."

Grainger nodded, not turning.

But Rob had to tell him again. "Because of Rachel."

"Then pray she last," Grainger said.

"I will."

By then they were passing through a long stand of woods that was Kendal land, a cool dense island of walnut and oak, old pine and poplar that had lasted the gradual selling-off of the draining years of Bedford Kendal's illness, still-standing money not yet redeemed—because they contained, deeper in from the road, the old Kendal house, Bedford's own birthplace.

It would be Rob's soon, had been given to him or promised at least a year ago. He had been down with Rachel for a week's vacation; his grandfather had been weaker than ever and confused for most of the week; but the day before they were planning to leave, he had sent Sylvie upstairs to wake Rob at seven. When Rob had come down in his bathrobe, groggy, his grandfather said, "Get Sylvie to feed you and come on with me." Rob said "Where to?" and his grandfather said "Wherever I lead." So Rob ate quickly and dressed without shaving and went to obey. By then his mother was awake and with her father, combing his hair. When Mr. Kendal saw

Rob walk in, he seized Eva's wrist with his one good hand and said, "You go on. He's come back to get me." Oddly Eva had accepted dismissal and left, simply saying to Rob, "Don't leave him in sunlight"; and Rob had dressed the milk-blue body, the sick scarce hairs, to his grandfather's orders and then leaned over and said "Where to?" again. His grandfather said, "Have you got a gentle horse?" Rob said "What for?" —"For me to ride. I'm a little weak today." Rob said, "Yes sir, I've got a sweet old plug"; and Mr. Kendal said, "Then lead me out to her." Rob, with no sure sense of where they would end, had bent and lifted the heavy body and carried it through hall, kitchen, yard to his car. Then he'd said "I'm ready"; and his grandfather said, "Ride out of here first."

When they'd passed through the center of town—August Saturday, the streets chocked with Negroes already at eight—Mr. Kendal turned toward him and said, "Listen here. I don't recognize one thing in all this" (he had not seen town for three or four years since Kennerly last bothered to give him an outing). "If you know anything at all, take me home." Rob had nodded and slowly boxed a block to go back; but as they stopped to cross the old Essex road, his grandfather said "Thank Jesus. Turn here." Rob said, "I thought we were heading home" (sun fell in the far side, all down Mr. Kendal); "I'm a little hot myself." His grandfather said, "I am asking you for rescue" and pointed right again; so Rob turned carefully and drove two miles down the rough Essex road, thinking, "Any minute now he'll forget and I can turn." But at the fork to Richmond, his grandfather pointed again to the right. Rob obeyed but said "Sir, rescue from what?" The flat eyes worked to remember—and remembered; they cleared and deepened—but he only said, "I want to see if my home is safe" and pointed onward.

Rob had understood then—the old Kendal place. He had seen it a time or two as a boy when they'd gone out for visits with a spinster half great-aunt and two distant cousins (old men, deaf as slate); but they had all died and the place had been rented to a man named Weaver who had once been a drunkard and killed his own son but had come round nicely and run the farm on half-shares and, old as he was (Rob remembered him as ancient), had started new children on a new young wife (the old one having left him at the killed boy's grave). Then he'd died and it passed through a slew of other hands, each sorrier than the last; and Rob had not seen it for oh twelve years.

It was safe when they got there—a high frame house nearly twice as tall as broad, on brick pillars high enough to let a school child walk upright beneath it, not a flake of paint left on roof or sides, every door and window open and a goat in the yard on a rusty chain. When they'd stopped and sat a moment and cut the engine, it meant nothing to Rob—the place, another millstone for some other neck—though he worked a whole moment at making it matter: one of the cradles of his life, one of the causes. Dead boards and bricks. He had turned to his grandfather then and found the old face feeding on the sight, through buggy plate glass, as if at a tit full of final joy. To break the long meal, Rob said at last "It's safe all right." Not turning, his grandfather nodded and made awful efforts to smile. Then the smile screwed downward into bafflement. Rob looked to the house. In the doorway—scared, big-eyed and staring—was a wedge of Negro children, four or five in view and the shadows of more, taller, behind them.

Rob had understood then; remembered in fact (Rena had mentioned it some months before)—Kennerly had brought in a Negro named Jarrel, a better deal. These were all his. Rob had assumed that his grandfather knew. He said, "They are keeping it very clean." His grandfather waited a sizable while; then only said, "Thank the goat for that." Rob said, "Do you want me to find somebody?" Another long wait; a tall woman stood in the doorway now, snuff-stick in her mouth. Rob said, "Do you want to speak to Jarrel's wife?" His grandfather watched her, not blinking once; but said to Rob, "I just want this—when I die soon, you take this place and fix it right and bring Eva here and look out for her." Rob had said, "She's happy in Fontaine, Papa." Mr. Kendal shook his head—"She won't be then. She'll need some place. Are you promising me or must I die in misery?" Rob had promised him simply to break his stare, then had waved to the woman and turned and gone home where his grandfather never once mentioned the trip. Neither had Rob, and forgot it till now.

Now he said to Grainger, "What about us living here?"

"In the road?—mighty dusty."

"In these woods, fool. I may own a farm back of here very soon, may own it already if my grandfather's died."

"I told you I didn't care much about the country."

Rob said, "I may be serious. Would you come here and help me?"

"You got a good job. What you know about farming?"

"More than you," Rob said. "No I'd get a good tenant. That job at the school is just to please Father. I wouldn't care if I never looked at a ledger-book in all my future life."

"What you want to look at?"

Rob said, "I don't know. I could sit still though till I'd thought it out good—maybe just at my children."

Grainger said "Where they coming from?" but gently now with real concern.

With his right hand, Rob cupped his own full groin. "From here," he said, also quietly. "Out from here into Rachel and out of her again." Then he looked up to Grainger.

"Is it time?" Grainger said. "Is she ready for that?"

Rob said, "The doctor told her six months ago she could try again. I asked her to wait; I still wasn't ready."

"How come?"

"Just scared. Scared to risk her again now I valued her truly. Scared to ask any child to bear me as father."

Grainger said "You ready now?"

Rob said "Since last night."

Grainger nodded. "I heard you" (his room was under theirs).

Rob said "You didn't *see*."

"No sir, I didn't. I was sitting in the dark."

"We were dark too," Rob said. "I was fixing to love her, rolling it on. She was flat there before me. I was up on my knees. She waited till I was full-dressed in the rubber, and then she said 'No.' I begged her 'Please'—I was that far ready—and she said, 'Surely. I meant *don't spare me*.' I said, 'You will have to let me decide that.' She said 'It's *my* life'; and I said, 'But you halved it; you handed me half.' She said, 'I did once and I will again; but *you* have got to give—you are hoarding back. All I promised was love; I never promised safety.' So I laid on her and went in her, bareback, first time in three years. It makes some difference. I had truly forgotten."

Rob had said it to Grainger, though not really for him. Grainger gave no sign of accepting, even hearing; but he took it as personal, intended to reach him with taunting and triumph. He drove as carefully as if they were lost in desperation—not three miles from town, their easy goal.

Rob said "Do you blame me?"

Grainger said, "You're rushing me. Give me time to think." He threatened to smile but in honesty he didn't, and he did not meet Rob's eyes again till they reached the Kendals' and stopped in the yard. Then Grainger said "I got you here" and extended his right hand as if for reward.

Grateful and needful (Rena rushed toward them now), Rob touched the hand, held it a long full moment. Faced with this day, this death and its duties, the risks of the night, Grainger's offered life—he had not been happier, would not be for years. He thought that now.

Then Rena was on him, begging "Hurry. Quick."

2

THOUGH Rena tried to pull him, Rob stopped in the door of his grandfather's room. It was full—the big bed, the wardrobe, the washstand, the black leather couch, Rena, Kennerly and Blunt, Min's mother Kate Tharrington, the doctor at the bedside holding a wrist. The arm was dead, the uncovered neck—violet and drier than any crisp paper, plainly dead. The blue lips were open on yellow peg teeth, the shut eyes had quickly rounded in their sockets to perfect little globes the size of great marbles. It seemed entirely permanent, a state that had lasted days or weeks; but Rob saw at once on every face but the knowing doctor's that he'd got here precisely at the instant of death. A killing presence.

The doctor said to Rena, "Where is Eva? Get Eva."

Rena said, "In the kitchen crushing ice. She's coming."

He said "Go meet her" and laid the wrist down.

Rena looked down at it, never got to the face. She shut her eyes hard once, then went past Rob up the hall toward the kitchen.

The doctor turned to Kennerly and Blunt and nodded. They sat on the couch in unison, axed. Then he saw Rob, two steps inside the room. He stayed by the bed but spoke at Rob clearly—"You are too late for him. Get ready for Eva."

Rob nodded. Quick steps were coming up the hall.

Eva rushed in past him, no notice of his presence, though her right hand brushed him like a strong bird's wing on his damp left sleeve as she oared to the foot of the bed and stopped. She studied what was left for a sizable moment—ten, fifteen seconds. Then she looked to the doctor and said "Where is he?"

He half-whispered "Gone" and offered her a hand.

If she saw it she scorned it. She stepped round quickly to the rag mat she'd hooked just the previous March for his feet when he stood (she hooked rugs in March, too hot a job for summer). In one move she dropped to her knees, touched the bed with both flat hands; and looking at her father, said low but plain, "Let me speak to him. I have got to speak to him."

Rob had never heard her pray before or speak of prayer (the few times he'd seen her at church through the years, she'd sat open-eyed through prayers and benedictions). He looked at the others; all but Kennerly's Blunt were fixed first on Eva, then (once she'd begged) on Mr. Kendal's face. Blunt was crying, had been crying since the first sign of death.

The lips moved first, a slow jerk to free themselves from drying teeth as if they would speak. Then the eyes were open, not focused on Eva but upward, dazed.

Eva smiled and half-rose, bent close above him to be in his stare. "I just went to get you some ice," she said. "Eva's back now. You rest."

Rob reached the foot of the bed in two steps. This was maybe for him, some word to warn or bless him, some hunt for his face. None of that, no. He was only in time to be all but sure that he saw a knowing nod, for his mother alone. Then the eyes clamped down again; and whatever last life had glowed up to answer that summons, take that message, guttered silently and fast.

Rena went to Eva's back and touched her bent spine.

Kennerly stood and opened a window eight inches and propped it. The first breath of air in the room for years. Blunt was still weeping, little puppydog yips.

The doctor moved up by the standing sisters and touched Mr. Kendal's wrist again, a mute wait of five seconds; Rob counted each. Then he nodded to Rena.

Rena held Eva tighter, one hand round her waist, and said "He saw you."

Eva stood only then. She said "I know he did." Then she looked to Rena; but Rob could see her plainly, lit by her triumph, dreadful and strong, her face young and lifting. He could not move toward her; she had not seen him.

She said to Rena, "I need a little walk, just a minute in the air." She faced the door, seeing it only.

Rena said to the doctor, "We'll be back shortly"; then to Kennerly, "Take over." Still holding Eva, who was straight and steady, she led them on a neat narrow path to the door, not pausing or speaking to anyone.

Rob watched them go.

Min's mother came to him and touched his left hand which was braced on the dark high foot of the bed. Her own round face, normally as boneless as a handful of veal, was firm and lustrous with the sights it had witnessed, the duties it must do now. "Thank God you made it in time," she said. "Min is coming, I know."

"Yes I made it," Rob said and answered her smile, sparing her the weight of his own recent sights, fresh harrowing up of his own oldest grief. Then he went to speak to Blunt and Kennerly, the only place to go.

3

WHEN the doctor had finished arranging the body (the washing and dressing were Eva's job) and packed his satchel, he left for the yard to find the sisters. Blunt and Min's mother left for the kitchen, so Rob and Kennerly were there with Mr. Kendal. They both were standing and had done no more than shake hands, speak names when they saw they were together alone, first time in years. Rob said, "I got here as soon as I could."

Kennerly said, "It was soon enough. He saw you."

Rob said "I doubt it."

Kennerly said "I doubt it matters." He stepped from the window to the spool-legged table by the head of the bed. Its top was empty of all but a glass lamp, an old corked bottle of codeine syrup, and the comb Eva kept there. He opened the drawer and brought out a gold stemwinder watch. Then he looked back to Rob. "This is mine," he said. "This is the only thing here that is mine."

Rob nodded as if his permission mattered.

"He gave it to me when I left home; I tried to leave here right after your mother. They called us both back. He gave it to me then in the depot, waiting—said, 'If anything happens to me while you're gone, ask your mother for this; say I wanted you always to know what mattered: just time, killing time.' I've had to kill a mighty lot of time to get it, ain't I?" He weighed its solemn roundness on his hard flat palm. Then he smiled at Rob.

"He had his own time, I guess," Rob said.

"Yes I noticed that too." Kennerly pressed the watch stem and opened the cover—six-twenty, it said, and had said all the years since his father's second stroke. "I will have to get it cleaned." Then he worked with his thumbnail at a small raised lip on the back; and it opened, a private compartment. He studied it quietly, then held it out to Rob. "Who is that?" he said.

Rob stepped up to see—an old photograph half the size of a stamp. A boy maybe four or five years old in a Wild-West hat, bandanna round his neck, smiling slightly. Some Kendal cast in the features but who?—the brother who had vanished to Missouri long since? Bedford himself? As a clear peace offering, Rob said "Is it you?"

"Eighteen and eighty-nine," Kennerly said. "Mother brought me the hat from a trip to Raleigh; and old Mrs. Bradley made a whole set of pictures—she'd got a big camera once she passed the change of life. I'd forgot all about it."

"He hadn't," Rob said.

Kennerly didn't smile again but he looked down pleasantly and touched the face with the tip of a finger. The spot of glue that held it to the gold flaked off, and the picture fell slowly to the mat at their feet. Rob bent to retrieve it but Kennerly stopped him. "I'll get it," he said. When he had it safe again, he put it in the watch-back and snapped down the lid. "He just kept it there. He'd forgotten it, I guess. Mother must have made him save it. I never knew it, see." He put the watch gently in the pocket of his cotton coat. "It's all that's mine here."

Rob said, "Can I have his pistol then?" and nodded toward the mantel.

"Ask your mother," Kennerly said. "Ask Eva and Rena. All this is theirs."

"Did he leave a will?"

"No he told me his wishes early last spring. The house and contents are Eva and Rena's, and all the cash from cotton and corn. The timber is mine and all the land except the Kendal homeplace. He said that was yours."

Rob said, "So he told me. He just told me once. I didn't know he meant it; I doubted he'd remember."

"He did. He said you had always wanted it."

Rob smiled. "Never. It means far less to me than this dusty rug" (he meant the mat beneath them). "What am I meant to do with a firewood house that Negroes have ruined and all those trees?" He had seen a good deal since his morning talk with Grainger, their ride through the cool stretch of woods now his—sights that made Richmond seem his feasible home or some place farther from here than Richmond.

But Kennerly answered. "You could kill time in it. He meant that by handing it on to you. Move your tenants out this winter, fix the house up a little, move Rachel in this spring, and you and Grainger farm it. You can also watch your mother. You owe her something better than worry, twenty-odd years of worry. She'll want you closer now."

"No she won't," Rob said.

"She'll need you anyhow."

Rob looked to his grandfather, no longer purple with the strain to live but lucid as a porcelain cup in daylight with the first short minutes of infinite rest. Who could blame him now? Rob found that he could. "Yes she may," he said. "She'll find it's too late."

Kennerly's face took receipt of that clearly but thrust it inward against future need. He didn't reply, didn't speak another word. He turned from Rob to his dead cold father; and not pausing once to study or fix his final picture, he bent quickly, neatly, and kissed the high forehead. Then he left the room.

Rob could hear Rena meet him halfway down the hall. "Eva's resting," she said. "She'll fix him when she can. You make all the plans, notify everybody."

"Does that suit Eva?"

"Those are Eva's instructions."

"All right. I will"—and he took two steps farther on toward the kitchen.

Rena said "Where is Rob?"

Kennerly stopped. "He was still there with Father thirty seconds ago, but he may be gone. He is planning to go, always a great leaver."

"Hush," Rena said and moved toward the bedroom.

Rob seized the last free moment he would have and also bent to the face, hard as plaster, and kissed the cool mouth. It seemed a kiss of gratitude; this man had freed him, not in death but in life—by twenty-five years of forcing starvation on a needy child till the child went elsewhere and nursed other dugs and stood now, free. Rob could see that at last.

Rena saw and heard nothing.

4

SHE came up beside him and took his hand, having not yet greeted him properly. "I never should have rushed you in here," she said. "Forgive me please. I thought there was some chance you might mean something to him. Nobody else did. He didn't know a soul after three o'clock this morning."

Rob said "He knew Mother."

Rena studied her father. "Let her think he did. Let her think that much. It was nothing but muscles though, settling round death. You've seen things die. It takes them awhile."

Rob said "Where is she?"

Rena pointed overhead. "I sent her upstairs. Down here will be bedlam in another ten minutes. Kate Tharrington is already sounding the call—and I made a caramel cake last night. There'll be six brought here by dark and you know it; I'll never be able to touch one again. Haven't touched a piece of bacon since Mother died." Then she pulled on Rob's hand and pointed to the door and whispered, "I need five words with you." She led him quickly across the hall, the old front parlor which had held Eva's bed for twenty years; and shut the door behind them. When she'd got them to the center of the old rose rug, she said in a firm voice one tone above a whisper, "Remember one thing and hold it tight through all that's coming. You are the only hope of this crowd, and I mean to see that you get the right share of whatever Father had. Hold tight to that now. Till blood springs out of your nails if need be." She had never turned him loose; she gripped him harder now.

Rob nodded and continued to take her steady gaze as locked as an ermine's, but he said "Hope for what?"

She did not understand.

"You said I was the hope—the hope of what though?"

Rena thought a long time, even lowered her eyes. Then she found that she knew. "Oh Jesus," she said, "just *rest*, my darling." Tears brimmed her eyes. She had not looked up again; they fell, a clean drop, small spots on the rug.

Rob had never seen that. He tried to remember when he'd last seen tears in the walls of this house. There'd surely been tears (since his own childhood storms); he could think of none—or had they all been hidden, choked back behind doors? Whatever, they had found a free channel in Rena, who let them run. When he saw they had spent their urgent flood, he said, "You can rest. You have got years to rest. Once we get through the funeral, you have got a long calm. You hold to that." He touched her at the shoulders, small handsful of strength (lean muscle, firm bone).

By then she could smile. "I didn't mean that."

"Tell me then please."

It was harder to say than any other thing, any speech she had dared in forty-one years of ready speech. But she partly knew, for the first time ever, what she'd meant to say (had meant for years); and though her eyes had dried, her brow and chin showed the reckless effort. "I mean that nobody in this house, nobody that ever slept one night here, has ever got the thing they wanted from life. I just mean that." What she did not say was what she did not know, not consciously—that she spoke for herself, that her hope was for him: his total return here, body and spirit, return to her own steady gaze and care. She could not admit, even far beneath consciousness, that this one strong boy could not put a whole hungry household to rest.

Rob nodded. "How can I hope to remedy that?"

"Did Kennerly tell you about the will?"

He said "No ma'm," a complicated lie, part sly child's wish to give her the chance to bring him fresh news, part canny man's scheme to check two accounts for consistency.

But she knew very little. "You ask him," she said. "Father told him last spring. It's in his head."

Rob was caught, shamed. "He did tell me this much—I get the homeplace."

Rena waited to think. "You mean this house." She pointed to the floor.

"The Kendal place."

She shook her head hard once and puffed a breath of disgust. "A readymade bonfire. One match would send it up."

Rob said, "He loved it. He wanted me to have it."

That turned her at once. The brief flight of yearning and anticipation which had borne her so high was wrenched down flat. "He wanted you to *die*—to sit in the country and die in the tracks of people whose names you never even heard, I never even knew: old selfish Kendals. You listen to me—" She checked her heat. "*Please* listen to me; drive out there this evening and beg that Negro to farm that place for the rest of his life and not bother you for any more than prayer. Beg him that if it means kneeling down in the dirt and scrubbing his feet."

Rob smiled. "Calm down. I'm staying put."

"In Richmond," she said.

"Yes ma'm. For the time. We have started being happy."

"Who is *we*?"

"Me and Rachel; you remember my wedding?" He smiled again, touched her shoulders again.

Rena stepped backward gently but out of his reach. "I remember very well. Can you remember *me*, what I told you that night?"

"Yes ma'm, I do. I have taken it to heart."

"I told you the life that I've had here, the life Eva's had, has been gristle and bone."

Rob said "She had Papa."

"And I had you as I said, twenty years."

Rob said, "Cheer up—Papa's all that's gone."

Rena laughed, a strip of sound like an issue of blood. "Not so," she said. She went to the door. But she stopped on the worn sill and faced him again. "Did it really matter?"

"What please?"

"What I told you—find another life and hold it, hold it; don't ever go single?"

"More than anything I think I've ever seen," Rob said. He had meant to say *heard*; but he'd seen Rena's life, all the lives of this house. The long sights had mattered. He let the word stand.

"Well, Jesus," she said. She was somehow grinning. "At least I touched bottom." She moved again to leave.

Rob was moved to stop her—one final offer, though he neither understood his need to say it nor the fact that he meant it as his largest gift. "I am going to have a child," he said.

Rena took it, nodded "Thank you" and was gone.

5

BY ten that night all the callers had left except for Thorne Bradley who stayed on the front porch with Kennerly and Eva (Rena had excused herself for the first time in memory and gone to bed at nine); so Rob went back to the kitchen where Sylvie was finishing and took a slice of cake and a glass of milk and sat at the big worktable in the center, too tired to think. He chewed on slowly while Sylvie moved round him, moaning now and then in her own exhaustion, addressing herself or the empty air with snatches of talk which Rob ignored.

Finally she stopped far from him by the sink and watched Rob, meaning him to look her way. When she'd failed to turn him, she said, "Look here. When they going to bed?"

Rob looked. Her eyes were heavy, mouth slack. "Go on," he said. "You've done a gracious plenty."

"She asked me to stay."

"Who?"

"Miss Eva."

"Stay where?"

"Where you think? In here. I'll lay down a pallet once they go to bed."

Rob had thought that the old arrangement would pertain; Grainger and Gracie had always slept at Sylvie's. "Is Grainger at your place already then?"

"You know," Sylvie said.

"I know very little about this place." He smiled but meant it.

"He gone in your car to meet Miss Min."

He'd forgotten entirely. Kate Tharrington had asked him early in the evening if Grainger might drive her the six miles over to meet the Raleigh train (she had phoned Min the news, and oddly Min was coming). He smiled toward Sylvie. "Guess she needed the rest" (Min had taken a job when school term ended at the State Library, searching family trees).

Sylvie also smiled. "*Rest* nothing," she said, "—she be busy struggling to watch you, Rob."

"Then I'll hold real still, make it easy on her."

Sylvie laughed but said, "If you smart you'll run. She get you yet."

"I'm *got*," Rob said.

Sylvie waited. "Miss Rachel?"

Rob searched her face quickly, no sign of mockery. "Yes."

Sylvie took a damp rag and scrubbed down the lip of the sink another time. She alone had rubbed it to rust through the years. Then she spread the rag carefully to dry and said, "How she going to hold you?" Still her face for all its tiredness was blank as basalt.

Half or more of what Rob had learned of his body—its growing and power, its offers of solace—had come from Sylvie. (The baths she had given him, stroking and laughter; the shards of her own life-story she would slip him when his mother and Rena had left a room—some fool that had sought her; some visitor she'd borne for the whole night before, to exhaustion and rest. *Vicellars Hargrove*—Rob remembered the name now: a short dark man who would wait for Sylvie at the kitchen door fifteen years ago. Gone like all her company. The night of his own high-school commencement—Sylvie's deep bed, old gold Money swimming, the dangerous darkness, dark Flora above him astraddle his horn more ready than ever in all nights since, more grandly assuaged.) But now tonight Rob could not read her meaning; was it kind curiosity or tired joke or a search for weapons to press against him? He gambled on hurting her. "Pussy," he said. "Simple as pussy. You know what that is."

Struck, Sylvie nodded before she really heard. When it reached her, she sat in her chair by the sink, no thought of leaving. While Rob drained his milk, she waited and thought. When he looked up and wiped his mouth, she said "Who taught you that?"

"What?"

"—That Rachel?"

Rob said "Who taught me what?"

Sylvie said, "Meanness. Never learned it from me."

Rob said "Excuse me."

She faced him level. "Too late," she said.

He waited awhile, then looked around. "Any more of that cake?"

"You get it," she said. "You just now told me I done a plenty."

Rob tried again. "Please, Sylvie. I'm dead."

"I'm *buried*," she said. "You sit there and wait till your nigger come back here with Minnie; they'll serve you, one of em."

Eva said "Something wrong?"

Both looked. She was straight in the door, one hand on the frame. Rob said, "No ma'm. We're resting our feet. Sit down; it's cooler."

She came forward quickly and sat.

Sylvie stood. "Miss Eva, you hungry?"

Eva thought for a moment. "I believe I am."

So Sylvie went to work—the clean blue plate that Eva favored, a large breast of chicken, half a fresh tomato, cold potato salad, rolls still warm from where she'd kept them nested, buttered and closed.

But before she had brought the plate to his mother, Rob said, "Are you going to be all right?"

Eva thought again. "For when?" she said.

He decided to tell her. "From now on. For good."

"The funeral is tomorrow afternoon at three; we just settled that after you left the porch. I can last through that, I honestly think. After that—" She stopped and turned back to Sylvie, "We'll see, won't we, Sylvie?"

Sylvie said, "Nothing but. What you want me to pour you?"

"Any buttermilk left?"

"A gallon."

"One glass please."

Sylvie went to the icebox, poured the thick milk, and set it with the full plate between Eva's hands, flat before her on the table. Eva thanked her and said, "You are staying with us, aren't you?"

"I told you not to worry," Sylvie said and sat again.

Eva ate two mouthfuls, swallowed with effort; and said to Rob, "If I've worried you, you can start calming down. I was tired just now. I'll certainly live." She took a taste of milk. "I can't say *how*—what I'll do, I mean."

"Come to Richmond," Rob said and touched her cool wrist. "Come visit me and Rachel."

Eva gave that a moment. "I may," she said.

"Come back with me Sunday. No need to stay here. Rena and Sylvie can hold down the fort till you draw breath—can't you, Sylvie?"

"Yes ma'm. Take Rena on with you. I do it by myself."

Eva faced him and studied. "Don't rush me," she said. "This is where I can breathe or *have* been breathing. I may strangle elsewhere."

"I'd be there," Rob said.

"I thought you were coming back here anyhow."

"No ma'm," Rob said. "Who told you that?"

"Father, last summer. After you and Rachel left, he told me you had asked him for the old Kendal place; so he said you should have it."

"No ma'm," Rob said. "It was his idea."

"But you promised him," she said.

He'd forgot the promise, his lie that morning to calm the old man. Could his mother know of it? "What?" Rob said.

She knew precisely. "To move there and clean it up and take care of me."

He felt cold fear for the first time since childhood (he was not a fearful person and had known it for years, no special virtue but a trait like his hair). He thought, "She is giving it now at last."

Before he could move on to ask if he wanted it, could use it any longer, Sylvie spoke. "God help him." She cast it as a mumble, but it rang clear as oratory.

Eva met his eyes, held on them a searching moment, then broke out laughing.

Sylvie followed higher.

Before they had finished, Rob managed a smile but a pale one, pinched.

Eva chewed a biscuit, swallowed it; then still smiling said, "What's so good about Richmond?"

He needed to harm her. All in him, a hot need to strike stood up. He tried to let it cool; but he lost and said, "You are not there mainly."

Eva's smile deepened, broadened. Before him again she was flying back to girlhood—his oldest sight of her, bent above him, baffled, genuinely searching him for answers and help. But she said, "No I'm not. You're safe; I never will be."

Sylvie clucked twice—"Shamed." She did not say of whom, knowing neither of them cared.

Rob said, "I'm sorry. It's been a long day. I'm too tired to talk."

Eva said, "Some people have been tired for years but have held their tongues." She was still pleasant-faced.

So he smiled in answer. "I'm working at that; that's what is in Richmond. I'm learning several things."

"Name us some," Eva said.

Sylvie said, "Same fool I've known from a baby."

Rob said, "All the stuff I had not known before. I am learning to love my wife and hope for children. I am—"

Eva's face had darkened and gathered through that. She stopped him with a hand. "Won't somebody *quit*?" She was white with the wish.

Sylvie said "Quit what?"

Rob waited only.

Eva's force had drained in the words themselves. She was left high, beached, ashamed of explaining. "I said I was tired. But I'm tireder than I knew. Sylvie, I have been tired for twenty years exactly."

"I know you have." Sylvie stood to check the plate.

Eva looked back to Rob. Her hand was still on him, his wrist; she flicked it lightly, hair lighter than hers, diluted by Forrest. "No reason for me to force others to rest though."

He waited till she knew he'd accepted the apology, then withdrew his wrist and covered her hand with his whole palm entirely. "There's not. You're right. No reason at all." He met her dry eyes that were working to hold him. For the first time in all his life, he merely liked her.

"Every reason on God's green earth," Sylvie said. "Get out of here and let me rest my tail."

The three laughed together.

6

Rob waited on the porch alone for Grainger. His mother had gone from the kitchen to bed; he had told her he'd sit with his grandfather awhile, then turn in himself. The oil lamp burned low and hot by his bed (Mr. Kendal had never let his own room be wired); and Rob had stood a minute by the still tallow corpse—composed, dressed, and combed by his mother this morning while some warmth remained in the neck, arms, legs. He'd known that a farewell of sorts was due; seemed expected even by the head, propped and waiting on the bolster from which it had fueled this house, these lives, for twenty years. But not Rob's, he saw then. He'd been unable to feel so much as simple relief at this final absence; not to mention hate or the various triumphs which might have been just, had surely been earned. He'd clenched his hands a time or two, nails deep into palms, to rouse some flare of pain or pleasure. Nothing came but the steady peaceful sight of an old man resting on his lifelong bed in his good black suit; so he'd turned down the lamp to the barest shine that would represent light—a watch till morning—then he'd gone to the porch and sat on the left in the old green swing, the place he'd stretched for so many empty hours, his head in Rena's lap, her long fingers scratching in his short hot hair.

It was cooler now, almost eleven; and he'd swung himself nearly to rest again when the lights of his car turned down beside the house and into the yard—Grainger. He must meet him, keep him out of the kitchen where Sylvie had already spread her pallet.

It was Grainger and Min. Min waited by the car till he'd got nearly to her; then she said, "It's later than I knew, Rob. I'm sorry. We let Mother out but I asked Grainger please just to run me by here; I meant to see your mother."

"She's gone on to bed."

"Is she all right, Rob?"

"I think so," he said. "Nobody knows yet, me least of all. I never have known her."

"Oh you have," Min said.

Rob laughed. "Still arguing. I hoped you'd outgrow it."

"I didn't," Min said. She looked back to Grainger, who was dark there behind them, awaiting his duty. "Thank you, Grainger. I'll walk on home now. It's cool."

Rob said, "Wait a minute, Min. —Grainger, Sylvie's in the kitchen; Mother asked her to stay. She said you could go on to her place tonight, said the little bed was clean and for you to use that. Take the car—just lock it—and be back by seven: a busy day tomorrow."

Grainger stood, no answer.

"Something wrong?" Rob said.

Grainger beckoned with his shoulder—"Let me talk to you please"—and turned to walk off.

Rob said, "Min, I will walk with you home, just a second."

Min said "I'd be grateful" and stepped on the running board and sat on the fender, dusty as it was.

Rob went after Grainger to the stand he'd taken far over by the hedge, past the reach of the one weak backdoor light. He stopped two steps short of touching him and said, "Are you tired as me?"

Grainger said "No I'm not."

"You need any money?"

"I'm all right, thank you."

Rob said, "Then I'll see you at seven in the morning."

Grainger came forward one of the steps between them. His clean high odor, cured hay in a loft, was firm as a wall. "You talk to Miss Rachel?"

"Three hours ago. I thought I told you."

"You didn't. I was waiting."

"She'll get here on the noon train tomorrow. You can meet her."

"—Miss Rachel," Grainger said. "You mean Miss Rachel?"

Rob remembered then. "So far as I know. She was still by herself at eight o'clock tonight."

"No sign of Gracie?"

"Grainger, I didn't ask but surely she'd have told me."

Grainger stood in place another long moment; then stepped back, forced by the ignorance that poured out of Rob in a sickening torrent. "Maybe not," he said, "if she thinking like you."

Rob said, "Well, she's not. She's better than me. I said I was tired; you know all the reasons."

Grainger nodded. "I've heard em."

Rob waited, hoping to outlast the anger. He searched to see Grainger's face—some chance that he'd misheard or misread the last two minutes; that Grainger was not now trying, as it seemed, to cut loose and flail with all his long hoarding of witness and knowledge, a dreadful weapon; then leave for good. But though Grainger faced the house and the light, Rob could still not read the face held level before him, a mirror which fiercely declined to reflect. So he said the beginnings of what was just—"I will beg your pardon, Grainger."

Grainger said "Now or when?"

"Now. This minute." Then Rob said in his own head silently, "I have saved my life." He meant his spirit, his chance of peace; and for now he was right.

Grainger also knew, had the grace not to thank him or mention the . moment which neither would forget in all their lives to come. He said, "I'll see you in the morning like I said." Then he reclaimed the single step he'd retreated and whispered the rest with a half-edge of laughter. "You take Miss Minnie straight home, no pausing."

Rob said "That's the plan."

"She tending to pause."

Rob said "Ease your mind" and punched him once lightly in the belly with the tips of his straight right fingers.

Grainger would have said "*Eased*"—it came to his mind—had he not had troubles that lay beyond this white boy in his path. He said "I'm working on it."

Rob turned and they went back in Indian file.

Min slid down to meet them.

Grainger said, "Good night, Miss Min. Sleep good."

"Thank you, Grainger," she said.

7

IN sight of Min's house, Rob slowed and said, "You didn't have to come all the way home for this. People prayed for this death; nobody's bereft."

"Just your mother," Min said. "I came to watch her."

Rob said, "Then you've wasted a good train ticket. You won't see a tear; she's calm as my hand." In the warm dark he held out a steady hand.

Min said, "I can see tears on any street corner. I came to watch calm."

"For what?" Rob said.

"Education," Min said. "I'm a scholar, remember?"

Rob said, "I do. What's your present subject?"

"*Calm* as I said."

"You writing a book?" He stopped and faced her smiling.

Min also stopped but could barely see him. "No I'm living my life."

"And that's hard?" Rob said.

She nodded. "Part of it."

"What part?" Rob said.

"Are you really asking or passing time?"

"Does it matter?" Rob said.

"This much," Min said, "—if you're asking, I'll *tell* you. If you're stirring a breeze, I'll say goodnight." They had almost reached the walk to her house. A porch light was shining and some dimness upstairs.

"Your mother's gone up."

"We can sit on the porch," Min said, "—if you're asking. Otherwise I'm tired." She was also smiling and Rob could see her.

"All right," he said.

So she led them up the walk and quietly onto the porch—the old green rockers. Rob sat in the far one; but Min stood on at the top of the steps till she heard her mother's presence at the upstairs window. "It's Rob and me, Mother. We're down on the porch. I'll see you at breakfast." Kate Tharrington agreed and Min reached inside and turned off the light and came and sat an arm's reach from Rob, though he did not reach; did not think of reaching. He gave her silent time to recall his question and plan her answer. Finally she said, "The hard part is solitude. I never asked for that; but I've got it, big supply."

Rob said, "You asked for it. I was present and heard you." His tone was pleasant.

"When was that?"

"Our commencement, the party at the lake, you and me by the water."

"I did," Min said. "I suspected you'd forgot."

Rob said, "I remembered and I honored your wish. I could see you meant it."

"I did," Min said, "but just for that minute. You were awful that minute."

"I was honest at least."

"Honest in what?"

"In saying I needed you to help me then."

"You needed help about as much as Jesus in glory. Rob, you were the victor through all those years."

"If that's all you know, you were blind and dumb. I was worse off than most."

"From your mother?" Min said.

"Then you understood something."

"No I didn't," Min said. "I was thinking of me, a full-time job. No your mother sat me down four summers ago and told me her story, right before your wedding."

"Her marriage?—all that?"

"All that."

"She mentioned me?"

"In passing," Min said. "That was how I knew; you were just in passing. You were worse off than me and had always been." She guarded in silence the rest of her memory, Eva's plea that she take Rob and hold him however.

"I'm better now," he said. "I am all but cured." His tone was joking but a joker would have thumped his chest then to show soundness. Rob extended straight arms to the darkness before him as if it would care for the last of his needs. He held there a moment, then withdrew them to his lap again and rocked on slowly.

There was just enough light from one hall lamp and the far street corner for Min to see him. She took the chance. He was facing outward, calm, a little tired. He had meant no harm, only simple truth—he seemed better now: this boy (twenty-five, no better than dozens within two miles of here and oiled as he was with the seizures he'd made from other human lives, the tolls he'd taken for his own selfish need); this boy was her wish. Her single wish, alive after eight years of earnest stifling and flight. She would have to speak or sit till he turned and found her. She said "You like your work," a fact not a question, though she didn't know the answer.

Rob considered that slowly, surprised as always to find that he did—at the edge of his mind where he might have liked a dog or a clerk in a store. "It helps some," he said. He regretted that at once; she could plunge on and force him to bruise her again. He'd allowed her to steer it her own old way.

She proceeded. "What else?"

He faced her in dread which he tried to wear as puzzlement.

"What other help?" she said. "You claimed you were well."

"Just better, I said. You knew me at the low point."

"Something's helped you though."

"More than one thing, Min."

"I'm asking you to tell me."

Rob studied her. Till now she'd seemed grave as she was when a girl, every instant a sum to be teased till solved, the solutions presented with laughing surprise (however brief). Now he saw she was wild—denied and baffled. It seemed a new sight, a fresh message shown by a dying fire. He would not receive it. But in silence and exhaustion and because Min still faced him, he went on watching till he knew that her offer was common as bread in his own short life—the only word he had ever had from women: Rena, even Sylvie, Hatt Shorter, Rachel. Polly at the daily will of his father. Della in her black room, her deep dry bed. The Hell they stood in and beckoned from (all but Eva sufficient in her own full place, arms down, or Gracie taunting Grainger). He had answered only Rachel, was trying to answer; had tried last night in their slow embrace, bare and dangerous. He did not know why and was not a man to ask; he felt now simply that he'd chosen rightly to put his lean strength into one strange socket—a girl named Rachel, as wild as any—that he had no strength remaining for others: Rena or Grainger or (a wonder) Eva. Or Min here now. He smiled and said, "Min, the answer is I'm loved."

"You were always that."

"Maybe so," Rob said. "Now I'm happy to be."

Min gave herself time; then she said, "Do you mind me watching you?"

"Help yourself," he said. But then he said, "Now or for years to come?"

"The years," she said.

"Yes I do. Yes ma'm. It's bad for us both."

She waited again; then laughed, amazed to find a laugh natural. "Then I'll stop," she said.

Rob said," You'll feel a lot better" and joined her. "You'll be a new woman."

"Praise Jesus!" Min said. That calmed them a little.

8

TIRED from the day (four hours on a hot train, a funeral, the crowd), Rachel went up before Rob and slept and dreamt before he joined her— she was on this bed on her back as now; but the bed was under heavy fathoms of water, and a dark girl (Gracie? she could not see a face) was far up above her bending over the surface of whatever pool this was and calling down to her, the words all muffled. Rachel thought in the dream, "I am safe from whatever that girl foretells"; and she did seem safe. She could breathe underwater, she could hold her breath and rest for long black hours, the dark girl would vanish. She was happy in the dream as she all but was in life, as life had begun to promise her she'd be. Soon. Through Rob.

He came up at ten-thirty, moving so lightly that Rachel didn't wake till he tried to raise a window. Then she surfaced from sleep and dream and saw him by the various dim lights that reached the window—street-lamp and moonlight, the odd passing car (he stood that long looking out, his side to Rachel): a boy a little shorter than she'd ever realized, his right hand hung on his sloped left shoulder, his weight on the left side, entirely bare. Since he seemed bemused and locked there, staring up the street, she took the chance to study him, a chance she'd seldom had since whenever he was naked he was generally in motion. A good while passed; he still stood on. Rachel fed on the offering he did not know he made. She understood nothing and was happy in the mystery; one portion of life encased in one form (particular, with all its own grandeurs and failures) had come through the dense world and stood here now apparently for her when she'd feared to the blank lip of certainty and farther that no one would come, not for her, not in time. She whispered "Good evening."

He did not turn.

"Good evening."

Still there, no flicker of notice.

She knew him well enough by now to stay calm. *He has not departed, he is cooling off, who's he here for but me?* But the calm was frail and raveled by the moment. *He'll turn now and tell me to go back without him. Go where? Away.* She clenched both hands—*Crazy; call his name.* She said "Rob" aloud.

His body stayed firm; his head turned slightly.

"Good evening," she said again.

He shook his head. "It hasn't been all that good so far."

"Your mother?"

"Everybody."

"That's why I came from Richmond."

"Why?"

"I thought you'd be down."

"You were right that far." Still looking toward her through the dark, Rob waited. Then he said. "Tell me how you thought you could help by being here."

She knew he'd been the fulcrum of the whole heavy day; so in spite of the chance that he'd taken some turn since touching her last, she said, "Relief. Maybe comic relief. I knew all the locals would be very solemn."

"Tell a joke," Rob said.

She was silent.

"Quick."

So she said, "All right—all I have is with me, my warm open skin. It was waiting for you. It will bear you to bliss."

He said "Please whisper"—she had spoken aloud.

She whispered *"Bliss"* and laughed once.

He turned.

By the light she could see he'd been ready awhile, for her apparently (who else was here?); for what she had brought, the little she'd brought. She felt it like that as he moved down on her and finally joined her. It seemed all she knew, all she'd needed to know through the bad time behind her or would ever need. She thought now of futures, a whole life ahead. What she didn't know—despite her plea of two nights before, despite Rob's second bareness as he came to port within her—was her other deep readiness: her body's fresh offer to accept his total gift and change it to a child, an actual child, that dangerous surrender, a long delight or death.

When they'd calmed and Rachel had drawn the sheet up to cover them, Rob said, "Tell me your idea of what comes now."

"Dreamless sleep."

"No from here on out, the rest of the time."

Rachel turned to her back—she had been facing toward him—and looked to the ceiling as he was doing. "Oh natural lives."

"What are they?"

"What we have, what we've had just lately—two people passing time, close and careful; eventually children, giving them room."

Rob said nothing.

"What's wrong with that?"

"It's harder than that. Two of anything is hard, not to mention fours and sixes—my mother, your father, any children that come. How on earth can we learn how to care for all that?" He still watched the ceiling, the string of the center light, a pale rope to nowhere.

Rachel said, "I think—and I think you will think if you look back a little—that Rachel knows at least as much of hardness as you."

He weighed that carefully as if it were urgent to know exact figures for burdens borne, payments earned—a rigorous fairness. Then he turned to his right side and faced her dark profile. "I think she does."

Rachel also turned—their breaths met and mingled, both clean and hot. "*She* is *me*," she said, "—Rachel Mayfield born Hutchins. I have given you my life. You can trust me forever. Nobody you have ever known could touch me for strength or for love of you. The rest of the time you can rest on me. I am more than you knew, ever dreamt I would be."

Rob could no longer see her; the moon had moved, all cars had passed. He tried—total darkness, though he knew she was there. Her breath brushed his face every five or six seconds; the voice had been hers, pitched upward by a fervor he'd imagined in her past but had not heard before—the lip-edge of wildness which till now only Della had recognized as *sight*, the visitation upon one girl in Goshen, Virginia of the gift of knowledge of present and future; the gift of *certainty* awarded for whole years of unbroken gaze toward cores of the world he'd barely glanced over, from weakness and fear. Sufficient home for heart and body, room in that home for whatever product of love might issue through its bloody gates (some risky child); the patience to plead those gifts from life, seize them if need be, honor them always—natural lives.

A hand touched his chin, stroked down to his throat, then the nape of his neck; then slowly downward.

He fully surrendered and slowly she brought him to readiness again. What he did not know of course as now he rolled on her—what she would not have turned back from had she known—was the near cold future: nine months from now this child's birth would kill her, this child started now in this lovely juncture.

9

WELL before day Grainger woke on his back in Sylvie's extra bed—a little corner off her big main room, no door, no air, not reached by the low lamp she burned by her own bed. He had slept untroubled since his head touched the pillow before midnight, but he knew the instant his eyes opened now that his rest was over. He must wait for day and Sylvie; she breathed on slowly ten yards away. He was fully dressed—just his shoes untied, his collar unbuttoned—so his watch was in his pocket. He quietly withdrew it in the small hope of gauging the time he must wait (it felt about five, the weight of the air); and though its steel ticking was the loudest noise for miles, he couldn't see hands; couldn't even see the face. He brought it to within five inches of his best eye and tilted both the watch and his head all ways to catch any loose light passing in the air. Not a trace, full-dark. It could be two o'clock; he could have to lie here on his back four hours and breathe Sylvie's used air (she wouldn't crack a window) and face his own facts.

It wouldn't be the first time—he had that at least; he'd had a fair number of wakings in recent years. And in the first minute or so of any waking, he would mention to himself what Mr. Forrest told him long years ago—"Never dwell on any grave matter in the dark and flat of your back. If you wake up worried or scared by a dream, take the bull by the horns and use your precious mind; use the knowledge you've gained, try to name all the states or the chief exports of the world by country or say all your poems. But don't ever pray, not dead in the night; you'll think you are desperate in fifteen seconds, not to mention rousing God." For years that had worked; he'd obeyed and profited—the names of the tongues of the Indian nations of North and South America, the battles of the Civil War in order by date and by casualties—but increasing years had brought him to this: all his recent knowledge, precious or trash, was hard and harmful. And now at thirty-six, his older knowledge—what he'd heard from Miss Veenie, Mr. Forrest, Miss Hatt, his captain in France—began to seem in danger, not so much of being lies but of having been always a grinning cheat, the meanest joke. What had they all ever told him but this?—*If you mind your step, stay clean and pretty, stay well and on-time, you can be our pet; we will see you through.* He'd liked them and listened; and they had seen him through—to this, this night: a middle-aged man in a hot nigger shack forced to wait till day till an ignorant woman, much darker than he, had slept out her stupor and woke (hacking, hawking) to feed her old dog and ride with him back to a kitchen where he'd help her make biscuits and breakfast for a table of the ones who were seeing him through, then drive two of them (the youngest two and best) up the roadmap to

Richmond where his own little clean room would swallow him in dumb dry silence, glad to have him.

Grainger went through that in the first ten minutes or so of his wait.

What saved him was this—*who had got any more?* The one voice that ever said another thing was Gracie (he'd known for some time now that that was why he'd sought her); and what she had said through all her going and coming, pitching and cutting; what she bellowed out clear in this latest last absence, what she'd said (he saw now) in her heat and light that first day he'd seen her in the churchyard in Bracey was no less than this—*I will have my life. Anybody that can help me, I will stay with awhile; I will lie underneath you long as you help. When you stop, I leave; when you run out of whatever I call help, that day, that minute. What I won't do is lie—I am hunting just this: what will use me up, what will burn me down (however quick it work) till nothing's left to touch, no spot of my grease, no rusty black hair, no slick bone to bury.*

Maybe Gracie had won, had got more than anybody else he'd watched. More what?—good life, good speed toward home. What was home?—well, rest. Who was headed elsewhere? Grainger thought for the first time in four, five years of the end of the story of the dark Pocahontas. He tested could he say it in his head in silence but working his lips—"She died of a broken heart beneath foreign skies with memories of the green woods of east Virginia, the swarming streams from whose sweet shallows she is still divided by the thousands of leagues of rolling salt deep by which she sleeps her longing sleep."

He wished Gracie speed on her way, long sleep; and by then felt the chance of dozing again, calm again anyhow.

But Sylvie spoke some hoarse quick sentence, clearly in her sleep.

Grainger rose to his elbows to hear if she repeated; he still had faith in the wisdom of sleep.

She said "Come here," low but urgently.

The last thing he wanted. He lay still and small.

She called out louder—"Here," in genuine pain.

Grainger said "Sylvie?"

A long wait. "What?"

"You sick or something?"

"No, fool," she said and scuffled with her quilt to return to sleep.

"You were hollering out."

Another long wait. "I got plenty reason."

He knew he'd been wrong. "You said come yonder."

"Won't talking to you."

"I know that," he said. Then he said "Who was it?"

"Seen a little baby in trouble," she said. She wanted to sleep.

"You catch it?" he said.

Sylvie lay back and told him. "I'm not sure I did. I was in this crowd lined up by the road, everybody watching something. Must have been a parade; you seen a parade?"

"Right often," he said.

"Where at?"

"Richmond. France. I saw more parades between here and France than I hope to see again."

"This was bad too," she said, "—everybody watching nothing but cars passing by. I was back from the road, lot of people around me; and I seen this baby crawl down in the gully and start for the road. Cars were still coming and I look around; nobody noticing so I leg out in the mud and catch him just before one big wheel grind him down. He not even dirty and grinning at me, not a year old yet. I bring him back over to the shoulder of the road, and there stand his mama. So I hand him to her, and she don't even thank me. I go on back to my place in the crowd; and next time I look, that baby on the ground again and that woman kicking him out in the road and cars still coming."

"You were hollering at him."

"I guess so," she said.

"But you woke up then."

"You called me," she said. "But he looked at me. He was looking up at me; he knew where I was."

"You'd have caught him," Grainger said.

Sylvie waited till he thought she had sunk back under; then she said, "I'd have tried. I'd have sure God tried."

Grainger said. "You'll catch him. You still got time. Go on back to sleep."

In a minute she was gone.

But her story stayed and worked on Grainger slowly. For reasons no stranger than necessity and patience, he lay and let it work—the harsh dream littered with hatred and hunger, not even his own. Yet it chose him as its object—he'd felt its arrival like a hand on his body—and bore in on him; and once it found home in his empty chest, it spread like streams and filled him with, of all things, happiness: a happiness that nothing else had brought him in weeks. Maybe months. No, years—twenty-five years nearly: a boy in a cold dark room in Richmond, Christmas, a gold ring, the promise of a life. He knew he was sane. He knew what those years had brought had been mostly pigshit and not of his making. He knew there was very slim chance of a change. Still he was happy. And could not think why.

But he didn't strain to know; he was glad to let it flood him, cool grace in the night. A grown half-black houseboy now abandoned by his field-nigger wife, a burdensome pet of the two white men who were now all he had (his actual kin), a man who could do nothing stronger than make

flowers grow anywhere or keep a car clean or drive it neatly and say a few
poems, who had made no children in ten years of trying—that seemed all
he knew, this one night in August.

Yet he did not feel it. He believed in blessing. This clearly was a
blessing at work in him now, Sylvie's dark dream intended for Grainger.
The dense dry earth was promising to bless him, as it planned to kill
Rachel and devastate Rob. It had saved him before; he would trust it
again. He had earned his keep and would not be refused.

Grainger smiled, a gesture as hidden as the work of the hands of his
watch, then raised his long legs and tied his loose shoes (a new gift from
Rob) and waited for day, rested and ready, his long life to come. After half
an hour, he thought of a question he should have asked Sylvie—was the
boy white or colored?—but her breathing was slow again, her welcome
stupor. She'd tell him tomorrow if he thought to ask her; if she still
remembered the message she'd borne him, the chance moving toward him
through time, time's amends.

THREE

PARTIAL AMENDS

JUNE 5-7, 1944

 They had slept four hours when the dream began, ran its slow course, and woke them—Rob, then Min. Rob woke in fact well before the end, to stop it. Naked on his back on the soaked narrow mattress, he had managed to refuse to endure the end again and he opened his eyes. But he didn't touch Min or turn in the dark to find her. He lay flat, waiting for the fan's next swing, and watched the low ceiling while she saw it through beside him eight inches away, suffering little yips and moans toward the end as she struggled to surface and took the first breath of consciousness, hot for early June. Then they both lay quiet, still separate though bare, testing in the rate and depth of breath how ready each was to speak, start a day.

 Finally Min said "Have you been asleep?"

 "Long as you, two minutes less."

 "What got you?" she said.

 He said "You know."

 "But tell me." She turned—in place, no nearer—and saw him by the streetlight filtered through shades: the line of his features like a map for the road of the rest of her life (she saw it that way, had seen it for years despite his refusal).

 Rob understood both her turn and what she saw; and neither from cruelty nor fear, he turned away—the need to focus on the story he'd seen and learn its demands. Then he put one finger longway between his teeth, a bridle should he need one; and said, "I was a boy. Fourteen, fifteen. We lived in the country and a war was on, around us but not near us. We were in the foothills, unharmed and green; and I had a sickness—my chest, my breath—though I felt well and safe and ready for my life. My father walked with me to the nearest town; and the doctor said—smiling, everybody was smiling, clear beautiful day—'T.B., very grave' and that, owing to the war, I must walk on up in the mountains to the springs. The good air, the waters. I left from there, not even going home—Father just vanished, no kiss, no wave—and I walked west for days through emptiness. Little towns in the distance, churches, trains; but not a living soul and I wasn't lonesome or hungry either. I just had the clothes on my back—a blue poplin shirt with the collar gone, big brown pants, old brogans—and a silver dollar to pay for my treatments at the end of the line. But I never ate a mouthful on the whole long trip, never felt the need. I was happy. All the way, every step of the way—all steep uphill—I was smiling to myself, needing nothing but me. Oh I touched a deer and saw most other kinds of harmless creatures; and every now and then I would hear the war, guns behind me muttering away. All the men were there, I guess; but old folks and children—where had they gone? And I never slept once. It was that far to go; and I wanted it that bad—the place, the springs, and not just my health but something beneath it, better than health: a magnet in the ground." Rob waited, the finger still in his teeth, still turned away.

Min said, "Are you telling me all that is true?"

He began an answer but only exhaled.

"Are you saying that happened?"

"It seemed to be," he said.

"But not to you."

"Maybe not," he said. "I'd have to think back."

"Think forward," she said. "Tell on to the end."

"I didn't let it end." Both their voices were as clear and clean as if they had never slept in their lives but had watched at doors steadily for arrivals.

"Tell as far as you went." Min watched him still, just the side of his head. He was beautiful and seemed calm now, which was why she urged him on—to learn all she could in the spaces of calm.

"The final night of the trip, all night, I walked through a storm like Hell on the rise. Night bright as day with lightning, trees crashing, rocks big as sheds falling at my feet—tame as dogs, sparing me."

"You were scared though."

"Was I? I don't remember."

"Yes."

"But I didn't stop, did I? That wasn't what it meant anyhow, the storm. It was not for me. I just went on—one foot, then the other, steeper up—into calm and morning which came together. And the first sight of people in all those days. I had come round a curve near the top of the mountain; and the road stretched straight before me, half a mile. At the far end were people all turned toward me—they'd been turned when I came into sight; they were waiting—so I went on toward them and knew I was there, my destination. Still I asked the first man—tall, old as my father—'Is this the springs?' He said, 'It was and it was mine.' Everybody else nodded—men and women, all grown but a girl a little younger than me, all sad but not hard. I said to him 'Was? I've walked days to drink. I'm dying, mister.' And he said, 'Well, die. The springs is gone.' I looked round at everybody there, all nodding, and said to them 'Help!' "

"You were scared."

"I remember—and honest, in earnest. Not a human moved. So I said it again; and the one girl stepped forward, just beyond being a child, a month or two beyond. And she said, 'Listen. We had the storm too, and it flooded our river and buried our springs.' I said 'Under what?' She said 'Six feet of dirt'; and I said, 'Hell, I'm dying. Let's *dig*.' The girl said 'Yes' but the first man said, 'How much do you cost?' I said, 'I'm free if you'll save my life.' The girl said 'No.' I said, 'You want me to die?' She said, 'No not that. But nothing's free. I just meant that; don't give away anything except for *return*.' So I said, 'Fair enough. I'll take you then'; and knew I was cured, healed down to the sockets and the springs still buried. The man didn't like it, frowned a lot; but all the rest grinned, and the girl led the way toward a little springhouse, white lattice work that was half under mud. And we dug forever. Days. Weeks more nearly. Every man but that one, who was my girl's father; and the women would cook us things and stand round and hum."

"This is much too pretty," Min said. "You're lying."

"I said it was a dream."

"—That you said was true."

"True the way dreams are, good stories that could happen."

Min waited. "My dreams have been literally true for thirty-nine years."

"I was coming to the true part next."

"That you were healed? That's never been the truth."

"—That I thought I was, felt truly that I was. Hell, I *was* then and there. The sight of that one girl had made me feel it, her voice saying 'Don't give except for return! Hell, sight and sound, just plain human words, have cured old lepers and lighted the blind. Who was I to fail? I was just weak-chested."

"In the dream," Min said, "—weak-chested in the dream. What would that be in life?"

Rob said, "I thought you were volunteering help. I can find mean bitches in any bus station."

She touched him, her left hand firmly on his belly.

He took it and moved it to her own side gently. "That's another thing available at every street light."

"Mine was free," Min said. She smiled toward his turned face.

He answered it fully as if smiles were as easy in his life as they'd been in the years she first knew him. "Nothing's free," he said, "like the young lady said."

"What else did she say?"

"She didn't speak again through all that digging. Not to me anyhow. I'd see her at a distance tell her father to smile; it was him we were saving more than me. I could read it on her lips. But all she'd do to me was grin and feed me and listen to my chest when we'd quit at night. I'd ask her 'What you hear?'—meaning *death*? or *what*? (I could still hear the war every day or so, no nearer but there)—and she wouldn't say so much as 'Hush' but just smile. I knew she was right, though I'd never told her I was sound as a dollar from the hour I met her—*because* I'd met her—and that all my digging in mud for a spring was just work for her, to earn my gift. She wouldn't have known a lung from a kidney anyhow; she was real in the dream, no magic girl. Real and waiting. So was I."

"For what?" Min said.

"Ma'm?"

"Waiting for what?"

"I told you once; this is nothing but a dream. Don't press it so hard. Just a story I made to pass one night."

Min waited. "But you know what you wanted from her."

"I do," Rob said, "—to love her, the girl."

"—For her to love *you*."

"I might have hoped for that in time; but no, the way I said it—I wanted her to stand there and bear my love."

"To sleep inside her?"

He thought it out as slowly as if it still mattered; it was still dark enough to take the question gravely. "I don't think I knew people entered each other or wanted to, even."

"Didn't know in the dream or in actual life?"

"They're the same, I told you. I was fourteen, fifteen; I lived in the country surrounded by animals. I still didn't know human beings needed that, to rub little tits of themselves on each other. But I knew there was something called love in the world. Most children do; it is God's main gift, once He's given blood and breath. It may be His last if you don't take and work it. I *knew* as I say not from hearing folks praise it or do it in my sight but from parts of my heart that had always been with me. A loving heart."

Min had waited for that; but she didn't try to touch him again, didn't smile.

Rob smiled and looked toward her quickly, then back.

"So you loved her," she said.

"Not yet, not at once. I'd made a deal. Her father stood there to keep me to it if I'd wanted to quit. So days, weeks later I found the first spring, a little ring round it of white flint rock. Everybody clapped but her father, and then we stood quiet till the water ran clean. I offered it to him, the first pure drink; and he came forward to me still frowning and said 'It's yours' so I drank. He said 'It's all yours' and showed with his hand the whole place, the people, the spring, the girl. It was his to give. I said 'Yes' and stopped."

"Stopped the dream?" Min said.

"Yes."

"You could stop it that easy?"

"By waking up, yes. I was happy enough."

Min said, "Mine lasted. Mine went on from there."

"I knew it would." Rob lay on silent through the pass of the fan, then silent in its absence.

"Ask me how," she said. "Ask me what I dreamt."

He said "All right."

"—That I was the one smiling girl and you killed me."

He turned to her slowly, to within four inches of her breathing face; then rose to his elbow, then to his knees, straddled her flanks, studied her face still dim and vague, then struck her in the mouth.

She gave no sound, never flinched or turned, never broke her own stare at his dim face above her.

He rode on another minute, bearing her look; then dismantled himself and lay down again, flat on his back.

No sound from Min. No move of response once her face had settled.

They both lay prostrate, staring up through the minutes till dawn—summer dawn, early. Then when daylight had clearly begun to replace the lamp outside and the dead-heavy weight of heat above them gave the first signs of new life, active pressure, Min turned to her side and faced Rob again. After half a minute, he accepted the gaze; and she said very quietly, "Listen to this. Please listen to this. I haven't ever dreamt it; but it's all I know, a story that could not only happen but did. I have used you in every way I could, every way you'd let me since I got old enough to have needs other than food and a roof and a few kind words. I have always known it was second-best—God, *fourteenth*-best. I've stood, don't forget, and watched you sucking on the ones you needed; that fed your craving. I could have turned and left. Well, no I *couldn't*; maybe even shouldn't. Where would we be, either one, right now if I'd kept my pride?" She paused, not specifically waiting for an answer.

But Rob said, "Dead. I at least would be dead. You'd be far better off, a real home, some rest."

"I might be," she said. Then helpless she smiled. "I also might be Eleanor Roosevelt and saving the world. I might be a high-yellow girl in heels at a Saturday dance in some shaky hall with my bosoms on fire and my razor fresh-honed—"

"You might have been some people's decent wife and mother."

"—Not a whore pushing forty with a poor drunk friend, school-teaching by day?" She had not intended to strike so soon or with so blunt a sledge. She hadn't intended to strike at all but to state the true past and plead one last time to have a true future, honest lives.

"*You* said that," he said. "But if that's what you think, if that's all it's been, I would still say thank you."

There was more to the story she'd meant to tell—the demand she had meant to make at the end: that at last Rob take her or leave her completely—but now he had stopped her with guileless thanks. She knew or had always chosen to believe that what she had loved and served in him through years of disorder, refusal, and shame was that one piece of the heart of the world—the precious meaning of life and pain, both cause and reward—which had been held toward her very early in her life (a small quiet life), the one chance for service and meaning and use which life had extended her. She half-rose now on her right elbow and looked all down him. Softened as he was, encased in his years, even a little rank from the heat, it was still buried in him—a perfect core which she'd once seen clearly in both their youths and reachable now in one last try. She knew of no other way to reach it but this—she silently climbed to the posture he'd taken: straddled him, kneeling but lower down, her knees at his calves. She rose there above him a long silent moment, her own surrenders to wear and gravity honestly shown; then her face sank toward him, and she brushed back her short hair with both hands carefully as if it were long and would hinder them.

He didn't touch her but he said "Please don't."

She shook her head No and loosened a forelock that hid her eyes. Then she used him as if he were nourishment; as if feeding on him would not exhaust any store he possessed but would honor, replenish.

So he didn't withhold but when she had roused him (his body which had never been all of him), he set both hands on the crown of her head and let them ride out her long careful act (too tired to ask was she giving or taking, healing or harming) till he'd given himself, again not all but a little hot clot that cut its way out more like death than pleasure.

Her face still hid, Min said her own thanks and rolled—never rising to his face—and slowly lay beside him, asking nothing more.

Rob waited to be sure, even offered her his own large hand to use any way she needed.

But she only pressed his fingers once more in thanks, then half-turned away and shut her eyes calmly as if headed for sleep.

Rob knew they mustn't rest; light was well underway. In another half hour he would hear his landlady cough herself out of bed, and then he and Min would be trapped here till eight when she might take her old scottie out for his walk. He must get Min out now and back to her place, get himself finally on the road he had planned and dreaded all spring.

He sat up quietly and propped himself to look round and let the room reel him up the last few fathoms into day and duty—a good-sized room, fifteen by twenty; all he had here at least, twelve dollars a month from a widow so lonely she made him feel lucky. But the room was still hers despite his long presence, going on nine years. One deep breath proved her ownership. It was drowned in the smell of her life not his, not to mention poor Min's—the dense dry smell of her dead kin, vanished children, as if in his absence at school or at meals she'd slip in to clean and, helpless, would grease every inch of floor and wall with glandular musk from the depths of her body. Even his clothes—two suits in a wardrobe, four shirts in a drawer—his worn hairbrushes, his pocketknife, gold watch, each day's small change: all conquered by her, it seemed to him now. Maybe even the pictures, unframed and curling by the dresser mirror. He stood and went to them and bent to see.

A girl fifteen, not smiling, long curls, staring fearless at the camera as if it might save her. A boy not twelve yet, still safe in childhood, brown-haired, smiling freely out from ample stores, the eyes a little crouched. The one of the boy was newer by years, raw and glossy, a school picture—Hutch his one child. The girl's was precious, though bare and unprotected—his picture of Rachel, the one she'd given him. Rob reached for them both; put them face to face and held them at his side, not studying them. They were still his at least. He looked to the bed.

Min lay jackknifed on her side; but her hair was well back and half her face showed. The eyes were still shut; and the good full line of her leg, hip, side was pulled overhill by her calm loose belly—"the abandoned melon," Min called it when he cupped her unawares at night.

Rob smiled and thought, "At my mercy. Offered. Unprotected, ruin or take." Then he went to the wardrobe and took out an old black Gladstone bag which had been his father's. He carefully laid the two pictures in the bottom; then covered them with two suits of underwear, black socks, two shirts. Then he dressed himself in his summer suit and shoes, tied his tie, combed his hair, drank a glass of stale water from the china pitcher. Then he went to his side of the bed and stood, trusting the force of his wait to wake her. In a minute it hadn't; out the open window a cardinal burst on its bossy song. Rob said "Time's up" pleasantly.

She turned at once; she had not been asleep but waiting for this. When she saw him all dressed, shielded against her, she knew she could say it after twenty-three years. She covered her breasts with folded arms, raised her knees toward her waist to hide her slit, nodded slowly, and said "It is. Sure is."

Rob also nodded. "Let me take you home, a working girl."

"Working woman," Min said. "Where are you going then?"

He still could smile. "To the moon, thereabouts."

"You don't understand what I just said, do you?"

"I thought I did, yes ma'm. I—"

She shook her head. "The *time* part, the part about time being up."

He didn't speak but sat, straight and neat, to listen.

"My waiting-time," she said. "I cannot wait on. You have got to find out soon and let me know. In words I can hear and understand—final words, Rob, soon."

"It's a bad time," he said. "Let me go see the boy; I've promised him a trip. Let me get some things settled. I plan to see the principal in Fontaine tomorrow; Mother thinks he may hire me. Let me check the old house; I doubt you could stand it."

"I'm too old," she said.

"It's dry," he said. "I could halfway heat it if it's not too ruined."

She shook her head again. "Not the house, Rob," she said. "I could live in the tomb of Cheops tomorrow. I am what's too old."

"For what?" Rob said.

"For waiting on you one extra week." She reached down and hauled the crushed sheet to her chin. "If you can't tell me Yes by a week from today, don't ever speak again, not to me. I'll be gone."

"Next Monday," he said. "I may well be in Richmond or Jamestown even."

"They have telephones and wires. Send me one cheap wire—*Minnie Tharrington, Raleigh. I accept. Come on.* Signed *Robinson, always.*" She had counted the words on her fingers as she spoke. "Nine words," she said. "A whole word to spare. You could even say *love.*"

Rob sat still awhile. Then he said "You mean that?"

"I do. I'm sorry. I know it's a bad time for you—no job and all your scattered families—but what you haven't seen is, it's gotten bad for me. Too bad to keep bearing."

"You told me you were strong. I asked you that—remember?—when we started this at all."

"I still am," she said. "I think I still am. But I'm also older and I want to be kind to me and to you. Another round of this and we'll both be worse, much worse by the minute. All the tides are going out."

Rob nodded. "Right now. I'm bad off now." He held out his right hand halfway toward her.

Min didn't take it but watched as he intended.

It shuddered in the air with a movement as delicate, as hard to see, as a struck bell's rigor or a bird's hot breathing and as hard to stop.

"Meaning what?" she said.

"Meaning *help*, I guess." He dropped it to the sheet.

She sat up, no effort to keep the sheet on her. "Rob," she said, "try to comprehend this. I am saying one thing and very little else—Min has not got any help left to give. Not in this situation. Not another day of this."

He let it all land, arrive deep in him; she meant it at least. He'd outlasted worse, he'd maybe last this, he could not think how—except for the boy. He thought of his son, who seemed a real goal. "I've got to go," he said. "Please get up now."

"You're not shaved," she said.

"You've seen beard before."

"For your trip, I mean."

He thumbed toward his landlady's room downstairs. "If we draw water now, we'll have her up, the damn dog howling. I'll take you and come back. I need to see her anyhow, explain about the rent. I need to write a letter. I'll leave by ten maybe."

Min nodded and wiped at her eyes with dry hands. Then she stood up and, not glancing once at the mirror, she quickly dressed. Then she took up her own handbag and went toward him, stopping two feet away so he could choose—precede her out the door or wish her goodbye.

Rob wished it but he said it; he could no longer touch her. "I think I'll be back. I think you can believe me. Let me just see Hutch and Mother and some others; I'll try to get us right. Believe that; believe *me*. And still try to help."

Min faced him clearly, calm in the knowledge that settled heavy on her—he must take or leave—but she lied again to save him a few days longer. "I'll try," she said. "I'll hunt for ways, no promise though to find them."

"I know that," he said. "I won't expect much. I just said it anyhow for old time's sake." He felt a smile and showed it; it spread up his throat and across his stale face like a slow show of broad firm wings from his youth, opened to morning. "I won't sink now. Men forty years old don't sink in broad day with the waters calm beneath them just because they've lost a job through a little weak whisky; just because they can't make up their mind to have a life, take the people who are present, and ignore the poor dead." The smile had survived. "They seldom sink, do they?"

"Every day," Min said. "Every day on every street." But she also smiled.

For the moment they stood there as willing mirrors, thcy seemed themselves again, their early selves, savable. Rob led her out quietly and safely down the stairs.

2

June 5, 1944

Dear Polly,

Are you well? You know that I hope so, though how would you know except on faith in light of my silence? I meant to write to you long before now. I've meant to do a lot of things since Father's funeral, but I've been much lower than I'd thought I would be. Not that I doubted I would be sad awhile, regretting the way he left so fast and regretting your loneliness; but you know as well as anyone alive how sizable people can leave your life and you stride on, not deeply struck (you and your father, all the tales you told me).

This has struck me deeply. I let him down so badly, from the day Rachel died; and since you called me with word of his death and I stood by you and watched him buried next to Robinson Senior, I have not once shaken the heavy thought that I've lost another last chance to recompense a person who only wished me happiness and worked to help me get it— worked to show me what it looked like, his life there with you.

Now because of that sadness and the drinking it caused and the anguish after that, I have been told here that I'd better go my way. You can teach something upward of a thousand children in nine straight years how to do long division and what life requires and still be shown to the back door fast if your own life skips any single requirement they've got for more than one day (I was absent six days spread over two weeks and paid my replacement; but I cried one day in the midst of explaining how you calculate the quantity of plaster needed to cover the ceiling of a hotel ballroom so big by so, and since thirty seventh-graders looked a little puzzled, I explained that too—what was needed by me: you won't need to hear, same old old story you heard years ago and answered so truly.

So now I'm fired, the last man but one in the Raleigh school system— all old maids now and one 4-F'er, an old maid too).

That brings me up one more time again to the starting line of a race I never even volunteered to enter. I know by now you are thinking "Boo-hoo"—you've sure God earned the right—but I trust you'll also know that I am lining up and will lurch off again once I draw four breaths, which is why I'm writing now.

I am leaving here this morning and will go to Fontaine for a day or so with them. I will also be seeing if the school board there can consider hiring me for their one vacant job, "shop" teacher. Picture that; I have seldom nailed a nail that didn't bend double. I will also be seeing if I think I could bear moving home after years. They are all healthy there so have never had the need to understand the poorly. Whatever happens anyhow I plan to strike out by the middle of the week and give Hutch the trip I've been promising him. Mother's brother Kennerly is on the county ration board and promised me the gas once I told him I would have to see you on Father's business. We will go up to Norfolk for a day at the beach, then to Jamestown and thereabouts as mileage permits. Then if you are agreeable, we'll come on to you by Saturday evening. Hutch can look around Richmond or go to the show for as long as it takes you and me to sort the papers and settle the estate.

I know you are not looking forward to that anymore than I am. My own impulse is to build a bonfire; but others are involved as you well know, mainly Hutch and Aunt Hattie and her one living son. Let me say this though in advance of our meeting—I said it at the funeral; but here it is in writing: as far as my part goes, I mean you to have it and will throw every ounce of strength I have, which is roughly one ounce, into seeing that the

*other Mayfields follow suit. They have all got lives of long ample standing;
there is nobody starving; if they don't already know the years of debt we all
owe to you (two generations' worth), they will when I've finished, if I can
keep afloat. Maybe floating's not the word. Anyhow I think I can with
Hutch along to watch me. And you have always helped.*

*I hope to be in Fontaine by suppertime tonight unless I'm wrecked
and dead (I have slept very little), so please drop a line by return mail to
say whether this plan fits in with your own convenience. You know I hope
it does since I feel the need to talk—far beyond the Mayfield business.
Soon, I pray.*

Love,
Rob

3

AFTER mailing the letter he stopped around town, paying all his May bills.
Then at once because he had never thought of breakfast, he went to the
Green Grill and ate a big lunch. He had not been there in the weeks since
Forrest's death; but his old waitress Luna was ready for him, smiling—a
short woman maybe four or five years his elder with the kind of permanent
good-spiritedness that bespoke in her either a mild feeble-mind or the grace
of God (Rob could never say which).

Once she got through the questions and regrets about his father, she
said, "Do you notice I am acting any different?" and stepped back to stand
and let him size up the change.

He looked a long moment and said "Well, *act.*"

She paused awhile thinking, then crossed her large arms on her low
breasts. "I'm a mother," she said.

Rob said "Who's the lucky boy?"

She shook her head. "No sir. This is serious," she said. "They called us
from the Welfare five weeks ago and said they had a girl and to come
down and see her. I cried all the way, begging Jesus for help—*Let her
answer our prayers; let me and Jess love her.* I've had this love all blocked
in my chest since Jess wouldn't use it, nowhere else to send it. So we got to
the place, and the caseworker brought out a three-months' baby. I took her
right then in my arms and deeper; and I knew the whole time of waiting
was over. She is named Rosalee; I let Jess name her—Rosalee was his aunt.
That was five weeks ago. Jess has not touched a drop—five weeks dry as
dust; four weeks was his record more than twenty years ago. You come
here next week and eat you a dinner; and if I'm not here and they tell you
I'm dead, you stand up and say 'Luna Wall died laughing.' " She laughed
full-eyed.

Rob said "God help him," meaning Jess her husband.

4

I⊤ was past two o'clock when he drove off for home, and the day was baking. He had gone three miles and was just past the final fringes of town when his old dread of lonely trips fell on him. *Places* in his life, his various houses, had been hard enough; but *roads* had been harder because so chancy, so glad to oblige. You could die on a road in utter privacy, secrecy of means; a road would conceal you, agree to your vanishing and yield no trace. Yet it would not guarantee your destination; if you took its offers, would you land in oblivion or punishment or just a cheap wallpapered room in a town big enough not to notice your face? *Imagine it's a tunnel,* Rob told himself—*a tunnel long enough to get you to Hutch the one living human that still needs to see you, still truly depends; the one human you have vowed God to live for. No windows in the tunnel but Hutch at the end.* He knew he was wrong and to this extent—there were windows for every regret of his life, and he had two solitary hours now to sit and stare through them at scenes he had made but could no longer mend.

He saw a Negro thumbing fifty yards up the road in an army uniform with a small canvas bag in the dirt by his feet. Negroes seldom thumbed white men in strange territory but stood as they passed, watching and ready. Nearer, Rob could see that this was no young boy—a short heavyset man, coal-black and glossy, great shoulders and neck but smiling frankly. He slowed the car and stopped precisely at the man, not forcing him to trot in the naked sun. All the windows were open. Rob said "Can you drive?"

"Yes sir."

"Got a license?"

"Yes sir." He reached to his khaki hip to fish out a wallet.

Rob said, "I believe you. Will you drive me to Fontaine, N.C. in guaranteed safety?"

The Negro smiled broader. "You lying," he said.

"Pure truth," Rob said. "I need a little help; been sick here lately."

"You got it," the Negro said. "I'm headed there myself. Didn't think nobody else in *this* world was going." He took up his satchel and came round the car. Rob slid to the passenger seat and watched as the man climbed in, set his bag on the back floor, and turned to check quickly for his benefactor's motives. When he saw he was safe, the man said, "Fontaine? You come from Fontaine?"

"My mother's people do," Rob said. "I lived there some."

"I lived there all my life," the man said, "till the army sent for me."

"Who are you?" Rob said.

"A Parker, Bowles Parker. I live in the country six miles out from town near what they call Beechleaf."

Rob nodded. "I know there're some Parkers out there. But Bowles, let's roll. This sun's out to kill us."

"Yes sir," Parker said and released the hand brake. They rode on a mile or so in silence while Parker got the feel of the '39 Hudson.

Rob wanted most to sleep. He had slept only minutes in the nights since his firing and would hardly sleep tonight after all his mother's questions and the supper they would give him. And he did feel drowsy; but he also felt the need to perform two duties now—be pleasant for a while and question his driver a little more closely before lapsing into unconsciousness beside him. So he said "How's the war?"

Parker said, "I ain't seen it, not yet noway."

"How long you been in?"

"Two years and two weeks."

"The infantry?"

"Yes sir. But my feet flat as pans, so they letting me cook. I can sit down and cook."

"You down at Fort Bragg?"

"Right now I am, yes sir. I been down at Fort Benning for more than a year, but they moved us up here three weeks ago. Said they giving us a change; but we know what it is—they fattening us up. They throwing us on overseas just as soon as they make that invasion." He smiled at the road.

"You still going to cook?—over yonder, I mean?"

"They still going to eat. So I'll be frying and the shells be dropping."

"You scared?" Rob said.

"No sir."

"How come?"

"I'- *certain*."

"W.iat of?"

"Dying early. No pain."

Rob said "Where?"

"In Germany."

Rob studied the black face—calm as a table, though not smiling now. "How are you so certain?"

"Jesus told me in the night."

"How? What did He say?"

"Said, 'You going to die in Germany easy, shot through the head, so tell em goodbye.' "

"You going home to tell them?"

"*See* em," Parker said. "I ain't telling nothing."

"Told *me*."

"You a stranger."

"How old are you, Bowles?"

"Thirty-seven last month."

"Who you got left at home?"

"My wife and three children; one of em is hers, oldest boy. He can keep her. Some cousins. My mama."

"Who is she?"

"Flora Parker. She just come back, been living up north since I was a baby."

Rob looked; searched the profile—smooth as pasture, nose and forehead. *Is he somehow my son?* was his first clear thought. No way, too old. Relief and disappointment. *It could have helped me now,* he thought, *to find I made a strong man my first night trying—a second good deed, one strapping black cook.* Still looking Rob said "Any brothers or sisters?"

"I wouldn't be surprised. Mama had a big life, but I never asked her much when she come home to visit—she come on my birthday every year but one. I didn't want to know; didn't want to crowd my mind, just think about her for the time I had (I lived with my uncle). And now she don't know. Her mind is affected."

"By what?"

"That life I told you she had. Doctor said her mind dead and will keep on dying, so she back home now."

Rob said "She's still young."

"No sir, she pushing fifty."

"I recall her as young."

"So do I," Parker said before he really heard. Then he heard and took his eyes off the road a long moment. "How you know her?" he said.

"Through Sylvie our cook. She used to visit Sylvie."

"Her and Sylvie fell out way back," Parker said.

"Will she know you?"

"Who? Sylvie? I ain't studying Sylvie. Sylvie come up to me one Saturday night when I was a boy in town just to look—big dance at the Hall—and she say 'You Bo?' I tell her 'Yes ma'm.' She step back and look and say, 'You ever see a orphan?' I tell her 'No ma'm.' I never heard the word; I was fourteen, fifteen. She step back to me and raise this little mirror right to my face—she been combing her hair—and laugh like a fool, 'You seeing one now.'"

"She was drinking," Rob said.

"I know it," Parker said, "—knowed it then; know it now. And I still don't excuse her. Anyhow she was wrong." He stopped as if exhausted.

So Rob thought he'd rest now; he leaned his head back.

"Still Mama won't know me."

Rob shut his eyes and waited; then he said "So you're dying."

"Yes sir," Parker said. "That ain't all the reason."

"For your country?" Rob said, no smile in his voice, though he waited to smile.

Parker said "No sir."

Rob decided not to press him—he seemed so earnest—and worked to clear his own mind for a doze. But Parker's great dignity, the weight of his voice announcing a doom as calmly as breakfast, would not let him rest. A genuine question formed in his head and seemed more urgent each moment he held it; he held it back though till he'd got it formed truly. Then he asked Parker quietly, "Tell me your reasons. I don't mean to drag you through anything painful, but I'm a man in trouble too. I'm looking for help." His eyes had stayed shut.

Parker said "You Miss Eva's boy?"

"Yes."

"Rob Kendal?"

"Mayfield," Rob said. "Mother married a Mayfield."

"I never heard of him."

"He lasted twenty minutes or so," Rob said, "—left before you were born."

Parker said, "That's the trouble?—the trouble you in?"

"Oh no," Rob said. "He got over that. I grew up and met him, and knew him till he died. He died this spring, had a very happy life. He found a good woman."

Parker said "You got one?"

Rob thought "He's turned the tables"; but tired as he was, he recognized a chance. A black army cook, a little cracked maybe, was holding out a welcome to the news of his life. Rob wanted to give it. He raised his head, opened his eyes on the road—deep country now: blank fields, black woods—and said "I had one." He didn't face Parker, afraid to see a simple fool or spite or abject courtesy. He focused on a hawk high above them up the road.

"She gone?" Parker said.

"Fourteen years ago."

"She dead?"

"All that time."

"You got anybody left?"

"A boy, fourteen."

"He kill her?" Parker said.

Rob considered that slowly, then said "No your friend Jesus."

"He'll do it," Parker said, "if it be His will."

Rob looked to him now, and Parker met the look for a quick close instant. "Listen to me," Rob said. "Listen here to what happened; and tell me why He did it, what your Friend was aiming at."

Parker nodded and listened.

"I had a good girl that really wanted me; really wanted to help me and knew a lot of ways, didn't just dream about me. She was also nervous and had had a little trouble with her mind before I met her. And she'd lost the first baby that I tried to give her which weakened her awhile and scared me off her; but when she felt strong enough, she begged me back on. So I started her again, summer 1929—"

"You speaking of a baby?" Parker said. "Just a baby?"

Rob nodded, looking forward. "It meant a lot to her. That had been her early trouble, wanting some child to love. Then she'd had me awhile till she saw I was a man and could not stand still but just so long for service, for her to decorate me like a tree with kindness, all she needed to give me." He turned to see Parker. "You know what I mean?"

"No I don't," Parker said. "I could stand still till Judgment, anybody want to touch me."

Rob smiled but thought it through. "So could I but years before, long years before my wife. By the time I met her, I was doing the touching."

Parker said, "All right. That didn't kill her, did it?"

"No I told you, the baby."

Parker said, "That used to happen a lot. I've known several die, couldn't nobody save em. My own wife drop em as easy as kittens; but I seen my auntie that was so good to me when Mama had left—I stood and seen her perish with the baby half in her. It died a minute later. I was right by her, watching; took the last look she gave. She say to me, 'Bo, help me back; help me back.' She thought she was slipping, thought she was falling. She thought I could reach her. I was fifteen years old." Parker waited.

Rob made no sound of consolation.

So Parker said, "Seventeen. She lived to be seventeen, just older than me. We all knew the daddy. He didn't aim to harm her; she let him in, smiling. Nobody blame a poor man for what Jesus do."

Rob said, "I'm to blame. Don't haul in Jesus. I caused her to die just as sure as you're causing this car not to wreck; you could kill us this minute, save yourself a trip to Europe if you just wanted to."

"I don't," Parker said, though he swung the wheel once to confirm his real power.

Rob leaned back his head and swallowed twice at nothing. "No I didn't either." He stopped and shut his eyes.

Parker said, "You telling me or asking me to guess?"

Still back, Rob said, "I'm telling you. Listen." Then he changed. "Please listen. Please drive and just listen. I once knew your mother."

Parker nodded again, knowing Rob could not see him.

"We were living in Richmond. I had a fair job at the James Institute; had a good solid house, a good man helping in the kitchen and yard. We nursed her through the months like a porcelain rose, barely let her cut butter, never let her touch a broom. We were giving her a chance; we were clearing the whole world to give her safe room so she could make her baby and walk on forward through the rest of her life. Nobody we knew till then had had much life."

"You mentioning *we*," Parker said, "—you and who?"

"The colored man that helped us. Lives in Fontaine now—Grainger Walters; you know him?"

"I've seen him from a distance. He wouldn't talk to me. I'm a little too brown."

Rob did not stop for that. "It mattered to us all, and for just the cause I told you; we were hoping for better, in various ways. And we almost got it. Everything was moving right, through the fall and winter. Wall Street failed of course, and word of that reached us; but nobody guessed for some months to come that half the world had ended, not at James Institute anyhow among people that had barely held a dollar much less lost one. So we got into spring—late April, green weather—and my wife's doctor said both heartbeats were strong, the baby's and hers, and that three weeks from then if our luck held out, we could thank God for blessings." Rob paused to wet his lips. "This is how much luck; this is what blessing came—I had an old friend I had grown up with. She was teaching school in Raleigh and came up to Richmond, chaperoning some children that had won a school prize to see patriotic shrines. Just a quick spring trip while a little money lasted. She never even warned me. I ran into her on Broad Street at noon; I had gone to buy a straw hat—I looked good then."

"You do right now."

"You ought to seen me then."

"I did," Parker said. "I remember you now. I seen you way back. You were standing on the street and telling some story to an old white man. You were waving your arms."

"And I'm telling *you* one."

Parker said "I guessed it."

"—That I met her that evening and did what I did? In a hotel room with two rooms of children on either side of us, listening like rabbits."

"And then your wife smelled it on you and hollered."

Rob waited. "No she didn't. I came home and told her I should wash before supper—it had been a hot day—and slow as she was by then with the baby, she came up and laid out my clean clothes for me. She liked to watch me dress; and until that day, I liked to have her watch me. It was something I could give her for all she'd offered; she had genuinely helped by just being present near the middle of my life. See, I've always been easy to help; wanted little, and most of that at home. But that one night like I said, she was watching; and I felt so scalded by her eyes that I rushed and was reaching for my pants still wet as a rat when she said 'Slow down.' I said 'I'm cold.' She said 'No you're not,' and I stood and faced her plainly. She looked for a minute, not smiling but careful as if I was teaching her facts she could use in a long hard life. Then she said, 'I doubt I will ever believe it.' I had to say 'What?' and she said, 'What's here—this room, us in it.' It was just a plain room, small and too bright for me; but I knew what she meant, and it burned on through me like terrible acid till it got to my chest. It settled there and stayed."

"You tried to swamp it, didn't you?"

"If *drunk* is what you're saying, I was drunk in two days—I stood it two days—and stayed drunk the best part of two weeks to come. Nobody knew why. They tried to protect me; told my boss I was sick, told my mother-in-law not to come down yet (she was coming from the mountains to help with the child). I'm a nice quiet drunk; I don't leave home. So at least they don't have to run me down; and I held my tongue—I never told them why, though she couldn't help asking: my wife, I mean. They always ask and I always know, but generally I spare them. Anyhow she stopped her mother; and my own father moved in with us for a while in the evenings after work to see me through the nights and to look out for Rachel—" Rob stopped, chilled and sick. He had meant to hold her name back at least from his tale. But because Parker drove on in large waiting silence, Rob could think of going on. He looked to the calm face, harmless as a child's, and believed now in Parker's own private dream—*This boy's bound to die, is sailing already toward a death as sure as evening. I'm telling a spirit.*

"You know when she died?"

"Very clearly. Very clearly."

"That sobered you up."

"No I'd done that myself. She understood me well enough to let me run my course. She would let Grainger go out and buy what it took to taper me off; and then she'd give it to me when I asked her for it or when she saw me trembling, just a taste in a ruby-red glass we had bought on our honeymoon four years before, my name etched in it and hers and the date. Then five days before her time to come due, she was reading beside me in late afternoon—I was down on a couch, feeling weak but cured for the time being anyhow—and she looked up and took my eyes and said 'Are you ready now?' I asked her 'For what?' and she said 'This child.' I thought and said, 'I think we should ask another question—is he ready for me?' Right off, she said 'Yes.' I said, 'If you know what you're doing, bring him on.' That was late on a Saturday. I'd gauged myself to be well for work on Monday (they believed I was sick; I had not missed before in my whole four years). She had told Grainger he could take the evening off; and when Father came by after supper to check, we sat and talked a little. Then I told him he could leave; he had a friend at home. I thought I was safe as I said. We'd cleared the house. I thought I could bear her again, full strength. What I didn't understand—it was her in danger; she was gone by breakfast."

"And left you the baby."

"Strong and happy," Rob said. "He had smiled before evening."

Parker said, "I seen him. I spoke to him once. Named Hutch."

"—For her father in the mountains, Raven Hutchins Mayfield; I gave her that at least. She didn't live to see him, but she knew his full name."

Parker said "Good."

5

THEY had lost two hours at a crossroads garage while an old man hunted them a used fuel pump in his acre of wrecks, well-hid in honeysuckle; then installed it as carefully as if it would last and earn him praise long years from now. That had put them past supper as they came to Fontaine; and since he had given Hutch no definite schedule and since all afternoon Parker had borne more weight than he'd bargained for, Rob told him just to drive straight through to Beechleaf, a ride to his door; and Parker accepted.

The house was old, not a flake of paint on it; but it stood two stories with a broad side-chimney of rose-colored brick as lovely as a human hand, in craft and service—big as the old Kendal place, which was Rob's, and as nearly ruined. The yard was all children, not a whole suit of clothes among the eight or ten, and all in quick motion despite the thick heat that hung on heavy, though the light was pale now and rapidly dying. They froze and watched the car, seeing Rob's face first. Rob said "Will they know you?"

"Some of em, yes. All of em ain't mine." Parker looked to Rob, not smiling. "You need a drink of water?—anything like that?"

Rob said "No but thank you."

"I thank *you*," Parker said. "I hope you do better."

Rob smiled. "So do I."

The children saw their father and bolted for the house; poured themselves through the open door, a single dog behind them, clean Eskimo spitz.

Parker said, "Step in here please and speak to Mama."

Rob thought a short moment. "It's been too long."

Parker looked to his own hands, still hung on the wheel; then back to Rob, begging. "Help me see em, Mr. Rob. Help me ease on in. God knows I hate to see em."

"Why?"

"—Me going like I am."

Rob nodded, touched the handle of his door, and looked out. A girl was in the door or a strong young woman. For a while it seemed Flora till he saw what she lacked—Flora's harsh thrust into unlived life and of course Flora's age. This girl hung back and children clung to her; she bore their grasp as calmly as a breeze. Rob said "That your wife?"

"Lena. Yes sir."

Rob stood to the ground and smiled to Lena. "I brought him home safe."

She nodded—silent, still—and one boy laughed and ran as far out as the top of the steps; then stopped and stared.

Parker reached back and found his bag and got out and stood. He put on his hat and said "Who you, boy?"

"*Your* boy," the child said.

"You talking," Parker said. Then he said "Hey" to Lena.

She said "All right" and smiled.

"Everybody doing good?"

"Pretty good," Lena said.

Parker said, "Where Mama? This man come to see her; he Sylvie's Rob."

Lena swept the big yard with solemn eyes. "I don't know," she said. "Ain't seen her since morning."

The boy at the top of the steps said "Yonder" and pointed to the woods. "She lying back yonder."

"Go call her," Parker said.

Rob said, "Bo, leave her. She's found her some shade. I better get home."

But the boy had run to call her. With silent speed he had run down the steps, bare feet in deep dust, and over to a big rusty bell on the ground, an old farm bell long rotted off its post. He took up a stick and beat the bell four, five times. It gave a sound, more moan than ring. Then he looked to his father. "She be here now. She think we eating."

Parker said, "Sit down on the porch, Mr. Rob. Cool off a minute. She be right here." There was one straight chair on the porch, bottom sagging.

Rob walked to the steps and sat down there, his feet on the ground, his back to Lena and the shy clot of children.

Parker came forward too and when he'd reached the steps and climbed halfway, the boy who'd rung the bell raised the same stick of wood and fired it like a gun, a single *Pow!* Parker dropped his bag and fell to his knees on the step above Rob, both hands at his chest. He groaned "Bull's eye."

The boy laughed and ran a straight streak toward the woods; then stopped a little short and watched the big woman come out and past him, heavy and barefoot and in a blue cotton dress pinned at every tear.

When she got to the steps she stopped at the bottom and looked up to Lena. "What you giving me now?"

Lena said "Not me" and pointed to Parker.

Flora didn't face him but he stood up and said "Hey Mama. It's Bo."

She looked to Rob instead, still seated on his step eye-level to her.

There was nothing here for him. He would never have known her, and he had a fine memory for faces once seen. She was padded in fat like Chinese quilting, a final fortress. He tried to smile but couldn't.

She said, "Did you ever see your little boy again?"

He said, "Not lately but I'm going to him now."

Flora shook her great head. "She won't let you have him."

Rob smiled, though it ached. "She will; she'd better."

She shut her eyes and shook again. "She need him too bad. She told me herself—'He won't never touch him, Flora. All this is mine.' "

Rob thought it out clearly. "She thinks I am Forrest. She saw him that once. I have got to get home." He stood up quickly but she blocked his way down, not by trying but by presence. She had swollen that large in twenty-three years; he had shrunk that much.

Parker said "Look, Mama." He had reached in his bag and brought out her present, a comb-and-brush-set in a celluloid box. She took it—not speaking, never facing him once—and climbed up between them through Lena and the children, out of sight in the house.

They came forward finally in hopes of their gifts.

6

AT the car Parker said, "She knew you at least."

Rob said, "No she didn't. She thought I was my father."

"She got the right crowd anyhow," Parker said.

Rob said, "What's the matter? She's not that old."

"Wore out," Parker said.

"Will she speak to you later?"

"—May. May not. She know I'm dying; she known for years. How come she left me—didn't want to watch, didn't want that grief."

Rob nodded, half-believing; opened the door and sat behind the wheel.

Parker came a step closer, ten inches from his ear; and half-whispered clearly, "You never let me tell you."

"What?"

"The reason I'm glad to be going toward my dream."

"Don't I know?" Rob said. "I know by now." He cranked the slow engine.

But Parker stayed on, his hands on the window ledge, his face still near.

So Rob said, "Luck to you. Take care anyhow. He may change his mind."

Parker smiled. "That's another thing you didn't let me tell you—why He done this to you?" Parker spread both his huge hands and gestured wide to include the car as if it were Rob's history, pressed down and portable.

"Is it short?" Rob said. "I'm long overdue."

"Yes sir. He love you. He calling you to Him."

Rob thought a moment, thanked him; then fished up two dollars from his own scarce funds and said, "Buy Flora some little thing she needs."

"She need a new life," Parker said and stepped back; but he took the money.

"Then something she wants," Rob said and rolled off.

The one boy ran behind him far as the gate.

7

By the time Rob had got back to Fontaine again, what he'd thought was the point of his hours with Parker (company and calm at the sight of others' trouble) had turned full against him. Bo and Flora had thrust deep fingers into flesh he had not known was tender. As he passed the first shacks on the black edge of town, he felt not exhaustion and despair as with Min but fear, hot fright as if a vein had been lanced in the soft of his heel or the back of his knee and was rushing to drain him before he could know or find helpful care. Eva, Rena, Hutch, Grainger—they did not seem this instant a possible goal: more hooking hands to grapple at a body now as fragile as a lidless eye. He could not head back to Raleigh—Min abiding his answer. He could not go to Richmond—his promise to Hutch.

He saw a light at Sylvie's, far back on his left. He slewed to the left shoulder, stopped and tried to see toward her. Two hundred yards through thick new leaves; he caught only light, no sign of her, no sound. (She had had lights a year now, having said one morning, "Miss Rena, I am scared now to live in the dark. I either got to get the wires or move in here." Since Grainger occupied the only quarters at the Kendals', there had been no choice for Rena but to take the news to Kennerly. He had got her house wired before the week was out and given her a radio; and that had helped to ease her, though she'd recently announced she'd be going home at six. Walking home too late, she said, made her realize her state—"Make me think I'm dying lonesome." So they served their own supper now, and Grainger washed the dishes.) Rob thought "I'll go to Sylvie" and cranked the car again; he had killed it in the sudden swerve.

He couldn't move though, not forward. He shook. In place on the dry dirt shoulder of a road a mile from the house which contained his living kin, all upright and strong, none contingent on him—the house in which he had known his first happiness, still whole in his mind and available for visits—he shook with a dry grief that rose from the deepest sink of his belly as if it were birth, the throes of expulsion, and rushed his chest, throat, mouth, skull, so broadly that he thought one clear thought—"Thank Jesus I'm *going*"—then fell to its power.

When it passed, he looked first to see if he were watched—no Negro in sight; he had lasted alone. He worked his dry lips loose from dry teeth, put his hands to the wheel and found they would grip, and felt a clear space at the front of his mind—a small patch, palm-sized, but clear and light.

With it, he saw his life and knew this much; could say it to himself— he had asked for one thing since he first heard of gifts, forty years ago; nothing far beyond any soul's just expectance: an ordinary home containing no more than an ordinary home. A decent grown man with clean work to push against ten hours a day that would leave him with the strength to come back at dark in courtesy and patience to the people who had waited—a woman he had chosen for their mutual want (who went on wanting and receiving as he did: courteous, patient) and the child they made (he had never wanted two, never trusted his own stores to stretch over two). Human beings had that, never millions but enough—in his sight too—to make it seem a plain hope, not howling at a beacon burning well beyond earth in the deep hole of night. He hadn't asked permanence, a set of frozen smiles; he'd granted grief and age long before most men. He had asked twenty, thirty years at most in the midst of a life which could water all the rest and firm it for death.

And if earning mattered, hadn't he earned it? What had he done in forty years worse than rub a small portion of his secret body on the secret of one woman not his wife? Nothing, he knew. If the rules of life were visibly posted (and he trusted they were; despite his not darkening a church for twenty years, he'd never once doubted that the rules were given, were just and plain and were followable), he'd done nothing worse than betray his promise to love Rachel only—betrayed it half an hour.

No, never. Not a moment. He had *loved* only Rachel; what he'd done with Min was rub at a starved little knot in his brain, starved by weeks of simple deprivation, his care for Rachel. Any hand could have rubbed it; Min was simply familiar, a willing friend, keen to oblige.

So keen she'd rubbed him now to blood and nerve and asked for his life. He might give it to her. No one else was asking; it had to go somewhere. Death was a place. He thought of his morning high above the James River, though he didn't remember the boys or the turtle. The trip was still easy. No, he wanted to stay.

Why?—Hutch and Grainger; he had shaken them enough. Eva and Rena—they had maybe earned their mother's foaming death (he had never weighed that) but surely not his; they had meant him well. Min so tangled in his own roots now that she couldn't tear free whatever she threatened—or promised (it seemed a promise: freedom, space).

None of them, no. They were not the brakes on him. He could grant that now; but he didn't understand what was deep under that, that he had a gift for pleasure, a true seed within him from Robinson his grandfather. That had grown once and for twenty-five years of its own strong accord till he'd cut it back to earth, let it be packed down. There were still live roots with their own patient will.

He went to see Sylvie.

8

"You got anything here to eat?" he said.

"They waiting for you down yonder," Sylvie said and pointed to the Kendals'. "I fried chicken all this afternoon, cooked butterbeans and squash. Hutch turning ice cream—"

Rob shook his head. "I can't." He was on her middle step.

She was broad in the door behind her new screen that had come with the lights (the lights had drawn bugs). She studied him well. "What you telling me, Rob?"

"I'm hungry like I said."

"No you ain't. What you done?"

"Lost my job," he said.

"Again?"

"Nine years."

"You drinking?"

"I was."

"Well, God—" Sylvie said.

"Can I sit down?" he said.

"You sure you sober? Don't come here drunk."

"Yes, Sylvie," he said. "When did you get religion?"

"Ain't," she said. "Just worn out with drunks."

"So am I," Rob said. "This one anyhow." He touched himself on the covered breastbone.

She searched him again as if she'd never known him or as if she'd known him well these whole forty years and was only now totaling the sum of the days. "No you ain't," she said. But she unhooked the screen and stepped back inward and waved him in.

The room was hot and bright; two naked bulbs pumped heat like hearts. The radio was on, some news of the war. Sylvie went back toward it and sat in her chair and leaned to listen. Rob had not been here in twenty-three years—his time with Flora—and since Sylvie hadn't invited him to sit, he stood and looked round. The real change was light and the radio's rattle. The two main absences, her dog and her fish, were filled by pictures in dime-store frames propped on every flat surface. No one they knew—moviestars and generals, all white and all smiling: Deanna Durbin, Maureen O'Hara, Kay Francis, Gary Cooper, Mark Clark, Eisenhower, Mrs. Roosevelt. Rob had given her his own picture some years before, one he'd had made for Rachel just after the wedding; it was nowhere in sight. Her news had turned into a singing ad for soap; so he said, "Where am *I*? Not pretty enough? My teeth beat Eleanor's." He gestured to the frames.

Sylvie turned down the volume. "You here but I hid you."

"I'm honored," he said.

"You know why," she said.

He didn't at all—he had been her choice—but he spared himself and didn't ask.

"Sit down there," she said, "if you ain't going home."

He knew he was not, not for hours anyhow while anyone was up who could question him. He'd face them at breakfast; they wouldn't probe in daylight. Sylvie's other chair was straight and against the far wall. He brought it over toward her, six feet from her own, and sat on the hard cane. "You doing all right?"

"I'm the same," she said.

"I like your new lights."

"Draw bugs," she said, "but they help keep it warm."

It was eighty degrees this minute, he knew. "That's company," he said and nodded to the radio, a mystery play now.

"Is," Sylvie said.

She did not want him here. Rob felt it like power. "You're mad with me."

"Just sick."

"With me?"

She gave it some time. "You the one turned up this evening," she said.

"How have I hurt you?"

"Every breath you draw." She had fiddled with her knee till then. She faced him. Then she laughed a little. "What you want to eat?"

"What you got?"

"Eggs and lightbread."

"Good," Rob said.

Sylvie heaved herself up and left him with the softspoken mystery on the air, an old man trapped in a shed by a stranger who smiles but never speaks.

She fried two slices of bread in bacon grease, scrambled four eggs with crumbs of cheese, poured him a glass of water from the bucket, and set it on the table which was now against the wall (no longer in the center; she had cleared the center years ago). Then she said "Help yourself" and went to her chair again.

Rob went to her basin and washed his hands quickly, pulled his chair up, swallowed two bites, and said "Fine." Then he ate on in silence through half the food while Sylvie seemed to listen, her eyes narrowed downward.

Finally though she said, "I ain't studying this mess. Talk to me if you want to." She snapped off the mystery with the stranger still strange.

Rob said, "Guess who drove me all the way here from Raleigh?—Bo Parker, hitchhiking."

"You lucky you alive."

"How's that?" Rob said.

"He been half-crazy ever since he a baby."

"How come?"

"Being Flora's. Watching Flora till she run."

Rob said, "She's back now; I took him by his house."

"You see her?"

"For a second."

"She *all* crazy, ain't she?" Sylvie smiled, first time.

"Seems confused anyhow. And she's put on flesh."

"Lost her mind," Sylvie said.

Rob said "What's the trouble?"

Sylvie freshened her smile. "No trouble," she said, "—she collecting her pension."

"She old enough for welfare?"

"Oh no," Sylvie said, "I'm talking about her *pension*, what she been storing up. It coming to her now."

Rob chewed that through; then he also smiled. "Yours coming in yet?"

She paused an instant to test his edge for power; then she nodded. "Come in torrents." She gestured all round her—her room, bed, life—but she went on grinning and said, "Like yours. Yours coming in early."

"What is mine?" Rob said. He believed her and waited.

"You told me just now," she said, "—the time you having."

"Will it get any worse?"

"May do," she said. "You got a lot of time."

"What way?" Rob said.

She actually laughed. "I'm joking you, Rob. I don't know nothing."

"**I'm serious**," he said. "You know me good as anybody, better than most—maybe all but Mother."

"Then go ask Eva. She waiting down the road with a freezer of cream going soft right now."

"I've asked," Rob said, "and God knows she's told me. She'll tell me again."

"Tell you what?"

"That I still have to learn to stand alone," Rob said.

"Like her—"

He nodded.

"She lying," Sylvie said, "—been lying forty years. Nobody lean harder than Eva, let me tell you—Mr. Forrest, Mr. Bedford, Rena, poor Hutch." She stopped and stared again at Rob as if she couldn't harm him. "You standing," she said. "You alone as me."

He saw she believed it, knew he had to correct her. "No I'm not. Wish I was."

"What you leaning on but liquor?"

"Min Tharrington," he said. "You know about that."

"I know what I see; I can't see to Raleigh. But seem like to me if she your leaning-post, you falling through space."

Rob smiled. "I am."

"And Min ain't," she said.

"She's stuck by me though."

"—What she wanted to do since she three years old."

"She did it anyhow," Rob said. "Wasn't easy."

"Eating *supper* ain't easy," Sylvie said. "What you want?"

"This is plenty," he said, "gracious plenty. Many thanks."

"—In your life, I mean, fool. You eat all my *food*."

"—What you and I and Grainger and Mother and Rena haven't got and never had."

"That's nothing but company," she said.

"No it's not; not *nothing but*, Sylvie, and you know it. Here you sit in this house—"

"On a happy tail," she said. "Got all this room, screen wire, new lights. This radio the best friend *I* ever had—cheap, clean, ever-ready, on all through the night."

"You'll die here at night by yourself," Rob said and loathed his sudden harshness, the last thing he'd meant.

She had lived her life with Eva; she decided not to blame him. "Suits me," she said. "Everybody I ever watched die died single."

"But we got years to go."

"May do," Sylvie said. "I'm ready for em now. You get yourself ready."

"How? I'm here to ask that."

"You seen it," Sylvie said, "—seen all I got to tell you. A satisfied mind." She showed the room again with one slow hand, then laid it on her knee. "Live in what you got. Too late to change."

Rob nodded. "How are they?"

"At the house, you mean?"

"The people we know."

"I know a hundred people," Sylvie said. "*Yours* all right. Hutch and Grainger waiting on you."

"Just them?"

"Well, you know—Miss Eva and Rena got they own fish to fry."

Rob smiled. "Such as what?"

"They business, big business; stay busier than you. Eva got Hutch, doing everything for him but sleeping and breathing. Rena got the garden and arguing with Kennerly."

Rob said "Grainger?"

"Grainger got Hutch. Everybody got Hutch—you got him; *all* you got."

"Does he love me?" Rob said.

"Don't matter," Sylvie said. "He yours anyhow."

"But does he?"

She considered it. "Somehow," she said. "He got a loving heart. Don't hate a human soul. Don't grudge nobody."

Rob said "He's fourteen."

"Shame on you," Sylvie said. "He had his life; good because he want to be. God love him that much."

"Thought you hadn't got religion." Rob smiled.

Sylvie didn't. "Still ain't," she said. "Who I'm speaking of is Hutch—your boy and Miss Rachel's, Eva's, Mr. Forrest's, Mr. Bedford's, Miss Charlotte's. Had to get his help from somewhere."

9

HUTCH slept on, though the room had filled with morning and the house was awake—Eva, Rena, Grainger all muffled in the kitchen. With school just out, they were letting him sleep; and despite his worry of the night before (Rob never appearing), he lay on his back on the white iron bed and bore a last dream. He was still too young and drowned too deeply to end it by will; and in fact he was held by the story, not hurt. He had seen it many times.

He was walking in the pine woods behind this house. He was simply himself—fourteen, his present age—and he walked with no purpose, no dog or gun, no friend, no secret. When he'd gone in as far as he generally went, through the woods and his uncle's field of early cotton, he stopped on the bank of the creek, the sandbar, and saw it was late. He would be late for breakfast (it was morning in the dream; this morning, clear and hot). So he went the last steps to the creek to touch water—that now seemed his goal—and saw the girl. She stood on the far bank eight feet away, his own age (maybe a year or so older) with hair to her shoulders, facing him not smiling. He said "Rachel" and was rushed by powerful pleasure; he had never called her Mother. She nodded, though there'd never been a shadow of doubt; they were standing mirrors of one another. He stood his ground on his side, not crossing, happy enough there. He only thought, "She has been dead but isn't. She's back for good." But he did not tell her to wade over toward him, and he did not think of going to get her. He did not think of taking her home. But he said, "Wait here. I'll get the others." Then he ran to the house which was empty of all but Grainger in the kitchen. Hutch told him she was back; and Grainger believed it and put on his hat and followed—Hutch running, Grainger stumbling with his morning rheumatism—and of course she was gone. Just the empty pillar of air where she'd stood, uncrossed by a leaf or branch or insect. He stared at the space and said "It was true." Grainger said "*I* believe you"; and with Grainger looking, Hutch knelt to the sand, rolled onto his back, opened his mouth to release the plug of grief. But the day, the morning sky through trees, poured in like water and lodged it in place, its permanent place. He had caused her to leave a second time.

Rob saw none of that, though he'd come through the door and walked without stealth to the foot of the bed and stood, watching his son. The boy's face was turned, but his neck and cheek seemed peaceful. His long bare chest was still, his breath slow and regular. Only in the gapped fly of his blue pajama pants was there visible sign of a fierce hidden act—the horn stood full as it ever would be, stronger than its bearer who would not grow to match it for eight or nine years. But Rob read that as a sign of his age, the stoked sleep of boys on the balked edge of manhood. He said the name "Hutch."

No move.

He spoke again. "Hutch Mayfield, arise."

The face rolled toward him, but the eyes stayed shut; and in three more seconds the breath was the slow breath of sleep again (deceitful peace—in the dream Hutch was plunging past Grainger toward the girl, his living mother).

So Rob slowly took off his jacket and tie, unbuttoned his collar, stepped out of his shoes, and took the last steps till his legs touched the bed. Then he laid himself—full-length, dead-weight—on Hutch's body, the bristles of his chin at the boy's warm ear (he had washed his face at Sylvie's but had waited to shave). He didn't speak again.

Hutch halted at the threshold, swapping the familiar misery of sleep for this scarce pleasure that waited all down the length of his body, joy that also threatened to kill him. The strongest, strangest memory of his childhood, four or five, when this same great body would enter at dawn and lie as now without mercy till he'd gasp in fear and happiness for air. Now he could throw himself free with one roll of his own strong hips; but he lay and bore the weight for thirty, forty seconds till the old desperation broke loose in his chest. With what air he held, he laughed and said "Help!"

Rob lay a moment longer, then kissed the boy's ear and rolled rightward onto the bed beside him (the bed in which he and Rachel had made him, though he'd never told Hutch and did not remember now).

Hutch rose to his elbows—he wore no shirt—and looked down, grinning. It was in his mouth to say "You came in time" (he was still in the dream); but he said, "You missed some Hutch-made banana ice cream. We waited till dark."

"I had a bad fuel pump. Took till ten to fix it, and I was dog-tired; so I stayed in a tourist court the other side of Wilton but woke up at dawn." (When he'd finally said to Sylvie, "Can I sleep here tonight?", she had thought a good while before saying "Dead-secret?")

Hutch said, "Ought to saved your money."

"Why?"

"Case we take our trip."

"Where to?" Rob said.

"Well, the stars would suit me but you mentioned Richmond. Are we leaving today?" Hutch noticed the gap in his pants and quickly closed it; he had lost the dream's force anyhow, a boy again.

"No, tomorrow; maybe Wednesday. I've got some chores here."

"Who with?"

"Mind your business." Rob smiled as he said it but too late; Hutch had seen—the old yellow teeth of his father's shame and flight. "About a job," Rob said. "What if I move home, back to Fontaine at least?"

"Or you could move to Richmond, and I could come with you."

"What's good about Richmond?"

"I was born there," Hutch said.

"Your mother died there."

Hutch hunted his father for blame, the final refusal he'd awaited all his life—*You killed her and must pay.* Not in sight, not now. "She's buried in Goshen," he said.

"So right."

"And I've never seen the grave."

Rob could smile and say it—"It's waiting, sweetheart."

Eva called from downstairs. "Breakfast served in two minutes."

Hutch was watching his father, no move to rise. He knew he was waiting for an urgent choice to be made on his life; he knew his father was the one who could make it—that his own strong body, for all its rush to fullness, was in the hands of others and would be for years yet. Might always be (he had had no taste of freedom in life or dreams).

Rob said "Invite me home." He was whispering now.

"Sir?"

"Invite me here to live."

"This house?" Hutch said.

"Just at first. We could move to the Kendal place by fall."

"We and who?" Hutch said.

"Grainger maybe. Maybe Min."

Hutch met his eyes, asking. They were genuinely asking Hutch for some gift at last. But he knew he couldn't give it. It was not his to give; it had not grown in him yet. Still he didn't say that; didn't say, "I'm still a boy. Nothing in me understands you." He shook his head. "No sir." Then he stood and went to the chair where his clothes lay and turned his back to Rob.

"I thought you were happy here."

"No sir, I'm not," Hutch said. He dropped his pants, stood naked with his back still turned.

"Son, I've got to feed us, understand."

"I'm *fed* here," Hutch said. "You could bring me to you. Feed me there." He faced round. "You've promised that forever."

Rob said, "Mother needs you. You're the thing she's got."

"I'm all *you've* got," Hutch said, still grave. He believed it as fact, as some children do—that he was both axle and wheel for his father—and was righter than most.

Rob wanted to say it out now for good—"No you're not; now listen"—but seeing the boy (his own eyes set in Rachel's face and hair), he said "Then never leave me."

"I haven't," Hutch said. "It was you left me. My mother, then you."

"None of us could help that. One day you'll understand."

Hutch had listened and made no move to dress. "I'm old enough, sir. I'm old enough to die. Boys die every day—drown, fall, run-over. Boys sixteen are dying in Italy this minute, babies being starved over most of the earth. I may not have *time* is what scares me. Tell me now; I'll understand." He believed himself again and felt he was desperate, though he'd gone to bed with expectations of pleasure, the sight of his father.

Rob saw more than heard, saw he'd made what was now in most ways a man (the ways nature honored). But he lied a second time. "There's nothing else to tell, Son. What I mean is just that you'll feel other ways when you're grown and look back—about a good many things, things you've always known but in part, Son, in *part*."

"I don't even know I can get through today much less thirty more years."

Rob said "*Hope*."

Hutch stood on a moment, then reached for his drawers and raised a foot; but he stopped and said "No."

"No what?"

"I can't wait. You owe me a lot. Pay me that little bit."

"Of what, Son?"

"—The story, why you left me with these women and still won't have me; why you still won't forgive me for Mother: I was young." He had stayed calm, unpetulant as a tree and as alien to any adult witness. And he'd won, just the face and body he had earned for himself in fourteen years had won for him now.

His father said, "I'll try. We have got our trip. All this time ahead."

Hutch said "Then you promise."

Rob nodded "I do," having no sense how, not knowing himself any single true answer or a whole true story.

Hutch proceeded to dress—his drawers, khaki shorts, a white short-sleeved shirt.

Eva called up again. "Hutch, you're failing. Bring your daddy."

"I'm bringing him," Hutch said.

10

Miss Hilah Spencer was at her old percolator, watching it pump, when Rob knocked once on the open door. She wheeled as if caught in something worse than office-coffee—a pencil flew out of her wild white hair—but she said, "A pleasure! I dreamed about you."

"Good, I hope?"

"Too good to tell." She laughed, the freest tongue in town. "Come on drink some coffee." She reached for another mug.

"Coffeed *up*," Rob said. "I'm nervous as a cat."

"Then you're in the wrong pew; this is Crazy House today. He's adding attendance figures from six county schools, and he may lose a teacher. Children stayed home in droves—the radio, I told him. Too much thrilling news." Hilah thumbed toward a shut door, the superintendent's office.

"I need to see him though."

She had filled her mug by now, disconnected the pot, and gone to her desk. She took a long black drink and searched Rob mercilessly. "Step through the door please."

He came to the desk, touched his legs up against it.

"You want to come home?" She had never mastered whispering.

"May need to," he said.

"That's not what I asked. Several may need *you*. What I said was *want*."

"I hope I do," he said.

Hilah held another long moment on him; then smiled so suddenly, fully, as to shock him. "Wait a second," she said. She stalked to the shut door, knocked once, and opened. "Cheer up, Mr. Bradley; a stranger to see you."

"What about?"

She turned to Rob. "The waters of life."

Thorne Bradley said, "Hilah, don't trifle with me"; but he stood and came out to his door and looked. He knew Rob at once, had known him from the age of four, five months; but he only said "Stranger—"

Rob said, "Mr. Bradley, I see you're busy. I can come back later."

Bradley drew out his watch and studied it thoroughly. "No, step on in." He smiled a smile as neat as the click of a boxlid.

Rob followed, smiling at Hilah when he passed (she said "Come home"), and entered the office he'd never seen before. A big bright room with a big desk and two chairs, a leather nap-couch, heavy wood filing cases, bookshelves on every wall and, above them, dark pictures of the ruins of Rome. As Bradley moved on to his own swivel chair, Rob stopped at one scene—*Venus Genetrix:* a tilted piece of pavement, the brown stumps of pillars.

"Take a chair please, Rob."

He looked to Bradley pleasantly. "My father had this"; he touched the oak frame, the wavy glass.

"I imagine he did."

"It's still in Richmond. I'm going up this week; may get it for Hutch. He had a whole set—Father, I mean—that a school teacher gave him."

Bradley sat. "Don't burden Hutch with Forrest's leavings, Rob. You be his last bearer."

Rob recalled his father as the kindest of men; had studied Latin under Thorne Bradley three years, years dry as desert sand. He wanted to say now, "We both bear him gladly"; but he came as a beggar and went to the free chair, six feet from Bradley. "I may need your help."

"What help have I got?"

"A job this fall."

Bradley shook his head. "Sorry."

"Teaching shop," Rob said. "I heard that was vacant."

"And may stay so," Bradley said. "I never thought it mattered one dry hill of beans, teaching good future farmers how to make fancy bookends for books that don't and won't exist."

Rob said, "Furniture maybe. I used to make furniture."

"Where? In High Point?"

"James Institute in Richmond. When my wife died I cast round for peaceful things to do, evening hours, days off. They had a shop there—old tools but they worked—and I'd go down and sometimes work till dawn. I made several tables, a big corner cupboard. I could do it again."

"What happened in Raleigh?"

"Sir?"

Bradley's face was clear, no sign of special knowledge. "You seemed well-fixed there. Eva told me recently she couldn't pry you loose."

Rob knew he'd gain nothing by partial concealment. He said "They've let me go."

Bradley sat forward slowly, knowing kindness was required. "Do you want to say why?"

"I will," Rob said. "I know you blame my father for what happened years ago, but I don't remember that. Once I grew up and found him, he did a lot for me."

"What?"

Rob had thought it out. Not *a lot* but one thing, a plain clear example, one kind of decent life in the face of difficulties. Love and generosity, sufficient patience for the slow stream of days. He could not say that here; and before he could frame some harmless answer, Thorne Bradley broke in.

"Was it drinking?"

"Sir?"

"Your trouble, why they let you go in Raleigh?"

"My father died in May. I doubt you know about it. They had let him go on teaching after seventy; they owed him more than they could ever pay and they knew it. They let him keep an office, and he was down there marking his examination papers; said he'd be home for supper. When he wasn't home by eight, his housekeeper took the bus and went down to see; she said she didn't phone for fear of learning at a distance. So she learned first hand. It was already night but his office light was out. She said she stood outside and tried to see through frosted glass till students passed and stared. Then she had to go in, switch the light on herself. He had turned his chair over as he fell but somehow had got himself composed and was over by the radiator, calm on his back. He had graded all the papers but three, the three best. He'd saved them to draw him onward, always did that. Once she'd felt he was gone, she set his chair up and sat at the desk to calm her own self. Then she marked the three papers, just the grade, all A (she had helped in the past and could imitate his hand). Then she went to get assistance."

Bradley had turned to his window through that. He stayed looking out but he said, "Tell me this—why come here and tell me this?"

Rob had not planned to tell it. "I guess because I've known all these years how hard you judged him. I wanted you to see he earned himself a pleasant death."

Bradley faced him. "I see it. So have many black hearts; Tiberius Caesar died grinning like a baby. But you've misunderstood me. I never judged him, Rob, whatever words I used. I *missed* him, understand. Understand I loved him deeply, and loved him several ways. He was older than me, eleven years older; and when I came home from Trinity to find him rooming at Mother's, ten feet from me, and working beside me at school every day, I loved him in a week, as friend and father. *Worshipped* him in time; I'm not ashamed to say it. Even now it seems right, seems a just response to him. He had lacked my luck in going to college; but he'd read more deeply than anyone I'd known—read because he needed to, fell on it like food, and turned it to strength and generous warmth. He wrote poems also—you may not know—and while they were heavy with standard

young sorrows, I thought he was happy. We would teach all day till I was
fit to slaughter; then Mother would feed us and we'd walk awhile out the
old Green road; then we'd do our preparations in separate rooms; and
sometimes after I had blown out the light (so dead I could groan), he
would open my door and sit on the foot of my bed in the dark and read
what he'd written—

> Can what I hope in dream prove, waking, true?—
> The long road of my life find rest in you?

I was totally deceived. I know I should have seen his secret rushing toward
me—he proposed to Eva with me just yards away, the class picnic—but it
was a sort of virtue after all that I didn't, that I bore more shock than
anyone except your grandfather when they ran off at last: I had buried my
attention in my own love of Forrest, that 'meeting of souls.' " Bradley
stopped to smile in irony, to show a smile was possible; and found he had
finished—that story at least. He said straight at Rob, "I'm glad he died
happy, glad the living know he did." Then he fished in his pocket, drew
out a key; and opened the bottom drawer of his desk, a careful hunt
through a black tin box, the right letter found. He leaned toward Rob.
"I've waited for you, see." He offered the letter.

Still calm from Bradley's story, Rob took it. Addressed to Thorne in
his father's hand, postmarked *Bracey* two months ago. The sight of the
script was still more painful than pictures or tales, a clear strong trail
secreted by a life now far past reach (but at rest, rest surely). "Did you
hear from him often?"

"Once in these forty years. *That* once," Thorne said and pointed to
the letter.

"Do you mean me to read it?"

"I think I do, yes. I think you'd better."

Rob opened it carefully.

Easter Sunday, 1944

Dear Thorne,

*A long silence. Please let me break it now; please read this through. I
break it because I honestly think I am soon to enter a much longer silence,
and I want to speak out to you on two matters that require some speech.*

*The first thing is pardon. I ask your full pardon after all this time for
deceiving you, young as you were, with my marriage. All I showed you was
true—I returned your full friendship; I wish I'd seen you daily for the past
forty years—but I had an older need that Eva seemed to fulfill; so I flew
toward that. You will understand by now. I was wrong about her of course
and harmed her by my error; but she had the mind and strength to throw
me off in time, and I landed (by a curious grace) in satisfaction. I have
had a good life. It has felt good to me, I mean, with three main excep-*

tions—the years till 1905, my lying to you, my part in Rob. You can help me twice over, it occurs to me now—say you've canceled my old debt, and help me with Rob.

Let me say what I mean in that second request. I have little sense of how well you know my son; but you knew me and know of my dumb power to harm, a power I neither intended nor learned of till far too late. My chief failure there was acceding to Eva's clean wish to leave me. By the time she'd convinced me of her firm resolve, I had moved on in my life to duties and dangers which made it unthinkable to claim a share in Rob (I was claiming my life, what had been kept from me). So he grew up with access to only a half of his natural rights, the less loving half. The Kendals have strengths that I crave even now—they have learned solitude—but they have sealed hearts. Maybe sealed because full—they have filled one another and require no one else—but firmly sealed: no home for a boy with the Mayfield doors in his heart flung open in welcome and positive hunger.

I found him too late; the damage was done. He married the first girl who showed she loved him, a choice in its own way more ruinous than mine—the one girl in all the world, no doubt, less fitted by health and her own legacies to make the belated amends. The strange thing is, he was perfect for her; he gave her all she'd dreamt of, including early death, though he's never seen that. And so since her death, he has been in confusion that nothing seems to clear. As you know, he left a good job here to take his child to Eva when I'd shown him that the best care was ready in my home with my own tried companion volunteering to serve. Then when that too failed him—Eva again, the whole shut house, the shameful job that Kennerly found him—he moved on to Raleigh and has taught there till now, a sad job with children who don't seem to prize him. I've urged him back here, but he says Richmond's ruined by his old bad luck.

Now I feel I won't be there myself much longer. They have kept me on kindly past the age of retirement at James Institute and seem quite prepared to give me a desk and some faces to polish till I pitch over cold.

That is what's coming soon. No doctor has told me; I know it too deeply. A bad siege of headaches some three months ago and a sudden loss of vision in both my eyes which is permanent it seems, though I still can read. Then the headaches eased, leaving one strong scar, a small globe of numbness in the midst of my brow just under the skull. No pain but a presence, something ripening there that will either spread or burst. I have taken pains in Richmond to order my affairs. I am spending Easter here in my boyhood home with my one sister Hattie who is older than me but will long outlast me—an open soul still, though occasionally addled from years on a hill alone, talking to her dog. She doesn't need me; I am saying goodbye but she doesn't know that.

What I think will happen when I die is this—Rob will suffer more than anyone, thinking he has failed me. To tell him **that** he hasn't would make him suffer more; I would have to tell him that he came too late, into my life, I mean. I had answered my questions or had them answered when he found me in Richmond. He became a young friend that I cherished, delighted in often, and regretted. But while his life in these fourteen years has saddened me often, it has not cut me deeply; so I couldn't tell him that, despite what I fear he will go through once I'm gone—a long bout of drinking and maybe unemployment (he has been warned in Raleigh, is on probation). If I'm right, he'll come to you. He has mentioned it before when he's felt pulled to Hutch, and has told me that you are the superintendent and may lean his way.

I ask you to refuse him. Not because he isn't good—he's a very fair teacher, and he shows them signs of life which they've never seen before—but because he will die, really die from the heart out, if he gives up and comes to Eva again. She would welcome him now, is my own distant guess. There are other places for him more genuinely his—my own house in Richmond, the Mayfield home, and almost surely a job at James Institute (he left a good memory, and I've spoken to the principal) or his aunt's place here (this was my mother's home—Bracey, I mean—and he was born here in the room where I'm writing) or even in the mountains, his wife's home Goshen (he has in-laws there with a small hotel). He can make himself a life for another thirty years if he wants to now and is not folded back into flight and ease—his mother and Rena, Sylvie and Grainger. He will make it hard on you if he does come asking; he was always lovable, a fact he's never known. All I'm asking you to do is urge him back outward into something more yielding, more likely to save, than his own old cradle.

You may think I am wrong as I guess you've done for years. And I may well be. But I've said my say with the gravity and hope of a man near the close; and I've called for the hand, over space and years, of an old friend who seems now a permanent creditor.

With thanks for your time and still in expectation

Yours as once,
Forrest Mayfield

Rob was calmer than before. He laid the letter unfolded on the desk and looked up to Bradley. "I'm begging still. He didn't understand."

"What?"

Rob said, "A good deal. All that's happened since I left him. He never could see that I'd made my peace with Mother, had truly left home. He didn't want to see it, so I didn't force it on him. He thought he had saved me. Then the other main thing, I kept from him too—for some years now I have leaned on Min Tharrington. She's given me a lot, and I have to thank her now."

Bradley nodded; the news was no news at all. "What way?" he said.

"Well, a life together."

"You seem to have that."

"A home," Rob said. "She has asked for that."

"You've *waited*," Bradley said. "I can hardly urge caution on either of you, can I?"

"I waited," Rob said. "Min was ready long since. I was held back by things."

Bradley reached for Forrest's letter and folded it slowly. "You're telling me you want to marry Min and bring her back, teach shop—and live where?"

"Some place of our own. The old Kendal place has been mine since Papa died."

"Ruined as Rome," Bradley said.

"No more so than us. We could all rise together from our own cool ashes." Rob laughed once, no strain.

Bradley said, "You're here now? You've moved out of Raleigh?"

"No I'm here to see you, see what my chances are. Then I'm taking Hutch with me to clear up things in Richmond—Father's papers to sort. Min is still at her job. I haven't told her anything sure enough to move her."

Bradley took up the folded letter again, inserted it into its envelope. "Then tell her," he said.

"Sir?"

"Tell her something sure."

"How can I?"

"Because I said so. If a job is what you need—a job here, teaching— and if you will give me solemn word that the drinking is behind you, then you've got what you need. I can almost guarantee it; I have to poll the schoolboard, but I think they'll concur."

Rob said "When will they meet?"

"Two weeks from tomorrow. But I'll see them all before then; I can let you know the drift."

Rob intended to thank him and give his solemn word (he'd given it before, always solemnly); but he said, "You are going against Father's wishes."

Bradley nodded. "I am."

"Why?"

"Because he was wrong. I knew before you told me, though I didn't know how. He was wrong all his life, Rob, in every big way; but he made his own home or so people tell me. Now you've got to make yours."

"Or what?" Rob said. He smiled. "What if I don't?"

Bradley thought it through awhile, then also smiled. "Nothing much," he said. "One more drowned life. But let me ask this favor on behalf of your people"—he leaned forward, grinning excessively—"Leave here. Get *gone*. Drown well out of sight. Don't ask Hutch and Eva and Rena to watch. Nothing's less amusing, less instructive than a drunk—a drunk never moves, never learns a thing; and he takes so long to drown. Don't ask Min Tharrington to stand on the shore and throw straws at you for thirty more years. Me, I don't really care. I am being polite."

Rob said "I know." It seemed all he knew and would ever know.

11

AT four o'clock when Hutch had gone to his piano lesson and the early heat had eased, Rob and Grainger went out to the old Kendal place, first time in a year (it was still farmed by Jarrel, who reported to Kennerly, who passed Rob his share of whatever came in). Rob chose the hour on purpose—to be alone with Grainger, whom he needed to question, and to see the place while Jarrel was still in the field, not wanting to scare them with the threat of eviction till he'd seen if the house were livable for Min. Grainger drove and when they had cleared the last edge of town, Rob turned to see him closely, the first chance since Christmas (he had been away at Easter in Bracey with the cousin who still lived in Veenie's house). Nineteen years since Rob had met him; he had aged profoundly without looking older—the skin drawn closer to the bones like varnish, uncrazed and clear; the straight nose sharper, the nostrils larger; the line of the broad lips more like a graven boundary (the mouth a foreign organ swollen with threat in the milder face); the black eyes slightly purple in the late sun now, opalescent in their depths as if in hopes of clouding into senile blindness. Rob wanted to ask his age, early fifties somewhere; but he knew Grainger had strong feelings on that (he'd worn his hair clipped to the skull for ten years since it first showed gray). So after they had praised a few things about Hutch—his school marks, his growth—Rob moved to the question he had held for two days: "Are you here now for good?"

"Here *where*?"

"Fontaine. Mother's house; you know."

"Why you needing to know?"

Rob said, "I've got to move, got to make new plans. I'm wondering if I can count on you?"

"For what?"

Rob waited. "Steady help, I guess. I know you've got your place in Bracey still. I know you've got Gracie when she turns back up, but you've been here seven years."

"You moving here, you saying?"

"I asked you first." Rob also smiled, entirely earnest.

Grainger drove half a mile (they were on dirt now, already thick dust); then he said, "I got Miss Veenie's place in Bracey; saw it this Easter, still in one piece. Gracie wrote me a letter eight months ago Wednesday; I sent her ten dollars for bus fare to here. No sign of her yet and no more word. She don't need me and I never needed her. I thought I did; people said I did. I'm here because of Hutch, like to watch him moving up. He been good to me, Miss Eva been good, Miss Rena good as gold, Sylvie don't bother me. You moving Hutch from here?" He faced Rob a moment.

Rob said, "He wants to go. He thinks he wants to go; thinks we'd have a good chance—him and me somewhere, you with us of course. But I'm caught again, Grainger. They've turned me loose in Raleigh; I may have to come here."

"What you going to use for money?"

"I can teach here, I think. I checked that this morning."

"And live with Miss Eva?"

"No with you and Hutch, I hope."

"Who's cooking?"

"Min."

"Miss Min? Minnie Tharrington? You giving in to her?"

Rob said, "I may have to; she's told me to decide. And Grainger, I was forty years old last winter. I'm not as good at loneliness as I used to be."

Grainger nodded and waited. "When have you been alone?"

"A good part of my life. It's got worse lately; you get tired of it, want somebody in your room."

Grainger said, "I saw you alone one time—the first day I saw you, in Bracey, Miss Hattie's. Every time since then you *swimming* in people."

"People aren't what I'm after."

"Young Della was people; you fed off of her. What did she get back? Miss Rachel was people. Mr. Forrest, Miss Polly, them children at school. Miss Rena, Miss Eva, Hutch and me. What we got to show?" He continued to grin.

Rob said, "I've tried to thank you. I've tried the ways I know."

Grainger said, "How much candy your thanks going to buy us when we walk in the store and show a handful of thanks?"

Rob said, "Not a piece. I never said it would."

"You sorry for that?"

"That's the main thing I am. You know that well. My main trouble always."

"Then change it," Grainger said. "Change it while we got time. You lost two of us already; too late."

"I've told you," Rob said. "I'm trying now."

"Marry Miss Min and come out here and live in a house too sorry for niggers and teach wild children—and think Hutch and me be glad of that?

You telling me that? You pull Hutch out, you kill Miss Eva; that's the start of your change."

Rob said "All right," which he did not mean. Then he looked to Grainger, turned firmly to the road, and said "Have mercy."

Grainger waited again. He was grave by now. He said in a voice barely more than a whisper, "Mercy all I had for nineteen years, mercy all my life. Now I mean to *cut* some. Listen here what I done. I watched your mess through all this time and cleaned it behind you. I let your daddy treat me worse than a dog when I was a child he promised to raise. Now he dead—God help him—but you still in sight with long years to go; and you ask am I staying? I tell you this, Rob—you come here and strow your old mess again round Hutch and Miss Eva, Miss Rena and me, I'll make you wish I had gone to the stars on a one-mule wagon." He finished, laughing. The separate mouth so odd in his face contorted in long, nearly silent laughter; but his eyes never changed—they had meant every word and would always mean them, would find strength not only to mean but do.

Rob said "Go tomorrow."

"I work for Miss Eva. You get her to tell me."

12

The yard was empty when they pulled up and stopped—no dogs, no goat—and the house had the tall solemnity of abandonment (a good deal less paint than when Rob had first seen it thirty-seven years ago, the porch steps swaybacked and two windows blocked with paper; but the whole shape unaltered, abiding this present, a minor pause). Rob leaned and touched the horn once. A wait—still no one. Then a black bantam rooster strolled out from the well. Rob said "Are you sure?"

"Unless they're dead," Grainger said. "Hutch was out here last Sunday, Mr. Kennerly and him."

Rob leaned for the horn again.

Grainger took his wrist. "Leave em alone," he said. "Your house; walk in."

Rob said "Come with me" and opened his door. Grainger followed him out and walked well behind him. Halfway up the steps Rob stopped and said clearly "Anybody living here?" A wait.

Grainger said "A whole family."

"Where are they now then?"

"In the field, your field."

Rob climbed on up, knocked twice at the shut door; then reached for the knob. It turned, no lock. He entered the long center hall and looked to Grainger. "Step in," he said.

"I'll wait out here."

It was his all right. He turned to the left through a half-open door—an empty room, entirely empty: the good white plaster ivoried with age but bound by pighair and barely cracked. His great aunt's bedroom, scene of a third of her life at least. Shut windows, damp heat. He walked through the room to its own inner door and opened that. The old dining room; the old table still there, eight feet of oval walnut, black and coated with age. But clean, wiped clean, no crumb in the cracks. The windows here were shut too, no screens on them ever; and late sun was pounding this side of the house. Rob went to the old glass to raise it a little. Lovely old iron lock, elaborate as a child's toy, some penny bank that did a short stunt to thank a child. The window cried hoarsely.

A woman said "*Who?*"

Cold with fright, Rob turned.

On a narrow cot against the far wall, a black girl craning up, face wild with sleep.

He said, "I'm Mr. Mayfield. Let me give you some air."

"Flies," she said. She waved a hand across her eyes, drew her long legs slowly off the cot to the floor; and sat up slowly round a sizable belly—seven, eight months pregnant.

Rob said "Where's your daddy?"

"New York last Christmas, the last I heard."

"I mean Sam Jarrel; I thought you were his."

She was waking by then. "No sir," she said. "His wife my auntie. They somewhere working."

"You live here?" he said.

"I have right lately. I been kind of low."

"When's your baby?" he said.

"I don't know exactly."

"You haven't seen a doctor?"

"I didn't want to ask em for the money, no sir."

"So you just sit and sweat?"

"Sir?" she said.

Rob didn't answer. He was studying her room (the cot seemed her bed—two pairs of shoes were under it; a round mirror framed in green celluloid stood above it on the molding with a nail-polish bottle). They had given her this, in the midst of their eating; why not his aunt's room or a place upstairs? He remembered now Kennerly saying that Jarrel stored his hay upstairs since the old barn fell—a great tinder box over all their heads, no other dry storage. And so she was kept here, her dry hot place. "What's your name?" Rob said.

"Persilla," she said.

"Will you have your baby here?"

"I hope so," she said, "if Sam let me stay. He want me to leave; say I'm a bad example."

Rob wondered *Of what?*

Coal-black as she was, she was bright with the force of her hope and dread. She turned it on Rob "You kin to Mr. Kennerly?"

"My uncle, yes."

She attempted to smile. "You tell him for me? You tell him, 'Tell Sam be good to Persilla. He all she got.' " Her smile dawned broadly like the pain of a thrust on her meager face.

Rob nodded. "This is mine."

13

AFTER supper and a slow hour of talk on the porch with his mother, Hutch and Rena, Rob excused himself and climbed to his old room—Hutch's room; there were two beds now. He sat at the table, switched on the student's lamp (an instant furnace), found a tablet of Hutch's, and started a letter as a pool to take the rush of the knowledge and chances that had boiled up today, the two past days.

June 6, 1944

Dear Min,

I got here safely, though I did stop at Sylvie's last night to brace myself and wound up sleeping there which no one here knows. I pled car trouble. They are all as ever except maybe Hutch who is showing his age, the worst age of all. When I was fourteen I used to ask God every morning and night to give me some sign that He wanted me to go on enduring such days. They were very mild days; I can see that now—just the total absence of nourishment and hope, no sense that I'd ever be of use to any soul (I could not notice Rena standing quietly waiting). I have had worse since— you have watched me have them: worse in the sense of causing real harm and knowing I'd caused it and could never repay—but always since manhood with the awful grace of hope, the knowledge of a future, that my body if nothing else at least meant to live and deliver me generally intact to tomorrow. Hutch is doubting that now and rightly so; he has no evidence which he can believe that says otherwise. And the hard question is, can anyone help him? Can I or Mother or Grainger or you say a word, do a deed, that will give him the chance you and I craved then, the word of hope?—the absence of which, when we needed it most, has brought us to where we were yesterday, two mornings ago, my dream, your demand. That is what I want to try—helping Hutch, my own last chance to make partial payment on some aging debts: among them debts to you. Can you grant me that, maybe wait awhile for that?

It had taken him a half hour to say that much. He had paused and switched off the hot light to sit in a little dark and think when he heard the front screen open, steps in the hall, then slowly up the stairs—Hutch. Rob stayed dark and waited.

Hutch stopped on the sill, tried to see into the room; but the downstairs light didn't reach the table. He said "Where are you?"

No answer.

"Rob?" (Hutch rarely called him Father; he'd seen him too seldom. He saw him as Rena and Sylvie did, a brief young visitor).

Rob still didn't answer, though his chair gave creaks and the sounds of his body were a hum above Eva's voice, rising through the window. He was not out to tease or scare his son; he was frozen, waiting for some better word than "Here" or "Telling Min *No*."

Hutch came on forward through the long warm dark, though Rob had known him to be scared of dark. He paused near the foot of his own bed and touched it, the familiar cool iron; then moved on again till his hand touched his father. "You should speak to me," he said, his hand still resting on Rob's folded arm, his voice grave but friendly.

Rob said, "Well, good evening. Tell me who you are."

Hutch stood in his place, no closer, no farther (Rob could see him slightly now against the dim window). He said "I was yours." He had not planned to say it.

Rob's right hand opened, an inch from Hutch's, and moved to take him. "I've counted on that. I was still counting on it. If I'm wrong, tell me now."

"What difference would it make?"

Rob waited and tried to think it would matter. This boy might vanish now, and what? *Very little*—provided he vanished in silence, no pain, in darkness as now. The words surged up in his throat, claiming knowledge, claiming simple truth of the sort Eva'd strewn in her wake all his life. But he forced them down unspoken, partly true yet much less than whole. Hutch had asked a whole question; Rob owed a full answer. He sat another long moment, holding two fingers of a hand as invisible as Rachel's when he'd met her in this room to start this. Then he said, "This difference. I doubt you know this unless Grainger's told you; he's the other one who knows, because he was there. Before you were born, when your mother still had you and we were both waiting, I let down and hurt her and was so shamed by that that I went back to something I had done as a boy—drinking as a way to excuse myself. But just to myself; I'd excuse myself. I was hurting all the others more every night—your mother and Grainger, your grandfather, you. Then a month or so passed, and it seemed I had killed you. Your mother tried to bring you into the world, for nearly two days, a terrible struggle. You were turned all crooked; you were trapped and strangling. I was out in the hall; but I heard your mother, weak as she was. A nurse came to me and said the doctor said you were both of you *going* and that I could come in the delivery room and say a last word. My father was with me, and I looked at him. He said 'Better go.' But I went outside. I just turned and left him. It was right before daylight and cold for May. I went to the car; my liquor was there. I had in my head to take one long drink and then go back where your mother was. But Grainger was waiting; I'd forgotten him. He had come down with us but couldn't sit inside; so he'd gone back out and was on the back seat, trying to sleep. I scared him, I guess; I opened the door and he sat up and said, 'You've had all you get.' I had caught him in a dream. I sat on the front seat and opened the glove box; and Grainger said, 'What are you the father of?' I told him 'They're dying.' He said 'And you're here?' I opened my bottle and took one swallow and said 'I'm going back.' Grainger said, 'Tell me this—Miss Rachel still conscious?' I told him she was when I left; I meant her moans. He said, 'Do this. You lean down and tell her, tell her slow so she hear—"You come back and live and bring a strong baby back with you, I'll *change*." ' I asked him 'Change how?' Grainger said, 'Pay your debts to everybody round you, every soul you *invited*.' I asked him who gave him the right to say that, and he said 'Jesus Christ.' Then he laughed one time. I turned and meant to strike him; but I couldn't, then or since." Rob waited for breath and released the hot fingers.

Hutch moved to his bed, sat there on the edge ten feet from his father. His father stayed silent till Hutch said finally, "You were telling me the difference."

Rob said, "Still am. It's more than I thought."

Hutch said "Did you tell her?"

"What?"

"The speech Grainger gave you."

"Oh no."

"Why sir?"

"She was gone."

"I was there," Hutch said. "You could have told me."

"You were there," Rob said. "They had pulled you through. You had never even cried, just came free and breathed, all weak from the hours, your head all torn (they had pulled you with forceps when they once got you turned); but yes you were there."

"And I'm here," Hutch said. "You can still tell me now."

Rob said "Son, I'm telling you."

"Not the difference," Hutch said. "You've told that already. Tell me what Grainger said you should tell my mother."

Rob thought that through; then sat forward slowly and felt for his letter; he had just now said it after all, but to Min. He could say it to Hutch. "All right."

"*Say* it please, sir."

"I will pay you every debt I know how to pay."

"Starting when?" Hutch said.

Rob stood and went forward to the boy and touched his head, the warm crown rank with the clean dried sweat of another long day. Then he kissed where he'd touched; the answer was *now*.

14

WHEN he got to the porch, they were both still waiting—Eva in the swing, Rena in the chair that was nearest the stoop and the old tubbed palm. They both said gladly "Sit down and rest"; Rob took the chair between them and sank. It was cooler and still, no car on the street for the first few minutes; so he did rest a little. (Hutch was in bed and sleeping; Rob had waited upstairs at the foot of the bed till he heard slow breathing, the safety of peace. Then he'd gone to the table and reached for the lamp to finish his letter but had heard Rena's laugh and decided to pursue it.) For all its withholdings, this house—porch, yard—had offered him as much calm as any other place. *More* it seemed now as he rocked here silently between his aunt and mother, his first and longest lover, his first beloved. Old forces had leeched away in time, old hungers been fed or starved into weakness too feeble to stand; they sat like a family in a child's dream of home. He could live here at last. He turned to Rena. "What was funny just now?"

He caught her half-dozing. She said "Very little."

"No you laughed. We heard you all the way upstairs."

Eva said, "At me—when you laughed at me, when you asked for the moon."

Rena said, "Oh the moon. Yes I'd been sitting here much admiring the moon. Hutch and I had discussed it; it keeps us awake. Then he went upstairs, and we sat on awhile; and when I next looked, it was nowhere in sight. So I said to Eva, 'Eva, where is the moon?' and she said, 'Don't ask me. I'm a stranger here.' "

They all laughed again and Rob turned to see her as they quieted slowly—his mother, not by moonlight (it was gone) but a lamp in the parlor, Eva's bedroom for years, that reached her right profile as she swung her little arc. No one on God's earth was less a stranger anywhere than Eva was here, this precise small axle rotating through space these fifty-seven years—a few boards and plaster, four dozen panes of glass. A life at home; had that been her whole triumph and the source of her power? It seemed so now (her face in the half-light, unyielding as ever, prepared as the marshal of an armored division for what lay in the woods—the ambush of age, failed mind, racked body or unchallenged march into harvest fields and river encampment, a slow drift to sleep).

She was watching the road not him or Rena, but she said "Where is Hutch?" in a whisper not to wake him if he'd already slept.

Rob also faced the road—nothing, still empty. One distant tired Negro. "Asleep, ten minutes. He seemed very tired."

"He was," Rena said. "We waited last night."

Eva pushed past the claim. "How long is your trip?"

"Oh long as my business and our little sightseeing." Rob had not spoken to her of the business till now. He had written Hutch a note just before his father's funeral, and he'd laid out his plans to Kennerly fully when he asked for the gas; so he guessed she knew of the death and the duties that faced him now.

But she didn't ask for more. "Less than two weeks?" she said.

"Yes ma'm. It's for him"—Rob pointed upstairs—"I have got to get back."

"To where?" Rena said. She had faced him all along, though he sat in full dark.

He offered it to Rena then. "What about to here? Can you find room for me?"

Rena said, "I did once. I'd try to again." She thought he meant the summer months from now till September. He had not told her or Eva of his firing or his morning talk with Thorne, and they clearly hadn't guessed. Rena said, "Plenty weeds waiting for you right now" and thumbed behind her, her half-acre vegetable garden just beginning. "Grainger's griping already; saw a black snake this morning. I'll get your hoe ready."

Eva said, "Hutch can move down and sleep in my room, give you space upstairs."

Rob still spoke to Rena. "I may mean for good. How would that sit with you?"

Eva swung on in silence.

Rena turned to the road, but her voice had the old rich puzzlement of hope. "Like sherbet," she said. She drew a long breath. "Lemon sherbet in the shade."

Eva said "Come here."

Rob looked over toward her.

She had moved to the dark street-end of the swing and was touching the vacant space. "Sit here a minute, Son."

Rob stood and obeyed.

But she spoke first to Rena. "Sister, what about your herring?" (Rena had bought salt herring to cook for Rob's breakfast; they would have to be soaked overnight, starting now.)

"What about them?" Rena said. "They were dead last I looked." But she sprang up in a moment and entered the house.

Rob said "Coming back?"

"When I've found the moon," she said and never broke step.

Eva said "And she *may*."

Rob gave a strong thrust with his heel to swing them. Eva said "Good!" and they watched one another, both smiling broadly as their cool arcs slackened and left them still again, the warm air close. The house was silent—Hutch asleep, Rena buried far back in the kitchen, Grainger in his own place fifty feet to the rear.

Rob said "How are you?"

"As I've always been."

"Then happy," he said.

Eva laughed once, high. "Has it seemed that to you?"

"To me, yes," he said. "I can't speak for others."

"You're the one who would know."

"Why me?"

"You've loved me. You're the last one who's loved me." She was smiling still but he saw she was earnest.

Rob couldn't deny her, not tonight anyhow. Any earlier night in the past ten years, he'd have said, "No, Hutch. You are leaving Hutch out." But after this morning and Hutch's plea to leave, he could only allow her claim unchallenged. He nodded. "I've enjoyed it, however much I moaned." Then he went on to tell her what he suddenly knew. "You are happy and have been ever since I knew you clearly."

"How is that?" Eva said. "It has never seemed easy."

"No I'm sure," Rob said.

"—I abandoned loving parents for a man I could please. I bore you in danger, and my mother killed herself. I left my husband, came here and nursed a dying father, leaving you to yourself—and rightly won your grudge."

"But you wanted it all."

"Why?"

"I truly think you did. Mother, that was what hurt me—that you had left me willingly to Rena and Sylvie. You left Father easily as stepping from a room. You had the best of Hutch, all his plain child's love. You have never been refused, I honestly believe. Very few humans are ever deeply refused, barring cruelty or sickness. Most people die smiling or are happy till the last. Most people get the lives they asked life to give; their needs get filled."

Eva seemed to smile again (she had faced forward now; he could not see her fully). "I have noticed through the years how good you are at inventing explanations for everybody else on earth but you."

"Maybe so," Rob said.

"No maybe about it," Eva said and touched his knee. "Here, answer me this—since most of us humans are happy tonight, how are *you*, sweet love?"

Rob waited awhile; they were still swinging gently enough to cool them. "Tonight I'm resting and am glad to be. Many days I'm not, most days here lately."

"What need have you got that is not being fed?" She had taken back her hand and had moved away slightly, just beyond the reach of light.

Rob did not think he knew. What came as his answer was the recent sad past. "I have not mentioned this by mail, understand. I've waited for the chance to sit here and tell you. But I've lost my job in Raleigh and am loose again."

Eva waited. "Son, why?"

"Father's death," he said. "It caught me so suddenly when other things were low. I stayed home and drank some and missed a little work. They said they'd had enough."

"When was this?"

"A week ago."

"Are you drinking now?" she said.

"No ma'm," Rob said.

"You and Hutch shouldn't go—"

"No, Mother," he said. "I have got myself together."

She faced him for proof and studied him as if there were plentiful light to show the degree of control in a man, the strength in his eyes. "I have never comprehended—what is drinking for?" she said; she herself had never drunk more than sherry at Christmas.

"Oh for ease, from shame."

"Shame of what please, Son?"

"Different things in different people."

"You're the one I know," she said.

"I've failed so many; Father's death showed me that."

"Any death shows that. That's the purpose of death. What did you owe Forrest?"

"What I've owed all of you, a useful life."

"Useful to what?" Eva said, deeply curious but almost whispering.

Rob knew at once. "God and all my family."

"Useful how?" she said.

"Just the usual ways—kindness, care, dependability. If nothing else, to furnish one rare lovely sight for other's eyes to rest on."

"You've done that," she said. "You have been more loved than anyone I've known—Sister, Sylvie, Grainger, Rachel, your father apparently, Min Tharrington, your son. *Me*—believe that at last. I've loved the best I could. Don't forget. I was half-wild from *my* mother's blood, all the fleeing killing Watsons. I had to feed myself. Once I had, I loved you." She reached for his hand; it was cool there beside her, palm-down on the swing. She traced a figure-eight in the curls of its back as if a slow figure would complete her message, detained forty years. The hand moved a little but stayed flat down.

Rob spoke though. "I believe you."

Eva kept her hand in place, riding his very lightly. In a while she said, still softly, "What now?"

"Sleep, I hope."

"No your future, your plans."

"I mentioned coming here," Rob said.

"To do what?"

"Teach school, teach shop. I saw Thorne this morning; he seems quite hopeful."

"Starting when?"

"This fall. I would come back sooner; get well settled in once we finish our trip, once I clear out in Raleigh—the rent's paid for June."

"You were not teasing Sister; I thought you were."

"No ma'm. I have had to keep it quiet like this till I thought my way through, till I knew if I was welcome."

"Who else have you told?"

"Min and Hutch, Thorne and Grainger. You now—"

Eva said "And you know?"

"Ma'm?"

"You know that you're welcome?"

"Are you telling me I am?"

Eva said, "I am asking if you are sure. You are too old to blunder here one more time."

"What would blundering be?"

"Failing again in sight of your family."

"You said it wouldn't matter, hadn't mattered all along."

"Not to us," Eva said. "I spoke for us—well, Rena and me; I can't speak for Hutch. No, to *you*. You would care; caring's ruined your life. I just meant that; can you welcome yourself? You are at home now; can you sit here and take it the way we have?"

Rob said, "No ma'm, not in this house here. I wouldn't try here. I would find my own place—the old Kendal place; I might go there—and take my own family: Hutch and Grainger, maybe Min. I may need to marry Min."

Eva faced the empty street and touched the swing's chain, old rusted cow chain. She carefully felt her way with thumb and finger up eight or ten links; she would smell of rust till morning. "Are you sure Hutch would go?"

"Yes."

"You already asked him?"

"Told him, yes ma'm."

"He would follow you out to that wreck of the past?"

"He'd like to go farther. He's growing up now."

"How did he tell you that?" Eva said.

Rob had never held a genuine weapon against her, never had one to hold. And because she faced the road and could not be seen, he was not sure he held one now, not sure she cared. Had Hutch been more than her latest job of nursing, ending soon and gladly? He did not wait to know; either way, he spared her. "Our trip," he said. "I just meant our trip. Hutch wants it to last, wants to go on to Goshen and see his mother's home."

"Will you go?"

"I doubt it. We've got the gas for Richmond, a day at the beach, maybe Jamestown at most."

"Let him go." Eva said. "Let him see his mother's home. Rachel earned that much."

He'd invented the lie—Hutch had not asked for Goshen—but she forced him on now. "Please say what you mean."

"I mean he asks about her, just lately, not before. For long years he never spoke her name. Then he started on Sylvie, oh a year ago. She told me one evening, 'Miss Eva, Hutch ask me how old is his mama.' I told her to send him to me next time, that I'd fill him in; but he somehow knew and didn't ask her again. I think he's asked Rena, but she'd never tell me."

Rob said, "I can tell him what there is to tell."

"But gently," Eva said. "Children suffer from blame."

"Yes ma'm," Rob said. "I've heard that, I think." He was suddenly exhausted—the restless night at Sylvie's, the tides of this day towing various ways, the thought of tomorrow and the hot drive north. He stood and said, "Excuse me please. I've just given out."

"Too early," Eva said. "You won't sleep, you know."

"I'll lie quiet though," he said, "and rest my eyes. Can I help you lock up?"

"Oh no. I'll sit here and wait for Sister. She's still in the kitchen. Those herring must have *fought* her."

"She'll win," Rob said.

"Little doubt," Eva said.

He did not lean to kiss her but faced her, raised his right hand; and gave a slow greeting—palm held shoulder-level and broad in the dark—as though to a stranger met high in dense mountains after long search in thin air on vanishing food.

Or as though at the bar, vowing truth with God's help. Eva read it that way. "Swearing what?" she said.

He held the pose, baffled.

"You are poised there to swear."

"—Amends," Rob said. "Even partial amends."

"You never harmed me. Come back," Eva said.

He could say no more, would never feel more certain that he had a claim on life, could continue and mend. He dropped his hand as slowly as he'd raised it and turned and went in and climbed toward his sleeping son, his chief good deed. He stripped and slept quickly, rest in a hot flood, palpable balm.

15

HE woke in early light awhile before six—no sound but birds, the downstairs quiet, Rena's room still shut, Hutch so silent that Rob craned up to check on his life. He was there on the near edge of his own tangled bed, hands clenched by his open lips which gave no sign of breath; but the rails of his lean sides swelled and sank every eight or nine seconds, so he'd also lasted. With his eyes on Hutch, Rob said the old prayer he had always said—"*Your will, Yours*"—then stood in his cotton shorts and top and went to the table and, not reading through what he'd written last night, continued his letter.

You have waited long years, I know very well—remember; so have I—and you've taken what few rewards I could give in strangling secrecy. Precious few. But I beg you for one last stretch of patience. Then I hope I can offer the best I have, a final answer. It will be one of two things you've asked me to say, firm Yes or No.

If Yes it will be for the simplest reasons—that most of our lives we have stuck together for what must be natural inclinations to mutual care, that now I can turn myself from old bonds and ask you clearly to take me openly for better or worse in what time is left us (for better will surely be my intention; you've had enough worse to hold you nicely), that I miss your company when you are not with me and always will. Lastly, that I'm much more grateful to you than you've ever believed. I could make you believe or could die trying hard.

If No the reason will also be simple—that I can't find a way to do both justices, to Hutch and you. Remember that I drove off nine years ago and left him age five in a house that nurtured my own miseries and have seen him since only as a brief Santa Claus (a poor one at that and occasionally shaky). I will try to know now on our coming trip how much I can give—what he needs and I have—and how much is too late. Or was never really wanted, just imagined by me.

You said one week. I will write you by then or maybe try to phone; but I won't have a whole sure answer in a week, maybe not for some weeks. Maybe not before fall when he and I have moved out of here and fit together in a separate place. So if that is too late, you can let me know now (care of Polly in Richmond); and if we should never meet in privacy again, I can say now I'll thank you well beyond my grave, not excluding

*here and now. You have been the best help. My continuing troubles were
not your fault and without you would have drowned me. Maybe we should
have let them. Hope we won't.*

Ever,
Rob

16

By the time he had got that sealed and addressed, he heard the single
cough that began Rena's day; then the quick sounds of dressing—his one
chance to see her. He quickly stepped into his own trousers, took his
shaving bag, and entered the hall. Her door was still shut; but he stepped
up and listened—perfect silence. Had she slipped out somehow? Or
dropped in her tracks ungreeted, unthanked? He opened the door. Her bed
was made; he couldn't find her. He drew a deep breath.

Rena whispered "Step in." She was over by the window in her cane-
back chair, her back to the door.

Rob stepped in and shut the door behind him. "I was headed down to
shave; I thought I heard you. Then your room was quiet."

She turned her chair toward him. "Come sit down," she said. She
leaned and touched the foot of her bed.

Rob went there and sat. "Are my herring ready?"

"They will be," she said. She had her Bible open on her lap; she let
him see it (he had never seen her go near a Bible before). "This is yours,"
she said. It was—his grandmother's, given to him by his grandfather thirty-
odd years ago as soon as he could read. "I borrowed it last year. It was in
your room."

"Should have been with me, shouldn't it? I'd have been better off."

"Maybe so," she said.

"Is it saving *you?*"

Rena looked down at it, the book of Romans. "From what?" she
said.

He remembered her father's death, their meeting in the parlor. "You
once mentioned rest. I was hoping you had found it."

She weighed that a moment, then looked up smiling. "Oh no," she
said. "But you don't have to find it. It comes; it comes." She looked to her
book and said him a verse—" 'For I reckon that the sufferings of this
present time are not worthy to be compared with the glory which shall be
revealed in us. For the earnest expectation of the creature waiteth for the
manifestation of the sons of God.' "

Rob said "Are you suffering?"

She thought again. "I'm hoping mainly. Hoping still."

"For what?"

"The sons of God, I guess. I don't expect much!"

"No really," Rob said.

"You know," Rena said. "Simple courtesy would serve till glory be revealed. You abused me last night—*Could you come back home?*"

"I was honestly asking."

"I honestly answered." She closed her book.

He reached out to touch her. She was just beyond reach, so he did not lean. "You left too soon; I didn't explain. I have got to go somewhere soon, a new job."

"What happened in Raleigh?"

"I broke down a little when Father died. They couldn't stand the sight."

Rena nodded. "He deserved it. He earned every tear."

Rob remembered her coldness to Forrest at the wedding, the cool smiling distance of her few meetings with him when she visited Richmond after Rachel's death. "From me, you mean?"

"From us," Rena said. "We ruined his plans. We all owed him something—the Kendals, I mean."

"I paid it," Rob said. "Too late of course."

"Maybe not," Rena said. "Anyhow wait and see. People sometimes cancel debts long after death; I know that for certain. Mother freed me through you."

"What way?" Rob said.

"From blame, real blame. I knew she was wild, and I went off and left her."

"The day she died? I thought you were here."

"In school," Rena said, "—and I hated school. She had asked me to stay, but I turned her down. The night before she died, she came to my room and knelt down before me to pin up the hem in a dress she was making for my school commencement (still six weeks off; she knew she was rushing). I had not cleaned my lamp; she had trouble seeing and worked very slowly till I finally said, 'Mother, I have got to *study*.' She rocked back then, sat flat on the floor, and wept bitter tears. I stood and let her weep them—never moved, never touched her (she was one foot away), never once said 'Why?' or what did she need? In a while she said, 'Stay home please tomorrow. Let's finish this thing.' I didn't say 'Why?' I knew she was nervous; we had heard of your birth the day before and Eva's weakness. I thought it was normal and that she would calm down. I was also too young to think I could matter; nobody had told me. So I said 'For what?' That was what she couldn't answer. At last she said, 'I thought you might enjoy it.' I said 'No ma'm' and you know the rest."

"It was not your doing."

"You were not here," Rena said. "It was mine all right. Anything you can help and don't is your doing."

"Who said?"

"Just God."

"And I helped you?" Rob said.

"You *freed* me, I said. You were Mother's way to free me."

"How?"

"I rescued you. When Eva turned to Father, I turned to you—with open arms; yours were open to take me. You'd have sunk otherwise."

"Are you sure I didn't after all?" Rob said.

Rena searched his eyes. "Not yet," she said. "Of course you still can. You have got years of chances. Even strong old boats have been known to plummet on calm summer days in clear sight of shore."

"You're telling me that I have got a chance of freedom."

Rena said, "I am not telling *nothing*, sweetheart. I was thinking my morning thoughts and you broke it."

Rob said "I'm sorry" and stood to leave.

She did not try to stop him; but she said, "Oh no. I was glad to see you. I hope to see you every day the rest of my life."

Beneath them, through the floor, they could hear Eva singing, softly but pure enough to penetrate walls—no tune they had heard, the product of a long night of tranquil dreaming.

17

ONCE he'd shaved in the bathroom, Rob passed through the kitchen—Sylvie rolling biscuit dough, no sign of his mother—and through the wet grass of the yard to his bathhouse, still the only shower in this end of town, though used now only by himself on visits. The once-mossy lattice of the floor was dry; and the few old threats—black widows, snakes—were represented only by a token dead spider in the low south corner, translucent from starvation. But the old pipes worked; and once he'd hung his pants on the single nail, the cold water rushed him—panic and pain. He bore it as always by a long high yell; then he wet the yellow soap and shut off the water and lathered his body from face to toes with serious care. All winter he had washed in his landlady's tub, quick shallow splashes to avoid a long stewing in his own scum and bristles, but now he lingered. Despite the shock of cold, he felt himself slowly; and was slowly pleased. This body which had borne him through some fifteen thousand days, through ninety percent of the pleasure he'd had; which had suffered the blame of Rachel's death, all the subsequent gifts to and punishments of Min, seemed young in his hands again, fresh and ready.

For what?—himself. Why not himself? Wasn't forty years of leaning on various others—rubbing on others—enough for one life? Hadn't Eva urged it on him twenty years ago in telling him the body had its own

private solace if he'd only accept it? A *strong closed world*—he seemed that
to himself now, the first time in his life. He could dress, walk out of here,
crank his car and leave—no word of goodbye, no prayer for pardon. He
could get a job in Norfolk at the shipyards or Baltimore. A plain rented
room with one single key. Who would suffer from that?—Min for maybe a
month till she'd raise up and know she was blessedly free; Hutch for
sometime longer, for some years maybe till he bowed to the fact of his own
composition (the potent bloods in him—Watson, Kendal, Goodwin,
Mayfield: all commanding his life, *demanding* it really); Rena forever but
she planned on that (how would she greet a true son of God if he came to
her now with a pledge of loyal presence?—she'd head for her garden,
leaving him in the swing). *Old Robinson;* whom had old Robinson
harmed in a lifetime of flight? Fewer souls surely than Eva in her one
place, Bedford Kendal in his, than Forrest even with his need to change
lives (fieldhands reading Ovid).

His sex had stood in his soapy hand, first time in two days. Rob
studied it, smiling. For all its hungers and humiliations, it had served him
kindly for thirty years. And never better than in solitude as now, the
uninvaded joy of self-dependence, perfect self-service. He could be his own
solace, had been the sole solace of his own life to now.

Cold and wet, upright in his bathhouse with slightly bent knees, Rob
honored himself. And his whole body thanked him with a pure flood of
pleasure that cleaned him more deeply than soap and cold water, than long
years of waiting on others (hunting them) in the hope of purgation,
eventual rest. He reached for the faucet to rinse himself.

Grainger said "Who is that?" and tapped on the wall outside behind
Rob.

"Your oldest friend."

"Is he clean?"

"Not yet."

Grainger opened the door as the water struck Rob. Rob's back was
turned. Grainger said, "Step to my house please when you're clean."

Rob turned in the freezing water to face him. "That may be years."

Grainger nodded. "I'll wait."

18

DRIED and dressed, Rob walked on to Grainger's beyond the bathhouse on
the edge of the garden—the old cook's house built for Sylvie's grandmother Panthea Ann when she was a young girl brought from the Kendal
farm, barely just free. The door was closed. Rob knocked once and stood.
The hyacinth leaves by the step had died, a dense mat of ycllow.

"Step in."

Rob opened the door and looked, the one dark room. He was blinded by the sun but was searching for Grainger.

"Step into the shade." He was in the far corner, squatting by his small trunk and locking it.

Rob entered the cool. "Am I clean enough?"

Grainger pointed to his one chair, a slat-bottomed rocker. "Rest yourself a minute."

Rob took a step toward it; then stopped, looking down. "You leaving today?" He knew he was not; his belongings were still in their old rigid places—on top of the small pine table by his bed, a battery radio, a Barlow knife, a dollar watch, the Irish potato Grainger normally carried for rheumatism (exchanging each one as it shriveled with poison drawn from his joints). No drawer in the table. Across the tan floor—boards scrubbed once a month—and against the back wall was a second larger table with a little stack of clothes (shirts, pants, underwear, all folded precisely), a graniteware pitcher and bowl, a bar of soap, a shaving brush worn to a stubble of fuzz, a shut straight-razor (its strop on a hook at the end of the table), a pocket mirror laid flat, a pair of nail clippers. The walls were bare as always—no calendar, thermometer, no nail or peg, no pictures of dogs, no human face.

Grainger stood and came toward him, no smile, no answer. He held a small box. "I need to talk to you; sit down here please." He went to his narrow bed and sat on the edge.

So Rob took the chair. "You've recovered?" he said.

"What from?"

"Yesterday. I thought you'd got rabies. I see you're better."

Grainger waited, watching Rob; then began on an answer. "I slept all night, first time in three months. Yes I'm—" He stopped there and held out the box, white cardboard tied with a cord.

"This a snake?" Rob said.

"You open it and see."

"Sing 'Happy Birthday.'"

"Your birthday's in March. This ain't for you anyhow." But he offered it still.

Rob took it and weighed it on his palm, feather-light. He loosened the cord and opened the lid on a bed of white cotton which he didn't move to touch.

"Lift it up, fool, please."

A gold coin, smaller than a quarter. Rob took it, strummed the thin milled edge, turned it over—Five Dollars, 1839. He looked up, grinning. "You're under arrest. Gold money's illegal for the past ten years."

"For Hutch." Grainger pointed. "That's for you to give Hutch."

Rob set it in its cotton and offered it back. "You give it to him then; he'll be up in a little."

Grainger shook his head twice. "That would force him," he said. "I don't mean to force him; he'll love me or not. You just change it, secret; and buy him some present, some thing he see on his trip and want."

Rob nodded and took it, closed the box, retied it. Then he moved to rise—breakfast, the day.

Grainger spread his right hand like a fan, meaning *wait*. "You wonder where I got it?"

"I *didn't*," Rob said. "People used to have gold."

Grainger said, "Mr. Rob your dead grandaddy. At the time I was born. He sent it to Papa in that same box to the state of Maine; said, 'Give it to Grainger to bring him luck.' "

Rob rose, stuffed the box into his deep hip-pocket. "Would you say it had worked?"

Grainger thought. "Off and on, like it did for him. He had got it at his birth; some cousin give it to him. It was made that year. Mr. Forrest used to tell me he made a good death."

Rob took two steps, then turned again. "You thinking of death?"

"Not much," Grainger said.

Rob came back toward him, all the way to the bed, and stood there above him not a foot away. "I am," he said, "—more and more here lately."

Grainger said, "You're a boy; you barely cut your teeth."

Rob showed his teeth fully in earnest, not joking, an unbroken set. "When He was my age, Jesus Christ had been dead seven years and some months."

"If He died."

"He died. Question is, did He rise?"

Grainger said, "Question is, what you mean about *you?*—thinking death."

Rob bent even closer. "We're leaving today; Hutch and I, this trip. If anything happens, if you get the word to come and help, tell me now if you'll answer."

Grainger said "What help?" They were whispering. "What thing might happen?"

"I might start drinking when I get to Richmond. I may fail there. God knows, I could die."

"On purpose, you mean?"

"I don't plan it, no; but you see where I'm headed—to tunnel through all Forrest Mayfield's leavings."

"You're coming back here. You're setting up house. I'm helping you out if Miss Eva spare me."

Rob nodded. "But answer; will you come when you're called?"

"If you're *live*," Grainger said. He laid his flat palm on Rob's breastbone and felt the heart adjacent. "You're live this morning; I'll swear to that. If they send here and say you're dead, I'll wait. Miss Rena can fetch you."

Rob covered the hard dry hand with his own; he smiled—"Breakfast served"—and made a waiter's bow.

19

AFTER breakfast while Eva was packing for Hutch, Rob walked the quarter-mile to Kennerly's house. His Aunt Blunt's car was already gone (the single woman in the family who could drive); Kennerly's truck was nowhere in sight; and when Rob knocked twice on the front screen and entered, no one rose to meet him—the cool dark hall: Blunt's paintings of dogwood, an Indian praying, the Angel Gabriel descending with lilies. Rob called out "Aurelia?" (the cook—he could hear her far back in the kitchen, already humming hymns).

No answer.

"*Anybody?*"

"Would your old uncle do?"—Kennerly in the parlor. He had said he'd be gone by daylight, cruising pulpwood.

Rob went forward to him; he was seated with the paper. "I thought you'd be covered with ticks by now."

"I thought so last night, but I waited for you."

Rob laughed. "I've never drunk a drop of your blood."

Kennerly offered his wrist. "Help yourself," he said. "Everybody else does. You may need it yet."

Rob sat on a footstool, a yard from his uncle. "I'm sorry if I held up your business," he said. "I thought you'd just leave the gas stamps with Blunt."

"I said I would; then I ran into Thorne and thought I'd better see you, hear the tale from you."

Rob nodded—"All right, sir"—but offered no tale.

"You mean to come home?"

"I mean to make a living; I'm out of a job."

"Why is that?" Kennerly said.

"Thorne told you."

"No he didn't and I didn't press him."

"Then don't press me please either," Rob said. "It's been a bad month, but I've not harmed a soul, and I'm looking for work near my own baby-cradle."

Kennerly nodded. "Just tell me one thing; you haven't been tampering with any child, have you?"

Rob smiled. "That was Forrest, Forrest Mayfield; I'm *Rob*."

"His boy."

"His boy, yes sir, who was grieving for him. I missed a little school from grieving for him. Us colored boys grieves worse than you white folks;

we feels things harder, things cuts us deeper; we takes the occasion to grieve when we can."

The joking stopped Kennerly. "You're settling his estate?"

"No estate," Rob said, "—just a house near niggertown and several bales of paper."

"Did he leave it to you?"

"No will, no sir."

"Then it's partly your mother's. She's his sole legal widow. What's Virginia law on that?"

Does she need it?" Rob said. "Tell me clearly right now; would a few thousand dollars mean a thing to her now?"

Kennerly shook his head. "She's fixed. Father left her well-fixed. What's fairly hers though ought to come her way."

"Then it won't," Rob said. "Nothing fair in her having one red cent of his. You watched that story; she chose her own life."

"Father chose."

"And she accepted, with a deep lasting smile. What's left should go to Hattie—it was her father's house—and to my father's helper: she's the one worked for this over forty long years."

"Give it to her," Kennerly said. "Eva wouldn't go near it. Then you're coming back here?"

"Did Thorne say I could?"

"Yes."

"Do you think I should?"

"Rob, you've never taken one piece of warning from me. I've stopped wasting breath."

"No, tell me," Rob said. "You've watched me close as any. Tell me what you know now."

"You're a very small part of what I know," Kennerly said. "I've watched you, sure, but not because of you. You were in my line of sight; I have watched all my people."

"Tell me that small part."

"Will you use it?"

"If I can."

"Come to life," Kennerly said. He had known it at once, had not paused to breathe.

"Sir?"

"Come-to-life."

Rob waited to think, then shut his eyes tightly, extended his hands; then looked again brightly. "Lo! I am," he said. "Feel my hands and see."

"No you're dreaming," Kennerly said, "—flat in bed still dreaming for the forty-first year."

Rob said "Dreaming what?"

"Perfect peace. You expect a happy life. You can dream that forever."

Rob waited till he knew he could speak without heat. "When did you wake up?"

Again no pause. "When Mother fell dead; I was eighteen by then."

"What had been your dream?"

"Same as yours. They all are, only dream people have. It's a way of dying young."

"So you woke up and saw?—"

"—That it's just a long wait, that your life is this wait."

"What for?" Rob said.

Kennerly hadn't thought. He had held his newspaper on his knees through that; he raised it now and looked, a random inner page. Then he put it down. "Oh peace."

"Have you got it?" Rob said.

"Don't expect to any more. That's the thing I mean to tell you."

"You could die," Rob said.

"That would get it," Kennerly said. He was smiling again. He folded his paper and laid it on the floor. "I appreciate your counsel. I'll give it sober thought." He moved to rise.

Rob stopped him with a hand. "If I come back here, would you call that a life?"

"Could be," Kennerly said. "You could have a life in Raleigh—Hell, in Boston, Massachusetts if you'd set your mind to have it."

"Should I marry Minnie now?"

Kennerly sat back to think.

"Should we move to the country, fix the old place up?"

"You set to drown some niggers?"

"Sir?"

"You dispossess Tom Jarrel, you'll need to drown his children or watch them starve before you. Drown a teen-age girl with a little nigger *in* her."

"Can't we find him a place close by? Tom could keep on working for us."

"*You* tell him," Kennerly said. "*You* find him the house. I quit right now if that's your main plan." He grasped the leather chair-arms and stood in one thrust, as strong as a boy. "I'll get your gas-stamps, and you get out of town." But he stopped at the door. "Let me tell you this story that you don't understand. You'd have known it all your life if you'd ever woke up. We are very plain people. We're the history of the world; nothing one bit unusual in any of our lives. You are just one of us; you have not been singled out for special mistreatment. Let me tell you my life; I can tell it in a minute, and it's sadder far than yours. I worshipped my mother—she was something very rare, she could charm the birds silent, she'd have set you straight in minutes—and she seemed to care for me, since I was the boy

and she was partial to boys. But I was dreaming, see—how to get myself
calm. I had hated school badly, Eva had all of Father, he could barely *see*
me. So I took a little job, little birdshit job jobbing brogan shoes two
counties away, to help me keep dreaming. I had a little rented room where
I could get my things straight. I had my combs and brushes laid as parallel
as tracks on the bureau top; and thought that was perfect, that I'd found
still harbor. Then Mother went under, was driven down simply by your
two parents and their selfish meanness. They'd have never succeeded if I
had been here (Eva didn't need Father by then, and Rena never); but I
was hunting peace, and my mother died in absolute misery—without so
much as a last word to me. I woke up as I said and came back home,
thinking Father would need me. He didn't, never had. But he'd taught me
one skill—how to estimate timber—so I did that for him, for myself (to
keep awake). Eva came home by then; and the first night she got there, I
knew she'd never leave. *She* was needed, all right, and wanted to be. She
had her a skill that would keep her calm forever—how to please one
precious human soul entirely, how to live on the interest of that once he'd
gone. I watched that for two years and decided to leave, just to here, a
quarter-mile. Leaving meant you got a wife. I had known the Powell sisters
since I'd known anybody; so I settled on them—both of them, couldn't
choose. One day I asked Mag which one must I take. She stood and
thought a minute; then she said, 'The high one's pretty but the squatty
one's the *worker*.' The high one was Sally; I settled on Blunt, and she's
worked fairly well. We have not raised our voices more than half a dozen
times in thirty-six years. She'd have liked to have children, but one of us
couldn't which didn't bother me. I've kept my eyes open, since Mother
tore them open; and let me ask you this—can you name me three children
that have brought their parents pleasure? I mean long-standing pleasure,
not a picnic here and there."

Rob said "Mother—"

"I said *parents*, two people. She breathed just for Father."

Rob said, "No I can't, no sir."

"You've had Hutch these years, you and Eva and Grainger; but he's
gathering to leave. I can see it in him more every day that passes over—
I am aimed out of here; God help the one that blocks me."

Rob nodded. "Why is that? He's had what I lacked."

Kennerly grinned broadly, walked halfway back. "I told you," he said.
"You didn't understand. That's the point of my story, mine and Eva's—
Hell, *Sylvie's*: nobody lacks nothing. Nothing special, I mean, barring rank
starvation and external torture. Everybody gets the same if you add it all
up; some a little more here but a little less there. It's a flat damn tittie
everybody gets to gum. You are luckier than most. You are luckier than
me; no you killed a woman too. So we're even. Come to life. Forty's just
about time. Most men wake up very naturally at forty. Few are called like
me, few as fortunate as me—Charlotte Watson foaming blood."

Rob also stood. "I do understand and I'll try to believe you."

Kennerly's grin reignited. "Don't matter," he said. "Don't let it get you down. The truth is something separate from you—pretty you!—and it won't lose a minute's rest, a particle of its power, to spit you in flames if Rob Mayfield can't believe at middle age." He left to get the gas-stamps.

20

HUTCH was seated in the car (they had told him goodbye); and Rob was standing at the open driver's door with Eva and Rena and Grainger around him when Sylvie came out the kitchen door, heading toward them with two paper bags.

She went round to Hutch's side and gave them to him. "Here's your lunch. Don't waste it; people begging for food."

Rob said "What's the news?"

Sylvie stayed at Hutch's window and spoke across him. "They killing em now; they killing by hundreds." It was just after ten. She had heard the war news on her kitchen radio, heard it all day through as each hour struck. France had been breached on Tuesday by a hundred thousand men, the final invasion.

Rena said, "Not killing them fast enough."

Sylvie said, "Plenty fast. Plenty of em to kill."

Rob leaned to face Sylvie. "Don't you want it to end?"

"I won't the one started it. *You* go help it stop." She had found ways before to deplore his freedom, though she well knew his age exempted him nicely (her one nephew Albert had been shipped to England, maybe on to France now).

Rob laughed. "Shall I swim? We could strike out from Norfolk; Hutch could tow me when I failed."

Sylvie searched Hutch closely all down his length—a blue polo shirt, khaki shorts, new sandals.

On the far side Eva said once firmly "Sylvie."

Sylvie touched Hutch's ear with her thick forefinger, gently on the top rim. "You leave Hutch safe on the beach; I'll come get him." She had said it to Rob, but Hutch took her wrist (he could still barely ring it). She wrenched free easily and went toward the house. After six or eight steps, she stopped and faced Rob; but at first she didn't speak. Everybody turned to watch her.

Rob said, "I'll pray, Sylvie; for Albert, this evening."

She nodded. "You pray. Then see do that save him."

Eva said again "Sylvie," milder now, and moved to Rob.

Rob said, "We'll see you, Sylvie. Anything you want?"

"Not a thing," Sylvie said. "Not a thing they got that you can buy." She went in slowly.

Hutch said "Let's go please," an audible whisper.

Eva said "She's worried," not wanting to expand in Grainger's presence (he and Sylvie had lived in armed truce for some years).

Rob touched his mother's shoulder. "We'll phone you tonight when we're settled at the beach."

Eva nodded. "I'll wait." Then she offered her face.

Rob was struck by the change. What had seemed, last night on the porch in darkness, a map of contentment—perfect and glazed—seemed suddenly the flayed drying head of a girl gravely assaulted and utterly puzzled but still uncondemning, a silent beggar. With his hand still on her, his wish was to flee; to pull back simply to the car behind him and drive till night, long nights from now where this face would be hid if not vanished, forgot. She had always loved him; he had failed her entirely. He bent and brushed his lips on hers—his carefully dry, hers wet as a wound. Then he turned and sat.

Rena held her ground three yards from the car; but she spoke up from there, having waited her turn. "We'll expect you," she said. With her big right hand, she managed a wave that was like a little spooning at the air, three times.

Grainger said "Let me know—"

Hutch again said "Please."

21

Rob had driven two hours—fifty miles north of that—and knew he must stop to buy Hutch a drink, let him eat Sylvie's lunch; but the deep chill of flight was still on his forehead, the five cold bits still cutting his mouth (Min, Hutch, Eva, Rena, Grainger straining to turn him five separate ways). At last he touched Hutch's leg. "Son, eat what Sylvie fixed you. I am not hungry yet; let me just push us on."

Hutch ate a dry sandwich and rode on gladly.

JUNE 7, 1944

Tʜᴇʏ had got to Virginia Beach in late afternoon and found a room at a cheap clean cottage called Abbotsford—two white iron beds like the room at home. Rob's headlong force had brought him this far, then abandoned him quickly; so he'd told Hutch to sit on the porch or walk while he himself napped. Then they'd find a fish supper.

Hutch walked half an hour toward the north sparse end, barefoot in wet sand, his own heart gradually lifting in solitude—the element he'd always suspected was his (both hoped and dreaded), though he'd known real loneliness of this sort only in half-hour scraps of wandering from home or behind a shut door. What he did not know from his fourteen years, and needed to know before all else, was a simple answer—could he live in the world, this world he'd had, the only world shown him by others in daylight, where grown men and women chose (apparently *chose*) to bind their own strong selves to others till they withered together and propped one another in permanent yokes? Could he live like that for sixty more years?

He had felt the substance not the words of such thoughts for nearly ten years. He had come to them slowly by witnessing the life of his grandmother's house, by guessing at the secrets of his father's life, and now through the sight of his friends whose bodies like his had burst into growth (loud with puzzlement and pleasure, new demands). The pleasure he'd accepted almost daily for two years, alone in his room or behind the house in woods. The puzzle of how such a large pure joy could be shared with another (the actual *method*—who would move how?—and stranger still, the *motive* for sharing an act so easeful, so healing and scarce): that puzzle he'd held deep in him, but by force and with shame; its demands were its own law and knew no place or time.

The fierce intermittence of hunger and surfeit had brought a new fear Hutch had not known in childhood. In the long years of being at the

mercy of others for care and kindness, he had treasured some hope that
once his body firmed (*if* his body firmed; he had seen his naked father and
older boys swimming, which were no guarantees that the process was
general), he would gain calm control of his world and his choices. He
would have his own way. Now the process had all but run its course in
him—and delivered him over to a far harsher power than any he'd faced.
(All the others had been people—his dead mother, Rob, his grandmother,
Grainger. This was in himself and wild.)

Then he came to a long clean empty stretch of beach and had walked
toward the middle of that, an old jetty. No human in sight, no houses
either way for two hundred yards. He had not seen the ocean for three
summers now; and though it was no large part of his wishes (he had lived
far from it), it seemed here this evening a possible mate, companion by
which he could pass through a whole good life alone, unwatched, his body
unchallenged except by itself beside this predictable wordless water. Behind him far back was a low grassy dune. He went there to sit while this
new calm lasted, to test it for good sense and possible endurance (he'd
never been sure any goodness would recur).

It had lasted whole minutes, and toward the end he had wished for
his father to walk here and find him and silently sit. No thought of the
dream of his mother's return.

Then he saw he'd been accompanied. Sixty yards to his left just
beyond the reach of water in a gray wool blanket, a man and a woman.
Only their hair and slick faces showed; the rest was covered which was
partly why he'd missed them. They'd also been still as a beached log or
shark. When he saw them he crouched, his chin on his knees. The move
had been soundless, he was downwind from them; but at that the man
looked, looked up toward Hutch, seemed to meet Hutch's eyes.

No man but a boy—seventeen, eighteen, short-haired, plain-faced.
Was his nod a greeting? He smiled very broadly, then faced her again, then
moved above her. He was lying all on her, though he held up slightly; their
heads didn't touch.

Hutch thought he should leave, but had he been seen? The smile was
uncertain; could have been the rush of pleasure, not intended for Hutch.
The girl had never looked. She was just the boy's mirror. To stand now and
go would be to make a speech they could not fail to hear—*I've seen you,
can leave you.* This was offered to him; they gave it to him—he chose to
believe that. So he rolled to his elbows, extended his legs in dry sand
behind him. Flat down in the sand, hopeful and dreading, Hutch watched
them closely.

They moved in their gray cloth like sleeping breath—steady, unstop-
ping, all but past detecting—and they moved so long that Hutch estab-
lished rhythms: the great joint heart made by their two bodies beat six
times for each slap of water on sand. And that never changed; that was

what reached Hutch as sweet confirmation—*This is simple as breath, a new rate of breath that will come to you soon in its own natural time like the hair on your groin, strong sweat in your hollows.* His pleasure in the thought and the sight that had made it did not call on him to seek their same goal; his own sex was calm. But he mimicked their beating with his narrow hips in the cool dry dune.

Then the boy laughed clearly, three high sounds quick but separate as beads, and looked up again to where Hutch had been. With Hutch flat down, their eyes failed to meet; and the boy then covered the girl completely—faces vanished. Their body was still. They might never move again, might never need breath.

Hutch went toward his father, searching some way to tell him and ask for more.

2

But Rob had still seemed exhausted through supper, asking Hutch only easy things about school and Sylvie and Grainger. Hutch had answered politely with part of his mind, a thin forward part. The deeper core still focused on the beach, the gift he'd been offered by two covered strangers hardly older than he. He had eaten his scallops and settled on secrecy—tomorrow maybe when Rob had rested—and the simple freedom of new air around him, new public food unburdened by Sylvie's visible labor, prevented impatience or mute regret. Then Rob had said, "Ready for a picture show?" Hutch said "—And willing"; and they'd walked a short way to an old brick building to sit through the last half of *Young Mr. Pitt.*

When it ended Hutch waited for lights to come on, the gap between pictures; but they darkened even further and from somewhere in front came the nasal whine of electric guitars, not Hawaiian or South Seas but generally eastern, maybe Japanese. Some collection for the war?—dead Japanese children? Hutch tried to see his father; he was sealed off in dark. So when the music went on and no announcement came, Hutch said "What is this?" A man on his right said "Shhh" and Rob was silent. Then the music built on toward a faster louder end. A spotlight struck the curtain; and a man's Yankee voice said, "Ladies and gentlemen, for your evening entertainment and patriotic pleasure, we proudly present—from across the salt Pacific and our grand ally China—the famous Ming-Toy to dance her nation's dances." The music came again, slow and soft. The spotlight widened. The curtain spread quickly on a short figure, swallowed neck to sole in purple cloth, hands flared to hide a face.

The hands oared slowly sideward. The face was round and pale, white as warm fish flesh. The mouth was straight and solemn; the eyes were

black, tip-ended, and stared out more fiercely than any Hutch had seen—
how did this dark room offend her? Who were all these hidden watchers?
(Hutch himself had entered darkly and had still not seen around him;
what was on his father's face?)

She began to tremble gently at her own veiled center, no relation to
the music. That grew to deep shaking which began to sway her arms. Her
legs began to buckle. She was finally all in motion on the net of the music
before Hutch could realize that this commenced a dance, that the girl
herself was willing.

For a while she danced in place, only raised hands and feet at the
edges of her purple—gold slits in a tent. Then she worked toward a fury
which involved long lopings and high straight kicks. Still her face never
broke its white glare at the room, never joined her body's turmoil.

Then her hair poured downward. It had been bound tight on the
crown of her still head; she'd loosed it someway. It reached to the waist of
her robe, lank black. She held still again, her head turned down, the hair
swung forward. When it covered her face, her hands moved inward to
work at the four gold frogs on her robe. She shuddered one time and the
robe fell off; a small white foot kicked it firmly behind her. The music had
stopped. She was in a gold halter and small gold pants, both tasseled with
gold. She was smaller than before, than the robe had made her seem; and
frozen as she now stood (her head down, hid), it did seem to Hutch that
she'd come to the end of her nation's dance—China starved and shamed
since before he could remember, a billion baffled children. She bore a long
look from all the dark faces, all silent as she.

Hutch again looked for Rob—still concealed but there: their arms
pressed together on the common armrest. Was clapping now in order or
was it too solemn? Would she just walk off?

A voice said "I'm waiting," a man behind Hutch.

There were two seconds more. Then her hands sought her halter,
slowly climbing her belly; and it fell too—she had hardly seemed to touch
it. Another kick backward, her head lifted slowly. In hiding, her mouth
had smiled very slightly, and it stayed smiling now. Her breasts were bare.

Hutch had never seen breasts in actual life. Since his own mother's
death, he had lived with old women who concealed themselves; so his
knowledge was confined to magazine pictures and the plaster casts at
school of Venus and Victory. Yet he hadn't deeply wondered; they were so
much a pendulous fact of his elders, denied still to all but a few girls his
age. He studied now though with wide-eyed quickness, certain that Rob
would lead him out any moment. They were perfectly round and while
they quivered with her—she was moving again to softer music—they defied
the earth as firm as white bowls held by magic to her chest and stained at
dead-center with brown aureoles the size of great flowers. What had made
her want to bare them? Why were people here watching? What secret was

shielded by such plain bulwarks that people would be drawn to pay and sit staring? Was another gift involved, his second today? A gift to use how, now that he could feed himself, had never fed here? What good was being done?

The lights began to swell, the music quick again. She accepted both changes and was starting to whirl, her arms milling wild. Hutch knew that if he turned he could see his father now; other men were forming round him. But now he didn't look—for fear a deeper puzzle would stare back, grinning: another secret offered, exposed without warning and no explanation. Had Rob known of this?—that they would see this, much more than a show? Hutch had noticed no sign out front, no word from Rob.

The girl was all naked. In the last gyrations she'd torn herself finally free of all cover and had stopped, back turned. A high flat behind like any boy's swimming. To the loudest music yet, she spread her arms straight like wings and faced them quickly. At the fork of her clamped legs, the short fold of flesh—as hairless as her mouth—was lined with bright stones that glistened three seconds. Then every light blackened.

Rob clapped with the others.

3

IN their room an hour later after seeing all the picture and eating ice cream and deciding they were tired, Hutch was in bed already with a light sheet on him, face turned to the pine wall, his mind still grinding.

Rob entered from the bathroom in his shorts and sockfeet and sat on his bed. The boy turned away. Rob tried by kind staring to force him to look. Or was he asleep? He was not old enough to have lost the child's gift of total surrender. "Did you say your prayers, Son?"

"Yes sir."

"Pray for Albert?"

A sizable wait. "I have now, yes sir." He didn't plan to turn.

"Are you mad at me?"

"No sir. What about?"

Rob had peeled off his socks and was kneading his feet. "Any number of things—the vaudeville show."

"No sir."

"Did you like it?"

Another long wait. "I don't understand it."

"What part?" Rob said.

"The whole thing."

"Do you want me to tell you?"

"Yes."

"You've got to look at me then; I don't talk to walls."

Hutch rolled over slowly as if it were work. He faced his father vaguely, no trace of a smile but entirely awake.

Rob said, "I didn't know it was going to be that. I thought she'd be an acrobat or some hula dancer. She was just pleasing men, just selling quick fun."

Rob nodded. "What was fun?"

"—That she showed herself naked, things people want to touch."

"Men, you mean?"

"Men and boys. You are not getting younger. It'll come to you soon."

Hutch had met his father's eyes through all that; now he flinched. He looked down and flushed in great splotches, neck and chest.

Rob saw that clearly and felt the cold burning of a child's shamed refusal to face the settled fact that he's left one room and walked deep into another, that doors have shut behind him. He had his own knowledge of Hutch's new body; his own fresh memories of the same in himself twenty-six years ago, the cold spit of torment. He knew Hutch prayed for the room to darken now, for them both to part and sleep. But he also felt as strongly the need to give a gift—what he'd never had in childhood; had scrounged from long years of waste, harm, and punishment: a partial shield composed of battered scraps but true at least. What old Robinson had known and refused to pass to Forrest. What Forrest also scrounged but hoarded till too late. He began his painful offer. "In a short while from now, Hutch, you'll need all of that. All she showed and all that's under."

Hutch rolled full over now and lay on his belly, face half-hid in pillow. Then he said "For what?"

"Your ease. So you'll think. See, you'll soon get to where you'll be twisted up with what will seem like desperate starvation. What you'll really be is *curious*; but you'll think you're dead with need and that what we saw will feed you—what was under that purple, what she'd stuck cheap diamonds on."

Hutch thought, then said "I doubt it."

"No you will. You're mine and Rachel's. You could not escape by trying. You could jump up now and start in your light cotton drawers and run like deer forever; and it would tap your shoulder in a year or so and seize you. You are mine and Rachel's child."

Hutch said, "Can we go to Goshen?"

"No."

"We'd skip the trip to Jamestown and go on to the mountains. I've read Pocahontas."

Rob said "Why?"

"To see Mother's place."

"I can tell you all you need. We would not be welcome, Son."

"Then tell me," Hutch said.

"What?"

"All I need." He rose to his elbows and met his father clearly.

Rob bore the look a moment, then walked to the door and switched off the light. Then he came back and spread down his own top covers and lay flat on them. He spoke to the ceiling but strongly enough to carry on the din of surf that pumped through their two open windows, mild but constant. "I've thought about this for some years now. I think this is all you will need or can use; I honestly do. When I was twenty-one years old at home, I thought I was unhappy. I had thought it long before but had not known I could act. I thought I'd been neglected by my mother, who was busy; and of course I'd never seen Forrest Mayfield to remember. I was hot after that, after all I'd been denied; so I struck out to find it, which meant to find another. I thought it lay in others and could be mined out, that streams could be dug which would fill me forever. Just by touching others, young girls my age, the size of that poor girl tonight. They were all hid from me; so I thought it was there, the ease I mentioned. I still think it is, but that's a later story. Well, girls grow on trees as you may have seen already; and quite a gratifying quantity of them thought the same thing as me and were ready to try. It *does* help—don't ever let a Christian say it doesn't; even Jesus never said it—but it helps very briefly, the length of two aspirin. Or until you wash yourself and the feel begins to fade in your mind with the picture and the words you and her said to bait each other out of hiding and look. So when I got to Goshen after wandering a little, I had had several little spells of ease as I said; but what had made me leave home was still far beyond me. Then I saw Rachel Hutchins, who lived where I slept; and she above every other human I've known believed what I did."

"What was that?"

"That you could live. That no power in heaven had ever intended for people to want one day of their lives, not for calm human kindness; that people could furnish each other all the needs of a good useful life if they'd set their minds to it; that some people's minds were already set and waiting."

"Rachel, you mean?"

"Rachel. Your mother. She was younger than me; but she'd run well past me in the hunt for her hope, had all but given up when I crossed her path."

Hutch said, "You are telling all that about bodies?—just bodies together? You still believe that? I thought it killed Mother."

Rob rolled to see Hutch. A window was behind him; and by the dim blackout lights of town, Rob could only see the compact ridge of his side—he was turned Rob's way anyhow and seemed to wait. So Rob said "It did" but could not follow that—no tears, plain blankness. He'd exhausted his knowledge, his pitiful gift that had meant to stretch miles. A fourteen-year-old child had dried him up in less than five minutes. He sat up quickly, no sense of destination. A little walk maybe.

Hutch said "Nobody blames you."

"Thank them for me," Rob said. He went to the chair and felt for his clothes, stepped into his trousers.

"Are you leaving?" Hutch said.

"For a while," Rob said.

"Want me to stay here?"

"You wait."

"For how long?"

"Till I tell you to stop." Rob had kept his voice calm, but the spine showed in it. He walked to the bathroom and shut the thin door.

Hutch rose and found the light and also dressed. When his father came out, Hutch was opening his bag.

"*You* leaving?" Rob said.

"Yes sir."

"Where to?"

"To the bus station first." Hutch had kept his back turned. He was taking out a light jacket; packing his book, *Swiss Family Robinson.*

"Have you got any money?"

"Grandmother gave me some."

"Would you go back to her?"

"To Goshen first maybe."

Rob walked nearer to him, two steps from his back. "There is nothing in Goshen but one girl dissolving six feet underground."

Hutch nodded. "Maybe not." Then he shut his bag and turned, his face white with purpose, taut with revulsion. "That's more than is here."

Rob struck him, not gently, on his left ear and neck; and even before the shocked face responded, Rob said to himself "A *second time.*" He meant the second irreparable harm he'd done in his life—Rachel, now her son. He was accurate.

But Hutch, when he'd swallowed astonishment and pain, said "You promised to stay."

"Where?"

"With me. Rob, I've *waited.* I've waited for you since I was five years old—to come back and take me to live with you, to find us a place. You said that to me plainly the day you went to Raleigh. Grainger heard you say it; I didn't dream it up: 'You stay here with Eva and Rena just awhile till you get school-age. Then we'll be back together and can hear ourselves think.' So I've lived with old ladies picking at me nine years, and you've had a good time. Now you say you'll come back to Fontaine and drop there. I won't be there to catch you."

Rob smiled. "Where can I find you?—just for Christmas cards and funerals." He touched the hot shoulder which stiffened in his grip, then pulled free and turned.

Hutch opened his bag again and reached deep in it. He found a short envelope and handed it to Rob. Then he went to the window and tried to see out.

Rob handled it slowly, the postmark *Goshen*, May of this year. To *Master Raven Hutchins Mayfield, Fontaine, N.C.* Inside, a single sheet of lined tablet paper.

May 18, 1944

Dear Raven

    I know you had a birthday a day or so ago; and since I saw awhile back in one of my papers that your other grandfather had passed to his grave, I thought you might be interested to have your last male forebear rise and wish you happy days.

    Happy Days.

Come to see me if the spirit ever moves you; I am here all but alone,

Rachel's father,
Raven Hutchins

Rob said "What did Eva say?"

Hutch had gone to the edge of his bed and sat. "She never knew about it. Sylvie brought it straight to me."

"Did you show it to Sylvie?"

"No."

"Or Grainger?"

"No sir. I was waiting for our trip."

Rob went to the bag, laid the letter in on top. "Did he write to you before?"

"The Christmas I was five, Rachel's mother wrote to me—just a card saying *Love*. Eva showed me that. But him, no sir. I remember him though."

"How?"

"He's all I remember. Was I three or four?—anyhow that time you took me up there before we moved to Fontaine."

"We were pulling out of Richmond; I had given up there and was hunting a place. 1933, you had just turned three; can you really remember?" Rob lay across the foot of his own tangled bed.

Hutch said, "A drink of water in a strong-tasting cup, that much anyhow. And that he seemed old. You were not with us, were you? I don't remember you."

"I may not have been. We stayed several days. I was looking for a job, and he used to keep you with him."

Hutch nodded. " '*Stay here.*' He asked me to stay. We had had the drink of water and walked out into sunshine. Then he picked me up and faced me and said, 'You can stay. You are Rachel to the ground.' I think he said that much; I'm sure he said *Stay.* I'm sure about the water. Was my grandmother there? I can't see her at all."

"Oh yes," Rob said. "She was very little noticed. Very kind and obliging, very ready to forgive; but she liked to fade back, till she faded completely. Rena heard that she died of some blood weakness the year the war started—Rena'd swapped notes with her; they had met at our wedding. Mr. Hutchins notified her."

Hutch said, "Why are you not welcome then?"

Rob waited awhile, working back through it. "I doubt you want to know."

"I do, yes sir."

"It's more of what you wouldn't listen to just now, what you cut me about."

Hutch said, "But tell me. I promise to listen."

Rob knew that the start lay a good way back. He could not tell it in another rented room. He sat up and said, "Come with me to walk."

4

THEY went down a block to the ocean in silence, Rob a little in the lead. He had kept his feet bare and walked to the extreme edge of the calm surf before breaking step. Hutch came up beside him. There was no real light— the town mostly black; no moon or stars, though the sky seemed clear. No bomber could have found them. Looking out Rob said, "Shall we swim on for Sylvie and join Albert fighting?" He pointed straight out to the unseen horizon. "Just three thousand miles; think we could find him?"

"Where?"

"In France. I'm guessing he's in the invasion if he's not dead by now."

Hutch said, "Sir, you're pointing at the Straits of Gibraltar; but sure, I'm ready."

Rob laughed. "Walk north first. Walk north to Nova Scotia; we'll need to aim for France."

So Hutch led them left the way he'd gone alone before in late afternoon. He walked on damp sand but beyond the reach of water; his father on the ragged edge of its fling, his ankles now and then phosphorescent with foam. When they'd walked some distance and Rob had not spoken, Hutch said, "About welcome—you were telling me that: why you can't take me there."

Rob said, "All right. I was still thinking back. It maybe starts here; anyhow this was early in the story. I first went to Goshen when your mother was away. She had had a nervous breakdown and gone off for treatment; so when she came home, I was already there—her father's hotel with a job of my own and Grainger in the kitchen and the form of help I mentioned (also in the kitchen: a colored girl who lived on the place, named Della). *She* welcomed me right off. I had gone to her most of the nights I was there till Rachel came back; she lived on the place, next to Grainger in the quarters. She bore me up through whole weeks when, Son, I planned to die—just by letting me in. You don't understand that now— you won't ever; I sure God don't—but you might start believing it and honoring it now just on your father's word. It is some kind of bridge, to bear you through life; and it bore me to Rachel. I have to tell you now; I didn't love Rachel till after we were married. We were natural mates though, as I said awhile back; we were both that reckless to have our own will, the same goal in life. But even after I had met Rachel and chosen her, I still went to Della. She was still helping out." Rob paused and, not stopping, walked rightward till the surf reached half to his knees (he had rolled up his trousers).

Hutch said, "And Grandfather objected to that?"

"Not at all. Not then. I didn't think he knew—Rachel never did at least—but it turned out he did and had helped us along, hoping I would be eased and could pass Rachel up. That wasn't Rachel's plan."

"What did Grainger think of her?"

"Very little, I guess. He was waiting for Gracie—she had already left him—so he'd taken me on as a spare-time job, but I never let him stop me."

"You just said he did."

"When?"

"The morning I was born. You said Grainger stopped you and sent you in to Rachel to tell her you'd changed."

"That once," Rob said. "And he's helped at times; of course he has—it has been half his life, thinking he saved us. It was Della that saved me, without even knowing."

"And Grandfather blamed you?—for lasting on Della, for getting through to Rachel?"

"I don't think he did. He'd given up on Rachel himself, I think; he saw he couldn't ease her however hard he tried, and he'd seen enough of me to think I might. No your grandfather only spoke hard to me twice— the night I asked him for Rachel's hand, he promised to harm me if I harmed her (he never knew I did, never blamed me for you) and the time you remember, 1933. After Rachel died I tried to stay in Richmond, keep my job at the colored school (I was head bookkeeper and by then was teaching a little mathematics). The first few weeks my Aunt Hatt came and nursed you along; and your Grandmother Hutchins and Rena paid visits, and Polly was always nearby to help; but after you were oh maybe six months old, you were just mine and Grainger's—we were what you had. And we did right by you. God never made a better baby anywhere than you. You would only cry for hunger or for actual pain. I could wake you up any hour of the night I needed to see you, and you'd wake up grinning. You sobered up later when you understood more, but you did a life's share of bellylaughing as a baby. I could talk like a duck and you'd answer somehow; that could last us an hour almost any night. And Grainger would read to you out of his book or play his mouth-organ, and you would dance circles. You slept in my bed from the time you could walk; and I'd lie down beside you in some dim light and watch you for minutes. You would always breathe through your mouth, wide-open, breath fresh as new milk. I'd let it wash my face, same smell as your mother. I never once blamed you; you were innocent as any clear pane of glass. I loved you till it drew great tears down my cheeks, and I stayed good for you—I'd made God the promise Grainger said to make Rachel. I had tried to change. I would lie some nights after you were deep asleep and whisper you questions up against your ear. One night after you had moved to my bed, as I put you to sleep, I said, 'When I come to bed will you wake up nicely and take a little leak?' and you said, 'Ask me. I'll answer you.' So for some time I asked you did you want to go pee, and you'd always answer in your sleep Yes or No; and were always right, never wet me again. That gave me the idea to ask other things. At first child's questions—'Hutch, growl like a tiger.' You'd growl in your sleep. Then I'd ask did you love me? You'd generally nod and once you grinned, but you never said Yes. And once after two years, I asked did you mean me to keep my promise? I don't think you knew what a promise was, not to mention *my* promise (unless Grainger told you); but you said Yes as clear as day."

Hutch said, "What was the promise?—just to change your life?" They had passed all lights now and walked in pure darkness, guided by waves and the faint earthshine; their feet bare to shells, rocks, rotting fish but safe so far.

"To stop harming people in the ways I had, by not touching one human body again (not for my old reasons), by not drinking liquor; I had drunk a lot of that since I was your age."

"Why?"

"A form of ether, deadens the pain."

Hutch said, "But you promised that *if* we two lived, Rachel *and* I. You got just half."

"That was why I asked you; you were all that was left. I thought you should say. I thought you might be taken if I broke it."

"And I told you Yes?"

"In your sleep, age three."

"Did you listen?" Hutch said.

"Obey, you mean?" Rob stopped in his tracks.

Since Hutch could not see him and was one step ahead, he walked on a few yards and came to a block. His foot struck a low wall; he bent and groped at it. This afternoon's jetty. He looked back for Rob.

"No I didn't," Rob said.

"Step here," Hutch said.

"We'd better head back."

"We can sleep late tomorrow. Step here please, Rob."

Rob went toward the voice and blundered into Hutch.

Hutch took his father's left arm and pulled him one way. "We can sit up here. There's a good dry place. I was here this afternoon."

Rob accepted the lead and they went up the beach to the low dry dune—the sharp dune grass—till they stood still, touching, in what seemed a bowl. Hutch pulled Rob down and they both lay flat on their backs looking up, both hunting lights in a sky that seemed cloudless but was also unbroken.

Hutch said "Why not?"

Rob was lost. "Not what?"

"Your promise, why you broke it."

Rob lay still awhile. "You are changing tack. I was telling something else, the story of Goshen."

Hutch said "All right."

Rob thought, then laughed. "It's all one story. It'll answer all your questions. I broke my promise from the time you were two, long before I asked you, by needing human touch and finding it in places that shamed me to drink. I was drunk when I asked you, more than half-gone beside you. You weren't enough, Son, though you tried to be. I had a taste for human touch, had it from the night I finished high school; and no young child, even one as kind as you, could help me ease that. This is nothing very strange or scarce at least, common as trees. You'll come to see that."

Hutch said "I don't yet"; but he also laughed and recited Rena's universal answer to *common*—Acts 10:15, " 'What God hath cleansed, *that* call not thou common.' "

"I don't," Rob said. "They were mostly good people, a girl at the school, an old friend of mine, the odd cheerful stranger. But I'd made that promise; and there you were to prove it, to warn me and shame me. So I shunted back and forth for a year or so between weeks of honoring you and Rachel's memory and backsliding weekends of gorging and puking. Grainger kept it from you very well, I think. I would stay out until I could come home calm; he would say I was working and take you to Forrest's, and Polly would feed you."

Hutch said "I don't remember."

"Oh somewhere you do; I knew you would and I still couldn't stop. Then I lost my job."

"Did they punish the girl?"

"She wasn't the cause; they never knew about her. No I started missing work—Mondays, Mondays and Tuesdays. It nearly killed Forrest or so I thought then. I guess it just embarrassed him; he'd spoken of me highly. He'd worked so neatly to keep his own life well out of their reach; and here I'd gone on show—I would drink on the job. So he didn't fight for me—I never could blame him—and we sold out in Richmond, took Grainger back to Bracey, and went on to Goshen: 1933."

"The time he said *Stay*, my Grandfather Hutchins."

"Yes. To you, not me."

"—The story you're telling."

"You and I went to Goshen in May. We'd been invited. Your Grandmother Hutchins had asked us for the summer ever since Rachel died, or for my vacation, and we'd never accepted. So when I was let go at James Institute, I wrote her and said we could come if she liked. I had made a new start in the mountains once before, my *only* start; I thought I might again. I hadn't been up there since Rachel's funeral and you'd never been. They might help; I was ready to slave, empty slopjars, anything. 1933 was miserable times for more men than me, even after Roosevelt—several dozen million men. We had two hundred dollars after selling all our stuff; everything but clothes and toys, a few souvenirs nobody else would want (though I tried to sell them, even pictures of Rachel), an electric fan. Well, we rested a day or two, eating and sleeping—the little I could sleep—and then I told your grandfather what our plight was. Half-told anyhow. I didn't give the reasons for me being fired but blamed it on the times. He said he was sorry and to let him know if you were ever in need, but he didn't offer any direct help or job. And I understood why; he was near-broke himself. Not a whole lot of people were seeking out a rest spot in Goshen, Virginia in those years then. He had cut back, no help in the kitchen but his wife and a white girl that came in to make beds and sweep; he did his own upkeep. And of course he dreaded us. We were signs of Rachel when he'd almost got her hidden. Dreaded me at least; you say he wanted you. Fair enough—I'd been the cause. But somehow I felt there was no place left; that if we couldn't stay there, we might as well die."

"Kill us, you mean?"

"No. Yes maybe I did. I'm pretty sure I did, just driving those roads that I'd helped build and knew like my body; one swing of my hand, we'd have plunged a quarter-mile over sharp rocks and laurel. But that was no plan, no big intention. I still planned to live, and I saw you did. So I asked him point-blank if he knew of any work in the county nearby. He could have said No and sent us on then; but he gave me a list of three or four slim chances—a dry-goods store, the local welldigger, the local high school. And I set off to beg, though I skipped the school, knowing they would want references. A beautiful day; I can feel it right now, air cool and dry as powder, miles of yellow leaf light. I left you with him and checked all his leads and a few of my own. They can't even say No with grace in the mountains. The welldigger said, 'For eight dollars a month you can stand and watch me piss; that's as much contact with running water as I've had since Herbert Hoover dried up the world.' He meant I could pay *him*. By late that evening, I was dismal as a blind dog. I knew I was expected— suppertime was bearing down—but I walked half a mile to the west side of town and stopped by the river. There are bad rapids there, rocks the size of whole houses. I was not thinking clearly, though I hadn't drunk for days. I could think of rest though; and it seemed a simple reach, just to grasp out and hold it. Or to fall down and cut myself to ragged pieces. You'd have never had to see me, they'd have raised you well as I, you were just as much theirs. Then I saw a colored boy walking slowly toward me, maybe younger than you are now, maybe twelve. He was barefoot and wearing the rags of rags, and he didn't want to cross the little bridge with me on it. He just stood and waited on the far side, looking. So I told him, 'Come on. I won't throw you in'; and he came on past me. I thought I recognized him, not him but something in him. I said—he was moving—'Have you got a name?' and he said 'Fitts Simmons.' I said, 'Do you know a colored girl named Della Simmons?' —'My auntie,' he said. I asked him did he know where she was that day."

Hutch said "Your old friend?"

"From my first time in Goshen."

"Was she there?"

"Slow down. The boy said 'No sir.' I said 'What about yesterday?' —'No sir' again. I said, 'I'm her oldest friend; I've come here to see her.' The boy said 'Too late.' "

"She was dead," Hutch said.

"So I thought. And I thought if Della was dead that would just about do it—clear my own way to go (not that I'd thought of her twice in eight years). But I asked him and he said she had been there to visit just a few days before and had gone back to Philly; he made it sound like Heaven not the tailside of torment. So I asked him was he heading to his house right then and could I come with him? He said, 'Who you know at my house but me and Della?' I said 'Nobody' so he said 'Come on.' It was just a short distance."

"Was she really not there?"

"If she was, they had her hid. No she'd gone to Philadelphia the day we came to Goshen."

"Running from us?" Hutch said.

"I doubt it; even asked in a roundabout way. It seemed she'd intended from the first to leave then, though the boy's mother did say she'd heard we were in town. She was some distant cousin of Della's, strange to me. Said she'd seen me years before; said she served at our wedding which I think was a lie. Anyhow she was ready to sit and answer questions; so we sat on her shaky porch and talked past dark. She was older than Della; the boy was her grandchild. She seemed to have memories of Della and me, little hints Della gave her; but she used them very gently, just suggested Della might come and work for us now since we were alone. She had known Rachel well, said she pitied you and me. Said Della was a day-maid in cold Pennsylvania, had still never married or had any children but claimed she was happy. Asked how happy was I. I told her fairly plainly—"

"And she gave you some liquor."

Rob stopped and rolled over to his side, toward Hutch. By then his eyes had widened or some light had risen; he could see the boy's shape. He bent over the face; it seemed to be smiling. "Are you smiling?" Rob said.

"Not to speak of, no sir."

"Well, don't yet," Rob said. "It'd be a little early; this gets even sadder."

"Tell on," Hutch said. "I'm ready as ever."

Rob also grinned. "It helped me a lot. It has always helped me to sit down with Negroes and smell their strangeness, let them bleed me with questions. They are either much worse off or so much better—I've never known which—that they soothe me at once."

"They are spirits," Hutch said, "—like angels here to guard us."

"I didn't claim *that*."

"Grainger does," Hutch said.

"When?"

"A week or so ago. We were listening to the news in his house late at night; and the man read a piece about Negroes in the war—how many had enlisted and what they were doing: building bridges, cooking meals. Grainger shut the man off in the midst of a sentence and said, 'You remember'—and pointed at me—'They are guarding people's lives, which is God's plan for em. They are spirits bringing word. You listen to a nigger if he ever bring you word.' "

Rob waited. "Grainger's aging, going hard like Sylvie. But that one in Goshen, Della's cousin, soothed me down. And I went to the Hutchins' after dark, still alive and sober as tonight, still jobless and broke but intending to live and to stay on there as long as they'd have us till I found us a place."

Hutch said, "I don't remember; I must have been asleep."

"You were watching," Rob said. "It happened in the kitchen. When I got there your grandmother met me, distraught. It was later than I knew, nearly half past nine; and you had been crying for me ever since dark, kept asking was I dead? (you had heard the word from Grainger—that was some of his *word*; had you scared you were orphaned). They had tried everything they knew and failed to calm you; so your grandfather had gone out, hunting me down. I calmed you, no trouble; and told Mrs. Hutchins that I'd been in the country and had had a flat tire. We three were eating supper in the kitchen when he came. He had found my car parked in town and asked questions; somebody told him they had seen me on the bridge before dark with Fitts Simmons, and he'd gone there to check. Must have passed me walking back, but neither of us noticed. He had known of Della's visit and thought that I had; thought I'd come there to see her and had met her several times in the previous days (he had just asked her cousin if she'd seen me at all, not for any details). So with you in the high chair, all spotty at my elbow, he let us both have it. I was nothing but a nigger-loving, ass-sniffing drunk who with your help had killed all he loved in the world. I didn't want to scare you two times in a day; so I asked him if I could just finish my supper—he had not said to leave; I doubt he meant us to. He walked out in silence and sat on the porch. She apologized to us, said she hoped I understood what Rachel meant to him and how sad he'd been. I told her I understood every single feeling any human ever had (I had had it before him); what troubled me was not understanding but excusing."

"How soon did we leave?"

"Soon as I got us packed. I finished my supper and took you upstairs and put you in pajamas and folded our things. When we got back down to the foot of the steps, she was waiting there for us with food in one hand and a lamp in the other; they didn't have lights. She whispered 'Step here' and led us back a little to the foot of the hall, the shut door of his room. I said, 'No ma'm, I won't speak to him'; and she whispered again, 'He is still on the porch.' Then she opened the door and pulled us in. He had moved in there alone before I knew Rachel, but I'd never passed the door. It was big and pitch-dark except for her lamp. She went toward a corner; and we followed her over through a smell thick as grease—old cloth, old medicine, all clean and dry as sand. Where she stopped was a dresser with a dark high mirror and a brown marble top. He had made a little shrine—several pictures of Rachel, her ivory comb, a petrified flower (most likely from her grave), a book she had used (*Evangeline*, her favorite). Mrs. Hutchins never spoke, never touched a single object but held the lamp steady. So I turned and got us out."

"Did we tell him goodbye?" Hutch said.

"Just the word. He was on the porch as she'd said, at the corner; so he saw us coming out. She was helping with the luggage; he didn't lift a finger. When I'd got us all ready and told her goodbye—she was dry-eyed but worried; she said she would write and that things would calm down—I called out to him, 'We thank you, Mr. Hutchins' and he said 'Goodbye.' I think you may have waved; you were very strong on waving."

Hutch waited awhile, then said "I don't remember."

"What?"

"None of it really. But his room—that's funny. You'd think I'd have kept that, remembered that much."

"You do," Rob said. "You did once at least."

"When?"

"A year or two later. I was still in Fontaine, still working for Kennerly, eating his meanness. I came home one evening from estimating timber. I was studded with ticks—always fascinated you; I would strip and let you count them, but you'd never touch one—and Rena had gone down to get the scalding water (I would sit in the tub, she would pour water on me, ticks would float like corks). I was still upstairs and you were still with me, counting—thirty-some was the record—and then you said, 'Rob, I need a picture of Rachel.' You'd never asked to see her; of course I had pictures, but I kept them wrapped up—they were still too painful. I said 'Why, Son?' and you said, 'For a show. I can make a penny-show like the one we saw of Rachel!' Somebody had made you a penny-show that spring, Sylvie maybe; dug a cradle in the ground and lined it with flowers, put a toy or two in it, laid a pane of glass on it, and hid it under dirt. For a penny you would sweep it clean and show your little treasure. You'd remembered pretty clearly up till then at least."

Hutch was silent.

"There are several pictures of her—Rena's got some, even Grainger; I have got one in our room in my grip right now. You can have it any time. I was trying just to spare you."

Hutch said, "All right, sir. Thank you. No real hurry though." Then he sat up slowly to face the black water. It was in a brief trough of calm, quiet as a pond; but it still gave a steady glow of light to eyes as open to the night as Hutch's now. Its horizon showed, a line curved downward at the ends like brooding wings. Day was far ahead though, still six or seven hours (Albert fighting now in daylight or dead or buried). Rob had stayed flat beside him; they had not touched since lying here. Hutch clasped his own hands. "You mentioned a bridge."

"When?"

"In speaking of Della. You called her a bridge."

Rob thought back to there. "Not Della herself but the welcome she offered."

"Letting you touch her?"

"It's a good deal more than that; it's all in your mind or eighty percent." He tried to see Hutch. "You know that by now."

"Maybe so," Hutch said. But he held the reins closely. "You also broke the promise after I was born and lived."

"I said I did, yes."

"Even after asking me."

"Hutch, by then I was a grown man scrambling to live. You were still a plain infant."

"I'm not blaming," Hutch said, "—not now, just asking. This is my first chance."

Rob knew that it was and waited in place.

"I mainly need to see how you've lasted; lasting worries *me* now. You've mentioned these bridges. They're years ahead of me if I want them at all."

"Son, I said they were bridges; not the only road."

"Name some others."

"People's jobs; many people live to work—my father, Rena's garden, Sylvie standing at the stove. That has been my great lack; I can see that now, twenty years too late. Or protecting a home with your wife and children in it and a good tin roof. Or comforting your parents when they get toward the end. Or hunting fat quail."

"You've lacked all of those."

Rob waited. "Yes I have."

"I thought you had *me*," Hutch said. "All this time. I thought I was standing in my room like a magnet, or reading at school or back in the woods, to hold you true and draw you to me. I thought you wanted that, thought you told me you did when you left me at Eva's."

Rob said, "I did. Son, it's taken this long. Raleigh seems close to you, two hours away; but I've had ten years of my life to wade through. I may be ready now; I told you that and you turned it down flat."

"No sir," Hutch said. "You are not being fair. You didn't say *me*; you said Fontaine, a house holding Grainger and Min Tharrington. If I've been the bridge to that, it wasn't what I meant—not to mention what I hoped."

Rob said, "I know that. But you've been a child, Hutch. What you hoped were child's hopes, you and me on a kind of safe boat in warm water. I've had my share of child's hopes all my life. I've tried to tell you that; they have damn nearly choked me. They're the only hopes that *are*. So I've tried to root them out. Now I'm trying just to live, one foot before the other. And I've asked you to help me. I've asked to help you."

"But with Min looking on. She has been the main bridge."

"Far from it," Rob said. "More the other way round. I have borne Min up since she was your age. She chose to love me when we were both children just for reasons of her own. I used her like dirt; she was none of my need. She tried to go her own way; I went off with Rachel. You know all that. Then when we were back at Mother's—'33, '34—and me a cowed dog, Min took her last hope and kept me close company the whole of both summers. I was very grateful to her—thanks will bind you to people more strongly than love—and I got used to her, her gentle steady help."

"Like Della? Della's help?"

Rob waited that out. "Min is still living, Hutch. We could hurt her past healing, just by talking here tonight. I can say this much; we never harmed a soul, Min and I, in anything."

Hutch said, "I think there were souls you never asked."

Rob could not answer that.

And Hutch had nothing else, no question, no blame. He lay back again in the sand and was still; and in three or four minutes, the long weight of day had pressed him to sleep. He breathed, slow and high, mouth open to the world (another Mayfield trait).

Rob also was still and nearly exhausted but calmer than he'd been since before Forrest's death. His only conscious worry, no worry at all, was that now they must stand and walk all the dark way back to their beds. Something brushed his right arm, surely Hutch. He raised slightly and bent toward Hutch—no, sleep: the slow pendulum of rest devoured with the urgency of hunger. Rob brushed his touched arm. A sand crab maybe? They were buried in night, as native to here as any blind crawler; but one another's own, one another's only mate in the swarm of strange feeders. Rob bent farther down till Hutch's breath brushed him, their only touch; and he said, half-whisper, "I am asking you now."

Hutch gave no response.

"I'm asking you to tell me."

The warm breath paused an instant, caught like a cough. Then with no other sign that he'd waked, he said "I will."

"What now?—you and me."

A sizable wait with no sound of breathing. Then Hutch, clear and natural—"We would go on from here, never go back home; but we'd let them know. We would stop first in Goshen. You could keep yourself hid; but I would see my grandfather, see Rachel's grave. I owe myself that; I owe her that. I could pay what I owe or show I meant to try—a good kind life. Then I'd come back to you; and we would go on farther up in the mountains till we came to a town that we'd neither one seen and where nobody knew us. We could change these names. You could get a job there; why would you need a job? We could sell what we brought and rent an old house and grow our own garden. We could watch each other, really watch all day. I would learn a good deal."

Rob said "What about night?"

"First, we'd be tired by night. But with any strength left, we could take long walks, steep climbs over rocks high up to clear air. There are more planets there; you can see more planets, make guesses about them. We would sleep out a lot." Hutch stopped and thought. "It would be like that whole years at a time."

"War and sickness?" Rob said.

"We'd take them if they came; but we'd both be healthy, and I doubt there'd be a war, not after this one's over, maybe fifty more years. We could both die there."

"Our people?" Rob said.

"They've lasted through worse. They would barely miss a day, Grandmother and Rena. I know Sylvie wouldn't; she would feel simplified.

Grainger might miss us; but then he might not—Gracie might come back, and he'd have her to tend." That seemed the whole vision; Hutch offered no more.

And Rob knew of no questions. He lay back for one last time before rising, the forced walk to bed. But he said "What for?"

"Sir?"

"What would it be for? Why would we do that? What would we be winning?"

Hutch waited through the break of three slow waves. "The thing we want."

Rob quickly thought "What?" again but held it, didn't say it. He knew that he knew. He said "Yes sir."

Hutch was uphill from him by maybe a foot. He rolled down silently and stopped against Rob. Then he raised himself on straight arms and moved above Rob. Then he lay down on him full-length, full-weight, the way Rob had lain on him many times—most recently a day ago at Eva's in their room: the room where Rachel and Rob had made him, in which he had learned (been given by them, warm funnels of the past) what he knew so clearly of hunt and capture, hunger and food, work and sleep.

Rob bore him gladly for longer than he knew—not thinking of Hutch, who seemed all safe, or of Min still waiting for simple word, or of Eva, Rena, Grainger, his dead father, Polly, his own vague future or of mute helpful Della with her accurate dreams but of Sylvie's Albert in the cold Norman dawn (maybe colder himself, all word now delivered) and of Flora's Bo still poised in Beechleaf for the death Jesus willed him. They did seem spirits, though stout, dark, and glistening with earthly sweat, emerging toward him and his growing son with word of strength, sufficient pardon, the promise of hope. Rob prayed his prayer for them.

The long way back, they were all but silent, knowing nothing was cured—nothing planned or settled—but already partly rested and pleased.

JUNE 10-13, 1944

Against Polly's protests, Rob had helped her clear supper and sat in the hot kitchen now while she scraped up and drew her dishwater. It was well past nine. He and Hutch had come at seven from their two days of looking (Yorktown, Williamsburg, Jamestown); and Hutch had gone straight up from table to bed, suddenly exhausted from newness and the sun. Rob was also tired—hours of poking round ruins and reconstructions, dead-weight on his feet—but as often in the past, the air off Polly trimmed his strength to attention, curiosity. Still he waited in silence, not wanting to quiz her on their multitude of problems. Let her find their way and show it.

She washed all the glasses before she spoke. "I hadn't heard that much about Pocahontas since Grainger was young. He was hipped on her somehow; and we never heard the end, till he left at least."

Rob said, "He still is and has passed it on to Hutch; Hutch can tell you everything about her down to her height."

Polly washed on awhile. Then she said, "Wonder why. I've always kind of blamed her."

"How's that?"

"For her life. Here she was, this pretty child—great king for a father, woods as far as you could walk, deer as tame as house plants—and she left her own people and sold it all away to a crowd of English crooks that turned it into this." She gestured round widely with her wet left hand—the space beside her.

Rob smiled. "But for *love*. It was love, Miss Polly. We were founded on love."

Again she took her time. "Then we ought to beg pardon and give it all back, call the deer in and say 'Graze here in peace' and go drown in the James."

"The James wouldn't hold us."

"Then the blue ocean would. It's a few miles east."

Rob studied her back, then laughed. "Good night!"

She looked round to face him. "I'm serious," she said. "It *must* have been for love, some pale white fool; and see where it got her (homesick in cold England, smallpox at twenty)—see where it got us." She waved round a second time as if this kitchen where she'd lived since a girl, a room only some one hundred years old, were the ruined world.

Rob did not try to answer.

So she turned to work. "I'm sorry," she said. "I meant to be cheerful; I promised myself I would meet you, all smiles. It's just that I've had time to study here lately—oh I've had it all my life; any woman minus children has a good deal of time—and all I can see is what a waste people make, choosing up like they do."

"Pocahontas or me? Are you speaking of me?" Rob spoke in earnest now.

"Yes both," Polly said, "but mainly Polly Drewry, Miss Margaret Jane Drewry."

"Why?"

She didn't turn again but she said, "You've got eyes. I had my own place that my mother died to give me; I could have stayed there."

Rob barely understood. "Washington, you mean?"

Polly nodded. "But I sold it, gave it up that easy"; she snapped a wet thumb.

"Now you've got this place."

"I haven't, no."

"I wrote you, Polly, and I told you in April; nothing I or Hattie or Hutch could ever do will half-repay all your goodness to Father."

"I came here before him."

Rob said, "I know that. It's part of our debt."

"How much do you know?"

"Ma'm?"

"You say 'I know that.' Just say what you know."

"—That you worked here for Grandfather, nursed him at the end; that you made a home for Forrest when Mother turned on him, helped him have his good life."

She had turned to hear that, her washing half-done. Now she drew her hands from water, carefully dried them, came to the table, and sat beside him. Through all that followed she cupped a salt cellar in her long red hands and made little swirls in the salt with a finger, eating the white grains in moments of pause. "Is that what you know? Be honest now."

Rob said "Yes"—it virtually was; all else had been guess. "You told me that first time I ever came here."

"There's a little more," she said. She watched her own hands, did not face him (he watched the clean crown of her head, still chestnut though striped with gray). "I started years ago, well before you were born. I came here from home for what I figured was love. It may have been that. You never saw Rob. Even sick, he was a magnet—to me anyhow (and a good many others; all before me, I can brag). And he may have loved me. He died there beside me in the old store room"; she pointed behind her. "That was our bedroom. Well, for what *that* meant; you can die in the street. What I'm sure of—he was grateful. Then your father came to get him, take care of the funeral. I mentioned that to you, as you say, the first time. I think I told you Forrest had his job here already; that wasn't quite true. He got it right then, morning after the funeral, February twenty-fourth, 1905. I had been here with Rob by myself three days—him lying in his bed; I kept the fire low—so you can imagine I was nearly worn out when Forrest turned up and made the arrangements. A very small funeral, just us and the preacher and one old stranger. Forrest had wanted to put it in the paper; but I warned him against it, knowing Rob had debts and a few ill-wishers who might seize the chance. Still this fellow turned up, short and red as a stove (and the grave all but frozen). We didn't speak to him, but he stood through the service; then he came up to me and smiled and was crying. He said 'Do you know me?' I said 'No sir.' He said, 'I am Willie Ayscue, Rob's fireman from the railroad days when we used to come to Bracey, your mother's hotel. I knew you from the start, same time as he did; I knew you would last him.' I didn't understand, I honestly didn't; but Forrest did and took over then, thanked the old fellow kindly (he'd been asked by the preacher as Rob's oldest friend; they had been boys together). He had thought I was Anna, Rob's wife, your grandmother; she'd been dead something like twenty years by then. I was eighteen myself, though I did look older. When we got back here, I cooked Forrest a meal; and right at this table, he looked up and said, 'If I come here for good, how long could you stay?' —'Well, for good,' I said; and it turned out I did. Till now anyway."

"No for good," Rob said.

Polly looked up at last and managed to smile. "I thank you," she said. "You've been more than kind. In all these years you've treated me like I was right to be here. But Rob, I'm not begging a roof for my age."

"I know that," he said. "You've got it, always had it. Hatt will say that too once I've had a chance to see her."

Polly nodded. "I have no doubt she will, and I'm grateful to all, but I doubt I can stay."

"Why?"

She searched his face. "Have you thought about this? Rob, think about this—I was here forty years with two men who saw that, however I *felt*, I never once *lacked*. I've taken in sewing sometime to stay busy, a lot since April; but I've never spent three seconds worrying for money. Now that has to start."

"No it doesn't."

"It does." She was smiling but firm. "I'm fifty-eight now; I could live thirty years. I could outlive you and Hutch and Grainger; my dad lived to eighty-six, and I'm much like him. These are hard times, I know, for you and most men; and even if they weren't, I couldn't draw on you—not yet anyhow, not till I'm blind and down."

Rob said, "It's my pleasure to do what I can."

"Don't tell yourself that till you've done it for years. I know what I'm saying, and you don't yet; *pleasure*'s not the word. No if I'm lucky I'll keep my strength for fifteen years or so, my working strength. So I plan to be a nurse, just a practical nurse, somebody's companion. People still need those and it answers my needs, but it also means I won't need a house. I'll either live in with the people I nurse or get a small place—one room suits me nicely; I like walls close round me."

Rob said "What's left in Washington?"

"Nothing, not a hair. The U.S. Government. By the time Dad died, he was on public pension (and the check Forrest sent him, fifteen dollars a month) so no that's out."

"Come to me and Hutch." Rob had not planned to say it and at once chilled slightly but kept it from showing.

Polly laughed. "Three of us in one room in Raleigh?"

"I've got to leave Raleigh. I wrote you that."

"Can you go to Fontaine? You mentioned work there."

"I can *go* there, I guess. I looked into that; the shop job was open." He was starting to tell her of Forrest's plea to Thorne but wondered if the premonition of death had issued in similar precautions for Polly, plans for her future. No sign it had, not to Rob anyhow; so he held that back. "Can I stay there though? Mother's there in full sail, Aunt Rena gazing at me, Grainger grudging me breath. Hutch is begging to leave, says I dumped him down there and left for my fun. You know how much fun—"

"Where is Min in this?" Polly said, "—anywhere?"

"Very much in the middle." Then he knew that was wrong. Min was out at the rim where he'd posted her, to wait his call. "That's another thing," he said. "I've got to decide. Min has been good to me through thick and thin, mainly thin; and I've used what she had. It's eased me at times; but it's harmed me too, and now I must tell her to come for good or go."

"How has she harmed you? I can't picture that."

"She has kept Rachel's memory raw, never healed."

"How? I thought Min was gentle the time I met her."

"She is," Rob said. "She's as good a soul as you." In fourteen years he had told only Grainger of his meeting with Min in a Richmond hotel just before Rachel's death—Grainger and, this week, Flora's cracked Bo. He could tell Polly now, of all living women, and bear her quick pardon;

she would pardon it surely, brush it off with a hand that had brushed things as heavy a far safe distance. When he looked up to tell her, she was facing him though, upright, waiting calmly. Her broad worn face—still damp from work, still burning in her flat seamed cheeks with the life that had forced her this far through the shames she had eaten and would haul her far onward—her face crushed his heart. She was still here waiting, still ready to serve. How could any man have borne to share space with her, to see each day—and offend—that face, with its grave health and hopes as fragile as shell (but daily reborn)? He said, "Polly, listen. I was not made for life, not the life people want."

Polly smiled. "You fooled me."

"Really. Listen. I wasn't. I may have known it always, but now I can see it."

"What life do people want?"

Rob laughed in protection. "The one you've had; you and Forrest, forty years."

Her smile survived but she said "God help them." When Rob didn't answer she said, "No I guess it was some above average; I try to think that. What do you mean you don't want it?"

"I want it, yes Jesus. No I meant I couldn't take it. Something's set wrong somewhere in my training or blood; it *costs* me too much. I can sit here with you, see you lonely and strong, know you've had a full life; but you know what I feel?—like running forever, like standing up here and bolting through that door and running through night and day till somewhere I reach a place as bare as my hand, not a person left to face me. You and Hutch, my mother's kin, Aunt Hatt, Grainger, Gracie—Hell, children in the road: I can hardly bear to see you. I have got a heart as tender as a baby's blue eye—"

"No you're scared," Polly said.

"—It must have come from Forrest; Eva's still as strong as you."

"No it didn't," Polly said. "He could bear anything. He bore, as you say, living here forty years and letting me serve him. He bore his own death—knowing of it far ahead; the doctor said so—and never warned me, never made one arrangement to see me through this. He was strong all right."

"And he knew you were. He didn't want to grieve you with maybe false warnings. He knew you could stand anything that happened, and he knew I would see you were honored and thanked."

"By being left high and dry alone in this house? I know you mean well, Rob; but that is plain torture. You can kill me tonight if that's your plan."

"No'm, it's not." He smiled.

"Well, I've told you mine. Once you've gone through his papers and made your arrangements, for the house and all—I'll gladly help with

that—then I mean to start over. A little place, a job. I may have a life yet."
She stood at the end of that and went to the sink. She was well into
finishing her dishes before Rob spoke again.

"You didn't find a will then or any instructions?" At the funeral he
had been so stunned by regret that when Polly had said, "Will you look
through his papers?" he had said, "Please let me just wait till June; it will
wait till then." But seeing her face, he had opened Forrest's desk and
checked the obvious places—a great many rollbooks, a notebook of his
poems, a lifetime of letters (or the ones he had saved, none of them from
Eva); no sign of a will or a letter of wishes.

Polly said, "You saw the desk. I haven't opened that; that was his one
place. I have checked his bureau, since I always stacked his clothes, and the
shelf in his wardrobe. I searched my own room from ceiling to floor; he
would sometimes leave me notes I would find days later, little gratitudes
for things. But no not a word." She dried the last skillet; then she turned
in place. "He didn't write to you?—any warning, I mean."

"No ma'm, just the news, the present daily news."

"I've wondered this," she said. "I may be foolish. Do you think he
wrote to Grainger?"

"I doubt it," Rob said. "He never wrote to Grainger, maybe sometimes at Christmas. Why would you think that?"

"Forrest loved him," Polly said. "He thought he was responsible for
Grainger somehow. He encouraged Grainger as you well know; then
because of me, he dropped him. So he brooded ever after."

"I never really knew the whole story of that—Grainger came here
with Forrest in 1905?"

"And stayed six months, helping fix up the house. He had his own
room, your grandfather's room. Forrest wouldn't sleep there but stayed in
the study then and moved me upstairs. He got a little spending money,
bought himself books; and when fall came and Forrest started teaching
Negro classes, Grainger'd go out and sit through every word he said. But he
never liked me—Grainger, I mean. I had addled his dream. He thought he
had found a real gold mine in Forrest, a kind white father or brother or
something that would need him forever and give him a home."

"I doubt he wanted money."

"I don't mean he did. By *gold* I meant care, just care. All *I* wanted.
Before long he saw I was cared for too, and he turned on me."

Rob said "How?"

"Oh at Christmas. I have always dreaded Christmas. You get too
expectant; it never lives up or *you* never do. Anyhow it was Forrest's first
Christmas here, my first since Rob died; we were both a little sad and felt
we needed calm (he had told your Aunt Hatt he would come there for
New Year). So well ahead of time, he called Grainger in and said he knew
Grainger was missing his people and should see them for Christmas—

either make the trip to Bracey to his old ancestor or all the way to Maine. Forrest offered him the ticket; he refused it right off, saying he had a home and Maine was too cold. Forrest meant to stop there, but I guess I must have pressed him. He had been rude to me since the day he came; treated *me* like the brown one (I washed his underclothes the first week or so till I said I just couldn't, and Forrest took them out to a woman at the school). He barely spoke to me, but he showed what he thought—they are first-rate *show-ers*—sitting round with that ring. You know about that?"

"Grainger's ring?"

"*Your* ring by all natural rights. Yours and Hutch's beyond you. It was your Grandmother Mayfield's wedding band. She had left it to Forrest. When Forrest found his father, he brought him the ring—some idea of his he had dreamed in a poem—but Rob wouldn't have it; said give it to Grainger. You know he was joking; but never trust Forrest to recognize a joke. He gave it to Grainger, who wore it like a leech. Anyhow Forrest told him he would have to leave for Christmas, that I needed a rest; so Grainger chose Bracey (he would never go to Maine; once he left he couldn't bear to think he had a real father who was not Forrest Mayfield). I packed him a lunch, and Forrest took him to the station. When they got to the colored cars and Forrest said goodbye, Grainger wouldn't shake his hand. He stepped back and took off the ring and held it out. Forrest asked him why was that. He said, 'For Miss Polly. She think it's hers.' I had never said one word about that ring to Grainger—or God. Forrest said, 'It's not hers'—he told me all this (his famous soft heart)—'I gave it to you.' Grainger still held it out; so Forrest said, 'Just throw it on the tracks yonder then.' That brought him to his senses, and he put it in his pocket. If he wore it after that, I at least never saw it; never saw him though. I never saw him again till you brought him back; he stayed in Bracey, pouting. When I saw that ring, it was on Gracie's hand. I guessed it at once, but I didn't ask Forrest. I waited till a day when I was over helping Rachel upholster a stool, and Gracie stepped in once when Rachel stepped out. I said to her, 'Gracie, I admire your ring.' —'Me too,' she said. —'It looks like an old one' (it was broad and thick, heavy). Gracie said, 'Bound to be. It come from Old Misery,' which I knew meant Grainger. She left that month, ring and all, last time."

Rob said, "There are lots of broad bands in the world."

Polly said, "I know that." She smiled. "I've noticed that. But if you ever see Gracie Walters again, you tell her to let you see hers. Engraved inside it will say 'Anna Goodwin from Rob Mayfield' not 'Gracie from Grainger.' "

Rob was exhausted; the day fell on him. He pushed back his chair and braced himself to rise. "I won't ever see her, and Grainger won't either."

Polly came to the table and wiped it with a rag. "I saw her last week."

"Where?"

"Here. This room. I see her every year or so. She comes back to Richmond; some kin of hers here over past the old icehouse, a cousin, Gladys Fishel. She begs a day's work, and I try to give it to her if Forrest is at school." Polly spread her rag before her and pressed it with her palms, then folded it neatly as dry Irish linen. She'd done it ten thousand times in this house. "It helps with her wine. I tell her the news, what little I know. She never mentions Grainger—just Rachel, you, Hutch. She asks for all of you."

Rob said, "Did you tell her we'd be here now?"

"No I didn't, didn't know."

Rob nodded. "Thank God."

Polly said, "You're dropping. Let me turn down your bed."

Rob said "Oh yes."

2

ROB stood at Forrest's desk while Polly turned back the fresh sheets of the cot.

"Rob, you're welcome to *my* room. I can sleep here fine; this is good for my back." She thumped the felt mattress.

"No ma'm," Rob said. "This will be old times. I slept here the first time I found this house." He saw in the quick assurance of her hands, folding, smoothing—even now this late—the willing skills of a life at work in its only home, in actual harness. To what? And why? He said, "Polly, why are you doing this?"

She didn't look back. "Doing what?"

"Caring for me; big supper, this bed."

"I work here," she said; but her voice was pleasant.

"I'm serious," he said.

She stood and looked toward him. "Rob, are you drinking?"

"No ma'm."

"Are you sick?"

"No I'm curious," he said.

"What about?"

"What I asked you," he said. "Do you really care if I live or die?"

She sat on the edge of the bed, at the foot. "I don't understand what you're after, Rob."

He sat on the desk by the picture of Eva and himself age five. "Just this," he said. "I would really like to know. Why would any grown human, any crawling child, spend a minute on me? Don't answer with praise; I can't use that. Say truthfully why you can sit here with me."

"I've known you twenty years. Why not?" Polly said.

"Because I only amount to this"—he rubbed his chest with his flat right hand—"a nice-hearted former boy (except if you cross him) who had a good face till his nature showed through it some ten years ago, whose mind and talents are little over average, who has never propped any other human ten yards on their way through life since he can't be leaned on (he drinks under pressure, so has lost three jobs of the four he has held, not counting family handouts) and has come up now at forty years old with less good credit on *anybody's* books, Lord Jesus included, than most drunk Negroes with a long razor scar laid out in the road come Sunday dawn."

Polly smiled quite broadly.

"That's true," Rob said. "A fair description."

"Maybe so," she said. "I won't dispute you." Her smile didn't fade.

"What's funny?"

"Not much."

"You're grinning," Rob said.

"No I'm answering you."

"Then say it," Rob said. "I won't guess right."

She said it to the white summer quilt she sat on, unable to face him. "You're the thing that's left of what I had."

3

THE next morning, Sunday, Rob and Hutch slept late; ate a big long breakfast; then in early afternoon set out to see Richmond, ending up downriver at James Institute. School was out for the summer; so they saw nobody whom Rob remembered but went to Forrest's office (Rob had always had a key) and checked his desk there—only neat piles of good student-work from past years and more class-rolls back to 1905 (several hundred Negro boys, some now old men whom he'd read poems at—had they called him a fool; and if so, did they still? had he known or cared?). There were some good books, one box full maybe, and his white bust of Byron. They would come for them later, give the rest to the school. Hutch asked for the Byron.

Then they went back to Polly, ate a light early supper, and took her downtown to see *Cabin in the Sky*. Then they bought ice-cream cones and window-shopped awhile before heading home to help Polly wash the cold dishes which she'd dreaded to leave. They listened to the nine o'clock radio news—Germans claimed to have captured fifteen hundred Allies—and turned in early. Rob would start his chores on Monday.

It rained about eleven which cooled the house nicely; and Rob was able to slide under then, a deeper sleep than any he'd been given in months, a slow dark stroking through cool thick waters. Toward dawn he dreamed this. He was walking through a field near the ocean in France. There was high summer grass that reached to his waist and made him feel safe, though the day was still and the war itself seemed a distant dream from which he'd escaped by skill and strength. He had a destination or his body did. It bore him straight forward; he didn't think *to where?* He was not hungry, not thirsty; clothes were clean; he did not need sleep. A woods loomed ahead, cool shade. He went toward it. A girl came out and started to him through the grass. At first he'd never seen her; then her skin and hair resolved—Della, still coming toward him. He stopped; Della stopped maybe six feet away. He told her her name; she nodded agreement. "You safe here?" he said. She nodded she was, then held up her left hand—"I got my protection. My ring you give me." He saw the gold band, freshly cleaned, on her finger and felt that it had some right to be there; but he said to himself, "I gave you nothing; you'll die before night." The war was all round them.

4

AT ten, after breakfast, he saw Hutch to the bus stop for a day in town— the Confederate museum, Hollywood cemetery, another show, the stores. Then he came back and shaved and was ready to work through Forrest's desk when Polly brought the mail, one for Hutch from Grainger, one for Rob from Min. He let Polly go, then sat at the desk to read it.

June 10, 1944

Dear Rob,
 You didn't believe me. I knew you wouldn't. You were wrong not to, this time anyway. I meant every word and have meant them some months now, longer than I realized. I can't wait, no (and it's can't not won't). I won't lie either; there is no other person or thing in the wings. There is just my long-delayed understanding that what I've been to you has been hardly unique and that, however much I believe you when you thank me, I know that any number of women could have done the same service and got the same pay.
 I'm humiliated, Rob. Or I've seen this spring, more clearly each day since your father's death and our trip to the funeral, that I've been humiliated most of my life. I'm not blaming you; I volunteered for it. (If you want a little blame, take thirty percent.) All I hope you can do now is try to understand that it's fairly bleak for a woman near forty to look back and see that the force of her life has been pressed against someone who really

didn't want that force at all, however he took it. I also feel foolish. Just
understand that please.

I understand it all. *That is my worst trait; I see all sides. I know that*
your own life has had its troubles, not all of your making; and I well
comprehend your present resolve to concentrate on Hutch and see him
through the slow woes of adolescence. But I also know how Hutch resents
me, and I see why clearly. He would not let us be, even if you were
ready.

Someday you may be; you are still saying that. But remember, Min's
not. And honor that please. Just leave Min alone for a long time to come.
Maybe years from now we could sit on a porch and talk it through again—
weigh it one more time, find it wanting once more—but for now I mean to
rest, just do my job and eat well, sleep long nights, and forget what a small
part I played after all in this story you seem to be telling yourself called
Rob Mayfield.

We will no doubt collide in Fontaine or Raleigh; I don't plan to
dodge you. If you grin so will I.

> *Strongest good hopes, Rob, and thanks for*
> *what there was,*
>   *Min*

Regards to Miss Polly.

Rob thought he was relieved, consciously thought that he had not had
such a great weight lifted since his Grandfather Kendal's death years before.
He would answer her tonight, warm thanks and parting; then honor her
plea for silence and absence. A *simplification,* whatever else. He laid Min's
letter in the top of his suitcase, stood Hutch's on the mantel (and recalled
he'd forgot to give him Grainger's gift, the goldpiece—well, something for
tonight). Then he sat at Forrest's desk and began to search the drawers.

The letters had been carefully weeded and sorted into neat tied
bundles, by correspondent. None from anyone in Fontaine; even Hutch's
thank-you notes at Christmas and birthdays had been discarded, not a
trace of Grainger. A few from Rob which he could not bear to read but
identified by dates—the announcement of his wedding-plans, a note from
his honeymoon, the long tale of shame and promised reparation which
he'd written from Goshen when he and Hutch had gone there in 1933,
two or three from Raleigh in 1939 begging small loans when Hutch was
suffering asthma (the loans had come on payday by telegraph, but Eva had
paid the doctor), a card in '42 saying only "Cheer up! I am too old to
draft. Happy Father's Day from Rob." Then three sets from students—
one a dentist in Portsmouth, a Bristol undertaker, an insurance man from
Chatham: mostly writing once a year with their stiff news of births and
deaths, their rising incomes, their formulas of thanks (script and grammar

sliding steeply downhill with each year). Four large stacks from Hatt—surely none was missing: every penciled note pleading company, covering gifts (iced cakes mailed in tins, beaten biscuits, a ham once that streamed grease from Bracey to here). Only three from Polly—single thin letters: one to Forrest in Bracey in 1905, one to Goshen in November '25 (Rob's wedding), one c/o Stevens' Hotel in Asbury Park where he'd gone to a four-day Negro teachers' convention in August '29.

Rob could hear her overhead, the treadle of her sewing. He would take these to her; but lulled by her steady work and curious of her needs, he read the one to Goshen, nineteen years before.

November 27, 1925

Dear Forrest,

I doubt this will have time to even reach you but you said write so here I am. I am safe of course like I said I'd be but there was a little excitement this morning once you left. It was bright and dry still so about ten o'clock once I finished the sweeping, I rinsed a few clothes and was hanging them out when the Pittman girl came running down her steps and through your yard to ask could I come quick, her baby was going. You know he has had those hard convulsions, three in a year. I thought he was gone. He was laid out flat on the bare kitchen table with the cook holding on. Blue as indigo and twitching with his eyes rolled back. She had fed him some egg. Egg is poison to him. I guessed that before when he had the last one after eating pound cake. He was hot as a kettle. I said call the doctor and she said they had tried but couldn't get to him. They use Dr. Macon. So I said I know a good clean Negro doctor at James Institute, do you want to call him? So she called Dr. Otis at the school and got him. Meantime all I knew was we had to break the fever. His head was scalding. I told the cook to draw me a sink of cold water and I stripped the baby right out of his suit like undressing a tree, he had gone that stiff, and commenced to plunge him in and out of that bath. In three or four minutes he was limbering up and his eyes were showing. I could see him sucking breaths. By the time Dr. Otis got there he was crying so I thought he would live. He said I did right, Otis I mean. He was giving him an enema when Dr. Macon came. I wish you could have seen Dr. Macon's face but he spoke to him nicely and called him Dr. Anyway they worked together and I came on home. I tried to eat my dinner. Then I tried to clean the stove. Then I broke down and boohooed for something like an hour. I thought it was for him being helpless and young and some of it was but it mostly was for me, I guess, and for joy. It was somebody else's trouble. I don't have to bear it and never will. Then I took my little nap and walked to the store and fixed a trash supper, a can of corned beef, and ate more than half! Now it's cooling off fast but I won't light a fire.

I hope you are fine. Before the excitement I worried all morning that I

used mayonnaise in those sandwiches and that it would spoil on you and
leave you in trouble. I trust you ate them early though and got through
alive. If you did I know you'll have a big spread tonight. You are greatly
missed here and will be till you're back.

Remember what you see and save it up for me. I have never seen a
wedding. I hope you've told Rob my message already, a life of good help to
each other forever as long as they last. He told me last summer the first
time I saw him that he had two girls and who must he pick? I told him the
strong one. Do you think he has? He will need that I know like the rest of
the world.

This will not even reach you if you come back tomorrow. Till you do
rest yourself, have a good birthday,

Very truly,
Polly Drewry

It reached Rob at least. He took up the envelope and saw what he'd
missed; the Goshen address had been struck through once and, in Mr.
Hutchins' hand, returned to Richmond. Forrest had been safely back here,
surrounded, when this had come to him—a luxury of patient care so large
as to stand like a picture of heart's desire, clear and attainable. Attained in
this house for days at least, whole human days.

The noise of Polly's work went on above. Rob stood and walked to the
study door and shut it. Then he sat again and tied Polly's letter in its
bundle and reached for the picture of Eva and himself.

Surely they'd been a sad joke to Forrest, their pale last offer to wind
his life again in numb coils of anxious perpetual need.

He laid them, still framed, in the bottom of Forrest's dry wicker
wastebasket and buried them with two generations of letters—the Negroes', the family's, sparing only Polly's. He would keep those himself
unless she should ask.

Rob worked through the morning on his father's business papers, old
bills, paid checks, tax assessments on the house, five thousand dollars'
worth of lapsed life insurance, a postal-savings account (sixty dollars).
When he heard Polly come down to start a cooked dinner, he went in to
ask her just to bring him a sandwich and a glass of tea. She brought it, no
questions; and he worked on till four in the gathering heat. He searched
the volumes his father read most (Vergil, the Psalms, Emerson, Browning,
Woodrow Wilson's history of America). He even read quickly through the
notebook of verse—some Latin translations, a few old laments for Eva and
Rob (1904), musings about the purpose of teaching, a memory of his
mother, a birth-poem for Hutch, a dozen clean limericks, but no clear word
of care or concern for any survivor. No burdens either; the largest bill was
for eighteen dollars, the early spring coal. Forrest Mayfield had had his life

and had known it was ending; aside from the letter to Thorne Bradley, he'd departed in silence.

As Rob laid more dense bales of waste in the pile, this much came to him—*That is his last intention.* A perfect silence after long years of talk.

Yet he'd also intended that *someone* speak, had surely known that silence would force choice and action on his leavings. Polly and Rob. They had already spoken, to opposite purposes—Polly's aim to leave and work, Rob's easy munificence (a useless house).

Must he speak again now? There were two more choices—make her some further offer or accept her aim, move her out, lock the house, and hope to sell it. With any luck (as was, with no repairs), it would bring three thousand dollars. He could give Hutch a third, a third to Hatt, the rest to Polly—a nest egg to start her on the life she planned. She would never accept it. Then what?—abandon her at her present age to the mercy of life: a string of old cripples with bedsores and money enough to keep her in rented rooms for fifteen years till her own self failed her, then a charity home?

He'd asked her to live with Hutch and him, the rush of impulse two nights ago. She had not forced it on him; and he'd dropped it gladly, a load he wouldn't even have to shoulder, much less unload. But two days had held the proof of Forrest's silence and Min's final letter. He could stand now and find her (on the backporch, shelling peas) and say, "Miss Polly, I am begging this of you—come to me and Hutch." Hutch loved the long tales of a life which, however plain, she made seem crusty with vigor and riot; Rob bore her only gratitude. She'd simplify their lives.

But where? Not Fontaine. Even granting that he'd repossess the old Kendal place, he could not bring her there—Eva's nearness, Rena's spite, Grainger watching from the yard.

They could come to her, Richmond. He could hunt a job here, even beg again out at James Institute; say he'd sworn a new life since 1933, come back as a teacher. Failing that, a salesman, a clerk—anything. Men as young as he were scarce, and the war would last awhile. He would have this at least—a house that was his, his growing son in it, a woman who had known him for half his life and who might ease the rest.

Would she want that at all? Would she want more than that?—and wanting, would she ask? Could he find some human way to say that her needs were as useless to him now as the needs of a good horse, a good yard dog that has served for years? Where would he take what Min had given for a steady eight years?—what no child or woman near sixty could give but his own blind clamor would go on requiring?

She'd moved to the kitchen by then and was filling pans. Rob did a little sum—the fifteen-thousandth-odd supper she'd started in that one room. She was working alone but she'd always done that. Since old Rob's death, she had spent the best part of each day here alone, no real friend but Forrest. It was one of her elements; solitude and quiet, as strange a part of her strength as any other.

The front bell rang. Rob kept his place and let her go but listened through the door.

Polly said, "Was it locked? That's just my habit; old hermits love locks!"

Hutch said "So do I."

"Was the world still there?"

"Ma'm?"

"How was the world?" she said. "You've been out in it."

"Oh I liked it," he said.

"Come tell me then," she said. "I'm getting supper on." She started down the hall.

Hutch seemed to stay put. "Where is Rob?"

Polly said, "Still working in the study. You come help me. He'll be out directly."

So Hutch went with her, not pausing at the study.

And Rob sat to listen. Though the kitchen door was open, they were ten yards away; and their words came to Rob as no more than smoothed sounds, worn counters in a long cool game of contentment they were offering each other—flat rocks in a gully, slow bubbles in a pond. What had it been for?—the whole of Rob's life, all that this house had held (and the Kendal house and the Hutchins' hotel)—if not to have this and to go on having it? The far rounded voices of a woman and a child who wanted your presence and wished you well.

Rob admitted to himself that Forrest had no will, that tomorrow he must go to the clerk of court and investigate the handling of intestate remains—would he need to be bonded? would they bond a jobless man? would the final disbursement after all be his? He named the questions over as a gray bottom harmony to Hutch and Polly's chatter, but the questions rode him lightly. He stood from the desk and walked to Forrest's cot and fell asleep with ease.

5

ROB waited at the dining-room table for dessert while Hutch took dishes out to Polly in the kitchen. There had been a quick storm while he had his nap, and the windows bore in light cool air. Through the open door he heard Polly—"What did Grainger say?"

Hutch's voice was puzzled. "Ma'm?"

"Your letter from Grainger."

Rob had not thought to tell him. When Hutch had come in to wake

Rob for supper, they had talked a few minutes (Rob groggy with sleep); then gone straight to eat. He called toward the kitchen now, "It's on the study mantel, Son. It slipped my mind."

Hutch came to the door and looked at him closely. "Did you read it?"

"No sir. That's a federal offense." Rob smiled.

Hutch didn't but continued to face his father, then turned and went through the kitchen to the study.

Polly came with lime gelatin and cold whipped cream, served it out in three bowls. She raised her voice—"Hutch?"

Rob said, "Let him be. He'll come when he's ready. Very touchy about mail. Eva's kept some from him; now he thinks I've started."

Polly said, "I'm sorry if I stirred up trouble."

"You didn't. Give him time."

But they ate on in silence and Hutch didn't come. When Polly offered more, Rob stood. "I'll go get him."

6

THE study door was closed. Rob opened it, no knock. Hutch was over by the window, back turned, staring down. Rob stood in the door. "Grainger living?" he said.

Hutch nodded, not looking, and folded the letter.

Rob said, "Son, it's simple. I was dazed from my nap; I forgot you had a letter."

Hutch nodded again but still didn't turn.

"How are Mother and Rena?"

Hutch began to say "Fine"; then his throat stopped on him.

Rob thought "He's tired" and walked over to him, gripped both of his shoulders, and buried his own broad chin in the strong hair of Hutch's skull. Though the letter was folded, Rob could see it was Min's. Grainger's lay spread flat on the desk at their left, a neat half-page. Rob raised his chin and reached round and took the folded sheet, Min's ribbed blue paper. He took a step back, stuffed it into a pocket, and said "Are you glad?"

Hutch nodded.

Rob said "Answer."

"Yes sir," Hutch said.

"Glad of what?" Rob said. He was filling like a narrow pipe with anger; it reached his throat, a cold sour cud.

Hutch turned. "—That now you're alone." He'd recovered the strength of his voice and was calm. Or hidden at least; all feeling was blanked from his features by the force of his hidden purpose—harm or spite or plain embarrassment or, again, balked care?

Rob thought of all that but asked nothing further, afraid to know. He said to himself what he seldom remembered—"He's mostly Rachel's. She works deep in him."

Hutch said, "Can I have my money please?"

"What money?"

He pointed to Grainger's letter, touched a line near the end. *"You can either spend your money on something you like or bring it back and save it. Rob will tell you what it is and why I passed it to you. Then you can decide. Anyhow now you got it. If you meaning to save it let Rob keep it for you in his safe place. It is too old to lose."*

Hutch said "What money?"

Rob went to his bag and found the small box. He gave it to Hutch and said, "Can I read the rest of his letter?"

Hutch nodded. "All right."

Rob sat in Forrest's chair; Hutch sat on the cot to open his gift. Grainger said,

Dear Hutch,

Everybody here is fine and wanting you back but glad you got a chance to see the world. Remember it and tell me but I don't guess it changed much since last time I saw it.

Miss Rena was painting the yard chairs this morning and I was weeding round and when she got done she said did I want her to paint my house, she had some left. I said "You hadn't got nothing like enough" but she said she could paint the south side at least and cool it from the sun. So I told her yes and she painted it white. It's after supper now and it does seem cooler. Still smell it though. Miss Rena is a case.

No more news I guess. You write me a postal card and say how you doing and anything go wrong along the way, you sit down where you are and call Miss Eva and I will come get you. Night or day, count on it. Tell Rob the same thing. But have a good time.

You can either spend your money—

Rob faced Hutch, who'd quietly thumbed the coin.

"Is it gold?" Hutch said.

Rob said "Five dollars' worth" and held out his hand.

Hutch hesitated, then passed Rob the coin.

"Grainger gave this to me last Wednesday morning as we were leaving home. He wouldn't give it to you directly himself since, or so he said then, he didn't want to press you for thanks or returns. In fact he told me not to tell you but to change it and buy you something you wanted. I was planning on that."

Hutch said "Something changed his mind." His face had resolved to its usual transparency; a boy was behind it.

Rob said, "Me taking you away, that's what. Grainger knows you might like it; he's scared you might stay."

"In Richmond, you mean?"

"We own a house here."

"You mean this house?"

Rob smiled. "I didn't mean the state capitol." He rubbed his right shoe on the floor as a touch. "This was built by your Great-Great Grandfather Mayfield—the first Forrest, anyhow the first known to me—in 1835, just him and two slaves. Then he found a wife for it."

Hutch had listened and nodded. Now he stood, reached out, and took back the coin. He sat on the cot again and said "Whose is this?"

"Yours, from Grainger."

"Whose was it back then?—1839?"

"It was given to Grainger by my father's father when Grainger was born, a good-luck piece."

Hutch calculated back. "That was 1893."

"People saved gold."

"Wonder where it had been all those years."

"In somebody's sock."

Hutch rubbed it for answers. "When was old Rob born?"

"Oh I don't really know. We could check on his grave. Or ask Miss Polly." He recalled Forrest's story of twenty years ago. "I know it was after this house was built; he was born in this house."

Hutch nodded. "That's it. This was his, don't you guess? Somebody gave it to him when he was just born, and he kept it for luck."

"Maybe so," Rob said.

"Why'd he give it to Grainger? Grainger lived in Maine."

"He knew Grainger's daddy and kept up with him." Hutch was facing him plainly, no sign of knowledge or pressure to know, though ready for a story if there were a story. So Rob started telling it. "Grainger was his grandson."

"Whose?"

"Rob Mayfield's."

"How did that happen?"

Rob smiled. "The way it always does; somebody laid down on somebody else. I don't know all that many facts about it; Forrest told me what I know. My Grandfather Rob moved from here up to Bracey and married a Goodwin; she had Hatt and Forrest. Then he messed with a Negro girl and she had Rover. When Rover got grown, he moved north to Maine and married up there and he had Grainger."

Hutch said "Why?"

"Why Maine?"

"No, messing with the girl. Why did he do that?"

"His nature. It seems he was a wheelhorse till T.B. curbed him."

"Was his wife still living?"

"Oh yes, lived for years."

Hutch said "Is that a sin?"

"A very common sin, Moses' seventh commandment."

Hutch said, "I don't understand. What you told me at the beach, that grown men want a girl who'll ease their life. Why would he want two?"

"More than two," Rob said, "—must have had a lot to ease." But he saw Hutch was earnest, still waiting on the numb puzzled far side of manhood. "Men and women are as separate as rabbits and cats. Just because we bear some resemblance to women—two eyes, two ears—and because women *bear* us, we think they are like us and have our needs. They don't, really don't—which is part of their beauty and most of their trouble. They know they're alone which men never learn (or way too late), and they set out as early as they can to hide—in a husband and children. They try to duck under, but men try to fight it. Once the woman is buried in all her work (and can barely see him), then he starts all over to hunt a way out. Or a way *through* at least."

"—Through to ease?" Hutch said. "Is it always ease?"

"No it's sometimes to harm her, to punish her for failing you, but yes mostly ease."

"And you never get to it?"

"For minutes, just minutes. I'm speaking for myself. And for my grandfather; maybe some have done better."

"Who?"

"Forrest—here maybe."

Hutch nodded, no question.

"Even old Rob maybe toward the end of his life."

"Did he ever see Grainger?"

"No."

"Does Grainger know this story?"

"Yes—or so Forrest told me. But in all these years with me, he never let on."

Hutch had repacked his coin in the box, retied it. "I think Grainger's eased. How is Grainger so peaceful?"

"What makes you think he is?"

"He just has his life out there in the yard. Never sees Gracie or anybody else very much but us. Never tries to harm people."

Rob had never thought it through. He took awhile now; then said, "Listen, Hutch, you'll never figure Grainger; do and you'll be a wiser man than me or Forrest. Father took him up, then dropped him—cut him to the quick—but never understood him no more than that doll." Rob pointed to the old bark doll on the mantel which he'd stood upright in a pause this morning. "I came along and Grainger took *me* up, really helped me out of misery for a while with genuine care; and I really meant to thank him, to give him a good home as long as I lived. But he'd married Gracie before I turned up and she changed things."

Hutch said "How?"

"She came back to him. She had run off once already when I met him. I never even saw her till the time I was married. He was with me in Goshen, and he'd begged and begged her back, and she came for the wedding."

"Why?"

"She always liked a big crowd, but that may not be why. I never knew her reasons, never gave them much thought. Anyhow there was Gracie, serving ham at the wedding—a good-looking tall girl with hair straight as yours—and she stayed two years. Came with us to Richmond and lived with Grainger and worked like a Trojan, was a big help to Rachel (who couldn't cool milk on her own at first). Then something broke in her or broke loose again, and she started drinking and vanishing nights."

Hutch said "Was it you?"

Rob said "Sir?" quickly before he really heard. Then he went hot in anticipation of anger but decided on patience. "Was it me *how* please?"

"Was it you broke Gracie?" Hutch's eyes were grave but curious not condemning.

Rob said "No sir."

"You didn't even touch her?"

"Not once." Then he smiled. "She touched me a time or two; she had strong hands and could work out a crick in your neck, a sore muscle. But no that was all and Rachel watched that."

"You didn't want to touch her?"

"I had Rachel, Son."

"You said men were different and would hunt other ways."

"Some men, I said. I didn't speak for all. I didn't speak for Grainger. He's lived minus women, minus anything but you and work for fourteen years. He's got his own strength."

Hutch said, "No but *you;* did you stay just with Rachel?"

Rob knew they were near the place he dreaded. Must they push on now?—arrive and see it clear, the tan square room where he'd failed once for all on Min, clenched and damp—or could he detour them, wait till Hutch had grown further toward his own needs and mercies? Eva, Rena, Min, Grainger, Rachel long dried to leather—they had all left him now, *had no further use.* Hutch was simply what he had; Hutch needed him awhile yet. He mustn't lie at least. Rob said, "All but once. One day in four years, part of one afternoon."

"But not with Gracie?"

"No." Rob was braced to answer the next and explain, to ask a child for the clean forgiveness no one else had given or ever could.

But Hutch said, "Then why has Grainger turned against you?"

Rob said, "Has he turned? I didn't think so."

"I do."

"Say why. Has he told you something?"

"One thing, several times in the past month or so—that some people leave you and some people stay, and that you should know which and lean on the stayers."

"Did he say I'd left?"

"No he never mentioned names."

"He could have meant Gracie."

Hutch nodded. "You and Gracie and Grandfather Mayfield; all his stories are about you, you and France in the war."

"Most of mine include him," Rob said. "We know each other. It's you he loves though. He has to love you; you have been there with him, and you're worthy of love. Now he's struggling for you; he sees you are leaving, sees he'll wind up with Sylvie grouching at him at breakfast and Rena whitewashing his south wall for coolness."

Hutch said, "He's a man. Why can't he change that?"

Rob said, "It's too late. Son, he bet on us; on Forrest, then me, and now on you."

"Bet us what?"

"What I've told you ever since we left Eva's, all I've really got to tell you about anybody—that we'd give him his home place, the few things he needed; that we'd do it all his life and that he would help us."

Hutch said "How?"

"The work he does, the company he gives us."

"Then he's won," Hutch said. "He's got what he wanted."

Rob nodded. "He's had it for three short spells—the few months with Forrest in a little house in Bracey when he was a boy, awhile with me in Goshen, this longer spell with you. Now he knows that's ending. You'll be leaving him soon, four years at the most."

"*You're* coming back, aren't you? Everybody wants you back."

Rob said "You don't."

Hutch smiled. "Now I do. It was Min I didn't want. Nobody wanted Min." He stood, the coin box in his closed left hand, and went to the mantel and reached for the bark doll.

Rob watched him—he seemed to have grown an inch today, a frightening speed in his size and knowledge—and waited for a new string of questions to come: who had made the doll and why? He tried to think ahead through what Forrest had told him—old Rob's last days, his family of dolls (and with Polly at hand, young, ready to serve) all burnt by Forrest but this one sample—yet his mind was stopped. The sight of that one boy's strong right hand making touch with an old man's desperate effort at help, the model of a father long powdered to dust, raised a panic of fear. A high wall of sadness, that he'd thought past coming, rushed toward him and fell. As Hutch turned to face him, Rob said, "I did. I still wanted Min. She helped me for years. None of you ever will." He took up his light coat and left the room, the house.

7

IN the kitchen Polly overheard the end of Rob's speech and the front door slamming. She worked on a little and waited for Hutch; but when he didn't come, she dried her hands and went to the study door and looked.

Hutch was flat on the cot, eyes open, looking up. He didn't turn to face her.

"War over?" she said.

Hutch shook his head No.

Polly came to the desk and stood by Forrest's chair. Hutch's eyes were dry but his cheeks were pale. "You forgot your dessert. Looks like to me you need it."

"No ma'm," he said.

She was tired and should sit, but she'd never sat at Forrest's desk since that hard morning when Eva sent the picture of herself and Rob, and she'd opened it here and sat a quarter of an hour considering the depth of the wound sustained and her chances of continuance in this one place that was home to her then. She went to the foot of the cot and sat. Hutch drew in his bare feet to give her room; but she sat all the way back against the wall, then lifted his ankles and laid them on her lap. She hadn't borne his weight, any part of his weight, for eleven years. She had not, she knew now, borne the weight of a boy in all her life. Two full-grown men but never a boy; she had missed knowing boys. Her hands were beside her, not touching him now; and she didn't look up at his face at first but studied the smooth knees, the blades of the calves slowly furring with brown, to find more signs of the men she'd known in the boy they'd made. Nothing, none. A lean neat boy whose joints gave promise of height and grace (six, seven years from now) but no marks of old Rob or Forrest in sight—all Rachel's maybe? (she recalled Rachel's face but no other part). Finally she laid one palm on his dry skin. "You're growing while I watch you."

Hutch said "I hope so."

"Growing up to what?" she said.

"Ma'm?"

"You'll grow up to something if you live and keep eating. Have you planned on *to what?*"

Hutch waited a good while; then reached up above him, both hands overhead, as if to find and pull down a firm destination. Then he offered it to Polly. "Yes ma'm, an artist."

"Well, you'll need you a smock. I can make one tomorrow." His eyes cut to her, and she realized her error. "No I'm glad," she said. "My father was an artist."

"Did he make a good living?"

Polly said, "Pretty decent till Herbert Hoover struck."

"Have you got any pictures he painted?"

"Oh no he kept everything. It was part of his living. When I left him, he had his museum still; and the pictures were for that—soldiers dying, an Indian cutting a baby, a white woman screaming. They went with the museum when he gave that to an Alabama college. He learned it from his mother; she was Irish and smart—I descend from her! Have you got one of yours?"

"No ma'm, they're at home" (they were with him but secret).

"This is one of your homes. You could draw me right now."

Hutch raised his head and looked at her profile awhile. "You would be hard," he said.

Polly laughed. "All the wrinkles? You could leave them out. Imagine me a girl. I used to be one. Wrinkles didn't use to be here when you first saw me anyhow."

Hutch said "I don't remember then."

Polly waited. "I do. I do clear as light. I kept you whole weeks at a time when you were little. We were good friends then."

Hutch said, "I don't remember much before I was three."

Polly said, "You will. I mean it's there in you. You saw it all happen; it will rise up in time."

"When it does, will I like it?"

She laughed. "Oh a lot. We had good times. When your Grandmother Hutchins and Miss Rena had left, Rob would bring you by here as he went to work; and I'd keep you till evening."

"I thought I stayed with Grainger."

"You did sometimes. But Grainger had his hands full watching out for Rob—he stuck by Rob like a guard that year—so you came to me."

"Would I talk to you ever?"

"At first you were a baby, three, four months old. But eventually you did; I taught you all you know! Really—Grainger and I. It used to worry Forrest that you talked like us. We were all in the kitchen one evening drying dishes (Rob had gone somewhere), and Forrest dropped a lid. You said 'Goddammit!' and Forrest nearly keeled over. But that came from Grainger; I only *praise* God." She squeezed his ankle, laughing.

And Hutch turned to smile. "What else would I say?"

"Oh a lot like that till Forrest set you straight (he brought you in here and read you a sermon on good words and bad). You liked for me to sing;

you were always calling out from two rooms away, 'Polly, sing all you know,' meaning all my many songs—I could make up songs. I'd sing till I parched or you fell asleep." She stopped there and waited as if he might sleep again now and leave her.

He was watching her calmly, his head propped slightly on Forrest's felt pillow from Asbury Park.

"We weren't just jokers though; it wasn't all laughing. I thought it was my duty to remind you of Rachel. Nobody else would—Rob, Forrest, Grainger. They sealed her off from you and I understood why. But I'd come the same narrow road as you, lost my mother before I could see; so I made it my part to tell you little things about her when I could, when we were alone."

"Like what?"

"Her expressions, the words she'd use, the color of her hair; just a lot of little things."

"You'd think I would remember," Hutch said, "but I don't."

"Don't worry; it's in you. You could start running now and run sixty years; she would still be in you, controlling your feet."

Hutch said "Is that bad?"

Polly hadn't thought of that, but she did and answered truly. "Part *no*, part *yes*. Rachel was more full of hope than any other girl, worked harder than any other human I've known to make her hopes happen; to hold and please Rob, to bring you to life. Which was also her main fault—she hoped too much. She couldn't understand that the best people get is a few peaceful breaks; they don't get their wants. So she died from pure wanting. You will have to fight that."

Hutch nodded. "Rob's in me," meaning Rob worked in him as surely as Rachel.

Polly said "Where is he?"

"All through me, I guess."

Polly smiled. "No *now*. Where's he gone right now?"

At first Hutch seemed not to hear her at all; but since he lay flat, he stood no chance of concealing the water that pooled in his eyes. Still he tried not to blink and flush it down his temples. Polly watched him though; so at last he confessed his misery, blinked, and said "I'm afraid."

"What of?"

"That he *is* gone."

"Where?" Polly said.

"Anywhere, but for good."

Polly said, "I doubt it. What happened in here? What did Grainger say?"

Hutch said, "Not Grainger—Min Tharrington. Rob heard from her today that she wouldn't wait for him any more, so not to ask her. I saw the letter yonder on the desk and read it and told Rob I was glad."

"Glad of what?"

"That she'd left him alone."

Polly said, "I would think that you'd wish your father well."

"I do."

"But he's lonesome. He's drying up, Hutch."

"He's got me now; I'm old enough to help him. He's got you too; we could come here with you."

Polly sat on awhile; then she lifted Hutch's ankles and stood from beneath them. She went to Forrest's chair and sat and faced him. "No you couldn't," she said.

"Why? I want to; Rob has mentioned it."

"He's young," Polly said. "Forty's still too young to settle for this."

Hutch said "What is this?"

"A house with nothing but a young boy in it and a woman fifty-eight years old, played-out."

"We would love him," Hutch said.

"Not the right way," she said.

"What would be the right way?"

"Maybe Min's," Polly said. "I liked her when I saw her; she has surely stuck by him."

"So have I," Hutch said, "except when he left me."

"It takes touching, see. Every grown man I've ever known, except my funny daddy, needs some amount of that."

"I touch him."

"So could I"—Polly smiled at her hands—"but I won't. We're the wrong beasts, Hutch; too old, too young, misshaped to his purpose."

Hutch was flat on his back again, facing the ceiling with his arms straight beside him; so she rose and took the one step and picked up the bark doll that lay by his hip. Then she sat and studied quietly, then said "You understand this?"

"—That it's Grandfather Mayfield's?"

"Great-grandfather's," Polly said, "—old Robinson's. He used to have several. When I came here to help him, he had a box full that he'd made in the months while he watched his mother die. He had names for them; said they stood for his people, different ones in his life—some white, some not, but all brown as bark. He wanted me to dress them, make suits of real clothes (I could sew then as good as I ever have since; I'm Singer's best friend). I told him that was crazy; that I had better work—this house was a buzzard's nest when I came here—but he said, 'Then just dress Mam and Pap.'" Polly shook the one she held—"He called this one Pap, the man that built this house. I said I'd dress his Mam, but I wouldn't touch this one. He said, 'Pap's the one needs dressing.' He'd made this doll of his Pap with a thing, a man's thing also carved out of bark and set on a little wire axle in the crotch so it could raise and lower. He thought that was funny, said it favored his Pap in every small way. I said it was the *big* way that I wouldn't touch; and he unwired the moving part, just carved this notch here to show it was a man; and I made him some breeches and a coat, long lost." Polly stood again and laid it on the cot by Hutch. "You keep it," she said. "When you get to be an artist, you can try to do better."

"It's Rob's," Hutch said.

"No it's not. It was Polly's; now it's yours till you lose it. Everything that was old Rob's, Forrest gave me—all his little souvenirs that Forrest didn't burn (he burned every doll but this one, even Mam). I've got them upstairs, what was left—razors, Bible, a picture or two. I left this down here because Forrest liked it."

"Did he give you the house?"

"Sir?"

"Grandfather Mayfield," Hutch said, "—this house; did he give it to you? It was old Rob's, wasn't it?"

"It was. And yes Forrest said it was mine. On the way to the funeral, Forrest said to me plainly that they thanked me for the care I had spent on his father and they wanted me to have everything that was his. Rob had abused him and Hattie by leaving; and they wanted none of him now he couldn't keep running. That was before Forrest knew he would move here, an hour before; he never brought it up again."

"But he never said different, did he?"

"No," Polly said. "Oh no, not a word. We just passed the time for all those years."

"Then it's yours," Hutch said. "You could ask me here." He sat up slowly and faced her, still grave.

Polly smiled. "I *would*."

"No, ask me," he said.

Polly said "All right." She spread both hands on the flats of her thighs, looked again at her fingers not withered or dry. Then she gave a short laugh to show they were joking, that she must stand now and finish her work.

Hutch said "Where has Rob gone?"

"To Heaven I hope but I very much doubt it."

Hutch waited awhile. "No *my* Rob," he said.

"Oh." She thought, then rose. "He has gone to find liquor. He'll be back late. We'll see plenty then but we have to wait here. You come help me."

Hutch stood to obey.

8

Rob found her well after dark, not knowing at first that he'd set out to find her. At first he had driven out to James Institute and parked and walked up to Forrest's office door before he remembered he didn't have the key (it was on the study mantel). He hadn't had a real purpose there anyhow, had brought no cartons to pack the books; so he'd gone back out and was nearly at his car when he saw an old Negro standing twenty feet away, staring at him through the late clear dusk, dressed neatly with a bamboo cane. Rob stopped and called out, "You love your country yet?"

The man took two slow steps and said "Sir?"

"I said I hope you have learned to love your country, with a new war on."

The man came all the way forward and studied. "Mr. Rob?"

"Hey, William," Rob said and extended his hand.

The old serpent took it in his cool horny palm and squeezed it, laughing. "You ain't lost nothing; remember *too* good!"

"Well, I never knew a better janitor, William. Haven't been really clean since I left here."

"You back?"

"Just to visit, just to pack my daddy's things."

William nodded. "Mr. Rob, nobody told me nothing. They retired me here June two years ago, seventy-five years old. Took my broom and give me this." He stirred a little maelstrom in the air with his cane. "Last time I saw Mr. Forrest, he was *standing*, strong and straight as ever; I come by to see him on Christmas like he told me. He give me my cigars and say, 'Look, William, you shining your wings?' I tell him, 'Yes sir, my wings is ready; but I'll be climbing and circling like a chicken long before you—you young as ever.' He looked real solemn and say, 'I doubt it. Place I'm going they don't let you fly.' —'What you done?' I say, and he say 'Failed my people.' I told him, 'Mr. Forrest, you talking about white folks, I can't speak for them; but you see I'm dark so let me just tell you, you sure God saved black niggers by the dozen.' Mr. Forrest say 'From what?' " William stopped there and stood, looking off toward a squad of wild dogs by the statue of Robert Burns (a Carnegie gift).

Rob said "Did you say?"

William came back slowly. "Say what?"

"—From what? Saved them from what?"

"No sir," William said. Then he faced the dogs again They had cornered a bitch; and the big male was mounting her or struggling to—she'd agreed to take him, but his haunches humped drily in the air between them. When William turned he said, "That light girl told me." His own face (the color of a good tan glove) was fierce with anger, suddenly young.

Rob was honestly puzzled.

"—Girl used to be married to that fool of yours."

"Grainger? He was Father's. It was Father spoiled Grainger."

"*Yours* when I knew him, hanging round to watch *you*."

Rob hoped to derail him and calm him at once. "You run into Gracie? I hear she's back."

But the eyes still glared. "Gracie, that's her. She run into me. I minding my business, heading toward the ice plant one evening last week; and she yell out at me, 'Mr. William, come help me.' She was setting in a slat chair right down in the road; I never would have known her, she aged so bad. But I went over to her to help *any* creature and saw she was drinking—Mr. Rob, she was drunk. I said 'Who are you?' and she told me to guess. I said, 'I'm too old to stand here guessing'; and she asked me what else was I too old for?"

Rob said, "You mean she was smack in the road?"

"In front of a house but right in the street, two feet from the cars."

"Did you tell her you were young enough to handle her still?"

William studied; then smiled, easing as he went. "No sir, cause I ain't. Old as she look, she could grind me dead!"

Rob smiled. "Maybe so. I'm tired myself." The need to stop William, to move onward now had stood strong in him.

William said, "No such a thing. You ain't even started."

Rob said, "Then God save me. Can I carry you home?"

William thought a moment slowly, checked the sky for light. "No sir, thank you no. Old woman's still awake. I'm walking till she tired, at least her *tongue* tired." He laughed; Rob joined him. Then he pointed with his cane. "I'm just over yonder where I always been, behind the old smithy. Little house still holding; they ain't made me move. I'm praying they don't; being real good—don't you know?—so they don't think about me. Come see me fore you go."

Rob said "I'll do it."

"You need any help?"

"All kinds; what you giving?"

"Packing up, cleaning out. My knees still good; I just carry this—give me something to do." William waved his cane again, a grinning flourish.

Rob followed its point to the feverish dogs who had somehow calmed and were spaced on the grass as flat and separate as folded bats, staring his way.

9

So it was full dark before he found the icehouse and bought a small melon and asked for directions to Gracie's cousin's house. As he turned into the steep dirt street, he saw a straight chair twenty yards ahead, almost in the road—Gracie's but empty (there was one street light at the far dead-end). He drove there and parked half into a ditch and walked through the tin cans of flowers toward the dark house and called through the screen door—"Gracie? Gracie Walters?"

"Nobody named that." The voice was from nearby and clearly was Gracie's.

He just said, "Gracie, it's Rob out here."

A sizable silence, some fumbling with metal; then a flashlight lit at the end of the front room and searched for his face at the screen.

He gave it, stood still with his face almost at the wire and smiled in the beam. "I used to work for you."

"Oh God," she said and rose from the bed she'd lain across and came to the door, bare feet on planks. She still held the light, still fixed on Rob. Then she said, "You sure did. Step in here and rest."

"I stopped at the icehouse to ask where you were and bought a little melon; it's in the car cold."

"You get it," Gracie said. "We cut it on the porch, but it give me the headache. What else you brought?"

Rob had not really seen her; she was still behind the screen. "What you see," he said, "—my last remains."

"You shaping up," she said. "Ain't you got no nip?" She threw her light down to his hips and pockets.

"Not a drop. I remembered that was your department."

She thought a long moment. Rob could not see her nod, but she did once quickly. "You got to pay for it."

"What is it?"

"Mean wine," Gracie said.

"How much you got?"

"Best part of a quart."

Rob grinned. "Not enough."

Gracie lit his face again. "Maybe not," she said.

"Your cousin here with you?"

"She work all night; nurse a old white lady."

"And you're by yourself?"

"Way I like it," she said. She turned half-away, half-intending to leave (he'd waked her from a deep sleep which pulled her back).

But he needed to see her. "I got a little money for you; sit down and talk."

Gracie halted. "Who from? You ain't still trying to find me for Grainger?"

"No I'm not. That's your business. The money's from Father; he asked me to give you a little when I saw you so you'd think kindly of him."

Gracie said "How much?"

"A five-dollar bill."

She was back at the screen; then she opened it enough to hold out her hand. "I'll remember just that kindly," she said.

Rob stepped back enough to see the one street light and took out his wallet, tried to see five dollars. (He thought he had only wanted to see her, hear her talk of the past, ask her one or two questions. But she'd caught him in his lie; now he'd tip her and go.) He could not really see. "Come here with your light."

Gracie unhooked the screen and brought the beam toward him. She moved fast and straight; and once she got to him, he could smell her slow breath, damp and warm but fresh. She had not drunk for hours at least, he knew. She stood in deep silence, aiming her light at his thin sheaf of cash.

He found five dollars, drew it out, began to fold it. "Can we sit down a minute?" There were rockers beside them on the porch and a swing.

Gracie switched off the beam. "What you want me to talk about? I'm low as a well."

Rob said, "Nothing special, thought I'd tell you the news; Polly said you were asking. You could tell me yours."

She thought it out. "Who you telling what I told you?"

He did not understand.

"I sit down here and tell you my story, who you carry it to?"

"Nobody you tell me not to," he said.

"Grainger Walters," she said. "You keep it from him." She went to the far chair and sat, sighing.

Rob took the other chair. He still held the money in his right hand, wadded. She had not reached again. They sat a good while, Rob rocking, Gracie still. It had been a mild day, and the evening was cool; so the breeze that suddenly rose on their right was almost chilling.

It started Gracie. "No *news*," she said. "Nothing you don't know or ain't seen me do; had a whole lot of jobs, a lot of good times, a lot of bad lately. Been drinking for my health. But you know that too." She stopped and asked nothing, didn't turn toward Rob but faced his car.

He tried to see her now, the damage William mentioned; but could only see the line of her features and throat. It perfectly matched his memories of her nineteen years before—silent, sullen at his wedding; a laughing help to Rachel their first year in Richmond; then the slack hurtful drunk whom he'd tracked down with Grainger so many weekends till she vanished entirely. She was still all those, in this light at least. For the first time he knew what he'd come here to ask (not for drink or the use of any piece of her body). He said "Gracie, what was wrong?"

"Wrong with what?"

"—That you left us, that you ran so far and tired yourself out. Did I harm you anyway? Did Rachel ever harm you?"

"Won't running," she said. "Nobody scared *me*."

"You left though."

"A lot of times. And came back a lot."

"For what? Was it us?"

She waited till he thought she was silently refusing or had dropped off to sleep or chosen at last not to hurt anybody else by word or deed. Then she raised her left hand, brought it down on the chair arm announcing a fact; and said, "I was pleasing my mind. That simple." She waited again; then gave a low chuckle, the liquid burble of a drowsy bird.

Rob said "Are you still?"

She was sure. "Nothing but."

"So you don't blame us?"

"I didn't say that." She waited a little. "Not *you*," she said.

"What was wrong with Grainger?"

Again she was sure, had known it for years and not been asked. "Not enough white blood."

Rob said "Meaning what?"

"Meaning Grainger couldn't ease his mind no way on earth. I was too much nigger to ever satisfy him. Oh he come back from France all hot from the sights and men blowing up round him; and I eased him awhile, thought he was easing me. But once I showed him every trick I knew—he didn't know *nothing*—he figured he'd got to the dead-end of Gracie; so he struck up, you know, to *staring at the wind:* hoping two suits of white skin would blow in the door and him and me be real kin to your dead daddy. Or *one* suit of skin; it was him he dreamed for, dreamed Gracie right on out of his life. You thought I was running; I was looking for home—some warm dry place with a black nigger in it that could use my butt when he come home tired from a hard day's hauling, not gazing at wind like the wind would blow in because you were pretty and bank blessings on you."

Rob said "He's still waiting."

"Not for *me*?"

"Not you. No I don't really know."

Gracie said, "*I* do—nobody but you. I told Miss Polly last Wednesday when I seen her and she asked me was I ever going back to the fool—'He don't want me no more and ain't for fifteen years since Mr. Rob walked in and halfway adopted him. He just want the rest of that.' "

"Of what?"

"The whole adoption, to be your whole brother. Rob, you all he waiting on. You the one can do the trick."

"What's the trick?"

"Where's he at? At your mama's place?"

"Still in her backyard listening to the war news, making her garden, watching Hutch grow up and leave him like us all."

"Then you go out to him when you go back home—that coffin he live in, two feet square—and you hold out your clean hand and say, 'Mr. Grainger, I know you at last.' "

"Know what?" Rob said.

"Whose people he is, what's rightfully his. He don't know you know, or didn't when I left him."

Rob said "How do *you* know?"

Gracie said, "Two things to know—how did I know he's white? how did I know you knew? Grainger told me the first part, the first time I left him—'You leaving a good man that's nearly half-white.' I threw oil at him (I was filling his lamp so he'd have light to read by when I was long gone, them dream books that ruined him—Pocahontas eating grief till it choked her heart because she was two shades too dark to know Jesus). Mr. Forrest told me you knew."

"When?"

"Years ago." She offered no more.

So Rob let her sit and rocked on another minute, telling himself that he'd come for nothing but the air, the change, and should stand now and tip her and go back to Hutch and Polly, face them. As heavy as they were, they were after all walls holding back deeper waters that were ready to pour. He sat to the edge of the chair and faced her. She still refused to meet his look but gazed on outward at his car, the road, her old chair beside it. Only her hands moved—long thin hands on the broad chair arms, still silently flapping in rhythm as steady as any fine clock. She was telling time. She wore the gold ring; Rob could catch its dull presence. Rising, he tapped it once with his finger—"You haven't lost that." Then he held out the money packed down through their talk to a hot wet bullet.

Gracie didn't reach to take it. "That's a lie," she said.

"Pardon me then. I thought I saw a ring, thought I recognized it."

"—What I said: Mr. Forrest. He told me you knew who Grainger was the same day he died, early that afternoon. Miss Polly don't know it; you tell her and I'll kill you. I had come down here from Newark, New Jersey to see my cousin; see would she let me live here with her. She say I could if I help with her bills, ten dollars a month, first payment due *then*. I didn't have nothing but a bus-ticket back to pigshit Newark (I hate that hole; freeze you inside and out) and was getting real nervous with no wine to help me; so I took my chances and went to James Institute and found Mr. Forrest. He give me fifteen dollars, no hesitation, all he had in his pocket. I told him once I moved back down here for good, I'd work it out for him; and he said all right, not to worry about it. Then he ask after Grainger; didn't try to make me feel bad for leaving or nothing, just wanted to know if I understood his troubles. I say, 'Yes sir, Grainger told me years back'; and he say nobody was to blame but his father for starting it off, not watching hisself; and nobody could help it now unless *you* knew a way. He said he'd told you."

"Help what?"

"Just Grainger. I guess he meant Grainger."

"I don't," Rob said, "—no way on God's earth."

"That's it then," Gracie said. "I told him it would be."

Rob said, "That last day—he seemed all right?"

"Same as ever but old, marking his little nigger papers like old times.

He did seem sad but that was old times too, saddest soul *I* ever seen. I offered him this"—she raised her left hand. "You know what it is?"

"Yes."

"You know everything; can't nobody help you." But she chuckled again. "I told him he could take it for the fifteen dollars. He say, 'I lost my chance at that ring. It's having its life; I can't stop it now.' "

Rob stood a long moment; then stepped up to her, laid the money in her lap. "Will you sell it to me?"

"This ring or my monkey?" (in the dark he'd brushed her more deeply than he meant).

Rob said, "Well, thanks all the same—but the ring."

"What you want to do with it?"

"Keep it. Maybe Hutch—"

"You want to get married? Where your Miss Minnie?"

"Wore her out," Rob said. "She gave up waiting."

Gracie tapped the broad ring on the wood of the chair. "You show her this thing, she come back snappy."

"You didn't," Rob said. "You took it and went."

Gracie said, "I'm different; I told you how different. I just wanted one thing men had to give; that's easy to get if you look good as me, good as I used to look—had em standing thick as pulpwood. Miss Minnie wanted *you*, that thing and all the rest—wet breath from your nostrils, white gristle in your heart."

Rob said, "She can have it. I planned to tell her soon; then she called time on me. Got a letter this morning saying she was past reach now, to leave her alone."

"She playing," Gracie said.

"No she's not. I've abused her."

"What she *want* you to do." Gracie sat forward quickly and struggled with her hands in the dark of her shadow. "Give her this," she said. With the hand that held his money, she offered the ring.

Rob weighed it on his palm. "How much would I owe you? I'm a little hard up now, out of work myself."

Gracie said "You been drinking?"

"Enough to get fired."

She thought awhile. "You keep it. Got your name in it anyhow; never had mine, fool Grainger's neither."

"You ought not to give it."

"It was give to me. I never worked for it. When time come to work was when I left."

Rob suddenly brought it to his lips and touched it. "*I* sure God have."

"You ever get a little bit ahead," Gracie said, "you send me a buck or so."

"How will I find you?"

"Miss Polly; she'll know me."

"She says she's leaving too," Rob said, "—to nurse. I feel bad about it, but she won't let me help her."

Gracie passed over that if she heard it at all. "Then send it to Jesus; He keep up with me." She gave a long laugh like a seam of fresh water she'd found in her chest, unsuspected till now.

Rob said, "I'll do it. He knows me too." Then he walked to the steps. "If you're over our way tomorrow, stop by. You haven't seen Hutch; he's two-thirds grown."

Gracie stood in place. "All right. I hadn't seen him—Lord—six years." Her flashlight lay on the floor by her chair; but she came on without it, stopped one step from Rob. "I ain't," she said, "so don't wait for me. Ain't coming nowhere where that child is."

Baffled, Rob said, "He's good. He won't tell Grainger."

"I know he's good," she said, "and he welcome to tell Grainger anything he see. No I'm sparing myself. I started doing that; you ought to try it too. I don't see children if there's any way to help it. Children break me down worse than anything else."

Rob touched her on the elbow, the flesh hot and dense in its slick dry rind. "Keep us posted someway. Try to keep up with Polly; you can help her a lot."

Gracie nodded—"She'll make it"—and gently freed her arm.

Rob went down the steps and straight to his car. At the shut door he looked up and said "I thank you."

"Glad somebody do."

He could no longer see her—she was shaded by the porch posts, her cousin's tubbed ferns—but he thought of one thing he'd forgot till now. "How about this melon? It'll still be cool; you could take you an aspirin."

"Can't do it," she said, "—give me dreams this late." Then she turned and went in; just the sound of the rusty screen opened, shut, hooked.

So Rob leaned in and drew the light melon out—still cool as he'd promised, striped with snakes of dark green—and set it in the straight slat chair by the street. She could face it tomorrow, maybe swap it for a drink; or her cousin coming home in the dawn could find it, or some early child—a gift from grace itself, the sky.

10

POLLY went up to bed at seven o'clock, telling Hutch there was no use in ruining themselves in a wait that might well last till noon (she recalled such waits by Forrest and Grainger after Rachel's death). Hutch had said he would stay in the study and read till he felt really tired, and he read till one in his grandfather's copy of *Martin Eden*. He was still not tired enough to face a dark bed; but by then he suspected there might be worse sights to face if he stayed to meet his father, so he quietly switched off all but the porch light and climbed to his room.

He didn't think he slept; but he did fairly soon, a frail speeding through half-formed visions of fear, assault, the chasms of final abandonment. He had raced himself to a deeper unhappiness than any he'd known—still faceless, embryonic, drawn from his own mind—when Rob's key woke him as it grated in the street door. Rob or someone Rob had sent or someone who'd killed Rob and come straight here—Hutch added all those to the chances around him. He raised to his elbows and strained to hear. The door had not shut.

At first there was only the breathing from Polly's room—her door was half-open; she slept on through even this, another abandonment. Hutch tried to see his watch—too dark: at the window there were no signs of day. Then downstairs the door shut firmly at last, then steps down the hall (not certainly Rob's; they were quick and heavy), then the brass light-switch clicked loudly in the study.

Hutch's arms went numb as wool from the weight of his urgent body as it waited for news. For a long time he took no notice at all of their lack of blood. Then when minutes on minutes of unstirred silence continued to pump from below like a flood, he fell back and let the cold blood pour through him, sour and scalding. He had heard all his life of his father's failures—in mumbled scraps from Sylvie and Grainger, a friend or two—but he'd never seen one. Till now something spared him; now he knew it had stopped. He must stand now and find his way downstairs to see—whoever, whatever, was offered and waiting. Nothing in his whole life had readied him for this; not his mother's absence or the warnings of Negroes that this lay ahead or the war that had run in Europe and Asia since he had been nine, consuming in hordes (as its food and fuel) the bodies of children as good as he, as worthy of mercy.

He stood in his cotton pajamas, barefoot, and felt his way like a blind boy down.

11

THE study was a blank plane of hot white glare from the ceiling light and showed no sign of containing more than when Hutch had left it two hours ago—furniture and light, the rank summer mold on yards of books. The one man here was his great-grandfather's bark doll on the cot. So he went there to sit and wait again.

Another man was huddled in the dark square yard of space between desk and cot—buck-naked, curled on his side like a fetus and silent as bread.

Hutch was stunned and scared but held his place, standing one step from the legs. Then questions poured on him—was it Rob? was he dead? was it Rob or a stranger waiting to spring? He said "Rob," whispering so as not to wake Polly (though what could wake her now?). No answer, no stir. He took the last step and crouched by the body, hoping it was anyone on earth but his father. The man had wet the clothes he lay on.

They were Rob's tan trousers; the legs were his, strong calves still thickly haired with brown when most men his age had worn their legs bald.

Hutch bent forward, holding his breath against the piss; and shook the flat hip—"Rob."

The waist was moving slightly to breathe, no other move.

Hutch pressed the hip hard, forced the body flat to face him.

Rob's eyes were half-open, though in fact he was dreaming. He'd started to dream before he lay here, had lain down only to ease its progress through his mind and eyes.

Hutch said, "Wait here. I'll go get Grainger." In his own shock and fear, he thought they were at home; that he and Grainger hauling together could lift him.

Rob said, "Understand. I want this rest," a speech from his dream. His sex was half-standing, still bore a yellow drop.

Hutch thought he understood. He rose and left.

12

In his room again, he shut the door quietly and turned on the one lamp beside the bed. Then he sat on the edge and tore with his nails at the rims of summer callus on both his heels. When he had a pile of dead skin the size of a quarter on the sheet beside him—his left heel was bleeding—he knew his course. He went to his open bag and found his drawing tablet. Near the back on the clean sheet that followed his portraits of Chopin and Liszt, he wrote this quickly.

June 13, 1944

Dear Grainger,
It is now three-thirty in the morning, and I am still in Richmond. I got your letter last night after supper. Till then I didn't know about the goldpiece or I would have already thanked you for it. Rob forgot to tell

me. I blamed him for that, and he went out and got what I guess is drunk and is lying downstairs on the study floor now, naked asleep. He wouldn't let me help him.

So I'm leaving right now. Where I'm going is to see my Grandfather Hutchins before he dies. He wrote me on my birthday and said he'd like to see me. Also I want to see some things near there. I will try to ride the bus. I have twelve dollars from my savings and from Grandmother. If that runs out, I have now got the goldpiece and can cash that in. I will leave in five minutes, meaning sometime tonight I hope to be in Goshen if you need to send me word. This is not any secret. From Rob, I mean. I will leave him a note. But don't tell anybody else in Fontaine.

Do you want to come join me? You could take a few days off and ride the bus yourself and show me the things you remember in Goshen. We could head home together when we had our visit. Anyhow think about it. I will try to stay till Sunday at least if Grandfather seems well and knows who I am and wants me that long. So come before Sunday if you're coming at all.

I am doing all right but really feel bad. I guess you know how.

Thanks again, I hope to see you.

> Sincerely,
> Raven "Hutch"

Then he took a last sheet and wrote

Dear Miss Polly,

You are fast asleep so this is to thank you for my visit here. I enjoyed your part of it and am sorry to leave early, but after our talk tonight I guess you understand why.

I'm going down now to try to get a bus to Goshen where my mother is buried. I have got enough money and will be all right. Boys younger than me around the whole world except here are fighting.

Rob is back downstairs, and since you have known him so much longer than me you will know what to do. He told me to leave him alone and I will. You can tell him where I am and that I will go to Fontaine as soon as I have finished.

I hope you will have a good time from now on. I would like to give you anything here that is mine, and I hope I will see you again some day when I know as much as you and can sit down to talk.

> Your friend,
> Hutch Mayfield

Then he packed his few things and, carrying his bag and his sandals, went out and left the note for Polly on the doorsill of her room. All the way downstairs he kept his eyes from the open study where the light still burned; but once he reached the hall he knew of three things that he could and must do. He set down the bag and entered the room; pulled the spread off the cot and covered his father, sparing Polly the sight. He took the bark doll, despite his gift to Polly in the note he'd left (she had never wanted this), and turned off the light. Then in pure hot darkness he found his way out.

JUNE 13-14, 1944

Sнe saw him take the first step at the bottom of the hill, two hundred yards off; and she paused only long enough to prove to herself that he climbed toward her. Then she bent again to chopping weeds between her rows of corn (corn she knew she'd never eat; she planted it for company). It would be time wasted to strain to know him yet, to look up again till he stood within arm's reach. She'd enter her seventy-eighth year next week and had long since surrendered curiosity and safety to the thickening veil of twin cataracts. She could still see the weeds.

And then she forgot him, thinking calmly but with dread fresh as warm milk of Whitby, her younger, in Belgium now at the mercy of nothing more visible than God—twenty-five years old, her favorite and her hope. If they killed him, she'd die. She had stood all the rest; she wouldn't stand that.

Hutch came to the edge of the garden and stopped; set his bag in the dirt and said, "Have I got to the Mayfield place?"

She rose and looked; still only a slim clot of color beyond her in the tan light of evening. "No the *Shorter* place," she said, "but I'm no Shorter. My husband was, my boys are. No Mayfield either but that's by choice."

Hutch said "Miss Hattie?" (he had never called her *Aunt;* never seen her to remember, not since 1933).

"Yes, Hattie," she said. She was straight as the hoe-handle upright beside her and could hear his short breaths, quick from the climb; but she would not say she could not see his face.

"I'm your nephew," he said. "I was trying to find you."

She smiled but said "From where?"

"Richmond last night. I'm headed on west but my bus stopped here, so I thought I'd try to find you."

Hatt spread her free arm, one bare bone wing. "You found what's left! What you want to do with it?"

"Good evening," Hutch said.

2

THEY had said very little through supper or before (when they'd gone to the house, Hatt had said, "You climb on up to your room. Wash your face, lie down, I'll call you when I'm ready"; so he'd climbed the strange stairs and found the bare open room that seemed not hers and washed with the pitcher of warm water ready by a white china bowl and then had fallen back on the bed in which his father was conceived and slept off an hour of the debt he'd acquired in the past hard night before Hatt called, "You can eat if you're ready"); but once they had got near the end of the baked eggs, four vegetables, and biscuits, Hatt said, "Now tell me how your whole trip went."

Hutch had not said Rob's name once till then—she had not asked for it—and he could not now. He said, "Everything was crowded, lot of soldiers; and I had to stand up a good part of the way, but it was all right. I'm glad to rest here."

Hatt said "I know you are." Despite her silences she'd smiled often freely, especially when he'd looked up and caught her in a squinting gaze at his face. She was smiling now. "The walk did you good."

Hutch thought she referred to his climb up the hill. "Yes ma'm," he said. "I'm used to flat country."

"No you're not," she said.

From that moment Hutch knew she had him wrong. He hadn't said more than that he was her nephew; he knew she had no other—her great-nephew really. So she thought he was Rob. Was she really that far gone? She looked clean and kept, no trace of the burning odor of age, the singed-chicken-feather stench of unwashed bewilderment which rose (he knew already) from a number of souls with years yet to live. He surely couldn't ask her, stop now and set her right—"I am younger than that; I am *Hutchins* Mayfield." What he'd seen last night could not be worsened. No news of the war, no one photograph of the hundreds he'd seen of children in torment had rushed on him stronger. He knew in his deep heart that then he had passed a trial which would never come at him again, that he'd earned a permanent safety from fear. He could wait and listen. He smiled at Hatt and said, "Well, it taught me some things—the walk, I mean."

"Like what?"

"Like nothing will hurt me, from now till I die."

"What tried?" Hatt said.

"Different people, things they said."

"Saying you were an orphan?"

"Alone, yes ma'm."

Hatt was opposite him at the big square table, four feet away. She leaned over suddenly and took his left wrist that lay on the clean cloth.

"You know the word *liar?*" Her face was pressed blank of its lines by the force of her question, nearly young.

"Yes ma'm, but I haven't—"

"Then use it," she said. She settled back again. "Words are meant to be used; they'll stand you in good stead when all else fails—eyes and hands'll *fail*. Words are what I mostly have now."

"Use it how?" Hutch said.

"In the teeth of any human tries to say you aren't cared for, loved as close as any blood-child that draws breath. Call em *liar*, plain *liar*." She was still lit and lifted by faith in her words, but she sat unmoving with her palms down before her like guards by her plate (she had barely eaten half).

"By who?" Hutch said, "—cared for by who?" He felt for the first clear time in his life that he played two games, both serious and funny, his aunt's and his. She thought he was someone he knew he was not; he deceived her in that. But himself, he was bent now on knowing her error; hungry to know could he wear her error as a useful disguise in this new life he'd started, today at dawn.

Hatt waited a good while, upright and still, no longer facing him. Hutch thought she was lost in confusion again; she was not. She was straining to bear his question, the fact he could ask it. Then she said, "Try Hattie. Try guessing it's Hattie. See how does that feel." She had not looked up.

He nodded "I'll try" but was faintly smiling.

And though she couldn't see it, she smiled again; let it open on a laugh to show how certain she was of her claim. She loved him enough; one human was safe. She thought he was Forrest her brother, age twelve, who for lack of a dollar had been unable to ride with his school-class excursion to Danville, two hours by train, so had walked there ahead and met them at the station and walked back alone, arriving just now. That had actually happened sixty-one years ago after their mother's death and had been a main cause of Hatt's own rush to marry James Shorter and bear him the two sons who'd left her entirely in the past two hours; left her memory, her worry. Soon she'd never be forced to shame Forrest again. They would be past shame.

She went on smiling. But something remained to block full pleasure and darken her hope. She stayed in her seat, and her hands stayed still; but she faced him again—his face one vague white globe among globes—and said, "Forrest, what I'm asking for now is pardon."

Before Hutch could know should he laugh or leave or ask *For what?* or tell her all the fresh truth in one quick stream, he said "That's easy" and touched the broad top of her right wrist with fingers that wanted to calm and were sixty years younger yet were cool as new sheets on her hot dry skin, the fervent meeting of utter strangers.

3

BEFORE it turned dark, Hatt had told him he should go on to bed; so with no more questions or answers, he had climbed to the bare room again and stripped to his underwear (the room was still hot) and looked out the window toward the dense black crest of the hill they were on. He settled his eyes on a nearer dead tree (stripped of leaves, branches, bark; of all the fittings and intentions of a tree but its need to stand) and thought of the string of new chances which spun from his choices today.

He had chosen to leave his father, huddled naked on a floor. (Or had he been *sent*, as he'd felt at first? He'd puzzled that all day, what Rob's speech had meant—"Understand. I need this.") At the station, when he'd found a bus to Goshen wouldn't leave before mid-afternoon, he had gone in to breakfast at the station cafe to consider if the wait would be fatal to his plan, whether Rob would recover enough to come and find him and, if so, what answer he would give to that. As he'd started on his peach pie, a loudspeaker called out a bus to Bracey, Danville, and points southwest; and though he barely noticed the name at all, the old waitress writing out his check before him had said, "There you go. Want your pie in a sack?" and he'd said "Please ma'm," taking that as his next choice, offered by luck—a step on, at least. Once in Bracey he'd asked for directions to his aunt; then had let her build her own confusions round him, let her suffer for that (unless the easy pardon he'd laid across the table had actually reached her and sealed some cut which his voice had reopened). He'd chosen in fact to be her dead brother, his dead grandfather, for an hour or so.

Could he go on from there? What would morning bring? Would her mind have cleared so she knew him as himself? If so would she probe where he couldn't bear probing?—Rob's whereabouts, his own unlikely future? Would she beg him for all she so clearly lacked? Could he say No and leave? Should he dress and leave now?—creep past her down the stairs and walk toward Goshen or the next bus station or lie here and wait till she slept and leave then? (she was still in the kitchen; a radio was on).

Or could he *be* Forrest, become Hatt's dream?—not just to ease her for the time she had left (surely he was safe here; they'd hunt him in Goshen, never think to look here—they'd all dodged Hattie since before he could remember) but to help himself, save himself from the coming life which flew toward him now: Rob and all his power to hurt, power to raise love and hope by his simple words and presence and crush them each evening.

Standing there all but stripped at a window which had framed his grandfather's face for years—then his desperate grandmother's, then his newborn father's—Hutch thought he could sleep here and rise and be new,

be Forrest Mayfield and live a life free of choices that would bring down
pain on himself and nine others. He knew (from Sylvie, Grainger) enough
facts of past years—Forrest running off with Eva and the main after-
maths—to think that ten lives were bent crooked by the choice: Eva,
Forrest, Eva's parents, Rena, Hatt, Grainger, Rob, then Rachel and
Hutch. He could choose to spare them all, save Charlotte Kendal's life,
save Robinson and Hutchins from having lives at all. What would flow out
from him would be calm satisfaction—his Aunt Hatt's old age accompanied and tended, his own great longing for freedom from others (from
love *or* pain) quenched daily by life in this bare room, bare house: hoeing
beans, climbing that hill there to its top, looking back on a dead tree, the
peaceful empty house, the road in the bottom, the far hill beyond, reduc-
ing each in order to a picture in his tablet. Lasting, useful, safe, harmless.

Knowing again that he played two games—only with himself now—he
thought he could stay here, be that. Could and would. He would be here
tomorrow and as long after that as his life moved safely.

The hill had darkened, the bare tree melted into dark grass behind it.
Hutch went to his suitcase, took out his tablet, turned on the one bright
overhead light; and sitting on the stiff bed before the old mirror, began for
the first time to draw his own face—an excellent likeness and a first firm
memorial of what he was leaving for this new life.

4

WELL into night, ten minutes past twelve when the last news had finished,
Hatt shut off the last light and climbed in black dark to the top of the
stairs, no need to feel her way. She stood still there till she heard steady
breath from Forrest's room. Then with no attempt at silence, she walked
to that door—half-shut—and pushed it open. What moonlight there was
reached her only as a thick screen of glow between her and her goal, the
boy she could hear and must touch now freely before she could sleep. She
hardly knew this room, had avoided it for years, only swept it spring and
fall; so she put out her arms and shuffled to the rag rug, struck the bed
with her knees. The boy's breath stopped awhile; then started, safe and
deep. She sat on the edge of the mattress and waited. She was not sure for
what—the comfort of a living animal in reach, entrusted to her, or for
some further answer. Yes a question remained.

At last she remembered. Sure in the dark now, she found his broad
hip with one reach of her hand and let it ride there till the breath stilled
again. Through the cotton spread and sheet, she pressed the flat bone. The
breath had stayed silent; he would be awake or nearly. She was sorry to
have roused him, but she had to ask now while she held it all clearly

together in her mind. "This Normandy," she said, "—is it anywhere near Flanders?" She knew he loved maps.

He said "Yes ma'm."

They stayed like that for a good while, quiet. He could see her above him, her face as young in moonlight as it had been with fervor at the table over supper when she swore how loved he was.

"That's it then," she said. "That's it. He's gone."

He was dazed from deep sleep, but he thought she meant the war. "You been listening to the news?" He could see her nod slowly.

"—Said the Germans pushed them back today right up against the water: Cherbourg, around there. Said they suffered pretty bad."

He thought he understood. He said, "Albert?—he's safe. He's never looked up."

"Whitby," she said. "I seem to know he's gone."

He thought he remembered she had lost a son; hadn't Rena told him something the day of Pearl Harbor when he'd asked, if it lasted, would he have to die in it? "Not likely," she'd said. "God seldom takes two, only rarely and for necessary reasons of His own. Your cousin died in Flanders. Makes you all but safe, however long it lasts." But he wasn't sure *Whitby* was the name, so he only touched the hand that was still on his hip.

Hatt bore the touch but did not try to hold it or press on it any dumb message or thanks. She stayed on beside him though, the hand on hers, and remained so silent in her certainty of loss that he soon slept again, this time beyond waking, if there'd been a cause to wake him.

After some long time she began to feel cold and thought she must go to her own room for warmth. Her down quilt was there at the foot of her bed, her mother's quilt really. She could wait under that. Since 1918 she'd slept very little and, until her sight had failed, had often spent night after night downstairs mending clothes, writing mail, making perfect preserves to send whoever—contentedly enough. Since her blindness the only thing to do was hear news, five years of war news—all the late bursts of short-wave news in all tongues, any one as sad as English—so she'd started lying down again in James's old bed, the one she'd shared with him where she'd never felt easy.

She would feel this child first. As hard as he slept now, and with his long day, he might be feverish. She found his face again in one sure reach—his brow dry and cool, his breath on her palm still regular and moist. Then her fingers stayed to search him for any other threats, any trace of shame or fear brought back from his trip and concealed in daylight.

No the whole face was calm, entirely surrendered—brow, eyelids, mouth, chin. But it wasn't any face she had ever touched before; a whole new country lay beneath her light hand, young and eased and trusting but new.

5

AT seven Hutch woke, clear sun through the window; and said his prayers and dressed. He thought he could smell bread baking downstairs and the smoke from bacon. They were only his hope; when he passed his aunt's door, heading straight for the stairs, he saw her upright in a black Morris chair against the far wall, wearing last night's clothes, her eyes on him. He walked to her doorsill and said, "Good morning. Have you been up long?"

She nodded, not smiling.

"I didn't hear a sound; dead to all, I guess. I needed to be." He took a step inward.

"Please wait," she said. She held out the hand which had studied him by night.

He waited, baffled.

"No it's all right," she said. "Just answer me this—have you ever known me?"

"I'm your nephew, yes ma'm. I said that, remember?"

"Not Rob," she said.

"No'm, Hutchins."

No light. She looked every instant of her age, spared nothing.

"Rob's—" he said; that burned him too deep. "Rachel's Hutch," he said; and knew he must leave now—his old life again, guarded round by the thickets which called themselves love but were hunger and fright.

Hatt understood nothing, remembered no Rachel; but she stood without effort and grinned and came toward him. "You can still stay," she said.

JUNE 14-17, 1944

June 14, 1944

Dear Min,

It's early Wednesday here, a little past six. Your letter came Monday and was one of the last straws the old camel bore before buckling under. You told me not to write, and you may just burn this without ever looking; but I've lain through the night, seldom closing my eyes, and Polly's still asleep; so I'll tell it toward you, hoping truly that it reaches.

In the week since I wrote, these main things have happened. The "shop" job at home had not been filled, and Thorne Bradley seemed inclined to give it to me if I'd sign The Pledge in blood. Mother, Rena, Sylvie, Grainger are each far gone at the ends of their tethers—no thought of coming back; they can barely hear each other and are happy as fleas—so I can't stay there. But with some fumigation and a week of whitewashing, the old Kendal place would be habitable once I locate the nerve to turn eight Negroes flat out in the road (one is not yet with us—the oldest girl is pregnant—but is well on the way). Hutch would not live with me if you were in sight and may well have gone for good now in any case. More about that. The sand and water of the Atlantic Ocean are holding up well, all recent things considered (two world wars etc., all the drowned young men, their effect on sharks). The shrines of colonial Virginia stand firm, as do all Virginians I have met so far—Miss Polly among them. She is Hell-bent on moving her duds out of here as soon as I leave and taking up practical nursing, age sixty (she is rightly mad and puzzled that Father left no will or instructions for her welfare, so has chosen me to punish in his unquestioned absence). I have offered her the house here and every stick in it; she still says No, which means I have to sell it all at auction or burn it or come here and live—using what for money? eating leaves from Father's Vergil, his deathless lines to Eva at sixteen? Also Grainger's Gracie; she's here and I've seen her, what's left anyhow. And I took some of that, her

*wedding ring which really was my Grandmother Mayfield's. Father gave it
to Grainger. I can wear it in my nose, but no one wants to lead me. Or sell
it if I have to—twenty dollars if I'm lucky (it is far out of style, wide and
flat, just gold). Hutch accused me of stealing five dollars from him, a story
in itself which you won't need to hear. And no doubt half a dozen boys I
have known, maybe some I have taught (maybe Sylvie's nephew Albert),
have died in France in fouled underdrawers shot square through the brains
while I bore my week.*

*As I said, I didn't bear it. Once I got the ring from Gracie, I found a
bootlegger and drank myself under but not far enough. I got back here
alive and lay down to rest on the floor in my skin—my floor, my skin—and
my son found me and fled the whole scene. That was yesterday morning.
He left a note saying he had pushed on to Goshen to see Rachel's father
and would head home from there. I have not gone in hot pursuit as you
see. He is fourteen years old, could father a child; so I guess he can cross
the state of Virginia without great risk. If he can't—well, I've hurt people
weaker than him and as dear to me.*

*In my last to you, I said I was trying to do Hutch justice alongside of
you. Maybe now I have, to him at least. I've shown him two things I never
could have told him—the stock he comes from, or half of the stock, and
how little he has actually meant to me. He's all I ever made that was half-
worth making, that stands some chance of redeeming the backed-up debts
of my life, Forrest's, Eva's, old Rob's. And I made God a vow on the
morning he was born that I'd turn and be a man, a decent man you could
lean on, if he and Rachel lived. God did half His part; I've never done
mine. If I'd loved that boy, I'd have done it, Min, you know—not to
mention God or you or Rena, Grainger, Sylvie.*

*So he knows he's on his own—age fourteen years, long before I
knew—and he's given up hope, of me anyhow. If there's anyone on earth I
should truly leave alone, I guess it's him now. My grandfather left my
father, age five; and Forrest died happy or gave that appearance, not seriously troubled by his failure of Mother or leaving me, age one, or leaving
Polly now as abrupt as a sneeze. We have all chugged on, some with more
smoke than others but no stopped hearts.*

*Will you marry me on Monday or as soon thereafter as law permits?
You have asked to go free and I understand why; but I'm also as sober as
the day I was born (woke at noon yesterday and have needed nothing
since, nothing sold in bottles); and I know I must beg you to come back
and stay now from here till the end, whoever ends first (and I just mean
death, for my part anyhow). I've known it long years, Min; but shame has
held me back—shame and my promise to be a good man, with Hutch as
God's hostage. God has taken him and gone, so I'm free to beg you. Take
please the man that's left. It is who you've always known, minus any sane*

reasons for further shame or hope or Pledge—except the hope to meet you
soon; the pledge to stay by you, such as I am, for all the time left (maybe
thirty more years if I'm like my ancestors in body as in heart).

What I hope to do is this—finish up here by Friday (start the no
doubt slow process of getting myself named executor of Father's intestate
estate and, failing any chance of Polly staying in the house, help her move;
lock the door; and think awhile of how to sell it, rent it, burn it, or come
back); then drive on to see Aunt Hatt who has rights in this, I guess; then
to Goshen very briefly to see if Hutch is there safe and wants a ride home.
I must do that for Mother if nobody else. And of course I wish him well. If
you write or wire Yes c/o Hutchins Hotel, I will drive down to Raleigh by
Sunday evening if my gas stamps hold out; and we can work from there—
though there's nothing else to say, as you've already said, except Yes or No.

You've tried to say No, and I'll never doubt you felt it with more than
good cause and meant it in your bones, but I'm begging you to change.
You have understood Yes all your life; keep on. I think I have also; it is my
single virtue—how few I've refused. I've damaged six or eight and killed
one girl; but who up to now have I ever refused but you? Pardon please.
Let me work at pardon. I may last your life.

Will you tell me by Saturday, Sunday morning at the latest? If Yes,
then we'll have other questions to face—do we stay on in Raleigh, you
keeping your job while I hunt for something (my rent there is paid
through July 1st and, with marriage license, I'd let you in)? do we go back
to Fontaine for me to teach there, assuming that's settled? do we head for
the moon in a '39 Hudson whose tires are badly showing their age?—

> Though no worse than
> Rob

2

Hutch had asked no directions but walked from the bus toward the west
end of town, past shut stores and houses and the bridge Rob had mentioned into sudden thick pines and high banks of laurel dark as wet snake-
skin and the sight of one mountain still catching the sunset, well after eight.
He thought he was lost and knew he was weak from not having eaten more
than five cents' worth of peanuts since leaving his aunt's (He was holding
his money back against the unknowns of himself and Goshen—how he'd
face his grandfather, his mother's grave). But he felt no need to turn and
ask. If he'd come the wrong road, he would lie down at dark and sleep till
light and find his way then. He had worked through to calm in the past

two days, a calm which he recognized and thought he had earned by his courage in making his own life at last, not knowing that it came more than half as a gift from the lives buried in him and the lonely day and whatever cared for him in the hidden world.

So he came up first on the servant's house and saw a light there (the main house was dark), but he knew he was right. It was all in his memory and rose now to match what stood here before him—the house, the spring-house, the broke-down quarters. The light showed dim at the one small window; and since he thought he'd seen a body moving there, he set down his bag and, barely raising his voice, said "Is somebody here?" He knew the walls were thin, two thicknesses of pine; but he heard no steps and no voice answered.

Then a face looked out—Negro, a woman, black as oiled slate.

Hutch only smiled.

And at first the woman answered—the start of her own smile, canceled at once by eyes as refusing as any his mother turned toward him in dreams.

He said "This is Hutchins," meaning his name.

She shook her head No, shut her eyes and was gone.

By then it was nearly dark where he stood. The main house was darker; he could not go there. Yet he knew he had come to the place he expected, that somewhere in this he would find his mother's father. The woman hadn't heard him; maybe he had scared her (she seemed all alone and might have thought he looked like his mother, a spirit). He went to the front door and knocked three times.

Finally she came, switching on a hall light—a tall woman wearing a navy-blue dress, two strings of white beads; her skin as dark as field hands', though she seemed above work.

Hutch said, "I'm looking for Mr. Raven Hutchins."

She shook her head again.

"This is Hutchins Hotel?" He pointed to the house. "I'm not lost, am I?"

"It was," she said.

"He's my grandfather."

She shook her head.

"I'm Rachel's son—"

"*Rob's,*" she said.

"—Raven Hutchins," he said, to clarify his name.

"Too late," she said. "He passed in May."

"Is anybody here?" He pointed again.

"Two ladies from Roanoke, on the far side, guests."

"No Hutchins though?"

"*You* if you telling the truth." She reached out as if to touch his right cheekbone, a test of his claim; but even in the new dark, her sight had confirmed him. "You tired?" she said.

"More hungry, I guess."

"Step in here," she said.

Hutch stooped for his bag but thought and stood. "Are you Della?" he said.

"I was," she said. "Step in and let's see." By then she had smiled, if only for herself, at the patience of years.

3

HUTCH had asked no more questions and Della had volunteered no answers through the next twenty minutes but had worked at eating. She had brought food out from the kitchen when she'd finished there—enough for her supper and something in the night—and she'd put off eating till she sat and heard the news; so she was hungry also and had enough to share and a spare plate to hold it: cold ham, macaroni and cheese, rolls and water. She had sat on her bed, Hutch in her one chair; they'd swallowed in silence but had studied each other in quick deep glances by the one hanging light—Della searching him for all the signs of his parents, the chance that their old claims on her and her life continued in him; Hutch picturing her younger and helping his father countless nights in this room.

She held on his eyes at last and said "How you know me?"

Hutch had cleaned his plate. He set it by his feet and said "Rob."

"You call him Rob?"

He nodded. "My father."

"I know him. What he tell you?"

"That you used to help him out."

"Out of what?"

"Oh trouble. He said he'd been very unhappy when he got here, and you were a bridge for him."

Della laughed. "To what?"

"My mother, I guess."

"And that made him happy? Well, Jesus be praised; I can die satisfied."

Two days before this, he'd have stood and walked out, proud of one more chance to refuse such a world. Now he was tired and, deeper than tired, knew he also needed help bad as Rob ever had (he was wrong, being safer than Rob at any time; but the two past days had made him doubt every landmark he'd relied on for fourteen years—people, houses, trees). He could not ask directly, not knowing what help or what she would give; so he said, "He thanks you. Rob does; he just told me."

"Where is he?"

"In Richmond."

"They let him back in Richmond?"

"No my grandfather died. Rob's there to settle things."

"Your Mayfield grandpa?—you're losing em, ain't you?"

Hutch saw she spoke earnestly, no taunt on her face. "I'm used to that," he said. "Rob said you knew my mother."

"Good as anybody did. She liked to be secret, but I grew up with her—she couldn't hide long."

Hutch said "She did from me."

Della said "What you remember?"

"Don't you know I never saw her?"

Della said, "I was gone. Excuse me; I was gone, left here when they married. I thought she lasted long enough for you to know her some."

Hutch shook his head. "No. I've seen pictures of her. I've had dreams about her."

Della nodded. "What she do?"

"In the dreams?—she leaves. I find her by accident, standing in the woods; and I ask her to wait so I can call Rob, but she always leaves then."

"You go to get Rob?"

"He's back at the house." Hutch pointed behind him, out of the dream.

"You leave her then; you leave Rachel *first*. That was what she was scared of; nobody would stay. She worked against that so hard it killed her."

Hutch said "I killed her."

Della thought a good while, then stood with her plate, and went to the bureau and set it there. She studied herself in the cloudy mirror, not reaching for her comb or touching herself but as long and closely as if all she knew lay in sight on her face, printed deep in the dark skin, eventually legible. She knew about Rachel what she knew about Della. So she went to the bed again, the far side now, and sat facing Hutch. "Somebody lied to you; I ain't asking who but I *ain't* lying. You hang on to this; I know it's God's truth—Rachel died doing all Rachel ever tried to do. She had her deep faults—I was one that suffered from em—but she wanted one thing in her life: to *have* something. To have it for good. And she wanted it *living*—no clothes or shoes, no ring you could turn. She wanted it *talking*— no dog or cat. She thought it was various ones that it wasn't—her daddy, little friends. They all cut her deep; no shame on them. Then here come Rob, with the same idea; and she thought it was him. Must have turned out it wasn't—I was gone like I say. So she dreamed it was you."

"Did she tell you that?"

"No, Son, I never saw her once she left that house. I cooked her wedding dinner, and she came in and give me the flowers she had carried and told me I knowed her and to come if she call. I told her I would, and I guess I was lying (I was aiming for Philly). She never did test me though so maybe I wasn't. But no, she dreamed all her life about you; you were something she knew she could truly have, make and keep by her. She died by accident or God cut her string. You stuck with her, ain't you?—you got her deep eyes; you back here now."

"But they're gone," Hutch said. Neither he nor Della had mentioned his grandfather once since she first spoke.

She smiled. "*We* ain't."

Hutch smiled, agreeing, but he needed more now. "Was he sick a long time?"

"Mr. Raven? Not long. I lived up north from the time I left him, but he'd been good to my mother long as she lived (I used to not think so, but now I see better); and every year he'd think of my birthday, never failed. Here would come a little check wherever I lived, no news, just the money. So when I would come back every two or three years to see my cousin, I would step here to see him; and he'd ask me this (after Miss Carrie died)—'Della, what will you do when I call you to nurse me?' I'd laugh and tell him, 'Mr. Raven, I'll be calling *you*.' I liked it up north and had some good jobs; but the weather didn't suit me, gave me arthritis so bad I got *crippled*, thought I'd sure have to wash up here soon and die. I come down this Easter at the end of a long spell, out of work since Christmas and broke as a honest man. I stayed at my cousin's for the first week or so, just drawing my strength up; didn't go to see him; so he finally come to me. Drove up in the yard and climbed out slow. I saw him out the window and knew he was sick—the way he lifted his legs too high, trying too hard, and once I could see him close, the back of his hands: yellow as gourds and shriveling fast. My cousin was gone and Fitts her boy; so I stood there alone and said 'Della, here it come.' I knew he had called me; and I had to answer—he buried my mother, paid every last penny when pennies round here were thinner than now. And I said, 'All you need now is one more dying'; a friend of mine had died on me back in the fall. But I went to the door and sat with him on the porch. He talked about business, never mentioned the past (only man I know didn't care for the past); said he had a good crowd due in July and August—people give up going to the beach, scared of Germans. Then he said would I come there and help him in the kitchen. I told him I won't what I used to be, that you couldn't lean on me like you used to could. He bent over then—we were setting in rockers—and said it to the ground: 'You everything I got. I got to lean on you.' So I asked him was he poorly. Said he guessed he was. He reached over then and took my hand that was still bad swollen and brought it to his left side and said 'What's that?' My mother used to rub his neck for him sometime (her right hand was healing), so I pressed on him gentle. He said 'Go deeper.' I probed down then and this tumor was waiting, the size of a near-born baby's foot but streaming roots. I tried to laugh and told him 'Feel like you expecting.' —'Am,' he said, 'so I'm begging you back.' " Della stopped there and looked toward the one window—pure night. She offered no more, thinking that was sufficient or that now Hutch must ask whatever else he wondered.

He said "Were you glad?"—last word she'd expected.

She knew now she had been, an order to rest; but she held that back. That would mean telling this child more than he needed or ever could use. She said, "I was holding the truth in my hand. I told him I would, and you see I did. I'm even still here."

"You said it was May?"

"Three weeks yesterday."

"Nobody had told me."

Della said, "He wrote you. I well know he wrote you; I mailed it myself."

Hutch said, "My birthday—to wish me happy birthday."

"To beg *you* too. He was begging you to come." Her voice was low but powerful within, firm with knowledge and her long need to judge.

"He never said that; he said *sometime*." Hutch pointed to his bag and half-rose to open it, prove his excuse.

Della waved him back. "You how old, you tell me?"

"Fourteen in May."

"You old enough to have two children of your own, old enough to die shot if you lie to the army like a lot of good boys; and you saying you thought that was birthday wishes?"

Hutch nodded. "Yes ma'm. I read it that way."

"Let me teach you something then—how to read between lines; that's the best book there is. He was here, going fast, no other kin but you. He didn't talk about you—you were part of the past—but he knew your birthday and wrote that letter and told me to mail it and made me swear I did when I got back to him. He wanted you present, you to *be* the present and all that come after."

Hutch went to his bag then and found the letter. He read it through slowly; then folded it back, no offer to Della. "Not there," he said. "Nothing there but good wishes, 'Come to see me sometime.' " He was still on his feet.

"All right," Della said, still gentle, still firm, "—sit down and answer this."

Hutch obeyed and faced her.

"How come he give me this?" Looking only at him, she touched the bed with her index finger.

Hutch smiled. "You were tired."

Her high laugh surprised her, a scared-dog yip. "Tired as God," she said. "Tired as waves in the water, but I mean the whole thing. He give me this place." She waved slowly round her with the hand that had pointed. "The hotel, the springhouse, the nigger house, all."

Hutch said "He did right."

Della nodded. "Thank you. I stayed to the real end. We put off the guests that were due to come in May, and Fitts and me saw him through best we could. I never saw him suffer; he could swallow all that, swallowed that all his life. And he wouldn't let me call no doctor for nothing, said doctors were the suckingest leeches on feet; had watched his mama, my mama, and Rachel die in their own blood and still sent him bills just for watching up close. 'They can guess about *me*,' he told me, '—no charge.' So I cooked what he'd eat—bread pudding, boiled custard—and Fitts bathed and shaved him when he couldn't raise his hands. Toward the end I offered to sleep in his room, but he told me '*Too late*' and laughed long minutes. The last time he laughed. After that it froze his tongue, and he could barely talk; so the little he said, he said dead-earnest. He thought I was Mama for two long days and begged my pardon. I never told him better, but he cleared up finally; and when I brought his supper on the evening he died, he said, 'Della, we've seen the whole story of the world.' I told him 'Yes sir'—he had had his own life; and I'd told him some parts of my own little business up north, up yonder." She pointed to the ceiling as if that were north—Philadelphia, Glenolden, tile kitchens she'd kept like the skin of her face, steam-heated dry rooms she'd slept stone-alone in, the men who had found her. "Then he said 'What you know?' —'Know I'm tired, Mr. Raven.' —'Then rest here,' he said. I thought he meant his room; he had his old couch he used to nap on. I told him, 'I'm going to go soak my feet and hit my old bed like a sack of dead birds.' He didn't say no more till I had finished feeding him and picked up the tray. I was heading to the door and he said 'Say thank you.' I said, 'All right. Now tell me what for.' He knew I hadn't understood—'I give you this place,' he said. I said 'You mean the house?' and he said 'All I'm leaving.' So I told him 'Thank you' and went on out, thinking he was just talking and would be there in the morning still waiting for you. He was there, cold as Christmas. Fitts went up and found him—God spared me that much—and we buried him next morning. Preacher asked me 'Where his people?' and I told him we had wrote you, and you never had answered—you nor Rob neither one. He said he'd notify you, but I guess he never did."

"Not me," Hutch said. "I was coming just to see him. It had been eleven years."

"Going to be a lot more." She smiled; trusting fifty, sixty years lay before him.

But he said "Maybe not."

"You sick yourself?"

"No, tired like you."

"I'm pushing forty hard," Della said. "I earned it. What you tired of? —candy? little girls coming at you?"

Hutch knew. "No. Waiting."

"Child, you talk about waiting; you ain't started yet—something else I can teach you."

"What you waiting for?" he said.

She started to tell him—she also knew—but she said "I talked enough."

Hutch said, "My father. I've waited for him going on eight years."

"For him to do what?"

"Find a place for us."

"You ain't got a home? I thought his mama had you."

"She's kept me," he said, "and she's been good to me; I can love her for that. But I wanted Rob—"

"Lot of people wanted Rob—"

"—I didn't have a mother; so I turned to him: he drew me to him, said he wanted me there. At least he showed me that, five years—three years in Richmond till he lost out there; then we tried to come here (Grandfather wouldn't have us, not Rob anyhow); then two years in Fontaine at my grandmother's. Then he left for Raleigh."

"Didn't take you with him?"

"He promised he would. He hadn't even told me he was going till he went. One late August morning I was in the backyard out behind Grainger's house, digging by myself; and Rob came to me and said, 'Sweetheart, I am going for a while to be in Raleigh. I've found a better chance for both of us and will come and get you and Grainger both by New Year's.' So I didn't cry then, but I might as well have and got him behind me. The chance was for just him; he never kept his word."

"What job he have?"

"Teaching school, high school."

"What's Rob know enough about to teach anybody? The stuff he was learning when he lived here, you can't teach children."

Hutch heard that and understood but saw no way to follow it on into her life, the memories she clearly theatened to show. He took up his own story, nearly as hard. "He has this woman in Raleigh that he needs. He's stayed there for her."

Della said "Who is she?"

"Min Tharrington, a teacher. He's known her all his life, since long before Rachel."

"You say they ain't married?"

"He says not, no. They spend time together—"

Della nodded. "All right. You grudging him that?"

"Yes ma'm."

"All right. Then you want him to die. Or grieve himself sick."

Hutch had studied her room through all of that. It was all but bare of the signs of a person—at the foot of the bed, a pair of white shoes, high-heeled and broken; a book on the shelf by the head of the bed, old, crudely covered in new blue cloth; a black alarm clock that had ticked on beneath them, loud in their silence. Otherwise a hotel or a hospital room, where people could twist in torment or die and then be wheeled out and leave no speck. He said "*You've* lived; you are sitting here smiling."

Before she had fully understood him, Della said "I'm smiling at you."

And Hutch said "I'm funny—'"

Then she saw he had rushed in and weighed her life and registered it wrong. The force of her feeling for his mother and father, rubbed raw now by their signs in Hutch, longed to slam forward here and tell him precisely *how* she had lived and with what little help from the world—strangers, kin, even those who had promised to pay her with care for the use of her kindness, her quick lean butt. With what little baggage she had come back to Goshen, to what meager welcome (her mother's sunk grave, a helpless ignorant cousin, a dead white man's house she knew she couldn't keep)— still smiling, sucking breath. But the sight of Rachel's eyes, reset in this face ten feet from her bed, recalled what her own dead mother had said when Rachel was wild and pouring abuse—"Remember that child don't mean to cut you, don't know you are here. You can't see it yet, but she's struggling to live *in the same world as you*—new clothes, big house, plenty coal in the shed; but the same hail of fire that'll scald you too is licking her now. She walked out early; your day'll come soon." So Della rose and came round the bed and stood at the foot, Hutch an arm's length away, though she did not touch him. She said, "It hadn't seemed that hard to me." It had seemed hard as pigiron.

Hutch nodded. "You're lonesome."

"A little, right now. But not for much longer; I'm heading north in June once those ladies leave. They just come Sunday, saying they didn't know; Mr. Raven wrote the others telling them it was over—somehow forgot those. They got another ten days; then I'm heading out."

"And leaving your stuff?"

"I can carry my stuff, one good handful."

"The place," he said.

"Place *yours*," Della said.

"He gave it to you."

"It won't his to give."

Hutch said "Why not?"

"Oh don't get me wrong; it's the Hutchins place and *been* that. I guess what I mean is, it won't mine to take even if the law let me and I could pay taxes—Rachel all over it (and all over you), your daddy's memory, old high-hat Grainger, my mama dropping dead out there by the spring and all us watching. It's yours, Son. *Take it.* You got your place now." She touched him finally, the first time ever, on his right ear and jaw. He was also Rob's; same good skin seamless as a pressed linen sheet, as warm and dry.

Hutch stood, took his bag, and walked to the door. Then he said, "Have you got any sort of flashlight?"

"Where you going?"

"To the house. I remember it now. I'll find a spare bed."

Della shook her head. "Nothing, no flashlight or candle. You go stumbling round over yonder tonight, you'll kill those ladies; two hearts'll stop. They already bolted in tight like they beautiful. Mr. Grainger's room right here next to me; you sleep here tonight, do your looking tomorrow."

He was tired to the sockets so he nodded acceptance.

Della went to a bureau drawer and found clean sheets and stood to come toward him; but again the sight stopped her—his active face, worked as surely by Rachel as if she were in him, still waiting her life. Della spoke to break the lock. "Say thank you," she said.

Hutch said "All right."

"For the place, I mean." She was smiling, dead-earnest.

Hutch nodded. "I knew. I thanked you for that."

4

TIRED as he was once she'd made his bed, Hutch had lain three minutes in close concentration on the name of his mother, his version of her face, in the hope of guiding himself into whatever corridor of sleep held the dream of his mother by the creek. He would wait this time till she spoke or called him.

But he failed entirely. For hours, it seemed, his mind only moved through lists of words, no people or scenes. The words were names of things he had wanted all his life, all actual things that could somewhere be got but had never come to him—a Noah's ark like the ones in child's books (two of everything living, the family of Noah, and the great houseboat with its loading ramp), a four-foot hollow stick for use as a blowgun, a set of real photographs of men's and women's bodies from which he could draw and imagine possibilities still beyond him (how the bodies could join and what would be proved or gained in their meeting), an accurate like- ness of Joan of Arc, a book explaining what was not told of Jesus in the King James Bible, Hitler's autograph. Then after more hours of deep blank peace, he made a full dream which lasted till dawn, not the story he wanted but the one he got.

He was walking on a flat dark field in France through hills of corpses, not a live soul in sight, no sound but his own feet and distant thunder which was sure to be guns. He was hunting for Rob, but he had no light. That forced him to crouch over man after man and feel cold faces for the traits of his father. The wet stumps of necks. Chests pierced more deeply than any girl. Boys smaller than himself. But no trace of Rob. Then he noticed a brown glow some way ahead and hurried to that—a good-sized tent with a light inside but all flaps laced. He scratched with his nails at the drumhead canvas till he started a tear which he slowly lengthened till he had a straight slit the length of a door. He slid through and found himself warm in kerosene light which showed two men, Sylvie's nephew Albert on a low pine stool and a man on a cot. The man was Rob and, though he was dressed in a clean uniform, Hutch knew he was dead. He took two steps forward into the light—not to touch, only study the resting face (calm as water in a bowl)—but Albert spoke low: "I found him, I'll guard him, you head on back."

He woke then, the first news of day at the window; still dark but the total silence of dawn. He did not remember the facts of his dreams but knew he had failed to reach his mother; and though he might well have lain and thought of Grainger˙ (his bed; this room that had held him, hopeful) or of Rob in Richmond (if he'd stayed in Richmond, had not gone to Min or called her to him), he returned to his mother whom sleep would not give him.

But now, even waking, he had lost her face. No memory would come. He stood to the cold floor and felt through the dark for the one light string, found it, scalded the room with sudden glare. He had wanted a mirror—Rachel's face in his—but the pine walls were bare: a long-dead thermometer stuck at 28. In his thin underclothes, Hutch held himself, shivering. The morning before, he had risen at his Aunt Hatt's, planning a new life to spare himself the debts of his kin, their designs to own him outside and in. Here—freezing on a dirty floor, miles from what he wanted, refused by his mother this final time (his sex half-hard still from dreams she avoided)—he saw he'd found nothing new and would never. The world was *made*. It had offered him space and a section of years, a full set of harness to which any number of people held reins, some of them stone-dead. At any moment, unannounced, the offer would vanish and his be a life like Rob's—unwashable shame, permanent flight. Fourteen years old. Children much younger this morning, this instant, were forced into harness as heavy though brief—unrescued death.

Hutch chose to wear it. No sound from Della. He crept to his clothes and quietly dressed. Then he turned out the light again and stopped for his prayers, the Lord's prayer quickly and the names of his kin, adding Grainger and Della. By the end of that, there was some daylight in the room, thin as mist but sufficient for movement. He turned the old door-knob, a rusty cry; if he woke Della now, he would simply explain. He waited on the sill but could only hear her turn once and settle into snoring. So he entered the hall and passed out the main door with no further sound.

The dawn air was colder than the quarters had been, but Hutch stopped and stood in the hope of finding memories to guide him on now through the scarce tan light. They came at him slowly and in the form of buildings—on his right the springhouse, cedar roof pale as pewter. He had drunk there once in his grandfather's arms eleven years ago. He could still taste the cup.

It was waiting there still—a long-handled copper cup, poison-green from its years of use in strong water. Hutch took it down and opened the lid of the spring and bent far down where no light had seeped yet before he found water. Then he drank a slow swallow, far warmer than expected. His Grandfather Hutchins had held it up to him and said, "Son, drink. You ever drink this, you'll need to stay here. It has cured some pain." Hutch found that now like a stone in his mind, covered but patient, ready to serve. He took more water and poured it on his hands and rubbed his face and eyes. Then he hung the dipper back by the working nest of two red wasps and went toward the main house to find the next thing Rob had promised he'd know.

5

HE did, though slowly. The big dark kitchen was strange in itself, but there seemed a path through it to an opposite door; and once he had eaten a biscuit from the bread box that stood on a cupboard, he went to the door and (silently again) opened on the central hall of the house, still all but dark. Its only light, through the transom window of the far front door, showed ranks of black doors in whitewashed walls, all closed but the two farthest from him—parlor, dining room. The path seemed to go to the nearest, beyond him. Hutch stood a moment, downing his last dry crumbs and thinking that the door might hide sleeping women or worse—Rob dead on a cot, Albert guarding. Then he took the four steps and opened it quickly and found that he knew—not only that he'd come here with Rob, led secretly, but earlier and freely with his Grandfather Hutchins. It was his bedroom. The shades were up and a window faced the sun.

There was one wide bed with a high carved back—little turrets and pillboxes, spindles and domes—and below at the foot, a smaller cot like a white dog resting. Both were smoothly made with fresh linen, not a crease in sight. But the path went on to the far wall, a dresser—tall mirror, marble top (a streaked liver-brown). He followed to that. It had been the goal of coming here at all, the source of dreams. It had been where his grandfather kept his mother; Hutch remembered he'd thought of it that way for years. Why? The marble was bare now of all but a yellowing crocheted mat and a pair of men's brushes, bristling dead white hair.

He had been brought here, direct from the springhouse still in his grandfather's arms, to this dresser. He recalled independently of Rob's own story two pictures of a lady, young with dark hair and eyes; his grandfather raising one picture with his free hand for Hutch to see—"This is what we lost. They take it all, Son. Come here and I'll help you." Now he was here. It all was his. Where was the help?

At least there was a mirror. He leaned toward that and searched his face. Though he'd drawn it two nights ago, it seemed strange as ever, unknowable. It had been two years since his Aunt Rena first said he had Rachel's eyes. Till then he'd assumed, when he thought at all, that he'd been and would always be a new thing, a fresh attempt by his parents and God at a thing which would *work* (as the whole world hadn't). But they'd been near the end of Sunday dinner two summers ago, the anniversary of Bedford Kendal's death; and Eva had picked at Rena all morning for having no decent flowers for the grave. Rena as always had waited her time, only saying she was sorry and blaming late frosts; then she had stared long at Hutch and said, "You're turning to Rachel before our eyes." Eva had said, "There are several eyes present; you speak for your own"; and they'd dropped it there. But Hutch had asked Grainger a few days later and Grainger agreed—"Plain as day; her eyes, for the past year or so." After that Hutch had studied himself with new hope—that the half of his life which had gone at his birth had in fact only slept and was waking inside him, molding his face in silence from within, offering the gift he had never had: absolute certainty of love and safety, a permanent shadow.

Now he leaned till his breath fogged the glass. Still strange. He recalled Della's speech—"She wanted to have one thing in her life: something living, for good. Something talking."

So he spoke. His dry lips brushing cold glass, he said, "You have got it, Mother. You could come back." He drew back then and saw reflected a woman in the open door, tall in a nightgown, a green bathrobe. Calm as at no other time in his life, he turned to meet her.

She said "Who are you?" but before he had answered, she saw and said "Hutchins."

"Yes ma'm. Do I know you?"

It took her awhile. "No you don't, I guess. I was your mother's friend, Alice Matthews." She pointed to her left. "I sleep next door and I heard footsteps. I thought it was Della."

"No ma'm," he said. "How did you recognize me?"

Alice waited again. "Your mother," she said. "You're hers all right."

Hutch said "Tell me how."

"Your face, I meant."

"Do you have her picture?"

"Not with me," she said. "I'm in Roanoke now. There are pictures here though." She came forward then the length of the room and knelt and opened a dresser drawer. "These were your grandfather's. Della put them away just yesterday morning; I was helping her clean." She held out two framed pictures to Hutch.

He suddenly dreaded to take them but did.

Alice rose and stood beside him while he looked.

Rachel, laughing broadly in both. One was blurred by her moving; she leaned far forward with her elbows propped on a high white railing and held her own chin in two long hands. Just the face was blurred; the body was still as a tree in August. It seemed to Hutch that some strange girl was pressing a happy mask to her own face, hidden and safe. But the same girl laughed clear as ice in the other (same dress, same day); the camera had seized her, though not her hair—it burned out round her and mixed with the dark leaves that pressed from behind. She was in the same springhouse that he had just left and beside her, four feet away, another girl stood and watched her closely. Hutch looked up and said, "What was funny, I wonder?"

"So did I," Alice said. "I'm the onlooker there."

Since Rachel faced outward, intent on the camera, Hutch said "Who took it?"

"Rob Mayfield," Alice said. "Is he here with you?" She looked to the door as if Rob might wait there.

"I'm alone," Hutch said. "I'm here on my own."

Alice nodded. "I'm sorry—" She meant his grandfather.

Hutch thought she meant his loneliness. "I am too," he said. Then he studied the second picture again. "What was happening here?"

Alice reached out to take it.

Hutch said, "I think these are mine now please."

Alice flushed and wanted to turn and leave. But twenty years of teaching art to children his age (and a childhood of living in her father's sanitarium) had taught her one thing at least—all children are desperate: boys more so than girls since boys seldom know it; girls taste it from birth. She looked at her watch and said, "Quarter to six. No Della for an hour. Come help me fix coffee. That's a story; I'll tell you." She pointed to the picture, but she did not touch it.

6

WHEN she'd poured their coffee and set it on the table, Alice said, "I would scramble you an egg but Della'd kill me." Then she sat at the far

end from Hutch and drank, scalding hot, no cream. Then she said,
"November 1925, the day before her wedding. I had come up from Lynchburg on the early train; and her mother had given a small lunch party, her
piano teacher and two local girls (Rachel didn't have many friends; she
kept them too busy). That was over by three; and her mother ordered naps
all round, to protect her. I was frankly delighted, having woke before day;
but as soon as I stretched out, Rachel came knocking and wanted to talk. I
knew she was wrought up and I understood why, but my father had been
her doctor and I'd nursed her; so I said, 'Talk to me for five minutes
straight, and then lie here and rest'—all the beds then were double; anybody slept alone was thought to be odd if not in worse trouble. Rachel sat
on the edge of the bed and laughed and said, 'Five minutes? I will need
one second.' Your mother was a well-practiced talker, Hutchins; she could
go on for minutes, hours if Rob was the theme. So I said, 'Praise God, take
two and then rest.' Rachel said 'I'm going to die.' I said 'Says who?' (my
father had seen her through serious trouble, though nothing too mortal).
She lay back beside me then and showed no intention of explaining herself. I assumed she was joking and dropped off to sleep. We were under a
down quilt—the upstairs was cold—and she lay there as still as a field
beside me for more than an hour till I'd got my strength back and woke up
and looked. Her eyes were open, just watching the ceiling. It was well past
four, and the light was failing. I had already put her joke from my mind; I
said 'Did you rest?' She said 'No ma'm' (I am one year her senior); and I
said, 'You missed your last good chance.' Rob had already gone to meet his
Aunt Rena; his father would get here at six-fifteen; wedding supper was
at seven. Rachel said 'Stop there' and turned her face to see me. Then she
said, 'Every string of my being knows this—*I will not last*. I have been too
lucky. I will rest much sooner than anybody knows. Let me have my way.'
I watched her through that and knew she was right. Some message had
reached her; I've never known who from. Till then, young as I was, I'd
really tried to help her, not humor her along as her poor parents did. I
loved her that much, and I thought she could change (children think
people change). But seeing her eyes then, I knew I was wrong. I said, 'All
right. Say what I must do.' She laughed again and said 'Oh nothing.' But
she sat up and thought awhile and said, 'Do this. Take some pictures of
me. There are not any good ones.' I said, 'All right but it's getting late.' I
had brought my father's antique Kodak which required blinding light. She
jumped up and combed her hair. I slipped on my dress and shoes, and
down we went. She wanted me to take her in the chair on the porch where
she always sat. I said she would have to lean forward on the railing to catch
a little sun, and that explains this one." Alice pointed to a picture.

Hutch said, "What explains the laugh if she knew she was dying?"

"My foolishness," Alice said. "I told her something funny."

Hutch studied the face again, then smiled at Alice. "Tell me," he said.

She flushed again, embarrassed but glad to recall. "I had got my first job two months before, teaching in South Hill; and I lived in the house of a widow named Key who had four roomers and one bathroom and severe constipation as her personal cross. The trick every morning was to beat her to the bathroom or we'd be late for school. The trick seldom worked; the general sign that the day had started was the sound of her bolting the bathroom door and running warm water for her enema bag. It was bright red and hung on the back of the door like an object of pride. By a week before the wedding, we were fed up with *that*; and the one male roomer—the coach, Peg Pittman—had planned a revenge and warned me in advance. He went to the bathroom late that night and poured a full tablespoon of pure turpentine in her enema bag. So morning came and she bolted the door, and we all lay and listened. Running water, long silence; then cries of '*Mozelle!*' (Mozelle was the maid), 'Mozelle, oh Jesus!' I was telling Rachel that."

Hutch also laughed and said, "Did she live?—your lady, I mean."

"Lived and was cured." Alice rose and poured her cool coffee down the drain and took a hot cup. "You ready for more?"

"No ma'm," he said, taking up the other picture, the one in the springhouse. "You say this is you?"

Alice came and looked again. "I regret to say. Don't I look like a witch?"

"Yes ma'm," Hutch said. "Who was holding the Kodak?"

"Guess."

"Della maybe?"

"Rob," Alice said. "I had taken four or five pictures there on the porch. Rachel said we had enough and took me to the spring. I had been here to visit just once before; and then she had warned me off the spring—it was old and dirty and, if I'm not mistaken, had given her Grandmother Hutchins the ailment that finally killed her. But this day she said, 'Have you tasted the spring?' and I said I hadn't. She said, 'That's part of what I want then'; so we walked over there, and I set down the Kodak on one of the railings. It had been cleaned up quite a lot since I saw it; swept out, new roof, the scrollwork painted. I didn't mention how she'd described it before but drank when she held that dipper out to me. As I swallowed I thought, 'This is all still a joke. Rachel won't drink now and will tell me *I'm* dying.' But she took the cup from me—I had drunk just a swallow—and downed what was left; and we sat on the steps of the far side in sunshine. She asked me to tell her what my life was like. I'd known her some months; she never had asked me; and I started to tell her, the serious part, no more turpentine jokes. Then a man's voice said, 'Now the world can *proceed*.' It was Rob, back from meeting Miss Rena's train. I was square in the middle of what she had asked for, my thrilling life; but she touched my knee and said 'Alice, please wait.' Then she stood and went toward him; and of course I did too, though a good way back. He had seen my Kodak and was aiming it at us; so he caught what was there, caught it clear as you see. I never knew how. All mine were blurred but his was clear—and Rachel vibrated in every cell from the moment he spoke. Miss Rena was behind him, not approving at all."

Hutch said, "Grandfather kept it. But he didn't like Rob."

"Who told you that?"

"Rob."

Alice took a long draught of her coffee, then faced him. "You're fourteen, aren't you?"

"Yes ma'm."

"Live with Rob?"

"No ma'm, with his mother."

"May I tell you my feelings?"

"Yes ma'm," Hutch said.

Alice hooked her own short hair behind her ears and showed her full face, her permission to speak plain, the license she'd earned. A fine calm face with whole long planes like warm ground in light, room to rest, little used. "Mr. Hutchins liked Rob well enough. So did I. What worried us all was the knowledge that he was as needy as Rachel in his own different way, as Hell-bent on food; that they couldn't feed each other for long without one finishing the other off. They were not big feasts; they were country children. Hutch, they could have been Albert Einstein and Madame Curie and still been in danger."

"Why?"

Alice thought she knew, had known for years. "They thought they had *rights*."

"To what?"

"Their wishes. Their wishes fulfilled."

"What's wrong about that?" Hutch said.

"Very little—provided people know that wishes are dreams, stories people tell themselves; that wishes aren't orders which the world will obey. Rob and Rachel didn't know that one simple fact. Rob may have changed since. Rachel never did, I know; never could have, however many years she got."

Hutch said, "Were you old enough to know what they wished?—this day, I mean." He still held the frame with the springhouse picture.

Alice said, "Son, I knew it from birth. So have you. I know it is all any human dreams of, no secret at all." She stopped there and watched him, smiling over her cup.

He also smiled. "You aren't going to tell me?"

"Tell *me*," she said.

Hutch knew she was a teacher and must work like this. At the same time he knew the old school-pleasure of the one right answer on his tongue, held ready. He said, "To be still next to someone you want in a place where there's no extra people in sight."

Alice laughed. She had not planned to hear it that way. She had thought he would somehow speak, like most, of courteous lasting mutual love.

"Then what is it?" Hutch said, a serious question.

She opened her mouth to say it her way, then could not. He had learned a truer wish—or one half-truer than hers at least. If nothing else had come of Rachel and Rob, this had; this lean boy five feet beyond her, waiting silently for what he already knew better than she. So she said, "No, *still*. To be still. Just the *still* part, I think. Other people come later and are mostly mistakes."

Hutch said, "Then Rachel's happy. I did her a favor."

"How's that?"

"That she died. That sounds still to me."

Alice laughed again but cut it down in midair.

"I don't believe you though."

"About what?"

"About people, not for me anyhow. I've wanted Rob with me since before I remember. Nobody else."

Alice said "Where is he?"

"In Richmond two days ago when I left there. But he was drunk then, so he could have moved on. He could be on the moon or in Normandy dead, but he's not wishing Raven Mayfield was there."

"That's you?"

"Yes ma'm."

Alice said "I believe you" and flushed with regret, to have told a child more truth than he required.

But Hutch only looked to the window behind her and said, "Can you say if you've got your wish?"

She could. "Yes I have."

"Will you tell me how?"

She thought awhile. "It has been very simple. Nobody tried to stop me! I've lived in a single room for nineteen years, a good single bed not as wide as this table."

"And you really wanted that?"

Alice waited again till she had the truth. "When I was a child, yes. And more and more lately. My father ran a private sanitarium in Lynchburg—at first for weak chests, then for weak nerves and dopers of various sorts—and I grew up in a house next door, a plain quiet girl who was no good at anything but watercolor drawings; so maybe you will know that all I prayed for till I was, say, your age was *me in a room* with a one-way lock and a window that would see *out* but not show me. I thought I could sit there and spy on the world, which was mostly Father's patients, till I'd understood its beauty—I was told it had a beauty, by God's design—and could draw that pattern down in color on paper so clearly and plainly that I could walk out then and people would love me as naturally as dogs had. I thought it would be pictures of people—the pattern, people clustered like plants in their proper native spheres—and that they would recognize themselves and thank me for it. And they did seem to praise me, when I was a child and walked out occasionally to where people were. Then I got your age and began to think I'd understood wrongly—that the world came *paired,* that the pattern was simple: one here, one there, the line between. And misery began. I thought I'd been bad off before! I'd been *blessed.*"

Hutch said, "Who was it? Did you know who it was?"

Alice nodded. "Clear as a needle through the eye, clearer than anything else I've known. Named Marion Thomas, a tall boy with eyes such a pale light blue that from ten feet away they seemed all-white; and he seemed a statue in warm tan marble. Ten feet was near as I ever got to him, and in Latin class. He was very good at it and smiled a lot but always toward the front (I was three seats behind in the next row over). I kept a full record for one entire year of what he wore to school—gray trousers, blue shirt, a stretched gray sweater; that sort of simple thing. It seemed a path into his secret heart. I still have the list and, you know, it worked. I grew to understand him deep down to the ground. I could wake up and look out my window at the day and know how he'd dress, the socks he'd choose. I could almost guess what he'd smile at in class. He said about eighty-five words to me in the course of that year. Then his father died and he had to work—at a general store on the outskirts of town where I never went. I hurt for two years; I would sit and draw the memory of his face by the hour."

"Did he know?"

Alice traced a peaked vertical line on the table; then repeated it twice as if summoning memory and hardening it, the line of a face. "I used to think not. As I said, all he ever asked about was homework; but then two years ago when my mother died, he came to the funeral. I saw him in the small crowd behind the grave; and it struck me like a great hand, harder than the death. He had barely known Mother, and I hadn't seen him in twenty-four years; so all I could think there, with Mother cold before me, was 'What can he say?' Well, the first thing he said after 'Alice, I'm sorry' was 'Meet my wife'—a thin woman plainer than I'd ever been, with several times more teeth than most humans have. Then he took my hand back and said 'See, I never forgot.' "

Hutch said "What did that mean?"

"I have no idea."

"And you didn't ask him?"

"No. He might have said something like he'd known and was grateful; and then I'd have seen we were both great fools, mooning down the years (though he'd had her standing by to fill in)."

Hutch said, "You were by yourself till then? He was all you wanted?"

Alice smiled and did a whole crowd of quick profiles around her cup, lost on the wood. "Oh no. Several others; I was seldom not pining. Or wishing at least. I was never really pining. They were all real chances, all possible people; no moviestars or princes, none already spoke for."

"Did you ever speak?"

"For one of them? Yes. I learned to do that once Marion was over clerking dried beans and rope. Never lose in silence. Speak up and then wait. I have told three people, in words more or less, that I wanted their lives near mine for good. One of them was Rachel. They all said No, politely but No."

"Who's here with you now?"

"My father's pet sister. I've given her this trip for three years now since your grandfather wrote and invited me up. She suffers from asthma and the mountains help. But I guess this ends it."

Hutch only said, "When did you change your mind?"

"To what?"

"To your old thought of just being still. You said you had come back to wanting that again."

Alice said, "I never really left it altogether. In my deepest longing, sitting two feet away from a human person that I had made God, I would hear the buried core of my mind say, 'Alice, you're lying and you know it.' No I tell you, Hutch, I guess I could forget again tomorrow and fix on some face, magnetize some perfectly plain human face and rush helpless to it; but I have long stretches now of what seems peace."

"When mostly?" Hutch said.

Alice laughed. "Good night! J. Edgar Hoover!"

Hutch smiled. "I'm sorry. But I really need to know."

She studied him again and saw that he did. "Are you busy this morning?"

"No ma'm."

"Then I'll show you. I've talked too much."

Hutch nodded. "What time?"

"An hour after breakfast; let the sun get up." She stood and went to the sink again.

Hutch said, "Please say what was wrong with my mother."

Alice kept her back to him. "In what way?" she said.

"Everything people say makes her sound too strange."

"What way?" Alice said.

"Every way she could go—wanting me, wanting Rob, wanting death that young, not wanting you when you spoke out for her life."

Alice emptied her cup, rinsed the brown dregs down; then turned, grinning broadly. "That was pure good sense. Every one of those," she said. She honestly did not think she lied.

The porch door opened and Della looked in; looked slowly round the whole room, then gravely at Hutch. She said, "Well, it wasn't mine long but I *enjoyed* it. Anybody need a cook? I'm a good bacon cook. Can't everybody cook good bacon, I tell you." She laughed and they joined her.

7

By noon Hutch was thinking he'd finished his picture. It was clear lines drawn with his best hard pencil, no smearing, no shadows. It was what he could see from the flat bare ledge on the rocky slope where he'd sat for two hours—the rest of the slope, the back and head of Alice who was twenty feet down on her own ledge under a big bent cedar, the distant bottom with the quick brown river, the opposite walls of sheer tan rock which (with laurel and some strange yellow flowers) bore the bright green mountain. He clamped the pencil between his teeth and studied the whole sight against his picture. It was not what he'd seen or was seeing now. Nothing he had ever attempted was that. It was what he could make, on this one morning (having driven out to here with his mother's old friend to sit in pure silence—only nesting birds, the fierce hot ringing of bugs in weeds: no word from Alice since she'd chosen her own place and settled to work). Not *could* make, even.

It was one thing he *had* made this morning, unaided, from what the earth offered of its visible skin—the surface it flaunted in dazzling stillness, in the glaze of rest, to beg us to watch; then grope for its heart. (He knew that much now, had known it some weeks; but would not have said it or felt it in words.)

The hard part as always was trees, not their trunks which were easy as human legs and as frank in their purpose but leaves—their hanging gardens in tiers. He had done those badly. The opposite rocks, the back of the mountain, the line of Alice's back and head, her farmer's hat—they were right and true, his own gift offered to the world in return. A peaceful likeness of a peaceful sight. The promise or the strong hope of long years of swapping, with mutual aim—a common stillness, common provisions.

Alice moved, stretched her arms but did not look back. "Want to show me now?"

Hutch looked again. The leaves were worse. "No ma'm," he said.

She returned to work.

If he'd left them out—assumed it was fall (there were days good as

this in mid-November) and drawn plain trunks and a few stripped limbs.
He reached for his new eraser to strip them. If he'd been on the porch in
Fontaine now, Aunt Rena behind him might have said "No, stop." She
had said that the Sunday after his birthday when he'd sat down to use his
new tablet and pencils on the yard-trees, the millstone, her shrubs, the
road. He had done it in clear lines, then started to shade. She had sat six
feet away and watched twenty minutes without a sound. He'd learned to
forget her—till his thumb scrubbed-in the first shadow (farthest first).
Then she'd rocked forward firmly and said, "May I tell you? The whole
world is waiting to see what you're ruining." He had stopped and said,
"Ma'm? I'm not that good"; and Rena said, "Not you—the secrets of God.
The whole world is waiting in expectation for the revelation of the secrets
of God. You've just now drawn their excellent likeness and are ruining it."
Hutch had said "It's the yard" but had stopped there and sat, not touching
his paper, not asking her more, till she stood and went in.

So he spared the trees now. He trusted to wait till the secret of leaves,
if nothing more, came into his power. First the power to watch one green
leaf in stillness; then the dark banked branches in all their intricate shifting
concealment—concealed good news (that under the face of the earth lay
care, a loving heart, though maybe asleep: a giant in a cave who was
dreaming the world, a tale for his long night) or concealed news of hatred
embellished with green (that a sight like this or a shape like Rob's was only
the jeering mask of a demon who knew men's souls and guided their
steps). It seemed, now at least, that any such power would come here if
anywhere. This place was an entrance. He'd need to wait here.

How nearly alone though? Della would stay, had already offered.
They'd have to go on taking odd guests for money. Della and Fitts could
see to that. And would Grainger respond to his letter and come and want
to stay? Would he be too many, not wishing them well? Hutch knew he
was dreaming Alice's dream—not his own or Rob's, surely not Rachel's—
but he felt what Alice had promised to show, plain peace. She had not lied.
Whoever else in all his life had not lied? He looked down toward her.

She was no longer painting but still looked over toward the mountain,
not moving.

He said, "Miss Matthews, could Rachel have sat here?"

"With us, you mean?" She didn't look back.

"Yes ma'm."

"Not really." She waited awhile, then said "Not at all."

"Have you had a good time?"

"This morning? Still am." She hadn't turned yet.

"You teach in Roanoke?"

"September sixth."

"Stay on till then."

Alice looked to the sky. "I might get wet."

Hutch laughed but after a while said "I mean it."

"And I'm grateful," she said.

"Look here please," he said.

Slowly Alice looked round. The sun was behind him but oh what was left of Rachel was clear, the hair and the eyes and behind them the passion for absolute pleasure, the soul's reward. She shaded her eyes then and saw him more clearly, a long-boned boy, young-faced for his age. She thought she could stay here by him for good. A person had asked. The chance was now. It would not come again. Rewards came in *their* time, undreamed-of forms. She thought she was going to say "All right." But Hutch looked away, down at his tablet.

He had taken his pencil and was signing the picture—one name, *Mayfield*. Then he stood and, not looking to the rough ground for safety, he half-ran toward her.

8

Rob said, "Excuse me for knocking this late but the hotel was dark, and I saw your light."

She nodded. "I was listening to the radio." It was on behind her, some grainy music from Cuba or Mexico, hoarse from its journey.

He said, "I just drove up here from Richmond. My name is Mayfield. I'm meeting my son Hutch Mayfield; is he here?"

She pointed toward the dark house. "Yonder asleep."

"Mr. Hutchins asleep?"

"Mr. Hutchins been dead three weeks, Rob," she said.

The only light was her overhead bulb which struck him fully but barely touched her. Still he searched at her face. "You know me?" he said.

"I used to, a little."

He still couldn't see and the voice was strange. "Is it Della Simmons' cousin?"

She waited in silence a good five seconds, then bent down laughing, then stood and took two steps back into light. "It used to be *Della*," she said, "—last I looked."

Rob followed her in but kept the same distance while he studied the face. Even in the white light, he didn't know her—an older sister who had had a harder life but no, not Della. Yet she'd known him on sight, and why would she lie? He looked round for some firm piece of the past. The bed, the table, the dresser were the same; but they were Mr. Hutchins'. He said, "Have you got your dream book still?"

"You dreaming too?" She pointed to the shelf beside the bed, the yellow edges of an old book wrapped in fresh blue cloth.

"Can I sit down?" he said.

"You didn't use to ask." She was no longer smiling, but she showed him the chair. While he sat, she stayed on her feet to watch him. Then she said "You sick?"

"I have been," he said. "No I'm mainly tired—old thin recaps, had to drive so slow the car boiled over. Had to wait two hours by the side of the road."

"You want you a shot?"

Rob faced her again. Was she really Della? "You keeping that now?"

"I got me a pint, case a snake crawl on me." She stepped toward the bureau.

"Is Hutch really here?"

"I told you he was sleep. Mr. Raven's room."

"And Mr. Raven's dead?"

"The cancer. In May."

She had found her pint, a little more than half-full. With pure concentration she took her one waterglass and poured in an inch of whisky, knocked it back in a single swallow. Then a pause, then again. Then she turned to Rob. "Speak now or hold your peace."

He shook his head No. "What is that for?" he said. It could have been cold tea; she hadn't winced once.

Della capped her bottle carefully and laid it away. "I heard you were some kind of expert on that."

"From Hutch?"

"N'mind who."

Rob smiled. "I am. Maybe not an expert but pretty well-trained. And you know why, you know every reason, you've known a long time. I was asking about you."

Della went to the radio and turned it down so the music was ghostly under what came after. Then she sat on the foot of her bed, facing Rob. "What you want?" she said. "You want me to tell you I died-off for you?—just rolled over sick when Rachel grabbed you, just started sucking bottles? You come to hear that?"

He still smiled. "No."

"Good thing," Della said. "You'd have wasted good gas."

"I came to get Hutch."

"You wasted it then."

Rob said "What are you saying?"

"I'm saying that child ain't letting you get him. He got what he say he always wanted, a place; and he plan on sticking with it."

"This place?"

Della nodded. "From me. I give it to him. Mr. Raven left it to me, and I passed it on to Hutch."

"And Hutch plans to run it?—fourteen years old, poorest hotel in Virginia?"

"We got two paying guests in yonder right now and more on the way once he tell em 'Come on' (Mr. Raven stopped a lot of folks by mail when he was dying). People like this place, old people anyhow—my age, don't you know." She seemed entirely earnest.

Rob said, "You staying here with him then?"

"He asked me to, this morning first thing. Come out here and woke me up at quarter to six—said he couldn't sleep for thinking—and told me he was wanting to live on here and us run the place and him go to school here and Miss Alice come back next summer and help him. Said old Grainger might come."

"Miss Alice who?" Rob said.

"Matthews. Rachel's friend."

"She's the one here now?"

"With her old aunt from Lynchburg."

Rob said, "She's in on this dream too? She putting up some money?"

Della wiped her dry lips with the back of her hand. "I told you too much. He swore me not to tell. I was all he had told till I told you. You go mock him now, I'll kill you, Rob."

She seemed half to smile but her face was so changed from his memory that he saw no firm landmarks for judging her now—not fat but a thick inward padding deep round her, held forward like a shield of air or feathers. Finally he said "You never liked Rachel."

"I never liked you."

Rob nodded. "All right. I meant something else."

"Say it then."

"You're helping Hutch."

"I never claimed that." She shook her head firmly.

"You talk about staying here with him," Rob said, "—that foolishness."

Della looked to her lap. "I'm helping *me* and about-damn-time."

Rob said, "I already asked you what was wrong."

She studied him a long time; then faced her bureau mirror—tried to cut down through meat to the old face he'd known, that had helped bring him here those eighteen nights in the summer and fall of '25: a girl all pointed with the will to *leave*, hot to the touch with the steady banked coals of denial and silence and famishment, eyes like a fox. She found her easily, then offered her to Rob. "I left here two days after you and Rachel; didn't give no word of notice or nothing, just walked out and went. Straight north to Philadelphia and my Cousin Tee. She was my mother's best niece, and I hadn't seen her since I was a child; but she sent me a

message when Mama died, saying, 'Come on to Heaven and live with me.'
Heaven was a cafe named The Delicate Teacup that she owned part of. I
went straight to it from the depot by asking, and she hadn't got my letter.
But she knew me by sight (I hadn't changed then; you'd have still recognized me) and started in hollering when I stepped through the door—'O
Jesus, *Lucy*.' I said I was Della; and she said 'Can you work?'—it was
Saturday night. Well, the hollering stopped. I cooked right on through
Christmas and New Year, cooked three years without looking up. Same
way I cook here. They didn't seem to mind; ate it all anyhow and paid
good money—colored people, understand. Then Tee got married. She had
had one husband that melted away but never no baby (and that had half-
killed her), so I had lived with her and managed all right. But here come
the new man, a whole lot younger; and here come a baby. She picked her a
baby right out of that man like a splinter from your finger. Forty-four years
old. I told her 'Be ashamed'; and she told me, 'All right but you can't
watch'; she meant 'Get out.' I was glad by then. I had a fellow my age
been asking for me, named Newmarket Watters. He come in The Teacup
on Saturday nights and wait till I finish, which would be near morning,
and carry me to ride or something like that. He worked out from Philly on
a rich man's place, gardener and chauffeur; and they let him take they car
on his night off. That meant they trusted him—ought to: they raised him
(his mama was their cook, and he grew up beside em; she died before he
saw me). I trusted him too; first person I trusted since I was a child.
Trusted him and started thinking my time had come, my *luck* had come.
So when Tee's baby started and I ruined my welcome, he asked me did I
want a job with his white folks; they were needing a maid, already had a
cook. I told him 'All right'; and he said I was hired—they trusted him to
hire me. Well, he moved me out there the week before Christmas; and I
knew I was blessed. Had a good warm room to myself in the quarters
(Newmarket next door) and never touched a stove; they had a man-cook
from overseas. I just swept up and polished floors. They were gone half the
winter—in Georgia, staying warm—and when they were there, they didn't
barely know you. I mean, they could smile if they bumped into you; but
they didn't want nothing they hadn't paid for, a good-smelling house.
Didn't want your whole life. I gave it to em, the sweet-smelling house; the
rest I was giving to Newmarket Watters." Della stopped and looked to the
mirror again. She could see her old face; it still seemed a gift. She turned
back to Rob. "You believe me, don't you? You know what I got."

Rob nodded he did.

Then she said, "No you don't. You don't know half. I was opening up
all grades of flowers down in me that you never got near and sure never
touched. Newmarket was four shades darker than me (I darkened since
then); and I thought he could last me; thought time would come when
he'd tell me by day, and in presence of company, what he told me by

night. So a year of that passed; and I thought it was Heaven, like Tee had promised. I still think it was, ain't never spit on it, nothing ever been as good. Then here come Hoover and his depression. My folks lost they money or the best part of it; and four months later he keeled over dead, heart split down the middle. But the lady was living. She still had the house, and I was still waxing floors; and Newmarket still come visiting me, no sign he had changed. Thing was, he hadn't. It was me had been the change; little temporary change, little snack of home cooking before he went back where he wanted to be. Two months after that old man's heart broke, Newmarket come in to me one evening extra early. We just talked awhile; then I rose up to touch him (he made touching him seem part of your duty; he was that fine to see), and he said 'Wait a minute.' I waited while he told how hard-up the lady was, how hard she had to save, how she had to let me and the foreigner go. I said 'What about you?' and he said 'She need me.' I said '*I* need you' (I wish I'd bit my tongue out); and he said, 'I've been here all my life. I can't leave now.' Then he reached out to feel me, and I struck him like a snake. He had told me to wait. I said, 'You can wait till the hills yawn open and show you Hell, you ain't even *smelling* Della Simmons again.' He never did neither. I was packed up and gone out of there in a hour, never got my last pay."

"That was 1929?"

"1930, May 1930."

Rob said, "Rachel died the same month."

"I heard it," Della said, "—people down here wrote me." She waited awhile; then she said straight at him, "I was telling *you.* You asked me the reason. If you want to tell your troubles, let me sleep. Go wake up Hutch or Miss Alice; they'll listen."

He said again "You know mine" and managed to smile.

She said "I know everybody's," then surprised herself by easy laughter.

Rob waited till she finished. Then when she didn't speak again but pleated her bedspread, he said "What's your joke?"

"*Everybody* know," she said. "Everybody know everybody's troubles; all the same. What am *I* telling *you?*"

"A story," Rob said.

"What about?"

"Why you're back here. Why you want to stay."

Della shook her head silently, still pinching the spread. She fell back heavily against the one pillow. Her eyes were clamped shut. Then she said "Wrong again."

Tired as he was, Rob thought he understood. With her story as a trowel she had dug back not only to her first young face, the face that had drawn him, but to feelings he'd tasted in her nineteen years ago—a girl's first craving to float a man's weight on what she has guessed is a great deep of water, the untested secret of her nature and strength. Aching and dazed, he found she'd uncovered his own old need—to ride such a deep and to probe its dark, its constant promise that the skin of a body, of maybe the earth, was only the veil of a better place where the soul would be *borne*. A sheltered bay.

He stood and went to the edge of her bed and sat on the small square of pleats she'd made, not quite touching her. He was speechless with thanks—for old help renewed with no prior claim of sacrifice or debt. He was not so much young and starting again as *himself* again. He felt what he'd always been in his depths (however long buried, drowned, assaulted, ignored)—a strong gentle boy named Robinson Mayfield, who meant only good to the world and himself and would live to achieve it as trees do leaves, in silent perfection, the absence of doubt, a natural skill. The back of his right hand touched her right arm.

Della's eyes stayed shut but she breathed on calmly, awake and permitting his nearness again.

So in that dream of faith, he was free to move gradually; dream farther onward, this minute sustained. He could live on here, with Hutch again. There was one school in town, four county schools; men scarce in the mountains as Negroes or flat fields, all broke-down or fighting. They could ask Polly here. It was Hutch's not Forrest's; she'd come for Hutch. She'd take to Della, another strong orphan with the courage of oak. He would last out his life now, forgiven and freed, his intended self.

Della moved her arm, separate from Rob, and laid it on her stomach. It did not jar his calm or hope. He said, "You're sure this will all go to Hutch?"

She nodded, not looking. "*Gone*," she said. "Already gone to him. Nobody else want it. Rachel getting him back here to keep like she planned."

Rob said "And you're staying?"

"Not for Rachel," she said.

"No for you."

Della chuckled. Then she looked up at him. "I'm staying in the hope I die soon in peace and can lie by my mother."

Rob could not speak to that; he silently believed her.

Her smile endured but with such a strong light as to show both her gravity and some hidden joy which even she had only guessed, the hope of rest. She said, "I've got a little burial savings. Not nearly enough. Will you see me buried right?—good waterproof box?"

Rob nodded. "Are you sick?"

"No strong as a bear. Just tired, tired out. But you done promised— Della buried in style." She laughed again and shut her eyes; crossed her thick hands on her puddled breasts, her picture of peace.

So Rob laughed also and took her right wrist and raised it in the air. "Look here," he said.

Della looked at his asking eyes and understood. "I couldn't. Not now. These bones wouldn't bear you."

He waited, their hands joined, suspended between them. "They have," he said. "We have not really changed." Then he said "I'm begging."

9

HUTCH did not wake till he heard the sound of running water. He had been deep asleep, not dreaming or hoping to but genuinely healing in every cell. Then he came awake cleanly, not shocked or scared. The room that opened off the far bedroom-wall was a small bath made from a closed side-porch. The light was on there, and the door was closed; but someone was filling the basin slowly, then slowly washing—Hutch could hear soap-on-rag, rag slapping skin, a toweling-down, a mouth rinsed twice. There was some faint light from the moon through blinds, enough to see there were clothes on a rocker which were not his own (too crumpled to know) but no sign of a bag. He knew it was Rob, no question at all—the rhythms of washing (Rob could never wash quickly; he'd rather go dirty than speed through a rite as solemn as any), the sound from the rinsed throat of grateful relief. Rob had come now and found him.

Hutch at first wondered why and what he would say to whatever came next, anger and orders or the old numb apologies, pledges, amends. He'd moved so far from Rob in these four days—Hatt, Della, and Alice; the chances of real life—that he'd planned no replies for what was now on him. Still he was not worried; and the hard revulsion of the last night in Richmond, though remembered, was distant. It occurred to him, waiting, that he must have wanted this. A man had come through his door and, whatever else, had undressed ten feet from his sleeping body; and he had not stirred. He liked to think he woke at the slightest change round him and generally he did. He thought now he'd known in the pit of his sleep who the change represented—his father—and had welcomed him by love's homeliest gift, the adjacent trust of untroubled sleep. Hutch also knew Rob had never surprised him, even drunk and naked on his own father's floor. He saw now how children learn the terrors of the world—by watching their parents, suspecting them of infinite power to turn in an instant into monsters, then confirming that suspicion. *And surviving it.*

Hutch knew, lying in the great black room that had been a recent temple to his vanished mother, that he had not vanished and would not soon, barring accident. He had had a life already, fourteen years of life, one-fifth of his seventy. At fourteen most dumb animals were long dead or blind with age; fourteen-year-old automobiles were relics. He smiled to the air.

The light went out in the bath; the door opened. In the new sudden dark, Rob could not see to move. He stood still to wait while his eyes responded.

Hutch could not see him. He was naked, still holding a small hand towel. He seemed to have thinned down, drawn himself inward to some firmer core that was Hutch's oldest memory—his father young beside him, asking questions through the night: all the years before them. Which now they'd survived—both, alive and here again, one another's goal (of all human destinations either one could see, that walked above ground). Yet Hutch couldn't speak, not from fear or uncertainty of how he'd be met— Rob was standing bare, free to be harmed or ignored—but because he could not think of what to say first. What had he said last? He could take up from there; but he couldn't remember—Rob had begged to be left alone; had he answered that in words? No he'd left. Could he say he was sorry then? He wasn't. He had walked straight forward into this, the socket for his life. Could he simply say, "Lie down. You are back with me now. This is mine and I've asked you"? Rob would say it wasn't possible, list a dozen reasons why the plan would never work, why they couldn't stay here—bills, taxes, rusted roofing, youth, age, the hurt feelings of a squad of bystanders.

He could say that he'd gone into Goshen that morning at Alice's prompting and seen an old lawyer who had known his grandfather and said that if no will actually existed, and the lawyer knew of none, then the hotel was Hutch's for what it was worth, which had been next to nothing since the early depression; that the Hutchins had lived on the income ·from timber Mrs. Hutchins owned near Suffolk, sold stand by stand (it had been her mother's); that some of it was left, he was almost sure, and might be Hutch's if there were no great outstanding debts, which of course there might be, and if Mrs. Hutchins had no kin in Isle of Wight who would file family claims. So he buried his head half-down in the pillow and said, "You are going to catch cold in your peter. Then where will you be?"

Rob jerked a little, startled; then laughed—"Better off." Then he came forward slowly through the dark to the cot, still there at Hutch's foot, right-angled to the bed (who had it been for?). He sat on the center edge and faced toward the boy; he could only see his outline. "I tried not to wake you up."

Hutch said, "I doubt you did; I wake up all night. Did you just get here?"

"I stopped and saw Della."

"Did she tell you what's happened?"

"Since your grandfather's death?—yes it sounds like a lot for you to have to deal with."

Hutch said, "It is. Did you get Richmond settled?"

"No I have to go back soon. Polly said she'd pack all the stuff we were keeping. She'll stay that long; then she'll go her own way. I can't even get her to consider staying on. She's had her pride hurt; first time in her life and it came too late. She refuses to take it."

"She could come here," Hutch said.

Rob waited awhile. "You can ask her—go to it—but I think you'd have better luck asking Mussolini. He's a man anyhow."

"Did you see your telegram? It's there on the dresser."

Rob said "What does it say?"

Hutch waited, then laughed once. "It says 'No please.' "

"Min, you mean?"

"Yes sir."

"Just those two words?"

"And her name, yes sir. I was going to mail it to Fontaine tomorrow."

Rob raised his legs and slowly lay flat on the cot, his face upward.

When he didn't speak for minutes, Hutch strained to see his father's eyes—open or shut? It seemed a piece of news necessary to proceeding; but he couldn't, just the clear line of head, chest, legs (both hands cupped his groin). Finally he said "Is that bad?"

"Yes. You'll live to understand."

Hutch said, "I do now. Don't forget I left Richmond."

"No I won't. Never fear. I'll live a long time—Kendals, Mayfields, both do—and I won't forget that."

Hutch said, "Might as well. I'm forgetting it soon."

"You've scheduled it, have you?"

"Yes sir. I'll be working so I won't dwell on things."

"Hotelling? Son, you won't have ten guests a year. You and Della'll be crazy as owls by Labor Day."

"—My drawing," Hutch said. "Rachel's friend Alice helps me. She thinks I'm worth the time." Hutch laughed but thought. He could tell her story now (Alice lonely and peaceful); Rob would like her better when they met in the morning. Might like her too much though. Hutch kept his silence.

Rob said, "I guess you have seen Rachel's grave."

"No sir." Hutch waited, then told the truth which caused him no shame. "I forgot to, really. I saw her picture, the one where you surprised her right before your wedding."

"All I did was surprise her. She never once believed me—that I meant to be with her, that I was truly *there* when I sat down beside her or touched her at night, that I would come back any time I left the house.

She expected me to vanish, doubted I was ever there. I surprised her to death; I could never see why."

Hutch sat up quietly to prop himself on pillows. "I can," he said. "I can see very well. It's why I need to leave you."

"Still?"

"I think so, yes sir."

"I was thinking you could hire me in your enterprise here; might need a good yard-man."

Hutch said "I've written Grainger."

"Oh well, I withdraw then. He outclasses me." Rob had kept his tone light, but he rallied no further.

They were silent a good while. It seemed Rob might have dozed off, no sound of his breath; and Hutch thought of getting up and covering him with quilts (there were two at his own feet; he still could see Rob's nakedness, the hands at the ears now).

But Rob said "You sleepy?"

"No sir, wide awake."

"Can I tell you one thing while it's clear in my mind?—it might fade again."

"Yes sir," Hutch said.

So Rob thought awhile. "You mentioned that wedding, your mother's and mine. It happened in the morning up the hall in the parlor; and then there was a big feed for everybody here, Della cooking and Grainger and Gracie serving. Then Alice and a friend of mine that died shortly after (Niles Fitzhugh from home) drove the two of us to Lynchburg to catch the train to Washington, our honeymoon trip. There had been an early snow somewhere in West Virginia; and the train was hours late, maybe wouldn't even come till some time the next morning. We sat in the depot with Alice and Niles till way after dark—Niles had to head on; Alice lived in Lynchburg, her people did—so I paid a Negro porter to come round and warn us when they got final word on when we would leave; and your mother and I walked across the street and got a bedroom in an old hotel, old drummer's hotel, old railroad boys (all about my present age, I guess, looking back). It had been a pretty tiring two days for us both, and Rachel had never been all that strong; so we turned on in, not a morsel to eat—"

Hutch said "Rob—"

"Yes?"

"Listen—" Then he held a good while. "Am I meant to hear this?"

"Meaning what?" Rob said.

"Do I really need to hear this? Things worry me a lot."

Rob said "I know they do." He was silent a minute. Then he said, "Yes you do. I really think you do. You've suffered not knowing."

Hutch said "All right, sir."

"We were tired as I said, and you always had to guard Rachel from exhaustion (she would rush straight to it; it was home to her); but I also didn't much trust that porter to give us fair warning, and I meant us to leave; so I said we would just kick off our shoes and lie in our clothes in the dark, all ready. She agreed to that and pulled up a thin blue blanket that was folded at the foot of the bed and lay right down in her traveling suit. I darkened us and joined her. She kissed me like a sister; and in under twenty seconds, I was rowing through sleep like I hadn't ever slept. We'd lived in neighboring rooms for some months, right overhead here; but I'd never slept beside her, barely touched her. The funny thing to me was, I knew I was resting. Far down as I sank, some eye in my mind could still see and register that I was being washed, being truly refreshed."

"Was Rachel?"

Rob waited. "I very much doubt it."

"What dream did you have?"

"None I remember, too far to remember."

Hutch said, "You generally dream. I just wondered."

"How do you know that?"

"You talk in your sleep."

Rob laughed once, then waited again a long time. "I did then too," he said. "Rachel had to wake me. I had almost scared her."

"Must have had a nightmare."

"Oh no," Rob said with the speed of certainty. Then it came back to him through the nineteen years like a spirit called up from the patient earth, bearing freight that the caller had not foreseen. When he'd seen its shape, though not its full load, Rob told it to Hutch. "I was sleeping in a bed like the hotel bed; and Rachel was beside me, only we had undressed and were naked under sheets."

"In the dream?" Hutch said.

Rob nodded in the dark. "I could see us stretched out. Day seemed to be breaking (light was rising round us); and I was in two places, resting in my body and watching overhead. Then the light woke Rachel, and she saw the tall man standing in the door. The light was from him. She didn't understand so she started shaking me, begging me to wake up. I struggled against her and said 'I *need* this,' but she kept on till finally I opened and looked. I knew right away. The man was an angel. He was dressed like a real man in common street clothes, but I knew what he was. Every really grand thing I ever encountered was wearing street clothes; but I don't fail to know them—I'm a student of eyes. This man had *eyes*. He was watching us calmly; and though he didn't speak, I understood clearly. It was Judgment; he had been sent to tell us that message direct. I wondered *why us?* out of all the world's souls; but I said, 'Not now. I need this please.' Then Rachel really shook me—in real life, I mean—and I woke up scared, thinking numbers of things: mainly that the train was leaving and we'd missed it. The room was dark and we hadn't missed anything as it turned out. She said I had been dreaming hard for some time (my arms and legs twitching); but that she had had to wake me when I called out twice, me begging the man. Whether she'd ever slept, she had us both awake then. The only light was from out in the hall, seeping round the door-frame; but I could see enough of her to want to proceed then, before any message, to thank her for her gift to me and show her she'd been right—I was all she had dreamt and would always be. I undressed us both as gently as babies; and though she had never even kissed a man but me, I managed to show her and thank her both and leave her not hurt or confused or sorry but smiling and ready. It was dawning by then, by the time I was through; and I could see her face. Till then I had had a lot of worries about her and whether I was right in taking her on, whether I would harm her—God knows I've had them since—but that one morning I could *see* I was right. Could have been right for years if I'd kept that sight foremost in my mind and worked to preserve it. Then the porter came to tell us the train was there, due out in five minutes; so we dressed and ran. First mistake we made and the worst; my mistake not hers. Should have lain right there in that old hotel till I really understood what my dreams had said for twenty-one years, what Rachel's face meant. Then angels could have come by troops with swords; they'd have found no mortal fault in me, no fault they could judge." Rob paused there to think, then knew he had finished.

But Hutch said "Finish."

"That's all, just some sightseeing up and down Washington. The story was over once that Negro knocked."

"No the meaning," Hutch said. "What you claim to understand—all your dreams, mother's face."

Rob said, "I claimed that I would have understood if I'd gone on watching Rachel closely as that. Or any other person that I wanted to watch and who held still for me."

Hutch said "Min."

"Min wanted *me* so she never held still. And now she's stopped."

They were quiet a short while; the house was still settling from the heat of the past day, groans that could easily have come from humans, any person from the hundreds who had stopped here briefly or lived out lives. Hutch said, "Why did you think I had to hear that?"

"Did it bother you?"

"No not yet anyhow but you need to explain."

Rob understood then. He said, "I was happy. I was happy that once. I could have kept on. I wanted you to know. People get what they need if they stand still and watch till the earth sends it up, most people I've known—Mother, Forrest, Rachel. What they need, not want."

Hutch said "I knew that."

"How?"

"It's happened to me."

"Already?" Rob said.

"Yes sir."

"Here lately?"

"Yes sir."

"Want to tell me about it?"

Hutch waited. "Not now."

Rob said, "Well, it's late. Got to rest for tomorrow."

"What happens tomorrow?"

"I'll drive down to Bracey."

"Aunt Hatt won't know you. I was there Tuesday night."

"She never has known me," Rob said, "—nothing new. Can she still sign a paper? That's all I need."

"What paper?"

"Just a form saying I can live in Richmond at Forrest's, that she won't claim it or her living son."

"She might want to live with you."

"Might let her," Rob said. "—little old-folks' home. Might be just the trick. I'm not moving backward through time, sure thing."

"Then you're staying in Richmond?"

"I think I may try it, beg Polly to stay. She could sew and support me!"

"When did you plan that?"

"Just now," Rob said.

"Have you looked for a job?"

"I'll start Monday morning. It's a big enough place. I could change my name, start a whole new life—pick a name from the air: be Newmarket Watters, a model of trust, credit to all my loved ones and friends." Rob was too tired to laugh. He reached behind him and molded the thin child's pillow to his head. Then he said "Say your prayers."

"Long since," Hutch said.

They lay without moving again for ten minutes, Rob bare on his back, Hutch propped in the midst of a bed his arms could not yet span. They were both too tired to think or plan, regret or hope; too tired to sleep, at least as they were—their bodies a great T-square in the dark room, but four feet from meeting.

Hutch could see more of Rob now; the moon had moved round. He tried to imagine his own life starting in that groin there, yearning out into Rachel fifteen years ago. Had it been as good a night as the first in Lynchburg? What room, what bed?—surrounded by what? (what house, what dreams?). He must think to ask at the next good chance. Ask who?—this boy stretched here at his feet? In the pale glare his father seemed nothing else but young and already cold (the mountain night was cold). He'd chosen that—Rob had; he'd just said as much. And Hutch had chosen his now, a gift from Rachel through his Grandfather Hutchins and Alice

Matthews (all he had of his Grandfather Mayfield was a bark doll, and that was made by old Rob and passed on through Polly); a place to stand in till the world showed its core, its secret news, its reward to his patient watch on its skin.

Rob moved, stood huddled on the floor to turn his covers down; then slowly climbed back in and lay on his left side away from Hutch. But in five more minutes, his breath hadn't settled to the calm of sleep. He was silently awake.

So Hutch said, "Why don't you sleep with the master?"

Rob said "Where is that?"

"Isn't this the master bedroom?"

"Yes."

"Well, here's the master bed." Hutch slid to the right half, a cold plain of cloth.

Rob came to join him.

They did not touch at first, of their own volition; but quickly slept in the warming depths of Raven Hutchins' bed, not thinking of his death.

In an hour Rob woke in new dense dark—the moon was gone—and found that he'd worked his way to Hutch's turned back. He had not slept a whole night beside his son since they'd first left Richmond eleven years ago and passed through this room (Mrs. Hutchins leading) on their sad way to Fontaine, Raleigh, all the time since. The mutual warmth of their bodies had stoked a feverish sweat down the length of their juncture. Rob's left side was damp against Hutch's damp back and pants. He flapped the top edge of the covers twice to draw in cold air and moved to turn back to his own empty half.

But the bedsprings were ancient and had puddled in the center. They lay in a trough; any turn was uphill. So Rob lay another moment, touching the boy, planning a gentle heave to free himself. The moment stretched till the touch seemed a graft, a natural bond. Hot as he was, Rob remembered a question he had not asked in years, since they'd last slept close—*should he keep his promise?* The promise Grainger told him to offer Rachel dying—that he'd change, starting then; take his present life and honor it, love it when he could (if never, then never: half the world had had that) but honor it daily. The actual present.

Supposing he planned to renew that promise, what was present now to honor? What had ever been present these fourteen years but this one child he'd volunteered to start on a girl frail as paper?—a child not sufficient to have held him true. Clearly not sufficient but present here now.

And clearly too these last few days—*the child had his own life;* was struggling free into plans of his own, however doomed and childish.

Leaving, aimed outward, no backward glance. But still here tonight. Here, anywhere in the breadth of the world, all he had was this child. Absolutely nothing else but a body that worked fairly well for its age.

Or so he thought now, and he knew he thought clearly. Della's deep welcome, as if they'd never parted but had gentled through long years of daily meeting, and the one hour of sleep had cleaned Rob's mind to a freshness as familiar as rare—once before. He had once seen, as now, with this perfect clarity; a quick space of knowledge, prophetic and true. Still against his back, Rob searched for that time. His first meeting with Grainger, Grainger quoting from his books as though books might serve a drunk boy bound for death? The meeting with Min in a Richmond hotel, the bleak aftermath of hunger and food when they'd still lain together, comprehending their future, their whole lives till now? His first morning with Rachel—Lynchburg, his dream of judgment? No, true as they were, something truer lay behind them.

Hutch shifted his back, spooned deeper into Rob.

It came to him, whole and clear as at its birth—May 1921, seventeen years old, his high-school commencement, creeping home in the morning from his drunk sleep at Sylvie's (the meeting with Flora) to find Eva, beautiful, waiting for him calmly to speak her own love and to prove his father's, despite barren years, whatever her reasons. That had been his life's height, Rob realized now—not the happiest time or the one he'd repeat but the literal height, the precipice from which he'd surveyed all his chances and seen them as good, subject only to his own will, the world's permission. A boy loved at last by the girl who had borne him, who swore to go with him through whatever might rise. A girl as needy as he'd ever been, and begging him.

He had never believed her. If he'd only confided in her offer that morning and bent his life to it—a job, their own place—what would he be now? An aging boy maybe, as dry as Thorne Bradley. He was that anyhow. For all his scraping, cutting, through the life of a man, what lay round him now—round his unchanged heart—but a middle-aged child's loose arms, legs, belly: an abandoned melon? He smiled to himself and saw Eva's face as he'd left her last week in the yard, a lost girl, still straining to grow toward a prop that would hold her.

Rob decided to believe her now at last—both Eva and Forrest, however untrue. Decided to believe they'd intended his life; that they met in him, only place on earth. That last at least could never be a lie. Had he not nearly killed Eva proving he was her need, proving Forrest's need to love and renew her? He could *let* them meet in him, even now this late; let them come to the restful harbor they'd sought, a son made from their lives but stronger—to perfect their purpose and transmit it. He'd refused them too long, and they'd torn him for it.

As they met in and tore this hot child sighing against him now. So did he and Rachel, both big-eyed with fear and hunger and flight. Bedford Kendal and Charlotte Watson, both wild. Anna Goodwin and old Rob, more famished than any. The child needed help.

What help on earth could Rob Mayfield give any living soul, much less his own son whom he'd left nine years ago to grow unwatched? Supposing he believed Eva's old claim now, Eva's and Forrest's—that they'd met above all to start his life, that their separate dreams had been the world's means of driving them together to start a further life (*his*, beating in him now in the close cold dark). Supposing that then and supposing they had loved the one life they made and wished it well, hung their main hopes on it, and supposing he could trust them through all remaining years—then how must he change and, once changed firmly, what help could he bring to his own child?

He could come back at least, starting now tonight, wherever *back* would be—Richmond, Fontaine, Goshen, or some fresh chance. He could stay in place wherever they landed and watch Hutch closely till Hutch said *Stop*, one still human face that had asked him to watch, that remained to be known. He could watch it at least. That might be help someway in time, for one child anyhow, the one he'd started. All the rest were beyond him or behind him, past help—Forrest vanished, alone. Polly bound for lone age, no child, no kin. Hatt addled by abandonment, too loving for comfort.

He saw for the first time in all his life how, though he'd been started (been aimed) by his parents, he had been steered and saved (so far as he was saved) by the single and barren—Rena, Sylvie, Grainger, Polly, Della, even Kennerly. They passed through his sight now like old Bible figures, tall forms in dark pictures on whom the sky leans—but sufficient to bear it. Any dog could start a litter; they had shivered alone. He honored their strength now and prayed for them, that they die in God's care.

His whelp was here now, a twin to his flesh. With his lips on the bone of the boy's left shoulder, Rob promised again, though he did not speak or forget as he promised how he'd failed other times after fervors of hope. Then he turned away and slept in a minute, a rest like warm blood, no scrap of dream. Rob did not know—no one alive knew, though his father had known till his dying day—that this same night forty-one years ago Eva Kendal, still mainly believing she was happy, was doing her own will, insuring her life, had borne Forrest Mayfield over her again and drawn from his joy the seed and permission to grow her one child.

Hutch dreamt of children, real children a little smaller than he, seated far apart in a bare Norman field, consumed by real flames—no man in sight or hearing, no woman. Real agony.

10

AT eight in the morning, they were still asleep. The muffled sounds of Alice and Della in the kitchen since seven had not disturbed them, but now Rob woke as the hall door opened slowly. Dazed and scared he sat up to see—Mr. Hutchins, alive? Some boy on the doorsill—Negro boy, well-dressed in a dark blue summer suit, a clean white shirt buttoned neatly at the throat. No smile, no recognition; he was not seeing Rob but was fixed on Hutch. Some kin of Della's?

Then the boy looked to Rob and beckoned him once with a long left hand, no words but a call to follow him.

Naked as he was, Rob almost obeyed; but the gesture, hand slow as if air were liquid, had waked him fully—Grainger, Grainger Walters in Sunday clothes, always younger in the morning before a day's toll (surely though he'd traveled through the night to be here?). Rob said "You can come in," half-whispering to spare Hutch. Then he propped on his pillow against the high headboard.

Grainger stepped in, shut the door, and walked to the cot. He stopped there and stood, then nodded toward Hutch. "He all right now?"

Hutch sprawled on his stomach, covered to the ears, his face toward Rob, mouth slack, no sound of breath.

Rob said "Fine, last night anyhow. I got in late but he woke up and met me. He's dead-out now."

"Della told me what happened."

"Mr. Hutchins?"

Grainger nodded, leaned to the cot, spread up the covers, and sat on the edge. "You mean to stay with him?"

"Della tell you his plan?"

Grainger said "I knew it."

Rob said, "We'll have to see. We may not can eat here, may have to eat leaves."

"He won't mind that." Grainger grinned toward Hutch.

Rob said, "Of course not. Little minor detail like life wouldn't stop him; he banks on the Lord. But I'll have to check round. I just came for one day to see was he safe; he left me in Richmond. I got to finish there."

"He told me you were drinking."

"I was. One night though, not a drop since. I had a partial reason; I killed that nerve. Or numbed it awhile."

Grainger pointed behind him through the wall, outdoors. "Ought to stay here and force yourself to drink from that spring; that'll cure all your nerves or break you from wanting any beverage again. Rinsed my mouth while ago when I got here—tell you, I'd forgot." He showed his clamped teeth still edgy from the water. "My roof lasted good."

Rob said, "Knew it would. It'll outlast you."

"You too," Grainger said. "Say you heading back to Richmond?"

"Today, maybe Sunday. Still clearing-up there. Polly means to move out. I searched high and low through all Father's stuff; no will after all. Her pride took a beating."

Grainger nodded. "She'll make it. You need me with you?"

"Thank you, no," Rob said. "She's packing things now. I'll sell all the rest if I don't stay here."

"Anything there for me?"

Rob did not understand. "No. I said no will."

Grainger shook his head once. "See Gracie anywhere?"

"In Richmond? She's there."

"Somebody said she was. I got word from Bracey."

"I saw her one evening. She lives with her cousin."

"She doing all right?"

"Drinking," Rob said, "but all right, I guess—little shaky but walking. Good as most of your friends."

Grainger nodded twice. "Send me any message?"

Rob shook his head quickly, then knew that she had; knew he was her messenger, duty bound. Not waiting to think what the full message said or from whom it had passed to miserable Gracie, Rob raised his left hand and pulled the wide ring from his little finger. He held it toward Grainger.

Grainger studied it a moment in the dim air, then leaned; then shut it in his long palm, hid from them both. He looked to the floor and understood it all, understood all its senders.

It hurt Rob to have done it—late, too late. But he honored his act and said, "Everybody all right at home?"

"Same as ever. Missing Hutch. Sylvie grieving all week."

"Over Hutch?"

"Kin people. Some kin of hers dead."

"Not Albert?"

"Flora's boy."

"The one in the army?"

Grainger nodded. "Car wreck. He was thumbing back to camp. Old man picked him up, let the boy take the wheel. They were dead in ten miles; dodged a mule, rolled over. Sylvie grieving all week."

Rob laughed, full voice.

Hutch raised up—"What?"—face stiff with confusion.

"Good morning," Rob said.

Hutch scrubbed at his eyes. "What's funny?" he said.

"Sylvie," Rob said. Then he said "Look there" and pointed to the cot.

Still flat, Hutch craned round and, once the sight reached him, grinned slow and broad. "How did you get here?"

Grainger smiled. "My wings." He stroked one shoulder with his shut right hand.

"Dressed *up*," Hutch said. "You brought your work clothes? Got work here to do."

Grainger nodded he had.

They all held a moment; something crashed in the kitchen.

Then Grainger leaned forward, half-over the bed. "What I brought—" he said. He held his arm to Hutch, far enough to make him rise.

Bare to the waist, skin creased by the stiff pure linen beneath him, Hutch sat up slowly and turned and looked—Grainger, Grainger reaching. So he met Grainger's hand with his own, slightly cupped. Hutch had never seen the ring, never known of its life; but it fit his left hand.

REYNOLDS PRICE

Born in Macon, North Carolina in 1933, Reynolds Price attended North Carolina schools and received his Bachelor of Arts degree from Duke University. As a Rhodes Scholar he studied for three years at Merton College, Oxford, receiving the Bachelor of Letters with a thesis on Milton. In 1958 he returned to Duke where he is now James B. Duke Professor of English. His first novel A Long and Happy Life *appeared in 1962. A volume of stories* The Names and Faces of Heroes *appeared in 1963. In the ensuing years he has published* A Generous Man (*a novel*), Love and Work (*a novel*), Permanent Errors (*stories*), Things Themselves (*essays and scenes*), The Surface of Earth (*a novel*), Early Dark (*a play*), and* A Palpable God (*translations from the Bible with an essay on the origins and life of narrative*). His books have appeared in fourteen languages.*